LIONHEARTS

ALSO BY NATHAN MAKARYK

Nottingham

LIONHEARTS

NATHAN MAKARYK

A TOM DOHERTY ASSOCIATES BOOK

NEW YORK

LIONHEARTS

A Forge Book
Published by Tom Doherty Associates
120 Broadway
New York, NY 10271

www.tor-forge.com

Forge® is a registered trademark of Macmillan Publishing Group, LLC.

The Library of Congress Cataloging-in-Publication Data is available upon request.

ISBN 978–1–250–19585–2 (hardcover)
ISBN 978–1–250–19586–9 (ebook)

Our books may be purchased in bulk for promotional, educational, or business use. Please contact your local bookseller or the Macmillan Corporate and Premium Sales Department at 1-800-221-7945, extension 5442, or by email at MacmillanSpecialMarkets@macmillan.com.

First Edition: September 2020

Printed in the United States of America

10 9 8 7 6 5 4 3 2 1

for anyone who has ever been afraid to be the first one to rise

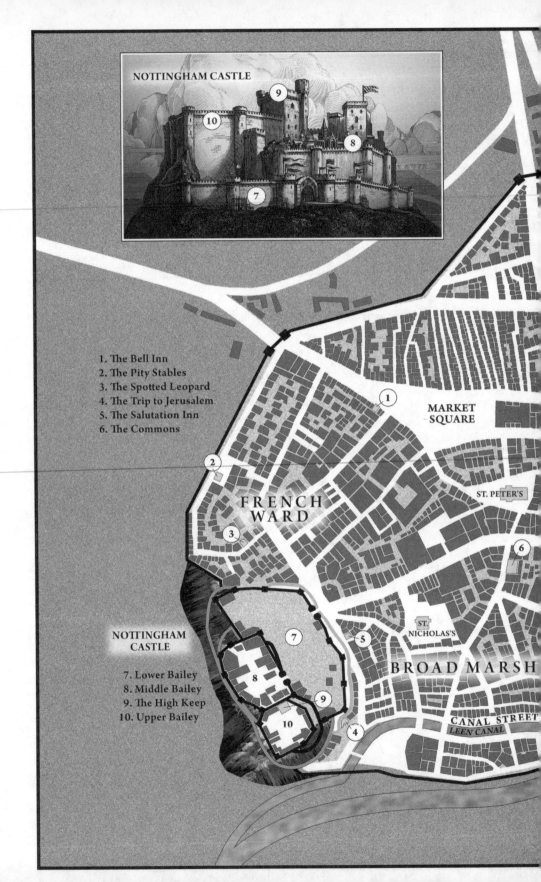

NOTTINGHAM CASTLE

1. The Bell Inn
2. The Pity Stables
3. The Spotted Leopard
4. The Trip to Jerusalem
5. The Salutation Inn
6. The Commons

MARKET
SQUARE

ST. PETER'S

FRENCH
WARD

NOTTINGHAM
CASTLE

7. Lower Bailey
8. Middle Bailey
9. The High Keep
10. Upper Bailey

ST.
NICHOLAS'S

BROAD MARSH

CANAL STREET
LEEN CANAL

NOTTINGHAM

PARLIAMENT
WARD

ENGLISH WARD

11

16

ST. MARY'S

12

14

13

15

WHARFSIDE

11. Zinn's Hovel
12. The Long Stair
13. The Dockmaster's
    Office

14. The Peach and the
    Pear
15. Red Lion Square
16. Plumptre Street

ONCE UPON A TIME

Robin Hood is dead, long live Robin Hood.

If you're starting this book without reading its predecessor, *Nottingham* (or if it's simply been a while since you read that book), you might need a quick recap of its events. After all, there are a handful of significant events you should know about—and the only characters who know the truth are dead.

In 1191, King Richard took all of England's men and coin away and named his mission a "Holy Crusade" because "A Really Wretched Idea" was just a hair too accurate. When critical supplies from home failed to arrive, he sent his two personal body doubles—**Robin of Locksley** and **William de Wendenal**—back to England to investigate. Their search led them to "Marion's Men," a group of outlaws and destitute peasants organized by **Lady Marion Fitzwalter**, who were living in the Sherwood and stealing supplies to survive.

Robin and William split up to effect a peace: Robin stayed with Marion's outlaws and tempered their outright stealing toward more *gentlemanly* thievery, gaining them the love of nobles and peasants alike, while William went to Nottingham to pacify the High Sheriff of Nottingham, **Roger de Lacy**, and the captain of the Nottingham Guard, **Guy of Gisbourne**. For a short but unsustainable time, things were slightly less terrible.

In that time, William was reunited with an old flame: **Arable de Burel**. The Burel family had once been prominent in Derby, until the Kings' War of 1174—in which the Burels followed the Earl de Ferrers to war, while the Wendenals refused. As punishment, William's brothers were kept as hostages in the Burel estate, where they were accidentally killed trying to escape. William's father, **Beneger de Wendenal**, blamed the Burels and destroyed their household—which obviously ended William and Arable's youthful romance, and sent her into exile. Now, seventeen years later, they could rekindle that relationship.

Violence ignited when Marion and Robin's crew tried to raid the Nottingham Guard's supplies in Bernesdale. Two Guardsmen were killed, and Captain Gisbourne unintentionally killed a young boy named **Much**. In revenge, two of the outlaws—**Will Scarlet** and **Elena Gamwell**—went rogue, snuck into Nottingham Castle, and assassinated Sheriff de Lacy. They were captured and sentenced to death.

In the aftermath of this, Robin embraced the persona of "**Robin Hood**," while William managed to claim the vacant Sheriffcy. When traditional methods of capturing Robin Hood failed, Captain Gisbourne devised a devious plan: he assaulted Arable and tricked her into releasing Will Scarlet and Elena

Gamwell from prison, and then trailed them back to Robin's camp. He also convinced Elena to poison Robin, but she mistakenly killed her friend Alan instead, and then drank her own poison in remorse for the betrayal. A brutal fight ensued, ending with the deaths of Gisbourne and most of his Guardsmen.

A few other notable names include: **Lady Margery d'Oily** and her husband **Waleran de Beaumont**, Earl of Warwick, who befriended Arable but eventually turned on her; **Gilbert with the White Hand**, a violent killer who left Marion's Men to join the Nottingham Guard; and a Guardsman named **Bolt** who abandoned Nottingham after his best friend Reginold was killed.

In the end, Arable guided Robin back to Nottingham Castle to confront William and save Marion, who he believed had been captured against her will. In reality, Marion had arranged her own wedding to William to increase both their power, in the hopes of creating a lasting peace. In the Sheriff's office, Robin and William confronted each other. Seeing no alternative, William killed Robin, but was immediately poisoned by the young new Earl of Derby: **William de Ferrers**. Ferrers seized the Sheriff's seat as his own, and publicly claimed that "Robin Hood" had killed Sheriff William de Wendenal.

In the Sherwood, Will Scarlet took on the mantle of Robin Hood, vowing to continue the fight against the new Sheriff alongside Marion, even as winter begins.

SARRA BILLINSGATE

THE FRENCH WARD

"GOD'S TEETH!" LITTLE HUGH tried—and failed—to wink. "I'm fucking Robin Hood!"

"Mind your tongue!" Sarra snatched his earlobe with a mother's precision and twisted it. Her son's joy vanished as he writhed between her fingertips. "I don't ever want to hear such language from you again, understand? Now go find your father, he's waiting on you!"

She slapped his bottom—always too hard but never hard enough—and his legs *flik-flacked* away down the alley slop. Sarra's shoulders slumped. *I don't remember ever having that much energy.* She was exhausted just watching him, and jealous of the simplicity that came with being a child.

Mindful of her bruises, Sarra tugged her roughspun shawl closer at the neck and winced. Above, the sky spat in little pockets and rolled grey behind the silhouette of Nottingham Castle, looming furiously over them. Thin waves of black coursed over its frame as the wind and water fought across the battlements. It gave the illusion of a castle with hair—long, uncontrollable wisps whipping out, vanishing, then lashing out again elsewhere.

"*We're going to starve either way,*" her husband, Rog, had explained, "*but it will be better in the city. You'll see.*"

You'll see.

It sounded like wisdom then, as hope always does to the desperate. And Rog had always held a clever sort of patience, knowing when to ignore an easy lure. It broke Sarra's heart to remember how Rog once kept their spirits high, singing at night for Hugh when they had nothing to eat, even just a few months ago. She'd always loved that toothy smile of his, especially when she could see it in their son. But now, Sarra's husband could hardly bear to look her in the eyes. There was no predicting each day if it would be rage or humiliation that made him keep his distance.

"Gack," some noise snapped for attention at her right—a dirty, bony thing reaching out from a hole in the alley's stone wall, a too-skinny old man covered in dried mud or excrement. Eyeballs shining but shrouded in dark. Panic froze her for only a moment, but long enough for him to grin black gums. "I'll trade you a dry place for a wet one." Clacking his few remaining teeth, he uncurled one finger out toward Sarra's legs. She busied herself away, to outrun her disgust.

Sarra wondered, again, if anyone else from Thorney had survived. Most fled after the fields had burnt, but some stayed behind. Rog's only brother, Hanry, swore he'd join them in Nottingham, but winter was halfway through with no sign of him.

She pushed away from the alley, and through the unwelcome clamor of the French Ward.

This place was an infected sore in the city's armpit. The French Ward had grown out of sheer spite to the north of the castle's hill, wedged between the foot of its craggy cliffs and the slope of the western Derby Road. The finest parts of the French Ward were an overrun lot of ramshackle wooden buildings and filth. The worst parts were appropriately worse.

"It's the only place we can go," Rog had explained, "but it's better than nothing. You'll see."

You'll see.

What she *didn't* see was *him*, not anymore. A year ago she would've gladly left Thorney for any place he suggested, so long as they were all together. But here in the city, he was always working—or *hoping* to work by waiting in lines, which rarely paid off—and they merely traded Hugh off between them, sometimes with barely a word. That wasn't *together*.

At the makeshift stairs up to Park Row, a commotion seized her attention. Splashing carelessly off the uneven cobbles and into another muddy alley, a pack of young street boys—just barely older than Hugh—chased at each other. Their faces were smiles and they laughed the way Hugh laughed, until one turned and swung the heft of his knapsack into the face of the boy behind him, who spun and fell into the muck. The rest pummeled the fallen boy with their sacks and fists and feet, then turned heel and sprinted right past Sarra. The last one barked in her face and laughed as she startled.

Ten paces away, the poor boy in the mud didn't move, his face down.

Get up, she thought at him, because she didn't want to know what she'd do if he didn't. At the very edge of her mind, her guilt replaced this boy with Hugh. Sarra tilted her face up to the rain and refused to think on her son being beaten so. *Or worse,* it came before she could stop it, *what if he becomes one of the boys who delivers the beating?*

The image of the barking boy's greasy, pock-ridden cheeks burnt in her mind.

Get up.

She suddenly regretted letting Hugh run to Rog on his own when she could've easily accompanied him. It didn't matter that Rog and his shovel were waiting with the other hopeful dayhands only a few buildings away. She could've held Hugh's hand and told him something important and true about making good choices. Something about character. Something that would stay with him. *Next time,* she promised herself. Again.

Get up.

The street boy didn't move.

She couldn't be late, she had a *gentleman* waiting. Well, they were rarely *gentle,* but she had no other word for them. *They have a word for you, though.* She hadn't said that word to herself yet, nor had Rog. At least, not out loud. His eyes screamed it, but they both knew their marriage would only last until its first utterance. So he stayed his pride and didn't ask how she came about the occasional coin that kept the three of them alive. When they spoke, it was only of Hugh, and of how to protect him from the city's grime.

Get up.

With a gasp, the fallen boy jerked and pushed up to his hands and knees. Sarra exhaled, hot tears mixing with the rain down her cheeks. She lingered to watch the boy shake himself off and limp away, when something smashed into her side.

She yelped as she turned, but the little familiar something wrapped its arms around her legs, and Sarra tugged her son's hair.

"You gave me a start!" she said—reminding herself of her own mother—and wrapped her fingers into his sopping mop. "Where's your cap, now?"

"He's here, Mum, you have to come!"

"Where's your cap, young sir?" she repeated, twisting him to see his face, cheeks pinpricked red from running. He pulled the thing from a pocket and tugged it over his head, along with a grumble of protest. Sarra grumbled right back at him and readjusted the cap over the tips of his ears. "Who is this, now? Who's here?"

Hugh pulled at her. "Come on then, and hurry!"

"*Who's* here?"

"I can't say."

"Well you'll have to," she chided him, glancing down the alley where the imprint of the street boy's body had already turned into a puddle of dirty rainwater.

Hugh's entire face squirmed. "I can't. You told me to never use such language again."

AN ANXIOUS CROWD GATHERED outside the Pity Stables—which, despite its name, hadn't housed any horses for years. The Pities had only a few upright wooden walls, but provided relative shelter for those with the greatest need. Today its open frame was packed shoulder to shoulder with soggy onlookers, but Hugh weaseled himself forward and dragged Sarra along until they were under its roof.

She'd heard over and again that Robin Hood had been making appearances inside the city of late, though she'd tried not to let that build up her hope. If this really was Robin Hood, and if he was giving coin out as he had last year, there was no knowing how many warm meals that might put in Hugh's stomach. *Or boots!* Or more realistically, to grease the right palm that might pick Rog's name for day work. Robin Hood's presence was a lucky turn, for certain . . . but it came with a price. Hugh was at an impressionable age, and it might not do for him to see how easily a thief could bring in coin when his father's honest work could not.

Inside, the musk of wet men was palpable. A few hands pawed at her as she squeezed in, grunting their objections to her slipping by, but Hugh found handholds in the exposed beams of the back wall and climbed until his head was above the crowd. Sarra found a foothold beside him and eased herself up for a better view.

"Quietly, all!" An unfamiliar man hushed them from the center of the Pities, and silence rippled outward. "I have a story I think you'll find most interesting." He pulled back a slick hood from his head and raked his fingers through blond hair, matted dark from the rain. One finger flicked water off his pointed nose as he sized up his audience. Young for a man, and dangerously handsome, but there seemed to be an age about his eyes. *Not Robin Hood,* Sarra knew, but probably one of his closest men. Here to rile everyone's spirits before the real man arrived.

Sarra spotted Rog's head bobbing up and down near the front of the crowd, but was quickly tisked when she called his name. So she wrapped an arm around Hugh's waist to watch with the others.

"I found some men on the road to the north," the handsome man drawled out, stretching the tips of his mouth wide and squinting his eyes, smiling with both. Behind them, the light rain turned heavier, as if to veil them from the outside world. "Well, not really *men,* I suppose. That's not what they'd call themselves, at the least. They'd prefer the word *looords.*" He treated the title like an insult, and received a collective groan of agreement. "These *looords* had everything a man could want. Why, I'd never seen finer clothing. Excepting yours, of course, love." A wink at a young woman whose dress was the definition of threadbare. Still, she blushed and patted herself down as a few others whistled. "These *looords* had not a speck of dirt on their breeches, white as their asses!"

That made Hugh snort, which Sarra hated. The last thing she needed was for Hugh to idolize a rebellious man with a thirst for danger.

"Found more than a bit of gold on them, too, didn't we?" the man asked, and at his side two larger men gave a *hurrah.* One stout and bald, the other with the long careful face of a greyhound, they both positioned themselves to create a respectful distance between the speaker and the crowd.

"So I reach out with my hand," he continued, "this one right here, and I pluck the ring from his finger and whisper, *'Is there anyone who might need this more than you?'"*

"Aye!" answered one timid voice in the throng, then another.

"Aye, sir!" was Rog's intellectual contribution, craning his skinny neck and grinning stupidly. Sarra was at once relieved to see his smile, and pained that it had been so long since he'd shown it.

"I wonder, Friar, is there anyone else who needs any gold?"

The bald man shrugged theatrically, while the crowd called out once again, louder.

"I said, is there anyone here who could use a shilling or two?"

And the answer bellowed back, packing the room with noise and anticipation.

The showman backed up in affected shock, as if their voices had thrown him off his feet.

"Not so loud, friends!" he laughed. "We wouldn't want our voices to travel all the way up to the Sheriff, now would we?" Laughter, now, all around.

"I thought you killed the Sheriff!" shouted a young girl not much older than Hugh.

"I did, my lady," he responded. "And the Sheriff before him, too."

"Then what's taking you so long with this one?" came a deep man's voice, and the crowd erupted in agreement.

"All in good time, friends," and his smirk was all charm. "For you are my friends, are you not? Who here considers themself a friend of Robin Hood?"

Every hand in the building went up, every man and woman and child shouted out their love for the man, even as Hugh turned to Sarra and whispered, "*That's not Robin Hood.*"

"*I know,*" she whispered back, surprised he remembered.

They'd met the real Robin Hood once, when he visited Thorney. Back when he was only a rumor, back when Thorney was a place to call home and not a patch of ash. Before the winter, before the raids and the fire brigades, before hunger and the French Ward. But that Robin Hood had a soft face and a curious sort of humility. It was hard to believe the stories that he killed the Sheriff, and had been hanged for it.

But Robin Hood or not, this new fellow had the people's love. They stretched their hands to the air and called out, "*Friends, friends!*" Even Rog seemed happy to call this stranger Robin Hood, so long as there was a promise of coin.

"Then never let it be said," the-man-who-was-definitely-not-Robin-Hood knelt down to the floor, whipping a wet cloak up to reveal a small wooden chest, "that Robin Hood has ever neglected his friends!"

His toe kicked the lid open, one hand reached in and then flicked a few coins out, one by one by one, each touching the air gently before falling into the crowd. Sarra instinctively pushed herself against the wall as the room churned inside out, grasping and pushing and tumbling over itself. Despite her best effort to hold him, Hugh slipped right out of her arms and dropped to the ground to disappear into the mash of arms and legs.

Sarra steadied herself on a post, frantic for any sign of her son. The boy in the mud invaded her thoughts again, freezing her with the same empty sense of indecision. But the crowd calmed as winners claimed their prizes, and Sarra pushed the image of a trampled Hugh to the back of her mind. *He knows to come back.*

"Don't worry, there's more for all of you," Robin called out, quieting the room. "But I have to ask for a little help first. Do you suppose you can help me out?"

"Aye, we can!" came the reply. Expectant faces and open palms waited upon Robin's every movement.

"Those of you who received a coin, could you come forward, please? Let them through, make way now!"

He gestured them closer, and a few lucky bodies held their coins up proudly and formed a row before him. Five in total, though Sarra only recognized one—a curly-headed friend of Rog's by the name of Dane, a dockworker who'd shown them rare kindness.

Robin smiled at the winners. "My friends, I am happy to help you. After all, who else out there is going to help you out?"

"No one!" Dane answered, instantly earning Robin's attention.

"No one!" Robin snapped his fingers. "Why not the King, why doesn't he help?"

"He's in Austria!" came one answer.

"He's in prison!" came another. Both were true. Somewhere on the other side of the world, King Richard the Lionheart had been captured. But those still at home were the ones suffering for it.

"Why not the Sheriff, then?" Robin continued. "Why doesn't he help?"

"He's too busy taking our money!" was a gruff answer, followed by laughter.

"You have the right of it, friend." Robin smiled. "One quarter of everything, to pay for Richard's ransom! You have to be careful these days. I have two hands and two feet, and the Sheriff's like to take one as my payment!" The grumble that followed had only an empty mirth. The collections for the king's ransom was no mere tax. For many, surrendering a quarter of all their worth was the brutal snap of a branch long bent to its breaking point.

"Well I wish I could give these coins to you and ask for nothing in return," Robin continued, "but even Robin Hood needs help sometimes. You understand that, don't you?"

"Whatever you need," Dane answered for them. "Just name it."

"It's very simple, it's nothing really." Robin paused. "I need that coin back."

Dane chuckled, as did the crowd, but Robin held his hand out as the laughter faded into embarrassment.

"This coin?" Dane asked cautiously. "The ones you just gave us?"

"The very one."

His next laugh was smaller, dumber. "Is this a trick?"

"A trick, no. Call it a curiosity!" Robin clicked his tongue. "Right now that shilling is yours, and you may do with it anything you like."

"It's a crown, sir."

"A crown?" Robin's eyes widened in disbelief. "My, but I'm more generous than I thought! But it's yours, I won't take it from you. You've had it all of a minute but I'm sure you've already thought well on how you'll spend it, no? What will you do with it?"

Dane looked to the other four coin-bearers, but the question was clearly for him alone. When he spoke, there was doubt in his voice. "Food. Boots, maybe."

"Boots, maybe, that's good. That's good," Robin looked down, kicking his own dark leather boots against the chest. "Would you like *my* boots?"

"No, sir."

"Don't call me sir, I'm not a knight."

"No, sir. Er, no . . . m'lord."

"Even worse."

"Sorry . . . sorry."

"Hm."

Sarra wished very much that Hugh would find his way back to her.

Robin leveled his eyes on Dane, who buried his attention into the ground. "Food, you say? Nottingham has a Common Hall, does it not? Why aren't you there?"

Someone in the crowd answered angrily, "You have to be on the lists!"

"And they won't put certain types of people on those lists, will they?" Robin prompted them. "Deserters, gang members, . . . *tax evaders*, yes?"

An unsettling murmur rumbled in assent, while a few other titles were called out—other types of people who could be refused the charity of the Common Hall. Sarra hated that she flinched when the word *whore* was shouted.

"And with this damned ransom, everyone's a tax evader, aren't we?" Robin Hood smiled. "A crown's a fine amount, I'll bet you could pay your way onto that list for a crown. Is that what you meant when you said you'd spend it on food?"

"I hadn't thought about it."

"I'm aware of that." Robin suddenly raced through his words with precision. "So think about it now. You have a choice! You can give that coin to Nottingham, and to the Sheriff, and pay your way and feed yourself and be considered a lawful man. Or you can give it to me, as I ask for it, and show that you can be as generous as I am. If you are my friend, as you claim to be, why would you refuse to do for me that which I gladly did for you?"

Dane opened his mouth to answer, but Robin silenced him with one finger.

"But if you *do* give it back to me, know that you're choosing my side. Know that you would be considered an outlaw, as I am. An enemy of Nottingham. I will not *take* the coin from you, friend, it is yours. I simply want to know what you'll do with it, when I ask for it back."

Robin's hand extended again, just as before, and the room was ever silent. Even the steady patter of rain outside had somehow faded beyond Sarra's ability to hear it.

Dane resolved himself, the muscles at his jawline flexed. "I don't think I will, no."

"You don't think you will, what?"

"I don't think I'll give it back to you."

Robin Hood smiled. "And why not?"

"Because when you gave it to me, it was a gift." Dane swallowed, trying his best to look tall and proud. "I didn't ask for it. It was your choice to give it. But if you ask it of me, that's different. You always say that nobody should be able to take anything from us."

"Is that what I always say?"

Dane pursed his lips.

The greyhound man's fist smashed bloody across Dane's face and brought him to the floor.

Sarra lost her footing, her heart pounded furiously, and she gasped for air as the crowd reeled in horror. They had all gone blurry—*no, there were tears in her eyes*—and she blinked them away. Looking twice, she realized the attacker had not used his fist. He was holding a short bludgeon. He flipped the tiny club about in his hand as he heaved Dane back to his knees and pried the gold crown from his fingers.

"Who else received a coin?" Robin barked out, and the other four cowered. "I ask for it back. Do you give it to me?"

In unison they dropped and held out their hands, desperate to be rid of their incriminating prize. The man with the bludgeon gently reclaimed the crowns from two more coin-bearers, then turned with horrifying speed to crash his weapon onto the tops of both their skulls. Sarra screamed, but threw her hand over her mouth to keep from drawing any undue attention her way.

Hugh. She searched desperately for him, but couldn't avoid watching what was next.

One man and one woman remained, quivering, on their knees. The others cradled their heads, rolling in pain.

"I ask for that coin," Robin's ferocity was naked now, "will you give it to me?"

"I don't . . . I don't know," the next man whimpered. He pounded the coin onto the ground and turned to scramble away, but the greyhound man bounded over him and twirled the bludgeon by a short rope at its handle, slinging it up-ward into the man's chin. His teeth cracked loud enough to silence the room. Robin seemed startled by something, then wiped the fine spray of blood from his face.

There was still no sign of Hugh.

"I ask for that coin," Robin growled at his final victim, a thin woman with ratted black hair. "Will you give it to me?" By now, the friar had brandished a thick knife that kept anyone in the crowd from pretending to be a hero.

The woman stayed at her knees but straightened upright and bore herself into Robin's eyes. "Don't pretend to give me a choice!" she bellowed back at him, her volume masking her fear. "You'll hit me either way. You'll hit me if I give it to you. You'll hit me if I don't. You'll hit me if I do nothing. So hit me. Because you're going to. You're going to hit me because you're a bully." She clenched her neck. "You're going to hit me because you're a coward."

"No." Robin held his hand up, staying the greyhound. He crouched down on the balls of his feet to bring his face next to hers. "You've got it all wrong, love. You *did* have a choice. But you already made it."

He stood.

"I'm going to hit you because you took my money in the first place."

The bludgeon came up but Sarra closed her eyes before it fell, the sound was enough. The crowd panicked at long last—they'd been frozen in disbelief but now fell prey to hysteria. A few fled into the rain, but the rest were halted by Robin's voice.

"Quiet!" he shouted. "We are not done here! Nobody leaves."

Eventually the entire room buckled down, curling into balls, to be as small and unnoticeable as possible.

Sarra slipped down from her post and hid as well, then burst with relief when Hugh splashed out of the crowd and flung himself around her. His face was white, and she engulfed him in her arms that he might see nothing more. She closed her eyes as the tears ran hot down her cheeks and into her son's hair. But she could not close her ears.

"These five of you took coin from me, and have been punished." A moment or two of silence, save for the moans of those five. "But I threw six coins."

The room shifted, Sarra peeked out. Robin picked his way with care through the huddled bodies, a wolf stalking in the bushes. The greyhound signaled— just a nod of his head, really—but it led Robin Hood to stop directly in front of Sarra's husband.

"Show me your hands."

"I didn't get one, none."

Robin turned back for confirmation. "He does," the greyhound stated. "I watched him pick it up."

Back to Rog, Robin's face was all smiles. "Are you calling my friend a liar? We know you have it."

Sarra didn't have enough hands to stop Hugh from watching and also to muffle the whine that rose in her throat.

Rog kept his face stubbornly down, away, his fists behind his back, his mouth tight. He didn't respond when Robin Hood repeated the demand. Nor when the friar grabbed his shoulders and wrestled him to the ground. Rog simply stayed where he landed, unmoving, as if he could ignore himself out of the room.

"It'll be better here, you'll see."

You'll see.

The friar handed his knife to the greyhound, then revealed an iron hatchet from beneath his cloak.

"I'm not going to pry your fingers open like a child," Robin said. "You either give me the coin, or we'll take a king's ransom from you. One in four. You hear me, friend? We'll take your hand."

Rog made noises, they weren't quite words.

"Try that again, friend. Use a language this time."

"I-don't-have-anything."

"It's either in your fucking hand or you gave it to someone else, and I don't think it's the latter. Open your fist, then."

"I don't . . . I didn't . . ."

"God's cock, man. Give me the coin."

Someone braver than Sarra shouted, "He doesn't have it!"

Robin looked sideways at the greyhound a third time, who nodded again. Small, but with an absolute and grim certainty. Sarra wasn't the only one who knew Rog was lying.

Robin hesitated, but his voice was strong. "Alright, Tuck. Do it."

White funneled in from all sides as Sarra's vision closed tight on her husband. She felt somehow twenty feet tall, her hands impossibly large and numb, her stomach churned as her balance span, but somehow she kept watching, noiselessly, breathlessly, as they held Rog's arm across the wooden chest, a strap of leather went around his wrist, the greyhound pulled it tight and stepped on it, Rog's mouth was open, in pain, maybe, but his hand still a fist, and the friar knelt on him, one knee on his chest, and nobody helped *and nobody helped and-nobodyhelped* and the hatchet split flesh and bone but it didn't cut the hand off, no, it was left dangling by a strip of slick bloody meat and the friar nearly toppled as Rog screamed, the greyhound went down and kicked Rog in the ribs, they fought and kicked him again until his arm was braced back across the chest a second time and the hatchet chopped down once more, just missing the wrist as he squirmed, gouging deep in his forearm, a well of dark red pouring out, it wasn't until the third try that the hand came off and Sarra stared at her husband's blood, it was so much blood, and nobody helped and *he didn't even have a coin* and it was so very much blood and *Hugh was choking.*

Her son was gagging at her breast, struggling to be free, she'd been holding him too tight. She let him loose but held onto his cheeks—always too hard and never hard enough—preventing him from seeing his father's mutilated arm. Hugh coughed a mouthful of spit into his hands and gasped for air, then buried himself into her chest again.

Friar Tuck was hammering an iron spike through the palm of Rog's severed hand, nailing it high on the back wall of the Pity Stables.

Robin Hood, his face white, thrust a finger at it. "That's *mine* now! And it stays there. I'm starting a collection. If anyone tries to take it down . . ." He may have picked anyone at random to focus on, but it was Sarra's eyes he found. "Well, you've seen how I deal with people who take what's mine."

She could only barely feel its tiny uneven ridge through the shawl at her neck, slimy but firmly held in her son's little hands, but Sarra knew well enough that Hugh had coughed out a gold crown.

PART I

BLACK SNOW

ONE

ARABLE DE BUREL

ARABLE WAS STARING AT nothing.

"I see nothing."

"Good," Arthur whispered, next to her. "Let me know if that changes."

Crouching in earth still stained from the black snow, the three of them squinted uselessly into the distance. Despite Arthur's warnings that there was *something-they-had-to-see* ahead, the Sherwood Forest looked the same in every direction—an endless expanse of barren spires, its once lush canopy shorn both by winter and by flame. If Arable was expected to see anything other than desolation, she doubted she'd find it.

Arthur a Bland, too, bore the signs of their winter's famine. His frame was somewhat leaner, his red mane and beard somewhat mangier. Where he once looked like the type of thug who might beat you to death for frivolous joy, he now looked like the type to stab you to death for the coins in your pocket. *Perhaps that is not so large a distinction, after all,* Arable thought. She was still comparably new to trusting men such as he.

As Arthur eased to his feet and crept forward, David followed. They were two sides of the same coin. Where Arthur was gruff, David was supernaturally kind—so much so that Arable often wondered if she'd become an object of flirtation for him. A smile always lingered within the long features of David's face, and he kept his thin horse-mane hair tied back into a long blond tail. One would never fear being beaten or stabbed to death by him . . . but simply because David of Doncaster preferred the longbow over the knife.

These were Arable's friends now, and the worst part was that she sort of liked it.

"It's up a bit more." Arthur lowered his voice even further. "Best we stay silent until we're on it, just in case."

"Yes, but what *is* it?" she asked.

"Wha'd I just say now?" he replied in shock, his frozen grimace signaling the very serious start of their silence. Arable threw her hands up in frustration, causing David to smile, but not speak.

The boys moved with caution, searching for silent spots with each footfall, pausing behind whichever tree trunks seemed thick enough to hide their bodies. David held his spindly fingers aloft—the middle two encased in his lambskin archer's glove—to signal Arable for a safe moment to follow. She couldn't decide if they were being exceptionally diligent, or honestly afraid that every tree concealed an enemy.

It didn't matter. They were hiding from nothing.

Arable de Burel had been many things in her life. A handmaiden, a servant, *a thief*. A lady, a fugitive, *a traitor*. She'd been both a lover and a mourner—recently, and to the same person. She'd been as close to the top of society as she was now to its bottom, and she'd been to both extremes more than once. She'd lost her family, she'd fled more homes than she could count, and was intimately familiar with the terror of each day's hopes extending no further than the morrow.

But she had never, not even once, been afraid of trees.

"There's nothing there!" she proclaimed, and both Arthur and David dove for cover.

Ignoring their attempts to quiet her, she trudged forward with no care at all toward the noise she made. A plume of soot billowed in her wake, weeks of ash stirred into eddies as she kicked through the forest's debris. The deep smell of smoke permeated everything, and most of the Sherwood's naked trunks bore weeping black lines where they'd been discolored by rainfall. But up ahead was the only meaningful marker in the Sherwood—an area where first the trunks were scorched black, then into cracked and broken shards, and then finally to ruin.

They were at the edge of the Sherwood Road, and Arable's breath halted in her chest. She suddenly regretted her flippancy—if she'd known they were coming here, or anywhere she might be seen, then she might not have joined them. She'd been so thankful for Arthur's invitation, and a slight adventure in the forest had sounded like a perfect distraction. But seeing it now, and the wide road that might bring any traveler upon them, was too harsh a reminder of why they were hiding in the forest in the first place.

Beneath her feet was the story of the last six weeks, broken into char and ash. After Sheriff Roger de Lacy's funeral, fire brigades from the castle traveled the Sherwood Road daily, setting ablaze the trees on either side of it. Arable had worked with the remnants of Robin of Locksley's men, sending every Guardsman they found limping back to Nottingham. Will Scarlet had claimed the mantle of Robin Hood—and though nobody within the group had yet taken to calling him that, the Nottingham Guard would never forget the name.

But for every brigade they stopped, there were three more they never even knew about. Mile upon mile met the torch. The brigades only ceased when the weather turned too terrible to bear, but ash rained for a month. Smaller streams became poisoned, killing much of the wildlife they needed to survive, and what little natural food could be found was rendered withered and deadly.

Still they fought on—even if sometimes that meant no more than spreading the truth of what the Sheriff was doing. The Guard could take resources, but in doing so they made themselves more enemies. Once winter was over, Will Scarlet promised they would regroup, regrow their numbers from sympathetic villages, and flourish again. Until then, the momentum was well against them, and they tried to keep their encounters with the Guard short and safe. They did their best to turn scouting Guardsmen back to the castle by being just nuisance enough to be more hindrance than worth.

As the earth beneath Arable's boots turned from snow to slush to burnt bark, the Sherwood Road revealed itself through gaps in the trees, extending off to the north and south. Though it made a serpentine path through the Sherwood, the fires had extended the margins of the road tenfold on either side, where at last she saw the subject of Arthur's worry.

A large square patch of dark soil.

Ten paces long on each side, the area had been leveled and cleared of any offending refuse. At its center were the remains of a makeshift campfire.

"Keep your eyes open," Arthur commanded, emerging slowly from the trees, wary of the open space. "Might be gords nearby."

If there was indeed some regiment of the Nottingham Guard lying in wait for them—*which there wasn't*—she would be in far more danger than Arthur or David. Theirs were just a couple of unknown, bearded faces, and it was no crime for commonfolk to walk the Sherwood Road. But many in the Guard would recognize Arable on sight. Even those that didn't know her personally could identify her by the two straight scars defining her cheeks.

In Nottingham, she was famous for stabbing Captain Gisbourne in the back.

In Nottingham, she was known as the traitor who freed Will Scarlet from prison.

Thankfully—she exhaled in relief—there were no Guardsmen here to point any fingers.

"I don't see any tracks." David's voice was singsong. He craned his lean neck about to investigate the area. "Rained some, last night. If anyone's been here since, it'd be obvious."

"Well you can still keep your eyes open," Arthur growled. "I didn't say *get ready for a fight*, I just said *keep your eyes open*."

"Were you worried I was going to wander around with my eyes closed?" David returned. "Good thing you told me to keep my eyes open, that was a strategy I had not considered."

"For fuck's sake!" Arthur spread his hands out wide, but there was a smile behind his scowl.

"So why do we care about this campsite?" Arable asked.

Arthur had clearly been dying to answer the question. He raised a finger and outlined its square perimeter. "I don't think it's a campsite."

"There's a campfire." She pointed, rather certain she'd perfectly solved the mystery.

"True, but nothing else makes sense. It's too large an area, and why bother flattening it all down like this? Why a square? And who would make camp in the middle of ash, when they could take a few fucking steps into the woods?"

"Because it's flatter here."

"Nobody camps right next to the road," Arthur said with finality.

"And yet . . ." She splayed her fingers out at the campsite, which was, quite obviously, right next to the road.

David laughed, but he seemed to understand Arthur's point. The two of them reminded her sometimes of Reginold and Bolt, two Guardsmen she'd befriended in Nottingham before that life fell apart. It was curious how life worked sometimes, when the same patterns and relationships appeared in completely unconnected people. Their banter, the way they'd both tease her and include her, she'd known it before.

"I think it's an *outpost*." Arthur's eyebrows bounced. "The size of this footprint, right next to the road? I think they're planning to build something, maybe a little tower."

"A little tower?" David snorted. "So they can see the trees a little better?"

"I said *maybe* a tower. Something, is what it is."

"It is certainly something," Arable confirmed.

"There were people here when I saw it yesterday," Arthur defended himself.

"Guardsmen?" she asked.

His mouth twisted. "Couldn't tell. They weren't in uniform, but could still be workers from the castle."

Arable raised her most skeptical eyebrow.

"Don't act like this was a complete waste of time! There were tents, horses, too. Thought they might've left some food behind."

"Admittedly, that happens a lot." David shared his grin with Arable. "*Oh we've got too much food, why don't we just leave it here in the dirt? Better than putting it back in the pack, innit?*"

"Fuck you both."

"The Nottingham Guard has never stationed anyone in the Sherwood before," David said, then turned to Arable for validation. "Right?"

"Right."

"Well I've never kicked your teeth in before," Arthur cocked his head, "but that doesn't mean I couldn't."

"Oh, I am very tall," David proved it, "and you are not so flexible."

"I could bring your head to the ground first—" Arthur moved to tackle his friend, and the two of them slapped at each other and vied for leverage. But Arable was drawn toward the campfire's pit, and the tiny flecks of trash lingering at its edges. She crouched down to look closer.

"You might be right," she said, ceasing the boys' bickering.

"What?"

"Could be coincidence . . ." She picked through the ash at the side of the fire ring. There was an unnotable piece of twine charred at both sides, barely a finger long. "But string just like this . . . it's what we'd use to tie up bundles of food for Guardsmen going out on patrol."

David made a face. "A piece of string, that's proof?"

"No." She brushed her hands off. "But it's plausible."

Arthur snapped his fingers. "Which is exactly why I asked her to come."

"Thank you."

She hated to say that. She shouldn't have to thank them for considering her expertise valuable. Her history within Nottingham Castle was an asset, not a scandal, and taking advantage of her knowledge should have been an *obvious* strategy, not a clever one.

"So they're building outposts . . ." David squinted down the road. "What does that mean?"

Arthur inhaled heavily. "It means Will was right. Gords are moving into the Sherwood, hoping for a permanent presence. We've got to make sure they don't."

"But Will thought we had another month at least," David said, his focus far away. "Didn't think they'd move until winter was over."

"Sneaky little shits." Arthur crossed his arms. "But we'll be ready for them."

No, they wouldn't be. It was a death sentence, Arable knew it. They weren't ready for this. They'd been able to turn most prying Guardsmen away with little acts—stealing their food, loosing their horses, anything that forced them to return to the castle for supplies. But if the Guard fortified an area *inside* the Sherwood, that was a new set of rules. Scarlet's group couldn't stop them—not now, at least.

They had barely survived thus far. Some of them hadn't. There were elderly in the group who had passed. Most of their time was spent scavenging to survive, and they were failing at that, too. They simply didn't have the resources to go on the offensive. Arable had cast her lot in with the group at their worst hour, at the cost of burning every other bridge she had. She did not want to die with them, but she had nowhere else to conveniently do so.

"Aw, *fack*," David said suddenly, his eyes narrowing. Then, just as quickly, "Keep talking, don't act anything strange now."

This proved there was no more certain way to make Arable act like an imbecile than to order her to act normally. She had no idea what to do with her hands, her body somehow made five different poses at once, all while she struggled to understand why it was doing anything at all.

During her unintelligible display, David knelt down and unslung his longbow, quietly readying an arrow. He raised its tip directly to Arable's navel, then he drew the string back forcefully and pushed the bow forward, ready to spear a hole right through her stomach.

Arable's mouth waggled open, probably trying to escape the rest of her imminently doomed body. She prepared a masterful argument as to why she should not be murdered like this, which escaped her lips in the form of a discreet squeak. She had apparently forgotten how to breathe, too.

"And . . . *move*," David ordered, so she did.

The arrow sprang from the bow with sickening strength, missing her by a hairswidth. Her attention snapped to its flight, down the Sherwood Road a good distance to then vanish unimportantly into dense black thicket.

For more than a few seconds nothing happened, which seemed like such a good idea that nothing went ahead and kept on happening for a good while more. Still David didn't move, his eyes sharp and piercing down the road. Eventually he relaxed, but only for a breath—a heartbeat later, he nocked another arrow and sent it screaming after the first.

And as it flew, the tiny distant silhouette of *a man's body* rose from the thicket in question and retreated south down the Sherwood Road.

"Fack indeed." Arthur shook his head.

Somebody had been watching.

David started chasing the intruder, but Arable snatched his arm and turned him around. "Let him go," she urged. "We need to get away. Now."

David allowed himself to be drawn back into the woods from where they'd come, while Arthur let an impressive slurry of expletives fly. If it was a Guardsman, then more were nearby after all. And if not, they would come soon anyway, to start building their outpost.

This instinct, again, was something of Arable's expertise.

She'd spent her life on the run. Ever since Lord Beneger de Wendenal had decimated her father's home and chased every last Burel from England, Arable had been fleeing. It was ingrained in her soul—only half of her ever able to focus on the present, the rest of her always looking for escape paths, calculating the things that could go wrong.

So when she said it was time to run, *it bloody well was.*

TWO

QUILLEN PEVERIL

NOTTINGHAM CASTLE

BARE CASTLE WALLS DEFINED the corridors through which Quillen Peveril was half dragged by Lord Asshole. Months ago, those walls had been appropriately furnished with all the resplendent tapestries and ornamentation that befit a castle of Nottingham's notoriety. But such embellishments had been systematically removed by Sheriff William de Ferrers in light of the king's ransom collections. Whether each adornment had actually been sold for coin or simply moved into storage, Quill did not know. He disliked seeing the castle so naked, but in truth he did not care about decorations at all in this moment. He only focused on the missing tapestries because it was such a favorable alternative to looking at Lord Asshole's big asshole face.

"I have a big asshole face," he growled.

To be fair, these are not the words he said, but they were certainly the ones Quill heard.

The man's bloated and puckered facial features looked as much like an asshole as could be possible before one would have to pity it as a deformity. His nose excreted out and away from the rest of the face—a wise move on the nose's part—but then drooped down until it nearly touched the man's lip. The abrasion across the bridge of his nose was still wet and red, and blood crusted at both nostrils. Frankly, the wound was an improvement on the man's appearance, but there was little Quill could give the man that would improve his personality.

Lords like this one thought the world was theirs to shit upon.

They barreled into the captain's room unannounced. The chamber was well lit by two tall openings to the east, revealing a maelstrom of unsorted parchment on the desk that spoke to Fulcher de Grendon's disdain for clerical work. The old Sheriff, the old Captain, and half his Black Guard had been slaughtered by the villain Robin Hood. Those that replaced them were all new to their office, or—like Quill—to Nottingham as well. De Grendon had received the dubious promotion to Captain of Nottingham's Guard a month ago, but his military skills had not yet translated into administrative ones.

Lord Asshole did not stop, more likely a result of momentum than decision, pounding into the captain's desk. "Your name Captain Grendon?" he demanded.

Quill was impressed—here was a man so important he had no use for verbs.

The new captain, who was seated at his table with a palm over his forehead, blinked exactly once. "Your lordship, my name is *Fulcher de* Grendon," he corrected, sliding his hands back to fuss with the leather tie of his ponytail. "And I do happen to be Captain of the Sheriff's Guard, Nottingham."

"That's what I asked you," Asshole complained.

It wasn't.

"It wasn't," Quill had to say.

"Guardsman." De Grendon's stare lingered into a harsh command for obedience.

Quill put his hands up in a simple apology. "Very well. I concede there are more immediate problems to be discussed."

The captain squinted. "Such as the blood on his nose?"

Quill nodded. "Such as the blood on his nose."

"Such as the blood on my fucking nose!" Asshole was quite pleased with his creative addition to the sentence. "I've brought your man here to be reprimanded."

"Which I assure your lordship, he shall be." The captain fidgeted at his doublet, clearly unsure if this meant the conversation was over. "Thank you for bringing him to me."

"I showed him the way, actually," Quill corrected. "As he did not know where your office was."

"*Quillen.*" This time, Quill could see the red in de Grendon's eyes. He needed no further aggravating, not from Nottingham, not from Quill, and certainly not from his arrogant lordship.

"Apologies," Quill said, and the man seemed genuinely thankful for it.

"Well then, Guardsman." De Grendon's beady eyes blinked twice and he summoned one of his more captainly voices. "What exactly am I reprimanding you for?"

"He tried to arrest me!" Asshole raged, with all the grace of a cow rolling down a hill. "With no cause!"

"Not without cause." Quill raised a finger. "Simply without precedent."

De Grendon quieted them with a wave of his hand. "I'm sure this was a misunderstanding. I hope you can accept the Nottingham Guard's sincerest apology." His tone, however, had shifted from irritation to curiosity. "What did you attempt to arrest this man for, Guardsman?"

"Public defecation."

"Don't you lie!" Lord Asshole erupted, waggling his arms about uselessly. "Wasn't anything like that. I was taking a shit, is all."

"My mistake."

"You need to reprimand him immediately!" Lord Asshole continued his arm waggling. "Do you have any idea who I am?"

"The odds are staggeringly against it," Quill pointed out.

"I'm Lord Asshole of York," Lord Asshole announced. Again—to be fair—this wasn't what he actually said. But Quill had already equated the man's real name, Lord Brayden, with *asshole* so completely that he could no longer hear any distinction between the two. "And if I need to shit in your street, then I'll shit in your street."

De Grendon nodded the appropriate number of times for a sensible person to digest such a statement. No doubt these were not the sort of disputes he thought he would have to settle as captain. "And why did you need to shit in my street again?"

"God's balls, have you never had to shit before?"

"I have to shit right now," Quill told the ceiling. "But you'll notice I'm not. I suppose not everyone has my self-restraint."

"Remarkable," the captain agreed. "And you're in some way responsible for bloodying his lordship's nose?"

Quill answered with truth equal to pride. "Not just in some way, but in all the ways. I punched him in the face."

"Ah." Fulcher seemed to expect that, the faintest smile tugging the corner of his lips. "You know, you could have waited at least a sentence or two after boasting of your self-restraint to admit that."

"Point taken."

Lord Asshole caught up and blurted out, "He punched me in the fucking face! He needs to be reprimanded immediately!"

He blustered and blobbered about, forcing Quill to think of new words to describe his blumbibbery.

"I must admit," Quill crossed his arms, "I have acted in a manner most unbecoming of the Guard. I agree, you should reprimand me."

The captain nodded. "For punching his lordship in the face."

"Oh no. The man worked very hard to deserve that. I ought to be *commended* for that, not reprimanded. I should be *reprimanded* because my doublet was unfastened at the time."

More billabusting and bollybrustles from Lord Asshole. "What? You're a fucking idiot."

De Grendon's eyes narrowed. "It's not against the conduct of the Guard to have your doublet unfastened."

"Point of fact," Quill straightened himself, "it *is*. When my grandfather William Peveril was Sheriff, he penned the current conduct of the Nottingham Guard, which included a clause that all Guardsmen be well presented with *'clean vestments free of stain or soil, fastened with tight discretion.'*"

The captain swallowed, unconsciously checking the buttons of his own doublet. "I've never heard of that."

"Regardless, it was unmannerly of me and I should be reprimanded."

"Immediately," Lord Asshole demanded.

"Immediately," Quill agreed.

De Grendon returned to his desk, sat down, and shrugged. "I hereby reprimand you. Fasten your doublet, Guardsman. What else would you have me do?"

"My grandfather's charter of conduct states that the reprimand should be publicly announced by the city's heralds thrice daily for a period of two days, both in Nottingham and its neighboring counties."

This delighted Lord Asshole in the same way that most shiny things would. "So you'll be denounced in York, then?"

"To my utter shame, yes."

"That's much better. Let his name be dragged through the fucking mud."

De Grendon shared a brief look with Quill before turning back to their noble defecator. "His name is actually very well respected, both here and in York, your lordship. The Peverils are a founding force in Nottingham."

Even that was an understatement. Though the last few generations had receded to their estate at the Peak in Derbyshire, the castle in Nottingham was practically the Peveril family signature.

"Never heard of them," Lord Asshole laughed. "Besides, this little shit-squeak is nothing but a Guardsman, so how the fuck important can his family be? Sounds like it's time his name gets what it deserves."

With a final burst of bragglebouting, Lord Asshole convinced himself he'd won and turned sharply to leave.

Quill let the man get as far as the door before he cleared his throat. "Oh, one thing in addition, Captain. The charter is quite specific about the phrasing of the reprimand."

Fulcher smiled. "Guardsman?"

"It states the entirety of the offending act be included in the announcement."

Captain de Grendon closed his eyes, finally understanding. He drew a quill from his desk and uncorked an inkwell. "Very well. I shall have it known by every man and child in four counties that Quillen Peveril of Nottingham's Black Guard did have his doublet quite unfastened whilst punching Lord Brayden of York in the face for shitting in the street."

Lord Asshole treated his pants as he had the street. "Wait, what?"

Fulcher dismissed him. "Lord Brayden, your consent in this punishment has already been recognized. I thank you for bringing this matter to my attention."

"You can't announce that!"

"Guardsman," Fulcher fake-scowled, "consider yourself reprimanded."

It was a punishment Quill would have to bear. "I am most embarrassed, Captain."

"You can't . . . I'll be . . . you both . . ."

"No point in trying to string words together now," Quill patted him on the back, "when you've gotten so far in life without them. Also, don't shit in my fucking street again."

There was a bit more commotion to be had before the man was finally escorted out of the captain's office, but Quill spent most of it being too utterly pleased with himself to note any of it.

When at last they were alone, the captain laughed. "You've got more brat in you than I thought, Peveril."

"Thank you, Captain."

"When I first came on, you had one hell of a stick up your ass." Fulcher stoppered the inkwell and put the quill away. "Turns out you're damned good at sticking it up someone else's, too. Not sure what you got out of all this, though."

"Oh, it wasn't for me." Quill didn't care for compliments. "That was for all the people who saw him do it."

"You know we have more important things to do than shame nobles for doing their business in public."

"Do we?" He raised his eyebrows, thankful that this captain—unlike his predecessor—was open to criticism. "We're preparing some of the Common Guard to build outposts in the Sherwood, to capture the rest of Robin Hood's crew, yes? But that's not where the fight is. The fight—the *real* fight, the one we lost—is the favor of the people."

De Grendon's eyes shifted, but he did not contest it.

"Robin Hood showed the people that they didn't need their lords. Taught them those same lords didn't care for them. When they see a visiting noble shit on their street, do you think that helps? And now we're taking a quarter of everything they make to bring back a king they don't think loves them."

The captain shrugged. "That's life."

"No," Quill matched him. "That's how rebellions start."

Outside the window, some noise swelled and left again. De Grendon seemed to take it as a sign he was right. "What do you know about how rebellions start?"

Because I know how to read, Quill almost answered, but thought better of insulting a good man. He had not brought the Peveril name back to Nottingham to play Guardsman, but to assess its stability. Quill could return home whenever the whim struck him; though his father would think unkindly if that whim struck prematurely. His father had no desire to coddle Nottinghamshire back to health, but Derby would suffer if Nottingham had an unstable leader. Reclaiming the sheriff's title could be the Peverils' prerogative. And as far as Quill could tell, the current sheriff—William de Ferrers—was a skulking little sapling who only made things worse.

"I'm sure you've heard the stories that there's a new Robin Hood," Quill said. "And this one's more teeth than smile."

"We'll hang him. Like we hanged the last one."

That strategy was exactly what Quillen Peveril was worried about.

"Which do you think the Sheriff will run out of first, then?" He paused at the captain's door. "Robin Hoods, or rope?"

THREE

ARTHUR A BLAND

SHERWOOD FOREST

IT WASN'T THE FIRST time Arthur thought about it, not by a fucking spit-shot. But it was the first time he said it out loud.

"I should leave."

He let the words slip out and they were suddenly real, though broken into meaningless grunts as he hustled through the Sherwood's understory. Arthur was tired, he was hungry, and he did not goddamned have to be.

I should fucking leave. But David would hate him.

Even now, even as they sprinted back to camp after being spotted at the gord outpost, David was smiling. *Fucking smiling.* He was, impossibly, always like that. Despite every fool adventure and brush with death they'd been through together, David still smiled at sunsets and sang to himself and told jokes. And if David could stomach more of this, then Arthur had no right complaining none neither. They'd been through Locksley together, watched it burn together, survived everything since together. They'd been tied up and gagged together, watched their friends die together, and they'd keep on pushing together until they got killed together, probably doing something fucking stupid together like *not leaving when they should, together.*

But the world was better when there was someone watching your miserable back, and David had his.

"We probably don't need to run," Arthur huffed out, without slowing. "Whoever saw us at the build site . . . I don't think they're following."

"They're not following," David answered, bouncing beside him, "because we're running. Why change what's working? Sides, running's good for you."

"A twisted ankle ain't." Arthur pivoted to glance behind. "And Arable's struggling. We can slow down for her."

With a shrug, David the stallion slowed from a gallop to a canter.

"You ought to put on some muscle," Arthur complained, "so you can be slow like me."

They continued on for a while, weaving through barren trees across uneven ground, following the distant line of the ravine that would lead them back to the camp. Once Arable caught up with them, she was the first to brave the question. "Any thoughts on what happens next?"

"That's for Will to decide," Arthur answered.

"I say this is a good thing," David said, his face calculating. "Well, not a *good* thing, it's clearly not *good,* you know, but it's a kick in the shin, innit?"

Arthur eyed his friend in silence until he was certain those were the actual words he'd spoken. "First you say running's good for us, and so is getting kicked in the shin? Someone raised you wrong."

"Well, we've been in a slump of late," David explained. "We knew things'd be harder as winter moved on, but right now all we're doing is surviving. Will might actually be thrilled about your little tower."

"I never said it was a—"

"Because we've got to do something about it, right? And *now*. Organize a group to watch it, disrupt supplies, maybe look for others like it, you know? This . . . this is what we're good at."

As always, David had a point. If the Nottingham Gord could be ready to go on the offensive again, then *damn it,* so could Robin Hood. Will Scarlet promised them, come spring, that he'd build a network of companies spread all across the Sherwood. Said he knew how to do it, they just had to get through winter first. But snow or not, the gords had just declared the end of winter. Which meant it was time for them to come out of hibernation.

Arthur picked up his pace.

Arable excused herself when they finally neared the camp. She kept her privacy away from the main group, and was likely only the better for it. More than a few times Arthur had thought upon living at the edges himself, maybe even spending time with Arable. She'd proven herself useful, and sharp, and able to take a fucking joke. The rest of the group thought she was the source of their foul luck, but the rest of the group were limp-wrist skivers who'd thought Robin of Locksley could magically make their troubles go away. Arable was more realistic, like Arthur. Though he'd learned long ago that women were not wont to enjoy his company unlessing they'd asked for it first. And he was ever too busy anyhow, given that he and David bore the brunt of keeping the others alive.

They came upon the first of the group in the ravine, half-naked and bathing in knee-deep water that was more like to kill than clean them. Nobody liked being dirty but neither had anyone ever died from it. The near bank was steep to the water, so he and David had to carefully pick their way down.

John Little, bare chested and tying his breeches as he walked, bellowed a greeting up as he heard their commotion. Despite their rationing, John was large as ever, his big wet belly slogged side to side. "Slap the wet off, ladies," John called to the others. "The boys are back early."

"We'll be down in a minute!" David yelled, one of his boots slipping a bit.

"You two should be glad you missed this!" Will Stutely shouted. He was nearly unrecognizable wet, the wild plume of his hair and beard matted down into some sort of bog beast.

"Indeed," John added. "Worst idea anyone's ever had!"

"Was your idea," hooted Charley. Skinny little Charley Dancer clearly took to the cold as much as one would expect from his nickname—the *frogman*. He grinned against the frigid air and splashed out to dry land.

"That's right, it was my idea!" John slapped both sides of his face. "A rare exception to a lifelong streak of brilliance. Not to be used against me."

"Come now, John," Charley was grinning, "you can't be cold if I'm not cold!"

John grabbed the frogman's little waist and shook him like a twig. "Of course you're not cold, there's nothing to you. Look at how much more body I have to keep warm! There are parts of my body, important parts, that I can't even feel right now."

Charley croaked. "John, you can't *see* those parts anymore neither."

Arthur was surprised to see Charley's bulgy eyes and squat face actually having fun. Ever the outsider, the man was skittish in a crowd and kept strictly to himself. Tuck was there, too, and the Delaney brothers, all shivering from their brisk morning dip. But Arthur had no intention of joining them in their latest fatal contest of idiocy. He and David made the final few jumps down the incline to flatter ground.

"We need to muster everyone." He was near out of breath. "We had a run-in with the Guard, and they're up to something."

It was met with groans and protestation, a bit of stomping in a circle from the oaf Stutely, but nothing that resembled surprise. Lately, *every* day brought bad news—it was really only a question of what form it took. The group begrudgingly dressed and ambled back upriver, toward the main bulk of the camp.

"How does it take to the cold?" Tuck motioned to Charley's lame leg as they made their way.

"Lovely." Charley squinted back. "Can't feel it at all. Your arm?"

"Hm." The friar touched his elbow that'd been broken last year and smugged himself into further superiority. Arthur sneered at him. It didn't feel good to sneer, he knew it made him an asshole to do it. But Tuck was cradling his arm as if he'd suffered worse than any of them. He was alive, at least. There were some who'd lost nearly everything and were still working day and night. The only thing Tuck ever contributed to the group was empty stories about some fucking God who loved them despite the daily proof against. Thought this meant he was pulling his own weight, rather than dragging them down further.

Tuck was the last of them that had right to complain.

And who was the first, then?

That was the real question.

There was one poor bastard who had suffered the most, and he was still here. Still leading them.

The camp was a camp in name only. An onlooker might have thought it the aftermath of a battle, and in a way they'd be right. Bodies were strewn slapdash across the broken terrain, easily mistaken as dead. There was nothing resembling organization or purpose. Those that bothered to build shelter used little more than a few branches and a stretch of tattered fabric.

John Little called them to gather, though most simply propped a head on an elbow, or did not rise at all. Arthur doubted they'd see this news as the *good thing* David did, but any change from their current situation had to be a good one.

Arthur summarized their encounter for those who were close. "They're invading the Sherwood," he finished. "So I'd say we've got to move quickly."

"There's no point."

Arthur startled, unsure who had said it. All eyes turned to the back of the crowd, where Will Scarlet shook his head numbly and said it again. Though his words were *"There's no point,"* they dripped with insult. He meant, *"It's hopeless."* He meant, *"We're going to die anyways."*

He pushed through the crowd until he was inches from Arthur, ignoring the others. "You were right, then." Not a question.

Arthur nodded. "Nottingham Guard is building."

And Will Scarlet's face sloughed, his body sat down on the ground.

He was having one of his bad days.

"You're not ready for my brand of outlaw," he'd promised back in December, when they thought the world was theirs to steal. And some days he lived up to that promise, driven with a crystal-clear certainty. But more and more lately, every day was a gamble. Some days he festered at the edges of civility, sniping comments with deadly accuracy. Some days he'd hunt with Arthur and David and garner their greatest spoils, but took little for himself. Some days he'd pay special attention to Arable's well-being, other days he loathed her very name.

But even on his good days, there was little of that invincible boyish brat Will had been before becoming Robin Hood. Before Much and Alan and Locksley. Before Elena. That man had crumbled, and what walked in his place was debris. He was barely even recognizable, hidden beneath a ragged blond beard and a month of grief.

The crowd waited to see if Will Scarlet had any more instructions. "We have to leave," he said at last, to the ground. "If someone saw you—as you say— we have to pack up and move camps. Again. We move within the hour." Then he burst up again and stormed away silently. People made room for him as though he were on fire. Some would argue he was.

David gave a piteous frown. "What do you think?" he whispered.

"He's in a mood," Arthur answered. "That's where he wants to be."

So John Little gave the order again, ignoring Will's lurk. "Get to it, then. Off we go."

With every knuckle of depression, the group dispersed, as if this were the final fall of the axe. They'd reacted the same way a week earlier, and before that, again and again. It would happen again a week from now—they'd gather whatever belongings they had, pack what they could into whichever sacks were still continent enough to carry weight. Existing only to break down whatever small amenities they'd built for themselves in the willowbank, to tie their shredded boots tighter about their ankles. To pick which items were no longer worth carrying and abandon them. To slog on.

"To hide," Arthur added, aloud. He'd thought this news would be a call to action, not the bell of a funeral dirge. They were in a loop of hell, an unrelenting repetition of misery.

And I do not have to be here.

* * *

IT DIDN'T TAKE LONG for Arthur and David to pack. They'd become experts at impermanence. He'd long learned that if they waited for every last person to be "ready," they'd be waiting a week. It was best to start their travel in a trickle, letting the strongest lead the way and force the others to hurry. This also gave those that harbored a desire to slink away the opportunity to vanish forever.

If they all left without me, Arthur wondered, *would I bother to follow?*

"We should build a castle next time," David said cheerily.

Arthur was familiar with each of those words, but they had no business living in that order. "What?"

"We should build a castle," his friend repeated. "Rather than move every week, we should just build a castle and stand our ground."

"I think castles take longer than a week to build."

"Hm." David chewed it over. "But you don't know?"

"If you're asking if I've ever personally—"

David clapped and folded his arms. "I'm gonna build a castle."

Arthur might have said more, but Will Scarlet made his way closer. His pack was full, and he pushed against his knees with both hands as he ascended the steep ridge. He didn't stop by them, nor so much as grunt a greeting.

"Gords are building," Arthur said after he'd passed. "We've got to stop them."

The figure climbed two steps more, and paused. "We can't."

"You said we could."

It was just Will's back, no more. "I thought we'd have more time, Arthur. Another month, at least. We could've recruited some more men from the villages, train them. But . . . but we're everyone. We can barely keep them alive, much less *fight back.* We're just . . . we've got to move."

Will Scarlet pushed off again, and Arthur exchanged an uneasy glance with David.

"He'll think of something," David urged, as if sensing Arthur's thoughts. "You'll see. I'm gonna get that castle."

Scarlet was first over the edge, and Arthur was halfway up the ravine bank himself when Friar Tuck's raspy nasal whine caught him. "You can't leave yet!"

Arthur didn't turn around to reply. "They'll catch up."

"You can't leave yet," Tuck repeated. "Lady Marion isn't back yet."

A shiver took a little romp through Arthur's body. It wasn't the idea of waiting that irritated him, it was the implication that Marion ought to make the call. She hadn't spent the entirety of winter with them. She'd frequently left for days on end—a week, even—while the rest of them froze. She ate well and did not suffer as they had. This day she'd gone out for a friendly walk as if the morning was made for picnicking instead of survival. Her bodyguard, Sir Amon Swift, also enjoyed a fairer life, rather than lending his desperately needed strength to keeping the group alive.

"She should be back soon enough," Arthur answered, and heaved up the incline.

"If the Nottingham Guard truly is nearby . . ."

"She'll be fine." He stared at Tuck's angry little face, his beard shooting out like an animal's whiskers. "Besides, isn't your god watching out for her?"

Tuck snorted. "He's your God, too, whether you like it or not."

At that, he had to laugh. "Well I wish he wasn't, then. Seems he hates us of late. Have you tried praying lately? That ought to make life a bit easier."

"We have to trust in Him."

"That's right, *he loves us all*, doesn't he? Has a terrible way of showing it."

It was the same helpless-maiden routine, with a different savior. People waiting for Robin Hood to save them. Waiting for God. Waiting to be saved rather than lifting a finger for themselves.

"He *does* love us all," Tuck insisted, because of course he had to. "Despite us, our faults."

"Well if I had a woman who loved me half the way your god loves us, I think I'd find me another woman."

"If you'd already found one woman," David chimed in next to him, "then you wouldn't have enough coin to find you another one."

Arthur wagged a finger at his friend. "First order of court, fuck you. Secondly, all I'm saying is that it must give you pause, no?" He threw what he hoped was a piercing gaze down upon Tuck's ugly little bald head, who answered by way of clenching his jaw. "Maybe your almighty man in the sky isn't there at all, or that he doesn't give the first fuck about you? Or maybe the gords in Nottingham prayed harder than we did last night? Or worse, that my grandmother's pagan gods are up there instead, laughing themselves to shit-all as they listen to you praying to the wrong jackass?"

Tuck didn't flinch, he just nodded and accepted it. He looked over his shoulder, the entirety of the camp behind him, readying themselves for another day's miserable march. The friar somehow seemed inspired by it.

"Any halfwit can complain about the hard times," Tuck said. "There's no genius in pointing out the very obvious. Our lives are not now what we'd like them to be, and you suppose it takes a brave man like yourself to blame someone else? Well that's fine. Do it. Complain all you like about how our troubles are proof the Lord hates us, shout it out as loud as you can. I'll listen to every word, I promise I will, if you make me one promise in return. For every good moment, for every bite you eat, for every night you sleep safely, for every healthy breath you take, for every day your friends laugh at your jokes instead of telling you how intolerable you are . . . give Him credit for that, too. Every time you want to blame Him for the bad, or say He must not exist since He hasn't personally attended to your every passing fancy, you must also thank Him for the fact you're alive enough to have such thoughts. You think the troubles you count outweigh the blessings you don't?"

Arthur would've responded, but he didn't have the hundred years it would take to get through the friar's skull. By Tuck's argument, if Arthur were to lose nine of his fingers, he should be thankful to still have the one. A fine theory for a victim, but a man who thought that way would never be anything else. Tuck couldn't see the shittiness of their truly shit situation because he'd spent his life blinding himself to reality. Arthur was happily miserable because he was smarter. To know misery is to know exactly what you need to fix.

Tuck continued, not realizing that nobody cared. "Of course I doubt, to answer your question. That's why we call it faith. And do you? *Doubt*, that is? Do you look at the arrogant little pile of bitterness you've built up in yourself and wonder if maybe there might have been a better path for you? Do you ever watch someone pray, amazed at the solace and comfort they find in the Lord, and realize you've never known that kind of peace? You have your laugh at me for keeping faith, and yet you seem so very very sure I'm wrong. What makes your belief better than mine? Tell me, Arthur, do *you* ever stop to wonder if perhaps *you* might be wrong, every time you open your damned mouth?"

Beside him, David put a fist to his lips to cover his laughter.

"I'm not intolerable," Arthur grumbled, but he plopped to the ground and consented to wait.

FOUR

QUILLEN PEVERIL

NOTTINGHAM CASTLE

FROM THE HIGHEST RAMPARTS, the city of Nottingham was too far away. The three-tiered baileys of the castle cascaded down Castle Rock, leaving even the closest structures of the real city well behind several barriers of curtain walls and gates. Good for protection, but terrible for governing. It was too easy up here to forget the troubles on the other side of those walls. Quillen's grandfather had famously left the castle every day to walk the city streets, something the opportunistic new Sheriff would be terrified to do. Quill leaned over the edge of the battlement as far as possible, loving the streams of white smoke that pulsed up from a hundred chimneys and braziers in the city, but hating the serenity they implied. This soft pleasant cloud of the city's breath gave no indication it was poisoned and coughing itself to death.

"Hello, city," he said, mostly confident there was nobody nearby to hear him. "What shall we fix today?"

The city, rudely, did not respond.

Fortunately, Quill didn't need it to. Like any decent physician, he could divine the source of a problem with or without his patient's help. Which was—like it or not—why he was here. *"Nottingham and Derby are sisters,"* his father had explained, *"and what ails the one will be caught by the other."* If Nottingham needed it, the Peveril family would reluctantly intervene. It was up to Quill to decide if that was necessary.

Along the keep wall he chanced upon Jacelyn de Lacy, another member of the Black Guard. Jac was a curious case—a hard woman with a face half-paralyzed by some childhood ailment. Older than him, he guessed, but it was hard to know if her deformity aged with the rest of her. Neither Quill nor Jacelyn had the peacekeeping experience to deserve their position, but such it was with beggars and choosers.

"Still here, then?" he asked, the customary greeting between them.

"You, too?" was always her response. "Help me with this."

She carried a long roll of burgundy cloth with gold trim, but she set it down and gestured to two chains draped over the front edge of the battlements, fastened to iron mounting rings on their side. They each took one, hoisting in unison the heraldic banner suspended below.

"Confound it, have we been conquered?" he asked.

"Just replacing it. Sheriff's orders," she answered, without even the smallest smile. "This one tore itself to shreds in the last storm."

Indeed, the king's standard they soon hauled up and over the battlements was in pieces, clinging onto its horizontal pole for dear life. Quill tried to ignore the obvious symbolism. "This is really the best use of the castle's coin? Pretty new flags for the Sheriff?"

She paused before untying the banner's knots. "I'm sure you'd rather I not remind you that you owe him fealty."

"You'd be right. I'd rather you not." Somewhere in the high keep, the Sheriff William de Ferrers was likely stuffing the soles of his boots. The youngest Sher iff in history by a decade at least, his claim to the title was only an emergency measure. Quill intended on sticking around to see who would replace him— either to influence that choice, or to determine if his father should politick for the seat himself. But Ferrers unfortunately also bore the distinction of being Earl of Derby—which made the Peverils his bannermen, as backward an ar- rangement as that was. "He can't keep the seat here for long. I think Chancellor Longchamp would have made a permanent appointment already if not for this distraction of King Richard's capture."

Jac just shrugged and concentrated on the banner. Neither of them, strictly speaking, should be doing such menial work. Serving in a guards' barracks— even the "elite" company of the Black Guard—was an inglorious life and well beneath Quill's station. But it afforded him the position to watch over Notting- ham's inner workings; and when two Sheriffs are killed in quick succession, those inner workings become suspect.

As for Jacelyn's part, the first of those two dead Sheriffs had been her uncle.

He shifted toward her. She'd pulled out a knife and was sawing at a par- ticularly troublesome knot. "You hear there was another *Robin Hood* sighting in Parliament Ward last night?" he asked.

"If I *hadn't* heard that," she glared at him, slashing through the fabric, "you'd be sorry you weren't the one to tell me." Her uncle Roger de Lacy had been killed by a simple thief named Will Scarlet, who escaped prison and took the name of Robin Hood, making minor troubles in the forest. "But I already looked into it. Wasn't him, just a bunch of children. Almost threw radishes at us until they realized they didn't want to lose their dinner."

"These sightings in the city, they're not all children," Quill said, unsuccess- fully prying his fingers into the stubborn ties of the old banner. "Sheriff Ferrers hanged Robin of Locksley, but he only killed the man. The name survived, and is ever more difficult to catch."

Would that a Robin Hood would show up and do unto this new Sheriff as he had done to his predecessors.

Jac finished with the ties and tore the banner free. "If someone new wants to call himself *Robin Hood* in the city, then he's FitzOdo's problem, not mine." The Sheriff had tasked Sir Robert FitzOdo and his men with hunting down any Robin Hood rumors, which were usually fruitless. "But Will Scarlet is hiding in the Sherwood, and he's the one I care about."

Quill suppressed any reaction. Both of them were only using their positions for their own devices.

She wasn't one for small talk, but as they went about tying the new banner to the pole, Jac allowed him to recall his morning's experience with the good Lord Asshole. Exactly half of her seemed to find it amusing. "Going for the little victories today, are we?"

"Any victory is a good victory," Quill quoted, assuming anyone important had said it before him. "They add up over time, as do the losses. Aim to have victories, then."

Jacelyn didn't argue it, she just stood and stretched her back, looking out over the city with him. "The tax certainly doesn't help."

"Not a tax," Quill corrected her. "A ransom."

"Feels like a tax."

"Try not to call it that, though. Taxes comes from within England, from the Chancellor. This ransom comes from Austria. The people have every right to be incensed about it. But if you call it a tax, they'll be incensed at the wrong people."

"I could call it bullshit," Jac suggested, "and then I'd be right?"

"That you would." Quill stared away again. "*Bullshit,* as we've already been bled dry by the war tithes. *Bullshit* upon Austria for laying hands upon any holy crusader, much less our king. *Bullshit* to set the ransom at such an irrationally high price, and the greatest *bullshit* of all that the Chancellor actually chose to pay it! If heaping bullshit upon bullshit could somehow make the former bullshit bullshittier than it was before, only then could it adequately describe the bullshittery of being a proud Englishman in times such as these."

"Or English*woman,*" he added hastily.

They placed the pole on the battlement ledge and—rather than lower it gently with the chains—simply nudged it to fall over the other side. A second later its tethers went taut and it snapped in place, the fresh new banner unfurling against the wall of the high bailey. A red sea with three lions rampant, the king's heraldry—no longer torn to shreds. "A waste of coin," Quill repeated.

"People need to respect it," Jac replied. "Lest they forget the king is still alive."

"Hm." He looked down at the crumpled pile of the old banner. "What should we do with this one, send it to Austria? Let them throw it in a cell?"

At this, finally, Jacelyn cracked a smile. "I heard that King Philip offered Austria half as much just to keep Richard locked up for another year."

Quill had heard the same. *Sixty-five thousand pounds of silver.* Higher than any man could fathom—equivalent to three years' worth of England's total income. "It's been a thousand years since France was known as Gaul, but they've apparently spent all that time practicing their gall."

She somehow didn't appreciate how clever that had been. That was her loss.

"Interesting." Jac cocked her head. "Derby."

Quill had no idea how the two were connected. "Excuse me?"

"Derbymen." She nodded to the east, where a half-dozen bannerettes from Derbyshire, full green with silver trim, were marching unexpectedly through the middle bailey. "Friends of yours?"

"Not likely." Quill reoriented himself from their idle banter into a tepid alarm. He squinted but could not see any further hint of the visitors' identities. Ten men, perhaps—enough for a single lord's retinue. He allowed himself the brief hope that the visitors were from his own family, from Peveril Castle. But he knew better; if his father had any actual desire to be in Nottingham, then Quill wouldn't be here watching it for him. The contingent below was a question mark . . . which happened to be one of Quill's favorite things.

"Shall we investigate?" Quill chirped brightly and started moving, inviting Jacelyn to follow.

IN THE MODEST TOME that should someday be written about Quillen Peveril's life, he hoped his intrepid chronicler could capture his skill at preparing for every circumstance. He certainly did not pretend to have any sort of clairvoyant foresight, but he was proud of his ability to anticipate different outcomes so that he might never be caught off guard. In the rare circumstance where he found himself genuinely surprised, he had learned to hide that reaction. His father had taught him chess at an early age, using an invincible defense of always appearing to expect Quill's every move. It was a ploy, of course, and one that Quill learned to master.

This is why he was so embarrassed to gasp and sputter for words when he descended the narrow stairwell halfway to the training yard, where he found himself face-to-face with a man he never expected to see there, waving a thick knife wantonly between them.

"I swear to every god, every one there ever was, that I will gut you like a fish if you don't remove yourself from my path."

The man was tall, and he had a knife, and those were his only two definitive physical qualities. The rest of him somehow flirted between extremes; his frame was lean but sturdy, his face was deeply weathered but had soft edges. Even his hair was both silver and black, including his tight beard. His eyes might have been gentle if they were not busy being so furious.

"Garble bobble," Quill's mouth said.

This is not an accurate account. What's important is that he did not use any of the greetings he'd crafted as he and Jac descended from the upper keep's ramparts. He'd prepared a subtle barb disguised as politesse if the visitor was William de Ferrers's wife, which he had calculated was most likely. He'd whipped up a wonderfully nonchalant greeting for any member of his own family, despite the low odds. He even had an easily adaptable jab he could customize for any notable knight returning home conspicuously early compared to their imprisoned king.

But Quill had no response for the breathtaking rage of a bereaved father.

"I don't intend on repeating myself," swore Lord Beneger de Wendenal. This man's son—*his last surviving son,* if Quill remembered correctly—had only been Sheriff for a month before Robin of Locksley took his life.

"Put your weapon down," Jacelyn ordered from behind, revealing a fat dagger of her own. She likely didn't know the elder Wendenal, nor realize how much she had in common with him. Both of them the surviving kin of dead Sheriffs—and the only real legacy of the name *Robin Hood*.

It was all Quill could do to summon words back to his command. Lord Beneger had no need to be armed at all—he could simply request an audience in the castle and be welcomed with the honorifics of his station. If he was *expecting* to be stopped, that spoke volumes of his reason for being here. "Your lordship, one moment please. You know me—"

"*What did I just say?*" Lord Beneger snapped, every inch of his face twisting red. He slashed his knife riotously across the stairwell where it sparked against the stone wall and shattered in his hand. He pushed forward, swinging the broken hilt and pressing into Quill, and Jacelyn heaved against them both until they clattered down a few more stairs. Lord Beneger's eyes were wide and unfocused, his hand bled freely, he clambered to his feet but slipped, driving upward, and Quill felt a pit of horror in his stomach. The man was untethered—but at the same time, driven with spectacular precision.

"Your lordship! Lord Wendenal!" he shouted, trying desperately to align his own face into the man's line of sight. "Look at me, your lordship! You know my family, I mean you no harm!"

"Family?" The word seemed to burn him, but his pupils constricted as they found Quill's. "*Family?* Who are you to tell me . . . who are you . . . who in hells upon hells are you?"

"Quillen Peveril, your lordship," he said, as calmly as he could justify. "The Peverils. I have been to your estate with my father many times. We went hunting together for midsummer, three years ago. You showed me how to lay snares when I was a boy."

He fumbled for other memories. He did not want to say, *I was at your son's funeral, and you were not.*

Wendenal fumed, but his senses returned. "Peveril, yes. I do know your father." But that swung him into a far more exacting direction. "And your father knows me. And if he knew that you stood in my way at this moment, in this very place, then he would not grieve to hear that I dashed your skull against the wall without a thought. So stand out of my way, boy, while you can."

Though his words were sharp, Quill knew the man to be a better arbiter of judgment. He was a true force of will in Derbyshire, with indomitable resolve.

A natural leader. With an ironclad purpose.

"*Move,*" Lord Beneger repeated.

"You misunderstand me, your lordship." Quill readjusted his stance. "I do not intend to stand in your way at all. If you tell me you're headed to Sheriff de Ferrers's office . . ." he took a breath to notice Lord Beneger's twitch at the name, confirming his calculations, ". . . then I intend to show you the way."

Wendenal stared at him, unmoving, probably wondering if the offer could be trusted. From behind him, down the short stairs that led to the training yard, a commotion simmered. The lord's name was being called with some immediacy. Curiosity forced Quill to glance out a slivered opening in the stone wall, where he could see a semicircle of Beneger's men protecting the entrance of the stairwell below. Their weapons were sheathed, but a crowd of Nottingham's Common Guard began to gather, wondering if they were expected to do something about it. The defensive circle tightened slightly, allowing three of its members to disappear into the stairwell, where they would come across Quill in mere seconds.

Their voices arrived before they did, but if they affected Lord Wendenal's decision in any way, he showed no sign of it.

"Please, your lordship," Quill whispered. "Let me help you."

A quiet eternity passed, and then the tiny space was all too crowded with intense men. But Wendenal raised a hand. "Alright, Peveril," he said, straightening himself. "Lead the way. Just the two of us."

Quill nodded solemnly to Jacelyn, who was left in the impossibly awkward position of staring at the three Derbymen in the middle of the stairwell, each of them unsure who was supposed to have the advantage. He led the way back to the high tower toward the current Sheriff's office, bringing along the man who—if Quill had calculated correctly—would command it next.

FIVE

MARION FITZWALTER

SHERWOOD FOREST

MARION KNEW SOMETHING WAS wrong the moment they returned to camp. The sounds were off, there was anticipation in the air like a lightning storm. At first she thought it her imagination—a paranoia that something would undoubtedly ruin the tremendous news she'd come to share. But Sir Amon clearly sensed it, too. His blade was already drawn, and he motioned for her to stay back.

Horrors filled her head, of course, that their day had finally come. It was only a matter of time before the Nottingham Guard crashed through their camp, ending with blood their winter chase—which was specifically why her news was so critical. To think that the rug would be pulled out beneath her now, when she was finally so close to saving them all, was more than she could bear.

But as the camp drew closer, Marion's alarm faded. The only terror evident in her companions' faces was that of surviving another day. They were breaking down their battered tents and tying meager bundles of food into their packs. Campfires were doused. Down by the stream, deerskins were being filled with water.

They were on the run again.

Yesterday, it might have broken Marion's heart. The pain of seeing her people suffer—despite her efforts to help them—had no name. Their nomadic status had degraded with each week, and the victories they'd collected at the top of winter did nothing to fill their bellies now. Most of this group had no quarrel with Nottingham, but suffered the Sheriff's wrath, nonetheless. Yesterday, moving camps would have meant they were one rung closer to the bottom of a ladder overhanging an abyss, the Nottingham Guard stomping down on their knuckles.

But today, it meant they'd be ready to travel as soon as possible, to the new home she'd found for them.

"Help me gather them," she commanded Amon, who nodded and went to it.

She craned her head to search for Will Scarlet, but he was already upon her. His mourning beard had overtaken his entire face, his eyes barely visible like two baby birds in a nest. He rushed through an attempt to bow to her. "Sorry to interrupt your morning stroll, m'lady," he said, all sarcasm.

Marion had never been a mother, but she suddenly had the urge to smack some sense into her child. "I see you're in a mature mood this morning."

"I see you're in a bitch mood this year."

She wasn't going to let him bitter this. She turned, searching for anyone less useless. "Tuck! What happened? Why are we moving?"

The friar's face flustered red as he explained, in short and accurate sentences, how the Nottingham Guard had spotted Arthur and David on the Sherwood Road. Marion considered it gravely, but it was only more reason to hasten. "We'd best be on our way then."

"You think so?" Will scolded her. "What did you think we're fucking doing?"

Marion balled her dress into her fists, but would not let him rile her. If this had been any other man, Marion might suspect him drunk. But Will Scarlet had been entirely sober since Elena's death—that which tore at his soul came from within. He'd been particularly combative with her for weeks, off and on, ever since they'd realized they were no longer on the winning side. He'd thought that simply claiming the name of Robin Hood would compel the world to bow to him, and had grown sour that life was more realistic than that. He was good at gravelly insults and a brooding lurk—but when it came to survival, their group was still very much *Marion's* Men.

Will smirked, for reasons only he could know. "Pack up, Marion," he ordered. "Unless you'd rather stay. Give my best to the Nottingham Guard. They'll be here soon."

A heavy moment passed between them. It was so difficult to forgive his grief, and to remind herself that everyone had their own method of coping with the unimaginable. Some people like Will let it out to attack everyone, while others . . .

. . . others preferred to stuff it into a perfectly round ball and swallow it, where it would probably kill her later.

He started up the hill, making a show of leaving. Their squabble had thankfully already attracted the majority of the camp, mostly packed and awaiting direction. Marion's eyes lingered on a solitary figure watching from halfway up the climb, who showed no interest in coming any closer.

Good, Marion thought. *First decision Arable had ever made that didn't get someone killed.*

She packed it into a perfect ball and swallowed it.

"I know that nobody wanted to travel today," she announced, even as a few people started up the hill to follow Will, "but the good news is that we have an actual destination. Someplace we can stay. No more running."

John Little, who had finally joined them, lit up. "Well that's ever good to hear! What do you have in mind?"

She didn't even pause. "We leave the Sherwood. We leave Nottinghamshire."

An unease rippled outward, infectious as a rumor. She'd expected that. They'd long decided against fleeing the county borders. Outside of the Sherwood, their group would be easy to notice, and they would be at every disadvantage. But those risks only lasted so long as they were impermanent.

"Where?" Tuck asked. "You said your home was too dangerous . . ."

"Not my father's estate, no," she answered before he could finish the thought. Her grandfather's lands were too far, and carried too many complications. "That will never be an option. But I've been communicating with Lord Robert, Earl of Huntingdon, and he's consented to take us in."

It had been no easy feat, and the news should have been greeted with celebration. But she knew the journey would sound daunting. Huntingdon was, as far as most of this group knew, on the other side of the earth.

"Huntingdon?" Will coughed.

"He seems downright eager to have us," she laughed. "Lord Robert has been one of your primary supporters, though most of you would never know it. He was the one who purchased most of the jewelry we took in the autumn. He loved knowing it came from his political rivals."

"Huntingdonshire is two counties away," Arthur said, somewhat delicately. "There's no way a group this size can travel that distance in secrecy."

"And the days are still short," warned David.

"You don't have to do it in secret," Marion answered, hoping to encourage them. Her group would need all the manpower possible to make the journey. "The Earl Robert will welcome you openly."

"Openly?" Tuck asked. "What is he offering? This Earl Robert?"

Marion wished there was a way to make this more exciting, but there was very little thrill in what lay ahead. "I won't lie, it won't be an easy life. You'll work. Huntingdon is struggling to pay its share of the ransom as well, make no doubt. But you would have safety as his vassals. Work his land, or his estate, each according to their ability. You would be . . . people again. Instead of outlaws."

Will had not moved. "You want us to give up on everything."

She didn't look at him. "I want you to consider your options. Your *real* options. This is a chance to live a peaceful life again. Not just what you had at Locksley, but before that. Lord Robert is being very generous with his offer. It is, without doubt, the best opportunity you will ever have."

"And all we have to do," Will's voice rose, "is pretend none of this ever happened."

"All you have to do," Marion matched him, "is walk away before anyone else is hurt."

"Walk away and let them get away with it."

Marion's temper flared before she could grapple it down. "Yes, Will. Actually, yes. They're going to '*get away with it.*' Everything they've done, they've already gotten away with it. There is no scenario in which we 'win.' They have the power, and it doesn't matter if you think that's *unfair.* That's how the world works. Grow up."

Unsurprisingly, he didn't. "Well then. You just said it. You don't think we can win."

It was hardly an opinion, and she was sick of pretending otherwise. "Look around. Where are your victories, Will? I wanted you to succeed, *God,* more than anyone! But I see burnt trees. I see starving people. How can you not see that?"

She didn't ask the rest of the question. *How could he not see that it was his fault?*

"Of course I see that. But I see the rest, too." He thrust a finger at the nearest tree trunk. "I see the trees that are still standing, that *would have* been burnt if not for us. I see the people still living, who *would have* died if we hadn't fought back. You're only seeing failures because they're all you're looking for, Marion."

That ball, she could not swallow.

Will cooed. "You don't understand. How could you? You come and stay in the woods with us for a week or so and then go home—or to Huntingdon, apparently! This is our life, that you choose to visit on holiday. You think of us as your little playthings, *Marion's Men,* for you to move around where *you* want. Fuck that. Keeping us on a short leash, keeping us from doing anything that will actually make a difference."

He started to circle her, playing to the crowd.

"God's teeth, you had us roaming village to village *giving* out coin rather than putting that money to real use. I wonder if we might be doing a bit better now if you hadn't made us throw it all away?"

She'd long run out of patience in correcting this particular argument. "*Put it to real use?*" she echoed his phrasing. "You never recognized that our charity was a strategy. It was a *bribe.* You're only as safe as the first villager willing to sell you out. When you stopped helping the people, you stopped giving them a reason to help you. And you wonder why you're hunted everywhere you go now, you wonder why you cannot steal as much as you used to."

All eyes returned to Will, who tapped his fingers restlessly. "Do you notice how she always uses the word *you* instead of *we*?"

"*Your insults don't feed people!*" she snapped at him. "You want to attack me, fine. But don't pretend that helps anyone. What's over that hill, then?" She pointed up and out of the willowbank, where he'd been headed. "Where were *you* planning to take them?"

Will shook his head. "A. Way. From. Here."

"Down the river a bit?" She frowned, and found a few sympathetic faces. "We'll find another beautiful stretch of mud until we get discovered there as well?"

At that, Will slung the pack off his shoulder and descended back toward her in contempt. "If you want to leave so much, then go home, Marion! We don't need you anymore. We aren't taking in any jewelry or necklaces anymore, so we don't need you and we don't need Huntingdon. The next time we start shopping for trinkets again, we'll find you." He snorted, eyeing her up and down. "Or are you worried we'd think poorly of you? If I had a castle and a featherbed waiting for me, you can bet I would've left a while ago."

Marion was undeterred. "Nobody doubts your willingness to be rid of us."

"Fuck you." He quivered. "Oh, fuck you so much."

"Stop it!" Tuck threw his hands up between them, as if there were a risk of violence. As if Will were a danger to anyone but himself. The idea had never even crossed Marion's mind.

Will's gaze was stuck on her, staring her down with alternating eyes. Marion ate up his spite. "My question stands, what better option do you have? I'm not being a *bitch*, Will. I'm asking you an honest question. I want to know what your plan is." She let a few moments pass. "Do you even have one?"

Will snorted again. "I do."

"Then why don't you try answering me when I ask you a question," Marion scolded, "instead of pissing all over the ground just to prove you've got a dick?"

Arthur a Bland let out a low whistle. "Holy mother of fuck—"

"Shut it, Arthur," Marion said.

"Never mind, then."

"You think I like roaming around the forest scavenging like this?" Will asked, his eyes moving quickly. "Barely surviving? Hiding from everyone just in case they might mean us harm? It's pathetic. We've got an awful lot of mouths to feed and there aren't many of us bringing in the food. But I'm still here, so don't you fucking tell me you think I'm trying to be rid of everyone."

"Fine," Marion consented. He was right. "I'm sorry for that."

"We need more men, is what we need." Will returned to a higher place on the hill, and it made him appear deceptively taller. "If the Nottingham Guard is building outposts on the Sherwood Road, we can't stay on the defensive. If they control the forest, we're done. But we know we can stop them in small groups, you all know I can deliver on that promise. So we can't let them build. We *have* to fight back."

"Fight back," Marion echoed. "To what end, Will? You've already tried violence, why don't you remind me how successful that was?"

That, apparently, struck a nerve. "We didn't draw first blood," he growled.

A perfect ball.

Swallow.

Will just laughed at her. "I don't know what kind of world you think this is, but you're fucking clueless." He paced away, then back again, speaking with his hands. "This is no children's story where the plucky underdog wins because he's just so plucky. This is reality, and we're dying. I thought we'd have more time, to recruit some men from the villages, train them. But we don't. We need men now, or we die."

"And so this plan of yours . . . ?"

"I go to Nottingham."

By the crowd's reaction, Marion was not the only one shocked by this. Nottingham was literally the last place any sane person would go.

"I have a lot of friends back there," Will continued. "Friends who hate the Guard as much as we do."

"Street rats," Marion translated.

"Talented men," he shot back. "Real thieves, who have the skills we need.

Right now we barely have enough men to keep ourselves fed. But if I bring back even a dozen of my old crew, then we can stop these outposts before they're built, and we turn the Nottingham Guard back cold."

"Gang members," Marion scoffed. "Loyal to nobody."

"You think they'll follow you?" Arthur asked.

"I know they will. When I led my boys out of Ten Bell Alley into Red Lion Square, we became the strongest gang in Nottingham. They're still there. They'll know about Robin Hood—and right now that's me. They're sure to follow the man who killed the last two Sheriffs. I get my boys again, we get a useful crew, we get back to making a difference."

He smiled, and for a moment it reminded Marion of the charismatic man he'd been a year ago. Confident. Cocky, perhaps, but only because he could back it up. It was good to see that drive in him. She honestly wished they could just slip back into their old ways. But even his boldest words didn't make his idea any less of a disaster.

"And what about everyone else?" Marion asked, searching the crowd. Women and children looked back at her—the very people Will had just labeled *useless.* "These families, they're supposed to . . . what? Wait here until you come back? *If* you come back? With no protection in the meanwhile?"

"I'll only need a few days."

"What if we have to run? How would you find us?"

"We'll work out the details. God's tits, I know it's not perfect, but we need the help. I can get the men, I can bring twenty of them back here, ready to fight!" Will humphed. "Let's let everyone choose. Those who want to run away and beg for handouts from some rich lord are welcome to do so. Welcome to go back to living like slaves, and wait until this all happens again. But those who have any amount of self-respect can follow me."

"And by *follow me,*" she clarified for him, "he means *stay here.* And hope he comes back."

"I'll be back," he said, with a perfect calm, "before you even get to Huntingdon."

She hated him in that moment. For offering them easy answers he couldn't back up. The group murmured with indecision. It was beyond reason that any of them even hesitated. She spat under her breath at Will, "Why do you have to be so stubborn about everything?"

"I'm not being stubborn, goddammit!" he said at full voice, halting the murmur. "I'm being faithful! Faithful to the people who died, that you clearly don't give the first shit about. I'm the only one trying to make sure they didn't die for nothing!"

Marion tried to hide her fury. She started one sentence, thought better of it, started, and stopped again. She tried to roll it up, but the ball wouldn't form, it resisted until she couldn't hold it back. "I didn't realize you had a monopoly on grief."

Stillness. Even the wind silenced itself, leaving nothing but the tall tree-spears around them and tiny Will Scarlet suddenly on the edge of madness. It was Will's voice, but his lips didn't move. *"Don't go there."*

She had to bite her lip to keep from breaking. "You're not the only person who lost someone they loved," she whispered.

"I didn't *lose* anyone!" Will yelled back. "Mine were *taken* from me. Ripped out of my hands, right out of my fucking hands! At least Robin died doing something he believed in, he died the way we all ought to die. He died fighting for you and you're just walking away from him."

She slapped him. Hard.

For a moment Will reeled, and then he slapped her back. Just as hard. Not harder.

It stung, and her ear rang—she must have been knocked backward because she was in Sir Amon's arms. Once she was on her feet again, Amon positioned himself between them, his sword whispered out of its scabbard. Will kept his eyes on Marion, utterly ignoring the steel point now trained on him.

"You have no idea how lucky you are." Will's voice was terrible, and his face even worse. Tears streaked down both cheeks, his skin was nearly purple, and not from bruising. "Robin died a hero. You have that, at least. What do I have?" He pounded his chest. "Elena died a *traitor*. You really want to compare scars?"

Marion touched Amon's arm, who obeyed without question. His sword vanished as though it had only been a thought. "Will." She reached her hand out, palm up, begging for him to join her. "You have to let her go. You can't do this for her, you can't. If you go to Nottingham, it will be suicide."

In retrospect, she should not have used that final word. It found whatever softness he had left within him and dried it to chalk. "You want to run away, then hurry up." His eyes looked through her, at nothing. "I'm not coming with you. *That* would be suicide. Because I wouldn't be able to live with myself."

There were no more words to be said after that. Will picked up his pack and marched himself up the ridge, halfway to forever. Something tugged downward inside Marion, grounding her where she stood, feeling even more helpless than ever. She had neither the words to unite her people, nor the ability to tear herself in half and go with both groups. The others were now loudly making their own decisions.

Arthur a Bland and David of Doncaster spoke in hushed tones, and Marion approached them. "You know we need you."

David bit his lip.

"I think Will needs us more," Arthur answered, and would not meet her eye.

She didn't want to lose them. "It's a long road. You two are the best hunters we have."

"But when you get there, it sounds like you'll be safe. And fed. And then what?" Arthur swallowed hard. "You're saving these people . . . that's good, it is. But the Guard is still coming, still going to look for us here. We'd be abandoning all the people who've helped us in the villages. They'll suffer for it. They're waiting for us to come back. I don't know. Leaving for this earl of yours . . . it seems . . . I think it seems selfish."

That hurt. *Selfish* was the last thing Marion thought she deserved to be called.

But by the end of it, *thank God,* it seemed there was no real decision to be made at all. Only Arthur and David stood by Will, volunteering to go with him to Nottingham. They tried to instill a sense of adventure and righteousness into some of the other men, but most had never developed the temperament for a criminal life.

"Come on then, Stutely," David coddled the bloated nomad whose mouth was as large as his belly, but Marion could tell that even he did not want to go. "You'll finally get a chance to show us how brave you say you are."

Will Stutely hung his head and followed Scarlet like a dog.

Charley Dancer struggled greatly with his choice, but Arthur took the burden away from him. "You'll be no good to us, Charley. That leg of yours will slow us down. It's not fair, I know, but that's the way of things."

David slapped John Little's back, trying to smooth over the tension. "Come off it." He smiled. "Let's not make a big deal out of this. We're splitting up, is all."

"It's good strategy, really," Arthur seconded. "It will make it harder for them to find us."

"*Splitting up?*" Marion was hardly able to hide the vile taste of the day. Losing four strong men would be devastating for what lay ahead. "Why don't you try counting, Arthur? There are three of you following Will, and a hundred of us that are not. This is not *splitting up.* This is you abandoning us. I don't care how you want to sell it to yourself."

David looked genuinely hurt. "We're not abandoning you, Marion. We're going to get more men from Nottingham, and we're going to rebuild. We'll come back, and anyone here can come back, too. We'll keep going like before."

The murmur from the crowd said they did not believe him.

"This isn't the end," Arthur insisted.

"It is," Marion laughed. "Will's a river rat. He's going home. And anybody who follows him is going to drown." She slung a hemp sack over her shoulders and nodded to John Little, steady and somber. "Let's go, everyone. We have a long way to go, and the work just got harder."

SIX

ARABLE DE BUREL

SHERWOOD FOREST

ARABLE LISTENED TO HIS words, but her only surprise was in how little they affected her. Will Scarlet was apologizing, in the same curiously whispered breath he always used with her, his eyebrows praying together for her approval.

"I understand," she said, because she did.

His eyes begged for more, maybe he wanted her to kick and wail. Maybe he knew what it meant that she didn't. She couldn't say, *It's fine*, because it wasn't. Nor could she say, *I'm furious*, because in truth she didn't feel anything at all about it, because how could she? She was a sailboat in an endless squall, weathering blow after merciless blow. There was no sense in being angry with any single wave.

"We wouldn't be more than a day or so, three or four at the most. You could wait for us," he suggested.

"That's not . . . no." Arable's vote had been the only one for staying in the Sherwood and waiting on Will's return. She had no desire to follow Marion's group to Huntingdon, but waiting alone in the forest would be a deadly price to pay for stubbornness.

"We'll get more men, then, and come get you in Huntingdon." Will shifted from looking off in one meaningless direction to another. "Huntingdon's actually a good idea for most of this group. You drop off the families there, and be free of them. And Marion. Then the rest of us, and the new crew I recruit from Nottingham, we'll get back to it. You included. First we stop them from building their outposts, then we start hitting noblemen again. But we don't stop at jewelry this time. We'll take back what we had, and then we go five steps beyond."

"I said I understand."

She understood better than he, how unlikely it was for them to find each other again. If he was delayed in Nottingham. If the Guard built faster than they could fight back. And through all of it, there'd be no way to communicate. The idea that Will would abandon this new fight of his to fetch her in Huntingdon was a fantasy. He would be the one free of Marion, while Arable would be trapped with her now more than ever. Even Arthur and David—the closest things she had to friends in this group—were leaving with Will.

"I wish I could go with you," she admitted.

His face tensed. "You could."

But she couldn't.

Arable de Burel could never return to Nottingham, not under any circumstance. Not for an hour, not a minute, certainly not "a day or so, or three or four at the most." The city was full of her ghosts. Her father, and her mentor, and her lover—all three murdered in Nottingham. Their memories haunted the land for a dozen miles in every direction. Even if she could bear its sight, she was wanted as a traitor there. And unlike Will, her scarred face was known by every Guardsman and scullery maid in the castle.

She knelt to pack up her bedroll, which was also her rain cloak. The flattened bracken on its downside she brushed away with a bare hand. The rest of her belongings, which hardly counted as plural, were already in her sack. That was all it took to pack her entire life.

Will clearly recognized the depravity of her action, and his face writhed to express some sort of sympathy. She barely recognized the gesture on him. His once youthful features were devoured by his unkempt mourning beard, and months of unwashed dirt stained his skin dark and turned his blond hair to russet. He looked now more like the feral murderer that she'd once wanted to believe he was.

"Thank you," she said, in case she never had another chance to. Through the bitter days of winter, he'd always looked to her comfort before his own. His care for her was practically religious, and appropriately born of equal parts gratitude and guilt. It might have been the only task that kept him sane. But aside from that penance, he kept his distance from her. Whether he associated Arable with the death of his lover, Elena, or if he simply couldn't suffer the guilt of spending any time alone with another woman, Arable couldn't know. His visits lasted only long enough to ensure her survival, and then he'd return to whatever cave of grief he had clawed into his mind.

Without him, there'd be nobody between her and Lady Marion.

Will practically read her thoughts. "I'm sorry to leave you with her."

She could only laugh. "She sure thinks a lot of herself. And she has a knack for riling sympathy from the masses, I'll grant her that. But it's all selfishness. Marion . . . cares about Marion."

His mouth tensed into a knowing nod.

"It's not just her, though. Everyone blames me for what happened to Robin, but if Marion had just been decent enough to tell her own people her plans . . ." Six weeks earlier—at Robin of Locksley's request—she'd led him and John Little into Nottingham Castle, from which Robin would never return. Nobody cared that their rescue mission failed because Marion turned them away. That she didn't want to be rescued. That she was chasing her own ambitions. They just knew that Arable was the one who took Robin there. Half the group saw her as a symbol of their troubles, while the others suspected she'd outright betrayed them. Some avoided her entirely, and she likewise kept to the outskirts and talked to almost nobody.

Even the villages within the forest who had once protected them now refused them sanctuary. Their crops were sick, their fields were burnt, but they did not blame Sheriff *Ferrers* who had done it, no.

They blamed the death of Robin Hood.

Whose death was really on Marion, not Arable. "But somehow *I'm* the curse."

"John Little likes you," Will tried. "And I'll ask the Delaney brothers to look after you."

"I hate you, you know."

The words caught both of them off guard, and for maybe the first time since autumn, Will looked her full in the eyes. She wasn't sure why she said it, aside from the ravenous feeling that it might be her last chance to ever speak with him.

So she opened her mouth. "The Sheriff, Roger de Lacy, he was dear to me. You took that." Will reacted as if he'd been punched in the chest, or harder somehow into his soul, exposed and raw. Tears came to Arable's eyes, but they did not distract her. "But Will, there's more than just hate. I can hate you and still be thankful for you. I can hate you and still wish you the peace you deserve. I can hate you and miss you, and I will. Hate doesn't destroy everything else, not if we don't let it."

His eyes were red, his face rifled through every emotion it knew.

"Why tell me that?" he asked.

"Because I think you need to hear it. You and I have a lot in common."

"Do you think I hate you?"

"No." She brought her hands up to his cheeks. "I think you hate you."

She kissed his forehead and stepped away, wiping her eyes. She could tell he wanted to say more, but he wasn't good at such things. There was no need for any grand farewells, it was better to whimper off. She crossed her arms and winced. Her stomach chose to split the silence, ripping a sickening growl that even Will had to raise his eyebrows at. Her body was not doing well lately, her hunger kept her on edge all the time.

"The Delaneys. I'll see to it. They'll make sure you eat, at least."

That was the only way he could show that he cared, this functional thing. He thought it was made stronger by repeating it. All she could do was shrug her shoulders. She recognized it as a kindness, but she wasn't in the mood for accepting any. Making sure she ate shouldn't be a favor. But to those she was left with, she was only a mouth to feed—she'd even overheard Marion once say exactly as much. Arable could hardly pretend she was much use to the group's survival, but if Lady Marion Fitzwalter alone was left to judge her value, then Arable wouldn't receive the last scrap of charred fat to suck on.

Whatever lay waiting for them in Huntingdon, Arable doubted greatly that it was safety. This Earl of Huntingdon would offer Marion some new opportunities to rise, to be certain—but Arable and the rest of the group were likely just stepping stones to keep the dear lady's feet out of the mud.

"Good luck, Arable," Will managed as he left.

She clicked her tongue, and sighed. "Good luck, Robin Hood."

His beard twitched, almost as if there were a smile somewhere beneath it.

SEVEN

QUILLEN PEVERIL

THE DOORS TO THE office of William de Ferrers—Fourth Earl of Derby, High Sheriff of Nottinghamshire, Derbyshire, and the Royal Forests—crumpled like paper as Lord Beneger tore into the room.

The Sheriff's official chamber was wide enough to encompass much of the upper keep's second floor, brightly lit by slender windows that looked out over the highest bailey. The previous sheriff, Lord Beneger's son, had never used the room. Ferrers had reclaimed it for its original purpose, presumably to aggrandize his authority; but it had the opposite effect on Ferrers's near-skeletal body. Quill had to look twice to even find the Sheriff, who was leaning against one of the room's thick support pillars and rendered effectively invisible.

To Quill's delight, the Sheriff made an audible gulp.

The Peverils were Derbymen, and no self-respecting Derbyman cared a stitch for the opportunism of the Ferrers family. Quill had been loath to see this young Ferrers sworn in on his first day of office as High Sheriff, and he was equally thrilled to be the sole witness to the beautiful transition of power that was about to occur.

"*I came to see my son.*" Beneger's words had the razor precision of rehearsal. "I received notice he'd been made Sheriff."

Ferrers's demeanor normally carried an affected deliberation, a poor facsimile of grace. This made it all the more rewarding to watch the little weasel stumble back in the face of Lord Beneger's rage.

"This is inappropriate," was all Ferrers could say.

"Imagine *a father's joy,* imagine *how proud I was.* My son, William, my last living son. My only *surviving* son." Indeed, the two elder brothers had died fifteen years earlier as hostages of the now-destroyed Burel family. Lord Beneger's hatred for the Ferrers family was second only to that for the Burels, whom he had neatly eradicated from England.

Beneger drove forward slowly, hunting Ferrers as he wound backward through the pillars of the room. Quill positioned himself at the room's entrance, a subtle implication that Ferrers would find no escape there.

This will be like watching a gladiator fight, Quill reveled, unable to contain his excitement. *Not the sort between two matched foes, no—the sort where a lion is unleashed upon some starved criminal.* He had never understood the attraction of watching a man broken on the wheel until this moment, when the victim deserved every ounce of what was coming to him.

Sadly, Wendenal was only here to take Ferrers's title, not his life.

"This is unmannerly," Ferrers was saying, still retreating. "You should re-cuse yourself, Lord Wendenal."

"My son had left to war," Beneger continued, driven, riven, "to put himself in harm's way, for our king. I begged him to stay, do you understand me? You can't know what it is to die every day, as a parent does. I begged him not to put me through the daily horror of wondering at his safety. Do you understand that word? *Begging?* It's a word with which you will soon become uniquely ac-quainted."

"I am the Earl of Derby," Ferrers flustered, backed into a corner. "Lord Wen-denal, I grant you an allowance for not—"

"*You grant me nothing!*" he exploded. Quill found himself in awe of the raw emotion. He mouthed the lord's words as they were spoken, in the hopes of memorizing them more accurately later. "There is only one thing from you that I desire, and I will *take it,* do you hear me? I will rip it from you, I will tear it out of you, you cannot grant it to me or bargain it to me because it is not a thing in your power to give."

"Guardsman!" Ferrers shouted at Quill, waving his hand limply. "Escort Lord Wendenal out of this room."

Quill chose to momentarily become fascinated by a mote of dust instead.

"So imagine my joy when I learned my son had returned safely from the war. Not only alive and healthy, but as a leader, as the High Sheriff, of all things. As *my* sheriff."

Ferrers tried for a softer tone. "Your son was, indeed, a remarkable man."

And Beneger met him with fury. "My son's character is not yours to judge!"

He'd backed the man into a corner, and his voice held the reckless abandon of one on the edge of violence, but Beneger was clearly no slave to fury. Quill was glad for it, lest he himself accidentally become an accomplice to an assassination.

But Ferrers seemed to recognize that same absence of violence, and he re-couped his nerves. The young earl straightened himself against the wall. "You have yet to state your point in being here."

"My point?" Lord Beneger cracked the air. "My point is at the end of the sword I will bury in your stomach!"

But Lord Beneger de Wendenal carried no sword. If his *point* was simply to swear empty threats, then Quill had sorely miscalculated.

"I came here to Nottingham to see my son, to swear my fealty to him. So imagine how I would react to find that he had been murdered, and in his place I find a *Ferrers.*"

"A Ferrers," the Sheriff said slowly, "to whom you owe fealty."

Beneger suffered a slight hesitation.

"You have traveled far, Lord Wendenal," Ferrers started casually, moving away from the corner and back to his desk by the tall windows. "It must have been a great distance indeed. Your son was murdered nearly two months ago, after all."

Lord Beneger startled, turning as if looking for a weapon. "I do not answer to you!"

"For someone who has only just arrived at the scene of a four-month-old crime, you seem unusually confident of its details."

"The details are obvious," Beneger countered, stalking Ferrers's path across the room with only his eyes. "William should have been safe here. He was home. Protected by a hundred men. I've played this game far longer than you, so don't insult me by pretending you invented its rules. The man responsible for a death such as this is always the next one to sit in the chair."

"I'm sorry, what? To sit in the stair?"

"The next to sit in the *chair*."

"Ah." Ferrers frowned sadly, as if to agree. "As you say, you're more familiar with it all than I. So you should know that politics is a far more dangerous place than wartime will ever be. For men such as us, that is." He fussed about absently with a ledger at his desk, smoothing over its leather cover with his fingertips. "But whether you like it or not, your son was murdered by a common criminal. I had nothing to do with his death."

"Go and lie, child." Beneger smiled. "Every lie is one more piece of your tongue I'll cut out before I'm done."

"Then I have no fear for my tongue. No, it was Captain Gisbourne's mismanagement of the situation that led to your son's death, though I do wish I could have prevented it. Gisbourne cannot be punished, sadly, as he was killed by the same man who killed your son. I suppose perhaps you owe him for that."

The accusation was stunning, and brought a grave silence. Quill marveled at the rebuttal. Ferrers had transformed from a cowering creature into one masterfully claiming dominance with every nuanced movement. The elevation of his desk, the sun at his back, his distracted mannerisms, all spoke to a strategic superiority. He made his opponent repeat his words as if he spoke unclearly. These were simple tricks that most amateur debaters knew, but Ferrers was effortlessly using them in the face of violent threats. It was a revelation to watch in action. Quill hated to admit the man any respect, but there was no denying an expert his craft.

Quill had bet on the lion, of course, and somehow he was going to lose that bet.

He eyed the door, wondering about his own chances for an unnoticed exit; but the door laughed at him, having quite rudely somehow moved clear across the room.

"I don't know how else to tell you this, Lord Wendenal." Ferrers looked genuinely sympathetic. "Your rage is entirely misplaced."

The painful part was that this was true. Ferrers had *benefitted* from William de Wendenal's death, but he had certainly not orchestrated it. Quill might have mentioned as much if he were not now actively pretending to be tapestry.

Beneger laughed. "Your family has been grasping for Nottingham for decades. My first sons were killed by your father's greed, and my last son was killed by yours."

"Oh yes, Lord Wendenal, your tenacity in the sport of revenge is the makings of legend. You blamed the Burels for the deaths of your sons, and have since extinguished every trace of their lineage from England. Those that did not die by your own hand have been chased into obscurity and poverty. So ask yourself, why would I risk angering a man with a reputation such as this? And to achieve . . . what?"

He spread his arms out open to the room. Wide and empty, its corners cluttered with dirt and cobwebs shining in the sunlight.

"This? This tenuous position as Sheriff? I am not so ignorant as I am young. I claimed this title as an emergency measure, with Chancellor Longchamp's blessing, which was within my right as the Earl of Derby. But my stay here shall be temporary at best, lasting only until the Chancellor deigns to appoint someone more appropriate. This is my great prize?" he whispered, his voice dwarfed by the emptiness in the room.

Quill tried to watch Lord Beneger for his reaction, but the man was unreadable.

Ferrers kept pushing. "For this sliver of bureaucratic semipower, I have risked the wrath of the most vengeful man in England? This is the grand scheme you think I've concocted?"

Quill rarely doubted his own assessment of a man, but he found himself swayed. Perhaps the young Ferrers had the makings of a Sheriff in him after all.

"Even a halfway clever man would realize that he'd have to kill you first in order to make a plan such as that work."

"But you're not a clever man," Beneger responded, grasping for straws, his voice weak.

"Nor am I a guilty man. In the matter of William de Wendenal's murder, that is. You came here looking for answers, and I have them. They're not the ones you came for, but they're true. They're delicious and true and far more interesting than the predictable power play you've written, casting your favorite villains in familiar roles. You pride your righteous revenge, Wendenal, but you see enemies where there are none."

"I see enemies where there are enemies." Lord Beneger's voice faltered. His eyes shone, not with fury anymore. There were tears there. "I see murderers where there are murderers."

"What exactly did you think would happen here?" Ferrers continued, tapping at his desk. "You haven't touched me, so you're sane enough to know you can't. If I had confessed to all your ridiculous fantasies, even then you wouldn't kill me, would you? You'd be imprisoned, executed for treason. Your lands would be claimed, your remaining family decimated."

Quill was wondering the same thing. Perhaps Lord Beneger didn't care. Perhaps he had lost so much that it didn't matter. Perhaps he wanted Ferrers to attack first. Or—most likely, he realized—perhaps he simply hadn't thought it out. Beneger had simply come to confront the man he thought killed his son. He wasn't trying to expose him, or depose the title. *There was no plan at all. He was just reacting.*

This was often Quill's blindspot. He forgot that other people sometimes made choices based not in strategy, but in irrational emotion.

"I don't care," Beneger finally answered.

"Really? So why haven't you killed me yet? If you are certain I have done you this great wrong, why talk at me like a woman?" Ferrers finally turned vicious. *"Why not wrap your hands around my neck and snap it? It is not much of a neck."*

And Lord Beneger did.

Like a crossbow bolt held at tension and finally released, he closed the distance between them in the blink of an eye. The contents of the table scattered in the air and held there as Lord Beneger grabbed Ferrers by the lapels, both barreling over the table's edge and onto the ground, Ferrers's skull meeting stone with a dull, terrifying crack. Beneger wrapped his fingers around his prey's throat and squeezed, the veins in his arm leapt to attention, both men's faces turned purple.

Later, Quill would recall that he could do nothing but stare.

"You murdered my son!" Wendenal screamed, spit raining down onto the Sheriff. But Ferrers did not fight back. In barely audible, strangled gasps, "I did not."

"You murdered my son!"

"On my life," the last of his air creaked out, "I did not."

"You murdered my William!" Beneger's voice was barely human. He put all his weight down into it. "You murdered my boy!"

Quill had to fight the lump in his throat, and the tears in his eyes, to stop it. "He did not! Your lordship . . . your lordship, he did not."

Lord Beneger's face snapped up, as if Quill had appeared out of nowhere. His grip did not lessen.

Quill shook his head, slightly, then more vigorously.

No.

And Beneger collapsed, releasing his hold on the Sheriff, whose skinny frame rolled over in agony. Ferrers sputtered for air, the greasy squeak of his breath matching his convulsions on the ground.

Quill talked, he wasn't sure why. "There are many solid reasons for you to break that man's neck, your lordship. But in the name of justice, the murder of your son is not one of them."

Ferrers, snake that he was, had been with Quill and the rest of the Black Guard when they were ambushed outside Bernesdale. Ferrers had ridden hard back to the castle, but was too late to stop Robin Hood. Everyone knew the story.

Quill's heart went out to Lord Beneger, rolling on the ground, wrought to the edge of his reason. His fists curled up and pawed at his own face. "Who, then?" he asked, his eyes closed.

"Robin of Locksley," Quill answered. "Robin *Hood,* as they called him. Son of a minor lord, took to leading a band of outlaws in the Sherwood. He snuck into the castle and killed Sheriff de Wendenal in his office. On the very eve of Sheriff de Lacy's funeral, who died the same way."

"He doesn't sound like a common criminal."

"Better than most, perhaps. He used terror to his advantage. But he was caught, and hanged for his crime. It was witnessed by hundreds of men and nobles alike. I saw it myself."

Locksley had not said even a single word on the gallows. His once-handsome face had been swollen and nearly unidentifiable. There were no sympathetic demonstrations or disputes in the audience. When Locksley's body dropped, there was applause all around.

"How?" Beneger asked, a shudder taking over his breath. "How did William die?"

Quill couldn't answer. He hadn't been there.

"He fought," Ferrers whispered, his voice coarse as two stones scraping against each other. "He fought as well as any man ever has. If he had not, we would never have caught Locksley at all. But his wounds were grievous." He coughed, straining his bruised neck. "He died as well as possible, given those circumstances."

"That's good." Beneger's chest shook up and down. "That's good. That's how a man should go. I had feared it was a knife in the back."

"Impossible." Ferrers put a hand on Beneger's shoulder. "Your son was too clever for that."

Beneger slapped the hand away, startling Ferrers and Quill alike. "I swear . . . I swear upon everything . . . I swear if you're lying to me, I'll come back here and throw you out that window."

Ferrers gave the portal an idle glance. "This is only the second story."

"Then I'll wrap a rope around your neck first!" Beneger screamed, his voice failing him by the final words.

Ferrers put his hands up mildly, as if granting Beneger the permission. But the matter was plainly over. At the door's crack, the tiniest noise caught Quill's attention, and he noticed a gathering of bodies down the hallway. They were still as stone, some in Derby green and others in Nottingham blue. All waiting to know who would walk out of the room alive.

"I forgive you your grief," Ferrers was saying. "And I hope you appreciate the mercy I give you by not throwing you in a cell for attempting to kill me just now."

Beneger simply snorted.

Ferrers, for the first time since asking for his help and not receiving it, looked at Quill. There was no way to ignore that the offer of amnesty had not included him.

"*Hello,*" Quill imagined himself later explaining to the Sheriff, "*I brought the man who strangled you into your office. My mistake. I thought Sheriff-killing was an acceptable pastime here in Nottingham.*"

Fortunately, Ferrers did not seem concerned with punishment yet. "In the interest of honesty, I should admit to one thing. Locksley was not alone the night your son was murdered. His companions, regrettably, escaped."

"What of it?" Beneger asked.

"So Locksley did not act alone. In fact, he was once friends with your son. I've long had my doubts . . . given the violence of his death, I've often wondered if Locksley was really the one who held the knife. Whereas Will Scarlet—the man who now calls himself Robin Hood—well, he was infamous for that very type of attack."

"You're saying my son's murderer is still alive." Beneger's tone was a dog's ear, raised at the dinner bell.

"We have no idea where he is, though," Ferrers said, waving ambiguously at the outside world. "He disappeared after that night. We hanged Locksley publicly, for the people. To put an end to the name of Robin Hood, as it were."

He tapped his finger on the desk, nervously.

Not nervously, Quill noted. *Not the man who had reacted so calmly earlier. This was another practiced tic.*

But Beneger de Wendenal bought into it. "What is it?"

Ferrers's laugh was embarrassed. "It was not so tidy as that."

"*Robin Hood* still shows up all over the place," Quill spoke up. "We think Will Scarlet's not the only one using the name, too. It's become something of a symbol for the discontented masses. Of which, there are many. They might even be working together, then . . . both adding to its reputation."

Beneger closed his eyes. "The reputation of the man who murdered my son."

"As I said, it was not so tidy." Ferrers chose to return to the shadows against the wall. "I have a crew hunting them down. Sir Robert FitzOdo from Tickhill, and his men. I've given them special license to investigate anything related to Robin Hood. But they, ah . . . have yet to capture anyone."

"Then your man is incompetent."

"You are correct about that, at least," Quill tried to joke. FitzOdo would be more at home with a yoke around his neck than at the head of an investigation. He was a brute of a man, but many in Nottingham still knew him as the Coward Knight for his shameful service in the Kings' War.

"As are you," Beneger continued, letting the light shine on his face. "When you hang a man in public, you glorify him. The people know his name because you *told it to them.* If you want to dissuade them from repeating these acts now, you have to make such behavior unforgivable. You have to shock them. You made Robin Hood a martyr when you should have made him a monster."

"You're very right, I do not contest that." Ferrers bowed his head. "I wonder if I might be able to persuade you, perhaps, to speak with FitzOdo? To guide him, as it were? You do have a talent for building such a reputation of violence, perhaps you could lend a hand."

Quill watched the puzzle pieces fall together too late, not fast enough to wonder if Ferrers had planned it. It was as swift and impressive as an expert swordsman parrying one oncoming attack into another opponent's chest.

"I'll do better than that," Beneger swore, and the walls of the room itself might have obeyed his command at that moment. "I'll find these animals myself and I'll do what you've failed to do. I'll find the man who killed my son, and I'll destroy him. And I'll put an end to anyone else claiming to use that name for their own. When they realize what the ramifications are, there will be nobody in Nottingham who will so much as whisper the name *Robin Hood.*"

PART II

TOO MANY KINGS

EIGHT

QUILLEN PEVERIL

THE STANDARD DUTIES OF a Common Guardsman were to stand, grunt, or occasionally—but only under the strictest supervision—do both simultaneously. Socially they were miles beneath knights, well beneath those placed in a specific regiment, and even potentially just beneath river slime.

But within the Guard there existed one tier lower than Common Guardsman. The most useless of men were reserved for those who stood the walls at night and squinted out into the black sky. Theirs was a critical role; the castle, it turned out, was actually lighter than air, and required people to stand on top of it at all hours to keep it from floating away.

The butt of many a joke, the nightwalkers of the Common Guard now had one more in their number: Quillen Peveril. It was his punishment for standing idly by while Lord Beneger attacked the Sheriff. His options had been between two different demotions: either to become a nightwalker, or a corpse.

He should have chosen death. At least hell was warm. All the furs in the world couldn't protect his skinny body from the cold. Most of the other nightwalkers had accumulated a lifetime of fat to help them survive their shift. Little instruction had been provided in his new role, because none was required. He was a scarecrow. To call his duty a *watch* was disingenuous, for there was nothing for him to watch. The fires they kept at each corner of the ramparts blinded his vision against the possibility of spotting any theoretical trouble scaling the walls. He might be able to notice something the size of an army, he guessed, but—*wait!*

There! Approaching from the north! An enemy army!

Quillen Peveril alone saw the danger, alerted the castellan, and saved Nottingham.

Ah, wait. He squinted. No, he'd been mistaken. It was just the horizon. Again.

Next time.

Ironically, no army had marched on Nottingham since the current Sheriff's father. The late elder Ferrers had lost the favor of half his county when he pledged his banner to the traitor king Henry the Younger, and had never recovered. By sitting now in the seat of Nottingham's power, the young Ferrers had thematically finished the siege his father had failed at years earlier.

Still, judging Ferrers's competence was moot. A new Sheriff would be appointed soon, if logic could be bothered to get up anytime soon and do its job.

"You could leave now, of course," Quill told himself, while unsuccessfully convincing his muscles to stay active. He did not say this aloud, of course, because opening his mouth would cause his tongue to freeze and break off, and he wasn't yet familiar with the protocols for requesting a new one. But leaving would be, arguably, even more embarrassing than walking the midnight wall. *Greetings, Father, I'm back,* he could say. *No no, I didn't do as you asked at all. It was too cold, see?*

His thoughts were arrested by a silhouette on the battlements. On the far end of the ramparts, the unmistakable skulk of the White Hand.

Just a glimpse of the ghost man, and Quill was reminded that his body could always become a little colder. He'd given little thought to what had become of Gilbert in the past few months. Both of them had survived the ambush outside Bernesdale, where half of Gisbourne's Black Guard were cut to ribbons. Quill still awoke to fever dreams of that night; there were times when the images invaded his waking hours, too, and his heart would race as if it were happening again. Gilbert had left the Black Guard immediately afterward, opting for the obscurity of the nightwalkers. Some thought the role was fitting for him, while others thought he'd turned coward. Either way, he had vanished from everyone's minds—and now here he was, hovering over the castle's walls like a grim spectre.

Quill reminded himself there was nothing unnatural about the man. Gilbert was tall and gaunt, but not nearly as ghoulish as some claimed. His lean, stern face invited nothing, but nor did it hide the paranormal. He had probably grown up in a street gang earlier in life—as he'd always had good instincts with how to deal with them. There was no great mystery as to why he never talked about his past. He was just another slack-jawed thug with a sad story and a boring ending. The same path Quill might find himself on: a cautionary tale, but not a supernatural one.

Still, he felt relief when the White Hand disappeared down a flight of stairs to haunt elsewhere.

None of this was what Quill had spent his life studying for. Some day he vowed to take over as Lord of the Peak at Peveril Castle, if he could only prove himself clever enough. The role would legally pass to his elder brother, Stephen, who was better at smashing skulls together than using those spongy things within them. Somehow his father treated his brother's *manliness* as a measure of his worth, as if the two had any correlation. Quill had nothing but diplomacy and problem-solving skills, correctly relegated to the bottom of the family trash heap. He was still seen as the little boy who'd gotten lost in the caves beneath the castle one year, not *strong enough* to climb his own way out.

"*Nottingham and Derby are sisters,*" his father had said. Odd that he'd import such a familial term, when Quill was his literal family and received none of his father's concern.

He'd prove himself, he would. But this—standing on a wall in the frozen night a county away from home—was not helping. He knew there would be frustrations, playing the long game as a second son, but he did not think they would involve this. At least in the Black Guard he'd been above such menial work as wall walking, but now his work felt . . . well, it felt like work.

"You could leave the Guard," he considered. "And volunteer to ride with Lord Beneger's team." But that presupposed that the ghost of Robin Hood was Nottingham's greatest danger, and Quill was anything but agreed on that.

"Or you could join a traveling troubadour group." Songs were good for people, weren't they?

"Or you could go on a murderous rampage."

"Or you could do what you're told, living in comfortable obscurity."

"Or you could make the most of this position, and try to help people."

He hated that last one, mostly for the fact that it was the "right" choice.

At least the nightwalkers weren't out in the city collecting ransom dues from people who were starving, to send to Chancellor Longchamp. At least he was still in the castle, where he could keep his ears open for opportunities to help. And the thing that nobody else seemed to understand was that Robin Hood—regardless of who wore the name—was not the *cause* of the city's troubles. He was a side effect. Locksley's legacy could only flourish because the people needed him to.

Quill just had to fix the entire world, is all.

So he pulled his furs closer and trained his eyes on the city, leaning against the wall and waiting for time to pass. His forebearers had stood in this same place, no doubt, as stewards of the High Sheriff's seat for generations.

While this particular Peveril would make his mark yet.

—*"You're asleep."*—

The words hit like a dagger in the heart. Quill jolted awake, gasping, shocked to realize he had dozed off. He instantly pulled his fingertips into his armpits, burning from the cold. He choked on his own breath, and then a chill worse than the air overtook him. He was not alone.

"And now you're awake."

Gilbert with the White Hand's voice was a smooth stream over rounded stones. He stood with a captivating stillness, while Quill's entire body shook. Gilbert's impossibly relaxed stance was not the idle permanence of a statue, but rather the tense beat before a leap. A cat in the instant before its pounce.

"I can't believe I fell asleep," Quill stammered, trying to sort out each of his limbs. He blinked away layers of confusion.

"I've been watching you for ten minutes."

This registered as the most alarming thing Quill had ever heard.

"Ten minutes I've been watching you," Gilbert tilted his head, "but you can't even believe it happened? Do you think I'm a liar?"

"I mean, I can *believe* it, of course, I'm not saying—"

"I know what you mean."

"Gerp," Quill said, his brain busy elsewhere.

"What are you doing here?"

"I'm being punished." Quill tried to laugh. He'd forgotten all the creative stories he'd concocted to explain his new assignment. "I'm not here because I want to be."

"Clearly," Gilbert said after a long pause. "You were sleeping."

"Gerp," Quill, against all odds, said again.

The White Hand scrutinized him for a while, then smiled, his thin lips reaching all the way back to his spine. "How do you want to die?"

Yes, Quill urinated at this moment, but that wasn't the reason he was no longer cold. His body lost feeling everywhere, his muscles slacked, he felt as if his hands were falling down past the ground, through the earth. His head clouded and the only thing in the world that was clear was Gilbert's half-lit face and an encroaching black fog.

When Gilbert grabbed him, he screamed.

"I've got you," he said, calmly, kindly. "You can barely stand. Why don't you get inside, Peveril? You don't want to die like this, nobody does."

"Like this? Like how?" Quill asked, his head flopping about as his legs became increasingly useless. He felt a good deal of his body weight slump away as Gilbert shifted to help him toward the nearest doorway.

"By the cold. Alone, without a fight. That's no way to die, is it?" His silken voice was next to Quill's ear. "Stay awake now, tell me how'd you rather die. What's a better way?"

"Old age," Quill's mouth answered. He couldn't see anymore. It was like a drunken stupor. "Old age, surrounded by very young women. Not *very* young. Not, like, children. You know."

"I know what you mean." The world swooned until he was propped up against a wall. "You don't get to die of old age if you die of cold first. Sleep, Peveril. You're not made for this sort of thing, are you?"

There was something about that question that was unbearably true.

"No," Quill answered quietly, succumbing to his body's need to not exist. "I'm not."

"*Sleep.*"

Somehow he was being lowered into his own bed, in the Guard's barracks, and its warmth made the world disappear.

Gilbert was no slack-jawed thug, his mind wondered, just as sleep consumed him.

Why would he volunteer for the midnight's walk?

NINE

ARTHUR A BLAND

ARTHUR WAS IN OVER his fucking head. Not in the funny way. Not in the way that David could make fun of him but everything would actually be fine later. Not even close to that way.

Instead he was suffocating, smothered by everything, all his own misconceptions and shortcomings squeezed around him and there was nowhere to escape. He'd been so eager for a break from Marion and her beggar's horde that he'd never truly considered the alternative. Now he knew a new version of terror—not the sporadic bursts of panic that came from moving camps every week, no. This was pervasive, something that sunk deep and chilled from within.

They would never get out of Nottingham alive.

There were too many people, too much to keep track of, and far too many goddamn *goddamned* guards. Every new corner revealed their deep-blue tabards, in twos and threes sometimes, patrolling the streets or watching at corners. He had no idea there were so many. Arthur kept his head low, even when Will warned him against looking conspicuous.

"You look like you're up to something," David said, flipping his blond tail behind his back with a nonchalant smile.

"We *are* up to something." Arthur had no idea how David did it. If his life depended on it—and it actually might—Arthur could never pull off *nonchalant.* Arthur was fucking *chalant,* is what he was. Chalant as all hell.

"Try to look like you're comfortable. Normal people don't scowl as much as you. Even angry people don't scowl as much as you. And stop looking to the sides as if you're being watched."

"We *are* being watched."

"Only because you look like you're up to something."

Arthur punched David in the arm, but tried to control his panic. There were different rules to sneakthieving here—it wasn't about how to get in and out without being seen, but how to be constantly seen without provoking interest. Safety in anonymity. It was the opposite of everything Arthur knew. Arthur was good with punching things until they didn't need to be punched anymore. This city . . . this city, he couldn't punch.

Will Scarlet led their way, crooking a path through claustrophobic alleys that cut through Nottingham's sprawling streets, spinning them around until the safety of the forest was a fantasy a thousand buildings away. The city was a riot's mix of strong stone buildings and ramshackle wooden hovels, fighting each other for ownership of every inch. Perhaps the city had once been clean and organized, but since then it'd been overrun by an infestation of humans. Even straight roads were made unnavigable by odd cancerous growths, rickety structures that devoured every open walkway. No crevice went unclaimed by some soul hoping to sleep or sell or shit in its corner. And everywhere, a hangman's fog filled the remaining pores. Arthur tried to mark the castle above to get his bearing, but he could only catch an occasional blurred whisper of it, as if it hunted them.

Arthur nearly froze from the enormity of it all.

David tried to calm him down. "It's just like Sheffield."

That was a laugh. Their old stomping ground—where they'd met—was merely a village compared to Nottingham. "How the fuck is this just like Sheffield?"

David's lower jaw thrust forward, a sure sign his friend was brewing some horseshit. "It's just like Sheffield, if fifty other Sheffields all fell out of the sky and landed on top of it."

"Oh is *that* what it's like?" Arthur groaned. "Don't know why I was worrying then."

"You're welcome."

Years before any Robin Hooding, it had been just the two of them pulling small jobs in a playground small enough for them to memorize. They'd learned Sheffield's layout slowly, every brick and crack, from without. But here . . . here they were already in the heart of the city—or at least he thought they were, only to discover again and again they could plunge deeper still.

"This city is just too big to *know*," he said, when next Will signaled for them to pause.

"We don't have to *know* it," David answered. "Will knows it. He knows where he's going."

But as far as Arthur could tell, they'd backtracked three times already. And Lady Marion's words echoed in Arthur's mind.

"Anybody who follows him is going to drown."

They'd prove her wrong. With any luck, they could recruit the men they'd come for and get out of the city by nightfall. Marion would eat her words, she would. Will had some rough edges to him of late, but they all did. And as long as Will's plan involved Arthur's fist getting some alone-time with some pudgy gord noses, he'd follow it.

So they continued—Will in front, Arthur and David next, and the monster Stutely bringing up the rear. When they did stop, it was suddenly and with meaning. Will would signal them to lean against a wall, or to engage in a drunken conversation, or to pretend to be asleep in the crotch of an alley. David seemed to understand quick enough, but Arthur was always a few seconds behind. Then, Stutely would harrumph and dive into a terribly affected position with enough noise to bring every damned gord in town their way.

"You're going to get us all killed," Arthur hissed at him on one such break.

"Thank you," Stutely responded confidently, prompting Arthur to wonder what the oaf had actually heard. He decided to drop to the back of their foursome after that.

After what might have been hours of this stopping and starting and *chalanting* in plain sight, they stood at the edge of a largish square plaza. Its centerpiece was a waist-high wall that ran in a great circle, two dozen strider's steps, but within that ring was nothing but mud and poverty. "This is Red Lion Square," Will explained as he massaged his forehead.

"We've already been here," Arthur noted, taking in the surroundings. "Twice."

"But we came in from the wrong sides," Will muttered. "Your faces aren't known here, which can be a disadvantage, too. Any gang that sees some new faces come into a market from the common roads will peg us as marks."

"This is a market?" David asked. There were a few tables balanced at the edge of the retaining ring with some pitiful offerings for sale, which was no more than every other street they'd passed.

"Once upon," Will answered. "This was the main fish market, they kept water in that ring for fishermen to keep their stock fresh. Popular place. Looks like the ring has been drained. They cut the trees down, too."

Stutely grunted in agreement. "Do you see anyone you recognize?"

Will shook his head no. "I don't think it'll be that easy."

Damn. The sooner they got what they came for and slunk out of this maze, the better. Will was hoping for a dozen men at least, but even if they only found six or seven, it'd be enough. Hell, they could start dismantling one of those building sites in the Sherwood *tonight.*

"So how do we find them?" he asked.

A coy smile crept onto Will's face. "They're right in front of you. Stay small."

Ten minutes or so passed as the scabskin market did its version of bustling, and Arthur's heart beat out of his fucking chest. Whatever Will meant, Arthur didn't know. Three pairs of gords strolled through, one of them even looked directly at them with disdain. Arthur felt very much like slinking away and finding his fucking way out of the city before the fourth pair chose to look harder. But at long last, Will whistled and inclined his head toward one of the vendors. A squat old wench with leather instead of skin, selling a basket of day-old bread rolls from a wooden stool nestled between the two longer tables. Arthur watched her sell a roll to a young boy who ran off, but nothing stood out as unordinary.

"She's *fencing,*" Will said.

That explanation was as useful as a knife without a hilt.

"Don't watch *her,*" David explained, casually enough for a passerby to not think it a secret, "watch who she sells to."

So Arthur did.

Another ten minutes passed before she had a customer, just another young boy. In that time, two more gords walked by and yelled at a disruptive onlooker for a bit. One even made eye contact with Arthur, and it was everything he could do to suppress his instinct to vanish.

"I don't see anything," Arthur said at last, eager to move along.

"Watch who she sells to," Will said, as if it were obvious.

"She's sold two bread rolls to two little boys."

"Wrong."

David schooled Arthur with the joy of an older sibling. "She's sold two bread rolls to *one* little boy."

But Will's smile said otherwise. "*Almost.*"

Arthur looked back at the baker wench, but could not figure out the puzzle.

"Do you see it, Stutely?" Will asked.

Stutely laughed, coughed a bit, then finished his laugh. "Of course! How could you not see it?" He twisted his beard with both hands and turned away.

At least Arthur wasn't the only one who was confused.

"Where does the boy get the money?" Will asked with distinction, clearly knowing the answer already.

Frustrated, Arthur turned to watch again. And it slowly revealed itself. The bread boy, a mop of charcoal hair and tanned skin, ran around the square playing with a few other children. But eventually, a different boy with a deep nose like a hawk's beak put his palm deliberately in the bread boy's hand as they played. Then the bread boy went back to the old wench and bought a third roll.

Bread boy ran off with his prize into a side alley.

And was back again all too soon.

Arthur started peeling the layers backward, shifting his attention to the hawk boy who handed the bread boy the coin. This one was skinnier and faster, and when he ran with the other children, it was not reckless at all. They chased at each other and slammed into the leg of a grown man browsing a fishmonger's catch. Arthur would have thought it an accident if not for Will's warning. But if they'd pinched anything off the customer, Arthur couldn't see how it was possible. They'd barely made contact for a second, and nowhere near the man's coinpurse.

"I'll be damned," David whispered, and nudged his head.

Arthur looked again. Not the boys. A young girl with erratic dark hair and a tattered olive-green surcoat walked coolly away from the commotion, as the hawk boy was still making his last—and unreasonably loud—apologies.

They'd been the distraction. She'd done the deed.

The girl in the olive surcoat spent a few minutes sitting by a gutter at the edge of the plaza before depositing her loot in a crack between two stones and disappearing. A few minutes later the hawk boy found a reason to lie down by that crack, eventually picked out her prize, and ran around a bit more before handing the coin to the bread boy. Who purchased another bread roll.

When Arthur finally spotted the little girl again, she had a roll in her hand, which she gave to the squat old baker wench, who added it to her basket of wares.

"She sold *one* bread roll to *one* little boy," Will grinned. "Over and over again."

"So what?"

"Simple tricks, really," Will explained. "Distraction, an easy lift, a quick drop. A couple exchanges. They fence their pick by purchasing the same stale bread roll over and over again. Old woman probably keeps half at the end of the day, selfish cooz."

"And then they eat the bread," Stutely said, nodding his head importantly.

David smacked him. "No, the girl brings them back."

"Well, the ones she doesn't eat."

"She doesn't eat any of them!"

Arthur nudged Will. "Why so many moves, wouldn't that make it more complicated?"

"Meh, they're just practicing here. Getting it into their bones."

If these were the fabled Red Lions, then Arthur would just as soon surrender himself to the nearest gords than continue. These were *children*. The oldest might have been eight years old. "These are the friends you brought us to recruit?"

"No," Will chuckled. "But they're a gang. Young, yes, but this is their territory. Red Lion Square used to be an important ground to control. Might not be as important anymore, but I'll bet the Red Lions still say who's allowed to work it. So we can go through these children to get an introduction."

An introduction. Will had bragged he was a big fish in this city, and now they were begging children to make a simple introduction.

Anybody who follows him is going to drown.

Even Stutely seemed worried. "We're going to ask a bunch of pups for help?"

"I was younger than they were when I worked the streets," Will replied, calm and sure of himself. "We were the Ten Bell Boys, out of Ten Bell Alley. We would've killed for a territory like this. They may be young, but they'll know what's what."

Arthur tried in vain to think of any subtle way to approach these children, and fell shy of short. Fortunately, the opportunity came to them. The hawk boy and his companions were chasing at each other again and came within arms-reach, and Arthur happened to be very good at snatching little whelps and shaking answers out of them.

"Hey boy!"

"Arthur, wait—" Will reached to stop him, but Arthur had already palmed the back of the hawk boy's neck and spun him around, which startled the bread boy and sent him bowling straight into David. David snatched at Stutely, Stutely grabbed the hawk boy, and damn it if the ground didn't go right out from under Arthur, too. Bodies and limbs and hair bumbled together as they dogpiled down to the ground.

The hawk boy was first to get out, his hands in the air, begging for forgiveness. "So sorry! So sorry!"

"Ho there!" Arthur struggled to get his feet back beneath him. David and

Stutely were still down, too—only Will Scarlet had stepped aside to watch in amusement. "Stay where you are, boy, I'll have words with you."

"Sorry m'lords!" he gasped, panicked, and bolted away with his companions.

"Wait!" Arthur heaved toward them but only got two paces before a hand at his elbow spun him wildly around. Will tugged his arm and pointed in the opposite direction.

"Wrong way." He smiled.

Arthur twisted, confused. The boys were fleeing across the plaza, and David was already giving chase. In the direction Will was pointing was nothing but an empty alley . . . and the back of a young girl with erratic dark hair and a tattered pale-olive surcoat.

"*Son of a whore.*"

Arthur's hands moved to his belt. He'd seen it with his own eyes, and still had been too dumb to know it was happening. The tip of his coinpurse, which normally hung inside his breeches with its lip over his belt, was gone. Stutely laughed hard at him, then pawed at his own belt in a panic.

"That little bitch," Stutely spat when he realized he'd been taken, too.

The little bitch turned back, saw Arthur staring at her, and ran.

TEN

ARABLE DE BUREL

"GOOD NEWS," JOHN LITTLE countered. "They don't know who we are."

That much was true. The Sheriff's men here were strangers, because they were in a new Sheriff's jurisdiction entirely. These Guardsmen even *looked* different. Each of them—eight now, by Arable's count—wore a red sash with a stretched golden lion across it, baring blue claws and a blue tongue. But the rest of their uniform was well shy of *uniform,* and seemed poorly suited for action. By the inconsistent craftsmanship, it seemed likely that each Guardsman was even encouraged to sew his own sash. Some of the handiwork looked less like a lion and more like a rabbit, hilariously terrified of its own existence.

This was the small but proud company of the Rutland Guard.

"Bad news," Arable muttered. "I don't think they like us."

They had been detained for over an hour. With the promise of a new life in Huntingdon, their group had made good time fleeing from Nottinghamshire. When they ran out of forest, their speed increased over the wide, flat lands, and even the slowest of their sprawling crowd had been encouraged by their progress. Open space made them an easy target, but they crossed overland and avoided roads, and miraculously remained unmolested.

But two relatively easy days had been deceitful. On the morning of the third, they were awoken by a small group of bandits, who were only barely chased off by the Delaney brothers after stealing some invaluable rations. Their group was too large and exhausted to properly protect themselves. John Little suggested they return to forest hopping to hide their numbers, which brought them to the poorly named Leyfield Forest.

In a century, perhaps, it would be a beautiful lush woodland. But now it was nothing but saplings, and used as a training grounds for the Rutland Guard.

"Good news," John twisted to watch their captors, "is Will Scarlet's gone. Arthur and David, too. The rest of us don't look much like outlaws, look at the state we're in! Old men like me and pretty girls like you aren't usually the thievin' type. I think they'll believe our story."

"Bad news," Arable's turn, "is Lady Marion is doing the negotiating."

John Little made a face at that, but he was welcome to make all the faces he wished—he would still be wrong about Marion. She'd been gone the entire hour, speaking alone with whichever member of the Rutland Guard was in charge. Marion had promised she could make a quick apology for their trespass using the considerable influence she was always claiming to have, but Arable knew better. Marion's status put their group in *greater* danger, not less. To anyone informed, she was entangled with both the infamous Robin Hood and the murdered High Sheriff, which made her a valuable prisoner. To anyone *un*-informed, she might well be the Sheriff's assassin herself. Even in their poverty, Marion couldn't help but swing her infamy around in the hopes of bettering her own position, at the expense of anyone unlucky enough to rely on her.

"Good is, there's only eight of them," John tried.

"How is that a *good?*" Arable laughed. John was laying odds on their chances in a fight. "Look at us. They could take us all with half that number."

The Rutland Guard was mounted, some circled their group like shepherd dogs around a flock of sheep. A few others gathered to the side, arguing about what they were supposed to do with this massive group of trespassers. Marion had used the wholly unorthodox approach of telling the truth—that they were merely passing through Rutlandshire to get to Huntingdonshire, where they were invited guests.

Since then, their whole group sat and waited—while Arable and John counted the good and the bad news. And if Arable had learned anything in her thirty-some years, it was that the bad news always outnumbered the good.

The truly bad news was that—as Arable had long feared—the world was closed off to those in need. For over a month she'd toyed with the idea of splintering off on her own, leaving this group that clearly did not want her, and heading south. There were still rumors—only rumors, but better than nothing—that she might find some of her surviving family somewhere in France. But she'd been too afraid of traveling the county on her own, and in some small way she was glad to see those fears validated by this day's treatment. On her own, she could never have dissuaded the morning's bandits from taking more than her valuables. On her own, she could not stop the first ambitious Guardsman from doing anything he wished.

Like it or not, she was safest among the sheep.

"Good is," Little shifted his weight, "I don't see enough of you. Iffing an armed garrison is needed to get you to talk to me, well, I'll take what I can get."

That was kind. A younger Arable might have blushed at the compliment. But a patronizing tone lay within it, as if she kept her distance for childish reasons.

"It's not you, John," she answered. "In fact, you're my favorite person in this group." She very likely owed John her life. He'd been the only one to defend her when she'd been accused of poisoning them. The two of them had ridden to Nottingham together with Robin that night. Robin had killed William de Wendenal—the man she'd once loved—and hanged for it the next day. Nothing would ever undo the mutual grief she and John Little shared on that return trip.

"Well I'm glad to hear it." He looked at her. "I thought perhaps you didn't like my jokes."

"Your jokes are awful," she responded. "So of course I like them."

That seemed to delight him.

"It's the company you keep." She let herself go for the insult. "That's the problem."

A slow, understanding nod. "Say what you will, but we wouldn't be where we are without Marion."

Arable raised an eyebrow at him. That was hardly an endorsement, given their current situation. Huddled on the ground, hungry and tired, awaiting judgment for the crime of trying to survive.

He shrugged. "You know what I mean."

"She ruined my life, John," she said, "but don't misunderstand me, that's not my grudge. My grudge is that she didn't *notice*. She never thought about who she hurt. She just wanted to get to the top, and she still does. You defend her because your boat is rising with hers. But make no mistake, John. That's just a coincidence. Her leadership has one goal only, and it's to help herself, not you. Keep your eyes open to it. Best you figure it out *before* she leaves you behind."

John Little's lips pursed, but he did not argue it.

"Good is," he offered, "you're not shy to talk of it. I thought I'd have to squeeze it out of you."

"Bad is," she smiled, "we're probably all about to be thrown into gaol cells. It's easier to open up when it's your last confession."

There was an optimism in John's face that said *maybe, maybe not*. It said he'd gotten out of tighter scrapes than this. But some day, Marion would lead them through a scrape just wide enough for her and no one else.

"You're heading to Huntingdonshire, then?" came a thick voice. Its owner was an equally thick Guardsman with one of the more bunnylike lion sashes, and his face was smashed into a small area beneath an endless expanse of forehead. Arable recognized him as the man Marion had been negotiating with, rejoining them.

John hopped to his feet, as quickly as his girth allowed. "We are."

"Best get moving, then." The man looked over their group, smiling widely. "No point in sitting around here all day, is there?"

Arable glanced at John in surprise. "So we're free to go?"

"We'll escort you to Stamford and see you across the Welland," the Guardsman said, clicking his tongue. His mount twisted underneath him, and he struggled to keep her still. "But we'll be setting the pace, and expect you not to fall behind, understand?"

John seemed relieved. "That's very kind of you."

"No, it's not," Arable said, with an intentional sharpness. It was better than a prison, but it was not mercy that guided their host's decision. "They're not looking after us, they just want to make sure we don't stay in Rutlandshire."

The forehead man continued to smile, unaffected. "If you've been telling us the truth, then what matter is it to you? You're right, we don't want you here, and we don't have room for you none neither. We could've turned you back where you came from. But we didn't, so that's a kindness, innit?"

"Very kind," John huffed.

"See that you remember that." The Guardsman seemed quite proud of himself. "Sheriff d'Albini is a kind man, and he's shown you kindness this day. Be sure to repay that kindness by staying where you're going, once you get there."

Arable scoffed. "I didn't see Sheriff d'Albini here. Did you run off to Belvoir Castle while we were waiting?"

That wiped the man's smile into a scowl. Rutland was a tiny and rural county, so William d'Albini ruled over the smallest lot of land of any Sheriff in England. Belvoir Castle was a day's walk north, where d'Albini resided in comfort and practically never left. Arable only knew these things because of her time in Nottingham Castle, but she didn't like being spoken down to by some self-satisfied Guardsman with an inadvisable amount of forehead.

"Sheriff's a busy man," he answered, more coldly. "I speak in his name."

John Little gave Arable a stern glare. *Back down.* And he was right. The man had given no cause for Arable to snap at him, but she'd been quick to anger lately. The hunger, the fatigue, her body's perpetual ache—she'd noticed her emotions were ever on edge. She tried to soothe whatever offense she'd given. "Thank you, then. It is *your* kindness we shall remember, not his."

"I'd rather you didn't," he said frankly, "lest you see fit to assign a similar blame upon me for the price of our escort."

She stalled. "The *price* of your escort?"

"Your lady and I came to an agreement," he explained, though Arable had yet to see Marion return.

John shifted uneasily. "What's the agreement?"

"One in four," he announced, with enough finality to be clear it was not up for debate. "If you're traveling through Rutlandshire, we'll have our king's ransom for it."

"*One in four!*" Arable balked, but John put a hand on her shoulder. "We already have practically nothing left to call our own, what is a quarter of nothing to you?"

"'Tis the price of our roads, and our mercy," the forehead man answered. "If you do not wish to pay, you're welcome to take the long road around, or to sit in a debtor's cell."

"We'd be fed better," she grumbled.

"We'll pay it," John answered heavily. "Though I hope that when you see how little it amounts to, that you might take pause at it."

"Don't worry," the Guardsman smiled again, "we'll only take a quarter pause."

Arable would have said more but John's hand touched her waist and ushered her away. She stared at the Guardsman over her shoulder. Some things were no different, no matter what county or country or world. The Common Guard back in Nottingham was full of ignorant bullies grown into ignorant men, who were given a morsel of power and thought they were the head of the feast. Here, in a tiny parcel like Rutland, even the smallest minds would find nothing but boundaries to push against.

"They're not collecting it for the king's ransom," she hissed. "They'll take it for themselves and Sheriff d'Albini will never even know we were on his land."

"I'd say you have the right of it," John grumbled. "But that doesn't change none that we have to give it up."

They started collecting everything they owned, they took stock of every crumb, every blanket, every bit of string. The horsemen loomed over them, grunting now and then when they thought someone might be hiding something, and occasionally being right about it. Their group had long been stripped of their dignity, but to have the last of their meager possessions thrown haphazardly into a pile was the last of it. It was dehumanizing. Arable had to stay mad just to keep the tears away. She wondered if a quarter of them would be expected to strip down naked to give the very rags they wore as well.

Friar Tuck, in a rare display of muted antagonism, gathered a small crowd and read loudly from his Bible. " . . . *and neglect not your hospitality to strangers, for in doing so might you have entertained angels, unaware.*"

The Guardsmen ignored him. They poked at the piles and took what they wanted, insulting the paltry offerings. One man tested a knife against a nearby rock and complained when it broke. They were hardly mathematical with their sorting. They took one in four, but only that which was worth taking. Cups, spices, sewing needles—but leaving the clothes that were falling apart and the baskets that could hardly carry them. Arable watched one man mess angrily through her belongings and pocket her only thimble ring, apparently thinking he'd stumbled upon a piece of jewelry. She hated him, hated the violation. She memorized his face, accepting a grudge in exchange for his theft.

"Between the bandits this morning and *you,*" she sneered at the foreheaded Guardsman, who didn't seem to find much he liked, "we might not even make it to Stamford. We'd hate to inconvenience you by dying on your land."

"Look on the bright side." The man smiled. "If it weren't for those bandits, we'd be taking even more. As you say, a quarter o'nothing is better than a quarter o'everything, innit?"

"That's not—"

"Wanna make a fuss of it?" His jovial voice finally turned dark. "Rutland needs to see to its own, too, you know. Last group of refugees from Nottingham looted their way through, and that wasn't fair much neither, was it? As I say, we're leading you through, which is more'n generous. We ought to turn you back, so don't make me doubt mesself."

It was a queer comment, and Arable abandoned her disdain for the man a moment. "Wait. Why are so many people fleeing from Nottingham?"

"Fewer Robin Hoods down here, I figger."

It was a solemn drum beat, that name, it brought dread alone now.

Fewer Robin Hoods?

There was only one Robin Hood now, and Will Scarlet had taken that name to Nottingham.

Whatever the Guardsman meant by that comment, it likely boded poorly for Will.

The man chortled at her silence. "Can't right blame d'Albini for staying in a castle neither, can you, when there's folks goin' 'bout killing every Sheriff they come upon. You're the ones fleeing, you tell me what you're running from. Naw, don't, I don't care. Just thank me, so as there's no hard feelin's, girl, or we change our minds."

She didn't need any nudging from John Little this time. Arable knew when to surrender, when to become meek, and when survival was more important than self-respect. She hoped that pride had some fat in it, as she'd been made to swallow an awful lot of it lately.

Eventually, to equal parts dismay and joy, they were off again—pushed forward at an uncomfortable jog by the Rutland host. Marion stayed ahead of the group, riding atop her horse beside her knight Amon amongst the Rutland's vanguard. *Too good to walk with us.* She did not even come to explain how the "negotiations" went, how she had masterfully cost them a quarter of everything they owned for a single day's passage. Even without Arable's complicated history with her, it would be impossible to like Marion Fitzwalter.

Arable slung her sack over her shoulder. It was one-quarter emptier, as was her stomach. She wondered if she was starving. She didn't know how to differentiate one pain in her body from the others anymore.

"We don't have enough food," John huffed. "Enough for a few tonight, perhaps, but practically nothing when split amongst all of us."

"Then some don't eat at all tonight," Arable answered. "And come morning, none of us do."

ELEVEN

ARTHUR A BLAND

NOTTINGHAM

"GET HER!" WASN'T NECESSARY to shout, but Arthur did it anyway and felt like a right fool for doing so. He launched himself after the girl in the tattered olive surcoat, fairly confident he'd overtake her quickly, forgetting he was at every disadvantage.

Little Bitch—she'd earned the name very quickly—darted in and out of an open stone building, then changed directions behind a hanging rug and clambered over a low wall. Arthur followed her at each twist, but just barely. She knew the streets, while Arthur had to spend half his energy watching out for obstacles. He overshot her when she disappeared behind a square stone column, but he caught himself and saw her trying to walk casually away in the opposite direction. He hugged the wall and backtracked, hoping she might not notice—but the crowd parted and they made brief eye contact, then ran again. She was not so young as he previously thought. Arthur guessed her to be ten or eleven, and damned if she wasn't a sharp one, and curious nimble.

A dozen yards ahead she slopped noisily into the mud in the middle of a lane, pausing at an intersection to pick her way, second-guessed herself, then plunged down another. It gave Arthur the few precious seconds he needed to gain ground, but his heart plummeted when he made the turn and realized she'd planned it. He nearly bowled into two heavy gords, themselves still reeling from Little Bitch's flight past them.

"Woah, now!" barked one as Arthur scrambled to a stop, inches away.

"Here's a man in a hurry, eh?" The other stuck an accusing finger into Arthur's chest, his breath spewing the stench of onions.

The first gord moved at a casual lope to follow Little Bitch. "That your daughter?" he asked helpfully, intent to join the chase.

"No, no," Arthur answered, too quickly, missing the opportunity.

"Only two reasons for a fellow to chase a girl down," the onion gord grumbled, repositioning himself as Arthur tried to move past. "So she'd *better* be your daughter."

"No, she—" Arthur didn't want to contradict himself, but he desperately did not want them to get involved. Down the curve of the side street, Little Bitch paused and looked back smugly, flipped him a crude hand signal, then disappeared. *Horsefucker.*

"You'd best walk away," the first gord coughed. "That cunny ain't worth your trouble."

"You're terrible," the other chided him, grinning onion teeth and thinking some onion thoughts. Arthur should have been thankful those thoughts didn't involve arresting the obvious criminal in front of them, but he was too preoccupied with a particular little bitch who had his coinpurse. Arthur craned his neck to look past them, but she was long gone. Even if he followed her now, she seemed plenty savvy enough to know how to disappear, and she'd had more than enough time to do so.

Arthur lingered a few extra moments and mumbled an apology to the gords, hoping to become utterly forgettable. Losing his coin was bad, but getting pulled in by the Sheriff's Guard would probably spoil the rest of his life— merciful short as it would then be.

Fortunately, the two gords seemed happy to move on, and Arthur moved back around the corner of the intersection where the girl had slipped him.

The hawk boy and the bread boy, both looking more shocked than the other, slid to a halt right in front of Arthur and turned to flee back toward Red Lion Square.

So he was running again.

The boys weren't half as clever as the girl. They ran loudly, slamming into and over obstacles, shouting at each other and anyone in their way. Arthur had little trouble keeping pace with them, bounding through the wake of their clumsiness. These two were improvising and neither seemed to trust the other's choice. If they had any cunning in them, they'd have split up. He and David had done exactly that back in Sheffield, practiced a dozen ways to separate and help each other if ever they were chased. Instead these boys clumped, and he followed them through a series of shrinking alleys until they ran single file down the crack between two buildings and then tumbled to a stop.

The passage opened up into what was once a small plaza, now blockaded across its length by the backside of a two-story wooden monstrosity. This left them trapped in a squarish little yard with not even a window to escape into, well away from the busy street and its casual eyes. Arthur stood in their only exit.

"Well that's that," Arthur laughed, trying to hide his exhaustion. The two boys weren't nearly as winded as he was, but they were panicked and nervous. They looked around for any opening, then resigned to retreat against the wooden wall. He smiled and ambled forward into the center of the plaza. "First order of court, you'll be handing me back my coinpurse, fuck you muchly. But second, I've got some questions for you, and you'll answer them, and that'll be dandy, won't it?"

The boys looked confused. Perhaps they didn't speak English.

"Let me try again." He cracked his knuckles. "If you don't answer my questions, I'll reach into the back of your skulls and pull out the answers one by one." He exhaled harshly, hoping he still sounded intimidating despite his lack of breath. "Either way, this starts with you opening your mouths. So how do you want to do it?"

The two boys looked at him, then each other, then him again, and snickered.

They stood upright, offensively comfortable, as if they knew very many things that Arthur did not.

And damn it all if they weren't right.

"Thought you had the upper, dincha?" The voice came from *behind* Arthur, thick with sarcasm, and Arthur whispered a little curse. *Fuck me.* He didn't have to look to know who it was, but he did anyway. The alley entrance bore the shape of one very cock-heady little bitch in an olive surcoat. Whatever sense of innocence she'd had back at Red Lion Square was replaced now by a confidence that shouldn't be possible at her age.

"Same offer to you. Let's talk, girlie," Arthur said.

"You just want to talk *now,* causin' you're surrounded." She tilted her head, letting her black hair tumble onto one side of her face. She wasn't ugly but neither was she pretty. It was as if she'd stolen all her features from various pretty people, but they didn't quite fit together properly on her skull. "I don't think you chased me down to have a talk at me, didcha?"

"No, that's up to you, if you—"

"We're playing a game!" She lit up and uncurled one of her hands to let something dangle out of it, snapping taut just before it hit the cobbles, bobbing in place by a long thin rope. "The only rules of the game are that you're not allowed to tell me *no.*"

She swung the thing slowly, letting its tip just nearly graze the ground.

The rope continued in several loops held loose in her other hand. At its swinging end was a short wooden handle with an angled blade hooking away, just a small paring knife really, but she began to spin it in precise, deadly circles around her own body.

"You've already told me no once, which means I get to take something from you."

She let more slack on the rope, deftly manipulating its direction around and behind her, letting it wrap around one of her arms only to bend its arc and redirect it again. It spun above and below her, sometimes she'd step over its path or spin her own body away, a graceful dance between her nimble little frame and the blinding sharp flash at the end of her whip.

Arthur really wished he had the time to be impressed with it.

"You don't want to play this game," he said, stooping to pull his own knife from his boot. But she tugged the rope and flicked it, sending the blade straight at Arthur's feet, forcing him to leap backward as the dart bit at the cobbles where he'd been standing. A moment later it bounced back into her hand. His heart skipped, and he glanced around despite knowing there were no exits to be found. The two boys, ironically, had climbed halfway up the wooden wall, poised in little crawlholes that had been previously hidden. Each had a handful of sharp rocks that they raised to throw at him, laughing at his instinctive flinch.

"Nowhere to run," Little Bitch singsonged at him, giving her rope an elaborate twirl that wrapped around her neck and off again. *Fuck*, Arthur thought. *She could kill herself with that thing, but she looks downright bored with it.*

"Girlie, this is normally the part where I say I don't want to hurt you," he settled into a fighting stance, "but I'm not so good a liar."

"Sorry," she whined, "couldn't hear you since you're all the way over there. Why'n'cha come an' whisper that in my ear?"

"Girlie—"

She leaned and let loose on the knife dart's slack, and Arthur's bowels ducked before he did. The blade snapped back before it hit him, but it sent him flinching to the ground.

He was on all fours, more than a little embarrassed to be there, and the little bitch was already skipping over her damn rope again.

She cocked her head to match him. "Call me *girlie* again."

"Alright," he sighed. "What do you want?"

"Everything you've got." She smiled. "All the way down to your billies. Don't worry, I've seen them before."

The thought of undressing in front of an eleven-year-old girl was appalling, and hiding naked in the streets of Nottingham until David rescued him was just about the worst thing Arthur could imagine. His mind started racing for alternatives, but it wasn't much use in its recently throttled jelly state. All he came up with were flimsy excuses he could later give David to explain why he'd be stark nude.

"Come now," he tried, but the knife leapt at her command again, straight for his head. He recoiled and fell backward even as he watched its point snap just shy of him, then fly back to her grasp.

"Oh sorry!" she crooned. "Thought you said *no!* Guess I shoulda been more specific. I don't have the best hearing. Iffin' it doesn't sound like *yes*, it sounds like *no*." She smirked, her face flickering back to the unnerving innocence and wide eyes of a young girl. "Now take your pants off, and stop being a puss about it."

I'm a grown man, Arthur reminded himself, trying to ignore the heckles from the two boys perched on the wall. He stared at the girl, hoping to find a flaw in her posture, all while untying his breeches until they dropped to the ground in a humiliating heap around his boots.

"Oh my god, he fucking did it!" the bitch laughed, letting the rope skitter to a halt as she buckled over in hysterics. "Look at him—!" She pointed at his legs, burst backward into laughter again, and nearly fell over.

Arthur just bobbed his head, accepting his defeat, not sure if this meant they were done playing with him. He bent over to tug his breeches up, but the girl stood upright quick as a lightning bolt and started another slow circle with the dart. "Those are mine," she said, eyes on his clothes. She snorted, but managed to finish with a straight face. "Now hurry up with the rest of 'em."

Arthur slowly bent down to pull off his fucking boots.

A sharp whistle broke their attention. "First of all, you should learn how to count."

The voice came from behind her, down the narrow entrance to the alleyway, and of course it belonged to Will Scarlet. Arthur had never been happier to see him.

"There were *four* of us you picked back at Red Lion Square, and you only have but *one* surrounded here. One—and I don't mean to shock you now—is less than four. That leaves three of us to surround *you* instead."

Will's hands were empty, palms out. He stood in the crack of the alley, just shy of entering the square. Arthur looked for any sign of David or Stutely, but found none. Perhaps they were hidden, or perhaps Will was bluffing. Either option was more strategic than standing around without any pants on.

Little Bitch didn't startle at the interruption. Instead she swept her leg around in a wide circle to set her eyes on Will, not stopping the momentum of her weapon and the steady whisper it made as it cut through the air. She let out more slack on the rope, giving herself a larger circle overhead to stay Will's distance.

"Second of all," Will continued, "you shouldn't play with your food. Don't toy with him. Take what he has and disappear. The longer you linger, the more like you are to be walked in on."

"Stay back," she warned, but Arthur thought her voice betrayed the tiniest bit of fear. *She should be scared,* he thought. *The things Will has done should terrify her.* She increased the speed of her blade's spin, making it impossible for Will to leave the alley's gullet. He was safe between the building's walls, but she made it clear he could come no farther. Arthur's stomach twisted, and he had to waddle to a corner to stay safe himself.

Fuck. He pulled his breeches up and hastily tied them.

"And third," Will said, taking a step forward, flush with the alley's mouth, "that scorpion's tail of yours isn't much good in an actual fight. It's only good for scaring people."

He took another step in, too close.

"That means it only works on people who are scared of dying."

Little Bitch leaned into it and let the rope fly, and Will stepped into its circle and grabbed at the tether as it reached him. It tangled in his hands and the knife slapped him across his chest, but its momentum was dead. Scarlet tugged the weapon with both hands, and it flew from the girl's grasp to flap uselessly against the wall. She stumbled to chase after it, then turned to run in the other direction, but Arthur was already there. He snatched one of her wrists and twisted it to bring her to her knees.

"Let me go!" she whimpered.

"No," Arthur said, embellishing the word. "No no no! I get to say it as many times as I want now. No no *no no!*"

"Fourth of all," Will said as he walked up to them, "your boys deserted you."

Arthur glanced up, and sure enough both boys were gone, ferreted away once they lost the upper hand.

"Limp dicks," she muttered at them.

"They weren't very good anyhow." Will knelt down in front of her. "But you're not half-bad."

Arthur could see a bloody streak across Will's chest and forearm where the knife had bit. *He'd walked right into it.* The long cut wasn't bleeding badly, but there's no way Will could've planned that. He could've sliced himself deep and bled out in the mud, all for nothing.

Anybody who follows him is going to drown.

"Will," Arthur said. "We'd best move on then."

Will kept his eyes tight on the girl, but there was thankfully no sign of animosity in them. "I want you to take me to whoever's running the Red Lions."

The girl laughed. "And what makes you think *I'm* not running the Red Lions?"

"I think you can run your mouth," Will smiled, "and that's about it. So if you can't arrange this for me, then I don't have much use for you. Don't make me get creative with the ways I have to threaten you, just trust that you wouldn't enjoy them."

She kept quiet, fidgeted a bit, but didn't struggle against Arthur's grip. "It'll take a little time," she conceded. "And I can't promise anything. The Lions aren't going to listen to me, they don't even know who I am. But I could get them a message. Why would they want to meet with you?"

"You just have to tell them who he is," Arthur said. "Tell their leader that Robin Hood wants to talk to him."

Arthur couldn't have expected the girl's reaction, and clearly Will didn't, either. It started with a choke, then rolled into a ridiculous giddy giggle that made Arthur let her go as she dropped to the ground laughing.

"Alright, I'll do that, shall I?" She stood up and mimed shaking hands with no one. *"How am I? Very well, nice to meet me!"*

"What are you going on about?" Arthur asked.

"Nothing!" She shrugged. "I can't wait to see what'll happen when I tell Robin Hood that Robin Hood wants to talk to him."

TWELVE

QUILLEN PEVERIL

Three little words that meant everything.

Are you important?

ONE WOULD HAVE THOUGHT, in a kinder world, that the unfortunate tale of the great defector Lord Asshole was over. Caring about any detail of Lord Brayden of York's life—including his real name—was a torture all its own. Quill didn't want to know how he attained his title, or anything about his family. But the odds seemed very likely that the man was dead, and Quillen Peveril was regrettably qualified to identify the body.

It was why the six of them had taken to horse and ridden out of Nottingham, following up on stories of an ornate carriage overthrown off the side of the Sherwood Road. A messenger from York had come inquiring about Lord Brayden, who was still expected at home even though he'd left Nottingham four days earlier. Searching for the man should have been procedural work, but the inborn fool that brought news of the abandoned carriage was also foolish enough to mutter the name *Robin Hood*.

Those two words escalated the matter to the attention of Lord Beneger de Wendenal, and the team of bounty hunters he'd enlisted to hunt for his son's murderer.

The Grieving Father of Nottingham, some called him, even though he was from Derby. *Lord Death,* another had whispered, but Quill found that name a bit melodramatic. Someone cleverer had come up with the rhyme *Beneger the Revenger,* although not to his face. But his loyal Derbymen—a dozen sword-arms who had garrisoned in the middle bailey, openly hostile to anyone who showed them attention—simply called the man *Ben.*

"Still here, then?" Quill asked of Jacelyn de Lacy, who was riding beside him.

"You too?" she responded, as always.

De Grendon had availed the Black Guard to Beneger's hunt and recommended Quill specifically for this search, given his familiarity with the victim. It was admittedly a nice break from walking the midnight wall, and Quill was happy to share stories with his stony-faced counterpart.

"I'm only here because Lord Beneger thinks we're friends," Jac huffed.

Quill hesitated to ask. "Aren't we?"

She turned enough that her good eye could squint at him, as if seeing him for the first time. "You're not the bottom of the list."

That oddly put him at ease. From Jac, it was practically a love letter.

The three others in their group kept the pace methodically slow. Lord Be-neger had recruited the Coward Knight and his two minions onto his hunt party, on account of their supposed experience hunting Robin Hood. Sir Rob-ert FitzOdo was an incompetent ox, granted the ability to speak through some sort of magic. He had joined the Nottingham Guard in the winter, on loan from the Baron of Tickhill Castle, along with his impossibly more useless assistants Derrick and Ronnell. Quill dropped his horse to the rear, just in case their brickheadedness was the result of something contagious.

"Are you important?"

"You've faced these traitors before," Lord Beneger said. He had not slowed his horse, but simply motioned for Quillen to hasten and ride beside him.

His words had an oddly accusatory nature. "I did," Quill answered, "but only once. Jacelyn was there as well, as was FitzOdo."

"And I've spoken with them about it. Now I'm speaking with you. Would you be able to identify Will Scarlet on sight?"

Quill mulled it over. He'd only seen Will Scarlet once, in the mist outside Bernesdale, during the ambush. Panic could do queer things to one's memo-ries. "Maybe. But if he's grown a beard out, or his hair, I think he could pass me in the city and I'd never know. But maybe."

"Very good," was all Beneger replied, as his eyes sharpened ahead on Fitz-Odo and his men. Quill could guess what the man was thinking. FitzOdo's group had been at that fight, too, though most believed they fled as soon as the arrows flew. Since then, they'd been "on the hunt" with literally nothing to show for it. The majority of FitzOdo's search was probably done in whorehouses and taverns, where they could have crossed paths with Will Scarlet a dozen times and never noticed. "If this mysterious carriage ends up having nothing to do with Robin Hood, I'm not interested in it."

"Alright." Quill swallowed. He didn't know what he was supposed to do with that knowledge.

"And don't make me fish information out of you. If you see something out of place, anything at all, you let me know."

"I will." Again, Quill had no idea what he might notice that would qualify as being *out of place*. "How will we know? How will we know if it's the outlaws, or someone else?"

"Don't call them outlaws," Beneger said sharply, though not unkindly. Be-neath the thin skin of his crow's-feet, muscles clenched and relaxed. "*Outlaw* implies they live *outside the law,* suggesting there's a place where rules don't matter. That is an appealing notion to those who endure misfortune. It glorifies the misconception that they have a choice—which they don't. We have words for people who live *without law*, words provided to us by the very laws they break. Thieves. Murderers. *Widowmakers,* Quillen. Anarchists. Their cause is not so attractive once you identify it as treason."

Quill nodded and made a note to try to change his own vocabulary around Lord Beneger. He looked at the man, and the deep lines of his face—telling the story of his life like the exposed rings of a tree trunk. Quill had only barely known William de Wendenal before he was killed, but he saw much of the son in the father. Not physically, perhaps, but in the quality of their personalities. *Driven,* and impressive. In Beneger it was tinged with something cold, slightly hollow perhaps—but then again, the man was still mourning his son.

If somehow he could interest Lord Beneger in claiming the Sheriffcy, Nottingham would do well.

Three little words that meant everything. "Are you important?"

THEY ALMOST MISSED THE carriage, only a half hour's walk into the Sherwood. Two heavy trenches carved off road through the ash, then down a short snowy embankment now littered in splinters. Flattened underbrush led to the carriage, which had been dragged over a shallow ridge. Quill wondered how heavy the thing was, and how many men it must have taken to move it. They walked through its aftermath, through charcoal tree husks that would never grow back.

Someone's life had ended here. Quill didn't exactly wish the Lord Asshole Brayden of York to be *dead,* but if the body was indeed his, then that would not be so terrible a thing.

The bulk of the carriage was mostly intact, although both of its exposed wheels had been removed—by a good deal of hatchetwork, from the look of it. There were chunks of wood all about, torn remnants of colorful fabric and paper scraps. Any ironwork and hinges had already been plied off, giving the impression that its frame would collapse if any of them sneezed.

On its far side Quill noticed something he couldn't quite place, then realized with a lurch that it was a man's leg. Still attached to the body, fortunately, but it would be wrong to call it intact. The sole of the foot and the calf both looked half-eaten, showing black pulp and bone.

Quill would have turned away in disgust, but a slight shift of his focus put him in a dead stare with two hairy men, hunched behind a fallen oak a bit farther off.

A sudden memory of arrows cutting through the trees in the mist. Of Captain Gisbourne's throat, torn open.

Dirty, bearded. Barbaric murderers, perhaps, or terrified travelers. Quill rallied his nerves and raised his hand to get Lord Beneger's attention, but it startled the two strangers.

One stood, frozen; but the other raised a wooden club and ran at them.

Lord Beneger yelled for FitzOdo's men to advance, and it was over with very little fanfare. Ronnell swung his sword down onto the attacker, knocking the club from his hand and slicing down into the shoulder, by the base of the neck. The man lumbered, reeled, then ran into the woods, clutching at his injury. FitzOdo and his boys pounded after in pursuit, but the going off trail was tricky, and their horses did not seem much faster than the man running.

Jacelyn de Lacy went only so far as the fallen oak before swinging down from her saddle. She pulled her sword out and commanded the other stranger down to the ground, then bound his hands behind his back and to his feet.

Quill realized exactly how useless he was, standing there motionless behind the carriage while everyone else had sprung to action.

Of course he walked the midnight wall. Three months in the Black Guard, and Quill's instincts were still to freeze in the face of danger.

"Are you important?" Lord Beneger asked.

BOTH THE LEG AND its body belonged to Lord Brayden of York, but Quill took no joy in it. The stench was ungodly, such that Quill's stomach rose into his throat and he turned away to keep from retching. Lord Brayden's eyes were bloody-black holes, chewed out. Half his face was torn to gore—eaten, most likely—and maggots now infested the exposed meat. His clothes had been shredded, revealing great fissures in his belly that leaked pink and yellow clumps of fat. The flesh was rent away, leaving a black discharge that assaulted the sense of sight and smell alike.

And next to him, a second body. A woman's. A week ago, Quill would have made any number of terrible insults about whatever type of woman would choose to spend her time with Lord Brayden. But nobody deserved to end up like this. Her body was thin—a young woman, probably; she lay on her back with her bodice ripped apart, half her chest devoured by animals. Her face was no better than Lord Brayden's. She was entirely naked below the waist, her legs spread profanely wide, her pelvis pushed halfway into the earth.

Quill vomited.

She had no name, and no face, and when he vomited again tears came to his eyes.

He looked away, wiping bile from his lips, his guts twisting. He had not thought it would be so horrible. He'd wanted to see Lord Brayden with a stupid look on his asshole face and a sword in his heart. But this . . . this he wouldn't wish upon anyone.

"Can you identify them?" Lord Beneger asked. He was still on horseback, as if he could not be troubled to stay any longer than necessary. FitzOdo's men had not yet returned with the fled assailant, and Jacelyn kept her foot on her bound prisoner, cooing commands at him to stay down. Quill stared at the two carcasses, ignoring the woman and focusing on the man's face.

There was no doubt.

Lord Beneger simply nodded. "Any sign this was done by Robin Hood or his gang?"

"Why don't we ask *him*?" Quillen asked, pointing to Jac's captive.

Beneger dismissed it. "He's just a looter. We'll see what they know when Fitz-Odo returns with the other one. Any insight, Peveril?"

He could only sigh. "I don't know that I'd be able to tell. It isn't as if they left a note telling us who was here."

"Who is to say? Perhaps we don't know what to look for." Beneger pulled his collar up to cover his nose and dismounted to inspect the bodies, eyes wide and poring over their wounds. "I'd say they were stabbed, both of them, in the chest, multiple times. With a wide blade."

He pulled on the remnants of the woman's arms and hoisted her to a sitting position, though her body made a series of horrific cracks at the movement.

"Nothing went out her back. So either a knife, or a swordsman with incredible restraint. And see where the blood has run." He pointed to her naked body as if it had never been a person at all. "Or rather, where it has *not*. Nothing dried on her front nor her back. The blood all ran down. So she was killed while standing, or sitting perhaps, and was moved prone after she stopped bleeding."

Jacelyn coldly presumed she'd been raped, to which Lord Beneger agreed—with the addition that it likely happened well after she was dead.

"There's no bruising around her thighs," he pointed out. "If her blood was still pumping when she'd been taken, you'd see the bruises."

Quill retched again, though there was nothing left in him to expel. His stomach muscles seized, and he thought he might choke to death, until at last he forced himself to relax.

"Would you say this is consistent with Robin's gang, or not?"

"Consistent?" Quill asked. If seeing sights such as this was a consistency in the Nottingham Guard, he would have returned home to Derby long ago. "No. They normally don't kill anyone."

Jacelyn hissed in a sharp breath. "Are you fucking serious? My uncle, and Lord Beneger's son . . . these are the people they *haven't* killed?"

"God, I'm sorry," Quill stammered. "I didn't mean—"

"No." Beneger held out his hand, pointed in earnest at Quill. "You had a point, go on and say it. Don't be shamed for thinking what you think."

It felt like a trap, but Quill said what he could. "Yes, they've obviously killed before. But that's not what I meant. When they rob people out here in the woods, they normally don't kill them. In fact, they normally don't hurt them at all. They just take what they can and disappear. This . . . no, it doesn't seem consistent."

Lord Beneger nodded, neither in agreement nor against. His face had once been kind, Quill thought, but had turned hard as the years whittled away at him. Even the stubble of whiskers on his cheeks seemed thicker and harder than a normal man's. "Thank you."

The prisoner tried to say something, but Jacelyn simply reached down and twisted the inside of the man's elbow until he gasped. "You'll get your turn," she promised.

"Until then," Quill added, "I guarantee you're better off pretending to be a rock or something. Be a rock, friend. Be a rock."

Lord Beneger went on a bit longer, walking around the corpses, scrutinizing things that Quill would never have imagined would be of any interest. It wasn't until Beneger stated, "You haven't been around many bodies," that Quill even realized he'd been staring into Lord Brayden's hollowed face for quite some time.

"No." He turned away, shaking the sensation off.

"What did I say about making me fish for information?"

Quill huffed, but he didn't know what else to say. "I'm not suited for *this*. The Guard isn't exactly the right place for me. I'm better suited as an advisor, but Ferrers wouldn't have me." He gestured limply at the horror of the scene. "Clearly not *your* first body, though."

Beneger frowned. "No. But I'm still disgusted by it."

"You don't look it."

"Not the body, no. But the injustice."

"Exactly. Nobody deserves—"

"No," Lord Beneger cut him off. "We don't know what this man deserved. Lord Brayden of York probably deserved to die, most people do. Most people have wronged someone else in an unforgivable way, and should be made to pay for it. But he didn't die for that. He died because some strangers wanted his coin. Someone out there, someone who wanted to see this man dead for very legitimate reasons . . . that person will never get what they want."

Quill could only open his eyes wide and hope he never saw the world in such a stark way.

"That's how it is with revenge, that's why you have to seek it out yourself and take it. Before someone steals it from you."

Beneger the Revenger stared at the bodies as if they had personally done him wrong. Quill wondered if Lord Beneger's stone heart was what drew him toward revenge, or if it was the natural result of pursuing it.

He might have said something more, to suggest that Lord Beneger might make a good Sheriff. But he didn't.

Three little words that meant everything. "Are you important?" Lord Beneger asked.

DERRICK RETURNED ON HORSE, with the injured looter walking in front of him. His right arm crossed over his chest and clutched the bloody wound of his neck. Derrick instructed him to move left, or right, and smiled at his prisoner's obedience. The poor man's eyes were empty, his face was pale, and most of his life was already soaked into his tunic. The other looter, who had done a good job of remaining rocklike under Jacelyn's boot, broke out in sudden grief at the sight of his battered companion. FitzOdo and Ronnell were shortly behind, wandering back from the trees as if they had all day for this one task.

At Derrick's command, the injured man finally lowered himself to the ground. His breathing was too heavy, and Quill could tell he was struggling to stay conscious.

"What's your name, friend?" FitzOdo asked the healthier man. He had to ask it twice more before receiving an answer.

"Han . . . Hanry. Hanry, my lord. That there is Munday."

"This is your friend?" Quill clarified. "His name is Munday?"

"Yes, m'lord."

"Your friend Munday isn't going to make it," Jacelyn told him. "Do you know why he's going to die? He attacked us, which was a very poor decision."

"He didn't know what he was doing." Hanry bit back tears. "He wouldn't have been a threat."

"We didn't know that." Quill knelt, hoping to help in this, at least. "You understand that, right? A man comes at us with a weapon, we have no way of knowing if he's a halfwit or a knight. And with you two hiding next to all this," he pointed toward Lord Brayden's body, "we have to protect ourselves before we protect you. You see that, right?"

Hanry shook his head as if to argue, but he didn't. He kept staring at Munday's face, which was growing paler and more distant.

"Did you kill those two people?"

"No. Just found 'em."

"Do you know who did it?" Quill asked.

But Hanry didn't answer. He just stared at his dying friend.

"Was it Will Scarlet?"

The man's muscles contorted farther, a silent scream.

"He's in a lot of pain," Jacelyn offered. "We can end it for him, if you like."

But still, Hanry gave no response.

Quill didn't want to watch Munday's final moments, but Hanry's face was almost worse. Everything was clenched and turned red, there was no telling where his eyes were, it was all just tortured flesh.

Eventually Munday was dead. A shiver rushed through Quill's body like a regret. It was the oddest sensation for a death to happen while so many people were calm. Nothing at all had changed, and yet somehow there were now fewer people there.

"Let's talk about what you're doing here," Jac was saying.

"We weren't doing nothing," Hanry answered, a bit too quickly. "We had just come across this when you arrived. We didn't kill them, and we didn't steal nothing none neither."

"You knew to come here, didn't you?" Jac added, her voice offering the man no concession. "The same reason we knew to come here. Something this bloody, left out for everyone to see . . . that gets people talking. So why don't you tell us where you heard about this, and we'll take it from there."

Lord Beneger was back atop his horse. "Out with it. Was it Robin Hood?"

Hanry just seemed confused.

"What are people saying?" Quill took his attention back. "Who is laying claim to this? Are people saying that Robin Hood did it?"

"No." Hanry shook his head. "No no, nobody thinks that . . ."

Lord Beneger did not even bother to reply, he simply bid his horse to turn away. "That's all we needed. Deal with him quickly, Peveril, and we'll make our return."

"Wait!" Quill yelled, feeling like a pathetic child. He had no clue how to *deal with* all these bodies. Whether he was supposed to bury them, or ride back to Nottingham to tell Captain de Grendon. Surely someone would have to notify Lord Brayden's estate, but would they even want to receive what remained of their lord and his lady? "How do we . . . deal with him?"

"He was stealing. He's a thief," Beneger said, with a naked sort of finality. "Stealing amongst the poorfolk is usually punished by taking fingers. Stealing from a lord, even one who's already dead . . . I would take his hand."

Quill's arm started twitching. He looked to Jacelyn for support, but she only shrugged in general approval. "That's fair," she admitted. "I would think we've seen enough severed hands lately, but fair is fair."

"It isn't about being fair." Beneger squinted. "It's the law. Make haste."

Quill pulled out of himself, he floated up and away and watched his own body draw his sword from the frog at his belt. He heard the dull scrape of its steel against the iron ring, though he couldn't feel its weight in his hand. His eyes, yes, his eyes were locked with Hanry's, but even so he wasn't really looking anywhere. He knew he had to do this thing or else the others would leave without him, and he was more scared of that than of doing the thing.

"Put your hand against the log," someone said, and it sounded very much like his voice. Perhaps he'd simply never heard himself speak before.

Hanry, this person, kept his hand clutched against his chest. He didn't understand—he needed to put it on the log. The sooner he put it out, the faster this would be over, and everyone wanted this to be over. The man begged, "No no no," just kept guarding his hand and huddling down into it, but Quill couldn't hear him.

"Take your punishment," Lord Beneger commanded, cutting through the haze. "If you pull it back, or try to run, then it will be far worse for you."

Despite his coldness, there was no cruelty in his voice. He was simply offering facts, as if he were stating that there would be rain later, or what sort of soup he preferred at dinner.

Somehow, Hanry put his arm out, quivering, until it touched the bark of the rotted log and then he leaned away. Suddenly he gasped and swapped hands, plunging his left hand there instead, relieved that he'd made the wiser choice in time. It made Quill feel a bit better but still he was nauseous as he raised the sword up over his head.

"Please." Hanry's eyes were small and wet and red. He was saying other things too, lots of things really, but the words blurred together and hung like a fog.

"I'm sorry," Quill said. "I surely wish Robin Hood had been here after all."

He pulled up, hard, quickly—

"What if he had?" Hanry blurted out, his beady eyes widening in horror.

Then I wouldn't have to do this, Quill answered.

"What does it matter if Robin Hood was here?" Hanry yelled.

"If Robin Hood was here," Beneger answered from the top of the ridge, "then you'd be talking with me. If he wasn't, then you lose your hand for theft."

"What do you want to know?" Hanry asked, shaking his head, begging. "I've met him. I've met Robin Hood. His real name's Will Scarlet. I've seen his people, he gave us coin before, and food, though not for a long time. What do you want to know? Tell me, please, I'll tell you anything. They say he's gone mad. That's why Munday left them, why we're on our own. I heard he abandoned all the women and children in his group, it's just him and his men now. They killed these people, for certain they did. They say that he . . ." He paused for a moment, eyes fixed on the sword that Quill still held aloft. "They say he went to Nottingham. They say he has a man inside the Nottingham Guard."

That was chilling news, but a relief that Quill could lower his weapon.

Lord Beneger looked down his nose at the prisoner. "You've taken money from this Robin Hood, money that you knew was stolen, food that you knew was stolen. Did you report any of this to the county Guardsmen?"

"Hm?" Hanry's face twisted. "No. No, of course not."

"You should have. You've seen these murderers, you know their faces, you've accepted their payments for secrecy. You say they planted a traitor within our ranks, and you kept that to yourself." A warm cloud billowed from his nostrils. "You are complicit in their crimes."

"Complicit? What does that mean?" Hanry looked from face to face, his own shifting from a frown to a smile, unsure if he was being chastised or rewarded. "I told you about them, that's everything I know. I can't help you any more than that."

The poor fool. Quill lowered his head. "You only talked at the edge of a sword. That isn't help. That's a confession."

"You're not . . ." Hanry cradled his arm again. "You're not still going to take my hand, are you?"

Lord Death may have been a proper name for Beneger after all. "You have abetted Robin Hood's gang in thievery and murder, assassination, and treason. You will be treated as one of them."

The air left Quill's chest, and he found himself pleading for the man's life. "He's shown some remorse. Ought that earn a man a bit of leniency? His friend is already dead, and we were going to take his hand, we could leave it at that."

Lord Beneger gave the tiniest shake of his head.

I should have taken his hand, was the last thing Quill would have thought he'd regret when this day began.

"I haven't done anything!" Hanry gasped, kicking backward, and coming uncomfortably close to Munday's body. "Please! I haven't *abetted* nothing, all we ever did was take some of his coin, and then you came and burnt us out of our own fields! I've been lost out here, Munday and I have had to survive on our own. I've got a family, somewhere, please!"

"If you can truthfully answer me *yes* to any of these questions," Lord Beneger crouched to eye level with the panicked Hanry, "we'll only take your hand. You've admitted to hiding secrets about Robin Hood's movements from the county Guard. First, do you have any proof that you have not helped Robin Hood beyond this, or that you played no part in the crimes here with this murdered lord and his mistress?"

"Proof?" Hanry gaped and looked for support. He wouldn't find any. After some amount of babbling, he slumped down in defeat and answered, "No."

"No. Second," Beneger continued, "can you provide any proof that you genuinely regret your actions and that you will make efforts to repay the damage you've done?"

"I am regretful," Hanry let out. "So very regretful. I see now that keeping silent was as good as helping them, I see that, I do."

"No," Beneger answered for the man. "You cannot provide proof. You show your regret now that you have been caught, but not before. You cannot trade us anything that we can hold in hostage until you repay your debt. You have only your word to give, which you have proven is unfaithful, so you can offer us nothing of real value."

It was a while before Hanry could agree, and admit it. "No," he said. "I can't prove it. But I didn't do it. And I didn't mean to help them, I was just trying to survive. Isn't that enough? What else can I do? What's the third question?"

Three little words that meant everything. "Are you important?" Lord Beneger asked.

They hanged Hanry by the carriage.

DURING THE RETURN TO Nottingham, Quill could not escape his own mind, which tumbled about his skull in search of an escape and, finding none, chose to boil.

There was privilege to a name. Lord Beneger would have let that man live if he'd been family to a lord, if he'd held any title beyond *looter*. Quill, if not for a quirk of birth that put him under the protective title of *Peveril*, would not have been able to answer yes to any of those questions, either. Everything Quill had was his father's, or his grandfather's. Except his cowardice, that was his alone. He thought himself clever for playing games with noblemen and dabbling at policy, but in the real world he was useless. By all standards that mattered, he was exactly as useful as Hanry, dead and hanged.

FitzOdo and his men left to spread word of Hanry's hanging to any local villages, that they might collect the dead and—more importantly—know why he hung there.

"Staying silent is no less of a crime," Beneger explained as they walked their horses. "It is fear alone that keeps the people silent. They're right to fear Robin Hood, but the only sway he holds over them *is* that fear. Overcoming fear, that is the mark of a man. Succumbing to it, makes a man nothing."

"Are you alright?" Jacelyn asked Quill a bit later, when Lord Beneger's horse was far enough ahead to be out of earshot. "You seem shaken."

"That looter," Quill admitted. "I feel for him."

"That's good." She reached out, but their horses weren't close enough to make contact. "That's the only way we can help them. You think FitzOdo and those two donkeys have any care for the people out here? It's good to have a heart, don't lose that. You're one of the good ones, Quill."

It was a startling compliment, considering the source. "What about Lord Beneger? Is he one of the good ones?"

"He is. If you find him cold, then he's the sharpest kind of ice. He knows to surround himself with opposing viewpoints." She studied his reaction—with her good eye, her soft side. "How many times did he demand that you speak your mind?"

That was true. Beneger had respected Quill's opinion, even when he hadn't respected it himself.

"You see things that curs like FitzOdo never will. You feel things. Emotions, you know, and thoughts. I'm not sure FitzOdo has ever tried those out."

That made Quill laugh, which surprisingly came with a wash of guilt. Four bodies lay behind them off the Sherwood Road, who would never laugh again.

As he thought on the day's carnage, a stray thought wandered to the front. "What did you mean earlier," he asked Jac, "when you said you'd seen enough severed hands lately?"

She shrugged it off. "Nothing. We've been running down leads on Robin Hood sightings. There's some old stable in the French Ward where a couple of severed hands were nailed to the wall. Some people claimed it was Robin Hood, cutting off the hands of people who had stolen from him. Damned creepy.

Severed hands? That sounded like Scarlet, but they'd already decided that he couldn't be responsible for any Robin Hood sightings inside the city. He was many things, but not a magician.

"What do you think about what that man said?" he asked. "About Will Scarlet having a man inside the Guard?"

"It's possible. Probably bribe a Common Guard to look the other way now and then. Happens all the time. I doubt it's anything more than that. Or we'd know."

The pieces fell into place. "Would we?"

Damned creepy.

Severed hands.

"Staying silent is no less of a crime."
"They say he has a man inside the Nottingham Guard."
"Overcoming fear, that is the mark of a man."
"How do you want to die?"

"Are you important?"

"I THINK HE WAS RIGHT," Quill told Lord Beneger de Wendenal. "Scarlet has a man inside our ranks, and I think he's responsible for the Robin Hood sightings in the city."

He described everything he knew about Gilbert with the White Hand.

His unknown past, his curious late-night activities, his utter lack of friendships. His choice to volunteer for the midnight walk. His perverse interest in hands. How he joined the Nottingham Guard at exactly the same time Robin Hood's men started killing Sheriffs. His strange familiarity with all the town's gangs.

"Good man." Ben lowered his brow. "Now help me prove it."

Quill had never felt more important in his life.

THIRTEEN

MARION FITZWALTER

HIS NAME WAS GREY Symon, and he was dead, and that, too, was Marion's fault.

That wasn't the worst of it.

Nobody had known him well, nor had they tried. Such was the way all winter. Stragglers joined the group for days or weeks and might speak to nobody. There was no point in growing attached to someone who was unlikely to stick around.

Grey Symon collapsed not so long after they crossed the river Welland and entered the royal forest of Huntingdon. The entirety of Huntingdonshire was a royal forest, which meant only the Earl Robert's men were allowed to hunt its game. So even when they saw a handful of deer or signs of a wild boar, Marion had to refuse those who begged to hunt. She couldn't jeopardize their new relationship before it even began.

So old Grey Symon fell, hungry, surrounded by food.

A young girl, one of the Harnetts, said he'd given her the last of his bread the day earlier.

That wasn't the worst of it.

They had to debate—good God, they had to honestly debate—what to do with his body. With everyone starving, they couldn't delay the whole group long enough to bury him. They didn't have the tools, much less the strength, to do so.

But that wasn't the worst part, either.

The worst was that they decided so quickly. Because the facts were against them. They couldn't even carry his body. So they left him, seated beneath a yew tree, propped up as if he were napping. Somehow that made it easier than leaving him lying down. Tuck mumbled a blessing, and they moved on.

Once upon a time, Marion convinced a group of refugees to leave their lives in the Sherwood Forest to find a new home in Huntingdon. They could have stayed and waited for Will Scarlet's reinforcements from the city. Instead they left, and an old man named Grey Symon starved to death along the way.

Once upon a time, Marion brought a group of debtors to the hermit lord, Walter of Locksley, who agreed to pay their dues in exchange for their vassalage. A community began to thrive, which thereupon brought the attention

of the county's tax assessors. They burnt his manor to the ground and Lord
Walter with it.

"You won't be very helpful if you fall off your horse," Charley Dancer whispered, with no small amount of sarcasm. "Your head has been bobbing off to
sleep for the last mile. You look drunk."

Marion opened her mouth for a witty response, but was sabotaged by an
unrelenting yawn.

There were six horses in total, four of them on loan from Lord Robert. If not
for that fact, the group would undoubtedly be eating horsemeat at this moment.
Instead Marion could let a few people ride by horse the final distance. Charley
was a healthy man, but his lame leg kept him slow. Three of their eldest members struggled even on horseback, barely able to stay saddled. Marion and Sir
Amon tethered those mounts behind their own, in the hopes of reaching their
destination before nightfall.

"We can stop, if only for a few minutes," Charley repeated. "You need it."

Ahead, Amon turned back, his hard jaw speaking to his disapproval.

Marion craned her neck backward but the sun was set, a dull grey blanket
muting any light the sky might offer. The trees in this part of Huntingdon Forest were thin and sinewy, which had a queer gossamer beauty in daylight. But
at dusk the limbs turned into knuckle-ridden fingers and spiders' legs, a maze
of unfamiliar shapes that beguiled the imagination. The rest of the group was
hours behind her now, and would be walking this path in near pitch blackness.

The sooner she made it to the castle, she could start preparing for their
arrival. Yes, she felt wretched for riding ahead while the others slogged on
through their endless trek, but she could help best by making sure Lord Robert
was ready to receive them.

That's what she told herself.

"I'm fine," Marion lied.

Charley's face pursed into something that probably started as a sympathetic
smile, but ended in a painful wince. It was almost enough to make Marion
laugh.

"Here come the infamous thieves of Nottingham!" she mocked, picturing
their beleaguered group limping up to the gates of Huntingdon Castle. "We
should have let ourselves be captured back in the Sherwood, just to shame
them into realizing who it was they were chasing."

Charley searched her face for something. "Well, we're not exactly all innocent." He grimaced. "We've . . . killed."

Once upon a time, Marion arranged a marriage for herself to the High
Sheriff of Nottingham, that she might influence the county's policies toward
greater tolerance to debtors. But she failed to tell her friends the details of her
plans, and they mistakenly tried to rescue her. Half of them died in the at-
tempt, including the man she loved.

"I wasn't there," Charley was saying, "when Captain Gisbourne was killed. Wish I were, though."

"You should be glad you weren't." She could only imagine how long Charley Dancer would last in a swordfight. "I'm not saying killing is ever the right choice, but when the alternative is death, I don't see how we can be judged for that."

"What about earlier?" Charley asked. "I joined on after . . . after Bernesdale. Didn't we kill some Guardsmen there, too?"

She closed her eyes. As if she needed more entries into the catalogue of destruction that was her life.

"I wasn't there, either." She preferred not to think about it. "John Little would know. Maybe Will or Elena killed a few Guardsmen, but nobody who's still with us should be punished for that. If you're saying we deserve this . . . no. It's just me. *I* deserve this. This punishment. The rest of the group, they're just trying to make it to the next meal."

He digested this solemnly, then tried at another smile. "We're not exactly a bunch of Robin Hoods, are we?"

The implication pinched at her heart, which could hardly suffer more damage. "Don't be so sure of that," she said. "Robin Hood was just a name. It's the name of anyone who tries to help another before themselves. Anyone can be a Robin Hood if they just pull their head out of their ass for a minute or two."

Charley's face tried to eat itself. "I wish I had known him better."

"Robin?" Marion tried not to react. "No you don't. He was the worst Robin Hood of all."

> *Once upon a time, Marion defended an elderly woman who sold salted meats from town to town, who had been accused of passing cat meat off as rabbit. To prove her innocence, Marion arranged for an inspection of the meat by an expert butcher from St. Albans, who then purposefully spoilt her entire stock to protect his business from her competition.*
>
> *Once upon a time, Marion championed an apprentice falconer at baronial court, who had been replaced after falling from his horse and injuring his leg. But to be present for his case, he needed to climb a staircase—whereupon he tripped and injured himself further. The injury, which might have mended if he had kept off it, worsened—and he lost the leg.*
>
> *Once upon a time, Marion thought she could make the world a better place. Even if it was a tiny improvement, for a few people, in a little parcel of land, it was something. But all her stories ended the same.*

"WE'RE ALMOST THERE. THAT spire way up ahead . . ." she pointed at the distant black spear, several rolling hillocks away, " . . . is the priory at Hinchingbrooke. Once we pass it, we'll be at Huntingdon Castle in no time."

The road would curve down to the north bank of the Great Ouse, where they would cross and rise up again to Huntingdon Castle.

She was riding beside Amon now, Charley and the three others lingering behind. The trees had thinned again and the last of the sky's lingering purple was devoured by black, but the path at least was certain. She'd traveled it a dozen times, though this would be her last.

"Lord Robert has promised all of us amnesty," she told her sworn protector. "*All of us.*"

Amon stiffened at her words, though he did not contest them. She knew he had many opinions on her exploits of late, made all the heavier by his own dubious standing in his knighthood. Though her father's charge was for Amon to protect Marion in any circumstance, that order had alarmingly uncertain edges. If Marion were truly an outlaw, it begged the question of whether it was lawful of him to protect her, even if he committed no crimes himself in doing so.

As if he were not already plagued by people unjustly questioning his integrity.

"If Lord Robert can forgive a group accused of assassinating the Sheriff," she pushed into the words, "I don't think *anyone* else has anything to worry about."

She knew he heard the words she didn't say. He pivoted on his horse to accept her attempt at discretion. "As you say, my lady."

"Lord Robert will protect you," Marion insisted. "And if he doesn't, I'll punch him, in the face, very hard."

He gave her a rare smile. "That's absolutely unbelievable, and yet oddly reassuring."

"I mean it." She arched her shoulders. "I may even call him a name."

"I wouldn't want you to go too far." Sir Amon's long face tilted her way. "Perhaps a withering gaze instead, I couldn't put you out."

"Withering gaze it is." She practiced one on Amon, which caused him to do whatever is opposite of wither. "But honestly, Lord Robert might as well be one of us. He's been our main benefactor. He's purchased so much of the jewelry we've stolen from traveling nobles that he must have . . . some sort of . . . treasure cave."

Amon raised an eyebrow. "A treasure cave?"

"Listen, I'm exhausted. I actually don't know what he's done with all the trinkets I've sold him. I'm guessing he trades them back to his political rivals in exchange for favors, but I don't actually know, and I definitely don't care. I don't have any necklaces for him this time. My only gift is a broken horde of sick and hungry people, and he's offered to take every one of us in. He's a better Robin Hood than any of us."

The earl was literally saving their lives, and Marion could never repay him for that gift.

While Robin . . . Robin had destroyed everything on his way out of the world.

Soon, her group would have safety again, and that wrong would be righted. But the passing of one fear gave immediately to another. She would stay with them in Huntingdon for a short time, to see them settled, but she would not call this home. There would be another cause, another calling, another foolish urge to do something lionhearted, and Marion doubted very much she'd be smart enough to ignore it.

Perhaps Charley was right. Perhaps it was time for her to rest, from all of it. *Will Scarlet, thrusting his finger at burnt trees.*

"We're almost there," Marion said again, not necessarily about the castle.

> *Once upon a time, Marion tried to use her influence—as a lady of a notable house—to help others. To do what other women never could, those who were voiceless by tradition or by servitude. Her family tree had King Richard himself, and wheresoever he chose to impose himself upon the world they called him Lionheart for it. For the same acts, Marion was called a nuisance. An agitator. She was left to wonder if her failures were truly her own, or the inevitable result of a world determined against her. For wheresoever Marion tried to be a Lionheart, the world was worse for it.*
>
> *Had she stayed silent, lived the life of a maid, how many people would be the better?*

RIDERS FROM THE CASTLE greeted them at the bridge over the Great Ouse, trailing green banners with gold trim. Relief poured over her aching body. Their escort led them up the long gentle hill to Huntingdon Castle, and she had to remind herself that this was real. All of it seemed impossible.

Huntingdon Castle was not much to call impressive, even in daylight. In the mottled darkness, it was little more than a black shadow wrapped around a hill. A single circular curtain wall enclosed the castle's lone courtyard and manors, broken only once by two squat, square keeps that framed a long stone ramp up a steeper hill. Upon that hill was the castle's lone tower, distinguishable now only by the flickering fires shining in its topmost stories.

"The Heart Tower," Marion whispered to Charley. "If you hear anyone call it the Tower de Senlis, don't let that stick. Three generations of men named Simon de Senlis controlled Huntingdon Castle, before Henry the Younger's rebellion."

Charley looked up at the thick silhouette of the tower. "And they supported young Henry?"

"Not at all. But they lost the castle to the Scots, and couldn't reclaim it on their own. After the rebellion was squashed, King Henry the Elder punished the de Senlis family for their failures. The earldom was granted to Lord Robert's father, who was known as the Heart of Huntingdon. He passed last year, and Lord Robert ascended to earl and rechristened the Tower de Senlis in respect to his father. So the *Heart* Tower now." Marion reinforced the words. "Calling it by its old name would be quite disrespectful to Lord Robert."

Another *heart*-ful name, she considered, for a man best skilled at cutting into them.

Passing through the gates of the castle might have brought tears to her eyes, if the cold night wind was not already doing so. Within the curtain wall was an open space lit regularly with braziers, warming the faces of the various buildings that formed its perimeter. Awaiting in the center of the courtyard was a small congregation, huddled around the largest fire. Though her vision was foggy from fatigue, Marion had no problem identifying Lord Robert, Earl of Huntingdon, who stepped forward to welcome her.

His frame was lean and tall, his pose was somehow always perfect, as if he were constantly prepared for the danger of someone painting a portrait of him. That was his way, he had the presence of a prince but a mirth that made him everyone's best friend. His dark golden hair and short beard had endearing touches of grey, and his face was most comfortable in a wide smile. This night he wore tall tanned riding boots and a simple green-and-gold doublet, half covered by an ornate brown demicape that clung to one shoulder and fell only to his thigh. He'd chosen it for her, Marion recognized, as she'd commented upon it favorably during a previous visit. He'd claimed it was purchased from an Italian merchant in Chipping Ongar—or Epping, maybe—and Marion had pointed out that it was very unlikely to be Italian. He hadn't cared, he just liked the way the cape looked.

"I was growing worried!" Lord Robert called as they approached, with no formalities or greetings. "Any difficulties on the road?"

"Nothing but," Marion answered, her lungs straining to raise her voice.

At Lord Robert's side was his wife, the Countess of Huntingdon. Lady Magdalena de Bohun was as tall as her husband, made taller by the nest of blond hair pulled sharply atop her head. Her modest blue dress had seen some work lately, and her thin face was full of scrutiny. Marion had not interacted much with Lady Magdalena during her previous visits, but it was obvious the countess held as much respect and power in the castle as Lord Robert himself.

"We have made terrible time, I'm afraid," Marion explained. "The rest should be here in three or four hours if they don't stop, or early morning if they do. I hate to bring such a burden upon you, but we have no food. Whatever you are able to spare—"

"We'll take care of them," Robert assured her, placing his hand on her horse's neck, clicking his tongue to calm her. "I meant *you*, did you have any difficulties?"

Marion wasn't even sure what the question meant. Her thoughts were too heavy. "Hm? No. A bit, yes, some nosy travelers. Nothing worth mentioning."

"Lady Fitzwalter, I'm glad to see you returned." The countess smiled simply, and snapped to her stablemen. "Let us take care of your horses."

"Thank you, she needs water more than I do."

A thick man in high boots—Lord Robert's horsemaster—took her mare by the reins, then paused and looked up at her in anticipation.

"Your ladyship?" he asked gently. "We shall take good care of your horses, I assure you."

Marion stared blankly for a moment, not understanding the problem, and then noticed that both Sir Amon and Charley had already dismounted, remitting their horses to Lord Robert's men. Her three elderly riders were already being shuffled off toward a nearby keep—*how had she missed that?* She completely forgot herself, and tried to shake it away, slipping down off the saddle. "Yes, I'm sorry. It has been a . . . harrowing week."

She stumbled as her boots found the ground, and Lord Robert moved to steady her, his hand at the small of her back.

"Thank you. There is so much to do."

"Perhaps you ought to rest first," Robert offered.

"They haven't eaten," she said to nobody, trying to blink away something in her eyes. "Some are wounded, we'll need to make room enough—"

If she fainted, it was for only a moment. Amon was holding her now, his arms supporting all her weight around her waist.

"My lady, I think it would be best if you lay down."

To him, at last, she conceded. Robert's voice faded away behind her, and Marion was dimly aware that she was being escorted away. Warmer air, then wood beneath her feet, then stone, then her weight disappeared as she sank into a mattress and sleep was upon her.

> *Once upon a time, Marion brought a group of starving outlaws to a castle in Huntingdon to start a new life . . .*

FOURTEEN

ARTHUR A BLAND

NOTTINGHAM

WILL STUTELY'S FACE POPPED up over the edge of the building, his mangiest edges chiseled out by the firelit windows of the open street below.

"What did you call me for?"

"We didn't call you none," Arthur answered. "Get back to your spot, you fuck."

"You clapped for me."

Only half his face was visible. The roof of the building next to them was lower than this one, just enough that Stutely could barely stretch tall enough to get their attention. But he was supposed to be five rooftops west, watching for the carpentry wagon.

"I wasn't clapping for you," David explained. "I was just trying to keep my hands warm."

"Well . . . don't." Stutely's head gophered down, then popped up again. "I thought you were calling me."

"Get!" Arthur started at him, more an excuse to exercise his legs than anything. They'd climbed up earlier than necessary, for fear of missing the wagon entirely, and all they'd earned for their caution was stiff limbs and cold bones.

The little bitch—who claimed her name was *Zinn*—had failed to arrange a meet with the head of the Red Lions. Instead, she'd brought back a demand. They had to *prove* themselves, of all the rotcunt backward things, before the Lions would ever talk with them face-to-face. So rather than recruiting men to their cause and giving orders, it felt a fucking lot like exactly the opposite of that.

"At the tenth bell," Zinn had explained, "a carpentry wagon will leave the castle and ride east through St. Peter's Square. All's you have to do is stop the wagon at Bridlesmith Street, an' Robin Hood'll take care of the rest. Easy enough?"

No explanation as to what the fuck their imitation Robin Hood wanted with a carpentry wagon. Didn't even matter *how* they stopped the wagon, just as long as it stopped. And oddest of all, Will Scarlet wasn't allowed to help.

"Lions already know who he is," Zinn had said, curling her face into an even uglier version of itself. "They want to know whether you three are any use without 'im around."

So here they fucking were, David and Arthur crouching on a roof in the black night, while Stutely kept his eyes on the road down the way, only occasionally risking fucking everything on account of David clapping his hands together before they froze off.

"This better work," Arthur grumbled, both to David and himself. "We've wasted enough time in the city already."

His friend grimaced, but in agreement. "Better than going back empty-handed, innit?"

"Not if the Guard's built a dozen outposts before we get back there."

"Will says this is the best way . . ."

David was a smart man, and he knew how to end a damn sentence. When he didn't, it meant there were plenty more words bouncing 'round his head than could fit in his mouth.

Instead, his lips pursed.

They were too close for any secrets to fit between them. "Say it."

David sighed, "Are you worried about him?"

Somewhere, a bubble of children's laughter died away. "I'm only worried if he doesn't get what he needs. With enough men, we're back to making a difference out there, sure as shit. That's what Will's good at. Stumbling about trying to keep families fed? That's not him. We need to get him what he needs, because right now all's he got is you and me. And we're not enough."

"And Stutely," David added, glancing to be sure the man was out of earshot.

Arthur didn't lower his voice. "As I said."

David twisted, probably hoping for a distraction. But it was just them and the cold air and the city of Nottingham sprawled out in every direction. "You said he walked into that knife."

"He did," Arthur answered, having thought good and long about it already. "But that's just the burnt trees, right?"

No response.

"Just like Marion said before we split," he explained. "She pointed at the burnt trees and said that was proof we'd failed. But Will points at the healthy ones, says they're proof we haven't. It's easy to see the burnt ones. Will's here, and he's fighting, and he's on the rise. He walked into Zinn's knife, sure, that's the burnt tree. He's damaged, no doubt. But he's still standing where any other man would've given up ten times over. That's his forest. Ignore the scorch marks, find the forest. That's where—"

Before he could say more, the tower of St. Peter's filled the air with a deep song. Stutely's whistle followed soon after, and Arthur looked to David in the hopes of him having some sort of final advice on how this was going to happen. Instead his cheeks just puckered in and he shrugged, picking up his ends of the ropes.

They had wanted a net, but all they'd been able to scrounge from the docks were three stretches of thick mooring rope. To the ends they'd tied small sacks with a single good-sized rock each, which they intended on dropping from the rooftops to tangle around the horses' reins and force its driver to stop. It wasn't a great idea. But it was the best of their other terrible ideas, because it hopefully kept their faces from being seen and they didn't aim to pick any fights.

Arthur gathered his ends of the ropes in his arms and walked across a narrow wooden bridge that spanned the street below. He lost his balance near the middle but caught himself. Which was probably a bad sign. He knew he'd die in some stupid manner someday, and this would have been perfect. Surviving this bridge meant his eventual real death would be even stupider than this, which was a tall fucking order.

Once situated, he and David shuffled down the rooftops on either side of the road, holding the three heavy ropes between them, suspended over the open street. They didn't need Stutely's whistle to hear the cart below, the clip-clop of the horses, the snapcrack of iron-rimmed wheels finding the occasional stone. The ropes were getting heavier, the cart was almost beneath them, and then David nodded at him furiously and they dropped the ends one by one.

It could have gone better. Arthur dropped the first rope when David dropped the third one, so both swung down and crashed against the building beneath them rather than falling evenly into the street. But the middle rope found its home, landing across the horses' harness and flinging the reins from the driver's hands. One of the rock sacks yanked and lodged itself into the gap between the cart and a wheel, grinding its motion to a halt and bringing a flurry of shouting from the men below.

Arthur and David both pulled back hard and away and ran to a better vantage, on their respective rooftops, hoping they weren't seen. There were only two men at the buckboard of the wagon, its open-top cart laden high but covered in canvas. *Probably not a carpentry wagon after all,* Arthur thought. *Something secret. Something expensive.*

With a small *thak!*, an arrow sprung into the canvas of that pile, and all eyes came up. On a third rooftop, across the way of Bridlesmith, stood a tall figure in a sharp, slender coat making a grand flourish of nocking a new arrow to his longbow.

"Don't worry now," came his voice like a wolf howl, every vowel long and elaborate. "We'll only be a minute then!"

That there, that's their Robin Hood.

At that came a loud crack followed by an even louder dull thud, and Arthur whirled his attention back down below. A second crack and thud, muffled only slightly by the useless protests of the wagon drivers, and then a third. It was damn dark down there but finally Arthur saw it. At the rear of the wagon were two more bodies. The first was someone massive, and the crack was the sound of an axe he brought round hard to bury longways into the spokes of one of the wagon's wheels. The second man was smaller, but strong enough to wield a thick log as a battering ram into the back of the axe's head, splitting the wood into sinew and freeing the axe again. After the third spoke splintered they barked at each other and vanished into the nearest alleyway.

And oddly, didn't steal a thing.

Arthur glanced back at the shadow of the archer, who was bowing to the men below. "On your way then, gentlemen!"

And he turned and loped away south, bounding over the rooftop to vanish into the night. The whole thing had been done in thirty seconds.

The drivers shouted another unkind thing or two as they finished clearing the mooring rope from their horses and prompted them forward. But when the rear wheel turned, its three damaged spokes took the brunt of the wagon's weight . . . they cracked, the iron rim buckled and deformed down with a piteous groan, and would never turn again.

David had taken the opportunity to dart over the wooden bridge and join Arthur on his rooftop. He seemed eager for them to escape, but Arthur wanted to see what came next. He expected the axemen to be replaced with an army of Robin Hood's gang, tearing the canvas off whatever it was hiding, hauling away that treasure in armfuls. But instead, what unfolded was nothing out of the ordinary. Some curious onlookers edged closer. Some offered to help, others seemed curious as to the cart's contents. A patrol of gords came by shortly enough and enforced a space around the cart, one of them ambling away with little urgency to bring more help from the castle. There was no fighting, very little yelling, and exactly zero thieving.

"What the fuck was the point of that?" he asked David.

"Just a test for us, maybe? See if we do as we're told?"

Arthur hated things he didn't understand. Admittedly, that usually meant he hated most of the world.

THEY HOLED UP FOR a fourth night in the crawlspace—filthy and narrow—within the second story of a wooden structure off Plumptre Street that seemed bone eager to collapse in on itself. This was one of those driftwood deathtraps built in the odd gaps of the alleyways, clearly constructed by hands that were not only unskilled, but likely now unfingered. This crooked pea-closet was Zinn's "home," though it seemed more likely to be just an architectural mistake. The walls on opposite sides, which could be touched simultaneously, were littered with nails that held all manner of odds and ends. No doubt all stolen. Two tiny straw mattresses on the ground took up the entirety of the room's footprint, but Zinn's place was apparently a shelf halfway up the wall just wide enough for her to lie down. Not that she was ever there.

Its claustrophobic confines were too small for even one man's musk, but all four of them were fucking contributing now. Zinn had insisted they wait there until she heard if the Red Lions had been satisfied with their performance. Arthur filled Will Scarlet in on their night's adventure, but he seemed disinterested, lying on his back across both mattresses. The bandages across his chest stretched as he breathed, and the blood spotting on them seemed fresh.

Whenever they left their crannyhole to piss or shit, they were always watched by either the hawk boy, the bread boy, or a third one that Arthur dubbed *dog scabs*. All three refused to ever speak a word to them, and Arthur was goddamned sick of it. Though he couldn't prove it, he had a gut feeling their wooden cage was the same one that had blockaded the alley plaza on their first day. He bet there was some hidden latch in the room that would cause the skinny wall to swing outward, as it had let those boys disappear into its cracks. If he opened it up, he'd still be able to see a puddle of his pride in the middle of the square alley where he'd stripped *"down to his 'billies'"* at Zinn's bidding.

At some point, either minutes or hours later, the room's door creaked open and the air shifted, and Zinn vaulted up to her little shelf, dangling her feet over its edge.

"Welcome back," David said.

"This is my room." She tilted her head at him in offense. "You don't get to welcome me back."

In a slightly better world, Arthur leapt to his feet, wrapped his fingers around Zinn's throat, and popped her head clean off like a fucking grape. In the unfortunate world he actually lived in, they fucking needed her.

"Do we have our meet?" Stutely asked from the ground.

"A *meet?*" she repeated, as if it was just a casual thing that had slipped her mind. "Depends."

"On what?" Arthur asked.

"You might try a little patience." She swung her legs back and forth. "The whole world isn't waiting to do what you want it to."

"You're a fucking philosopher," Arthur balked at her. "Depends on what? What'd the bossman say?"

"The *bossman?*" Zinn mocked his choice of words. "You sure think you're important, doncha? I've already explained this, but I kind of enjoy it so I guess I'll try it again. You're *nobody.*" Her shadow wiggled about on her little perch, proud of herself. Thin slivers of moonlight played over the erratic features of her face, making her even more goblinlike than normal. "You're nobody! That feels great, don't it? I'll explain it as many times as you want. You're nothing. You're not even nothing. When nothing feels awfully down on itself, it cheers itself up by reminding itself that at least it ain't you."

"Get on." Arthur closed his eyes.

David, of course, was laughing.

"*Depends,*" Zinn relented, "on whether or not you know why they had you do that thing tonight."

"I don't have a fucking clue," Arthur snapped, but caught himself. David clicked his tongue as if he was a horse that needed calming. Arthur hated that he was right. "I don't know. You attacked a wagon and didn't take anything from it. Seems like your version of Robin Hooding ain't exactly the same as ours."

Zinn's nose twitched. "How many wheels did they break?"

Arthur looked at David, wondering if this was some sort of puzzle. "One."

Little bitch clicked her tongue, imitating David. "Uh-huh."

"So what?"

"Out of how many?"

Arthur blinked, hoping she might disappear while his eyes were closed.

"Fack me." David rolled forward to his knees, and snapped his fingers. "One in four."

"What?"

"One in four," he repeated. "Same as the king's ransom. It's a . . . it's a message, then, right? One in four doesn't sound so bad, but it's as good as everything. Wagon with three wheels is as good as one with none. And taking one in four as a tax . . . that's as good as death."

"Look at you." She rolled her tongue over her teeth. "Only half as stupid as you look."

"Thanks."

But Arthur felt a tap at his boot, and looked down to see Will Scarlet shaking his head, small. He mouthed something meaningless, then again, and on the third one Arthur made sense of it. *Bread boy.*

Bread boy?

Bread boy.

"That's not all," Arthur said, just as he pieced it together. He craned his head up at Zinn's perch. *Bread boy.* "It's a message, alright, but that's just half of it. That crippled wagon needed to be guarded. More gords came from the castle to watch it, even more to unload it all into another wagon, and keep people at bay. That's a lot of men."

Zinn raised her eyebrows, waiting for Arthur to finish it.

"A lot of men that weren't somewhere else. The wagon was the distraction."

"There you go!" Zinn's voice was as condescending as possible. "Get some sleep then. You get your *meet* with *the bossman* tomorrow night."

There wasn't much more to talk about after that, and one by one they shuffled around the tiny space to find their way into some comfortable positions to nod off. Arthur replayed the events of the nonrobbery in his mind, wondering exactly what else the Red Lions had been up to while Bridlesmith Street was full of gords that night.

Though one detail stuck with him, which he didn't feel like voicing in front of the little bitch. For a city full of patrols, their mysterious host had known exactly when and where to hit that carpentry wagon when nobody was watching. Tenth bell, on the dot. Might've been a lot of careful planning for that . . . or might be they had some eyes inside the Nottingham Guard.

And *that,* well that was something maybe even more valuable than what they'd come for.

"*I* like your hair." David's whisper broke the silence, defending Zinn against an insult that nobody had spoken.

"It's not for you to like," she hissed at him, slipping her head over the lip of her shelf to give him a full snarl.

David just shrugged.

"But thank you," she finished. Leaning in a shaft of moonlight peeking through the hovel's slats, she combed her fingers through her hair, which was shorn significantly shorter on the right side. Dirty and dark, it fell just past her shoulder on the left side but was—

"*Damn*," Arthur cursed when he saw it. "What happened to your ear?"

She flicked her hair to tumble back over the scar. "Remind me to tell you when I give a shit. You'll know it because my foot will be two feet up your asshole."

"Oh, come on," David whispered. "We won't tell anyone."

Zinn hissed back, "It fell off when I was fucking your mum."

She said it through a giggle, and David cackled and kicked his heel into the wall. He caught Arthur's eyes and pointed at Zinn above, gesturing with his eyebrows to express exactly how impressed he was with her. Arthur wondered if David would still enjoy her so much if he'd been the one who had to dress down *to his fucking billies*.

"Does that even work?" Stutely asked at full volume. "'*When she was fucking your mum?*' I don't think the joke works that way."

"Shut up, Stutely," Arthur said, and twisted to find a more comfortable position.

"It's just . . . she's a girl. And she's what, twelve? She couldn't . . . we shouldn't . . ."

Zinn cut him off. "Shut up, Stutely."

FIFTEEN

MARION FITZWALTER

MARION AWOKE TO THE sound of work. Hammers, saws. *Guilt.*

Face wet from her own drool, she had not budged from the position in which she first tumbled off to sleep. The room was pitch black, but its window gave a dull glow behind thin curtains, which she pushed aside to reveal the castle's courtyard below. An army was at hand—people wrapped in heavy coats to fight against the night's cold bite, working by firelight to prepare for Marion's group. There was no sign yet of dawn in the sky, which meant the castle's complement had worked through the night.

She heaved off to the door and pulled it, pushed it, only to discover that it was—against all logic—locked. She shook her head. There were still cobwebs in her thoughts, she couldn't quite think straight, and she fumbled about to see if there was a lock on her side. But the door clicked and opened on its own.

"Lady Fitzwalter," came a voice from the other side. "Do you require anything?"

"Out," was the only word she could form. "Was this locked?"

"We did not want anyone to disturb you," said the young man, a fragile-looking thing with a shaven head.

That didn't seem to explain anything, but Marion dismissed it. Her mind was still grappling with why it was expected to exist at all.

"I can get anything you need, if you'll let me."

"I need out of this room," she repeated, perhaps a bit too sharply. "I need to help outside."

"Of course, if you'll follow me."

He set down the hallway at an unusually delicate pace, which Marion only followed until they descended the stairs and exited the Elder Hall. The moment she was in the castle's great courtyard she mumbled a thank-you and surged forward into the business at hand.

A number of makeshift structures were half-erected, covering the makings of bedding and an area for the infirmed. There were huge baskets of clothing being sorted, and cookfires smoking. An impressive endeavor, and it was beyond humbling to realize how much work had been done in expectation of their arrival. Huntingdon was alive, while Marion had been asleep.

At the center of the commotion was a tent that appeared most important. Halfway there, she was intercepted by the countess of the castle, Lady Magdalena de Bohun. "My dear Lady Marion!"

Marion stumbled her momentum to a stop and curtsied a greeting. Lady

Magdalena had exchanged her earlier attire for something more fit for labor, her hair now collected in a tail, her face flush and sweaty.

"I hope you are somewhat recovered," the countess said expectantly.

Marion let out one coarse laugh. "I had hoped I'd be *fully* recovered, but I shall settle for *somewhat*."

"Oh my." Magdalena put a hand to her breast. "I didn't mean . . . that is, of course I, too, hoped you would fully recover."

"I know, I'm sorry." Marion realized her rudeness. "I didn't mean to . . . *thank you*."

The countess smirked. "You didn't mean to thank me?"

"No—not . . . I meant—"

"I'm teasing you. I shouldn't, I know. You must be exhausted." Lady Magdalena reached out and fussed at Marion's clothing, the firelight making a haggard skull of her features. She had a sharp nose and bright eyes, the muscles in her cheeks well defined. "Would you prefer to return to bed? There is an hour still, I think, before dawn. We have preparations well underway."

"I am quite fine, you are too kind."

"Some of your companions arrived a few hours after you. We realized your situation is more dire than you described. So we . . . set to work." The countess brushed her hands off, presenting the courtyard proudly.

While Marion had slept. It was practically freezing outside, and yet so many people had labored regardless. She searched for familiar faces—within the central tent were a few shapes that might have been the Delaney brothers, and a smaller frame with a mess of curly locks . . .

Arable.

Marion sighed in frustration. "I should help with the preparations."

"Walk with me." The countess slipped a gloved hand through Marion's arm and gently drew her away. Marion could hardly deny her, in the face of her formidable generosity. "I find the cold air a relief on weary mornings such as this. Here." She swooped her hand down to pull a pair of cloaks from a nearby bundle, and offered one to Marion.

"Thank you." Her eyes lingered on the bundle. Piles of blankets, boots, shawls. They must have collected every last available item within the castle and beyond. The sheer goodness of it was overwhelming. "I feel terrible."

"Still?" Magdalena stopped. "Perhaps you ought to return to bed."

"No, I meant . . ." Marion shook her head, frustrated with her own lack of clarity.

"Oh, forget your apologies." Magdalena pulled the fur's hood on, and pushed them through an open archway of the first square keep by the Heart Tower's bridge. Inside was a staircase that took them up to the long battlement that wrapped all the way around the great bailey, one continuous stone path that eventually terminated at the second square tower adjacent to them. "You were in such a state when you arrived, Lady Marion. I'll have some of the men begin heating water for a bath for you."

"No, please." Marion fidgeted, uncomfortable with the attention. She would happily be rid of the title of *Lady,* if that was the reason the countess seemed so insistent on entertaining her. "That's not necessary."

The countess shrugged and drew them onto the open walkway. With so much commotion below, it was largely unmanned—save for a few sentinels in the arrowhouses that divided the walkway into regular segments.

"We saved a plate for you from dinner," she continued. There was an edge to her syllables now. "I could have my cook prepare something hot instead."

Marion hesitated, unsure how to react. She felt rude to continually deny the countess's offers. "No," she answered, quietly. "Thank you."

"It would be his pleasure, he adores the art of it, you know? Cooking, that is."

But Lady Magdalena continued along, forcing Marion to follow. It was not the clearest of skies, but the moon had found a healthy opening between swollen clouds to bathe them in a soft glow. Below, the inky shape of the Great Ouse snaked its way beside them, around the circumference of the castle. A jagged curtain wall of sheared timber nestled its base, and Marion considered with horror the damage it would do to a body, were one unfortunate enough to tumble from the walkway.

"This is beautiful," Marion said, "but I am eager to get to work."

"Are you? I should warn you that it is *exhausting.*" At this the countess stopped, and bore her eyes into Marion's. "Are you certain you don't wish to lie down a while longer while we figure out how to accommodate your people?"

Marion's throat tightened. "As I said, I feel terrible."

"That must be so taxing on you, to feel so terrible. Perhaps you ought to lie down."

That was clear enough. The countess was making a point, and Marion very much deserved it. "Countess Magdalena, I cannot apologize enough. I'm afraid I have given you a most wretched impression—"

"No, stop it." She waved away the moment as if it were a joke. "Consider it forgotten, it was my rudeness to mention it. *I apologize to you.*" She thrust her head into the wind as if impervious to its chill, while Marion had to pull her own cloak tighter. Not that any shawl could ease her sense of discomfort now.

The countess kept a painfully slow pace, as if there were not a thousand concerns to be addressed, on display for them in the bowl of the courtyard within the curtain wall. Marion followed in a wide-eyed stupor, full of a child's dread of impending punishment.

"Hm. Your sworn man must be well paid."

Marion turned to notice Sir Amon, keeping step with them below by walking the perimeter of the courtyard.

"He seems intent on catching you, should you stumble from the battlement."

"Sir Amon Swift is a godsend," Marion answered. "And very dutiful."

"*Dutiful,*" Lady Magdalena repeated, with an affected taste of idle gossip. "I believe you misspoke, the man is *beautiful.* Surely you cannot complain about having such a pretty thing waiting upon you every day? Anxious to fulfill your . . . every command?"

Marion might have laughed at the implication, if the question did not feel like an interrogation. "I assure you he has sworn his sword to my father in my defense, and no more."

The countess's entire body perked up. "I knew it."

"Knew what?"

"Don't be coy." Magdalena flashed a vibrant smile over her shoulder. "Your knight's secret is safe here. I see where his eyes land. You are an attractive young woman, but you don't seem to have . . . exactly what he's looking for."

Marion stiffened. That answer was not Marion's secret to share. She had long felt rotten that her own infamy carved a path for Amon's rumors to follow him. "I'm sure it's not my concern."

A few moments passed in which the countess seemed to expect more, but she let the subject drop. "As you wish. I should also compliment your companion, who arrived after you. The girl with the scars. Arable . . . Arable *de Ravelle*? Was that her name?"

Marion made a noise that was not an affirmation, but neither was it denial.

"Arable doesn't seem to have a single stitch of her body that is worried about herself so long as there is work to do. She has proven herself more than competent in a very short amount of time."

Marion wasn't proud of the bitter little ball of jealousy that suddenly formed in her gut, but she could not pretend it was not hers to own. "Yes, she is a remarkable young woman."

"She is. I just remarked upon her."

If the countess was trying to agitate her, that struck her core. Marion had said something similar to Robin once, when he called her *remarkable*. It was a cold knife in her chest now, which she could not hide.

The countess noticed her pause. "What is it?"

"Nothing," Marion lied.

Magdalena stopped. They had come halfway around the circumference of the great bailey, and at last she dropped her pretense of civility. "Why didn't you accept my offer of a bath and a hot meal?"

"I don't know what you want to hear from me." Marion practically collapsed. "Your hospitality is enormous, and I am ashamed of myself for having wasted the last few hours."

"You didn't accept them," Lady Magdalena ignored Marion's response, "because you knew you did not deserve them."

"Yes. As you say."

"You were weak, and my husband took pity upon you, and we took care of you. While others, who had equal reason to be as weak as you, toiled on. Those who are the strongest have received the least reward, whilst we have pampered those that could not carry their own."

Marion struggled to contain her reaction. "With all respect, I think you have worded that unkindly."

"The rest of your people that arrive tomorrow, they have had a difficult time in the last few months, on account of the taxes and the ransom, no? Not more difficult than anyone else, though, is it? Chancellor Longchamp did not make them pay double, did he? For a generation, Huntingdon has carefully picked partnerships and business ventures that prevent any single catastrophe from sinking us. We've endured difficulties here as well, by no small feat, mind you. We chose sacrifice and parsimony—while you made other choices, reckless choices. And now we take on the weak, because my husband feels charitable. While you sleep and recuperate, we work doubly hard to take care of you ... well, there is no doubt that *you* are the better for it. But what exactly is the benefit for us?"

Every word of it was true, and Marion had no more ways to apologize. "We will earn our keep, I promise, and repay this kindness."

Magdalena scoffed. "My husband tells me you are ever pragmatic, so perhaps you can answer for me. Remove yourself from the situation. Not everyone can succeed in life, regrettably. Is it wiser to help those who have failed, or to help those who can thrive? When your own survival is dependent on the outcome, where do you place your wager?"

Marion bowed her head. She knew the answer. She knew they offered Huntingdon nothing, she knew that any sensible person would have turned them away for the dead weight they were. "I'm sorry you find our presence so displeasing," her voice creaked out. "Lord Robert assured me we would be most welcome. If that is not so ..."

"Don't be so dramatic, Marion." The countess calmed her. "No one would be so cruel as to turn a group such as yours away, especially with them practically upon us. Unless they carry disease, of course. I was speaking extemporaneously. I'm sure my husband will uphold any promises you two have made each other."

"What?" Marion stumbled slightly and whipped around. "No, Countess ..."

Such a thought had never occurred to her, but it suddenly explained the Lady Magdalena's tempered hostility. Marion laughed now, relieved to realize this animosity was nothing more than a misunderstanding.

"I am so sorry, I never thought about how this might look to you. Little wonder that you have been so sharp with me! I swear, I have no intention whatsoever of ... abusing a relationship with your husband. That was never a thought— you have absolutely nothing to worry about."

Lady Magdalena froze, her jaw literally dropped.

Marion twitched. "Countess?"

She bristled, unhinged. "I have legitimate alarm for the welfare of my people, of our limited resources, of the dangerous precedent of opening our gates to a host of unknown strangers—*criminals,* actually—who bring a very real threat to our household for harboring your acts of terror," she breathed in deep, that she might spit out the rest, "and you assume that my issue with you is over a *man?*"

Spiders crawled all over Marion's skin. "I didn't—" she gasped uselessly, but Magdalena bore down into her again.

"I am the Countess of Huntingdon and I bear every responsibility of that title. I have educated many men who thought a woman too weak for command, but *you are no better than any of them.*" Marion shrank. "I am neither my father's daughter nor my husband's wife. I am myself, and that is reason enough to respect me."

Marion stammered to respond. She had borne the sieges of misogyny her entire life, starting from an age so young she believed they were true. For every accomplishment she ever won, it was always sidled with the dubious caveat of being impressive *for a woman.*

"You are right!" Marion blurted out, desperate to be understood. "You are absolutely right, I did not mean to imply any of that. As you say, we both of us are women who have worked hard to be respected. We should be working together, rather than squabbling."

"Ha!" Lady Magdalena took another step back. "And how is that any less insulting? Do all men agree with each other based on the fact they all have cocks? My issue with you, *Lady Outlaw,* is that you bring danger and carelessness and bad politics into my home. It is no more complicated than that. I told you this plainly and to your face, but somehow you thought I was talking to the slit between your legs."

Marion closed up and turned away. "I think it would be best if I left now."

"*No.*"

The words stopped her.

"You had every opportunity to come tonight and be impressive, to work hard and intelligently. But instead you seem intent on making the very worst impression you can. Do you think I'm being unfair?"

"I . . ." Marion's mouth opened and closed again, futilely. "I am at your mercy. If you don't want us here, then I don't know that we will survive. You have every right to be unfair to us, and we'll accept it."

The countess tipped her head back. "Would you prefer that I trust you?"

"I was hoping we could earn that trust."

"Then you should not have lied to me."

Marion's heart hammered in her chest, another wave of guilt washed through her body. "When did I lie to you?"

"Arable *de Burel,*" Magdalena enunciated quite clearly, "is working very hard to make your arrangement work, and for her sake I welcome your people tonight. You should thank her. Why lie to me about her name, if you want me to trust you?"

Marion closed her eyes and bit her lip. "Her secrets are her own. I hope you can respect that."

The chill of the wind cut in deep now, slicing in from the west, whipping the bannerettes over the wall into a frenzy. The Great Ouse lounged away to the south, and the pitiful little spring they called the Cook's Backwater branched off and below them, under the castle's only entrance.

One great river, strong and permanent, and the other an insolent distraction to it.

"I can tell you exactly how you will contribute." The countess's voice was indistinguishable from a far-off rolling thunder. "You'll do as I demand, when I demand, without question."

Marion, for the first time since leaving, missed Will Scarlet very much.

"Do you have anything specific in mind?" she asked.

"I'm certain, with enough time, you'll be able to decipher the meaning of the phrase *without question?*"

Like any good maid, Marion shut her mouth.

The lady of Huntingdon leveled her eyes on her. "You were leaving."

"Countess." Marion curtsied.

"Outlaw."

She rushed to the stairs that descended back down to the courtyard, glancing at Sir Amon below as he worked to keep time with her. From behind, Lady Magdalena spoke just loudly enough that they both might hear her. "And don't bring your pervert inside the castle grounds again. He is to stay outside our walls."

Marion was shocked. "What?"

"You heard me. I don't like the way he eyes my men."

Marion was defenseless. She couldn't fight back, she owed everything to Huntingdon. She swallowed the last remnants of her pride and bowed her head. "I'll see to it."

SIXTEEN

ARTHUR A BLAND

IN THE MIDDLE OF the night, Arthur startled violently awake to a strange weight on his chest. It was Zinn's crooked little head, tapping him with her chin.

"Wake up, Grumbles." She flicked the long half of her hair against his face. "Come get what you came for."

Arthur briefly wondered whether he could punch her face all the way through to the back of her skull, or if it were made out of some gargoyle stone that would just break his knuckles.

Scarlet and David were instantly ready, but it took some amount of work to pull Stutely from a groggy slumber. Eventually Zinn touched a finger to her lips and they left the room, descending the narrow wooden stairs that vomited them back into Nottingham's streets.

The city was unusually still this night, quieter than Arthur would've expected. And darker. With buildings on either side to smother the barely-light of the night sky, he found himself navigating by looking up at the ghostly shapes of the rooftops around them. Zinn didn't backtrack or try to confuse them this time. She made a direct path, keeping to the sides of the streets and through the cracks between buildings whenever possible.

"This is good," David's voice squeaked.

"Stop saying *'this is good,'*" Arthur whispered. "Every time you say, *'this is good,'* you start to worry me."

"Why?"

"It's called a liar's nail," Will Scarlet answered, keeping pace beside them.

"What's a liar's nail?" David asked.

"It's you, saying *'this is good, this is good,'*" Arthur said.

Will chuckled and followed. "When you're trying too hard to convince someone of a lie, you keep repeating it. Someone who tells you the same thing over and over, they're probably lying about it. Someone who tells the truth tends to only say it once."

David humphed absently.

"So it *is* a lie?" Arthur asked.

"No." Will breathed in long, slowly. "This *is* good."

Arthur exhaled a sigh of relief. It was still absolutely fucking beyond him how anyone who'd followed Marion thought traveling to Huntingdon was the better idea. An unfamiliar county where they had no allies, knew nothing, had no backup plans—all on the rumor of a promise from some fool lord none of them had ever met. It had taken longer than expected, but Will's plan was the one bearing fruit. And if these Lions indeed had someone planted within the Guard, that was worth its weight in gold. Huntingdonshire was a fantasy, while Nottinghamshire was *home*. They knew the lands, they knew where they were wanted and where they weren't, they knew how the Nottingham Guard operated, they had *history*. That was the difference between Arthur and— somehow—everyone else in the entire fucking world. Arthur believed in things he could touch, things that he knew, things that were certain.

Everyone else wanted to believe in their imagination. They put their stock in empty hopes, in religion, in rumors. In Tuck's stories, and his *"give Him credit"* horseshit. If Marion's group got themselves killed before Arthur saw them again, he could drop just as much blame on the friar's little ass head as on Marion's.

"Why's it called a liar's nail?" Stutely asked, huffing to keep up.

Will groaned. "Comes from carpenters, I think? A good carpenter knows to stop once he's driven a nail down to the wood. A bad carpenter would keep on hammering. Smashes a big ugly hole into it."

"Why would he be a liar?"

"What?"

"Well, I get why a liar keeps on selling his lie," Stutely argued, "but what does being a liar have to do with being a good carpenter?"

"Maybe he lied about being a good carpenter," David suggested.

"He keeps on hammering . . ." Will repeated.

"Yeah, I understand it. Just seems like the name doesn't make any sense."

Zinn reeled around on them and halted their group. "Who the fuck cares why it's called that? Shut the fuck up and keep your heads down."

Stutely's face turtled down into his own beard. Once they were moving again, he muttered to himself, "Just think it ought to have a better name."

The wharfside alleys ended abruptly against a small rise of rock to the north, only a few stories tall, which ran long and level to the east and west. From his small talk with hawk boy and dog scabs, Arthur had learned it was a natural divider between the broad march of the dock slops and the finer wards above. A ramp had long ago been cut at a gentle slope on the side of the rock face—*the Long Stair*—wide enough that merchants could cart their goods up to sell to betterfolk who had real coin to spend. Up and above the Long Stair, the shadow of a huge church with a square tower looked down on them all. Tuck would've fucking loved it.

But Zinn led them—rather than up the ramp—against the rock wall until buildings began to nestle against its craggy surface. Here she tugged aside a piece of canvas at the corner of the rock and building, revealing a thin crevice that slipped behind the stone structure. It was barely wide enough for a man to squeeze through, and only then by wedging sideways and scraping uncomfortably against the walls.

Stutely might not be able to fit at all.

Arthur peered into that crack, feeling something fucking stupid for squinting.

As if he were going to notice, just barely, some trap that would otherwise have killed them all. Their only real choice was to trust that Zinn actually knew half the shit she talked.

Will paused before they entered. "Zinn, how long have you known your Robin Hood?"

"Longer'n I've known you," she sneered back.

"Thank you for that sass, it was delicious. How about a real answer?"

She humphed. "Long enough."

"You knew him before he called himself Robin Hood, then."

She shifted her weight.

"What was his name before?"

Zinn pouted for a bit, seemingly torn between her instinct to be a little bitch and some long-buried drive to communicate like a normal fucking human. "Red Fox," she answered at last, as if it were a dare, and then slipped into the crack.

Will made a noise.

"You know him?" David asked.

"No," he exhaled. "At least, I don't think so. But everyone takes some kind of *red* name when they move up in the Red Lions, so could be."

"Red Fox," Stutely mumbled. "Robin Hood as a fox? Who's supposed to be afraid of that?"

Probing his hands forward in the pitch blackness, Arthur clenched his neck and went in first, finding nothing but the dust of sandstone to his left and cold stone on his right. He bumped his head twice and cursed each time, resorting to placing one hand on his forehead with his fingers outstretched like antlers. Eventually the rock opened up and he didn't have to stoop to stand, though he could still see nothing and had to tap blindly to find his footing. Zinn's hand found his and she pulled him a few feet farther.

By the hollow sounds of his own breath, he could tell the space had widened into a small cave. Behind him, the grunts of his friends muffled anything else.

"This is just one of the entrances," Zinn whispered. "They lead down, these tunnels spread across half the city, let the Red Lions disappear and move about unnoticed."

"They can see in the dark then?" Arthur asked back.

"Havin' a hard time, Grumbles?" She snorted. "Doncha worry, someone'll meet us here in a bit with a big bright torch an' everything."

"Hey Zinn," Will's voice came, cutting off Arthur's urge to throttle her. "I wanted to mention this—you're a sharp one with that scorpion's tail, you know? Very good, nobody wants to get near you when you keep it moving like you do. But when you strike out, you're forced to drop your guard. You have to catch the tail when it comes back, and for a moment you're defenseless."

"I'll be sure to put that on a list—"

"And you do the same thing with your tongue," Will interrupted her. "You're sharp, you're quick with the little insults and jaded barbs. You put up a good defense so nobody wants to get close to you. But when you lash out at someone for no reason," his sentence lingered, "you show your weakness."

The little bitch shuffled. "You all sure love to talk, doncha?"

"Do what you want," Will chuckled. "You'll figure it out someday. There's a time and a place for that brat you've got in you. But if you don't balance it out with something else, it isn't a tool anymore. It becomes a crutch."

He was talking about himself, of course. And *goddamn* it was good to hear that kind of advice from Will. If nothing else, Will seemed to discover himself again in this city, reclaiming the confidence that had fettered away to grief in the Sherwood. Perhaps Lady Marion was wrong.

Perhaps he'll teach us all how to swim.

"Alright, girl," Will finished. "You'd best be off now."

She laughed in protest. The noise disappeared down some nearby tunnel. "I'm going with you."

"You are not." Will's voice was cold. "What's to follow is for us men. You're too young for this."

"I'm the one who *brought* you here."

"I'm not fucking playing you," he replied, still evenly, his tone giving away nothing. "This isn't pinching errant coins and buying stale bread. You've got years, God willing, before you should be dealing with the level of shit we barter in."

"If I'm so young and useless why did you need me to get you here?"

"Don't be sour, girl," David said, softly. "You did us right, and we appreciate that. But we'll handle it from here."

Arthur tried to aim his voice toward hers. "That's just the way it is."

"You can't make me leave."

"You don't want to test that." Will's words were too precise, and they left nothing but silence. "It's for your own good. So if I have to hurt you to get you to leave, I will."

Arthur wondered if that were true. He didn't care much for the little bitch, but he wouldn't *actually* hurt her. He just liked the idea of it.

Her voice tried to mature. "Maybe I'll hurt you instead."

"*You're too young!*" Will snapped. "It took me ten minutes to figure out your game at the fish market, and following your slights through the streets was a joke. I disarmed you in one move. How long do you think you'd last against someone who actually means you harm?"

She started to say something, but a commotion between them meant Will was probably pushing her back toward the crevice.

"Get over yourself and learn your fucking place. I'm done putting up with your shit. You open that mouth again and I'll close it for you."

There was a quick breath, maybe a gasp from Zinn, *or the beginning of a whimper?* She was, despite all her bramble, just a young girl who thought it was fun to play at street rat. And Will was right, this was over her head.

Out of a curious sense of protection he hadn't expected, Arthur knew it'd be best for her if they chased her off. Like a dog. "Go on, off you little cunt!" he growled, and her noise shuffled out the way they came. A few seconds later the heavy flap of the canvas snapped back in place, and they were alone in the black cavern.

"You didn't have to be so harsh with her," David muttered.

"Yes I did," Will said with finality.

Those three words spoke volumes, as Arthur knew full well what the rest of the sentence would have been. *I should have been harsher with Much.*

He pictured Zinn, held aloft by a blade in her throat, tumbling to the ground. *No more children helping out.*

This was no game they were playing. It was no place for those who couldn't handle it.

As a slog of time passed, Arthur could begin to make out the outlines of their cavern. The chamber they were in was even smaller than he thought. Eventually a light jumped harshly around the curve of tunnel, and a torch crackled into view and blinded them. The deep ribbons of the cave wall wrapped around themselves at the flame's whim.

"Come along then," said the torchbearer, and they did.

Down and away from the children's playground, and into the bowels of men.

SEVENTEEN

CAITLIN FITZSIMON

THE LIONS DEN

FOUR STRANGERS, EACH STRANGER than the last, darkened the floor at the foot of the Lions Den. Not true strangers, no, Cait grinned. Not as much as they thought. They formed a diamond and the one in the front—the short little bushy creature—well, that was Will Scarlet.

"Greetings," he said, and the battle had officially begun.

His history with the Lions earned him a parley, and not an inch further. Not a black crag of an inch further, no. There was only so much room at the top, and not a bit of it was for Scarlet. One king, which was Alfred's title now. And Cait at his side, no other. There was a time when Scarlet had the opportunity to claim leadership of the whole gang, and instead he walked away. In some ways, Caitlin FitzSimon wondered if she ought to thank him for that terrible decision. His departure left an empty hole that she and Alfie had filled, like water flooding through sand. Her father would call that a *change of the guard,* to replace the old and tired with the fresh and new.

Two years ago, that was.

Five days ago, they received word Scarlet was back, and wearing the wrong name. The Lions had watched him and his men in that time—used them, tested them—while Cait learned everything she could about Will Scarlet. Now she knew it all, except for what in sweet hell he was doing here.

"Hullo?" Scarlet tried again. This boy who called himself Robin Hood looked as impetuous as the stories described. He looked about the cave, but none of its many inhabitants gave him any heed. The Lions Den sprawled over three mismatched tiers of empty slag in the hollows beneath Nottingham, a slanted cavern of granite and sandstone. Its harsh walls constantly changed shape at the whim of the braziers, whose smoke drifted up into wormholes in the rock and out to the streets of the Parlies above. The den was filled with assorted tables and chairs they'd pilfered from the topside city, where they were no longer welcome. Wretched, that *this* was what she was defending.

Scarlet's fingers lingered at the knives sheathed in his belt, and Caitlin wondered who she should punish for letting him in with weapons at hand.

"Oh look," Cait announced at last, as bored as possible. "Guests."

She made a labor of strutting forward, dragging the heel of each boot against the uneven rock floor, telling their visitors exactly how unimportant they were. Inside, her guts were roiling. If Scarlet meant to take the Lions from her, from her and Alfie, then hell would ope its jaws. Some in the room would side with him. Even if he stayed in Nottingham, he'd find enough support to be a rival.

Even if they warred, even if she killed Scarlet, her group would be split. They'd only survived this long by avoiding infighting, and Scarlet would ruin that. No, the only way to win was to win completely—and that started with pretending that Scarlet wasn't a threat at all.

"Did you hear, love?" She dropped her hand onto Alfred's shoulder as she came 'round the back of his throne. No doubt the intruders wouldn't call it a throne, they'd see it for the ramshackle pile of scunner it was. They'd probably see the Red Lions the same way. What Will Scarlet probably didn't see was that he was to blame for it all.

"Steady on, lads!" Alfred, ever the showman, clapped his hands several times, calling the room to attention. The hubbub settled, if reluctantly. The whores silenced themselves first, since, being whores, they were good at doing what they were told. The men at the horns followed, swallowing down their ale and abating their arguments, then the boys at the dice games threw their last grumbles. All of them were hers for now, but they were all up for grabs. The upcoming conversation was the game, her cubs were the wager . . . the room, an arena.

"Steady on, I say," Alfred cooed again as the chamber settled. "I've been looking forward to this all night." He unfolded himself from the throne like a spider, snapping his long duster down as he stood at his full height. In better light the duster was a rusty red, but down here so was everything else. The blond of his mane positively glowed, making a halo of his drawn face. "A bit of entertainment for us all, if we be lucky! If not, then I promise we'll put a fine hurt upon these strangers. So, entertainment either way, now that I think on't!"

"Oh no," Will Scarlet moaned.

"*Oh no*, he cries!" Alfred span theatrically.

"Not this."

"This, indeed!"

"I was worried about who I might find down here. There are brutal, violent men in the Red Lions, some of the very worst . . ."

Alfred raised a finger. "You are lucky we consider those words compliments."

". . . but nothing could be worse than being *talked* to death!"

Alfred reeled backward to Caitlin. He was a master of faces, though his features were ever handsome and sharp. "'*Talked to death!*' That had a mean-spirited quality to it, no?"

"He's a tiny little thing," Caitlin responded, not to them, but to Alfred directly. They were not yet worth her attention. "Look, he's only got room for two knives on his belt."

She spread her own coat open, proud to show off her size. *Cow*, they probably thought. *Pig. Fussock.* She'd heard it before, from every arrogant bawbag she'd smashed down on her way to the top. And these arrogant bawbags before her were particularly arrogant and particularly bawbaggy. She stared Scarlet down for an extra few seconds, refusing to give any ground. Not now.

"Look, love," she said, pointing at their guest. "He's even shorter than you described."

"Not true!" Alfred shot a finger up. "If my account of the man did not paint an accurate image, that is the fault of your imagination, and not my description. I think I described him thusly: he is exactly one head shorter than any man should be, and one head taller than he is like to remain."

"God's balls," Scarlet replied dryly. "That's so clever."

"I'm saying you're going to get your head cut off someday," Alfred explained.

Will nodded over and over. "Yeah, I got that."

"Just making sure."

"It was pretty clear."

"Really?" Alfred squinted. "I was afraid it might go over your head."

"No, it—goddammit." Scarlet's shoulders slumped. A few Lions let out their laughter, and eventually Scarlet succumbed and did the same. Cait inhaled deeply—she wanted to look around the room, catalogue reactions, to know if anyone was already falling on the wrong side of the line. But she couldn't. This Scarlet runt couldn't be seen to crack her composure.

So far, so good. He'd taken his insults, and had yet to demand anything. Maybe he wasn't here to play king after all. Maybe he just wanted to join again—*and backstab them later.* She couldn't allow that, either. The boy had to leave Nottingham, tail between his legs. It was the only way. If she and Alfred had refused him parley, it would have reeked of cowardice and played to his favor. No, no, a smile was the best way to disarm him.

Alfred was Red Fox, and the throne was his. Scarlet would learn it, in his bones if he had to. Of course, Alfie wore the crown only insofar as that Cait let him, and every one of her cubs knew she shared that power as much as he. But a ship needed both a captain to love and a first mate to fear, and Cait was better at the latter. Any fool cub who thought her word wasn't an equal with Alfred's was quick to get learned.

She wasn't giving that up.

Alfred slapped his throne. "I'm not going to lie and say it's good to see you, Will. But still . . . it's not the worst."

"Thanks. Same to you, Freddy."

This elicited a gasp that went around the cavern. Caitlin chased its path, stalking it in a circle, daring any one of her cubs to so much as breathe that name. That was a child's name, from his time as a pup in Severn's Yard. But now, reputation was everything.

"The first man here who repeats that name," Alfred craned his neck back, "will be given one far worse."

Caitlin snickered. "The first *man?*"

"Or woman!" Alfred followed quickly, and the edges of his lips gave way a smirk. "In this, at the very least, let the sexes be equal."

The whores cooed again, being whores. In their middle was Clorinda Rose, wrapped in red and sex, hoping for an errant glance from Alfred. It was hard to tell, but it looked as if her whore lips mouthed the word *Freddy* as if it were her own little secret. *Calm your thighs, slag.* Not to some painted knob-gobbler. Not to some chest-beating weasel.

"So you knew it was me?" Scarlet asked. "How?"

Alfred bent over like a toy doll and rippled his spindly fingers before his face. "*Inklings,*" he proclaimed, as if summoning some dark magic. "Your name carries a lot of deeds on its back. Not many are either brave enough or ignorant enough to call themselves Robin Hood."

"Also," coughed Rob o'the Fire from the dice table, "I saw you in the street."

Scarlet turned his body sideways and drawled out the side of his mouth, "Raaaaaaahb."

"Wiiiiiiill," Rob returned, turning to match him, and they both laughed at something only they found funny. Caitlin hated that familiarity, but she knew some here had been friends with Scarlet from his life before. Stomping that out would only make her look petty, so she had to allow it. So she smiled—*permitting it*—as if the choice were hers.

If she actually had a choice, she'd shove her fist down Scarlet's throat until he finally revealed what he was doing here.

Rob sauntered closer to Scarlet. He was the friendly sort of fellow who liked everyone, and was impossible to hate—which was generally why Cait hated him. "Scarlet, still? You kept your red name out there in the forest?"

"Of course, wouldn't want you taking it. Still Rob o'the Fire then?"

"Of course!" His face lit up. "I never left, so why should I give it up?"

"Red Fox!" Scarlet snapped his fingers, returning to Alfie. "I get it! That's cute." He explained to his seconds, "I knew Fre—*Alf* . . . *Red Fawkes* here, when he was in a gang in Severn's Yard, just behind Ten Bell Alley. Our gangs would scrap now and then, but Alfred and I . . . we sort of, I don't know, we made a game out of it."

Caitlin twisted a finger into Alfred's hair. "That's not quite how you described it."

"Darling, we've already established that my descriptions are impeccable," he replied, reaching up to take her hand with his. "You only hurt yourself in saying such a thing."

She pinched his hand in retribution. It was a fine bit of repartee in private, but she didn't need him talking down to her in front of outsiders. Whether he even realized how tight a line they were walking, she couldn't tell. She dug a nail into his palm, which he accepted. He'd apologize later.

"And this," Alfred put his hand at his breast, "is my better, Caitlin FitzSimon."

She greeted the guests with an icy stare, daring any of them to give her so much as a *hullo.* No red name for her. These strangers didn't know what *Fitz-Simon* meant, didn't know how it had saved the Red Lions from destruction, didn't know the double life she lived. The only thing her father had ever given her of any worth—his name, beast of a thing that it was.

Scarlet inclined his head. "So, Alfred Fawkes! Red Fox! Which are you, brave or ignorant?"

"Must I choose between only those?" he mocked offense, leaving Cait to meander toward the dice table. "Pray let me add handsome as an option."

"You said one must be brave or ignorant to call himself Robin Hood," Scarlet explained. "And isn't that the other name you claim to have right now?"

"*Claim.*" Alfred seized the word, breathing it into a tankard he found.

"That's a perfect word for it," Caitlin followed. "We did indeed *lay claim* to it. The title of Robin Hood fell out of Robin of Locksley's body along with his breakfast when he dropped from the gallows. We were there, in the very front where it landed, and we picked it up for our own."

Alfred wiped his lips. "I don't recall seeing you there . . . ?"

Scarlet didn't react. "You're right, I wasn't there. Nor would I have considered it entertainment. You see, I was busy in the Sherwood, fighting off fire brigades."

Cait nearly laughed. "Ah, yes. Must have missed a few, then?" A permanent black cloud had lingered over the northeast for most of winter. "If you think that counts as a victory, you must be using your diddle as a measuring stick."

"Come now." Alfred placed his tankard down, failing to contain a chortle. "Let's not *scrap,* Will. The name of Robin Hood garners us respect, and fear, and we're not like to quit using it on account of your jealousy. Tell me this is not the drum that drove you here tonight."

What he meant was *get to the point.*

"No." Scarlet shook his head. "But that name, it wasn't for you to take."

"Robin Hood is a thief, isn't he?" There was a seriousness now to Alfred's voice, his theatricality discarded. "I took it. Ergo, I'm Robin Hood."

"But you didn't know him. You don't know what it is you're stealing."

To Cait's surprise, Alfred actually softened. "I understand if you think I'm disrespecting your friend, but under—"

"He wasn't my friend." Scarlet looked down, he tapped his own forehead, over and over, absently. *Unstable.* "I hated him. But he was better than me. Whether I liked it or not, he taught me a thing or two . . . he didn't steal something because it was valuable. He stole to put it to better use."

Caitlin was careful with her words. Not for Scarlet's sake, but to make it clear for her cubs who was in charge. "We *are* putting it to better use. Your friend was no longer in a condition to use it at all. We're Robin Hood now."

When Scarlet clenched his fist, the room coiled with tension. Every Lion focused, every hand that had been pretending at casual now fingered a weapon. The silence of mutually held breaths was deafening. And though it may have been a promise of violence, to Cait it was the first moment she could relax. The room had turned against Will, which meant the day was hers.

Every goddamned day like this, constantly scratching to keep what they had.

Watching their backs, knowing the day would come.

Hell, she should let Scarlet have it all.

"An ugly subject, this," Alfred breathed. "It's fouled up the room like a plate of spoilt meat. I'm afraid it's distracted you from your purpose here, no?"

"Yes, why *are* you here?" Cait finally braved the question, now that she felt safer. "Been a lovely chat, but we don't have all the day to dally."

Will Scarlet didn't answer, he just twisted and fidgeted. One of his seconds whispered in his ear, and he shook it off. When he turned again, his boyish smile had returned and his voice filled the room. Cait held her breath, and hated that she had to.

"You know me, Alfred," he boomed, strutting through the space before the throne. "We grew up in these alleys together. I see plenty of old faces here who did the same. Those of you who don't know my face must know my name. Will Scarlet is half the reason why the Red Lions are what they are today. I snuck into Castle Rock and killed Sheriff de Lacy. Do you know anyone else who's broken out of the prisons beneath Nottingham? Killed the Captain of the Guard?"

A smirk was rippling 'round the room, and it ended in Alfred's lap. "No one here denies your . . . accomplishments, Will."

"I just want to be clear you know what I am, and what I get done," Scarlet puffed himself up, "so you know what I'm offering. Everything I've done of importance—of *real* importance, mind you—I did after I left the Red Lions. Squabbling over territory in the slums, slip picking in the Parlies, it doesn't amount to anything. And for some of you, that's fine! All you want is the next drink and a good fuck and I fully support that, so drink and fuck on."

This earned him a burst of approval he probably didn't want.

"But if any of you are looking to do something a bit more important, I could use you." Scarlet shifted his attention back to Alfred and Caitlin. "If you want to call yourself Robin Hood because it's impressive, feel free. If any of the rest of you would rather be the reason *why* it's impressive, you can be. Robin Hood's gang is my gang. I led them before Robin Hood was even a thing. We have campsites all throughout the Sherwood, we have people in influential positions, we've got the Sheriff's Guard chasing themselves in circles halfway to York and back again."

She eyed Alfie. *That was it? He'd come to borrow some men?*

A few grunts and laughter here, but he received nothing like what he must have hoped for.

"And if you're not interested in the glory, well . . . we gave away more coin last autumn than I saw in my entire life here in Nottingham."

This, at least, was the correct language of the room. Scarlet had come to the wrong place if he had nothing to offer but a sense of importance—but coin knew no master. Whether it was true, though, Cait had her heavy doubts. If Scarlet had coin to boast of, he wouldn't have dallied five nights in the slums. "Odd that he waited so long to mention that," she chuckled to her boys at the dice table. "If someone has enough money to buy a horse, they don't start off by explaining why the horse's life will be better. They just ask the price."

One of her favorite thickskulls—the Dawn Dog—laughed, made a ruckus of rising to his feet, and cleared his throat. He did them all proud by asking, in sincerity, "What do you . . . what do you *do?*"

It seemed to strike Will Scarlet off guard. "What do we *do?*"

"That's right." Cait picked it up, giving Dawn Dog a smile. "What do you do that's so important and impressive and what?"

Scarlet scoffed. "We're living life on our terms. Not beholden to the Sheriff's Guard and certainly not to the Sheriff himself. They're the real criminals, you know. We're the ones fighting back."

That was as empty a breath as ever Cait had heard.

"Lofty," Alfred mused, "but not much of an answer. I second the question. What—specifically—is it that you actually do?"

For a moment, it seemed he had no answer at all, which would have ended it there. But then Will laughed and rubbed his temples. "Well we don't spend our time hiding in caves getting drunk, if that's what you're asking."

"Hey now." Dawn Dog stiffened.

"Where are you going to be *tomorrow*, big fella?" Will bit into it. "Under the horns at that table again playing blind man's hazard? Me and mine'll be sacking a gord outpost, eating their food, breathing fresh air, and actually using our knives rather'n just sharpening them all the time."

Sitting amongst the whores, Ricard the Ruby—who had been audibly sharpening his knife the entire conversation—went still.

"You'd be better off asking if there's anything we *don't* do," Scarlet continued. "God's knuckles, did you miss the part where we killed a couple of Sheriffs?"

Cait exhaled. He may have gained some ground for a bit, but he'd just made the worst mistake he could.

"We did *not* miss that," Alfred noted delicately, "but would you remind me why you're *proud* of it?"

This seemed to stun all four of the strangers. They really had no goddamned clue.

Alfred clicked his tongue. "I was in such a good mood, I don't want to spoil it by being cruel. Darling, would you be cruel for me?"

"Gladly." She took three heavy steps forward. "You hang quite a bit of expectation on that deed, don't you? On killing the Sheriff. Are we to *thank* you? Is that our response? We are, then, most grateful, that is. Grateful for the increased number of gords in the streets. Grateful for their stricter punishments and lack of tolerance, grateful for the men we've lost to the prisons for petty crimes that were once ignored. We're grateful to be forbidden from eating at the Commons. For the fear the people have of working with us."

Her cubs echoed her at each point, riling their disapproval.

"Particularly grateful we were run out of Red Lion Square and into these tunnels, we did ever so hate seeing the sky." The Lions Den still stank of the desiccated piss and shit of tanner's pits. They'd never used it as anything more than a hideaway before October. It was a cave, and they did not *live* there, they *hid* there. Because of the squinty blond cockstain who stood before them.

"And these," Alfred added, brushing his hair back on the left side of his face, "are we to thank you for these as well?"

One by one around the room, each Lion tilted their head to the side, swept back their hair, took off their cap. All to reveal Will Scarlet's legacy.

"Oh you don't know, do you?" Alfred simmered. "You raised the stakes last year. Sheriff's Guard swept through the city, arresting anyone who was even barely associated with a gang. And they branded us all thusly." He traced his fingertips across the side of his face, down the scar that twisted his ear into red meat.

"And how exactly is this our fault?" Scarlet asked.

Alfred chortled. "They punish us for the things you did. You bore all the cause and none of its effects. And what was once an emergency measure has now become policy."

"Anyone caught for anything, *anything*," Ricard mimed a knife through his own ear, "gets clipped."

"If they're lucky," added Dawn Dog.

Rob snorted. "Right. Sometimes they won't wait to pull you in, they'll simply do it on the street. They're not exactly careful."

"Supposed to just be the tip," growled Caitlin, "to mark us. But what if their knife ain't sharp enough, or they've had a shit bad day? Well then it's a bit more. And if you fight back, then it's accidentally your neck, ain't it?"

Her own ears were intact, on account of her father being who he was. As the daughter of the *great* Simon FitzSimon, armsmaster of Nottingham, she was effectively invisible to the Nottingham Guard. A few others in the room too were lucky enough to be clean, and careful enough to stay that way, so they could be used for certain conspicuous jobs. But for the rest, that nub of their ear had become a sign of pride.

"We've taken to do it ourselves of late." Alfred walked over to a young wicker named Ginger Twain, whose ear was cut clean at the bottom but was otherwise healthy. "Rather than wait for a gord to do it to us. Better we do it here, and burn the wound shut. Lest we come back one day with full less an ear. Or a blackrot that kills as sure as the blade."

Some solemn hums made their rounds in honor of the victims. Caitlin poured the blame for this on Scarlet's head. "So you were correct, Will Scarlet. You are half the reason we are what we are now. Or perhaps better said that you are all the reason we are half what we once were."

And that was that. Scarlet had no answer. His body slumped. His failures were obvious. There were no recruits to be found here, not for one such as he. Even his men averted their eyes, rightfully ashamed they'd come here in the first place.

"I didn't know," Scarlet nearly whispered. If he left the city, he might recover and try again. But cowed as he was, he might have his uses. After all, he had exactly two things going for him. *He was short, and he was expendable.* Cait would eventually have a job that called for exactly that, if everything went right with the greenbeard.

"So no, you don't get to call yourself Robin Hood," Alfred finished. "That name lies with us now. Whatever damage you choose to do to yourselves out in the Sherwood is of little concern to us. Here in the city, here in the heart of Nottingham," his words had a ferocity to them now, "*this* is where Robin Hood lives. This is where he is known and feared and loved, this is where he makes a difference. We get to keep his name, because we also bear the consequences of his choices. That you think you can affect any sort of change from the middle of the forest, safe from the repercussions of your own actions . . . that is a specific and new insanity."

"Get it?" Caitlin asked, throwing an arm around her lover's shoulders, pulling the hair back from his scar. "No man or woman in Nottingham is like to follow a Robin Hood that still has both his ears."

EIGHTEEN

ARTHUR A BLAND

BENEATH NOTTINGHAM

DESPITE THE CRUSHING DISAPPOINTMENT they'd been served, there was dinner to be had and Arthur was grateful for it. There was no way of telling the hour, as no church bell could reach them down here beneath the city. Red Fox proved himself the better man by inviting them to share in the meal before they left. There was some sort of stew that smelled of fish but had little meat to it, but plenty of hardbread and heavy wine.

Arthur spent the earlier part of dinner exchanging uneasy glances with David. Every part of Will's plan had failed. Unless Will miraculously knew of another city where they could recruit men less hostile than these, then this was all an epic mistake. As soon as their meal was over—hell, maybe earlier than that—they needed to get out of Nottingham. Whether that meant they were going to try to tackle the gord outposts all on their own, or if they were going to limp all the way to join Marion in Huntingdon, Arthur didn't know.

"Is it strange that I sort of liked them?" David muttered, when Will disappeared to find some more drink. "They seem like a good outfit, no wonder they don't want to join us."

Arthur eyed him over the lip of his ale horn. "Then again, you're known for liking terrible things."

David seemed to take offense to that. "Like what?"

"You like to mix wine and ale."

"I do." David grinned. "But not because it tastes better."

"This," Arthur put his finger in the air, "is why we shouldn't trust your opinion."

"Well maybe you're right. Maybe these people are terrible things. But there's a lot to like about terrible things. I trust bitter before I trust happy. A terrible thing is at least a thing that knows itself. You were a terrible thing once, and I chose to like you."

"No one chooses to like me." Arthur smiled back. "People like me because I'm so fucking likable."

David always found something to like in everything. Even when they first met years ago in Sheffield, when Arthur had been trying to smash David's face into a flatter version of itself—and for good reason—David chose just to smile and introduce himself.

Arthur sometimes wished he were like that. Wished his first instinct was to trust. Admittedly, some of the Lions who came to mingle with them during dinner practically proved David's point. A great hulking barbarian named the Dawn Dog brought them a horn of a darker beer, and took delight in their reactions to its harsh bite. Two of the ladies lingered to tease them, and gave as much barb as Arthur could dish back. Arthur honestly couldn't remember the last time he'd had any cunny he hadn't paid for. But his drinking and laughing was half-hearted at best, his mind was set on how soon he could be anywhere else.

"At least eat up," David urged him, once he realized Arthur's mood. "What, you think they're playing us?"

Arthur just grimaced.

"What're they gonna take from us? If Red Fox means to kill us, he missed his chance."

Arthur took another spoonful of the fish soup, then paused. "This stew does taste a bit like poison."

"It's not poison, *c'est poisson,*" David laughed.

"Is that French? Are you talking French at me again?"

"Je ne sais pas." He ate another spoonful of the stew. *"Je suis trop mort."*

Arthur ignored him and surveyed the room. Scarlet poked at his meal, but seemed uninterested in talk. He was wide-eyed and distant—rightfully so, after his failure. Stutely stood the whole time with an odd vigilance, as if to prove himself by staying ever at his highest alert.

After some time, Red Fox ambled over to them along with his cow-woman Caitlin. They stood on a rock tier that was thigh height beside them, so Fox squatted to be at their level. Caitlin's body was not likely capable of squatting at all.

"Accept my apologies," Fox said, without his earlier grandeur. "You came here with a lot of assumptions."

Will Scarlet puffed out his cheeks. "It doesn't matter."

"You should have broached the matter with me privately, Will. Perhaps I could have helped you out then."

Caitlin literally looked down on them. "Did you expect us to let you win, here, in front of everyone?"

Will just shrugged. "I didn't know you were the man, Freddy."

"You *should* have known that."

"Should have spent the *time* to know that," Caitlin threw in. There was something about the Scottish dialect that always made a person sound crasser to Arthur, and Caitlin was particularly Scottish. "But you didn't bother to ask. You sent us a demand to meet with you, rather than a friendly inquiry. Then you demand we help you with what *you* want. But you don't know us. You don't know what *we* want."

"You were always ever impulsive, Will," Red Fox sighed. "I would like to help you, I would, but a lot of these men don't know you, and have no reason to trust you. Heavens, some that *do* know you don't have reason to trust you."

"You could have vouched for me." Will looked up. "Instead of calling me *careless.*"

Red Fox stood and straightened his long coat with a single motion. "You insulted us, and challenged my authority. And now I offer you our home and our food, rather than beat you merciless and send you away with nothing but bruises. They see this. Actions are something ever finer than words."

Will pursed his lips. "What good is that now?"

"Depends. Were you planning on giving up so easily?"

Oh fuck, Arthur could see exactly where this was going. "We can't stay any longer," he spoke up. "We have to get back to our own people."

"This was your plan?" asked one of Caitlin's neck folds. "Drop on by for a night and see how many people will follow you blindly?"

"Stay." Red Fox knelt again, placing a friendly hand on Will's shoulder. "Work with us, if only for a bit. I know you, and you're better than most of this lot, and that quality will shine clearly enough. *In time*. Let them see it on their own. Let them *choose* to trust you."

"We can't stay," David insisted. "Nottingham Guard's building outposts in the forest, we can't let that happen."

"Then you'd leave with nothing," Caitlin mocked, an insulting smile stretching wide. "Is that what you want? Or'd you come for help? We can give it to you, if you're done chewin' on your pride."

"Cait and I talked it over," Alfred picked up, in gentler tones. "Let me pair you with one of my seconds. Work together for a week or two, prove your interests mirror ours. Prove you have the humility to take orders as well as the competence to issue them. Actions and words, Will. Win yourself what men you need with actions."

A week or two. Arthur had never heard a worse set of words, in any order. He looked to Will, but his eyes were buried in the table. David seemed proper alarmed at least. If they waited that long to get what they'd come for, it might be too late. *But if they left with nothing, how was that better?*

Stutely cleared his throat. "We can't do anything in the forest with just the four of us. If we go now, we can't stop them. Outposts or not, we need men."

Arthur hated that Will Stutely of all people was probably right. He turned to their host. "Why help us now? Seemed eager to trounce us earlier."

Red Fox gave a dismissive snort. "Do not assume this transaction favors you. I have as much to gain from such a partnership, but unlike you I won't announce my motives for all to scrutinize."

Will still gave no answer, and Arthur couldn't guess what was brewing in his head. Arthur half hoped that Will's spite would get the better of him, that he'd say something perfectly vicious that would burn this bridge forever. It'd just be easier if they didn't have to make the choice, because he knew that whatever they chose would be the wrong one. They should have left before dinner.

Will stood up to look Red Fox in the eyes. "It's funny, you were one of the people I was hoping to find here."

"Well, you found me."

"One of the ones I was hoping I could convince to come with me."

"That, I cannot do." Fox clasped Will's shoulders briefly, and made to leave. "Would have been fun, though. It's been a long time since we've been in a scrap together."

"It'd be nice to have you next to me rather than across from me."

"You never know." Fox cocked his head. "Maybe we'll get that chance yet."

Fucking hell. They were staying.

Arthur didn't want to stay in Nottingham one more night, be it above or below the streets. *"This is you abandoning us,"* Marion had said, and she might yet be right. It hurt to think that Arable might assume they'd betrayed them, or that fucking Tuck would speak ill of them at a sermon. He tried to look for a bright side. Maybe it would still pay off. Maybe they'd get so many damned men it'd be worth the wait.

He wanted David's mind on the matter—he'd find something in it to be happy about. But they were distracted by a clatter from one of the tables. Rob o'the Fire, who became louder and clumsier with each drink, seemed to have found his limit. He made a good go at approaching them from half the room away, though the chamber's uneven ground worked against him. "Will! Wiiiiiill. So, anyone else we know with you out there in the forest?"

"Old Lions?" Will asked. "No."

"I always sort of hoped that's where Crimmy ended up."

"Fucking Crimmy." Will shook his head, though Arthur had never heard the name before. "He's either dead or sitting on a mountain of gold crowns."

"What about the ghost?" Rob asked.

"Gilbert left before winter. Don't care where the fuck he is now."

"Really? We thought he was still with you." Rob slurred his words, loud enough that most in the room started to watch. "Rumor is he joined the Guard."

That grabbed Arthur's attention. Gilbert had vanished after Much's death, without a single word.

But Will just laughed. "Wouldn't surprise me, he'd be right at home with those fucks. Again, he abandoned us when things first went bad. Or maybe he was the one what sold us out. Could be anywhere, I suppose."

"What went bad?"

Will bit his lip, having said too much. They'd become the center of attention. "Nothing. Nothing."

"Huh." Rob rolled his tongue in his cheek. "What about Elena?"

Arthur stopped breathing.

"I thought she went off with you?" Rob pushed. "She disappeared right around the same time. She's not with you?"

Not anymore. Arthur winced. Elena Gamwell had betrayed them, then killed herself for it. Arthur had watched it all, on his knees, gag in mouth, sword at his throat. Watched the whole hideous thing, unable to make a noise, as Will held her body until it shook its last. The memory froze Arthur to the spot, he couldn't think at all, let alone draw the conversation elsewhere.

Will didn't move, but his lips just said, "She's not with us."

"Damn." Rob shrugged. "If she was there, I would join you right now. That girl . . . mmmm. Best fuck I ever had."

The room was silent, Arthur had no air at all, too slow to stop it.

"She liked it from behind," Rob continued. "She wanted you to grab her hair and pull . . ."

The first punch broke Rob's jaw. Arthur caught a flash of Will's face that chilled him to the core. Not because of the hatred or the fury within it, but because it was absent. Will wasn't there. His features were relaxed, his eyes elsewhere, even as he drove his knuckles down into Rob's neck, his cheek, his teeth. He grabbed the man's head and wrenched him away, down to the floor so that he could drive his boot into it, and Rob's nose burst bloody from both sides.

Arthur stood and grabbed a knife from the table, at the ready, though frankly he wasn't sure if he meant to defend Scarlet or help take him down. There were, very likely, only seconds left before they were all killed, so it probably didn't fucking matter what Arthur did.

But somehow, the Red Lions didn't rush them. They stood at bay, perhaps waiting for instruction. Rob o'the Fire's body was motionless on the ground, a grotesque whistling wheeze the only proof he was still alive. Will stared at each of them, off kilter, as if he had not yet seen what he'd done.

Then suddenly he was back, casual and smiling. "Oh shit, look at this fellow."

He nudged Rob's body with a toe, but didn't seem to care any further than that. Instead he turned to the crowd.

"I came here looking for men, and all I found were little boys. Crying about their fucking ears. I've watched my friends die, the best people I've ever known, murdered by the shitholes who run this city. We're trying to make a difference, to bring some sort of fucking justice . . . and here you all are, doing your best to *not be noticed* and calling that bravery. You're right, you *do* deserve to be called Robin Hood, because that's the same bullshit he tried to sell us. You're hiding in these fucking caves and blaming it on me? Fuck that. You put yourselves here. Me? I'm the only one who can lead you out of here. Out of these tunnels, out of the slums, all the way up to the fucking rock."

He reached a hand behind his back and slipped one of his twin blades out, a long fat guardless dagger. "You don't get to wonder if I'm good enough to be with you . . ." he said, reached up and *holy fuck*—

Will stretched his own left earlobe out with one hand and drew the knife up to its base, then slashed up and forward, ripping the flesh in a long red streak that tore halfway up the side of his ear before it snapped off in a bloody lump that he flicked down onto Rob's chest.

" . . . I get to decide if *you're* good enough to be with *me*."

He put the knife away without even wiping the blood off, turned, and walked out of the Lions Den.

THEY STAYED ANOTHER DAY.

At Arthur's insistence, they spent their last good coin on a single room at a not-too-sketchy inn called The Peach and the Pear, named after the streets on either side of it. Their window was Pear-side, and looked down into a small courtyard that stank of gutted fish. Down the street, a blanket of smoke rose from cooking fires that littered both sides of the wharfs. Arthur tested the sill of the window, eased some oil into its hinges, and memorized the quickest path out and down. His gut told him he'd be fleeing through that window in the middle of the night.

By staying, they invited retaliation.

"They'll come," Will said.

That's what Arthur was afraid of.

"They don't know where we are," David answered.

"They know."

Will had refused at first to let them treat his ear, until Arthur forced the matter. They boiled water over the hearth in the inn's main room and used it to wash off the dried blood. The bottom lobe of his ear was gone, along with a thin strip around the outside that lashed gruesome all the way to the top.

"Or as I like to say," David described it, "all the most sensitive bits."

"Your ears were always too big," Arthur tried to joke, but not to be funny. It was because—he realized—he was now afraid of Will Scarlet. Had *David* cut his ear off, Arthur would've sat him down and torn him in half with reproach. But Will Scarlet was something else now, and Arthur didn't want to risk waking whatever demon it was that lurked in his soul. Like an unruly child, it was better to simply pacify him than to try anything resembling reason.

Somehow it fell on Arthur to burn out the wound. He was more experienced with such things than he wanted to be, but certainly not enough to know what the fuck he was doing. He had to pay a full shilling for a bundle of incense at an apothecary in the part of town they called *the Parlies*. But no spice could hide the sting of burning flesh as he touched the flame into each part of the exposed wound. Will kicked and bit into a heavy glove, and even passed out before it was done, which at least made it easier to finish. The wound hardened well enough—there was no blood or pus, though it was wicked to look upon.

"Is he . . . ?" Stutely asked, watching from the door with horror.

"No, he's not dead." Arthur blew out the incense. "I think he'll be okay."

"No, I mean . . . is he . . . insane?"

Neither Arthur nor David answered, which was very likely a bad sign.

Maybe he'd been wrong, earlier. Maybe Scarlet was nothing but burnt tree. Maybe the forest was gone.

"I'm not cutting my ear off," Stutely announced, though it seemed to take most of his bravery to say so. He shut his mouth tight, sealing his beard together in a great mess. "Not because I'm afraid to, but because it's smarter not to."

Arthur wanted to explain that none of them were going to follow Will's particular lead on this one, but there was no point. He was tired, and the room smelled of acrid flesh, and he was trapped in an unfamiliar city where they'd just made enemies instead of allies. Once Will was capable of leaving, they would.

Anybody who follows him is going to drown . . .

YOU'RE DROWNING, ARTHUR.

Arthur startled awake, not even realizing he'd laid down. It was a quiet knock on the door that roused him, which whispered open before he could move. But it was not a burly bunch of Lions come to pay their due in blood, just a tiny little frame that slipped in and closed the door behind herself.

"Sounds like it didn't go so well," Zinn said, tugging at her own hair.

Arthur rolled back down. "Oh you heard that, *didcha?* Word travels fast."

"Hiya, Zinn." David smiled. She opened her mouth at him comically wide, then kicked at Will Scarlet's foot as a somber greeting.

"How'd you know we were here?" Arthur asked.

She responded with an eye roll for the ages.

"Never mind. So what have you heard?"

"Half the Red Lions want to kill you, sounds like. But the other half think you're pretty fucking slag."

Pretty fucking slag? Was that a thing? Arthur suddenly felt old.

"You're not just checking in on us." Will said it from where he lay, eyes still closed. Arthur hadn't even realized he was awake. "Are they using you to send a message?"

"They are." She did not, however, elaborate.

"Well?" David asked.

"I'm deciding if I want to tell you."

"Why wouldn't you want to tell us?" Arthur asked.

"You said some pretty nasty things to me."

"Aw, fuck me," Arthur grumbled. "We were trying to protect you."

"You called me a cunt."

"Well you *are* a cunt." Arthur made a face at her. Still, she was the closest thing they had to a friend in the city. "But you're *pretty fucking slag* for a cunt. Now out with it."

That actually seemed to please her quite well. "Red Fox says his offer stands. You work with someone of his choosing, help out on a couple of particular jobs, and they'll decide later if they'd rather work with you or kill you."

"Fack." David rolled his eyes. "He already offered us that. Fat good your little stunt did us, Will. What about the outposts?"

"Forget the outposts." Will's voice had an odd calm. "Marion's not in the Sherwood anymore, and neither are we. So let 'em waste their time looking for us there. Like it or not, Freddy was right about one thing—if we want to make a real difference, we can't do it from the forest."

"So . . . what?" David asked. "We join with them?"

"No. They join us."

Zinn snorted again.

"They will." Will seemed unnaturally sure of that. "I like Freddy, but I don't trust him, and I don't think his men do, either. They're just waiting for a real leader. He wants us to work with one of his seconds? I guarantee whoever it is will try to play us, but we can play him right the fuck back. Pretend we're going along for the ride, but when the time's right, we take control. Trust me, the only way to rise in the Red Lions is to fuck over the person above you."

"So . . . we're staying again?" David's question was really for Arthur. For the thousandth time, they begged each other for agreement. If he wanted to leave, Arthur would go with him right now and leave Will behind. As far as he was concerned, David was the goddamned moral weather vane of the world. So if he somehow thought they ought to stay, then Arthur couldn't jump ship. They couldn't watch each other's backs if they weren't right next to each other.

And again—if they left now, this was all for nothing.

"Yeah, I think we're staying," Arthur answered, each word tasting worse than the last.

"Fack." David scratched his head. "Well, Zinn, you've been decent enough to us so far. Looks like we're joining the Red Lions. Care to tag along? You want a lift up the ranks? We could use help from someone who knows the city."

"No," Will answered before she even opened her mouth. "She's too young. Sorry, that's just how it is, sweet pea."

She stared at him, some dark fire inside her burning, but she was thankfully smart enough not to argue back.

"So when do we meet our new bossman?" Arthur asked.

Zinn's eyes didn't leave Will, but she curled her lip and threw him every inch of her twelve-year-old spite. "Oh, you've already met her. You cunts are mine. Welcome to the Red Lions. You do everything I say, exactly how I say, or I'll cut your balls off. Learn your fucking place. Sorry," she winked, "that's just how it is, sweet pea."

PART III

INCREASINGLY FOOLISH ACTS

NINETEEN

JOHN LACKLAND

"YES IT'S ALL VERY interesting," John explained, "I just don't understand why we're currently talking instead of having sex."

He poured all his considerable talent into keeping a straight face. One hand folded delicately over the other atop the smooth stone tabletop, and John looked both of his visitors in the face earnestly. Each opened his mouth, gaped at the other, closed it again, and repeated.

"I am not certain I understand you," one of the Frenchmen finally answered.

"Having sex," John replied, and reached across to the platter of fruits and cheeses in the center of the table. "If we don't have sex now, I won't be hungry again by dinner. We might as well do both."

He popped a grape in his mouth, and the two Frenchmen inhaled.

"Perhaps they misunderstand?" John turned and addressed his host, the ever-prickly Roger de Montbegon, who stood dutifully nearby. "What's the French word for it, Baron?"

"*Manger,* Your Grace," he replied, thankfully wise to the game.

"*Manger!*" John snapped his fingers. "You should *manger,* while we speak."

Both visitors practically melted with relief, and reached out for an item to eat. "I am so sorry," one of them frowned, "I thought you said . . . *having sex.*"

"Yes, that's what we call it here," John answered. "I think perhaps your English is not as good as you think, friends. Very well, now that we're all having sex together, what were you saying?"

John knew perfectly well what they wanted. They had been petitioning an audience with him for a month, which had launched a round of John's favorite sport of ignoring important things. He'd already made them sail all the way to Lancaster just to meet with him, admittedly with the hopes that the river Lune would be frozen and prevent them from docking.

He'd long discovered that Frenchmen came in only two shapes—walrus or rat. Both of these were walruses, with bulbous noses and untamed whiskers, to say nothing of their teeth. They brought flowery words and painted eyebrows and black promises. King Philip of France wanted to take advantage of England's misfortune by filling its absent throne with as much of his own influence as he could.

And he wanted the name of that influence to be King John.

"England will waste away trying to purchase Richard back," the first walrus explained, slapping his flipper on the table. "Philip would hate to see your great country wither away so. England needs a king, and I think there is no knowing when Austria will release Richard, if ever."

"How dare you!" John mocked offense. "There's no need for such coarse language!"

"I—" The second walrus looked to the first. "Coarse language?"

The first barked, "What did I say?"

"Well I shall hardly repeat it." John widened his eyes. "Honestly, *who* tutored you?"

They had come to woo him, and John was so very intimately familiar with the hoops a wooer will leap through to stay in favor. He would have made a finer point on how they should study their English if they meant to do business beyond their borders, but his brother was the King of England . . . and *his* English was ten times worse than any walrus.

When they continued, every word was impossibly deliberate, lest they *misspeak* again. "Philip wishes to support you, in Richard's absence, for England's stability."

"Well." John pretended to think on it. "We would have to have an orgy first."

They went wide-eyed again.

"A *meeting*, that is. You've never heard the word *orgy* before, really? We'd need to have an orgy, I can't make that kind of a decision without my brother present. We'll have to wait until he's back."

"That's not . . . I think perhaps we have not explained ourselves properly."

"Oh! There is that word again!" John recoiled. Admittedly, *think* was already a foul enough word when used by most people, but doubly so by these two. "You're mispronouncing it quite embarrassingly. You're saying *think,* which means . . . well, something inappropriate! The proper word is *fuck.*"

Even Roger de Montbegon had to stifle a laugh at that.

"I apologize, Your Grace," the man said, slowly. "As I said . . . I . . . I *fuck* you misunderstand us."

This had just become John's favorite day.

The first walrus fidgeted, likely due to some fish stuck in his flesh rolls that he might be saving for later, so the second took his turn. "King Richard was betrothed to Philip's sister, the Countess of Vexin, before he so rudely took a wife in Cyprus. Philip now extends that same offer to you."

At that, John could honestly balk. He was used to the regency throwing daughters at him, which was just the most delightful side effect of being a prince. But the *Countess of Vexin* was not half as attractive as her title sounded. King Philip's sister Alys was already over forty years old, and if John was purchasing a new mount he'd prefer a young filly over a broken and beaten plowhorse. So here he fell back to his usual excuse. "Oh, I'm married already, and I love her very deeply, whatever her name might be."

The first man cocked his head. "Isabella?"

"No, a human, actually."

"What?"

"As I said, I will fuck on this." John stood, forcing both dignitaries to match him. "I will fuck on this long and hard. Thank you for this orgy, gentlemen, it has been good having sex with you both."

Eventually they left, the crisp staccato of their heels echoing in the chamber. Lancaster Castle was full of crisscrossing black-and-white stripes—the sigil of the High Sheriff of Lancashire, Richard de Vernon—which apparently confused their already befuddled walrus bodies as they searched incorrectly for an exit. The conversation wasn't over, John knew. They would not return to Paris without trying several more tactics. They'd abandon the marriage proposal and offer him lands instead. When he refused those, it would be ships and money. Then they might start getting creative. After that . . . after that, they would offer trouble.

"Thank you for watching, Roger," John said, when at last they were gone. "Sometimes I just need an audience, you know. Entertaining myself becomes increasingly redundant as I grow older."

"Do you fear at all they may be right?" the baron asked, hunting for a treat from the table's platter.

"Well of course they're *right*," he said, hopping from his chair. The far side of the vaulted chamber had a doorway that opened to a balcony, he knew, which looked down upon the Lune below—and it was times like this when he wanted to see as much of the world as his eyes could hold. "But King Philip is being right for the wrong reasons. He wants to fund my ascension to the throne? I fuck not. You tell me—what sort of favor will he eventually ask in exchange?"

"Something hideous," de Montbegon answered, accurately.

"Indeed." John opened the door, felt the wicked chill of the outside slap him in the face, and closed it again. "I'd rather have nothing than to owe what I have to someone else."

"And if Richard does not return?"

That was a nightmare scenario. "I am fortunately immune to flattery. Philip does not mean to endorse *me*, he means to endorse civil war."

If Richard died, the throne could go either to John, or to Geoffrey's son, Arthur Plantagenet. Though Geoffrey died before ever being king, he was the eldest of John's brothers and his bloodline was strongest. But Arthur was five years old, and a ward of King Philip. The barons of England would rightfully see Arthur as Philip's puppet, and half would revolt—by supporting John instead. Then, there would be an awful lot of fighting about it. Which would very much interfere with John's plans of wasting his life drinking wine with young fillies.

Whereas if John accepted Philip's offer and took the crown himself, it would be seen as a coup. He'd be quickly killed by someone he once thought loyal, and nobody would complain when Arthur became King—puppet or not.

"Richard is much better than me at most things, but I really wish I had taught him a bit about fucking."

De Montbegon laughed. "Thinking?"

"No, actual fucking. If he'd just tried a woman out once or twice—just for the novelty of it—we wouldn't have to worry about who becomes king after him."

"He is married."

"Not by choice. My mother shipped a woman off at him when he left for the Crusades, demanding that he marry her, specifically to avoid something like this. But unless she's a very strange breed of woman who has a man's mouth between her legs instead of the usual bits, then no—I doubt my brother's tried making an heir with her."

The tightening of the baron's face said he'd rather be at his home in Hornby than continue that conversation. John abetted him by opening the balcony door again, wincing at the brisk air, and closing it behind him.

The world in front of him was one without King Richard, and that very much needed to change—and soon. From this vantage he could see the river docks where the French ship had moored. After another few days of antagonizing his guests, that vessel would leave without even a fraction of what it had come for. John did not know what King Philip's response would be, but he had no doubt it would have more teeth than four tusks.

And for the first time since losing his virginity, John had absolutely no idea what to do.

TWENTY

QUILLEN PEVERIL

THE FRENCH WARD, NOTTINGHAM

FIVE SEVERED HANDS IN a row, in varying stages of rot, were nailed to the wall. Something black and putrid stained the wood deeply beneath each one, dripping down and collecting flies, maggots. Quill would have retched anything left in his stomach, but he'd already vomited at the entrance to the stables when the stench first assaulted him. He pulled his quilted doublet up over his nostrils, keenly aware there were a handful of onlookers who probably expected him to behave in at least a vaguely more official manner.

"I'm not really a Guardsman," he didn't tell them. "I'm just a pansy nobleman's son playing pretend."

He doubted they would care much about his sense of self. All they saw was his blue tabard, which meant they saw him as *Guard the Guardsman*.

"Cut them down," he ordered, his voice muffled well past the point of any authority.

"*You* cut them down," returned Potter. A gentle man with a wild beard, Potter had been a member of Nottingham's Common Guard for years. He normally came with the jovial sort of spirit so common in the happy ignorant masses. "You ask me, I'd sooner put a torch to the place than touch those things."

As would I, Quill admitted. But this ramshackle building had a history, so he understood, as a place of mercy even amongst the poorest folk in the French Ward. These mutilations were a dire shadow over them, and a terrible thing for the commonfolk to suffer.

"We're here to help them," he explained to Potter. Gilbert with the White Hand was using the name of Robin Hood and acts like this as leverage, and leaving the severed hands hanging would make the Nottingham Guard complicit in that fear. "If people see a couple of Guardsmen come burn down the Pity Stables, they're not going to take it kindly."

"I wasn't serious," Potter muttered. "But still, I ain't touchin' them none neither."

It was easy to forget that Quill had no authority over Potter. He'd hoped his aid in Lord Beneger's hunt would have granted him some leniency, but instead it had worked against him. Ben had assigned him right back to the nightwalkers, to keep an eye on the White Hand. To *stalk* him. It had been ten nights already, and Gilbert had yet to deviate from his regular schedule of haunting the castle walls.

Quill could hardly keep an eye on him at every minute, so the rest of Ben's team kept records of Gilbert's movements when he wasn't on patrol, as best they could. *"Patterns,"* Ben had insisted. They needed to find the patterns that would let them catch him in the act. He was undoubtedly working with Will Scarlet's crew, and watching Gilbert would eventually lead to them. And then, Lord Beneger de Wendenal would exercise some of his legendary vengeance.

Quill was still doubtful that catching Robin Hood would actually help the city, but it would undoubtedly catapult Lord Beneger to acclaim. If that victory led him directly into the Sheriff's seat, as Quill was betting, that would in turn help the city, which was a worthwhile endeavor.

Instead of sleeping, Quill had taken to spending his days taking extra shifts in the Common Guard. After all, catching the criminal was only part of the work. The side effects of Robin Hood's destruction infected the city; and while Beneger was content to let that eventually settle itself, Quill knew that hole in the dyke would do far more damage to Nottingham in the long run.

"Don't take them down," came a whimper from his right. A young boy, seven or eight perhaps, was standing in the doorway. His thin frame hung loosely, his skin nearly black from dirt.

Quill didn't have a breadth of experience with children, outside of working for William de Ferrers. He tried to keep his voice light, nonhostile. "Why shouldn't I take them down?"

"He said he'd come back," the boy's voice wavered. "Said we had to leave 'em up, or he'd be angry at us."

"Robin Hood? Did you see him?" Quill asked, aiming for a casual tone. The boy didn't answer, which was as good as a yes. "Had a glove on? The man who did this?"

A confused squint. "What?"

Of course it wouldn't be that easy. Nobody knew why Gilbert kept his one hand in a glove, but such a feature was certain to identify him if he were to leave it on while in the mantle of Robin Hood. Taking it off was his disguise.

A little whine escaped from the boy's lips, and his face clenched. He was afraid, and had no idea how to deal with it. Quill suffered a brief thought of the vagrant Hanry's body, hanging in the Sherwood Forest. Hanry had probably once been a young fearful boy, too, and he'd grown into a fearful man, who got himself in trouble because he didn't know what to do about it.

Quill crouched down.

"I'm sorry he's been mean to you. There are lots of folk who are just mean, and they want to scare you, because that's the only way they know how to get what they want. But there are other people out there who want to help you, people like me, and my friend here. His name's Potter, and I'm Quillen."

The boy didn't offer his name.

"We live in the castle, and we have lots of friends who want to help. So if ever you see the man who scared you here, just run up to the castle gates and ask for Lord Beneger. Say that name for me."

"Lord Benja."

Good enough. "Say it three times now."

"Benja Benja Benja."

"Good. I'm going to take these hands down, and you can forget all about the man who put them there, alright?"

He reached his palm out, but the boy spooked and ran—leaving nothing but a rise of dust and a patter of footsteps.

"Gad, it stinks," Potter complained.

Quill stood, stared at the hands on the wall, and raspberried his lips. "Find me something I can use."

A quick search of the room garnered an iron horseshoe pick, and soon enough Quill was holding his breath on a small wooden ladder against the wall beneath the hideous display. He struggled just to keep his balance two rickety rungs up. The ladder, admittedly, would have collapsed under Potter's weight.

The stench up close was horrific.

Why not today? Quill wondered.

Today was a fine day to return home, to report to his father that the Sheriff's seat in Nottingham was in good custody. What did it matter if that wasn't true? Ferrers would be replaced eventually, whether by Beneger de Wendenal or someone else. Quill could move on with his own life, to something worthwhile, to bettering himself. He couldn't fix every wrong in Nottingham, not with a thousand lives and a thousand allies, and nor would any of it matter. He'd already made his contribution, by deducing Gilbert's identity as Robin Hood. That was a job well done, and Lord Beneger could take it from here. There were a thousand boys that would still be afraid, with or without Quill in the city. If he went back home to the Peak, he could at least focus his efforts in Derbyshire and make meaningful improvements to a place that actually mattered to him.

But he—again—chose to stay. And he was starting to wonder if there was something deeply wrong with him, at a fundamental level.

The first and freshest hand pried free easily enough, falling like a stone to the ground and sending a cold shudder down Quill's spine. But the older hands rent hideous when he tried to wrench them away, sloughing off in pieces and somehow Quill was vomiting again.

THEIR NEXT STOP WAS a tavern near the Market Square, whose carved placard featured a hunchbacked traveler and a dog that was dressed far fancier than any dog had reason to dress. The Bell Inn was either a local gem or an obnoxious wart, depending on who was asked. Its walls featured an eclectic assortment of trinkets from all over the world—or, at least, such was the claim. Many of the drunken conversations in its hall centered on the veracity of those stories, and everyone fancied themselves an expert on the matter.

Quill had only visited the Bell once before, to satiate his curiosity. But this day the door was locked despite it being a very drinkable hour. There were no patrons at the Bell Inn, not since it had been visited by Robin Hood.

A groggy male voice refused them entrance when they knocked a third time. But after Potter barked out, "Sheriff's Guard, come on now!" a barrel rolled behind the door's thick frame and it opened to reveal a woman with a wide, textured face.

"Doesn't matter who you are!" she growled. Quill tried to realign everything he knew to make sense of how she could be the owner of the groggy male voice. "I can't serve to you. Lessin' you want to buy a whole barrel."

"We're not here to drink," Quill said. "Heard you had a few problems. Mind letting us in?"

The woman shrugged and flung the door open. "Can't get worse. Might as well let the whole city know you're in here."

He noted the queer comment and ducked his head through the doorway, blinking to acclimate to the low light. Within, the stools and benches were piled upon the tables, and dust lines on the ground spoke to a morning's sweeping. There were two windows that would normally light the room in the day, but both were boarded over with recently milled timber. The normal human musk of a tavern was overwhelmed with the vinegar stink of wine, mixed with lye.

After some brief introductions, the woman—who identified herself as "Nissa, but most call me Niss"—explained what had happened. "Last night, a group comes in looking to make trouble for themselves. Normally chase 'em out, don't need that here. My husband deals with that, and he's a sight to reckon, but these ones wasn't interested in leavin'."

"Is your husband the proprietor?" Potter asked.

"Offie's the Bell, and I'm plumb-goggin' the opposite."

Quill recognized some of those as actual words. "Offie's your husband?" he guessed. "And where is he now?"'

"He's upstairs, but no good tryin' to talk to him. They put a beat on him, feckless cocksuckers, he's still in and out."

"Now, no need for language," Potter balked.

"Ain't no language, just fact. Each one of them had a cock in 'is mouth and not a single feck amongst the five of 'em."

"Alright then." Quill tried not to imagine what that meant. "Let's talk about them. Five, you say? Rumor has it that Robin Hood is claiming responsibility for it, does that sound right to you?"

"He said as much. Standing right here when he kicked Offie's head to the ground."

An odd shiver took Quill's spine and he stepped away from the spot. Beneath him, a large circle on the dark stone floor had been cleaned free of straw and dirt. It was freshly scrubbed, where Niss had probably cleaned up her husband's blood.

"Would you recognize him again? Or any of the other four?" Quill asked. "Any obvious scars, or gloves, anything like that?"

He felt a tinge of confusion from Potter at the second mention of the glove. Nobody outside Lord Beneger's force knew yet that Gilbert was suspected as a traitor.

Niss shook her head, and busied herself at wiping the cobwebs from some of the wall's ornaments. "Kept their hoods on, hardly saw their faces. Robin Hood was a tall skinny fellow, I can tell you that, and not much pack to his kicks, at least. Otherwise Offie'd be in worse shape."

Not Will Scarlet, then. Too short. This one was likely Gilbert himself.

Potter grunted. "And you're closed until your husband recovers?"

"Fuck on that. I can run the place on my own, but they smashed all the horns."

Quill looked around the room, scrutinizing it again. "They smashed the *horns?*"

"Every cup, every flagon, anything they could find that'd hold ale. Either smashed to pieces or put a hole in it."

"That's ..." Quill walked carefully about, noting the lack of servingware, and tiny shards of debris in the cracks of the tables and cobbles, ". . . strange. Were they drunk?"

"No. They came for that. Had hammers with 'em. Said it was punishment for us serving to Guardsmen like you. So thanks for makin' yourselves so visible comin' in, I'll bet they'll be back for a third round tomorrow now."

"*Third* round?"

"This was the second time. Same thing a week ago. Horns aren't too hard to replace, though I'd rather not spend the coin on 'em. Bought a handful in the Square after last week, had a few other taverns kind enough to bring me some of their own. Then last night they smash 'em all up again, and this time my windows, too. While, might I add, they was suckin' on cocks and fully feckless."

Quill would have laughed if he wasn't busy trying to piece it all out. He took a moment to be impressed with Nissa, who was able to find the humor in her husband's beating and the attack on her livelihood. She seemed the sort of woman who'd weathered far worse, callused against everything but the chore of having to clean up after life's inevitable obstacles.

And if that fact was obvious to Quill after only a few minutes, it would be equally obvious to anyone else who encountered her. Nobody was dumb enough to think she could be intimidated.

"Do you recall what times they were here? Both last night and last week?"

"Course I do. Last night was just after midnight," she answered without hesitation. "Week before ... Friday. Half after tenth."

Bless her memory. Quill could compare notes with Ben's team, to see if Gilbert had any time unaccounted for in those periods. Look for the patterns, and then be ready for him. It was good news that people like Nissa were finally willing to talk about it with the Guard. Back in the autumn, the commonfolk took a protective secrecy about Robin Hood's activities. But when he roughs up a whole alehouse just for serving to Guardsmen—or chops off people's hands—then he costs himself allies.

As Potter wrapped up the discussion with Nissa, Quill found himself staring behind the bar at three large barrels of ale, mounted on their sides. Her earlier comment about selling the whole barrel stood up in his mind and stretched its legs.

"Niss." He aimed a finger at them. "You said they smashed your horns and flagons, but they left the ale barrels?"

"That's right."

"They take anything else?"

She shook her considerable head no. "Didn't *take* nothing. I had a couple bottles of mead they broke, but mostly just the horns. Just broke what we can pour into."

"And they said it was for serving members of the Sheriff's Guard?"

Her face twisted, as if to say she couldn't care less about their motivations. "I'll serve anyone, s'long as they don't break the place. An' I'll continue to do so, so come back whenever you're thirsty now. I could use the coin. You can be sure we'll be ready for 'em next week, iffin' they dare to come again."

They left the Bell Inn behind, though Quill paid special attention upon exiting to scan the street for any conspicuous faces who might be watching them. Potter seemed eager to return to the castle, and Quill could not argue against it. If he was lucky enough to quiet his thoughts, he might be able to catch a few hours of sleep before his night's shift on the wall.

"What do you suppose they're after?" he asked as they turned south on Hollows.

"What do you mean?" Potter returned. "They hate the Guard, they hate anyone who caters to them. Seems simple enough."

"Why smash the horns, but leave the ale? They could've broken the taps off those barrels with their hammers, spilt everything she had onto the floor. They could've cut the wine skins, but no. They left the *merchandise*. That would've put poor Niss and her husband back a good ways further than her lot of horns."

Potter shrugged. "They also didn't kill anyone. You're angry at them for not doing the worst possible thing?"

That was true. Robin Hood had killed Lord Brayden and his mistress, raped her in death, and mutilated five poorfolk just for sport. Here he had just crushed some drinking horns and left a man with a few days' worth of bruises, no more. It was hard to find any parallel to the attacks, since they seemed so stubbornly unassociated with each other.

"They was sending a message, is all," Potter dismissed it. "Not to sell to Guardsmen."

"Then why go back?" Quill wondered aloud. "One visit is a message, two is a purpose. Everyone knows an innkeeper can't refuse service to Guardsmen if they want to drink, so what good is punishing them for that?" *And especially someone as hard-boiled as Nissa.*

"And why this tavern?" Quill added, just speaking as the thought came to him. "You ever drink here, Potter?"

He shook his head. "Usually the Trip, or the Salutation."

"Me too. This place, this is hardly known as a frequent stop for Guardsmen."

"Maybe this is just their first stop. Maybe we'll see similar attacks on other taverns soon?" Potter raised an eyebrow. "I don't see the mystery. They told her why they did it."

"Which is only the first reason to doubt it." Quill wasn't in the business of taking thieves' words at their face value. "If we look strictly at their actions, it seems . . . it seems like each time, Robin Hood simply wanted the Bell Inn to be closed for one day. No more, no less."

Potter clearly didn't care anymore. "Then why beat up the husband?"

Quill had no answer. "I don't know. But I'm starting to think there are a lot of things I don't know, and that is not a position I have any experience with."

TWENTY-ONE

ARABLE DE BUREL

"This," Marion prefaced, "is a tale of increasingly foolish acts."

And one half of the story started thusly.

John Little had three heads, and somehow the middle one looked sadder and lumpier than the two beside it. Arable had never seen him look more uncomfortable, despite their winter of living in poverty. But this was a new version of misery on him, stuffed into a pompous orchid cote-hardie that ballooned massively at his shoulders and vomited lace upward about his neck. It was too fancy for their purposes, but it was all Lord Robert had been able to find that fit John's impressive size. He and Peetey Delaney rode on their own horses beside her, while Marion and her group were off on their own.

"Somebody made this on purpose," John grumbled, flicking at the floof. "That's the baffling part."

Arable tried with little success to pat down the coat's more obnoxious accents. Her own dress fit surprisingly well, excepting a deep soreness across her chest. But that was little different than the rest of her body, still recovering from months of neglect. Her stomach had become so unaccustomed to food that it reacted oddly to the most innocuous meal, and she often fell asleep at inopportune moments as her brain forcibly reclaimed all its lost slumber. But instead of tending to herself and caring for her ravaged nerves, she was in a dress finer than anything she'd worn in years, riding a horse, preparing to do *this thing*.

"You look the part," John approved. In some small way, the disguise felt like redemption. *Important* felt good after so much time without it, even in pretend. "Better than me, at least. I think they might laugh me off."

"You're an intimidating man." She gave up trying to fix his costume. "I guarantee that nobody will argue with you if you try your very best at being surly."

If John had seen his outfit before this began, he might have refused to participate in Lord Robert's scheme entirely. But the Earl of Huntingdon had this way about him, a cloud of personality that drew one in and made the impossible seem effortless. When he described this mission it sounded like an afternoon stroll, and Marion had insisted that occasional adventures such as this were now the price of his hospitality.

"I need you to steal something for me," Lord Robert had explained the night before, his smile wider than his actual face. *"Don't worry, it's rightfully mine anyway."*

In exchange for their new home, they had agreed to the unknown—and this was the first payment. *An open-ended favor. That was his real price,* Arable knew.

He had not sheltered them out of generosity—he had purchased himself a toy. *He wanted his own private little team of thieves.* If there was one single thing Arable had learned from her time on the run, it was to always agree on the details of a trade first. Otherwise, the innkeeper might decide one drunken night he'd rather take his payment in something softer than coin.

But since Marion had never known fear in her life, she'd never learned lessons on how to protect herself or the rest of them. And so, Arable was now in Grafham pretending to be an important lady, while the earl Robert of Huntingdon did his best impersonation of a thief.

"Put on your angry face," Arable suggested to John, trying one on herself. "Let's go."

It was night, but a clear sky and the mirror lake behind the de Senlis manor made a silhouette of its features. It had only two stories, but if this was *humble* then Arable doubted she knew what the word meant. By now, the others would have found their way around it, hopefully avoiding the attention that Arable and John were trying to attract by carrying lanterns and riding horses.

The plan had been crafted, cast, and rehearsed, and they had traveled for hours of a brisk but dry day from Huntingdon Castle. Grafham was unfamiliar to most of them, but Lord Robert led their small group with certainty. Arable's trio was in charge of the lying half. Meanwhile Lord Robert and Marion—along with the other Delaney brother, Nick—would get the more interesting bits. It all involved a feisty lord, unpaid monies, and the manor in Grafham that hid them both.

None of them, excepting Lord Robert, were comfortable in their roles. But Will Scarlet had taken the only men who were actually good at this sort of thing with him to Nottingham, while Lord Robert expected them all to be experts on the matter. And so Arable—who admittedly at least had a lifetime's experience at lying—was now in charge of the first part of the night's plan.

Two young watchmen met them on the approaching lane, and Arable spoke before they could ask a question. "We'll see the lord of the manor, or the chamberlain, if he's indisposed."

They snapped appropriately to attention. "Shall I say who is to see them?"

"You shall not." John gave his voice a gruff lilt. "And we'll be asking the questions."

"Pretend you're in charge," John had coached her. *"Most people just want to do what's asked of them and be done with it."* But he also explained that he'd learned this advice on sneakthieving from Elena Gamwell, who was now very dead.

Arable's heart raced, and she hoped she was hiding it well. Every instinct told her to disappear in a situation like this, to shy away from unwanted eyes. This was the opposite of everything she'd become good at. She wondered idly how bloody her death would be, and prayed she would at least not see it coming.

The obedient watchmen led them to the front entrance of the de Senlis manor. Within they would find the Lord Simon de Senlis, fourth of his name, but the first who had never held the title of Earl of Huntingdon. Lord Robert had explained it all—three successive generations of Simons de Senlis had called Huntingdon Castle home until they were overrun by Henry the Younger's forces in the Kings' War. Unable to reclaim his castle back on his own, the earl enlisted the military help of Lord Robert's father. When the war was over, King Richard gifted the earldom of Huntingdonshire to Robert's family as a reward, inadvertently turning the Senlis family into their bitter rivals. This youngest Simon de Senlis was now effecting his minor revenge by refusing to pay into King Richard's ransom, which put an enormous financial pressure on Lord Robert to pay the Chancellor by making the difference himself.

"*It's too much politicking for me,*" John Little had huffed. "*Just tell me what to steal.*"

"*You don't have to steal anything,*" Lord Robert repeated. "*You just need to find out where his money is, so I can steal it myself.*"

"Could you repeat that?" the baggy-eyed chamberlain asked, after blinking twice and staring into his own soul.

"I said, hullo. My name is Petrus, and I'm a bodyguard."

This was—unimaginably—what Peetey Delaney actually said both the first and second time. Arable practically yanked him backward before he made a blunder of all their prepared aliases.

"My apologies," she said, wrinkling her nose. "My attendant is quite weary from the road. Allow me to introduce Lord Jonathan of Hastings, officiant en parole of the royal treasury, an honor which I share with him as benefactor adesso. My name is Lady Arabella Colonna, and we appreciate your inviting us inside."

None of those words, strictly speaking, made any sense. But the chamberlain stammered and stepped aside, nonetheless. "I didn't—yes of course," he cringed, and held the door ajar for the three of them.

She reminded herself of William—before he became terrible, that is. Or rather, before she *learned* he was terrible. He'd been clueless how to act as a Sheriff, so instead he just did his best impersonation of Roger de Lacy. "*I just say a lot of complicated words,*" he'd described in bed one night, "*and I use them confidently. Most people don't have the first clue how anything works, and are far too embarrassed to admit as much.*"

Arable could say she's the *first priorate of bullshitshire* and they'd smile and bow.

And still the best Peetey had come up with was "*Hullo, I'm a bodyguard.*"

They filed through the door into a small foyer, whose arched walls gave way to the manor's main reception hall. Its sunken gallery was met by short staircases on all four sides, and a series of elaborate ringed chandeliers filled the emptiness above. The manor likely held a hundred rooms at Arable's guess, built with two stories in a great square design around a central courtyard. This reception hall alone could have hosted a festival. Arable immediately surveyed

its layout, trying to account for every detail. Three balconies loomed—one at the top of each of the other staircases—all currently empty, making several exits aside from the main entrance behind her.

The chamberlain was an older gentleman with a thick mash of white hair about his neck—a stocky-strong man, but his posture hinted that his able days were well behind him. Arable dared herself to look him square with a haughty disgust. "We have immediate business."

John grumbled in assent. "You'll kindly fetch the Lord de Senlis."

"And for reasons that don't concern you," she added, "my man here will escort you to find his lordship."

Peetey stepped forward and motioned for the chamberlain to lead the way. *Confidence at all times.* It was their only strategy.

The wary chamberlain experimented with a few different expressions, but submitted. "Stay with them," he commanded one of his men, while bringing the other along with Peetey to unintentionally show him the layout of the de Senlis manor.

It was one of the last things that would go well.

A GOOD AMOUNT OF time passed before Lord Simon de Senlis joined them in the foyer. In that expanse, only three things happened—Arable and John exchanged a few furtive but assuring glances, Arable shifted her weight from foot to foot to relieve whatever bloating was apparently taking place in her costume boots, and a naked young woman ran the full breadth of the room.

It should have been an obvious sign that things were not going their way.

Before either Arable or John had a chance to comment on the naked woman, the lord of the manor was upon them. He was surrounded by a crowd of his entourage on the adjacent balcony, who whispered and pointed at John Little as if he were even more ridiculous-looking than probably had been described. Peetey was at the back of the group, looking exactly as perplexed to be there as would a giraffe.

The Lord Simon de Senlis was a well-trimmed young man with a smooth chin and a pinched nose, and he dismissed a few of his servants quite kindly. Arable would've felt poorly about robbing the man, but what they meant to steal today was no more than what was already owed for his part of King Richard's ransom. They were less like thieves and more like tax collectors.

"*One in four,*" *the foreheaded Guardsman in Rutland had demanded.* "*Everyone pays.*"

Arable tried to ignore the comparison.

"I present Lord Simon, fourth of his name, master of the house de Senlis and rightful heir to the earldom of Huntingdonshire."

The chamberlain's bold announcement echoed through the entrance gallery. John Little and Arable descended the shorter stairs into the hall proper and gave their best dignified bows to the lord of the manor.

"Your lordship. We apologize for arriving unannounced." John Little's mouth twisted hard to keep his diction clean, or perhaps to avoid swallowing the pillowing lace of his collar. "We understand this is unusual, but we appreciate your complete cooperation."

"You have my complete *attention*," Lord Simon said cautiously, eyeing both of them in turn. "I'd suggest you make the most of that before I reallocate it."

"As you say." Arable gave her warmest smile. "We are in the course of a financial investigation, which I . . . my apologies . . ." She put her hand to her breast. "Perhaps your lordship would prefer we continue in private?"

"If I have such a preference," Lord Simon answered, his lips barely moving, "I will make it known. I beg you to continue."

"With pleasure." She cocked her head. "The investigation to which I refer has led us to your estate. If we find you less than accommodating in its satisfaction, some might find suspicion in such behavior."

The balcony's railing took Lord Simon's elbows. "I cannot accommodate you, Lady Colonna, until I know what you ask for."

"We've come to investigate counterfeit coins," Arable answered him with a cool stare. "Which we have traced to your manor."

If that had any effect on the man, it was only to further calm him. "That's quite an accusation."

"It's not an accusation at all," she replied. "You might easily be its victim, not its architect. Although it is interesting how instinctively you associated yourself as the latter."

"Frankly, I'd be more offended if you intended the former. Calling me a victim would imply I am ignorant of the coin that passes through my estate. At least if I were an *architect*, as you say, you'd be accusing me of some sort of criminal genius. That is, at least, something of a compliment. Unfortunately for you, I am neither."

The lord rapped his knuckles on the balcony rail, eyeing his guests as though they were an unfavorable offering of hors d'oeuvres. He showed no interest in descending the stairs to join them.

"I suspect my insistence alone will not be enough to satisfy your . . . investigation."

"I'm afraid not," John humphed. "We'll need to have a look at your treasury, and see if you have any of the counterfeit coins in question. And iffing you do, we may have more questions for you."

Arable winced at his use of the word *iffing*, giving away his low education. They only needed to be believed long enough for Lord de Senlis to reveal the location of his treasury, where they would of course discover no counterfeit coins and make their apologies. Then Lord Robert and the others outside could sneak in and steal from it.

It was never exactly a *good* plan, but Lord Robert didn't seem to mind.

"I could bring a chest out for you to inspect . . ." Lord Simon lulled, clearly anticipating Arable's interruption.

"... which of course we couldn't trust," she finished. "Let's not make this any more difficult than it is. We'll need to see your storeroom, as it is, and immediately. The longer you delay, the longer your men could be—hypothetically—busy hiding any evidence. That would be precisely what a *criminal genius* would do. If you have nothing to hide, you have only to prove it, and immediately."

The lord made a few quiet clicks with his tongue, irritated to be at the disadvantage. "With great respect, I must decline you. I am not in the habit of leading strangers into my secure room."

They had made one plan for this. If it didn't work, they'd be freefalling.

"Do you think we're here to steal from you and run away?" Arable shared a smirk with John. "I should hope your guards are capable of handling me and my associate. I don't know that Jonathan is even capable of *running* any more, are you?"

"The word alone makes my knees quiver," John balked, overacting it a bit.

"And if you're worried about my bodyguard," Arable continued, gesturing up to Peetey, "then you are welcome to keep him here. You should buy his service from me, in fact. You must be desperately understaffed if the three of us present such a threat to your security. You could even pay him in counterfeit coins, I doubt he'd recognize the difference."

Peetey bowed his head awkwardly, clearly unsure if he was supposed to contribute some witty little barb here or not. Arable was grateful he did not try.

"Entertain me," Lord Simon rolled his head about, "with what would happen if I were to refuse you."

Arable shrugged. "We would leave. And report back to the Earl Robert of Huntingdon that you refused to help us. I imagine our next visit would be accompanied by a great deal more men, and perhaps the earl himself."

Simon shifted. "He'd love that, wouldn't he?"

"So please," Arable idled herself by picking at a seam in her sleeve, "consider this minor inconvenience a service to your earl."

"*My* earl!" Simon cursed, curling his lips back. "Oh, his fingers are all over this. I expected some sort of retaliation, but this is more than a bit underhanded, don't you think? My apologies Lady Arabella, Lord Jonathan—but I do believe you're being used. Tell me, how much of this investigation have you personally overseen, and how much of it has been dictated to you by my good earl?"

Arable did not respond, and instead turned uneasily to share a frown with John. They exchanged some harsh nonsense whispers.

Perfectly performed.

"Let him find the flaw," Lord Robert had counseled them. "*If he thinks he's outsmarted you, he won't look for the real play.*"

"I knew something was wrong with this," John eventually shouted, breaking away from Arable's fake protests. "Lord Senlis, I apologize. I had my doubts about this before, and you're beginning to confirm them. Something rang untrue about this whole thing, but Lord Robert insisted on it."

"He knew I would refuse you," Lord Simon laughed, buying into John's act.

"He just needed to concoct an excuse to come raid my estate himself, to take by force the money he's been trying to extort from me this last month. Oh, it rings very untrue indeed, my friend. You were wise to trust your instincts."

"How did he know you would refuse us?" Arable asked.

"Because it's a preposterous claim. So let's surprise him then, by giving you exactly what you've asked for."

A few minutes later, Lord Simon was doing precisely what they wanted him to, and he thought it was his idea.

They moved down the vaulted hallways in a single file. At a corner, Arable met Peetey's eyes for a hard moment. Once they had seen the secure room, he would find an opportunity to disappear, open a window to signal the others waiting outside, so they could slip in for a good bit of pilfering.

"I wish I could say I was surprised," the young de Senlis was complaining, "but apparently our false earl will do anything to hold onto his power. At least he's shown his hand in doing this. He proves himself to be the sloppy, power-hungry thief I know he is. And he's not even good at it. I'll have my men set up some rooms for you, with a hot meal and wine. I very much look forward to hearing about this *investigation* he's set you up on. This *perversion* of justice."

"It is indignity at its worst," John Little bellowed. The more they fed the lord what he wanted to hear now, the more he would be blinded to what was actually happening.

Their path led to a simple wooden door at the base of a stone spiral staircase, unique only for its heavy bolted hinges and barrel locks that were notably sturdier than its neighbors. No bedroom or sitting room lay behind this door, not at all.

One stubborn bolt split hairs as it screeched open, but an entirely different sound interrupted their focus before the second bolt was touched. A burst of noise and riot cracked open from a door halfway down their corridor, followed by a couple of men who seemed to be fleeing for their lives. One of them stumbled like a drunkard as he tried to unpuzzle himself from a wooden stool lodged around his head.

Arable glanced backward, at the way they had come. *The escape route.*

The stool-headed fellow and his companion vanished down another branch of the estate, replaced instantly by two people who shouldn't have even been inside the building yet.

"Holy damn," Marion Fitzwalter cursed, staring dumbly back at them.

And damn it all to hell if Lord Robert, Earl of Huntingdon, didn't pull a rapier from his belt and literally shout "*Ha ha!*" as he flew down the corridor at them.

TWENTY-TWO

MARION FITZWALTER

GRAFHAM, HUNTINGDONSHIRE

"This," Marion prefaced, "is a tale of increasingly foolish acts."

And the other half began the same way.

Once the very last bit of sunset's violet died away, they broke off from the others. Marion waved to John, saddled on a horse beside Peetey and Arable. Those three would make their way to the front of the Senlis manor shortly, just as soon as Marion's group made their long secret path to its rear. Marion's stomach twisted fierce worrying about everything they couldn't predict. But Lord Robert was quick to remind her that this was—for all intents and purposes—free of consequences.

"Hopefully we succeed," he shrugged, readjusting the cape at his shoulder, "but if we don't, what's the worry? Who's Senlis going to complain to? His earl? Why, that's me! He could take it all the way to King Richard, but he'd have to break him out of an Austrian prison first."

Marion wished she could be as flippant with her choices. So far as Lord Robert was concerned, there was no amount of trouble they could get into here that he could not avoid by grandly revealing his true identity and waltzing away. This worst-case scenario netted him the exact lack of coin from the Senlis estate he was currently receiving, so he risked nothing. Robert had an air of invulnerability to him that reminded Marion of easier times, when their escapades were frivolous. When they stole only from those who could afford it, and never when it was dangerous. In some ways it was reassuring to think their winter's lament was over, and they could finally return to light adventuring.

But when last life had been like this, it had descended quickly into tragedy. And history, as historians are prone to repeat, is prone to repeat itself.

"Let's at it, then."

Lord Robert drew from his belt a floppy, thinly brimmed hat that came to a crisp point in the front. He claimed it made him look like a mysterious bandit rather than an earl, but in reality it only made him look ridiculous. His disguise was as useless as the sword he'd selected—a thin little sliver in the Italian style that was only good for poking holes in practice dummies. But Lord Robert fancied its lightness and how quickly he could move with it, and didn't seem to care that it would shatter the first time some other sword came its way. He had dressed up how he imagined a provocative burglar might, and concocted the entire plan as if it were a game.

For him, it was.

But Marion wondered if he could protect the rest of them as well as he claimed. Or whether he would continue offering his protection if they failed to meet his expectations as notorious thieves.

"Nick, this side is yours," Lord Robert called out, even though they all knew their positions. The three of them would each watch one side of the manor for a signal from the others within, ignoring the front. Robert flourished his cape as he turned and skipped into a run. "If either of you see the signal first, you'd best find me. I do not intend on missing out on this skullfuckery."

That brought Marion to an abrupt halt. "*Skullfuckery?*" she repeated.

"Is that not . . ." Lord Robert looked for support from Nick. "I thought that sounded sort of dangerous."

Marion wondered briefly if this was all a trick. "Are you inventing words to sound more like a thief?"

Robert smiled. "I have some other ones I'll try out later then."

"Please don't." She winced. "If you try any fuckery on someone's skull, I'm leaving."

"What if this turns into a fight?" Nick asked, trying to find a discreet place to hide. "I've never killed anyone."

"Nor will you have to," Marion responded with a confidence she would later regret. "If it comes to anything like that at all, you surrender yourself and we will come for you."

"Or," Lord Robert whispered, his eyes bright, "disappear in a puff of smoke!"

Nick stared, incredulous.

"Is that . . . can you . . . isn't that a thing all thieves know how to do?"

Marion shook her head.

"Ah. Well then, yes, surrender is a good second choice."

With that, they left Nick behind and waded through waist-high grass into straight rows of spruces, beyond which the moon's reflection glimmered in the lake behind the manor.

It was queer to miss Will Scarlet. He had been the heart of any Robin Hooding they'd done since autumn, along with Arthur and David, but all three were long gone now. The very fact she was involving herself in an endeavor like this said everything about how unqualified they were to do it.

She equally hated that half this plan depended on Arable de Burel doing something right. Her talents in this world lay in doing the opposite.

But they had to go through with it. "*If you disappoint him in any way,*" the countess Magdalena had whispered before they left, "*I'll see to it that you pay, with something you hold dear.*"

MARION AND LORD ROBERT ended up hiding near each other at the far corner of the manor, where they could each spy upon their designated side. There lay a low stone wall, fallen to disrepair, which offered them a convenient shadow from the moon's gaze. Footmen paced the balcony atop the building—three in total, by Marion's count—that made irregular passes around the roof's perimeter.

"Do you actually think this will work?" she asked quietly.

"I think it will annoy Simon de Senlis greatly," Lord Robert answered. His tone was more honest now, less of the showman he took in front of the others. "Which, I can guarantee you, is only a fraction of what he has coming to him. He's a Simon de Senlis, and he's been told all his life that Simons de Senlis are the earls of Huntingdon. But you know how it is when you give a child something he hasn't earned."

"They take it for granted."

"And grow angry when they lose it. Also I think they might all be inbred. The Senlis family, that is—not all children. That's just a guess, given their slow declination of intelligence from his grandfather to his father to this sludge bucket. Could just be coincidence, but I like the *idea* they're inbred. It explains a lot, you know?"

Marion hated that she smiled at that. "I'm sure I don't."

The signal came far earlier than expected. A window on the ground floor creaked open, a quarter-length of the manor away. The moon glinted across its glass and Marion whistled. "That was fast."

"Hurry then." Lord Robert glanced up to see if he was clear before loping out from behind their cover.

"Wait!" she tisked, but he was gone. With his demicape pulled dramatically over his head as if its magic would render him invisible, he made a dozen long strides and jumped the final few feet to flatten himself against the manor wall. Marion craned to see if Nick was visible so she could signal him, but didn't want to draw any attention. Torn between going back for Nick or following Robert, she crouched back in the semisafety of the stone wall. The watchmen above lingered, and might easily glance down upon her.

Lord Robert signaled that he thought she was clear, but she wasn't. So she waited, ignoring his increasingly flamboyant hand gestures.

When finally the watchmen rounded the balcony corner, she rolled to her feet and walked, calmly but swiftly, directly to join him. He waited in patience, offering her the corner of his cape. "You could have borrowed this."

"I took the risk." She played along. "Maybe next time."

"No, the offer is over," he said smugly. "*My* cape."

"We have to get Nick."

"We will. But they're waiting for us inside, and they may not have much time. With haste!"

The open shutter was five or six windows away, a distance that they closed as quickly as silence could allow. No light came from the exposed room, which was likely a good sign. The bottom of the sill was nearly as high as their heads, and Marion was just about to suggest that one of them give the other a boost when Lord Robert sprung up and found a foothold in the stony wall, from which he pushed away and vaulted to bring one boot perched perfectly in the window frame. Marion was amazed. The earl was not young, but he moved as fluidly as a traveling contortionist, with the reckless abandon of a child.

Marion, instead, could barely jump high enough to get her elbows on the ledge, and scrambled with her feet noisily against the stones just to slide her belly onto its rough lip. She was instantly greeted by a feminine squeak, and a panicked bit of commotion. Then an orange rectangle of a doorway opened across from them and two shapes flew from the room, both naked.

When last she checked, Arable and John had entered the manor wearing clothes, which meant they were probably not the two people who had just fled the room.

"I don't think it was the signal," Lord Robert whispered, inches from Marion's face.

She wobbled there like a dying fish, half in the room and half outside. "What makes you think that?"

Lord Robert sniffed the air. "It smells like sex."

Regretfully, Marion agreed. "It smells like sex."

"Just a couple servants, likely, in a place they shouldn't be. They probably opened the window to hide the evidence."

Marion frowned, still teetering on the window sill. "I'm smelling someone else's sex right now."

Thankfully she did not have to slide in headfirst. She eased backward to return to their hiding spot.

"Where are you going?" Lord Robert whispered. He had already crossed the dark room and was leaning out into the manor's hallway.

She tisked him. "Get back! We need to get outside to watch for the real signal!"

"Don't you suppose we ought to follow them?" he asked, far too loudly for discretion. He lowered his voice after she cringed. "What if they tell someone they saw us?"

"Then they'll send someone, and they'll find us, because *we're still here.*" Marion gestured for him to return. "Whereas if we were not here, they won't find us. So let's be not here."

"But we're inside," Lord Robert countered, "and outside is outside."

Marion blinked. "Yes, I've noticed that."

"And inside is better than outside. So if you don't think we should be here, then we should probably be . . ." he glanced around the room and flashed a mischievous smile back, ". . . *there.*"

He pointed at another doorway to an adjacent chamber, and before Marion could protest he came to her, braced her by the arms, and pulled her through the window.

"What about Nick?" she whispered.

"He'll wait for the real signal. Shh!"

This wasn't the plan, ran a scream through her mind.

"If you disappoint him in any way..." the countess's voice answered. *"Lady Outlaw."*

Marion brushed herself off and followed the earl's every inadvisable move.

LORD ROBERT BOUNDED PLAYFULLY, one hand at his rapier's hilt, deftly maneuvering its tip to avoid any unwanted collisions. Its name was *Tesoro,* he had earlier explained, because the only point in naming a sword was to tell people about it. They moved through a cozy reading parlor which led to some smaller dining nook that reeked of garlic, and the door after that opened back upon the main corridor. He glanced twice in both directions and tugged her along, gliding past a few closed doorways before pointing at another to indicate his random target. He pulled open the simple wooden door and spun as he entered it, flashing a child's grin.

This fool of a lord will be the death of me, Marion thought, but followed him into the small room, where she stared directly at two bearded guards dining at a wine barrel, neither of which looked pleased about the interruption of their evening.

In a single but admittedly dashing move, Lord Robert yanked the stool out from under one of the guards with one hand and threw up the loose tabletop that contained their dinner with the other. It was startling in its ferocity, impressive in its creativity, but downright idiotic in its volume. The table plank, the pewter goblets, the dinner—not to mention the guards themselves— exploded in a crash of noise that was sure to bring the entirety of the manor screaming down upon them.

Lord Robert pushed the fallen guard onto his back with his foot as he twirled the four-legged stool with both hands and brought it down with frightening accuracy over the man's head, the legs creating a cage that pinned his skull to the floor. Robert sat himself on the stool's top, one foot lounging lazily on its rungs, as he slipped Tesoro from his belt and touched its point to the remaining guard's chest, who was now soaked in ale and reeling from the commotion.

"Holy *fuck!*" the guard swore, trying to push away from the steel tip but finding himself already pressed against the room's back wall.

"Kindly don't curse at me," Lord Robert cooed. He wiggled as the man beneath him flailed to gain leverage against the stool. "I didn't curse at you, and we may still have the opportunity to be fast friends."

"Who the fuck..." the guard started, but Robert raised an eyebrow at the vulgarity. "Who are you, what are you doing here?"

"I can understand you wanting to know that, but I'm afraid I can't tell you. I'm nobody, really, definitely not worth your concern. What you *should* be concerned about is your family. You have a family?"

"What?" The guard shook, breadcrumbs escaping the brown-red mess of his beard. His eyes were trained on the rapier, which bent very slightly from the pressure it kept against his chest. He wore no mail, and whatever strength it might take to pierce his outer coat would certainly be enough to slip through skin as well. "A family? Yes."

"They sound lovely," Lord Robert sighed. "They'd like to see you again. So I can kill you if you'd like, or you could promise to stay in this room and pretend you never saw us."

Marion was baffled at the display, but she thankfully saw no weapons for the guards to fight back with. "We're just going to leave them here?" she asked.

Lord Robert seemed to be genuinely confused. "Are you saying they're not trustworthy?"

Marion honestly couldn't tell if he was serious. "Maybe we should tie them up."

"You should probably tie us up," the upright guard gulped. "I think we'd catch hell something fierce if we just let you walk off."

"Stop them, Fed!" growled the trapped guard from under the stool.

"No, don't stop them, Fed," Robert grumbled, then shrugged his shoulders. "Alright, Marion, tie them up. I don't know that I really have any rope . . ."

Marion looked for anything to use, while the guard on the floor jerked his stool and tried unsuccessfully to wrestle it away from Robert.

"Now settle down there! We'll tie you up as well, just wait your turn."

"Fuck you!" the pinned man growled, kicking his legs uselessly about.

"I can make you the same offer." Robert turned his attention downward, though he kept his rapier against the man named Fed. "You have a family?"

"No," replied the guard on the ground.

"Oh. Hm. Well you have friends, at least."

"No."

"No?" Robert frowned widely and looked to the first guard for confirmation.

"That's true. Nobody really much likes him."

"What about you?" Marion joined in. "You wouldn't call him a friend?"

"A *friend?*" Fed fidgeted. "Well, we . . . I mean, we work together."

Robert exchanged shocked looks with everyone he could find. "You're having dinner with him, but you won't even call the man your friend? That's . . . that's awful, I'm sorry. Well how about, interests, then? You have . . . other things . . . that you like to do? When you're not . . . guarding?"

The man twisted against the wooden legs of the stool. "No."

"Good God, man, help me out here. Do you have anything in this world that you like? I'm looking for a reason why I shouldn't kill you."

"Fuck you. Go on and kill me."

"We need to move." Marion poked Robert's arm. "Someone will have heard us by now."

"I can't . . ." Robert shook his head, baffled. "I can't believe this. I'm really trying here. What am I supposed to do with him?"

"Stop them, Fed," the friendless man gurgled again, "or I'll tell Lord Simon you gave up without a fight."

"Well that's not very nice!" Robert snapped, prodding his prisoner's belly with a boot. "If you want to die I can oblige you, but don't make me kill your friend."

"They're not friends," Marion couldn't help but note.

Fed whimpered. "Please don't kill me."

"We're not going to kill you," Marion whispered back.

"Y'hear that?" yelled the second guard. "They ain't gonna kill you. So stop your whining and push him off this fucking stool."

Fed's eyes shot open with indecision, fused to Lord Robert's in a bit of a stalemate. Robert couldn't move without freeing the man beneath him, and Fed couldn't move without risking his favorite vital organs. The situation might have remained deadlocked for some time if not for the two additional guards that suddenly barreled into the room behind Marion.

THEY WERE RUNNING AGAIN, a riot following them, and Marion barely had the time to even think about how ridiculous the situation had become. They had spoilt their own trap before even setting it, and all she could really hope for was to stumble into an empty room with an open window that had a bunch of horses waiting conveniently saddled nearby.

Robert dragged her down one corridor and another, then quickly ducked through a small archway to hide in its recesses. "Are you enjoying yourself?" she chastised him.

"I am," he said, fumbling to resheathe his weapon.

"And you think this is going well?"

"Oh, this is the height of embarrassment." He winked. "But I think I know a way out!"

With that he led her through the other end of the room into something that could absolutely not be called a way out. It was the main corridor, clogged by a small host gathered outside an unusually sturdy door. One man was dressed far better than the others in a crisp white outfit. Next to him was a woman wearing one of Lady Magdalena's old dresses, beside a large man with three heads.

"Holy damn," Marion cursed.

John Little and Arable de Burel looked at her, their eyes as wide as the hallway.

And damn it all to hell if Lord Robert didn't pull his rapier again and shout, "*Ha ha!*" as he flew glibly toward the Lord Simon de Senlis.

TWENTY-THREE

ARTHUR A BLAND

NOTTINGHAM

FUCK. THIS.

Fuck. This.

Fuck the slums and fuck the stink and fuck the shit and fuck the this.

Every left foot was a fuck, every right foot was a thing worth fucking, and, fuck by thing, Arthur made another pass around the Spotted Leopard. It was a whorehouse, insomuch as it was a place where whores sold themselves, but there was nothing exotic about it. There were stories of whorehouses in the big cities that catered to noblemen, elaborate parlors with silks and secret passwords and rows of virgins.

This was not that.

It was all stink and grime in this area of Nottingham, a place called the French Ward. Everywhere were doorless, uneven wooden buildings that leaned into each other and the sky, covered in horizontal swaths of mold and murk likely made by floodings from years past. The French Ward was the lowest point of Nottingham, both geographically and morally. Even though it was well away from the river Trent, it was probably beneath water level and not designed with any sort of drainage in mind. It didn't seem designed at all, actually—it seemed like the random, inevitable result of a bunch of poor fuckholes trying desperately to pretend they were a part of the city. But that filth was probably exactly what attracted the man with the velvet cap.

The man was inside the Spotted Leopard now, though his velvet cap was not. He'd taken to disguising himself in the dirty rags common in this area, as had the rest of them. Will Scarlet was inside as well, trying to get information on their mark, while Stutely stood like a wart on the face of the building, keeping watch. Arthur was left to make watchful rounds about the block, doing everything he could to navigate around the puddles of questionable content and everywhere a consistent layer of caked shit.

Fuck the *gangs* and fuck the *whores* and fuck the *man with the velvet fucking cap.*

They didn't even know his name, but Arthur knew their mark's life was boring. Not the normal sort of boring that came with most folk, but a far more boring sort of boring. He spent his mornings inspecting food shipments that came by the river, he spent his afternoons inspecting food shipments that came by the roads. He lived in a humble but safe area of the Parlies, entirely alone. He never deviated from his schedule, and Arthur had never seen the man laugh. So when this boring man changed into a dirty smock and snuck away to a French

Ward brothel, Arthur had reported the information back to the Red Lions as quick as a pup.

"*Fascinating.*" Red Fox had drawn out the word. "*But most of the better half of Nottingham finds their sport between a poorer woman's legs. Come back with something useful, or don't come back at all.*"

Tonight was the third time the man with the velvet cap had visited this brothel, and it was still the only scandalous thing they'd learned about him. Which was, apparently, not nearly good enough.

David was off with Zinn today, on another errand or gathering supplies— whatever lesser gruntwork it was the Red Lions assigned her. Technically she *was* a Red Lion, albeit one of their lowliest lieutenants who managed a small outside gang. That was apparently how the Lions controlled the whole city—not by stomping out their rival gangs but by recruiting those gangs' leaders. Zinn had been a dockside runt with a tiny crew until the Lions brought her in, in exchange for a percentage of her gang's work. She was just a child, the little bitch, but somehow she was now Will Scarlet's gangboss.

Anybody who follows him is going to drown.

They were all Zinn's pawns for the moment, thanks to Will's recklessness. If Zinn's gang got bottomwork from the Lions, she doled the bottommost of that bottomwork to them. Moving packages from the docks to the caves, counting traffic through the gates of the city, following nobodies and reporting back on their movements. Today's bottomwork was to follow the man with the velvet cap again, as they'd done every day this week.

They'd become a joke, and leaping at every one of Zinn's commands was the first and worst of their shame. This was not the glorious rebellion they were supposed to be sparking. This was just humiliation, and trying to scratch any success out of Nottingham now would only likely carve a gullet so deep it would become their grave.

"See anything?" Stutely asked, too loudly, as Arthur made his next pass by the Spotted Leopard's entrance.

"I see fucking everything," Arthur responded, pointing his fingers erratically to demonstrate all the fucking things he could see. He was the last person qualified to notice anything out of the ordinary. Because he didn't know what the fuck ordinary looked like here. He was increasingly aware that the only thing that didn't fucking belong here was him.

He needed to talk with David. Zinn often split their foursome up on different tasks, and at night they all shared the same room at The Peach and the Pear, which made it tricky to have a private conversation. If he could convince David, then maybe it was time to leave Will Scarlet behind. Will could stay, and earn his men, as planned. Once he did that, would it even matter if Arthur and David were still around? Instead they could make their own way to Huntingdon, and at least be with people who respected them. Stutely could follow or not, based on how intelligent he felt like being at the time. But Arthur wouldn't go anywhere without David.

"Have you thought about what name you'll take?" Stutely asked as Arthur passed the entrance, forcing him to slow his pace.

"What?"

"Your name," the beastman repeated, then hunched up his shoulders as if to imply secrecy, while doing nothing to lower his voice. "Your red name. When they take us in."

"What? No." Arthur hated even the idea of the question. Everyone in the Red Lions took a *red* name. Zinn's name was apparently short for *zinnia*, which she claimed was the name of some red flower nobody had ever heard of. That's not what they were here for. "We're not staying here."

Stutely responded with a roll of his entire face that implied the opposite. It implied it so heavily that Arthur almost felt the fool to think otherwise. *No. We're not staying here.* That wasn't what Elena had died for, for them to go backward.

"I was thinking *Bloodly Stutely* at first," Stutely explained. "*Red Stutely* is nice but too obvious. But now I'm leaning toward just *The Blood.*"

"Stop thinking about it," Arthur said.

Fuck by foot he pushed forward.

"Nobody would ever make fun of *The Blood* behind his back," Stutely grumbled to himself, behind. "Nobody will ever tell *The Blood* to watch the door."

Arthur slogged on, making his pace around again.

Fuck. This.

Fuck. This.

It had been a long time, a *damned* long time, since Arthur wondered what it was that he actually wanted. For most of his life, that question was suffocated by the base need to survive from day to day, and the last few months had been no different. But at least all the hungry mouths in Marion's group—useless though they may be—had something they were trying to stay alive for. Arthur assumed his mother was from Yorkshire, since that's where his earliest memories were, but he didn't even know if she died or abandoned him. If there was ever a time he hadn't been begging for scraps and stealing his sleeps in the backs of stables and churches, he couldn't remember it. And frankly, until he met David of Doncaster he hadn't had anything to even call a friend in his wretched life. If anything, he'd actively avoided the burden of knowing people. He'd work odd jobs until the moment he became valuable, the moment someone *needed* him. That was his bane, and he'd move on to another job, another town, stealing when he needed to, surviving another day just to claim he'd done so.

After meeting David, there'd been joy in the wretchedness, and there was something infectious about David's optimism. It had been the two of them against the world, but sometimes *with* the world, too. And then Locksley Castle, and Marion's Men, and Robin Hooding. He'd bought into Elena's belief that they were building toward something, something none of them could quite define, but they knew it was a better life.

This.

This did not feel like that anymore.

Two nights ago, for instance, he and Stutely had accompanied Fawkes and a few others to a tavern near Hollows Lane, ordered to break all the drinking horns within. Zinn told them nothing as to why they were doing the thing, and it was likely that she didn't know herself. But breaking things actually felt good, compared to watching a boring man live his boring life.

He wondered if that's how good men turned bad.

If the simple thrill of breaking something was all it took to turn that particular corner in life. Stealing for survival was one thing, but breaking those horns had been nothing but someone else's business. At some point, the next command would be to break more than horns. Bones, maybe? Skulls?

How soon until he was just following orders? How long until he was a fucking *gord*?

When he made the next turn back to the Spotted Leopard, Stutely and Will Scarlet were waiting for him half a block closer. Arthur twisted his nose away from the stink of the street, brought up by a cold wind that hushed through the alley and stung his eyes.

"He just left," Scarlet said, meaning the man with the velvet cap. "Did you see anything?"

Arthur just shook his head, too irritated to even give a scornful response.

"Twenty-seven men walked by, seven women," Stutely reported. "But most of them were walking east, so I think that—"

"What?" Scarlet cut him off. "I don't care."

"You told me to watch the door."

"Yes, but I don't want to know about every last person who walks by it." He wrinkled his nose and shook his hands into little fists. "God's nails, this is fucking stupid." He was angry today, and ugly bitter. Scarlet took one step into the street and landed in a cake of shit, cursed, and scraped it off against a rock. He kicked at a puddle in fury, obliterating it amongst the cobbles. In a rare moment of camaraderie, Arthur found himself exchanging a look of unease with Stutely.

"Are we following him?" Stutely asked, inclining his head in the direction the man with the velvet cap had taken.

"Fuck no," Scarlet grumbled. "We already have everything we're going to get on him. He pays shillings for cunny, always asks for the same girl, Saddle Maege. That's it. I thought maybe I'd try to get some information from *her*, but the madame of the house laughed me off. Said that Saddle Maege wouldn't like me, so fuck her."

"I'll try," Stutely offered.

Arthur laughed, which seemed to offend Stutely. But the funny thing was that Stutely would probably do a *better* job. If Stutely went in there to *impress* the madame, at least he'd do so in a way that wouldn't involve *cutting off his fucking ear.*

"No." Scarlet pointed deliberately away from the brothel. "It doesn't matter. This mark of ours, we got nothing on him. He doesn't gamble, he doesn't drink, he doesn't have any family. There's no leverage. He's the *opposite* of a mark. I don't know what the *fuck*..." he emphasized this by kicking at another puddle, "...Freddy wants us to find, but it's not here. This is a waste of time. This is not what I wanted."

After a pregnant pause, Stutely huffed in defense. "Well it's not what I wanted, either! I'd rather be in Thorney pushin' the barrow, but nobody gave me any say in whether they torched it all to the ground. You hear me complaining about that? No point in wasting good breath, if it won't improve your lot none. Only way to make life better is to be good at it, and that's all I ever tried."

"He wasn't saying you weren't trying." Arthur hoped to calm him. He wished David were there. "What are we doing, Will? Are we really trying to prove ourselves by starting from the bottom? How long do we do this until Fox gives us some men? At this rate, feels like it'll be years."

"No. I'm done with this shit. Tell them we're done." Scarlet scratched at the dark mess that used to be his ear. "Tell them to put us on something worth our time."

It was the first good idea Arthur had heard all week.

Stutely crossed his arms. "That's Zinn's call."

"Zinn's a little shit," he spat back, "I'm making it my call. Go back and tell the Lions, tell them we're fucking done."

TWENTY-FOUR

ARABLE DE BUREL

GRAFHAM, HUNTINGDONSHIRE

THE GUARDSMEN REPOSITIONED TO defend their lord, while the earl Robert leapt down a side passage that led to the manor's central courtyard. Marion was dragged along, leaving Arable standing by the reinforced door with Peetey, John Little, and the appropriately scrutinizing face of Lord Simon de Senlis.

"Was that . . . the earl Robert?" he asked, using the condescending tone a parent uses with a lying child.

"Hard to say," John improvised. "Given the hat, and all. Could be."

Lord Simon directed his attention upon Arable, and she found that she could not lie. She offered a silent frown, and nodded in concession.

"You want us to stop them?" a heavy Guardsman at his side asked.

"I couldn't possibly say," mused the lord. Again he turned to Arable for confirmation, but she could give nothing other than a half shrug. Simon copied it for his Guardsmen. "Sure."

Off shuffled his men with little urgency, past the delicate decorations of the Senlis manor, following the inner path and mumbling orders to each other. The ruse was obviously over, but there might still be some diplomatic way of salvaging the situation. The Lord de Senlis did not seem a man taken to overreaction.

Arable opened her mouth. "So—"

"No." He spared her no look this time, just a raised finger. "I don't . . . no, I don't have any interest in a single word of what you were about to say."

"But—" John Little tried.

"Just . . ." The man was a father, more disappointed than angry. "Just no."

There passed a terrible amount of inactivity so awkward the hallway itself seemed likely to slink off for mercy. The only sounds were the echoes of the chase going on throughout the manor, floating back to them through the hallways but impossible to hear distinctly.

"Is he dangerous?" Lord Simon asked at last.

"No, no," Arable answered instantly.

"There's that, at least."

He clicked his tongue.

The earl Robert took this moment to burst from a doorway halfway down the hall, whipping his needlelike blade in front of him and aiming it theatrically at Lord Simon. "A *ha!*" he exclaimed again, clearly short of breath. Then he vanished into another side room.

"I didn't see Nick," Peetey Delaney muttered.

Lord Simon sighed. "Should I ask who Nick is?"

"His brother," Arable answered. "Hopefully he's still watching, outside."

"Hm." De Senlis cocked his head toward her. "How many of you are there?"

"Just six, that's everyone."

Another long silence stretched, in which Simon de Senlis seemed to digest every bit of what was happening.

"Maybe I ought to go look for him?" Peetey offered.

Arable exchanged an apologetic look with de Senlis. "Would you mind?"

"Of course, how could I . . ." He blew out his lips, then took in a sharp inhalation. "I mean, what's really the point in trying to . . ." He ran out of words again.

"Thank you."

"I'll send some men after you, of course."

"Of course."

Arable motioned for Peetey to leave, which he hesitantly did. Lord Simon threw a limp gesture to his last few remaining Guardsmen to accompany the man, though they did not seem certain if they were supposed to chase him or help him.

"I really am sorry about all this," Arable said as the three of them stared blankly down the hallway.

From somewhere far off, the sounds of an entire kitchen being dumped upside down let them know that Lord Robert was still having fun.

Eventually Lord Simon resigned himself to the fact that he would have to get involved. "I suppose we ought to go find him. Did you have . . . was there an escape plan?"

Arable shook her head and started walking. "There was never any plan."

They traveled at leisure back to the main reception hall. Along the way they were met with the echoes of shouts and vague insults, doors belched open here and there and eventually a bell rang out its dull dirge. This seemed to awaken everyone in the entire manor who had not already been roused by the clamor. It was hard to tell if Lord Robert and Marion were being chased, or if his reckless warscreams meant he was now on the offensive. There were a few moments when Arable was almost tempted to smile, to enjoy the sheer audacity of it, but instinct kicked away that urge. Life had recently conditioned her to recognize there were always consequences to frivolous misadventure.

Along the way, John Little tore savagely at the balloons of fabric on his shoulders. "Didn't like the color," he explained.

The main hallway followed the great square shape of the building, and eventually spat them back onto one of the three balconies overlooking the original reception hall. To their right was the entrance foyer, where Peetey had already found his brother, Nick, and apparently a few more of Lord Simon's men. The doors behind them were, impossibly, wide open and unguarded.

"He's insane," one of the brothers was telling the other. "We have to get out!"

To the left, an eruption of noise announced Lord Robert and Marion, popping onto the adjacent balcony. Robert spun and slammed the double doors behind him, then whipped out a long purple sash with which he bound the handles together. Seconds later the doors swelled but could not open, and he took a moment to catch his breath.

His efforts were in vain. Across the room—from the fourth and final door-way—a host of Guardsmen and servants alike all poured into the sunken gallery, armed with swords and knives and improvised weapons. At least thirty or forty bodies flooded down into that receiving hall at the foot of the staircases. The arrivals quickly assessed the situation and arranged themselves in obvious defense of Lord Robert's only path to the front exit.

Arable had no idea what to do, so she waved a greeting to Nick Delaney, who waved back.

Lord Robert may have been trapped on his balcony, but he made it clear he was not interested in company. He drew his rapier in front of Marion and sliced the air at the top of the staircase in dancing little sweeps, then perched one foot on the railing and called across to Arable's balcony. "Lord Simon! Stand down, your men are surrounded!"

Lord Simon took the bait and walked forward to his own rail, openly laughing. "Oh, Lord Robert, what a gift you've given me by coming here today. Lay your weapon down, and perhaps I'll treat your people with kindness."

"I've come to take that which is owed," the earl flourished. "And I'll keep you in fetters one day for every shilling short!"

"There are but six of you, and you're the only one that seems armed. Whereas I have twenty trained fighters, and fifty more who could stop you with a dishcloth. One is something smaller than seventy, Lord Robert. If this is your proficiency with numbers, I'd rather not rely on you to do any more of my accounting."

"Your seventy is meaningless," the earl laughed. "You can come one by one up this staircase and I'll dispatch every man. Which of you below chooses to throw away your life first for your rebellious lord? And Lord Simon, will you stand there on your balcony and watch your vassals die for you before turning over the first coin you rightfully owe your king?"

Lord Simon's body tensed at that, and he lowered his voice to a man standing near him. "Clarence, do we have bowmen?"

"We *do* . . ." the moustached man answered. "Do you mean to let loose upon the earl within the manor?"

Simon's face contorted, as if he were struggling to find the downside of this choice.

Posturing. Preening. Neither man would back down, until one was forced into something foolish. Then this light-hearted romp would end in someone's tragedy. Arable took a brief moment to consider how incredibly easier her life would be if not for men and their need to be men. Every damned second of the day.

Across the expanse, behind Lord Robert, a single sword thrust through the thin opening between the bound doors and started to saw at the sash.

"Marion!" Arable exclaimed in warning, surprising herself.

Once the two saw the sword, Robert gave it a sharp kick that successfully snapped the blade clean off. But its owner realized that the jagged broken edge was actually more effective at cutting. Lord Robert spun around, his head looking in every direction at once for an exit. Then he whispered his rapier away and jumped onto the thick railing where it joined with the stone wall, his hands finding an iron ring lashed with ropes.

Arable's eyes followed those ropes across the ceiling of the gallery, where they pulleyed down to hold the great chandelier that hung over the crowd below.

Good God, nobody could be so idiotic . . .

With both feet planted against the wall, Lord Robert heaved away, and the iron ring wrenched off the hook moored to the stone, and the chandelier's weight sent it screaming down. An epic crash split the air accompanied by horror on all sides, and Arable flung her attention over the balcony's lip to see the damage. But Lord Robert was not finished—he had kept ahold of the ring during its crash down, dragging him to the very edge of his balcony but no farther. There he slipped his foot into the iron circle, wrapped his arm around Marion's waist, and—*Arable gasped aloud*—he pushed off from the balcony's ledge, swinging over the trapped throng of guards below, his arc ending exactly on the opposite ledge where the Delaneys could receive him. He released the rope at the peak of its arc, landing in a deft roll, he turned and—

—"COMPLETE BULLSHIT," THE Countess Magdalena interrupted. "I won't hear another word."

"It's all true, dear." Lord Robert smiled, tracing his hand down his wife's back, but received nothing in return. "At least, the parts of it that were true were true."

Admittedly, they had all exaggerated their bits of the story. But the really shameful thing was they had not elaborated *by much*. Their participation in the tale was another favor Lord Robert had requested of them during their long defeated trek back to Huntingdon Castle from Grafham. They had spent the night in the city, too proud to take Lord Simon's extremely charitable offer of housing them in the manor they had meant to burgle. By midday they were back in Huntingdon, explaining their absence to the countess.

"How much of that was a lie?" the lady asked, then shook her head in a fit and flurry. "No, I don't even care. I don't want to know."

John Little bowed his head, the rolls of his neck bulging out. "Apologies."

Lady Magdalena buried her face in her fingers.

"It was always a longshot," Lord Robert crooned, stroking his wife's hair. She flinched, but let him. "I can hardly make Simon de Senlis hate me any more than he already does. And perhaps my other bannermen will hear of it. If they think I'm a little wild, a little unpredictable, then maybe they think twice of following de Senlis in this embargo."

Lady Magdalena met his eyes coolly, but sighed. "It doesn't matter."

That much, at least, was true. Their escapade had gained them no surfeit, no advantage.

"It matters for my people." Marion's tone was soft. "Countess, we upheld our end. We did everything we could to help—"

"Oh stop it," the countess cut her off. "Consider, for once, that there is a world beyond the petty things that only you care about." A tiny gulp escaped Marion's mouth, which Arable could not identify as relief or shock. Lady Magdalena continued, "I say it doesn't matter, because it simply doesn't. It wouldn't matter if you brought back every penny that Simon de Senlis owes us. It wouldn't be enough, not even close. While you were out galivanting, dear husband . . ." she somehow said with only a slight tint of bitterness, ". . . I took a closer look at the ledgers."

Robert sighed. "We have been over this, my dear."

"No, *we* haven't. You regurgitated to me what your coinmaster told you, but I wanted to see the numbers for myself. Our new friar has a head for mathematics, I don't know if you knew that. There's no way we can raise enough coin to pay what is being asked of us, it's not possible. The king's ransom would bankrupt us twice over. It simply isn't there."

"It's true," Friar Tuck said quietly from the far end of the littered table, his bald head reflecting the room's fire. By the look of him, spending the last twelve hours with the countess was as difficult as their trip to Grafham. "The taxes, the war tithe, and King Richard's ransom, there's no way to pay them all. We've been over everything."

He raised some pages loosely in his hand and let them tumble back to the table.

"I'm sure you mean well," Lord Robert gave Tuck a cute smile, "but I have men whose sole purpose is to manage my coin. They've told me—"

"They'll tell you what you want to hear," Tuck cut him off. "To keep their status, and their position, because the numbers tell them the same thing they tell me. Numbers, Lord Robert, numbers can't lie. Your worth on paper is far higher than what you actually have, and that discrepancy cannot be bridged. You can't pay your share of the ransom, not by any rational means."

"Short of indiscriminately burgling every single one of your bannermen's estates, *which I trust is out of the question . . .*" Lady Magdalena eyed the room heavily to ensure the severity of that choice, ". . . then our only option, dear husband, is to not pay. And *that,* at least, is something we *have* discussed."

Arable hoped Lord Robert felt as foolish as he should, returned home in defeat on a quest that was doomed from the beginning. Like a child, come home from slaying invisible foes in the forest to the harsh reality of survival. He fidgeted, unpinning the cape from his shoulder and letting it fall onto the table. Perhaps it was that easy for him to transition from an adolescent perspective to that of an adult.

Arable didn't know the details of how much money Lord Robert had given to Robin Hood's crew before her time with them, but it undoubtedly made a difference in his ability to pay his royal dues now.

"What is your option, then," Marion asked, "if not to pay?"

Robert did not answer, so Lady Magdalena took the reins. "We should stop referring to it as the *king's* ransom. It is not Richard who demands it, but Chancellor Longchamp—and he is a fool to do so. Or, more likely, a tyrant."

That word tiptoed around the room, stealing breath and raising eyebrows.

"We are not the only ones who have come up short. Chancellor Longchamp has abused the king's power, and thrown the country into poverty. These laws, these taxes, this ransom . . . they are beyond any reason, they are an overreach of the blindest kind. The punishments for not paying are extreme. Longchamp claims lands and titles he has no right to, he takes property and livelihood with equal apathy. He'll take this earldom from us, my dear, without a thought. He'll replace us with anyone who promises to take more drastic actions. The chancellor's grasp at power while King Richard lies in captivity is the ruin of us all. The solution is not to find clever ways of paying these outrageous demands. The rules are rigged, so it's time to change the rules. And it's time to change the man who makes them."

The room expanded. Arable's skin shrank. She suddenly longed for the smaller, sillier world she'd been living in seconds earlier.

"You're talking rebellion," she said.

"It was only talk," Robert defended it. "Consider it a war game. We were speaking hypothetically, weeks ago. Any good leader would be wise to prepare for the worst scenario."

"Which is where we now find ourselves." Lady Magdalena touched his shoulder. "It is not rebellion to discuss our options. We made a list of those of similar mind that we might rally. My father has spent a generation building alliances of barons and earls from all over England of sympathetic ear, who have no direct ties to the Chancellor. My sister's husband, Waleran, has a similar network of loyalties we can call upon. If this is not the moment, I don't know what could be. Our king, captured—and our country ruined from within. The need has never been more dire, and the opportunity never more tangible."

"You'd hold this . . . *rally* . . . here?" Marion gasped. "It's too dangerous—"

"I did not ask if you had objection," Magdalena barely said. "Your agreement is not required."

Arable was shocked to see Marion cow herself, biting her lip rather than fighting back. Her own instincts screamed the same thing, but she was in even less of a position to object than Marion was.

After watching Lord Robert run childishly through a manor all night brandishing a sword as if there were no consequences in the world, she suddenly now had to wonder if his half of the marriage was truly the reckless one.

The Earl of Huntingdon touched his fingertips to the table, a calculating demeanor now that bore no hint of his earlier levity. "Suppose I were to agree with you. We would have to proceed very cautiously."

The countess kissed him on the cheek. "Oh darling, your agreement is not required, either."

He stammered. "Maggie . . . we need to discuss this further. If we wrote invitations . . . well, talk is empty air, but putting ink to paper is taking a stance. I do not think—"

"I penned the invitations weeks ago."

Robert's jaw was not the only one to drop.

She smiled. "As you said, dear, to prepare for the worst."

"To even have those letters in our possession is criminal. You must burn them at once."

Her fingers wrapped around his. "I sent them out this morning."

TWENTY-FIVE

CAITLIN FITZSIMON

THE LIONS DEN

ALFRED FAWKES WAS MOSTLY drunk, which meant he'd be inclined to fuck. Which was, after all, why Cait had encouraged him to drink. But only *mostly* drunk, lest the liquor get a hold of his cock before she did. It was a fine balance that she'd generally mastered—getting him drunk enough to forget about the bone-skinny whores like Clorinda Rose, but not so drunk that he'd fall asleep against the cave wall again. Men were like crabs—it really did take an exacting amount of work to get what little meat she needed from them.

"I've got a surprise for you," Alfie slurred, every syllable a different note to a song he invented as he went. His attention was not on her, though. He was busy waving his arms in concentric circles, oblivious to the tight confines of their "room." Their little nook was just another cramped tunnel in a network of barely navigable passageways. It had the luxuries of a flat bottom and a few worming holes in its top that let in a drip of light during the day and let out a bit of stink at night. To have a preference of one of these mole holes over another was the miserable extent of how far the reign of the Red Lions had fallen.

They'd be back. That's what she told the cubs, that is. Bears were known to hibernate, and no one thought the less of them. Springtime, the Lions would prowl again.

"What's the surprise?" she asked, though Alfie seemed to have forgotten already. Caitlin rolled to the side of the dingy straw mattress they'd built months ago, which long stank of mildew. A plate of butterbur leaves and incense was burning, and she threw a pinch of panta in to smolder amongst the embers. Pantagruel herb was said to keep a man's seed from quickening, and the last thing she needed in times such as this was one more human to care for, especially a little one.

Maybe someday. But Caitlin had nothing to give to a child right now, aside from the promise of becoming an orphan. The recent months had been such a brutal setback, and it didn't matter that there was nothing Cait or Alfie could've done to prevent it. The first ambitious little cubs who got the taste for blood might make a play for the ramshackle throne, thinking they could sit it better.

Hell, they might even be right about it.

Until then, it was all about the performance.

"Shhhh." Alfie froze his arms in the air, pressing one long bony finger to his lips. "I've got a surprise for you."

"You mentioned that." She reached out to pull him down beside her.

But he wouldn't move, and instead cocked his head up like a bird. "Listen." His finger pointed upward.

There were the normal sounds of this underground abode—the stifling return of their own voices summed upon themselves, the muffled low rumblings of the cubs in the main room, still arguing or throwing dice. But there was something else *beneath it* . . . Caitlin closed her eyes and found herself cocking her head the same way he had. A consistent heartbeat, more a feeling than a sound, pulsing within the cave walls. And then above it all, just the tail edge of a shifting whistle, slipping in and out and impossible to notice until the moment it was gone.

"Music," she said once she identified it.

"I finally found where *that* leads." Alfie's finger stretched up to the wormhole at the top of their little chamber. Nothing but a black hole right now, but it carried a faint glow in the daytime, and brought in a few drops of water when it rained. "T'other end's in Crof's Plaza."

"The Parlies, really?" Cait found that surprising. "Didn't realize we were that far north."

"And I paid a little troupe . . . a little musical troupe . . . to stand on top of our little hole while they play tonight."

Alfie had his moments.

She closed her eyes again and angled her ear up to the wormhole, desperate to make out any of the notes. Her mind filled in the rest, connecting the dots and creating a melody where there was nothing but vibrations and ghostly whistles. Alfie had brought musicians into the den once, to keep the boys entertained, but that had brought a nearly disastrous amount of attention their way. The tunnels carried sound much farther down here than in the open air, and the whole of Nottingham leaked their music into the streets like a sponge squeezed of its water. There'd been almost no music in Caitlin's life since that night. And though she'd only complained of that fact once, Alfred Fawkes was ever a man who listened to his woman.

"Thank you," she whispered, drawing him in and sliding her hand down between his legs. But after half a minute or so with no reaction, she gave up. *Too much ale tonight,* she sighed, regretting the waste of panta.

"There's also this," Alfie continued, oblivious to her disappointment. He drew open his red duster and revealed a flat, rounded bottle from a deep pocket. Its top was still sealed with a cork and dirty golden wax dripped down the bottle's length, both of which carried a sweet smell of honey.

It was kind, but not productive. "Oh, Alfie."

"Courtesy of the Salutation Inn."

"This doesn't help us," she chastised him, raising the bottle of mead up to the lantern to inspect its liquid within. "Put it with the ones we took from the Bell."

"Just one bottle," Alfie defended himself. "Just enough to celebrate."

"We have nothing to celebrate yet. We ought to give this to the greenbeard."

"We have everything to celebrate. This is a promise." He reclaimed the bottle victoriously, cradling it in his hands like a father holding his newborn son. "This is evolvable . . . this is invulvable lillity . . . this is evulnerable . . ."

"Invulnerability."

"*That.*" He snapped his fingers. "My lips preceedeth me."

It was hardly invulnerability. One bottle was only worth one visit—those were the greenbeard's terms. Even a dozen visits wasn't nearly enough to do what they needed. They'd have to find a more permanent way to get the greenbeard his mead, something that didn't involve roughing up the other taverns every week. She hated that tactic anyway. Even pretending they were punishing places that served to Guardsmen, they were risking their reputation with the barkeeps. And the reward was not a guarantee—once it was all done, it likely meant little more than a pair of aces as their hole cards. Might literally save their lives someday, so worth the effort . . . but it was merely a shield, not invulnerability. And one they could likely use only once.

"What's the real goal?" she asked aloud. Any thought of sex had fluttered away, leaving the damned idea of a child lingering at the back of her mind. "Stay alive another day? More coin, more coin? Until we're too big and we get chopped down? We're already the head of the Lions, where do we go from here?"

"We get the Lions back to where they once were," Alfie said harshly, his fingers jabbing with each stressed word. "If Will Scarlet could do it, we can do it, too."

"But he walked away." Dumb little rogger that he was, she could still see the wisdom in what he'd done. "Once he was at the top, he left. Because he needed somewhere else to rise."

"And now he's at the bottom."

That was true enough, at least. But he'd risen further, first, before the fall.

"I hate that he thinks he's Robin Hood," she said, staring up into the wormhole that led, eventually, to a real world. More than anything, she hated the idea of *owing* the name of Robin Hood to Will Scarlet. When it was just some stranger's title she had no qualms about claiming it, but now that she'd seen the whiny little mess in person, she didn't want any of his inheritance. "I know it was my idea for you to take the name, but I'm having doubts now. Why not let him keep it? We don't really need it."

"But I like it." Alfred smiled, his thin lips stretching to ribbons. "It *fits* me. And we've gained as much from it as we've . . . not."

Cait's brows furrowed themselves at that. "That's not an argument for keeping it. That means we've come out even. That's a business that fails, that comes out even."

"Just because you don't know the argument, doesn't mean it's not an argument."

"You're drunk."

"I am! The air has forsaken us!"

She sighed, even as he tumbled down into the straw and took her calf in his hands, massaging her muscles. He knew he couldn't please her tonight the way she wanted, but he was also wise enough to know he could try to make it up to her.

"Will's an old friend," he cajoled her. "I'll send him away if you tell me to, but I think he'll be useful. He just has to learn his place."

Will Scarlet wasn't interested in learning his place. The job Cait had in mind for him was too dangerous to give to anyone she cared for, but it couldn't be done until their work with the greenbeard was complete. Until then, Scarlet was festering like a sore in their ranks. Might even be a threat. But it wouldn't help to have that conversation while Alfie was shy of his senses.

Her thoughts had darkened. "I'm worried about this Lord Death."

He shook his head and kissed her knee. "Stupid name, that."

"And *Robin Hood's* such a good one?"

His lips moved up.

Rumors were that Lord Death was the last Sheriff's father—that he was Revenge in human form, come to hunt his son's murderer. Alfie had dismissed it as drunken haver earlier, but Cait knew there was some truth to it. "We don't want to be mistaken for the man he wants."

"All the more reason to keep Scarlet. When it's pouring outside, you can only control that which you bring inside your home."

"The fat man said something strange, too," she said. She'd meant to tell him tomorrow, when their heads were clearer.

"When did you see the fat man?"

Cait just waved her hand, since it didn't matter. The fewer times she was forced to see her father, the better. "Says they think that Gilbert's tied with Robin Hood."

"The White Hand?"

"They wouldn't be wrong." They hadn't had any dealing with Gilbert since that business with the Guardsman Jon Bassett last year, and they were only the better for it. Gilbert had turned traitor and joined the Guard himself, and he was welcome to any punishment coming his way. "Gilbert used to work with Scarlet. Might still be."

The music breathed down through the walls, barely there.

A hum, Alfie's head shook no.

"Ask him about it. If they're watching Gilbert, and Gilbert's working with Scarlet, then they might keep going and find us, too."

His lips moved, slowly, up her thigh.

"No, you're not."

Caitlin didn't even bother looking up as she said it. She had no desire to stare at the hairy oaf Will Stutely, but that was not why she kept her head down. Scarlet had sent the lowest of his men to report back on their work, and that simply wasn't how they did it here.

"Ah . . ." came Stutely's bloated groan. "Maybe I should talk to someone else?"

"Maybe you should do what you're told, and realize how lucky you are to even be here," she snapped. "I told Zinnia that I wanted *Scarlet* to report back to me, and you don't look like Will Scarlet to me. Which is good for you most of the time, but right now very bad. Why do you suppose he sent you?" she asked.

"I'm reliable," he said, and Cait almost laughed that he did so seriously.

The rest of the Lions Den had less restraint. A dozen of her boys were playing dice at the tables and stopped to laugh at Stutely's response. Alfie was topside, dealing with some particularly conservative priests at the Commons who'd become troublesome. Whenever he was out, Caitlin sat the throne. But this mouth-breathing rambag somehow thought he should *talk to someone else.*

"It's true," Stutely doubled-down on his answer. "I always do as I'm told, the best I can. Don't see how that's something to laugh at."

"Scarlet sent you because you're shit," Caitlin said, finally raising her eyes upon their visitor's beastly face. "Don't wrinkle your nose at me—open your ears and learn a thing or two. That's not an insult, calling you shit, that's just fact. Shit slides downhill, so whoever's at the bottom is shit. *Someone* has to be at the bottom, and it just happens to be you. Lookin' about this room, I see at least . . . three more pieces of shit."

At the horns, Skinny Pink stood up and raised his ale. "I am definitely shit."

"That you are," growled the Dawn Dog and pushed him down again playfully.

"But here in the Lions, we *protect* our shit." She heaved up and off the throne to wander closer to her cubs. "Skinny Pink here is Pink because he's not ready to be red. He gets the shit jobs because he's shit, but if he fucks up then we don't yell at him, we *teach him better.* Because we all know he's still learning. On the other hand, if Ricard the Ruby makes a mistake . . ." the lean Frenchman stretched his neck out in anticipation, ". . . then he gets my entire holier-than-God leg up his ass."

Ricard nodded with bemusement, though he quickly raised a single finger to silence his seconds, who cackled a bit too eagerly.

Stutely, standing alone at the foot of the slab beneath the throne, seemed mortified by the idea.

"That's how lions work, the leader protects the pride. You hear stories about our king the *Lionheart* and you get it in your fool head that a leader is supposed to be all important, and his followers are supposed to protect him. That ain't it . . . here, the king's only job is to protect those beneath him. All the way down the line." Cait watched Stutely's head shake into a frown. "Not how Will Scarlet does it, is it? He's the top of your fetid little pond, so he takes that to mean he can do whatever he wants, yes? Cut his ear off, kill the Sheriff, doesn't matter who suffers beneath him, does it?"

If Rob o'the Fire were present, he would have *whooted* in support. But Rob o'the Fire was still in bed, choking out scabs, recovering from the unprovoked beating Scarlet had given him.

"A real lionheart puts himself *last,*" Cait continued, swiping a horn of ale from the boys. "Here, we demand *more* discipline as you rise, not less. More accountability for more responsibility. That's why everyone wants to be a Red Lion, because we take care of our own. Here at the top, everyone's mine to protect. Their victories are theirs," she pointed at the crowd, "but their failures are mine. But Will Scarlet sent you to represent *his* failures today. Doesn't seem right, does it?"

Stutely stared for a long time, but not an inch of him seemed like to deny it.

"He sent you today to tell me he wants to be 'done.' Because he knew I'd be angry. Suppose for a minute that you were successful, instead. That you found exactly what we needed. Do you think Scarlet still would've sent you? Or would he have claimed that victory and told me himself?"

Deep in the hairy thicket of Stutely's face, his beady little eyes blinked.

"So no, you're not 'done.' You'll keep following the man with the velvet cap until I tell you you're done."

If they could just find some dirt on the trademaster, that would speed up everything with the greenbeard. And like them or not, Scarlet's outfit should be more than qualified to find that dirt, if it was there to be found.

Stutely's head bobbed. "Got it."

"And when I ask for Scarlet, Scarlet better goddamned be here. And you want to know something else?" She moved closer now, letting a full belly of disgust roil up into her words. "I've already had to come down hard on Zinnia a few times for how poorly you all are doing. But I'm going to *guess* that she hasn't come down as hard on you, has she?"

He shook his head.

"'Cause she's a goddamned lionheart. She accepts the blame, to protect you. That's the cost of leadership. What you've come here today to tell me, that you want to be 'done,' that you've found nothing . . . well I regret that I'll have to take a piece of that out of her. So think on that. That's the cost of Scarlet's pride. That's the cost of you coming here to whine like a third whore. That's the cost of *being led.*"

If a full face could swallow, Stutely's did.

"Get your fickle candied ass out of here, and stop dealing in excuses," she barked. "Follow the man with the velvet cap until you find something useful."

Ricard the Ruby, smoothing out his moustache, was the first to stand before her when she was done. "What do you need, *mère?*"

"Bring Zinnia here," she answered, and the Frenchman left to do so, because that's what good dogs do.

Back at the mouth of the den, Stutely's feet hesitated as he sloughed away. Somehow, he had the balls enough to speak before leaving. "I *am* reliable, you know. I know I'm shit, as you say, but The Blood'll do what needs to be done."

It would have been an admirable defense if not for that last bit, which caused Caitlin to bellow. "*The Blood?* Well shit, guess it'll be a slow week for whoring. The blood normally only comes once a month."

She didn't bother to watch him sulk off in defeat. There were far more important things for a lioness to do.

TWENTY-SIX

ARTHUR A BLAND

DAYS ROLLED ON LIKE this, became a week. Sometimes they trailed the man with the velvet cap, even when he didn't wear the velvet cap. Sometimes they did whatever other busybody work the Lions wanted. When they worked in twos, Arthur tried to claim David as his partner, though Zinn usually broke them up. He wasn't sure which of the others he hated pairing with more— Stutely or Scarlet. Stutely's refusal to bathe had turned into a constant source of argument, given the unfathomable stink his body had collected. He was of-tentimes denser than Arthur had ever realized, and of late he'd become increas-ingly stubborn.

There was a sense of being trapped now, that none of them mentioned. Ever since Cait had rejected their attempt to quit, working for the Lions felt less and less like a choice.

And Scarlet was Scarlet. Every day, as before, was a gamble with him. His swings were wider now. At his best he was incorrigible and brilliant, outthinking whatever mission they'd been assigned and completing it in half the time, or for twice the reward. At his worst he was a silent storm, violent and uncaring. Left to his own devices, Arthur had even seen Scarlet talking to himself, scratching at his skin, taken to sudden bursts of crying that he could hardly disguise. Ever sober, but ever drowning.

David, against all odds, had only become increasingly fond of their little runt captain Zinn. Her petty little street gang—the ones responsible for the con of the endless bread roll—was full of equally rapscallious little cunts that David also apparently loved. In some other kinder life, David of Doncaster might've made a loving father. But in this actual rotgut of a life, Arthur would sooner chop his own cock off than have to care for a child.

Will's plan now, in short, was obedience. They did their work, and well, and hoped to earn some allies. Arthur didn't like life at all, but then life wasn't supposed to be liked. He did what he was told, bit his tongue, and then did so some more. Sometimes they'd pinch pockets, or study the rotation of the guard, and sometimes they did practically nothing. If that was earning them the respect they'd come for, he hoped it would pay off soon. Because saying "yes mum" to Caitlin FitzSimon felt like going in the wrong direction. And the more they mixed with these Red Lions, the more Arthur saw what kind of men and women they were.

These were the type who thought they were allowed to do whatever they wanted until life was likable. That sort of thinking was the short way to a quick death, Arthur knew. Arthur went beyond their orders and bothered to wonder *why* the Red Lions were so interested in the man with the velvet cap. His name was Gerome Artaud, and he was one of the city's trademasters. He inventoried every parcel of food that entered or left Nottingham, be it by road or by boat. The Red Fox clearly meant to blackmail him.

Which meant they were aiming to take that food for themselves.

More food for the Lions, is what it meant. And less for anyone else.

He'd caught rumors of similar actions, that *Robin Hood* had done. Beatings at the Commons, for people who gave out food to the wrong people. Hardly seemed like a *Robin Hood*-like thing to do.

Artaud was back at the brothel today, which was a regular stop for him. But this day, Zinn had chosen to accompany them. *"Sometimes you have to send a man to do a little girl's work,"* she'd complained in her usual carefree manner. She'd made some dismissive joke about the size of Arthur's cock when he asked her about the fresh bruises on her face.

Zinn was inside the Spotted Leopard with Will this time, and Arthur didn't want to think about what depraved story Will would concoct to explain her presence. Arthur's role was to make the rounds again, while Stutely was on the door again, and to his knowledge, David was back in the Red Lion Fish Market singing songs with gang children again.

Damn it all, he missed David. David was supposed to be his consolation, that at least they were in the muck of this together. But he rarely saw his friend anymore. David's stupid fucking jokes were no longer there to balance things out. *Thank God for every good moment, too,* Tuck had urged.

There was no fucking God in the world, but there was even less of Him in Nottingham.

"Are you with any of the others?" He heard a woman's voice around the corner. "Is Hanry with you?"

Arthur had just rounded to the front of the brothel, where he was surprised to see a waif of a woman speaking with Will Stutely. She leaned forward, as if desperate to claw the clothes from his body, which was alarming on its own. Most anyone gifted with a nose was more like to lean *away* from Stutely, so this woman must have a powerful reason to do otherwise. Arthur's first instinct was that she was a whore, but she was ever on the wrong side of the brothel's door.

"Haven't seen anyone," Stutely was answering, his face obscured by the entrance wall to the Leopard's walkway. "He's not with you?"

The woman shook more than her head. "You're certain?"

"What about Rog and . . . little Hugh?"

Arthur angled to the left, where he knew there would be a skinny stretch of mud between the neighboring building and the whorehouse, from which he could continue to listen without being spotted. There was, apparently, an advantage to having walked this block exactly five thousand times.

"Rog is dead." The woman's voice quivered. "He died of the greenrot, a few weeks ago. Never should've taken that fucking coin. Never should've come to this fucking place."

"Sarra, I don't . . ." Stutely stammered for a response, as if he'd never had any cause to show sympathy before. Through the slatted fence and a bit of foliage, Arthur could see them well enough. The girl was beet red, her eyes puffed in distress, and every inch of her malnourished body seemed on the verge of breaking.

"What about Hugh?" Stutely finally asked. "Your son, little Hugh?"

"He's somewhere," she said with a hopeless gape. "He doesn't come home most nights. *Home!* Whatever that's supposed to mean. Oh God, I don't know what to do. You can help, though, can't you? You can help?"

Stutely leaned forward to look down the lane. *Probably checking for me,* Arthur thought, and held his breath in curiosity. "I'll help you, but I'm busy right now. Where would I find you tonight?"

"You're busy?" Sarra's question reeled with insult, and a snide sneer snatched up her face as she took in her surroundings. A hurtful smile made it quite obvious she recognized the Spotted Leopard for what it was. "You're *busy?*"

"Not that," Stutely chortled. "I'm protecting the door, see. For someone inside. Sort of a bodyguard, you know, for an important person. Very important." He emphasized the word *very* with an eyebrow, in case she didn't know the word's meaning.

But Sarra curled her lips, baring yellow teeth. "You don't have to lie to me."

"I'm not lying." Stutely clamped down hard. "A very important man, he comes here a few times a week, always sees the same girl, Saddle Maege. Pays me to watch the door while he's in there, nothing unrespectable about that."

Arthur found that last addition interesting. Because the truth was that their work here was indeed something less, something south of respectable. Working for Scarlet, working for Zinn, working for the Red Lions.

Not working, really. Fetching. Watching.

"Working for Robin Hood," Stutely gulped out, finishing Arthur's own thoughts. That, at least, was true enough. And it was supposed to be *good*. Working for Red Fox, the new Robin Hood, was supposed to mean they were helping people. But that wasn't it anymore, not at all. The only people Red Fox helped were Red Fox's people. And Arthur's life had devolved into helping Red Fox do whatever the fuck it was he was doing. But where people had loved Robin Hood in the Sherwood . . . here they seemed just as like to recoil at the mention of his name.

Sarra, for instance.

Sarra spat in Stutely's face.

The glob of brown splayed across his nose, thick. He instantly wiped it away, but a long strand stretched to his whiskers, and as he tried to shake it off, Sarra filled his face with another. Arthur stopped watching and ran back to the exit of the mud alley, to foolishly add himself to the situation.

"*Robin Hood killed my husband!*" Sarra growled, a naked, shaken sound. "He chopped his hand off and left him for dead. And Hugh . . . whatever happens to Hugh, that's on Robin Hood, too." She spat a third time, but had nothing left in her mouth to spit.

"That's enough now!" Arthur barked with his deepest voice. He didn't think it would take much to scare off the beggar woman, but the last time he'd walked into a situation with any amount of confidence, he'd ended up with his breeches in a ball around his feet. "Get out of here!"

"I'm going!" she shouted back, twitching nervously away. Her eyes danced up and down Arthur's body, twice, before she made the decision to leave. *She was looking for his uniform*, he instantly realized. She'd mistaken him for a god-damned *gord*.

It stopped him in his tracks, as sure as an arrow. *Was that what he'd become? Guarding the door, and chasing away the poor? Taking orders because he didn't care enough to say no?*

"Don't go," Stutely called after the girl. She stopped in the road, but didn't turn. If anything, she was buckled over, her body giving way to a wail. "I'm not with them, he's not really Robin Hood . . ."

"Stop lying!" She twisted, her tortured face wrenched in knots. "If you can't help, then you can't help, that's fine! I'm used to it. But you don't have to be ter-rible about it, you don't have to add to it. Always out for yourself, Will Stutely, nothing ever changes. You think I don't know this place? Go inside and get your cock sucked, rather than stand out here lying to me!"

Arthur tried to help. "It's true, he wasn't lying."

"He's not lying?" Her smile was wicked. "Is your Robin Hood in there right now, is that who you're protecting? He's fucking Saddle Maege for a crown? Who—*by the way*—is a man, so don't *fucking* tell me you're not lying to me. He probably pays double for Maege to fuck him back." She laughed and cried in a single burst. "Why'n't you let him know he's wasting his coin, since you're so eager to do it yourself!"

Stutely moved but Arthur managed a hand onto his shoulder, letting the poor wretch trip off down the lane, cursing at the world and whichever god she felt had deserted her.

"She's drunk," Arthur said, though Stutely was agitated beyond his ability to hear it. "Who was she?"

"Her name was Sarra." His eyes focused on the last place she'd been before disappearing. "We lived in the same village, 'fore it burnt."

Arthur squinted off at the same spot.

"Thorney, right?" he asked, recalling the name.

Stutely's head bobbed. "The fire brigades, at top of winter. Last time I saw Thorney was when you all came by, asking for helpers. I almost didn't join, but seemed it was the right thing to do. Those fire brigades weren't so tough, only one or two Guardsmen each, you know? I could take one out on my own, maybe two." His jaw tightened. "But I couldn't stop the ones that come when I'm not there."

Arthur had never bothered to ask the man's history. He was just an arrogant strongarm, and even David wasn't shy about having a laugh at his expense. "Did you ever go back?"

A long, knowing grimace. "Nothing but black and char. So I stayed with Marion's Men. I guess that's when I 'joined,' seeing as how I didn't have a home to go back to. Never saw anyone from Thorney again, but she saw me standing here and recognized me. Her husband's dead now, I guess. He wasn't much of a man, but he didn't deserve that. Hand cut off? She said Robin Hood did that?"

Red Fox was the man who called himself Robin Hood, and here they were doing his beck and call. It tasted sour, every goddamn drop of it tasted wrong.

"He's not Robin Hood," Arthur said, since it needed to be said.

"I joined because I thought I'd be helping Robin Hood," Stutely muttered. "But he was dead before the fire brigades even started. And I hate to say it, and I hope you don't hate me none for doing so, but I don't think Will's got his head together at the moment."

The fact that Arthur agreed with Stutely was enough to show that the world had gone upside down.

At the edge of his senses, there was a commotion brewing.

"I used to tell stories about Robin Hood to that woman's son by the campfire. If I were to talk about him now . . ." Stutely's face turned into a fist, ". . . I'd tell little Hugh to run like hell."

At that, the wooden door of the brothel exploded outward.

Four or five bodies tumbled over each other, clattering out and collapsing into the slop and mud of the street. Arthur braced to move out of their way too late—someone's shoulder smashed into his chest and he went down with the rest of them. He winced when he hit the ground, feeling a questionable wetness soak into his elbows and knees. He was not surprised for even a moment to see that it was Will Scarlet at the center of the brawl.

"Get off!" Will shouted, scrambling backward through the muck, blood speckling his face. But his opponents ignored him. Arthur recognized them— the brothel's muscle, probably throwing Will out for coming too many times and not buying. There was still something wilder and violent happening there, and as Arthur regained his own feet he was able to make sense of the chaos.

The two bruisers were grappling at a third body between them—which of course was Zinn. One man would snatch her ankle just to receive her other foot in his chest a second later. Her neck was trapped in a hold until she sunk her teeth into the man's forearm, and she fell to the ground as the man cursed in anger. The bruiser smashed his good arm across Zinn's face, but she was too quick and rolled away with it. The long half of her hair sprayed water in an arc about her as she slipped to her feet.

"Let's go!" Scarlet yelled, moving away, waving for them both to follow. But Zinn had something feral in her. Arthur could see she had no intention of leaving this be. One man was distracted with his injured arm, while the other— dark skinned with a ponytail down to his chest—pulled out a knife.

Zinn moved forward, and Arthur's heart skipped.

Behind her, Will Scarlet gasped and reached out, too far away to help. He screamed her name—

No, not *her* name.

He called for *Much*.

> *Once, as a young man, though Arthur hated any story that started that way, he'd watched a dray horse go berserk. It was a godlike thing, the strongest animal Arthur had ever seen—a Brabant, bred to pull a plow through frozen soil. Arthur was little more than a spare horsehand at the stables, earning one coin for every two he stole from the head groom. Something spooked the horse, and whether it was a fire or a snake or an unkind word, Arthur couldn't remember. But he remembered the stunning power of the horse's legs when it kicked. If every single sinew in a normal horse had been wound tight as a crossbow wire and compacted, that was the strength of just the Brabant's thigh. It crushed a stableman's chest in the blink of an eye and sent him soaring backward. It left young Arthur awestruck, and in another second the beast kicked again, its every muscle perfectly concentrated into a single pinpoint where its hoof cracked a second man's skull open, dead before he even began to fall.*
>
> *That's what it was like to watch Stutely in full rage.*

It was over before Arthur could blink. Only later would he be able to piece together what he saw. Stutely closed the distance that Scarlet couldn't, screaming primal, hulking forward and smashing the knifeman across the face with a single fist, all his weight behind it. It was no punch, it was a Brabant-powerful explosion that likely popped the victim's eyeballs from his head. Arthur felt the impact in his own teeth. Without hesitation, Stutely turned and clamped his hands together, swinging down onto the top of the second bruiser, whose neck all but snapped as he crumpled lifeless to the ground.

The third punch was for Will Scarlet, square in the face, and then it was over.

Stutely slung Scarlet over his shoulder as if he were a sack of onions, and grabbed Zinn by the scruff of her neck. He barreled away from the whorehouse, dragging both of them, dripping alleyway filth, not even caring if Arthur had sense enough to follow.

THE REDHEADED COW CAITLIN was making noise, complaining that Will Scarlet ought to be apologizing for the brawl at the Spotted Leopard. Arthur nodded, and he apologized, or at least his mouth did. Scarlet was sleeping off the worst headache he'd ever had, so it didn't matter how much his "presence was demanded." Arthur eyed every member of the Red Lions with suspicion now—the whore Clorinda Rose whispered things into Alfred Fawkes's ear, lounging as was his style on his beggar throne. He caught a glimpse of Ginger

Twain and Ricard the Ruby snickering to themselves at the table, not playing any real game of dice.

These were the people who *chopped off hands.*

Who sought to steal the city's grain.

Who wanted to waste their time rather than help others.

David hadn't believed Arthur's story at first. *"You must have misheard him,"* he said. *"He wouldn't have called out for Much."*

But that didn't make any of it the less true. Wherever Scarlet's head was, half of it was in the past.

So far as Arthur could tell, that wasn't what had set Will Stutely off. Maybe he just felt protective of Zinn. Maybe they'd had a laugh at him one too many times. Or maybe he saw clearer than Arthur where all this was headed, and hit his breaking point sooner.

Whatever it was, he left. Just walked away. Arthur doubted he'd be back.

Which meant that Stutely was the smartest of the four of them.

The three of them, now.

Based on Scarlet's state of mind, the *two* of them.

Arthur had helped Zinn recover, too, who'd earned yet another swollen jaw at the hands of the brothel doormen. She had cruel things to say about Stutely's disappearance, ignoring the fact that he was likely the only reason she was still alive to shit and grin above her age another day.

The rest of the evening Arthur spent back in the French Ward with David, looking for the strange beggar girl Sarra. He hoped perhaps to find Stutely there as well, but they found no sign of either of them, nor nary a tale of the girl's name. But in asking for her they found more about her husband, and his hand, and the others that'd been nailed to a wall in a place they called the Pity Stables.

Arthur and David brought coin, what little they could spare. They brought food, what little they could steal, and they gave it to the desperate in exchange for stories of the villain Robin Hood. Most were wary—fearful, even—for the trade. But some they found, huddled in corners and darkness, thankful for the feast and the company. They told their stories begrudgingly, as though it were their last act on earth. Arthur and David nodded and listened to it all, of the impostor Robin Hood, of the legacy that Alfred Fawkes was destroying. How he took the hands of those that accepted his own charity. How those who spoke well of him, or who were known to have helped him before the winter, were beaten in the night. Or their names stricken from the Common Lists, left to starve. Or chased from the town entirely. Whatever good Robin Hood had once been, Alfred Fawkes and his Red Lions meant to turn his name into a threat, into fear.

Arthur had been a part of that. Smashing a few horns, breaking a few windows, was just where it started. They were still doing the smallwork. Someday, they'd be asked to wield the axe. He couldn't even tell if that bothered Will, or if it was all "part of the plan."

On their own, Arthur's fingers flexed.

"Did you at least find anything new?" Caitlin brayed, bending over as far as her cumbersome body would allow. *Anything new* meant anything she could use as leverage on the man with the velvet cap. That they could take his grain, that they could control more people. Behind Caitlin, Alfred Fawkes smiled oily and plucked an errant hair from the cuff of his sleeve, his slit eyes focused on the lioness even as Clorinda's lips breathed into his ear.

"*Saddle Maege is a man,*" Sarra had said.

Gerome Artaud was taken to lying with other men in secret. That more than counted as *anything new.*

"No, mum," replied Arthur a Bland, the last honest gentleman-thief in Nottingham. "Nothing."

TWENTY-SEVEN

QUILLEN PEVERIL

NOTTINGHAM CASTLE

MOSTLY, QUILLEN KEPT HIMSELF awake by playing out scenarios of his own increasingly grisly demise. It required little imagination to think he might freeze to death one night on his midnight walk, but then he started considering the many unnatural things Gilbert with the White Hand could do upon discovering his body.

Quill had coordinated his watch schedule such that he preceded Gilbert at each station along the bulwark; this was intended to make it less obvious he was studying Gilbert's movements, but actually made it all the more unsettling that Gilbert was *following* him instead. So when Quill inevitably succumbed to the night's cold and collapsed into an icy heap on the parapets, Gilbert with the White Hand was guaranteed to be first to stroll upon his body and the endless options it offered.

Cut off a hand? He could probably break off Quill's frozen extremities with a simple snap of his boot.

Throw him over the edge? There would be pretty pieces of Peveril scattered all the way down to the Trent.

Thaw him over a fire, then wear his skin like a glove? Sweet God, Quill hated his own imagination.

When he grew bored with these creative concoctions, he found his mind trapped in the even less enviable fantasies of how to fix all of England. Because this is what Peverils did with their free time; rather than throw dice or drink or find women to paw at, he took on every problem in the world as his own personal challenge. The frustrating part was the hypocrisy of his answers. Truth be told, his advice to Chancellor Longchamp would be to refuse to pay the first farthing of King Richard's ransom—*for the good of the country*—and yet his advice to every struggling commoner was to do anything necessary to pay their share—*for the good of the country*.

He didn't care much for the moral chasm between those two stances, so he returned to the idea of Gilbert lancing him through the heart with a spear and eating it raw.

The other curious side effect of his position with the nightwalkers was a new skillset—or rather, the *absence* of one. His was a mind that abhorred being idle, and so he normally found all manner of subjects to study or languages to learn or puzzles to unravel. If Quillen Peveril was not accomplishing *something*, he grew easily frustrated; this he knew about himself. But upon the Nottingham battlements, he became intimately familiar with the sensation of contributing exactly nothing to the world.

And that was, surprisingly, a useful feeling. Because he recognized it, too, in Lord Beneger's hunt for Robin Hood.

Yesteryear's Robin Hood was something worth hunting—two separate Sheriffs had died at his hands, after all, not to mention the political and financial upsets he caused across the entire county. But the stories they chased now were scattered and dimensionless. Behandings were terrible, yes—but when coupled with petty thievery and street brawls, they amounted to a withering pile no taller than somebody-else's-business.

Footsteps behind him, the White Hand approaching him like an arrow.

Quill had just enough time for a gasp, and then opted to spare the man his villainous victory by diving over the edge of the wall and plummeting into the rocks below.

"I'll be in the privy," Gilbert said to Quill's stubbornly stationary body.

Down in the rocks, Quill's skull cracked against many things, his brains spilling hot steam into the night air.

"Ten minutes," the ghost man added, without slowing.

Quill's mind eventually returned to his control, and he stammered for any appropriate answer. "You don't need to tell me."

"Just making it easier on you," the man slowed, pivoting by the braziers until his face was entirely in shadow, "for your records."

Quill ripped his own face off with both hands and shoveled it down his throat, to choke and die as quickly as possible.

"Yesterday there was a full hour after seventh bell when nobody was watching me," Gilbert continued, in his atonal lilt. "In which I visited the seamstress in the middle bailey and mended my own tabard. Ask for Wilmot if you need to corroborate it. For your records, as it were."

Lightning crashed through the clouds and incinerated Quillen Peveril's body, his ashes floated away in the wind where Gilbert could never re-collect them.

Once the ghost man was gone, down the stairs in the legitimate direction of the privy, little pieces of Quill's corpse recongealed into putty and gave one last stab at this whole living thing. *Gilbert knew they were watching him* was the first sentence his primordial brain invented, followed shortly by: *He doesn't care that we know.*

How long he stood there digesting that particular meal he could not say, but it seemed shorter than ten minutes. As footsteps grew closer, it occurred to him that he ought to pass this information on to another breathing human before he died again—but that opportunity was now gone. Gilbert returned with a crossbow loaded with a flask of Greek fire, and Quill was very thankful for its warmth as it shattered against his sternum and he blistered into a shriveled black ball of goo.

"Quill?" came an unexpectedly deep voice.

His eyes opened, and focused on a larger shape that was not Gilbert.

"Thought you should know," Potter grunted, bracing himself against the crosswind, "Lord Beneger has a couple of visitors."

"I'm not Lord Beneger," Quill answered, fairly certain that was true. "Why are you telling me?"

"Because they didn't ask for Lord Beneger," the man huffed. "They asked for *Benja Benja Benja.*"

THEY MET AT THE narrow table the next morning, a long skinny dining space that was more *hallway* than *hall.* Quill had spent the evening with Lord Beneger and his two unlikely visitors in his private quarters, before sending them on their way again. At first light, they summoned his crew.

The bells from St. Nicholas had long sounded nine when their group was fully met. Captain de Grendon stood by Lord Beneger's side, his eyes shifting nervously about as if to remind himself that he was supposed to be in charge of things. His entire Black Guard was present, including the brute Kyle Morgan and Ludic of Westerleak from the gaols. Even the armsmaster Simon FitzSimon settled in, raising a particularly scruffy eyebrow at the rest of them. Jacelyn de Lacy stood notably in front of the five men in Derby green tabards that rounded out Wendenal's task force. Last to join was the Coward Knight FitzOdo and his two lemmings, Derrick and Ronnell.

"There he is," Lord Beneger moaned, clad in a flowery grey doublet with tongues of red. "Ever the latecomer, FitzOdo."

For most it may have been an innocent jab, but Quill recognized the insult nestled therein. It was an intentional reminder of FitzOdo's shaming sixteen years ago, and his role in the failed siege on Nottingham during the Kings' War. Quill wondered how many in the room were knowledgeable enough to even know the details.

But if FitzOdo took offense, he did not show it. "We had a late night."

"At a tavern, no doubt." Beneger did not hide his disdain. "While you were out drinking, we received our first actionable information in weeks on Scarlet and his crew."

"Really." The knight seemed unimpressed. "What is it?"

"We've learned he frequents a brothel in the French Ward called the Spotted Leopard. Even more so, we know the name of his favorite whore—a man who goes by Saddle Maege."

"A *man?*" FitzOdo recoiled. "Where'd you hear this?"

Beneger gave a brief account of the late-night visit from the woman Sarra and her son.

FitzOdo gave an ugly sneer. "She's playing you."

"We've considered that," Quill answered. She had not been shy in asking for compensation for her service. "But we found her story compelling. The circumstances are believable."

"Bullshit. I've been following Robin Hood for months, since before you showed up. We've never seen any evidence that he does any whoring, much less that he's a fucking pillow-biter."

Quill had to laugh. "I don't think you're making the argument you think you are. If this information is true, it is indeed surprising that you never uncovered any of it."

"Oh fuck on you, Peveril." The knight dismissed him. "You never heard it none neither until last night. You didn't uncover fuck all. It came walking up to the castle, wrapped in a bow. All you did was listen. And why do you suppose this girl felt comfortable talking to you in the first place? I've—"

"I met her son last week, helping with another issue." Quill stood his ground. "That's why they came to us. The more we actually *help* people, the more they trust us. Chasing ghosts all day doesn't do anything for the people we're supposed to be protecting. They need to see us helping."

"I agree," the captain said, though he added nothing else.

Eventually Jacelyn inclined her head. "Are we still thinking this is Gilbert?"

"No," Beneger answered. Quill had already discussed it with him, that there were no patterns at all in Gilbert's schedule that matched their sightings of Robin Hood—and absolutely none that ever put him near a whorehouse. If there was any truth to the rumor that someone in the Guard was working with Robin Hood, it certainly wasn't with the man who openly welcomed documentation of his trips to the privy. Quill's embarrassment at being completely wrong about Gilbert was thankfully overshadowed by their new lead. "We're no longer considering him a threat."

"Well he's still a damned nightmare of a person." Ronnell's eyes grew. His brother, Derrick, shook in agreement.

"You have new orders?" Jac asked Beneger.

"We move everyone onto this whorehouse. We need to know every soul who comes and goes."

One of his Derby host squirmed. "I've never been in a wh— . . . in a house of ill repute."

"*Ill repute?*" Quill smiled. "Why, that's my favorite type of repute."

"*Everyone*, you say?" asked Morg, glancing to the captain.

"We've discussed it, yes," de Grendon confirmed. "Lord Beneger needs as many Guardsmen as we can spare. There will be a lot of people to track, and we have to determine which ones are threats. There's also rumor that Will Scarlet's in the city—Sherwood's been quiet for a few weeks, but I'm sure you've noticed things are louder here."

"Smart money says they're working with one of the gangs, Red Lions most likely," Jacelyn said.

"Agreed." Beneger tapped a map of the city that had been spread across the table, gesturing vaguely at its scope. "And there's not enough of us to simply raid a gang that size. They could move their Robin Hood—whoever he really is—beneath our noses all day. We need confirmation of his whereabouts."

"I've seen no proof they run with the Lions," FitzOdo growled out.

"Proof?" Beneger turned on him. "You've been responsible for tracking Scarlet for months and this is the first time you've braved that word. Are you to tell me now that you have a single valuable morsel of knowledge you've obtained from your long search?"

"Red Lions were the obvious guess," FitzOdo continued, his teeth ground tight. "But I hear it's not them. In fact the opposite, I hear that group hates Will Scarlet, blames him for everything sour that's ever happened to them."

Morg flexed his muscles. "But no harm in finding out for ourselves."

"There is, actually," countered the bald knight, finally rattled. "Could be that the Red Lions are the only things keeping Robin Hood's gang at bay. We take out the Red Lions, we've just given Robin Hood control of the city."

"We're not giving him anything," Beneger snapped. "We're taking. We're taking everything from him. We know where to find him, he cannot be hard to find now."

"But he has proven to be," countered the captain, cautious to contradict Lord Beneger. "FitzOdo has been searching for him for months and found nothing. I would not underestimate Robin Hood's ability to evade detection."

"That was Gisbourne's downfall," Simon mumbled. "Thought it would be easy."

"We won't make that mistake." Beneger's jaw tightened. "All eyes on this whorehouse, and he cannot slip by."

"*No.*"

This new voice came from behind, small but certain—as if he shouldn't have to even raise it at all.

Every face turned to see the thin frame of William de Ferrers in the doorway, covered in a blustering black fur that he had undoubtedly selected to make him appear more suited to his sheriffcy. But some men were born to lead, and others were whelps made for whipping. It was a sucker punch of a reminder as to why Quill lingered in Nottingham, to see this spindly runt replaced by a worthy successor.

"I have a lead," Lord Beneger explained, barely hiding his disdain for the man, "and I'm following it."

"You're *not.*" Ferrers walked carefully into the room, as if half the stones in the floor were traps. He held their silence until it was uncomfortable, daring anyone to speak against him. "It does us no good to catch another Robin Hood in the dark. The people will simply think we're lying again."

He spoke smooth as silk, concerned mostly with the fingertips of his arrogant gloves. To anyone educated in the art of politicking, these were basic tricks. But some of the men in the room were of simpler minds, and mistook the caricature of strength for the real thing.

"We could hang a Robin Hood every day of the week and it would only make him more dangerous," the Sheriff continued. "The people need to see him captured, they need the proof that it's really him—that's what we failed to do at his hanging. More importantly, they need to see him fail. His story needs a definitive—and public—end."

He paused, but nobody bothered to ask him to continue. It was too obvious that he wanted it. At last he placed his fingertips on the table and looked up at Lord Beneger.

"I'm arranging for a great archery tournament, to be held here in the castle. It shall coincide with the commemoration of the martyr St. Valentine in two weeks. Participation is open to the commonfolk, and the prizes will be formidable. Coin, of course, but land, too, throughout Nottinghamshire—and a building here in the city. The sort of prizes that no man could chance ignoring. It will be too tempting a target for the hubris of our dear Robin Hood. We keep a strict eye on its participants, and we ensure his victory. Up to a point. Then not only will we best him in archery, but we'll capture him before a crowd of people and denounce him for his crimes immediately. The legend of Robin Hood ends there."

The silence that met him was not the awe that Ferrers probably interpreted it as. It was more the stunned silence of watching an invalid fire a crossbow bolt into his own eye. The idea was as flawed as it was misguided, with too many obvious things that could go wrong, too many things for them to possibly track. It was exactly the sort of idea that a young man would dream up, a fool's plot to lure an enemy in and then prove himself the hero. A lord's fantasy, based on nothing but fancy.

But Ferrers was Sheriff now, and Quill was just a Common Guardsman on the midnight shift. He should have summoned his father a month ago. He should have done what he had come here for, and used his family's influence to put someone worthwhile in the sheriff's seat. Instead he'd grown content to wait it out, not realizing what damage this child might do at the head of the table. He would write his father this very night. He had to.

With the absolute smallest possible bow of his head, teeth set hard in place, Lord Beneger complied. "As you say, Sheriff."

TWENTY-EIGHT

MARION FITZWALTER

MARION BOWED AGAIN, OFFERED her glove for the next kiss, and welcomed yet another visitor to this castle that was not hers to present.

The Countess of Huntingdon had been far too reckless, in Marion's estimation, with her list of invitees to this council. It was no secret that lords and earls across England objected to Chancellor Longchamp's rule generally—and the payment of King Richard's ransom specifically—but those protestations were rightfully private. Lady Magdalena assumed that gathering like-minded people in one room might lead to something profound, but Marion knew better.

Filling a room with murderers would not coerce any single one of them to admitting a crime.

But Lady Magdalena's family sprawled wide, and some would say they'd been preparing for this moment for years. The great Henry de Bohun, Earl of Hereford, had spent his lifetime spreading his influence across the country. In want of sons, Henry de Bohun had married his daughters strategically, investing in a network of silent dissenters to royal corruption. Magdalena was his youngest, married to the Earl of Huntingdon. Another daughter had wed the Earl Robert de Vere of Oxfordshire. The eldest, Lady Margery d'Oily, was with Waleran de Beaumont, the Earl of Warwick. The entirety of that family was now gathered in Huntingdon's walls.

Rebels.

Marion ought to love them. She was, theoretically, amongst friends. But there was a bit of a problem with the other invitees.

Yes, they had come in full splendor, in every banner and color—a population of prestige that swarmed to Huntingdon Castle from as far as Magdalena's letters had carried two weeks earlier. It reminded Marion of the assembly in Nottingham for de Lacy's funeral, a map of arms riddling the bailey like a carnivale. Most prominent were the neighboring counties: the gold-and-maroon crosses of Northamptonshire, the waving blues of Cambridgeshire, or Bedfordshire's red-and-yellow motley. Farther counties were present, too. Marion could spot the ermine sash of Norfolk, the acorn-laden field of Rutland, even the loggerheads of Shropshire. It was a bouquet of colors and sigils, festive as a traveling performance troupe.

And twice as disingenuous.

"Thank you for accommodating us," came the wan smile of a man who was not Richard de Montfichet. "The baron sends his unfortunate regrets that he could not attend personally."

"I offer apologies," was the husky greeting of a plump horseman who was not William de Fors, "as I am a poor substitute for the Count of Aumale, but I must needs suffice."

"I humbly submit myself in the earl's stead," followed an elaborate bow from a moustached man who was not Roger Bigod, "and promise to report back to Norfolk the full details of our meeting here."

Every banner was a lie, every crest was a costume. A collection of attendants and cousins, dressed up in the guise of their lords and earls, come to *observe*. Nearly every invitation that went out was returned by a nameless servant whose prominent characteristics comprised obedience and expendability.

"Nobody wants to risk attending this council in person," Marion complained behind her smile, watching the man who was not Geoffrey de Say make small talk with the man who was not Geoffrey de Mandeville, oblivious to their masters' mutual hatred of each other. "They're afraid of being labeled traitors and collaborators, so they send these useless attendants instead."

"Do you blame them?" asked Lord Robert, his face plastered with a well-practiced grin. He wore his olive half cape over one shoulder, his head cocked confidently backward as if the event had not already been an epic disappointment. They stood between the two squat buildings that held sentry to the Heart Tower's bridge, welcoming their visitors after each was stabled and quartered. "These sort of talks are supposed to be held in secret, in wine cellars and closed stables. There ought to be a blood sacrifice, and a bone shrine to justify our sinister cabal. To receive a friendly invitation instead . . . would be understandably intimidating."

"Not just intimidating," Marion replied. "*Suspicious*. I'm imagining Sheriff de Ferrers, opening the gates of Nottingham Castle, unfurling a banner that reads *Free Food for Thieves*. This council must look like the least clever trap in history."

Robert drew his breath in sharply. "Well, Maggie is few things if not bold. And if nothing else, this will be an adventure."

"An adventure that ends in a prison cell," Marion mumbled. It did not take a great leap of imagination to think that one of the letters might be intercepted by an ally of the Chancellor, or that a recipient might find profit in selling the others out. Even an ambitious page or unruly stableboy might undo them all, if sufficiently disgruntled. "There is a reason the word *rebellion* is traditionally whispered, not shouted."

"This isn't a rebellion," Robert tisked her, abandoning his flippancy. "It's a conversation."

Marion smiled at him. "Oh, my dear, dear Robert. That's how rebellions start."

More servants came, introduced themselves, and apologized for not being their masters. Marion would have much preferred to hide in her room until the entire debacle was over, but her position as welcomer was yet another demand by the countess. *Servitude in exchange for hospitality.* The Lady Magdalena had a particularly dead stare she reserved for Marion each time she made a "request." Marion had not talked about this uncomfortable relationship with anyone else, though John Little alone seemed to guess as to the sacrifices Marion was making for their survival.

At the moment, the countess herself was effectively hiding. Once her family members realized they would be the only attendees who actually arrived in the flesh, they secluded themselves at the top of the Heart Tower. If there was any justice in the world, the Earl of Hereford was currently giving Lady Magdalena a proper scolding for her political ineptitude. Marion doubted they would even show their faces at the council tomorrow, given the disappointing turnout.

"It's *you* they're afraid of," Lord Robert said, in between guests. "You're famous for your rapscallious exploits."

"That's not a word." She elbowed him. "And none of them had any idea I would be here, so you certainly can't use that as an excuse."

"It only takes one person to notice you, and talk," he mused. "I think rumor has traveled. I think you might be famous."

Marion hated the idea. As she extended her hand to a fidgety man who was not William de Mowbray, she wished very much that she could send a facsimile of her own—a woman who was not Marion Fitzwalter—to play her part.

"My lord deeply appreciates your invitation, but he regrets that he could not escape his responsibilities in Rutland," came the capitulating voice of a man who was not William d'Albini. *Sheriff d'Albini of Rutland,* Marion squinted at him. The man whose forces had waylaid them on their travels. *"Responsibilities in Rutland" indeed.* She knew fully well that he stayed at Belvoir Castle and probably never even saw the invitation. If word had spread that Marion was in Huntingdon, it was very likely the men of the Rutland Guard who had started it.

"All the same, we welcome you in his stead," Robert was saying, treating the stranger with all pomp.

"My appreciation, Earl Robert, and Countess Magdalena . . ."

"Oh!" Marion interrupted. "My apologies, you mistake me. The countess is unavailable, but shall join us for dinner this evening."

"Ah." The servant apologized, and continued on.

It was not the first time today she'd been mistaken for Robert's wife, given that Magdalena should obviously be the one at his side. Robert had begun to enjoy the misconception and stood intentionally and increasingly close to her, prodding at Marion's embarrassment like a schoolboy.

"Just pretend you're her," he snickered. "None of them know the difference."

"Perhaps you should play her yourself," she pursed her lips to keep from scowling, "so everyone here can report back to their lords that Lady Magdalena is exactly as mad as her letters implied."

"She's not *mad*," he balked, but cut himself off. "But yes, she might have handled this more delicately."

"More accurately, she *couldn't* have handled this *less* delicately."

"I won't speak ill of my own wife." Robert's tone sounded more like careful conditioning than actual wisdom. "Besides, you've been helping her prepare every detail for the last week. I thought she had your full support."

"Hum," was all she could say. She recalled Magdalena's sneering features on the castle ramparts their first night. *"Don't bring your pervert inside the castle walls again."* By failing to stand up for Sir Amon, Marion had given Magdalena complete power over her.

Amon. Sworn to protect her, now forced to camp in the villages outside the walls and wait for her. To satisfy Lady Magdalena's bigotry, her self-righteousness. *If that was it at all.* Marion's instincts told her that Magdalena's issue with Amon had nothing to do with Amon. It was simply control, a way of manipulating her.

But, she reminded herself, the sacrifice was worth it. The rest of her people were flourishing in their new home. There was ample work to be done in and around the castle grounds, and they were eager to earn their way. A season of fleeing from the Nottingham Guard had destroyed their spirits, but here the opportunity to contribute in meaningful ways brought life back to them. That was Marion's reward, and it made the trade for her obedience equitable. Friar Tuck adopted this larger community of Huntingdon as his own. And the Delaney brothers, as always, were incomparable in their kindness, ever diligent toward making this home permanent.

"She means well," Lord Robert said suddenly, in sober defense of his wife. "And merits results more oft than not. She's just impulsive at times, which can be its own asset, you know."

Marion nodded, though she could not agree. *Impulsive, with no thought toward any consequences.* That description was a familiar one. Will Scarlet was gone, and Marion could only hope she had not ended in debt to someone even more destructive.

Not that this council has been particularly impulsive, she reconsidered. Magdalena had planned it in secret for weeks behind her husband's back, before sending her letters out when the opportunity arose. There was another word for Magdalena, something worse than *impulsive.*

"Surely I would have remembered giving my granddaughter away," came an oddly familiar voice, "but I cannot fault her choice in husband."

Marion turned to the next guests, several generations older than most of the other attendants. The elderly couple was struggling with the incline of the courtyard, aided by a few attendants on either side. Her heart leaped at the sight of their emblems—the three swords of Essex. Marion's grandfather's face bore every year with a grudge.

She had not been informed that they'd been sent an invitation. Their presence was an utter shock, as if the great hand of God had just yanked Marion from a dream of adulthood and thrown her back into a child's body. She could suddenly smell her grandfather's parlor, where she and her sister Vivian had learned to stitch. She remembered a particular flaky baked bread and some game with beans and pebbles. It had been years, perhaps, since she had seen them. The very idea that there was some very normal world where Marion could idly chat with her grandparents in comfort rather than spend her time assassinating Sheriffs was almost too much for her mind to grapple.

"The honor of your granddaughter's hand is not mine to claim," Lord Robert answered smoothly, giving a cordial bow to the Earl of Essex. "But the Lady Marion does me the service of welcoming our guests in my wife's absence. I am ever grateful for her presence."

"What a pity," Marion's grandmother cooed, holding the crook of her husband's arm, bundled to exhaustion in elaborate fabric. Her face was puckered plum, her lines deep enough to define the edges of her skull. "This one's handsome. Marion never had an eye for that. Do you remember Jeremiah, the fishmonger's son?"

Marion did. "I was eleven."

"Eleven is a fine age to be unwed." Her grandfather scowled. "And how old are you now?"

"Lord Robert," Marion pivoted, "allow me to introduce my grandfather the Baron Walter FitzRobert, Earl of Essex, and my grandmother Rohese."

"What a beautiful name, Rose." Lord Robert continued his saccharine courtesy. "Named for a flower as beautiful as yourself."

"*Rohese*," her grandmother gave the subtle correction. "Named for my own grandmother, who was anything but beautiful. It's been forty years since anyone has called me that, and ten more since it was not said in jest." She shifted her weight. "I should scold you for trying to flatter me, but instead I'll accept a kiss."

She wobbled forward and craned her neck out, paper-thin skin threatening to tear apart at the gesture. But Lord Robert smiled and brushed her cheek with his own, to her inestimable delight.

"I'm surprised to see you here," Marion admitted. "It is a long journey for you two. You could have sent an observer, as many of the others have."

"It was coincidence, and curiosity," her grandfather responded, feathering back his rogue eyebrows. "I was already planning a visit to York to discuss relations with the new High Sheriff there, and this was a convenient stop along the way."

"The High Sheriff of York?" Marion worried at the implication. Osbert de Longchamp was brother to the Chancellor, the very man this council was formed to conspire against.

Her father clearly sensed her hesitation. "Indeed. I don't much like the man, but that has little bearing on whether I must work with him. I hope that is something this council of yours will keep heavily in mind."

"Oh it's not *my* council," Marion said, pulling back. Being mistaken for Lady Magdalena was bad enough, but this was a misassociation she certainly could not abide.

"We're weary from the road," her grandmother smiled, hiding her fatigue, "and anxious to settle in. There will be time enough for us to talk later. Give us the shortest version you can, dear—how have you been?"

What a question.

Marion had never been particularly close with her grandparents. There was love there, yes, but its interest reached no further than the most cursory information. It was the same with her parents, who had done nothing to hold her hand through life. Marion wasn't bitter, as it had afforded her the independence she felt had defined her, letting her become her own woman. But there were times when she felt desperately disconnected from the prestige of her family. Her grandfather was the Earl of Essex, her father the castellan of London, and Marion was an outlaw in the forest.

"How have I been?" she echoed the words. She had spent the winter hungry and frozen, in constant flight. She had buried friends, been abandoned by others. She incited a grassroots rebellion, and watched it fail miserably. She had arranged her own marriage to William de Wendenal when he became Sheriff, only for him to die at the hands of her only love, Robin of Locksley. How could she describe that epic expanse in her soul? The guilt of his death, the caustic reality that she could have done more? Her mourning, her failures, her tenuous scratching at the world?

"No matter," Rohese answered her own question, when it grew obvious Marion would not. "We'll speak at dinner. You're welcome to call on us at any time, you know."

Once they ambled off, escorted to find their room by one of Lord Robert's men, Marion finally exhaled.

"Well at least we have one real attendee outside of my wife's family," Robert said. "So this wasn't a complete waste of time."

Marion watched them suffer the climb up to the Heart Tower. This visit would be brief, and utterly inconsequential to their lives. The summation of everything Marion had ever done amounted to no more than idle small talk to them. "Are my people secure here, Robert?" she asked, still watching them. "You wouldn't cast them out now, would you?"

"Of course not," he answered, his eyebrows a question mark. "And they're not *your people* anymore, Marion, they're Huntingdon's."

"Even if I were to leave?"

She could feel him hesitate. "Are you thinking of leaving?"

"I don't know," she answered, which was the truth. In many ways, she'd finally succeeded in what she'd long sought—she'd found a safe harbor for her refugees. How long would she have to suffer Lady Magdalena's dominance to pay for that? There was little else for her to accomplish in Huntingdon, aside from that penance. And if Robert vouched for their safety, then the only thing keeping Marion here was a few friendships, and painful memories.

If she wanted to continue to try to make some sort of difference in the world, it wouldn't be in Huntingdon, or at the countess's failed council full of absentee spectators.

She wondered if her grandparents could be bothered to let her accompany them to York, and their meeting with the Chancellor's brother.

She wondered what more she could do, were she not so confined by the walls she'd built around that thing she called her life.

TWENTY-NINE

CAITLIN FITZSIMON

WEST OF NOTTINGHAM

GOD'S TITS, MEN WERE ever the dumbest of beasts.

Caitlin smashed the palm of her right hand across Skinny Pink's face, startling the merry diddy out of his lopsided smile and causing him to drop the longbow in alarm. "Maybe someday the Sheriff'll throw a contest for chicken dobbing," she yelled at him, "and then you'll be the pride of Nottingham. But you hold a bow 'bout as well as your liquor. Give it up."

"You'd be surprised," Ricard the Ruby raised his flaring eyebrows one by one, "at how good a lover a chicken can be. You could probably learn *une chose ou deux*."

"Maybe I could!" Caitlin laughed, never shy to take as much as she dealt. "You, on the other hand, never gave *'learning things'* a try, did you?"

That was met with cackles and catcalls, and Ricard laughed out a few more barbs in French, taking the longbow from Skinny Pink and passing it to the next Lion cub.

They'd left the city for this, walked for a full hour upstream by the Trent to find some secluded wooded area long and flat enough to have their hand at archery practice. They weren't doing nothing illegal, but still it was best to be safe from curious passersby. Caitlin didn't like it one damned finger, but she'd long learned that liking things held little parley with doing them. Traveling in groups larger than three was always dangerous, especially in daylight, as any roving gord was certain to whet his lips at the sight of young men with clipped ears.

But Alfie had made his mind up on this one. He was determined that one of them would win the Sheriff's archery contest.

"It's our way out," Alfie had insisted, in the privacy of their cave beneath Crof's Plaza. "Out of these tunnels. We've been driven underground, and we can't crawl out again without braving something ever larger. This could be our chance. Think of the prizes—not just the coin, but the land! Something beyond the dirt that we make ours."

He had traced his finger across the ceiling of the sandstone, letting a small crumble of pebbles follow his fingertip's path. "I'm sick of the tanner's stink down here, sick of living like gongfarmers. I'll leave Red Fox and Robin Hood behind and become *Lord Fawkes*, wouldn't that be something?"

"They'll never let it happen." She shook her head at him.

He had let his hand drop gently, his fingers intertwining with hers. "I do what I can to keep the boys brave, but . . . but I don't know what other choice we have. I just . . . I just don't know."

"*Lord* Fawkes," she used her cruelest tone, the one they used in front of the Lions but rarely for each other, "I will not let you sacrifice yourself for them. You don't owe them a goddamned thing. You organized the Red Lions when they were leaderless, you pulled the gangs together, you ended the petty territory skirmishes, *you*."

It was an exaggeration, as she'd done as much or more to restructure the Lions than anyone, but neither did she have a man's need to be congratulated about it all the time. "They'd be nothing without you. Don't you worry your damned head about what more you should be doing for them. You've done enough."

"Enough?" His whisper had brought his head into hers, their foreheads touching.

Caitlin knew what he meant.

Enough didn't mean hiding in tunnels. *Enough* didn't mean being rounded up in the streets and mutilated. As Red Fox, Alfie saw himself as a failure. But as Robin Hood he'd found new strength. And admittedly, the idea of a piece of land for themselves, or a building in the city . . . well, that could be the start of something huge. And so they were here now, out in the daylight a few miles west of Nottingham, shooting arrows at trees and—very occasionally—actually hitting them.

Most of her cubs didn't have a lick of talent at archery, which didn't surprise her in the least. Knives and clubs were the weapons of the street. Hell, they didn't even *own* any bows. It had taken the gang a week just to procure a full quiver and the two longbows they now took turns at. They were losing arrows at a worrying pace, as half their shots went careening in laughably wrong directions—so much so that it was too dangerous to even keep a few men at the far end of their range to collect the arrows back. Even those that found their mark would oft splinter or break against the tree's hard bark.

"We should have made a straw box," David of Doncaster complained. The only one of Will Scarlet's men who wasn't a useless skiver, David had immediately become their longbow trainer. His own skill was practically offensive for making it seem so easy.

"You should have told us to make one," growled the Dawn Dog, struggling desperately to keep his arrow straight as he pulled the line back across his chest.

"I . . ." David's mouth waggled, aghast at Dawn Dog's terrible form, ". . . you're right. I should have. I was not prepared for . . . I should've asked how comfortable everyone was first. I just assumed that . . . I assumed the average level of training . . ."

"You're saying they're a cross cudgel sorry lot of shit," Caitlin helped him out, heaving herself toward Dawn Dog and snatching the arrow from his hand before he lost it. "You can go on and say it, no point in finding a fancier way to say they're all helpless."

"Not *all* helpless," David defended, but he was right. Alfie, for instance, had proven unnaturally canny at slinging arrows, despite his insistence he was as new to it as anyone.

"Of course I'm good," he had scoffed, *"I'm Robin Hood."*

"Ricard's got an eye for it as well," David added, "and Clo."

This was emphasized by a sharp flight and a sturdy *thunk.* Clorinda Rose, lowlife whore that she was, tied up in sashes and belts that squeezed her waist tight for every man to slaver over, was apparently a born archer. She whipped her head around to make eyes at Alfie, letting her goddamned fountain of blond hair splay around her like a fucking cat thrown against a wall.

Of course she'd be good at it, Caitlin cursed to no one, *just one more thing for her to try to have in common with my man.*

Some days Caitlin fantasized about coming across Clorinda in the tunnels all alone, and smashing the girl's skull against a hard wall or strangling her with her own hair. Clorinda Rose had the big sultry eyes and perky little breasts that made men swoon, and Alfie was just as man as anyone. But it wouldn't matter how lithe her hips were if Caitlin chose to break her cock-gobbling jaw off.

She was just Alfie's favorite diversion lately, but this Clorinda was the hundredth Clorinda in a long line of Clorindas who had come before. They flirt and they fuck and they're forgotten about, having never left anything more memorable than an itch between a man's legs. Caitlin had suffered them before, and this one was no different than the rest, no matter how many of her giant empty doe eyes she batted at Alfie. It didn't matter how many times she sucked his cock, because Alfie's heart was Cait's.

Outwardly, Cait made sure to never show any spite at Clorinda for fear of it reeking of jealousy. Cait had long been accustomed to being the ugliest and the heaviest girl in any group—which, for social reasons she would never understand, meant she wasn't allowed to complain about it.

"I'd say the day is a waste," David was saying. "I hope there's more to this plan than hoping one of you is genuinely the best archer in Nottingham."

This was confirmed by a grand slap on his back as Alfie joined them. "Mark my words, one of us here will legitimately win the Sheriff's prize! But there's legitimate . . ." he gave a wink, ". . . and then there's *legitimate.*"

They didn't have to be the best archers in Nottingham, they just needed to be the best ones to finish the tournament. The attendance roster would be public, which gave them seven days to track down their most talented competitors. The next week would be full of "accidental" street brawls resulting in dozens of bruised ribs, twisted draw fingers, and the like. For anyone they missed, there would be plenty of opportunities between competition rounds to whisper gruesome threats into other archers' ears, until the thought of winning was too terrifying to risk. It wasn't a sure thing, but the more Lions in the rosters the better—not just to give themselves better odds, but to put some muscle behind those whispers.

"We were hoping more of us would pass as decent," Cait grumbled. "But then, I also assumed anyone who tries to call himself Robin Hood ought to have a half a knack for this."

This remark she aimed across the glade at Will Scarlet, who had come along for seemingly no reason. He sat, digging holes in the ground with his knives, continuing his career of being utterly useless. At least he'd finally cowed—his need to be combative faded into obedience, which he apparently thought was supposed to be impressive. Theirs was hardly a unique tale. The Red Lions had long grown bigger by absorbing their rivals rather than fighting them. Scarlet's men were just another acquisition, now smoothing out after their bumpy start.

Alfie squinted. "Only one of us needs to win, the rest just need to get in."

"But they'll have to be good *enough* to get in." David chewed at his lip, as if he were afraid to give the bad news. "Contests like these, there's usually some sort of qualifier. They won't just let anyone onto the field, or the thing would last for hours, and be boring as all get out. There'll be a test at the sign-ups to weed out the raff. And quite frankly, we're the facking raff."

"Well," Alfie leaned back, watching with interest the flight of a bird from the nearby trees, "who is in charge of these sign-ups?"

Cait groaned, already hating her life so much more.

"You know I hate talking to him," she explained as calmly as she could.

"But he likes talking to you," Alfie sang, leaning farther backward, as if he were waiting for her to say yes to save him from falling.

"My father," Caitlin explained coldly to David, "is the master-at-arms of the Nottingham Yard."

"Fack me." He whistled. "That sounds useful."

"It's not. Every advantage you're thinking of right now has two disadvantages that come with it. I mostly try to forget that he exists."

David made a face. "Not the most generous of fathers, eh?"

"Oh he's got plenty to give," Caitlin spat back, feeling the old familiar suffocating anger, "as long as you're a young girl who doesn't know how to say no."

She spat at the ground and twisted, hoping to shake the fury off. She could tell by David's reaction that he'd misinterpreted her, but she didn't give shit one. Her father may have never touched her personally, but the same couldn't be said for her childhood friends. The mighty goddamned Simons, they called him. In charge of training boys to become men. How many would still respect him if they knew he had a thing for little girls? By God's cunt, they'd probably like him all the more.

David of Doncaster whispered an apology and wandered off, back to teaching the cubs how to hold a bow without hurting themselves.

She'd lived with her father in the castle as a child, even until womanhood. Then a drunken gord had been dared to flirt his way into her dress, and she'd been young and stupid enough to let him. Her father moved her into the city after that—paid for her housing, her food, wanted to provide her a safe life outside of the castle. Said he didn't trust his own men around her, and he didn't even see the damned irony in that. Nor did he see the insult. In all her life, she'd never had to suffer a man's lustful looks, or unwanted advances. Didn't understand that it hurt when he insisted she was beautiful, since he was the only man who'd ever said as much. Even Alfie could admit it wasn't her body he loved.

Unbeknownst to The Simons of Nottingham, Cait had found her real family in the city—her lion family. Someday, undoubtedly, he'd learn everything about her . . . and no matter how soon or far away that was, every day brought it closer.

If she was lucky, they'd all be caught trying to travel back into the city today, each of them thrown into separate cages, and she'd never have to talk to her father again.

Alfie touched her shoulder.

"Yes, I'll talk to him," she answered. Each word felt like a knife. But of course she would do it. Her father, as blind to how she felt about him as he was to his own indecency, insisted on visiting her every few weeks. She played along, teased information from him they could use, happy to take his coin and spend it on whatever hell the Lions could throw back at the Nottingham Guard. "But you have to wrap up the other side of the Trip to Jerusalem. We need to finalize things with the greenbeard."

"I know," Alfie said, tying his fingers into her hair. "If something goes wrong at the tournament, we need that as a back out."

"We were hoping for a trial run," she scolded him, but he just met her seriousness with raspberried lips. "Zinn's pups have been going every day, but they have a long way to go still. And the greenbeard wants more. We need to make a deal with the dockmaster."

"He won't deal." Alfie clicked his tongue. "And we have nothing else on him."

"Then it's time for a different kind of deal," she said, drawing out her words. "Make sure he knows exactly what's at stake."

Alfie's face was a statue. Breaking windows and bruising ribs was one thing—both were fixable. Even blackmail was a gentlemanly sport, given a victim that'd brought his woes upon himself. But weeks of tailing the impossibly virtuous Gerome Artaud had given them no leverage to use. They'd run out of options, and ideas. If they couldn't get what they needed from the dockmaster by playing nice, then it was time for the opposite. Alfie hated that, she knew. Always preferred clever tricks over violence, but he was a fool to think that both didn't have a time and place.

"We don't do that," he said, and gave her a kiss. A moment later he rejoined the others in a burst of showmanship, donning the grandstanding gangmaster act he was so good at. His show of confidence was all that kept the Lions going at times, most of them unaware how close they all were to ruin.

Clorinda Rose let loose another shaft that found its mark, and she gasped in feigned surprise, putting her hand to her breast and then onto Alfie's chest, purposefully tripping over her own feet to let him support her. Cait had nothing to fear from the harlot, but still she said, "*Just die*," out loud for the fun of it, and damned if it didn't make her feel better.

THIRTY

ARABLE DE BUREL

IT WAS JUST BARELY possible that Arable had died several years ago and was now trapped in some wicked hell, forced to repeat her own mistakes again and again.

Every visitor to Huntingdon Castle was assembling for a welcome dinner in the Elder Hall's main room. It boasted a tall ceiling but a relatively slim width, allowing for one extremely long line of tables that would not have been continent enough if all the invited guests had actually arrived. That was by design— or by the *countess's* design, at least.

"It is a careful line," Lady Magdalena had explained. *"If we appear too wealthy, then our proposal to refuse the king's ransom will read as greed. But if we appear too poor, then the decision would appear to be born from desperation, rather than political acuity. The image we project must be one strong enough to warrant respect, but also humility. We must strike an exact delicate balance of unsustainable comfort."*

Such was the plan, at least. Arable had worked side by side with the countess for two weeks to prepare for the event. They needed to accommodate the guests and their retinues, as well as entertain them, impress them, and feed them . . . just enough. The *delicate balance* might have been perfect, if not for the embarrassingly poor turnout.

Instead of a proper complement from each invited house, there had arrived only a single servant per invitation, or a duo or trio at best. No house demanded more than a single room, and the Elder Hall's modest banquet qualified as a magnificent feast for their paltry number. Two full tables had been removed from either end of the hall and still there were unused seats and a glaringly empty void that could have fit a crowd thrice the size now gathered.

Arable had somehow fallen into a familiar role of a castle servant, though that was not the hell that had come back to haunt her. In many ways, it was comfortable. Her time working for Roger de Lacy in Nottingham Castle had been stable, at least, compared to much of her life in the decade prior. No, her hell was the Lady Margery d'Oily and her husband, Waleran de Beaumont, Earl of Warwick. Margery was the countess's sister, and Arable had effectively been in hiding ever since their arrival.

"She once called me an *insipid little cunt*," she complained of the Lady d'Oily to John Little, whose size was an absolute advantage to hide behind.

"My goodness!" he grunted. "I don't think you're insipid."

He gave her an elbow and a wink, with a tongue in his cheek to hide a smile. They were in the corner of the room, mumbling beneath the hubbub of the growing audience. None of their group would have been invited to this welcoming dinner at all if the countess had not—at the last moment—demanded their attendance to increase the size of the crowd. They had all done their best to bathe and clean up, which is to say they were slightly less dirty than normal.

"There was a time when I thought Lady Margery considered me a friend," Arable continued. "But she was only using me for information, and she turned on me the moment I failed to deliver. I was meant to follow her to Warwick and serve there, had she not been so cruel to me. She's the reason I'm here."

"Well then I aim to thank her for it," John said, with a heavy kindness. "As should you. Would you have really wanted to serve a family as wicked as all that?"

Family.

For the third time in the last hour, Arable's gaze lingered on a particular girl—a servant to the countess's father, the Earl of Hereford. She was somewhat thin and mousey, which reminded Arable a bit of herself, but that was not the comparison that so consistently drew her attention. The servant was obviously pregnant, her swollen belly making a challenge to her duties, and she would often hold her hands to her back for relief.

Arable tried not to think about it.

She had thought the changes in her own body had been a result of their starvation. The weakness, the coldness . . . the absence of her normal cycle. She had simply thought it was the body's way of dealing with their perpetual emergency. But life had settled in Huntingdon, while her body had not. She absently touched her own belly, wondering if it was just her imagination that she felt a bit of roundness there. *It was because she was finally eating again,* she convinced herself. *She was still recovering.*

But still, she counted the months backward. To the last time she had been with William.

No, she pushed it aside, forcing herself back into conversation with John.

"If you want to stay in a bed tonight," she said, "let me know. We cleaned out every room in the Elder Hall and the Heart Tower, and barely a quarter of them are being used. I could sneak you into one where no one will think twice on it. You deserve it."

John Little's lips turned into a straight line. "I think my *sneaking* days are over. We had one last chance at it with Lord de Senlis, which was ever shy of useful." But Arable sensed a droll disappointment in his attitude of late. Planning parties was a comparably pale task to their adventures in the autumn, and he probably felt as if he was being domesticated. There was a dangerous sense of retirement to it all.

"I'm having trouble keeping track of what we are," she said absently. "Am I a thief? A refugee? A servant?"

A mother?

"I don't see a need to define it." John's face warmed. "You're Arable, and I'm tired."

She smiled. "Then sleep in a bed tonight, tired," she urged him. The dwellings they had built by the Cook's Backwater still had a great amount of work to be done before they could be called a home.

"Naw," he rolled his head, "no need. 'Sides, last thing I want to do is get Marion in any trouble."

Arable nearly scoffed, but hid it. *Wouldn't want that, would we?*

Perhaps she had spent too much time with the countess in the last few weeks, but her opinion of Marion had only grown worse in their time in Huntingdon. Most of the group, like John, still saw Marion as some sort of savior who had plucked them out of the forest and found them a new life. But it was Lord Robert who had done this, and he alone took all the consequences of that decision. Marion, as usual, took no risks on their behalf. Lord Robert and the countess absorbed enormous responsibility by housing them openly, but never expected to be thanked for it as Marion did.

They stood for a bit in silence, and Arable found herself actively looking for the pregnant servant. *Busy,* she needed to keep herself busy. Spying a glimpse of the countess, Arable excused herself to see if there were any tasks that needed tending.

Lady Magdalena lingered at the edge of the foyer, speaking with her father. Henry de Bohun was an old man, though not a withered one. There were yellow spots in his face and the small amount of hair he had was long past silver and gone to white, but his eyes were sharp and his jowls took quicker to a smile than a scowl.

Magdalena granted a curt nod to Arable, but was midconversation. "I thought more would come," she said sadly.

"Would that you were right," the earl answered. "I think perhaps it was the messenger, not the message."

The countess was slightly taken aback. "You mean to say this is my fault?"

"Only insomuch that you were born a woman. Which I suppose is my blame, or your mother's, but not yours. You are lucky to have Robert, who sees you as an equal, but you forget yourself outside of these walls. To the world, you are an outspoken wife with dangerous ideas. I wish you had spoken to me first, that I might have sent these invitations myself."

"It shouldn't matter that I'm a woman," she scoffed.

"I agree," he answered, his voice catching. "But that is a great deal further down on our list of things we hope to improve of this world."

Lady Magdalena composed a smile and gestured for Arable to join them. "Father, this is Arable, one of our guests from the Sherwood. She has proven herself in character and fortitude. If you still wish to get a sense of them as a people, you should look no further than her."

"Ah, yes." Henry's eyes squinted to understand what an Arable was. "A pleasure. I would very much like to speak with you, though not tonight. I'm curious as to the conditions you've been enduring."

Arable was barely sure how to react. "Oh?"

"I am fortunate to have been successful in this life," the Earl of Hereford continued. "At the expense of an unfortunate detachment. It is difficult to improve the quality of the commonfolk if I am unfamiliar with their details, you can understand?"

Arable gave a curtsy, hiding her surprise. She had rarely heard anyone of the earl's prestige give such consideration before. "I'd be happy to speak with you."

"I'm grateful for it. There ought to be enough time. I should think this council may be over before it has begun. Shall we?"

FOR THE THOUSANDTH TIME, Arable felt like an impostor in her own skin. But this particular disguise got to eat at the table. There was quail and duck with sliced parsnips, and she was benefitting far more from the countess's *delicate balance* than the others were suffering. They sat at the farthest end of the long feast, helping to fill out a visual lie, thankfully far from the only truly notable guests at the other end.

"My third carriage needs a new silver axle," John Little joked, with affected snobbery. "I shall have my manservant Euphestio attend to it at once!"

"I'm sorry, I can't hear you," Tuck added, "I have too much gold in my ears!"

Admittedly, he didn't have a lot of practice at humor.

The Delaney brothers snickered and joined in, eating their food in increasingly "fancy" ways, pattering their lips together and hum-humming in delight.

"Where's Charley?" John asked after choking down a laugh. "He would enjoy this!"

"He was here for a second," Nick answered, "then left."

"Huh." John's eyes widened. "He ought to eat."

Arable swallowed a bite of duck. "It's probably me."

"Hm?"

"The boy's never said two words to me, nor I to him," she explained. "I think he belongs to those of the mind that I'm to blame for all our woes. Avoids me at all costs."

"Charley?" Peetey balked. "Surely that's your imagination."

"It is not." Though both of them had kept to themselves outside the rest of the group, Arable had noticed that the frogman would always leave any circle upon her approach. "And he wasn't the only one."

"That's yesterday's problems," John said, making a point of it with his fork. "Yester*life*. I'll have a word with him on it."

"Please don't. I understand it. We were on the run," she said, almost unable to recall the misery. Perhaps they had all just shut off, locked themselves away to wait for an inevitable death. "Was no point in making friends that you were like to lose."

"Well here's to changing that," Nick Delaney said, raising a goblet of wine. His eyes were on her, and his small smile seemed to be just for her as well. She suddenly blushed, wondering what other friendships she had missed out upon.

Nick Delaney was a man handsome beyond measure, and she could not recall the last time she'd been comfortable being looked upon without feeling anything but fear.

She braved a smile back for him, and his eyes danced. "Cheers."

They ate as if they'd never eaten before, and for a short time she was almost able to forget the many terrible troubles that had brought them here. The hardest of their work was over, and though Arable feared for whatever the fallout of Lady Magdalena's failed council might be, she was comfortable in knowing that—for once—the spotlight of immediate events was on people other than themselves.

As she licked her fingers clean, the phrase *eating for two* floated about her skull and refused to die, which soured her enjoyment of the meal a good deal.

Shortly afterward, a bell caught all their attention. Its bearer stood upon the raised dais of the head table, where Lord Robert and Magdalena had gathered with a small handful of the castle's notables. They calmly awaited order in the room, that they may address their guests. Lord Robert dressed somewhat less grandly than Arable would have expected, well shyer even than the *delicate balance*. This meal was meant to be simply one of introduction rather than policy—that unpleasantness would wait for tomorrow, after a night's solid rest. Arable had half a mind to stay in bed the whole day.

"Welcome, all!" Lord Robert announced, after his castellan had introduced him. His voice bloomed to fill every dark corner of the tall chamber. "I am most happy to share my castle with each of you, and hope you will call it home while you are here. We are humbled to have so many of you tonight. I never hoped to have the entirety of England beneath my roof!"

He went on, listing every visitor's banners by name, excluding the obviousness of each liegelord's absence.

"How's it going?" came a whisper nearby, and Arable turned to see that Marion had joined them, squeezing into the bench beside John Little. Arable buried her attention in her plate.

"As well as possible," John whispered back. "Where have you been?"

"Hiding!" she replied. "Robert had me greeting every guest this afternoon, and it's altogether too much for me! I've only come to sneak a plate of food, then it's back to my cave, thank you very much."

John Little suppressed a laugh, for fear of distracting from the earl's announcements. "I'd say you're fine. Robert is very good at keeping things lively. By the way he speaks, you'd think this was a spectacular success."

"Who is to say it isn't?" Arable asked, giving Marion a cold stare. "After all, this turnout is better than a regiment of soldiers led by the Chancellor, come to arrest us all."

Marion didn't respond to that, but instead just eyed her. "You look healthy," she said, as Lord Robert droned on with the requisite introductions. "Huntingdon has done you well, I'd say."

Her fake smile said more. *You ought to thank me,* it boasted.

Arable almost rose to it, but again their attention was arrested by the far end of the room.

"—and to the *Lady Marion Fitzwalter*," the name rang out clearly. Lord Robert and Lady Magdalena held their goblets high in praise as the entirety of the room craned their heads to the table where Marion suddenly stood upright, startled and alert.

Even from this distance, Arable recognized the smug smile that hid behind the countess's politesse. She'd seen it in Lady d'Oily before, and it apparently ran in the family. It was the satisfaction of someone springing a trap.

Lady Magdalena continued, once the murmur of surprise rippled back her way. Her bright voice held no tint of derision. "Many of you have already met Lady Marion upon your arrival today, but she was gracious enough to allow me to welcome you to our dinner this evening. My husband and I are, after all, merely her hosts for this council."

Arable's eyes widened, while Marion was barely able to hide a gasp. *Merely her hosts . . .*

"We owe her a heavy debt of gratitude for her assistance in the last few months, but I hope we can consider that debt paid by availing our walls for this event of hers."

Arable could do nothing but watch, stunned. They were throwing all of it, every last burden of responsibility for this misguided council, squarely on Marion's shoulders.

"I deeply apologize to any of you who might be alarmed by her presence. I meant no deception in omitting her ownership of this council before now, although I think you can agree that fewer of you might have attended if you heard her name!" There were a few uncomfortable chuckles at the countess's joke. "As always I would prefer to be straightforward with you all, but you know what they say about beggars and choosers. And for those who may wrinkle an eyebrow at her, you should know that Lady Marion has promised me she will refrain from killing any more Sheriffs for the duration of this council."

Another round of awkward laughter came here, enjoyed in particular by the little muskrat man from Rutland who had come in the stead of Sheriff William d'Albini.

Magdalena angled her body sharply, like a predator before a pounce. "You all may depend on the hospitality of our house for the remainder of the event, but Lady Marion alone can answer in regard to the council itself. And while we will not begin those discussions until tomorrow, I am certain she will be happy to answer any of your questions, starting immediately."

The Countess of Huntingdon raised her glass across the expanse of the dining hall, which had now officially become a battlefield. "*Cheers.*"

The room erupted.

PART IV

CARTA
PARVUM

THIRTY-ONE

MARION FITZWALTER

"I CANNOT APOLOGIZE ENOUGH," Lord Robert said, so much later that Marion could scarce believe it was not yet dawn. He brought a cold plate of roasted chicken to her room, arriving only minutes after she had finally retired herself. It wasn't until she smelled the food that she even realized she'd never eaten, and took some small solace in the knowledge that Robert had kept track of her.

The evening had bled into night, the night bled into midnight and later, with Marion pulled in every direction. The countess had thrown all the onus of this ill-advised council onto Marion, and every soul in the castle wanted her attention first. Her grandfather was aghast at the announcement and threatened to disappear early, for fear of being identified as an accomplice to what he perceived as Marion's inept political hackery. There was no way for her to explain how Countess Magdalena had ambushed her, nor was there any time. She was beset by all manner of the castle waitstaff as well, as the countess had disavowed even organizational duties to her. There were a hundred details to arrange that Marion couldn't possibly care about, for an event she had never wanted to even exist.

The only two people she wanted to speak with—or, more accurately, *scream at*—were Lord Robert and Lady Magdalena, both of whom had become conspicuously indisposed the moment after the announcement was made.

Until now, when Lord Robert came and apologized. His eyes were strained, every muscle in his face tense, as if his very life depended on her forgiveness. "I fought against it, I promise you, but mine was the only voice against. They would not let me so much as warn you."

Marion did not have the energy to do anything but stare at him. "Henry de Bohun."

Robert's lips pursed in confirmation.

She had guessed as much. The great Earl of Hereford, and father to Lady Magdalena. He was by far the most important man who had actually answered the invitation, bringing with him his other two daughters and their husbands— the Earls of Warwick and Oxford. Marion had no difficulty imagining the heated family argument that must have taken place upon their arrival, chastising Magdalena's negligence. The answer to their dilemma was so obvious Marion couldn't believe she'd been blindsided by it. By shifting the blame of the council onto Marion and her already infamous rebelliousness, they maintained their protection from the council's fallout while still exerting their control over its purpose.

And Marion was sworn to continue playing the puppet.

"You've a wretched family," she accused Lord Robert.

"They're not *my* family." He threw his hands up in a polite surrender. "They're Maggie's. But yes, sometimes, *wretched* isn't inaccurate."

He did not elaborate, so she stared at him until he realized he should.

"Lord Henry made it clear that no one in his family could be tied to this. I thought Maggie would have fought him on that, she's so hard-willed at times, but she was more than happy to abandon her own plan. Part of me wonders if she expected it to fall this way."

"I have no doubt," Marion answered, because of course she had. It was why Marion had been asked to greet the guests. If the invitations had garnered greater attendance, no doubt Lady Magdalena would have gladly welcomed each one personally. "She admitted that she penned those invitations weeks ago. Why do you think she waited to send them until I was here? She knew I'd make an easy scapegoat in case her plan faltered, which it did."

"It's not so bad as all that, though, is it?" His neck twisted, as if he might look further down her eyes into her very brain. "This council, isn't it something you want, too? The Chancellor and his corruption, that's why you were out there, doing what you do."

It was Marion's favorite thing—*her very favorite*—when men explained her own motives to her.

"You may very well be the best person to rally this cause," he continued. "And it doesn't put any additional danger on you. In the eyes of many, you're already an assassin and a traitor, aren't you? It can't exactly get *worse*."

She hated that she laughed at that, but he was right. And she didn't have the energy to argue. His intentions seemed genuine, if poorly aimed. Hopefully it was true that he hadn't known his wife's plan beforehand. "Thank you for coming, I do appreciate it."

Robert stood and straightened himself, but his face slacked. "I was afraid you'd be angry with me. If I could have sent you a warning, I would have. Lord Henry is a wise man, but holy God is he stubborn. Maggie has clearly learned it from the very best."

He sighed softly, as a moment of fatigue washed over him. For a man who always seemed poised and performing, it was a relief to see that he too bore the burden of human frailty.

"Tomorrow will be difficult, to say the very least." He fidgeted. "You should know that they won't participate—any of them. Lord Henry, Maggie, Warwick, Oxford—they've all decided to watch and listen but not contribute. I am . . . obligated to do the same. It's all on you, Marion. But anything I can do to help . . . you know, behind the scenes . . . you know I'm there for you."

"You could beat them to a pulp," she suggested, only barely joking.

"Oh." He grimaced. "I just washed my hands."

She stared at him. "What?"

"I can't beat them to a pulp, because I just washed my hands. I'd get blood on them. And have to wash them again." He blinked. "Don't make me explain it again."

"You know you're not very funny, don't you?" she asked.

"I don't, actually." He grinned. "If I knew that, I'd probably stop trying at it. Anyways, I'll leave you to eat."

"No, stay," she said before meaning it, her fingers reaching out to the empty air between them. It brought a tear to her eye to realize how much she needed a bit of basic connection with another human being. "If only for a bit. I have no idea how to handle this thing tomorrow. I am desperate for advice."

"Now *that*," he smiled, pointing a finger and a smirk at her, "I don't believe. In all the time I have known you, I've never once seen you helpless."

A gasp pushed through her, a tear escaped to roll down her cheek. "Are you making fun of me? I was the very *definition* of helpless. Why do you think I came here? Why did I bring my people to you, starving and dying? We had no-where to go, I had nowhere to take them, I had failed them in every way."

"You led them here," he said, his voice broken with admiration. He caught her eye with such sincerity that she could not look away, while a lump caught tight in her throat. "You saved them, every one of them. You convinced me to bring in a group of outlaws during already difficult times—and for the life of me, I'm still not sure how you did that. You are . . . a *bear*, Marion Fitzwalter. You are ferocious and unrelenting, you find possibilities where others would find surrender. You're the type of born leader that I constantly only pretend at. People are drawn to you, they're drawn to help you, to believe in you. If you ask me, you're the *only* person to lead this council tomorrow. If Maggie were to lead it, it'd be a prickly business, or her father . . . ? He'd bore them to mass suicide. You can light them afire, Marion, you're good at that. You don't need my help."

The compliments deflected away, she had no use for them. "I *do* need your help," she replied, pained that he couldn't see that. "Now, as I did then. I needed you to lift me up."

"But not because I reached down for you from on high." He smiled wide. "All I did was let you step on my back. You're above me, Marion, you always will be. Just speak from your heart tomorrow, and see how they fall in line."

It could have been the late hour, or the tireless day, or the merciless winter, but Marion's heart clenched and she let herself cry. It almost shamed her to re-alize how much she'd needed to hear something like that.

"You're sweet," she said once she was able, sniffing. "Right until the point where you called me a bear."

He laughed. "You didn't like that?"

"Don't ever call a woman a bear, there's literally no woman alive who would appreciate that."

"Bears are strong!"

"Bears are huge and hairy," she exclaimed, wiping her face. "I don't know how on earth you've managed to keep a wife."

His hand, gentle but certain, found her shoulder. She startled at it and he retracted, but he was only saying a goodbye. He chuckled and gave a mocking apology, and left Marion to her thoughts.

She could only hope he was right, that she might find the words to turn the next day into a success. She had to pivot away from the mindset of a hostage, she knew that. It was blinding her, this feeling of being cornered. If she took on this task as a responsibility rather than a passion, she would fail. If she did little more than help Lady Magdalena save face, then she would deserve this subservient position she had found herself in.

But if she met this challenge fully—as a lionheart—she might just flip the tables on the countess entirely.

THIRTY-TWO

CAITLIN FITZSIMON

NOTTINGHAM CASTLE

"FIND THE SIMONS." CAIT stared at the gord's teeth. "Let him know his daughter has come to see him."

The greasy watchman rolled his eyes into the back of his head, where there was plenty of room. It was a look that said *look who thinks she gives the orders here,* and Caitlin hated with every inch of her soul that he was right. She had made a demand instead of a request, forgetting to play the sad helpless daughter.

The walls of Nottingham Castle in the morning sun were the golden color of piss, and the three scruffy Guardsmen that manned its pedestrian gate had attitudes to match. Still, one of them swallowed his pride and shuffled within to go find her father, while the other two snickered from a distance.

"We'll have to open the main," one muttered to the other, gesturing to the wide carriage gates to the right. "This one won't be big enough."

Caitlin pretended not to hear.

"Get off it," the other grumbled back, making a particularly guilty eye contact with her. "That's The Simons's daughter."

"Wonder who the mother was?" the first giggled under his breath. "A fuckin' . . . a fuckin' horse, or . . . a fuckin', a fuckin' pig? I dunno, what's a big fat animal?"

Caitlin ground her fingertips into the palms of her hands. This fannybaws couldn't even make a joke right.

"My mum's dead," she said loudly, affecting what she imagined was her saddest, poutiest face. "An' I can hear you."

"Oh get off it," the first one snapped at her. "I didn't mean nothing. Fuckin' crying at the gate now."

The other caught her eye again and mouthed *sorry,* but as soon as he turned away his chest shook in stifled laughter.

They motioned for her to pass through, thinking it was a favor. She glanced upward at the carved stone castle crest over the entrance, which depicted two stags standing on their hind legs, fighting over whose cock was bigger. The passage through the gatehouse was nestled between two bulging, round towers that housed small rooms, and she had heard every euphemism there was for the entrance. Whether the two towers were breasts or thighs, every goddamned gord found some way to turn a simple gate into something carnal.

Just stepping back inside the castle was enough to remind her of every small freedom the Red Lions afforded her that was unthinkable within these walls.

"You'll have to wait here," the more-terrible Guardsman mumbled. "Can't let you into the castle proper without accumpament."

"*Accompaniment,*" the other corrected him.

"Without *company,*" the first balked. "I know what I meant."

If that exchange had taken place amongst her cubs, she would have smacked them both upside the head. Here, she had to thank them. Here, an idiot was considered the top of the barrel. She idled in a circle, taking in the long-familiar sights of the inside of the walls. The great lower bailey wrapped around nearly half of Castle Rock, its rolling terrain currently filled with tents and cookpots, wares and craftsmen—the same makings of any village, excepting the curtain wall that kept out the danger of a real world. A path to the left would eventually ramp up to a narrow bridge that reached the barbican to the middle bailey, where her father would be busy training the next generation of entitled rapists and murderers.

Today, this section of the lower bailey was organizing into a market, though poorly attended. These vendors must have won some favor to set up here. Even if they lost money for a week waiting for the day of the contest, they'd make it all back and more in one afternoon. Some would sell food and drink, others were amateur craftsmen making flags and hats in a dozen colors and combinations to support the various competitors. Beyond, Caitlin could spy the makings of the wooden audience stalls being built off to the north, the din of hammers and saws providing a steady footprint under the heckling of the marketmen. One pocky woman pushed close, loudly claiming that Caitlin could probably eat her entire supply of dates in a single sitting. Caitlin huffed and moved away, hating how much effort it took to bear the hill.

The archery field was built at the end of the lower bailey, where the long curve of the outer curtain wall took a straight turn inward to meet the higher walls of the middle bailey above. At the far side of the range were ten huge stuffed straw targets, already lined in a row. Any rogue arrows would crash against the stone, and if any sailed high they would leave the castle grounds entirely and fly off the backside. Down below was the French Ward, which could only be improved by a few falling arrows.

But all Cait really saw was the danger. If anything went afoul—*anything*—there would be no escape from the archery contest. Battlements surrounded them on three sides, with towers regularly spaced within them. There was only one exit, which was the main gate she'd just entered. The moment Alfie entered these grounds, there was no guarantee he'd get out again.

Mixed with those fears were memories. She'd been in this bailey a thousand times as a girl. When she might have been daft enough to call this place home. The occupants of the lower bailey always adapted to the castle's needs, and she'd learned a new skill with each transformation. She'd sewn hems for tailors when a market like this one was in tilt, but she'd also learned to shoe a horse, or dig a posthole, or lie her way through a game of blind man's hazard. The strangers to the castle were more valuable in her upbringing than her father ever was.

And damned it all if that didn't make the memories all the more bitter now. Because like or not, there was one opportunity she had that Alfie never would. If everything went sideways in the tournament and the gords started arresting them . . . Caitlin's beast of a father could protect her.

That fact scratched at her soul. Something fouler than death, there, something fouler.

When her father found her, he was visibly angry. He apparently thought she must be in danger to call on him at the castle, and so he carried some large piece of firewood as a club to kill whatever her troubles were. As if some pervert had followed her and was still nearby, patiently waiting to be cudgeled to death by The Simons.

As if even some pervert would ever think she was worth his time.

Once he calmed down, they exchanged pleasantries, such as one would call them. But Cait couldn't even remember what she said a moment after the words were spoken. She was somebody else, playing the role of a daughter, and she thanked God that none of her cubs would witness her dealing in such heavy bullshit.

"I just worried at you, Cay," he said, after she gave him grief for the firewood. "I don't know the last time you came to see me."

Never, was the answer, though she didn't say it. "I can't stay long, it's why I came. But nothing to worry about none, I just had some questions for you."

"Questions?" He curled a lip into a smile. "Can't promise I'll be good at them. How about clubbing someone? I'm better at that."

If he thought a club could save her from her troubles, he would best start by smashing his head upon it.

"Stop it." She feigned embarrassment, knowing he'd seize the chance to laugh and pose a bit. *Had that ever worked?* Was there ever a time when she was young enough to be impressed by his braggartry? Probably when she was four or five, earlier than she could remember, she was like any little girl who laughed and smiled at her father's antics. She hated that girl, and wished she could go back and save her.

Some men thought that being the biggest and strongest was what made them men. Others like Will Scarlet thought they were made manlier by the amount of spit and spite they could throw at the world. But someone with grace and tact like Alfred Fawkes knew the truth—that anyone who measures themselves in terms of *how much man they are* can never be more than half a person. Man is, after all, only half the world.

"I have questions about the archery contest," she said at last, enjoying the look of disappointment that crawled over his face. "About how to sign up for it?"

"The St. Valentine's tournament? You want to be in the contest?" He nearly burst in laughter. "Since when do you know how to throw an arrow?"

She had to bite her tongue. As if he knew the first shit about what she was capable of. But instead she answered meekly, "Not just for me, for some friends, too."

"Oh, I don't think you should want it." He turned serious. "It'll be dangerous, that. I know the prize is something, ain't it, but you'd be better off telling your friends to bandy wide. Ought to make for a good show at least, but you wouldn't want to be on the field."

"Why is that?" she asked with every drop of dumb she had.

"Well it's who we're expecting, see." He twisted his head about to both sides, the universal symbol for needing secrecy. "You've probably heard about this gangman, Robin Hood, and his games of terror?"

"I've heard the name." Caitlin scratched at her head. *I've fucked him, too.* "He's pretty bad, then?"

"The worst." Her father spat at the ground. Alfie would eat up every word when she had the chance to tell him later. "Thief and a murderer, he was behind the deaths of both Sheriffs last fall. Someone else is usin' that name now, stealing and killing whomsoever he please."

That word was a splash of cold water. "*Killing,* you say?"

"A couple of nobles, the Lord and Lady of Brayden, or something, a month perhaps back. Raped and murdered them both, sick fuck."

Cait's mind reeled with the information.

It had to be Will Scarlet.

Fucking Scarlet.

"You should watch with me!" Her father grabbed her shoulder in excitement. She recoiled from his touch by instinct. "Cay, if you want to watch the contest, you ought to do so from safety, with me. We'll be *there.*" He pointed to one of the battlement walls above, where canopies had already been constructed for additional viewing. "Just like when you were a girl, you used to watch the boys training in the yard, you remember?"

She didn't. It roiled her stomach to even think of being a young girl around her father. To think of his massive paws holding her close to him, against the sweat of him.

"I'd rather be on the field," she pouted. "I know I won't win, I just want to feel what it's like. It may not sound interesting to you, but I'd never have a chance to do something like this in a thousand years, not without your help."

"I'd rather you stay out of it," he said, a bit more firmly. "As I said, we expect there to be a dangerous element down there with you."

"You don't think you can protect me?" she asked, knowing that would be as effective as kicking him in the groin. "With every Guardsman around, and you too? Just for me to shoot a couple of arrows, and get a little applause?"

He made a face. It was hard to tell what the face meant, since every one of his faces was uglier than the last. She wondered which face he made when he pawed at the servant girls.

Eventually he relented. "You'll need a range necklace." He shook his finger at the far end of the field. "We'll be giving them out all week. Just have your friends show up, and if they can hit two out of three targets we take their name and give them a necklace that lets them in. Anybody with a bit o'training can do it."

That was probably true, but it wouldn't be good enough. Cait could hit a target at a short distance, but not all of them could. And they couldn't just steal range necklaces or make forgeries, on account of the names of the participants being written down as well.

"There's the part, then, wherein I was hoping you could help," she said, as softly as whores like Clorinda spoke when trying to woo someone. "I don't think my friends will be good enough to earn a necklace on their own. They don't stand a chance, either, but it would mean the world to them just to have the opportunity. They've never even been inside the castle walls, you know. I know it's a big favor, but . . . well . . ." she fought back the bile of forcing this last bit, ". . . we don't see each other very much. And we don't have all that much in common, either. Maybe this would help?"

The tangled red pubic hair of her father's face split wide to show his yellow teeth, the perverse result of him smiling. "I'll need their names. How many friends, then? Two? Three?"

Caitlin shot for the moon.

THIRTY-THREE

MARION FITZWALTER

HUNTINGDON CASTLE

LADY MARION FITZWALTER HATED *exactly two of those three words.*

Growing up in a family of moderate prestige, there was often someone hovering over her and her sister, reinforcing their manners. To keep their backs straight and their lips pursed. To bow their heads slightly when responding to an elder. To speak distinctly, succinctly, and only when asked.

To be better than a common maid—to be a lady.

"It's true that my name is Lady Marion Fitzwalter, though I suspect many of you have heard that name coupled with another. *Outlaw.* Now, I have yet to be arrested for anything, and not so long ago I was nearly married to a Sheriff, so I would argue that I still have some work to do to truly earn that title. But still, titles have a certain persistence, don't they? They tie a pretty bow around a thing, let us decide everything we wish about it, rather than see it for what it is. Titles are comfortable. And *outlaw*, I admit it, is an alluring one."

The reception hall at the base of the Heart Tower had been reorganized such that the tables bearing her audience formed a single unending line, folded into a horseshoe. Marion stood in its center. The middle section alone had an elevated second row, whereupon sat the Earl of Hereford and his extended family. Those on the floor level were the impostors, the forty or so assistants who had come in lieu of their invited masters.

Come to report back that which Marion had prepared all night to say.

"Well if I have earned this title, then I wear it proudly. For what I have accomplished as an outlaw, as a *thief,* as a *rebel*—whatever name you may have heard thrown my way—may surprise you. Peace. Security. Tolerance. Perhaps not the adventurous words you might normally associate with criminals, but that is a sobering reflection of the laws we break. Laws that do more to turn good men into criminals than they do to protect them. Laws that threaten our ability to care for ourselves, and our families, and anyone who depends on us. Laws . . . that are not even laws. If there is any one thing I hope we can decide on today, it is this very distinction."

While young Marion and Vivian were taught to exude grace, their male cousins learned how to exude authority, how to command. The more Marion was taught to fit into society, the more she realized she could also master the same things the boys were taught. It required little else than taking everything involved in becoming a lady, and doing its exact opposite.

"In the last year, we have been subjected to an unbelievable strain—first to pay for King Richard's departure, and now to pay for his return. Make no mistake, I love Richard. He is my kin. If he were not, I doubt very much you would be listening to me at all right now, or if you were it would be from the audience of my gallows. Much of England's struggles would be better if he were returned to us, and so I understand the desire to pay this ransom. Richard is a good man, and a good king, and we do him honor to wish him back.

"But we also honor him by tending to England's needs in his absence, by helping our country thrive. And this ransom . . . this ransom cripples us. By accepting it, we do the nation irreversible harm. Thus we are bound to break our honor to Richard one way or another, whether we like to or not. It is an impossible and piteous position, but given that we must forsake him, we are lucky in that we get to choose the manner in which we do so. We can choose to either abandon his body or to abandon his kingdom. As I said, Richard is a good man, and a good king. Ask yourself which of these options a good king would have us do."

There was nothing terribly creative about her rebelliousness as a child. Every noble had that one daughter who hated to practice etiquette, tomboys who preferred running with the boys over sewing with the ladies. But that was not quite Marion's path. She did not hate learning to become a lady at all, she simply hated that she was not simultaneously learning how to become everything else. Being a lady had its absolute advantages, as does a hammer. But one cannot become a carpenter by only mastering a single tool.

"I wish I could say I would give anything to have King Richard back with us, but we've tried that, and it doesn't work. Austria has captured him. Austria has done us profound wrong, demands unpayable sums, and somehow we roll over like a dog and take it. I don't know how any of you are even sitting, it makes me so angry my blood turns, it scratches at my mind that we would even consider paying them for hurting us. Our king is captured, and it is a tragedy! But England has borne tragedy before. We have weathered worse, we will weather worse again.

"But do not be tricked by Austria's offer to think that this tragedy is ahead of us, and that we might still somehow avoid it. No. It has already come upon us. For anyone here who has ever lost someone—a child, a parent, a friend—you know that the worst pain comes from refusing to move on. Believing that you could have done more. Destroying yourself with grief, with regret. This is what we do in paying the Austrian ransom. It is a higher sum than we can ever raise, and in trying to do so we starve ourselves. We sell the very land beneath our feet, we cripple the next generation of proud English men and women."

What she hated about the word Lady *was that it was restrictive, as if that were all she was, all she could be. Yes, she embraced it when she needed to, when she wanted to, when she chose to. Being a* Lady *was a weapon to flourish, not an anchor as the tomboys thought. It opened the door, where she could then reveal her other titles. Her other weapons.*

"And for what? Do we actually think that Austria, who has shown the color of their character by capturing our King and crusading army, will *return* him to us? Should we trust in a nation that has already defiled us so completely? Are we fools enough to give them exactly what they ask? The nobleman who gives in to the demands of a thief only invites bolder demands from bolder thieves. Trust me, I've known a few thieves in my time. Anyone with a shred of wisdom knows it is folly to pay Richard's ransom. We're not here to argue this, it is simply too true to be debatable."

Fitzwalter, too, she hated. What did it matter that she was her father's daughter? What did that describe about her character that was so important for a stranger to know upon first meeting her? What qualities of her father were assumed to be passed down to her that made it critical for half of her name to be his, rather than her own?

"What brings us here is the question of whether we are bound to follow Chancellor Longchamp's demands to pay the ransom. If a king makes a terrible choice, yes, it is our duty to obey. Call it our English privilege. But what of William Longchamp, who would lead us to our own deaths? William Longchamp is not king. Is it our duty to obey his command and let ourselves suffer? William Longchamp *is not king.* It is well known that he purchased his position with coin, not experience. His contributions to Richard's war chest were his only qualifications. *William Longchamp is not king.* His power is a measure of his pockets, not his prestige. His orders reflect his own desire to stay in power, and not what is best for our country. Was anyone here surprised when he chose to pay the ransom? By paying it, he prolongs his tenure as Chancellor. The longer it takes to raise the capital, the longer he holds his grip onto power. If he bankrupts the nation and successfully brings Richard back alive, he will be in royal favor for the rest of his life. Is his comfort worth starving your subjects? Is this worth your wealth and resources? For Longchamp to keep that which he has never deserved? He knows he will be replaced the moment anyone else wears England's crown, and rightfully so. By keeping him there, we have become his lackeys."

No, of the three words in Lady Marion Fitzwalter, *only one of them told her story. Only one word contained all the information someone needed to know about her. One word unique enough to contain her victories and failures, her moments both public and private, the maze of her experience turned upright that it might be considered and admired for both its complexity and simplicity.*

"Look, then, at what he has done, this William Longchamp who is not king. Look at his demands, at the things we might otherwise call laws, if we did not know better. Look at the punishments he imposes for refusing the ransom. Requisition of land. Deposition of power. These are things a king might claim, but William Longchamp is no king. These are not the Chancellor's to demand. Those who refuse his payments have lost their seats, have had their castles taken from them. Imprisoned. This is not justice, no one can even pretend as much. These punishments have not been indiscriminate—they occur only to his political rivals. He knows the ransom is unpayable, but he uses it to replace prominent men with his own, to sow his seed of corruption into the very framework of England's power. And *we are letting him*. And every day that we do not resist, his influence grows."

Marion. Just Marion.

Know my name, and you know who I am.

"This is not a political question, it is moral imperative. Every day that we sit back and hope it will get better, we are actively helping him. You've essentially declared yourself his allies, because even your neutrality helps him. We have come to the point where inaction is more dangerous than action, where complacency is equivalent to death. All of you, every one of you, is currently on the Chancellor's side by virtue of your silence. In helping him, you help Austria—for what is Chancellor Longchamp if not an extension of Austria's arrogance? I had invited Englishmen to join me here, I hope I have not received Austrians instead. If you don't like being called an Austrian, then you're in the right place.

"The solution is self-evident. In want of Richard, the crown must pass to its next rightful heir. We are here to support John, son of Henry, brother to Richard, and next in line to England's crown. It is his hand that should be guiding us through these dark times, it is his leadership we should seek rather than kneel and capitulate to the demands of Austria. If Austria had murdered Richard, we would be at war with them, with John leading our armies. Instead Richard is merely imprisoned, and so we *reward* Austria for doing it? No.

"No, Richard isn't England. *England* is England. If they think they capture all of England by capturing one man, that is their misjudgment to make. England endures no matter who you take from us. By letting ourselves be crippled by Richard's absence, we admit that we are nothing without him. Tell me, are you nothing without Richard? Or are you . . . endlessly, inconsolably, inestimably, and unforgivingly . . . still England?

"We can bow to foreigners, or we can bow to our prince. We can give in to the demands of those who wish to enslave us, or we can look to the future. We can destroy England, or we can rebuild it. I know where I stand. Who stands with me?"

It was her absolute best. In her head, in her rehearsal, it had stirred them to riot.

Instead, nobody stood.

Every member of her audience, who had stared blankly at her through every word, now looked down into their hands, or nodded absently, or blinked. Only Henry de Bohun met her eyes, a stern look that spoke to his disapproval.

Marion, the impostor.

Marion, the helpless.

Maid Marion.

THIRTY-FOUR

ARABLE DE BUREL

HUNTINGDON CASTLE

A YEAR EARLIER, ARABLE had been washing laundry in Nottingham Castle when her friend Gunny approached, with a grin and a torn piece of parchment. On it was a hastily drawn sketch of a bird's head, and Arable had no idea what was so exciting about it. Gunny asked her several times to describe the picture, as if she were a blind old woman who needed help reading, and Arable explained over and over that it was a boring old bird and that they needed to return to their work.

Eventually Gunny pointed at the picture and said it was a hare. Arable thought she was insane, until a moment later her perception shifted, and the drawing transformed into something it wasn't. The beak became ears, the head snapped around, and Arable suddenly had difficulty seeing the bird that was so obviously there a second ago.

For the past few months, as far as Arable was concerned, Lady Marion Fitzwalter had been a bird. A bitter, vindictive little bird whose arrogance would get them all killed.

And now she was a hare.

"I am eager for your thoughts," Marion continued, as if the silence that followed her speech had not been devastating. Her words had moved Arable to tears, she was still wiping them from her face. But apparently nobody else in the entire room could be bothered to so much as look up from the table. "This council is met to discuss *all* our ideas, not just to listen to mine."

There were no ideas. The same faces, empty, waited for Marion to either continue speaking or dismiss them with seemingly no preference. There were neither approving nods nor angry head shakes. No laughter, no grumbling. Arable had watched it all from the side of the room where she stood with the other servant girls, ready to pour from her decanter of wine should any of the attendants be brave enough to drink.

"I'm afraid this will be a very boring day if no one else has anything to contribute." Marion tried to laugh, earning herself absolutely nothing. Arable saw in her now the cunning politician rather than the shrew.

Marion picked a face, seemingly at random. "Norfolk, you are all too familiar with the danger that faces us. Roger Bigod struggled for years to claim his rights as earl of your county, after King Henry refused to confirm his earldom for utterly political reasons. It set Norfolk back a decade, which you have only now begun to recover from. That was a clear overreach even for a king, but it's the same overreach we allow daily from the Chancellor. Do you wish to see Norfolk suffer more, when Longchamp chooses to steal your master's title again?"

The man who represented Roger Bigod remained silent, as if he did not even realize he was supposed to answer. When it became painfully obvious others were waiting upon him, he startled innocently. "Oh, my apologies! I am here only as an observer."

A motto for the man's life, Arable considered.

But Marion did not seem rattled, instead pivoting to another. "Lancashire. The Baron of Hornby has long been a friend to Prince John, making him an obvious target for someone such as Longchamp. This meet is in your favor, too, it would promote your allies and secure your own barony. Surely you cannot claim to be impartial."

Roger de Montbegon's portly surrogate raised his hands in abstention. "I cannot claim anything, I am afraid. My instructions are simply to listen, and to report back to the baron the results of this council. I dare not presume to speak for him, nor his intent."

"There will be no results of this council," Marion smiled, though her tone did not, "if everyone refuses to have an opinion. May I ask your name?"

"I am here on behalf of the Baron Roger de Montbegon . . ."

Marion silenced him with a raised finger. "I know that. I don't care. I mean your name. *You.*"

The man only fidgeted, as if an acorn had suddenly appeared between him and the plush seat.

"Yes, you. I am looking at you. You have a name. It simply isn't possible that your parents forgot to give you one."

After an awkward swallow, "Roger."

"Roger?" Marion's face slacked. "That's your baron's name, and it's also your name?"

"Yes."

Arable had to stifle a laugh. The whole country was full of Rogers and Roberts and Richards and Williams and Johns. Her hand moved down to her belly, to the slightest curve she was now actively ignoring. She had not considered any names yet, because that would make it too real. But she took this moment to remind herself to name her child something exotic, like Clytaemnestra—or something equally mundane, but at least unique. *Table.* She could name her daughter something like Table, and then at least no one would ever have to wonder which damned Table she was.

And just like that, there was now a daughter in her belly rather than a question mark. And in her eyes, hot tears.

"Very well, Roger, forget that you are here to represent your baron," Marion was saying. "I promise we will not mistake your own opinion for his. I ask for *your* thoughts on this, which no one will hold against you. Do you believe Chancellor Longchamp should have the authority to take land and coin at his whim in order to keep his position, acting as king? To appoint his own undeserving men to positions of power while the king rots in an Austrian cell? Or do you think that power should return to the royal bloodline, to a rightful heir?"

Roger's mouth opened and closed. Twice. "I haven't thought about it," he said.

Arable had not much thought about it, either. She hadn't thought about what life meant five months from now. About what the world would be like that she would bring her daughter into. About what life she could provide.

About what sort of person Arable would be proud to watch her become.

"I'm asking you to think about it," Marion said to Roger.

"I don't know."

"What don't you know? What questions do you have? I am eager to help you understand."

"I don't . . . I'm not the right person to ask."

"Are you *human?*" Marion attacked him, barely able to contain herself. "Do you breathe? Have you somehow blundered your way through life without ever harboring an opinion, or a thought, on anything at all? I am not asking you for the *correct* answer, I'm asking for *your* answer. You have lived for years, and in that time you have felt something nobody else here has—you have experienced something unique and captivating, your life is utterly yours. At this moment, right now, I want the sum of your experiences, the result of every decision you have ever made to give one informed opinion. Is it *right*, Roger? It can be yes or no or a thousand brilliant shades between, just open your damned mouth and decide!"

Roger opened his damned mouth, but he had nothing to say.

Someone had raised that Roger from a child, just for him to become a useless sack of man who had nothing to say. Nothing to contribute.

Arable could do better.

"This is not a performance," Marion lamented. "You are all of you only invited because your houses have every reason to be allies. This is not a hostile environment. It should not be a profound act of bravery to agree, not in this room of friends. Will no one so much as admit that their house is sympathetic to this cause?"

"I will," Arable said, stepping forward.

Heads turned, chairs groaned against the stone floor, to look at her. Once they saw her, the usual bevy of reactions broke the silence. Snickering, haughty scoffs. *A servant girl*, they laughed. *Who is she?* A few whispers about the scars on her cheeks.

"My house supports you," Arable said, tilting her head back slightly.

Marion was a statue, her eyes alone burning an intense fire across the room.

"Most of you do not know me, but my house was once as notable as any here represented. My father, Lord Raymond de Burel, lost his life in service to his king in 1174, and our estate was unfairly seized from us as a political punishment for my father's failures. It was gifted to Lord Beneger de Wendenal, who razed it to the ground. We lost everything, because a man like the Chancellor simply decided as much. Any one of you could lose everything, as my family did. Any one of you could become the next servant at the edge of the room, rather than a voice at the table. But since none of you are willing to exercise that right, I will."

She took one second to turn and take in the room's reaction, finally making eye contact with Margery d'Oily, perched in absolute alarm at the elevated table. That gave Arable all the courage she needed to finish.

"My name is Lady Arable de Burel, I am the head of the once-great house of Burel of Derbyshire. And though we have no land, no soldiers, no coin, and no power, we do have our dignity. I pledge my house to this cause."

Marion had not moved, though her jaw was locked tightly forward, her teeth bared. It would not have surprised Arable in the least if she leapt forward like an animal and tore Arable into tiny unidentifiable pieces, set to a deafening applause.

"Lady Arable," she said, one eyebrow flinching upward. "You should sit down at the table with us. Roger, go get her a chair."

THIRTY-FIVE

ARTHUR A BLAND

NOTTINGHAM

"WHY DOESN'T HE DO any of the dirty work?" Arthur asked, crossing his arms.

"I'm not an expert," David answered, "but I think that's why they call it dirty work."

Alfred Fawkes stood by the open doorway of the Commons, greeting every man, woman, and child in line with a wide smile and an elaborate welcome, flourishing his red duster. This dull square of a stone building was known for giving out charity meals to those who had earned the Sheriff's leniency, which normally meant fuck all. Arthur had seen how the Commons lists were "earned" during his time in Nottingham, and it was far more a method of control than kindness. Two gords always stood at the entrance to check the names of those who entered.

Those two gords were there today, but wrapped in fishing nets and lying on the ground, moaning beneath Alfred Fawkes's feet.

"Courtesy of Robin Hood!" Fawkes bowed to the next young woman in line, waving her inside to the rare promise of a full belly.

Arthur and David were on the other side of the plaza, warming their hands at a brazier. They'd stood on watch while the sacking had happened. But now that the dangerous bit was over, they had their own orders for the evening. Arthur hated it.

"We have to go out busting heads for this damned archery tournament, while he stays here glad handing, pretending he's some sort of hero? A free meal and suddenly they forget he's also the one chopping off hands?"

"Actually, yes." David looked at him importantly. "We've been hungry before."

The worst part of being David's friend was how he was always right about every fucking thing. They'd looked in many a different direction in order to keep themselves fed over the years. Arthur's belly never once cared where the food came from.

As if to put an edge to that point, a mother rushed up to the line and dragged her children out of it, whispering into their ears.

Maybe they weren't all so forgiving after all.

"Let's go, then." David stood. It wouldn't be long before word of what had happened here spread, and more gords would arrive to scare off the line. If even fifty people got inside before Fawkes was chased off, Arthur would be surprised. But he knew the way of it—this wasn't charity none neither. Tomorrow and the rest of the week, there'd be twenty gords standing outside the Commons rather than two, which meant twenty fewer men on patrol nearby whatever else the Red Lions had planned.

David held up the parchment roll Zinn had assigned them, a list of names who were likely to best Alfred Fawkes at the archery tournament come Friday. A list of people who needed inconvenient injuries that would prevent them from competing.

"I fucking hate this." Arthur didn't even whisper it anymore.

THEIR FIRST STOP WAS the sixth name on their list, and farthest from the center of the city, but it was the only one that Arthur thought he'd enjoy. There was a chapel at Heth Beth Bridge, whose groundskeeper was their target. David had upturned his nose at why Arthur would want to start with a "man of God," when frankly that was the best reason to do it. Arthur couldn't think of anyone else who more deserved a good bit of smashing.

"*Asher*, I think?" David studied the parchment. He was better with his letters than Arthur, but that didn't matter when the person doing the scribbling was even worse. Red Fox was using all his resources on this. He had people watching the sign-ups at every hour, noting the names of anyone who seemed like a legitimate threat. The smaller gangs were used to track down information on them, so that muscle like Arthur could pay them a visit.

"Tall," David continued reading, "brown beard. Or maybe *bard?*"

"Why would they write *brown bard?*"

"I'm just reading what's here. If you start clobbering the wrong man and then a brown bard comes out of nowhere with a sword, you'll feel sorry for that comment."

"I'm going to feel sorry either way." Arthur pushed forward. He felt sorry his life had spiraled down to this, sorry that he didn't know how to fix it, and sorrier still that David was ever at his side, never complaining. "If you have to do something you don't want to, best to get a drink on first. Or, wanting that, punch a priest."

"He's not a priest."

"I'm going to close my eyes and pretend he's Friar Tuck."

"Friar Tuck's not a priest, he's a friar."

"Probably because somebody already punched the priest out of him."

David scrunched his face into a ball, but Arthur paid him no mind. On the far side of Heth Beth Bridge was a little garden surrounded by a low wall, maintained by the chapel. A less-than-tall man with a less-than-brown beard was there shoveling dirt into a barrow, who inclined his head when he realized they were headed his way.

Arthur waved him away. "Looking for Asher."

The man motioned down the bank toward the Trent and resumed his duties, not saying so much as a single word. Arthur wondered if he ought to ask the man's name, and bring it back to the Lions. Just in case he was on the lists, too, on one of the other assignment rolls gone out to others in the group. Save them the time of coming back here. Maybe Arthur ought to take a swing at every damned man in Nottingham, just in case they meant to be in the way someday.

Down a short footpath through the reeds came the clear sight of a tall man with a beard. If the sun were on his face instead of reflecting in the water, turning him into a silhouette, odds were strong that beard would be brown. He was calf deep in the river, raising a large basin with both hands and straining the water out, and part of Arthur reminded himself that if he didn't do this thing now, then the Dawn Dog would be back tomorrow and he wouldn't know when to stop.

"Asher, right? Question for you."

The man startled, but didn't stop what he was doing.

"About heaven, that is. An' what happens when we get there."

"I'm sorry?"

"Let's say a little boy dies—killed—no fault of his own, he goes to heaven, right?" Arthur stopped at the water's edge just long enough to pull his boots off. "Does he ever grow up in heaven? Or is he stuck at eight years old for all eternity?"

"I'm sorry, what's this about? A boy who died?"

"Nobody else grows old in heaven, right? So what about the little boys?" Arthur stormed into the river, wanting nothing other than for it to be over, and soon. "They stay young and curious forever and ever? Never actually learn anything? Never mature? Never fuck a girl? A hundred years go by and they're still bright eyed and make mistakes, never get to be a man, never get to learn what that means?"

Asher took a step back, but he was too late. Arthur splashed through the water straight at him, kicked the back of the man's knee, and pushed him down backward, barely enough time for him to gasp. He sputtered and hacked out water, but Arthur had already grabbed the wooden basin, raised it over his head, and hammered it down into the groundskeeper's side. The leading edge cracked at the impact, which would be enough for Asher's ribs to complain about it for weeks. He wouldn't draw a bow to full length for a month.

"Sorry 'bout that." He pulled the man's arms until he was sitting upright, keeping his head out of the water. "Maybe you ought to pray harder next time."

Arthur kicked the water, he kicked the world, he kicked at every god, and didn't feel any better for it. His body was a shell and he'd come back to it later.

"Are you alright?" David asked quietly, when Arthur made it back up the embankment.

He didn't answer. He couldn't.

Arthur.
Back across the bridge, back to the heart of the city.
Arthur.
Another name on the list. Another job. Another task.

Arthur.

A trade. They'd get something later, if they did this today.

Arthur?

It would be worth it.

Arthur.

"Arthur."

"Is that him?"

"You're worrying me." David stepped into his vision, though he was focused on someone else. A cob named Jefferey hauled his water buckets up the Long Stair to deliver to some better establishment in the Parlies for pennies. The buckets were braced by a framework of light wood around his body to keep from spilling, his arms suspended outward to hold the thing up. Water carriers like him grew stout and strong, and Jefferey was no exception. His face was a mask, long accustomed to the grimace of his work. Arthur tried to find something to hate in him. Some foreign features, maybe. That'd be enough.

"We don't have to do this. We can say we couldn't find him."

Arthur shook David off, aiming to intercept the man once he made it to the top of the landing. Jefferey had been easy enough to find, which meant that any Red Lion could do it, too. They'd go for his arm, likely, not caring a shit about what that meant. This cob needed his strength for his living. A bruised rib or a sprained wrist meant he wouldn't work for a month, which was a death sentence. Arthur could spare him from that, at least.

"Start a fight with me," he said.

David sighed, but relented, as Arthur plowed forward.

He wanted to fight. Deserved to be fought. Deserved to be hated, though David wouldn't do it. But he should.

"Hey!" David yelled from behind, pretending they were at odds. Maybe not pretending. "Don't you walk away from me, Norman!"

Norman was always their name of choice for each other when they needed the other to play along.

"Go fuck yourself!" Arthur answered, steering wildly closer to the cob. He gave himself a drunken stumble. David yelled another few things and drew closer. Arthur sidestepped toward Jefferey, who pivoted absently to steer clear, not paying them no mind. It was too easy, Arthur rolled his fingers, already wrapped with a leather strap, and drove every bit of his weight into a punch that landed square and high on Jefferey's right cheekbone. The man went down with a grunt, his buckets unloading river water everywhere. "Out of my fuckin' way!" Arthur finished and ran off, leaving David behind with his hands outstretched, helping the water carrier back to his feet.

His eye would swell shut in the next few days. He could still haul water with one eye. But he couldn't aim a bow.

He also couldn't escape a fucking cobber's life.

Maybe Jefferey was the best archer in Nottingham. Maybe Friday would have changed his whole life. Maybe he'd be paying someone else to cob for him if he'd taken the grand prize.

Maybe now he'd go the other way. Ask the gangs for help. Make a trade. Do a job.

Get dragged down.

Maybe next year, Jefferey would be the one punching fucking cobs on the street, lying to himself, lying to his friends.

One horn for the groundskeeper.
One for the cobber.
Another for the tanner's assistant.
Two for the hooper. That one had gotten sloppy.

"Let me help you with that." The last horn was only half-empty, but it slid away from him into someone else's hands. Will Scarlet picked it up and drank it to the last drop. He wiped his mouth with his sleeve and pointed to Arthur's hands. "Rough night?"

"Yeah," David answered for him, still nursing his second. Ale and wine. Arthur didn't need to answer, because the nicks on his knuckles already told the evening's story.

Arthur's memory swam to figure out when Will had arrived. David had disappeared for a couple of horns, come to think of it. Gone to get him, no doubt. "Still one on the list," he mumbled.

Scarlet nodded. Maybe. Hard to tell. Could have been the whole world that dropped down for a bit. Arthur hadn't stood up in a while. Wasn't sure how drunk he was. *Not enough,* that was the answer.

"Just one more," Scarlet said, "then we'll sleep it off. You know who it is?"

Arthur nodded yes, and turned his head. He forgot the name of the tavern they were in. Forgot which borough they were in. But he knew who he was here for. On the other side of the room was a young woman named Roslyn, serving out drinks, with auburn hair that fell to her waist, bound in yellow ribbons. She was apparently quite the archer.

Scarlet followed his gaze, confirmed with David, and sighed. "Best to get it over with, then?"

Arthur scratched at a splinter in the table. "What the fuck are we doing?"

"Don't think about it," Scarlet answered. "Let's just get to tomorrow."

"Is this what we came here for?"

"I hate it," David said. "I hate this."

"I hate it, too," was Scarlet's answer. "But it'll be worth it."

"When?" Arthur didn't want to keep his voice down. Wanted to make a scene. Wanted a fight, maybe she'd run. "We've been here over a month. Nobody's going to follow us. There's nothing in the Sherwood for us to go back to anyway. Robin Hood isn't even ours anymore. We lost. We should've gone with Marion."

Will tipped the horn back again, hoping for more. "You're drunk."

"I am." Arthur pulled at the splinter. "And we should have gone with Marion."

The crowd was thinning, not that it had been a jovial group to start with. This wasn't a tavern where people sang and laughed, this was one for men to stare into their drinks, and the abyss. To spend what they didn't have. Nobody was looking for a good time here. There wasn't coin enough in Nottingham to buy that anymore.

"I bet they think the same thing." Scarlet gave a hollow laugh. "You think Marion is out there changing the world right now? They're probably still starving in ditches, if they haven't been arrested yet. I guarantee you they wish they'd come with us. The whole world wishes they were somewhere else. You want to go? Walk away like Stutely did? What's stopping you?"

The splinter jammed under his fingernail. Drew blood.

Across the table, David lowered himself and tried to catch his gaze.

Arthur sucked the blood.

"It wasn't as easy as I thought it'd be, I admit that." Scarlet lowered his voice. "But we're getting there. David's training the Lions at the bow. If they win, it's because of us. Freddy won't forget who delivered that victory."

"Why the fuck do we care?" The edges of the table blurred. "What does that do for us?"

"Are you serious?" Will squinted. "If the Lions take this tournament, they'll be the strongest they've ever been. And we're riding that with them, straight up. All that coin, all that land . . . you think they'll have any idea what to do with it? All they know is the city. But we know exactly how to make the most of it, and Freddy will see that. We'll end up taking everything the Sheriff gives at the tournament and using it right back against him."

Arthur heard all the other words Will hadn't said. "So we're Red Lions now. We're not here for men anymore. All this . . . was just for us to join up."

"I don't think they have to be two different things. The Red Lions are about to expand, in a way they don't know how. I can carve a piece of that off for myself—for us. Whether that's with Freddy or not, I'm not sure. But it's exactly what we wanted, and it's happening, mark me." Will and his plans, and his plans. "We wanted to organize . . . not just in Nottingham, but in every city across the county. Knock the Guard on its ass, take as we please, live like kings. Its starts somewhere. It doesn't come easy. This will pay off, I promise."

"Or maybe it doesn't." Arthur stared into David's eyes. "And maybe we're just hurting people for the hell of it."

Scarlet snorted. "Have you gone soft?"

"Got no problem fighting someone who wants to fight back." He wondered if that description fit Will Scarlet. Cocked his head. Ground his jaw. "But this isn't that."

"Keep the goal in mind." Words. "The Sheriff."

Arthur shook his head, but it wouldn't clear up. He hated the Sheriff, too, for everything that had happened. For Much, Elena, Alan. For that ambush in the woods. For Locksley. Arthur hated the Sheriff because he loved his friends. "But you . . . you hate the Sheriff just because you hate."

The girl named Roslyn looked at them, an eyebrow up, asking if he needed another. He shook his head no.

"We win this tournament, and it's the start of something big," Scarlet said, as slowly as he could. "I promise."

"You sure of that?"

"I am."

"How sure?"

He raked his fingers through his hair, some of it snagging on the black ridge of his ear. Will Scarlet's head bobbed several times, then he pushed off from his chair. He took a few steps toward Roslyn with his hands spread wide, some smiling lie pouring out of his lips. She rolled her eyes, damn but she had a pretty face, but extended her hand for him. Will took it in his own, bent to kiss it, and instead grasped her middle finger and snapped it backward until it touched the back of her hand in one swift jerk. She shrieked and fell to the ground.

"I'm that sure," Will said.

Arthur was on his feet without realizing it, and he shoved Will Scarlet halfway across the room.

The room emptied—*had it been empty already?*—except for the girl on the ground and the barkeep who was suddenly very close and armed with a club. David was at Arthur's side. Across Scarlet's face was absolute shock. Shock, of all things—not that he'd just broken a girl's finger, but that his friend had a problem with it.

"How long until we're chopping hands?" Arthur asked.

Will's mouth stayed open.

"You'd better be right about this," he said, all fists. "If we don't win on Friday, I'm . . ."

He took a moment to look back at David. Bless his fucking soul, he agreed.

"We win on Friday, or we're out."

Arthur knelt to help the girl up before he left, but she panicked and backed away from him. She saw him as something monstrous—and for it, she was the smartest person in the room.

THIRTY-SIX

ARABLE DE BUREL

HUNTINGDON CASTLE

THE COUNCIL PROCEEDED AT a snail's pace. Arable had hoped her act would open the flood gates, inspiring a rally to the cause and progress made. But instead of an eruption, she at best started a trickle. One by one, Marion teased the tiniest concessions out of each participant, the first baby steps toward anything resembling thought. She had to backtrack heavily, far from the concept of rebellion or the decisions to pay King Richard's ransom, back to the very basic structure of society. To the nature of their government, to the simplest of laws, to the inherent and perceived rights given by civilization and by God. Arable agreed with Marion as often as she found her courage, especially when it seemed that Marion was at her words' end. But they never spoke directly to each other, and frankly it appeared that Marion was avoiding eye contact with her entirely.

All the while, Henry de Bohun and the members of his family watched silently. Even more useless than the others. Every time Marion tried to pinpoint one of them, a curt shake of his head warned her away. Whenever Arable turned, Lady Margery was there with a blistering scowl. They could not be intimidated as some of the others could, and gave no ground. The Earl of Essex, too—Marion's grandfather—seemed entirely in line with Hereford on the matter. He was stoic and unreadable, refusing his own granddaughter's pleas for help. So instead Marion instructed the others, leading them down simple paths of logic, in a way that was not unlike teaching stubborn children how to juggle.

When they finally broke for a midday meal, Arable seriously contemplated murdering one of them, if only to elicit a reaction. Instead she hurried behind Marion, who retired from the reception hall for her own quarters. Only the slightest moment of connection between them let Arable know she was welcome to follow.

The instant Arable closed the door behind her, Marion burst with emotion, already on the other side of the room. "What are you doing?"

"I'm . . . I'm trying to help," Arable stammered. "Is that not obvious?"

"I don't know!" Marion returned, her face flush red as her hair, her entire body leaning forward as if she might leap out of her spine. "I don't know what on earth you're doing!"

Arable had no words, and suddenly regretted everything. "You needed . . . it seemed like you needed someone to agree with you. I thought I might . . . start the ball rolling, as it were. I know my house is nonexistent, but I thought it was better than nothing."

"To what end?" Marion's eyes bulged forward. "Why would you suddenly want to help?"

Instinct told her to leave. Arable turned and put her hand on the door, but she forced herself to not grab its handle. "I didn't. But you convinced me."

"I *convinced* you?" came a laugh. "I was there. I convinced *nobody*. I'm supposed to believe that you alone had a change of heart?"

"It's the truth," Arable said, and turned to look back at Marion. She sat on her bed, her hands clasped over her forehead, her eyes begging for the world outside the window. "Why else would I speak up? Why do you think I did it?"

"I don't know! I imagine there's some trap at the end of it all, I expect you're setting me up just so you can tear me down again at a moment's notice."

That was a feeling Arable knew all too well. It was the suspicion of the beaten, the permanent alarm that treated every act of kindness as a threat. It had been her default state of mind for a decade and a half, and it was chilling to share that moment of understanding with the woman she thought she hated. Where she had long blamed Marion for stealing power at the expense of those beneath her, she saw it now as scratching for prestige in the face of a world that afforded her none of her own.

"No," Arable said, as gently as she could. "It's no trap."

Marion's face was a fist. "Well you've chosen a hell of a time to decide to be useful."

And all Arable's sympathies threw up their hands and walked away. "Are you actually angry at me for trying to help?"

"If that's what you're actually trying to do ... then ... no. *No*." Marion squinted at her, as if she were a puzzle she could decipher. "But I have no reason to trust you. You have been nothing but combative with me for months. Now you're surprised I can't—"

"*I've* been combative with *you?*" Arable burst. "You have been *wretched* with me!"

"Yes! You—"

"I came to *help* you, and I have been outcast and shunned for doing so. By you, more than anyone!"

"Your 'help' has been disastrous!" Marion stood again, her hands flung to the sides, trembling. "You led Gisbourne directly to our camp—where Alan died, where Elena died, a dozen others. The fire brigades, all of this, only happened because you were too selfish to realize he was using you—"

"I know!" Arable gasped, her breath suddenly whisked away. She knew every bit of her failures, they haunted each second of her waking life, and a thousandfold more so in her dreams. "I know, I know! You think I don't know that?"

"And still I let you stay with us! When anyone else would have kicked you out, or punished you. You said I have been 'wretched' with you? I say I have been *generous*. I gave you protection, and food, and—"

"*Grief,*" Arable interrupted her, the word sharp on her lips. "And grief, Marion, you gave me grief. At every opportunity. With every look, you remind me how unwelcome I am. And the others follow your lead, don't you see that? Nobody knew how to react to me, so you set that precedent for all of them. And you're angry I didn't thank you for that?"

For a moment it seemed Marion would fight back, but when her mouth opened it drooped and then puckered tight again, the redness of her face moving into her eyes. She sniffed and looked up at the ceiling. "I am . . . a human, too," she said, her voice betraying her. "Am I expected to be above all emotion? I lost everything, and I'm supposed to be invulnerable to that? When I see you, I see everything I lost, I see so much pain and needless death. I show a little honest reaction, and you will not even allow me that?"

Pain and needless death.

"I take the blame for the things I've done, I do. But not . . ." Arable's throat caught, unsure she should broach that one name they hadn't mentioned. Too late—she could see the recognition in Marion's eyes. "But it isn't my fault Robin died."

Yes, she'd released Will Scarlet from prison, which brought Gisbourne upon all of them. But not Robin, that wasn't on her.

"I did as he asked, at great personal risk. I brought him back to the castle, because he wanted to rescue you. I didn't kill him, but you act as if it was me alone. And you're right, Gisbourne used me to find your camp. He *used me*. You don't think that is terrible enough for me to endure? Don't you see how unfair it is for you to judge me for that, to blame me for *being used*? Why would you choose to hate *me* instead of Gisbourne? Have I not suffered enough for what he did to me?"

A long pause settled between them. Outside, a horse whinnied, and a smith doused his metal in water, leaving a soft hush to replace a constant clanging Arable had not even noticed.

"Could I not say the same?" Marion asked at last. "Have I not suffered enough? Do I deserve your scorn?"

"You literally took my life from me," Arable answered.

Marion took that, she nodded long and hard to herself before looking up again. "I never even knew you existed until after it was all over. William never told me he had a lover. I proposed a marriage to him, to strengthen our positions, and he said yes. He never mentioned you. I didn't take your life, *he* did."

Arable had never pretended otherwise. But still, there was no *untangling* that. There was no *talking that out.*

"If you ask me to blame Gisbourne instead of you," Marion finished, "surely you can see that you should be blaming William instead of me."

What a mess. Her and Marion and William and Robin. Four terrible people, who knew nothing other than how to hurt each other. Robin and William went into a room one night, and Robin was hanged for William's murder the next day. Be it by sword or by noose, those two men had killed each other. For some time, Arable had wondered if she and Marion were destined to walk that same path.

"I wish I knew what happened."

"As do I," Marion echoed.

The last time Arable had seen William, she'd called him worthless and walked out of his office. The last time she saw Robin, he was stealing away from the postern gate into Nottingham's middle bailey, ready to smash the world. "I want to know who drew first," she whispered. "I want to know what they said."

Marion nodded. "But would it matter? The damage would be the same."

The damage.

"I'm with child."

Marion's hand went to her mouth, and might have stayed there for a lifetime. "It's William's?"

Arable nodded.

"My God. That almost seems impossible. That seems so long ago."

Arable gave a sad laugh. "Well there hasn't been anyone else—"

"No, that's not what I meant," Marion added quickly. "I'm sorry, I didn't mean that."

She had never heard Marion say *I'm sorry* before.

"I do blame him." It wasn't nearly as terrible to say as Arable had thought it would be. "William. I hate him sometimes, I hate him more than anything. For thinking he could fix the world, for swooping back into my life and then throwing me out into the streets . . ."

She didn't have anything else to say about it. She'd said it all in her mind a thousand times, but the words made it seem trivial, it was a thing that died before it could be born.

Marion tilted her head up. "Then hate me."

Arable matched her, finding her face utterly sincere. "What?"

"I was wrong. Don't blame William. Don't carry that. Don't carry that into your baby. Find a way to forgive him, for your child's sake. Whatever's left, that you can't forgive . . . fine. Yes. Put it on me. I'll take it."

Somehow that was so much more meaningful than an apology ever could be. "I can't hide anymore," Arable said. "I can't run in the forest anymore."

"I know."

"We need a life."

"That's what this is supposed to be about," Marion answered. "And I can't do it alone."

Arable looked at her, reading the history of lines in her face. The things she spoke of, the ideas she'd presented at the council so far . . . it was a world Arable wanted for her daughter. So very, very much. "You're not alone. Like I said, I'm here to help you. If you'll take it."

Marion closed her eyes as a tear rolled down her cheek. When she opened them, her face was full of thanks. She reached out her hand, Arable took it.

Outside, the smith started his hammering again. The world was still moving, along with all its problems.

"Well," Arable huffed, trying to transition to the matter at hand. "You can work all day and night to draw an opinion out of these people, but for what? They'll report back to their masters what they've seen here, what they've heard—just with facts, not opinions. Every absent earl is only interested in the attendee list, to know where the battle lines have been drawn."

"I know," Marion answered, her eyes suddenly alight. "But I couldn't just let the council be done after a few minutes. Then they all report back that this was a waste of time. But if they report that we debated about it for days . . . perhaps that gives it more merit. Maybe that will turn a few heads."

Arable studied Marion's face. "I saw you in there. You're not just trying to turn heads. You want to win."

Marion considered it. "If only for the change of pace."

"You're making more ground than you realize, I think," Arable said. She'd seen the hesitations, the urge to participate. "They're just . . . waiting."

"For what?"

"Your grandfather," she said, with a certain amount of disgust. "It's as if they cannot take you seriously if he does not agree with you. Or Hereford. With those two sitting silent at the back of the room, the rest are terrified to speak up. If they were gone, of course the others could admit to an opinion or two. But they need someone to . . . to *validate* this. Probably just because you're not a man."

Marion rolled her eyes. "Well they all came to hear from Lady Magdalena, so it can't just be that."

"And I imagine they only would have trusted her if her father stood by her side as well. It's always been this way, you know that. If a woman has a good idea, then it's seen as empty girlish chatter, until a man has the same idea. Then it's genius."

"So you're saying," Marion breathed heavily, "that the reason I feel like a dancing monkey is because that's how they see me."

"In as many words," Arable admitted. "Get your grandfather involved. If you get him to speak up, I think they'll all follow you."

Marion bristled and blew out her lips. "It's insane to think I've somehow become the spearhead of this movement. A year ago I was content with small acts of charity around Nottingham. Months ago I could barely survive persecution. Now I'm the face of a rebellion."

Arable took a moment to look at Marion with new eyes. She looked as powerful as the stone walls around them, as if her feet were tree trunks with roots that stretched down into the heart of England. The face of a rebellion, indeed.

"I have an idea," Arable said, scratching an itch that had been nagging her all morning. "Remember when you told Roger to fetch me a chair?"

THE RECEPTION HALL WAS still empty and lifeless, which was not necessarily a departure from how it felt even when filled with these people. Marion's speeches had not gained her any traction, nor pleading, nor informed debate. In the history of the world, these had always been the weakest of stimuli. If Arable's time in Nottingham had taught her anything, it was that action brought much more tangible results than words ever could.

She had only a short amount of time until the meeting reconvened, but it would be enough. Arable left the Elder Hall and the castle entirely, off the main grounds to the villages that speckled the hills down to the banks of the Cook's Backwater, where John Little and the others had made their new homes. John Little greeted her with a smile that warmed her soul, but she had no time for idle talk. She gathered as many of them as she needed, explained her plan quickly, and by the time they were regrouping up the hill by the castle gate, the bells rang out from the Heart Tower that signaled the council to resume.

Somehow, they were still the first to gather in the hall. Marion awaited them in the central space, affecting as natural a position as she could. John Little and the Delaney brothers lingered at the doorways, ready for her summons.

But ten minutes later, they were still the only attendees.

As time crawled slowly on, Arable strained her ears for footsteps, or voices, but it seemed nobody was even in the building. John Little gave a befuddled shrug. At the edge of her senses she thought perhaps there was some commotion, which prompted them to investigate. Pushing out the heavy doors of the Elder Hall's main entrance, Arable instantly noticed the throng of activity away at the castle's exit. All their audience and their retinues had bottlenecked, packed shoulder to shoulder.

Friar Tuck was hurrying closer, clearly relieved to see them.

"What is it?" Marion asked in a panic. "Why are they leaving?"

"They're not leaving, they're trying to see him!"

"See who?" Arable reached for Tuck's shoulder. "Has another guest arrived?"

"Yes." The friar smiled eagerly. "Prince John."

THIRTY-SEVEN

JOHN LACKLAND

HUNTINGDON CASTLE

JOHN WAS EMBARRASSED ON their behalf, the amateurs! He wanted to scoop them all up in his arms like children, sit them down, and explain the proper etiquette of throwing a revolution. The first rule of sedition—which was also the second, third, and probably only rule—was to keep it secret. But instead there was a verifiable throng of people come out to greet him in increasingly unsecretive ways, each one wagging their tail in expectation of praise.

"Well, we've found the right place," he muttered to his swordarm, Hadrian, on horse beside him. "But I forget the bet. Does that mean *I'm* right, or that *you're* right?"

"I am," Hadrian answered from the side of his mouth. "I'll add it to your tab of all the other things you know you'll never pay me."

"See that you do, thanks," John answered. Hadrian had grumbled mightily about traveling out this way—but Hadrian grumbled about everything else too, which was nine of the ten reasons John kept him employed. "Get Wally."

With his signature grumble, Hadrian peeled back to fetch Gay Wally. Whatever was about to happen here would undoubtedly be populated with people whose names John simply didn't have the capacity to care about. Gay Wally's swollen head was unusually large precisely because it was filled with all the little useless facts of the world that men like John were expected to know.

Huntingdon Castle was not much of a castle to look upon—a long circular curtain wall rounded the hill ahead of them, within which a singular tower rose from a motte. These defensive measures were rendered impotent by the massive open gate and the outflow of the aforementioned inexperienced revolutionists pouring from that hole. The group struggled in fairly comical ways to react to him. Some bowed, before realizing that not enough of the others were bowing to justify it. Others stood with their mouth gaping open, their souls perhaps departed for an afternoon nap. John had been bowed at and gaped at before—for most of his life, really—but those platitudes were generally instincts from commonfolk, while this group was dressed formally. And rather than a sea of shining pates and white whiskers, these onlookers were all curiously young.

"Alright then," John announced, after failing to identify anyone who seemed competent enough to receive him. "Who's the man in charge?"

He might as well have asked for the meaning of life itself, so stupefied were the responses. But one by one every face looked to another, until the grueling process of cowardly elimination ended at a short but full-figured woman quickly joining the group from the rear. "I suppose that's me," she answered, and the throng parted for her.

This "man in charge" had rolling red hair, pinned back, and an ample chest—and John took a moment to wonder if he'd later get an opportunity to verify her sex in private.

She bowed her head. "I am glad to see you, cousin."

Cousin. That was a bucket of cold water on his previous thought.

"The Lady Marion Fitzwalter," Gay Wally explained, who had sidled next to John. "Daughter of the castellan of London, granddaughter of the Earl of Essex. Her father married—"

"Thank you," John dismissed him, not wanting to appear uninformed. "Though frankly half the country could claim some relation to me. It's become a popular pastime. But I do remember you, Marion," he added, recalling her face from a few important functions that he had spent ignoring his responsibilities. "And I suppose I should apologize for my tardiness."

Marion's face lit up. "Tardiness? Why, we did not even realize you were coming!"

"That's because I wasn't invited!" he returned, throwing her an exaggerated grimace. "I do hope that won't be a problem. Admittedly, I'm not sure I understand exactly what the goal of this council *is,* aside from a vague promise to aggravate the Chancellor. But if that is on the agenda, you would do well to have the world's expert on the matter at the table."

He placed a hand to his own breast, mostly for the rabble who were almost certainly too thick to catch his intimation.

"That is," his cousin answered, "the *entirety* of the agenda."

"Brilliant." John clapped his hands. "Well I don't know if you've lined up some egregious scandal against Longchamp, or if you were thinking of doing things a bit more bloodily—*which I wouldn't recommend, so much laundry involved!*—but either way I would like very much to wave my princely hand to help determine whose name should next follow the word *Chancellor.*"

An aggravatingly attractive smirk claimed her lips. "Have you someone in mind?"

"Several, but I suppose that is the point of the meeting, is it not? Under pressure, I would say Gay Wally would be my first choice."

That smirk took a turn. "I don't know who that is."

"Nor does the world," John answered, without even giving Wally the kindness of an introduction. He would be a perfectly hilarious choice for Chancellor, in that he was the exact opposite of Longchamp in every way—young, knowledgeable, and loyal to John. "Or Hadrian," he added, gesturing to his hired muscle, "though he'd have to trim his beard."

"Ah." Marion's eyes tightened when she finally realized he'd been joking. "As you say, shall we leave the details to the council?"

"Oh, I *am* invited then?"

"Indeed, that was entirely our mistake." She clasped her hands. "We erred on the side of discretion."

"Did you?" John laughed back at her. "I'm curious how you thought this might be considered *discreet*. Coups and rebellions, they're normally conjured up in back alleys and the backs of taverns . . . anything with the word *back* involved, really. Here you are, front and center, announcing it in a prominent castle before everyone. I suppose it's possible you're brilliant, but that generally only lasts until the first person lops your head off."

"There is nothing to hide here." She spread her arms for all to see how certainly certain her certainty was. "The necessity of this action is undeniable, it's nothing to whisper about. It needs to be yelled, and it needs to be seen."

"So sayeth many a martyr." John looked into the crowd, found a pretty face looking back at him, and gave her a wink. He was rewarded with a shy blush.

Marion exhaled, hesitating. "May I ask how you heard of this?"

John gave one of his many well-practiced glares. "You may, and you have, but I won't tell you."

It was Roger de Montbegon, the Baron of Hornby, who had alerted him to it—undoubtedly thinking he was proving his loyalty in so doing, and had since found a thousand less-than-subtle ways of reminding John of his deed. *Jockeying for Chancellor himself, perhaps.* So long as they replaced Longchamp with anyone John approved of, he could happily slink off into obscurity for a few years longer. But John did not see his sycophantic friend here in the crowd, nor any other notable face.

Just this cousin, Marion. "Please, Your Grace, follow me."

He was mildly offended that she had not offered him an opportunity to rest first, but as a rule he was generally delighted by anyone bold enough—or foolhardy enough—to purposefully offend him. She led John and his small entourage through the castle grounds, which were sparsely populated and boasted all the ordinary makings of a castle's necessities. He wasn't quite sure what he was expecting, but somehow its sheer normality was disappointing. Every eyeball was upon him, which was as good a sign as any that there was nothing uncouth planned within. The moment that somebody attempted to play casual around a prince's sudden appearance would be the moment John raised an eyebrow in alarm.

One figure stalled his approach, that of a breathtaking lady in a stunning blue dress, fabric whipping violently about her in the wind. She stood on the solitary footbridge that led from the main grounds up to the tower's entrance, poised like an ancient statue, and showed no signs of joining them. John nodded to Wally, who took note of the woman and blinked several times as he conjured up the appropriate knowledge.

"The Countess of Huntingdon, Lady Magdalena de Bohun," he said, rather pleased with himself for a puzzle well solved. "The author of the invitations, so we've been explained."

"Hm." John led his horse forward, noting that her eyes followed them. "She looks less than inviting now."

"It's worth noting that I've recognized no one else," Wally added. "Unless they all await you in the council room."

"Sit by me, then. I think I'm going to need you to whisper quite a number of things into my ear. I'll do my best not to let it arouse me."

While Gay Wally's face crumpled into some delicious concoction of revulsion and confusion, John dismounted to give his horse to the approaching groomsmen.

"She's a prince's steed, no one else is to touch her. See that she's ten-flatted, immediately," he demanded of them, to which they nodded and retracted. He would sadly not get to enjoy their ensuing manic debate as to what being *ten-flatted* meant—as he had invented the phrase on the spot—but it put a spring in his step, nonetheless.

In little enough time, he was welcomed into a wide room with a generous ceiling, lined with green-and-gold banners. Fading tapestries of hunting scenes and falconry lined the walls, threatening to bore any lingering passerby to death. A circlet of half a hundred chairs was arranged about a few long tables, while another table was raised behind the middle section and filled with the older type of dignitaries that John had expected to find. Wally identified their titles as quickly as John could forget them.

A breathless fascination hovered in the air, aimed at him, and it dawned upon John that his every action was becoming the source of incredible scrutiny. He selected an unimportant pair of chairs for himself and Wally, and the decision received the same amazement as if the roof had torn away and rainbows had poured into the chamber from on high. Every chair in the room was quickly filled, no man wanting to be the last for John to wait upon. A servant girl half a table away poured wine into a glass until it overflowed, as her focus was entirely on John.

He crossed his legs, and felt the room inhale in anticipation.

He uncrossed them, the murmurs rippling outward.

He held his breath, the room held with him.

He parted his lips and whispered to Wally. *"What exactly have we gotten ourselves into?"*

When Wally didn't have an answer, that's when John knew something was amiss.

"Please," John said, loud enough for the entire gallery, which basked in the all-mighty glory of having been addressed, "pretend I'm not here. I've arrived offensively late, and am eager to simply listen for the time being. I'm just an observer—a breathtakingly handsome, but humble observer."

A ripple of laughter burst from a hundred lips, finally easing the room.

"Just an observer," Lady Marion echoed his words, gesturing to him as she took the center of the stage. "Now that's something, isn't it? This room is already full of them. The servant-who-is-not-Richard-de-Percy sits beside the

page-who-is-not-William-Malet, who sits beside the prince-who-is-not-the-prince!"

John pursed his lips, having no idea if that sentence was supposed to make any sense to him.

Marion swept her hand across the audience. "I'll let you draw your own conclusions. But I wonder if the Chancellor would be so modest? Can you imagine William Longchamp sitting amongst you, asking to be treated the same as any man? I lack such imagination. I would think he would have demanded the head of the table, and a throne for it, too. I don't imagine he has ever been *eager to listen* to anyone at all. It says something about the measure of a man, don't you think? And whether or not he should rule."

Whether or not he should rule. That phrase stood instantly erect.

John had misjudged them entirely. This was no friendly marcher rebellion, of finding clever ways to disenfranchise a rival, no. They were not simply planning on replacing Longchamp. Their aim was higher.

Much like the two French walruses he'd met in Lancashire, they meant to put a crown on John's head.

And suddenly, his cousin Lady Marion—who, to his knowledge, was no walrus—had every single drop of John's internationally envied attention.

THIRTY-EIGHT

CAITLIN FITZSIMON

THAT WAS THE THING about Caitlin, some thought she was *tough* or *cruel*. *A hard woman,* she'd heard that used before, as if it were supposed to mean something. She was no harder or tougher than the environment she lived in, but she weathered it better. Caitlin had the opportunity to take all the bitter stings the world had given her and turn them into something else, rather than *be* turned into something else herself. Some people shrank in the face of calamity, they withered and died under its pressure. Not Caitlin. When life gave her shit, she took it out on something else.

Right now, she was taking it out on Will Scarlet's face.

She felt the impact drive down her forearm, right to her elbow with a long reverberating squeal. She had wrapped her hand in thick leather straps to protect her knuckles, but she could still feel every blow in the ache of her bones. She wanted to stretch her fingers and massage her palm, but she wanted to punch Will Scarlet more. So she went for that second option.

His head recoiled from her fist and hung limp—some pathetic expletive dripped from his lips, but she couldn't hear him. His body sagged from his shoulders, which were suspended up by Dawn Dog and Ricard the Ruby. Neither could conceal their discomfort very well, which was for the better. Nobody liked this sort of thing—she would have worried if either was still smiling. But punishment was punishment, and did Will Scarlet ever deserve more of it.

"You want to lie to me again?" she asked, hoping he would.

"Fuck . . ." was all he could say, little bursts of blood spittling out. But his head started bobbing up and down. "Yeah, yeah it was me."

Caitlin frowned. She was really looking forward to giving him one more square. But she knew how to train dogs, and you can't punish them for doing what you wanted. For most mutts, you had to know exactly how to hit them.

One hit makes you a joke.

Two make you serious.

Three make you an enemy.

She didn't want Will Scarlet's fear, she wanted his obedience. But with men, it was always hard to tell how many hits it took to be taken seriously. And Will Scarlet ran on the more rabid side. She'd thought he'd taken his blows already, that he'd become a content little sheep—which was far more useful than her original hopes to kick him out of the city on sight. But apparently this little sheep had been up to no good.

"I know it was you," she said, handing him a rag to wipe his face. "I need to know how many others there are out there. What other surprises are waiting for us."

"Why does it matter?" His voice, weak, barely louder than his breath. The rag, held to his eye. Blood, dripped black and red across half his face, which was already swelling and turning blue. Cait took a moment to enjoy it. She'd brought him deep into the tunnels for this, far through their sandstone mazes that he might never find his way out if they were to leave him here alone. They were in the sphere of a cesspit, long ago farmed out for manure, but forever retaining a stank of bile. They were far enough from the Lions Den that his screams would never make it back there. Alfie wouldn't approve of her doing this, necessary as it was.

"It matters because of who you claim to be," she answered, signaling for Ricard to bring a bucket of well water. They had passed several low tunnels to get here that had holes down that were always filled with water—clean water, the only good part of living beneath the city. She dipped her hands in, to scrub the blood from her fingertips. "And since you seem to keep forgetting, I'll say it another time. Red Fox is Robin Hood now. So when I find out you're murdering people in the name of Robin Hood, that danger lands on us. Not you."

"I didn't do it in the *name of Robin Hood.*" His blood dripping on the floor. *Pat pat.* "I just . . . did it."

"Why did you do it? Who were they?" she asked, dully, because she didn't really care. She already hated that she'd learned something valuable from her meeting with her father. "Who were these two nobles to you? This *Lord of Brayden,* what the fuck did he do to Will Scarlet?"

"Nothing." His voice was a whisper. "We came upon them on the way to Nottingham, Arthur and David and I. And Stutely. We took what we could, nothing special. Nothing we hadn't done a hundred times . . ." His sentence lingered like a guilty child. She flexed her fingers, letting the faint sound of the stretching leather speak for itself. "And then I went back. I don't know why. I went back . . . and opened their carriage . . . and just . . . just *bam bam bam* . . . in the chest . . . and that was it. Barely a few seconds. Then we were on our way."

"Just you?"

Pat pat. "Just me. The others didn't know."

Caitlin took a full breath. "I hear the woman was raped. You do that?"

"Wha—?" His face keeled up, a seemingly genuine confusion across it. "No, no. I just . . . I just killed her. Both of them, in and out, fast. On my own. I don't know why."

She exhaled. "You don't know why."

His body slumped, heaved, slumped. "I don't know why."

She'd been pulling her punches before, but this time she followed clean through. Her momentum was almost too much to stop, and Dawn Dog had to take her weight even as he flinched from the shock of the sudden violence. For a bear of a man, he could be surprisingly weak. Nobody would ever call the Dawn Dog a *hard woman.*

She could see it in Will Scarlet's face, through the blood and bruises, that this was the hit that mattered. His adolescent spark was gone, replaced with fear, cowardice in his eyes, his jaw quivered and blood drained from his burst lips. "I wanted to kill them . . ." The words were nearly indecipherable, bubbling through his breaths. "I wanted to kill them for being alive. For being happy and alive. Sometimes I want to kill everyone, I want to kill everyone who isn't dead."

"Why?"

"Because it isn't fair . . ." tears came down, following the path of the blood down his cheeks, ". . . it isn't fair that they're alive, and she's dead . . ."

His breath choked, his shoulders seized. Cait signaled for Dawn Dog and Ricard to let him go, and then Will Scarlet wept on the floor, oblivious to their presence. Silently. He did not wail, his body just crunched into a ball and he moaned out whatever breath his body could take.

Eventually he slowed, he held his head in his hands and breathed in deeply, bringing himself back to reason.

"Grief is a bitch," Caitlin said, knowing from experience. "But so am I. You can't kill anyone you want, whenever you want. This happened before you came to Nottingham, so you're lucky. If you'd done this after we'd met you, I'd carve you in half, from asshole to throat. Unless you admit to it, right now. Don't make me ask twice. Anything else you done I should know about?"

He shook his head and squinted. One of his eyes was now swollen shut, and he had to twist to see her with the other. She stood up again and clenched her fist, but his hand raised limply to defend himself. "Nothing, no, no . . ."

"What about the hands in the stables?" she asked.

"The stables?" His hand fell. "That's not you? Heard about them, yes . . . thought it was Freddy . . ."

She repositioned her fist, but he didn't move at all. He had nothing left in him to lie, and she believed him. It was a stretch to think Scarlet was behind the behandings, since the first had happened before he came to the city, but it was worth asking. Someone else was out there soiling Robin Hood's name, but Alfie had already dismissed that. Probably just another rival, trying to make hell for them, better ignored.

"Alright, your men, then?" Just to be sure. "Do I need to ask them a few questions, too?"

"No no," he said. "They're not like that."

"Like what?"

"Like me." Will Scarlet's arms seemed useless to him, they tried to do something but flopped around instead. "They're good people. They're not like me. They're not . . . they're not broken."

Cait exhaled heavily, as if the utter truth of it had swept through the cave tunnel and taken away all the tension and danger. She nodded solemnly to Dawn Dog and Ricard, for both of them to leave. They eagerly scooped up two of the three lanterns from the floor to hobble back down the tunnels to the Lions Den. They did so silently, they made haste.

"I haven't told Alfred," she said, once she was alone with him. "And I'd rather not. He has a soft spot for you, fool that he is, but because of it he'll treat you far harsher if he finds out. He'll kill you, I mean." She spelled it out, realizing he was in no condition to put two and two together. "I'm willing to keep this secret, if you're willing to keep a different secret in exchange. I've got a task for you I'd prefer he not know about."

Scarlet snorted, black goop shot from his nose. "You want me to do something behind Alfred's back?"

"Quit drooling, this secret's nothing compared to yours. Just a difference of opinion between me and him on how to proceed on something, so I'd rather have you take care of it so we don't have to argue about it no more. If he finds out you did it at my command, he'll only be upset at me for all of thirty seconds. So don't pretend you can use this as leverage on me, you shit bag."

"I wasn't thinking that," lied the shit bag.

"Yes you were. If you weren't, you'd be too daft to be here at all."

He had no clever retort, just a slight catch in his breath. "What's the job?"

"Gerome Artaud, the saint of a trademaster you've been following— apparently the only man in Nottingham with no vices. We would've preferred to blackmail him, but since you can't find any dirt on him, we'll have to get what we want in more creative ways."

Scarlet nodded. "You want me to threaten him?"

"Not good enough. He's clearly not very imaginative, so he needs proof of what we'll do to him." She bent lower to match his eyes, making sure he felt every word that followed, as something that could just as easily happen to him. "Take a finger. Let him pick which one, then take a different one. Pull the fingernail first. Then flay it to the bone, draw it out. But cut it clean off and burn the nub when you're done. Don't want him to die of the rot."

With only one lantern left, his face was half-black, shadows filling the sockets of his eyes like his blood in the crags of the ground. "And this would make us square?"

"It would mean I don't have to put you down, at least." She wiped her hands on his shirt. "If Alfie finds out you did it, you say it was your idea. You know him, he means too well sometimes. He's not like you. He's not like us."

"I know." Will shivered. "The real Robin Hood was the same way."

Pat pat. She froze until he stared back at her. "Alfred Fawkes *is* the real Robin Hood. That's the last time I tell you."

Pat pat. "Got it. Sorry."

"Don't bring your men on this, either. I need David focused on teaching us archery. You'll do this alone." He nodded, and at last she helped him find his footing. "Get gone. Clean up. I'll get you details shortly."

His shuffle down the tunnel was piteous, but Caitlin felt nothing for him. Will Scarlet was a weapon too dangerous to use, he was a knife whose handle was wrapped in iron barb. Rather than wait and see what more damage Scarlet could do before the greenbeard job was ready for him—as she'd been doing for weeks—she could simply use him to expedite it. This job would take care of the Artaud problem, the greenbeard problem, and the Scarlet problem all at once. It was something of a shame there was only one person around to enjoy what she'd done.

"Sorry I didn't let you in on that," she said to Rob o'the Fire, still watching from the dark cranny on the other side of the cesspit. "I hope watching was something, though."

"It wasn't the worst," he said. "But yeah, I would've liked to give him back just a little of what he gave me." Even as he spoke she could hear the wheeze in his lungs, the lingering damage Will Scarlet had done him that first night. How Alfie had not seen the danger immediately was absolutely beyond her. But that was why a good man like him needed a hard woman like Cait.

"Pushing hard on the trademaster then, eh?" Rob asked, coming closer to look at Scarlet's blood on the cave wall.

"Don't see another way." Cait scraped her boot on the ground. "We need Artaud to get mead to the greenbeard, so we can get all the access we want to the Trip, and wrap that up. It's been dragging on too long."

"Yeah. But it's just . . . I mean, cutting off his finger? I don't want to second-guess you none, but he hasn't crossed us, right? Why so bloody?"

"Don't worry, those were just threats for Scarlet. He'll barely even touch Artaud. Just going to scare him enough to know we can get to him, so's we can make some proper demands."

Rob inhaled deeply, trying to figure it out. "What? So Scarlet . . . *isn't* going to hurt him?"

"He's going to try." She looked him square. "But I've got a job for you, too."

THIRTY-NINE

MARION FITZWALTER

HUNTINGDON CASTLE

WITHOUT VOMITING EVEN ONCE, Marion continued from where they had last left off. They had been discussing peerage and precedent, and the inequity of noncommensurate taxes. It was a tricky thing to focus on such ungodly boring topics while Prince John was electrifying the room with his presence. His arrival was the greatest gift she could have hoped for—after all, she didn't need to convince her grandfather or Henry de Bohun of anything if she could win the prince instead.

He was dressed simply and might have easily passed as any commoner, but there was an indefinable quality that drew one's eyes to him. His skin and his red-brown flop of hair were visibly healthy, his eyes bright and alert. Prince John carried himself like a man who was always slightly amused at a world that could never touch him. He'd always been that way—their mutual family had put Marion in the room with him half a dozen times over the years, though they rarely interacted. But whether seated on a dais or skulking in a corner, John was a man with only one foot in the world, judging every little thing for its audacity of existence. In a lesser man it would have read as brat, but in him it was a welcome strength, a cult of leadership.

Marion was doing her best to describe the advantages of levying a carucage tax over the geld, fully aware that the room was more interested in whether the prince would eat a grape or a fig first. But she didn't care. She was still going through with her plan, and the prince was the best audience imaginable.

Friar Tuck entered at the edge of the room—as requested—and Marion interrupted herself. She turned to a young man with a stiff moustache who had barely said a single word the whole council, the man-who-was-not-Eustace-de-Vesci. "Oh, I'm sorry, before we continue, would you mind if I borrow your chair?"

He perked his head as she motioned for him to exchange places with Tuck.

"He has an injured arm, you see, I'd appreciate if he could have your seat, thank you."

"Oh, of . . . course . . ." the man stalled, clearly wanting to ask why an injured arm would necessitate his seating comfort. But Tuck gave an exaggerated wince as he massaged his elbow, and the man-who-was-not-Eustace-de-Vesci toddled sheepishly to his feet, looking for another chair elsewhere that Marion had ensured would not exist.

"Thank you. As I was saying, regardless of one's support of Chancellor

Longchamp, we have identified multiple exemptions he's given for the geld that were unquestionably . . . well, unquestionably *questionable*."

And so they went into it again, her slow process of getting these messengers to admit to the existence of obvious facts without pledging any official stance. It was all the same infuriating neutrality they had shown in the morning, despite the prince's presence.

But earlier she had waded in hypotheticals, and this time she posed a specific opinion quickly. When she asked for anyone to agree with her, they of course remained silent. So she turned sharply to the friar, who was sipping glibly from his predecessor's wine goblet. "What do you think, Tuck?"

"I agree with you entirely," he said without hesitation, folding his arms. The man-who-was-not-Eustace-de-Vesci's mouth gaped open, still standing awkwardly to the side where he had found no place to sit.

"Well then at last we are getting somewhere!" Marion clapped her hands and considered the matter settled, moving on to the next. She stole a moment's glance at Prince John, whose pursed lips and half-cocked eyebrow seemed to indicate he knew exactly what she was doing. And, perhaps, even approved.

Another few minutes passed as she detailed more of the Chancellor's actions, two otherwise unconnected land seizures he had demanded in very different counties. "These are nearly identical issues, don't you agree?"

She posed the question to a disheveled young page who was certainly not Saer de Quincy. He of course refused to either admit or deny any equity between the two events, but Marion swatted away his protest. "Never mind. Could you stand, please? I'm afraid I need your chair as well."

The page's lips trembled, but any objection disappeared at the sight of the mighty John Little rounding the corner, who had every intention of sitting in the page's chair regardless of whether or not it was vacant. The young man barely got out of the way before John dragged the chair sidelong, lowered his frame into its seat, and sighed tremendously at the relief.

"What do you think, John?" she asked before he was even settled.

"Whatever it is you want me to think, Lady Marion." His smile split across his face. "I'm so very comfortable."

"Excellent!" She turned to the disposed page and summoned all her derision into a single smug grin. "Well then, we'll no longer need you here at the council at all."

The page's cheeks twitched. "I'm sorry, what?"

"I'm not interested in your opinion—or lack of one—and so I've replaced you. This man now represents Earl Saer de Quincy in your stead. I'm removing you from the chamber."

She nodded toward an exit, where Nick and Peter Delaney—along with their unreasonably athletic shoulders—suddenly stood in wait and moved into view.

"You can't do that!" the useless man protested. "I'm here as a witness, to report on the findings of this council and report back to Winchester!"

"Curious how quickly you object," Marion kept her tone as cold as winter iron, "when the thing being taken is yours. But don't worry, your earl will get his report. John, when the council is over, do me the favor of riding to Winchester and let Saer de Quincy know that everyone here has rallied their strength behind me."

John Little answered by way of popping a fig into his mouth.

"You're insane!" The page folded his hands in acquittal. "You can't keep me from telling my master the truth."

"I can't," Marion admitted, "if he chooses to come visit your prison cell here. Otherwise, I think it would be quite easy."

She snapped her fingers and the Delaney brothers moved, to the obvious horror of more than a few at the table. They were at the page's side in seconds and did not hesitate to nudge his knees out from under him, catching him at the elbows to drag him away.

"That's enough," came a grumble—at last—from Henry de Bohun. His family members seemed far more alarmed that he chose to speak than at the display itself. Marion enjoyed her first victory, but braced herself for the next part. "Your point is made, you've been anything but subtle at it. Can we dispose of the cheap theatrics and return to policy, then?"

"You use the word *we*, Earl," Marion rounded on him, "as if you have been participating. But you have remained silent through every question of policy, just as you remained silent when you watched me start taking chairs. So why do you speak up now?" She took in each of his family's faces, noting curiously that the Earl of Warwick, Waleran de Beaumont, was missing from the room.

Henry de Bohun's answer came slowly, scraping along the floor. "Because this council is dipping dangerously into the territory of being a farce."

"As is the country," Marion agreed. "But rather than merely take chairs, Longchamp takes *titles. Land.* This is not an empty exercise, it is happening all around us already! Men of worth are being replaced with Longchamp's corrupt lackeys, while we sit by and do nothing! I wonder how many more chairs I could have taken before someone else stopped me? But Lord Henry de Bohun was wise enough to see the danger, anticipate where it was headed, and so he spoke up. Why then are we afraid to do the same against the Chancellor?"

The silence that followed was different than the silence they had given her all morning. One was the simple silence of abstinence—but this was a silence that comes with the axe, at its height, ready to fall. At the next table, her grandfather and grandmother watched with extreme scrutiny, but did not look away.

"I was seconds away from dragging this man into a prison cell," Marion continued, hitting her consonants like an expert swordsman, "and every one of you made it possible. By staying mute in the face of oppression. But when *one voice* speaks up . . ." she dared the room to look away from her, ". . . the injustice stops."

A few seats down from Hereford, Lord Robert bit off a smile that his eyes could not hide.

"You cannot equate the two," old Lord Henry objected, before the gravity of her point could sink in. "You act as if there are only two choices—such a simplistic polarity of thought is the *cause* of our problems, not the *solution*. You would protect us from the lion by feeding us to the bear. It is perfectly possible to object to the Chancellor's activities without demanding his head in payment. I do not agree with an inch of his decisions, but nor do I think it wise to abandon King Richard to this Austrian prison. I shall joyfully support our beloved prince, but only upon his *rightful* ascension. Politics is not all or nothing, my dear girl, something your grandfather should have taught you."

That chilled the room a bit, as eyes careened from one esteemed earl to another. But Marion refused to let it rile her, nor would she let the focus be stolen from her. She was nobody's *dear girl*.

"You may be right," she said casually. "If we had all day, we could potentially find a happy middle ground. But keep in mind that every minute you waste pontificating about it, one more of my men will be sitting in a chair. Who will agree with you when you're the only one left?"

The earl's smile was *dear girl* without the *dear*. "But we do have all day. Is that not the point of us meeting here?"

"*I* have all day," Marion answered. "You have approximately fifteen seconds. Nick, Peter, please take the earl's chair."

He cackled once and the Delaneys hesitated for a split second, but Marion gave them no reason to pause. There was intentionally no one from the Huntingdon Guard present in the room, nor had any of the few actual lords seen a need to bring their personal protection into a debate hall. So when the Delaneys moved, Henry de Bohun's smile dropped. He glanced to his sides where his daughters and their husbands pushed back from the table, clearly unsure of how they were supposed to react. Each Delaney brother, by all rights the most impressive men in the room, barreled down either end of the hall until they converged on the elderly Lord Henry. They reached down to scoop his chair back and away, and the earl only barely lurched to his feet in time to watch them whisk it out from under him.

The great wise Earl of Hereford gasped for air and teetered, reaching blindly at the table, his lips wiggling in a breathless protest.

"At last," Marion smiled at him, "I've got you to stand for something."

The Delaney brothers, as she had instructed them earlier, smashed the earl's chair down hard onto the ground, cracking its frame in half. Each of them tore a hefty leg from the base and brandished it like a club, challenging any man to so much as bat an eye at them. There was commotion, an instinctive reaction to the possibility of violence, but Marion's voice was louder than their fear.

"If we wait, we lose! If we try to negotiate, we lose! You're all trying to be *honorable,* to obey the king's law, to figure out what is *the right thing to do.* That's how good people die. They're dying out there right now, your people *are dying.* This ransom—this damned ransom!—is taking the food from their mouths and the clothes off their backs, and the very people who are supposed to protect them are being replaced by those who would happily ruin their own land in the name of a little power. This is not a threat down the road, we are in its midst already. And we may very well be at the point of no return.

"Take it from me, Lady Marion Fitzwalter, leader of Robin Hood's men, that there is a time when laws must be broken. The alternative is death. So here's what each and every one of you is going to do. You're not going to give some passive report to your masters about *who said what* here, you're going to *demand they join us*. No rebellion was ever born of soft words and apologies. You won't ask nicely, or beg, you're going to yell and scream until you're red in the face. Because if you don't, if they sit back and try to *wait this out*, then you'll be to blame for the end of England."

She could feel the fire in her own words, the crystal clarity that pierced through the fog of ignorance that had otherwise smothered the room. But now, men who had come as messengers and who saw themselves as little else, were stirred toward something more. Not because her grandfather had endorsed the plan, not because Henry de Bohun had sanctioned it, but because she had shown them something true and real.

The danger of their own inaction.

"Huntingdon stands with you," came a confident voice, and to a great disturbance Lord Robert stood from the raised table, pulling his hand away from the countess. "Oh please, they all know the truth of it. We called this council but were too afraid to stand by it, while we let Lady Marion risk everything."

He stood taller, casting a private smile across the room for her.

"She's right," he proclaimed. "Silence is complicity. Every day we fail to stand up to the Chancellor, there will be fewer of us in position to do so. Every man represented here may find themselves replaced on a whim."

"Is that an argument you are truly prepared to make?" asked de Bohun, still quivering without his chair. "Your own earldom you owe to exactly such a whim of King Richard. You gained everything from his royal prerogative. But now you decry that power when it is aimed against you? Ought we give your castle back to the Senlis family, if you are suddenly so concerned with fairness!"

"Perhaps we should." Lord Robert shrugged. "But if I can do anything with the power I have, while I have it, it should be to protect others rather than myself. Why do you remain silent, then? For England's interests, or your own?"

"We must be careful!" Marion's grandfather finally rose to emotion. "If we act as a mob, and claw down that which we disagree with, then we invite the next mob to do the same to us. The Chancellor is corrupt, yes, but he does nothing that is not within his power to do. He is a fetid disease, any man can see that. To which we ought to prescribe medicine. You are suggesting we wield a hatchet. If we wish to support Prince John—as all of us here do—then we must do so from *within* the system, not by burning it down. There is no point in putting a new monarch on the throne if we destroy the monarchy to do so!"

"I agree," answered Hereford. "You speak as if you know Richard's mind on the matter, when you do not. Your kinship to him does not make you a Lion-heart."

Marion caught his gaze and held it captive. "That is true, it does not make me a Lionheart. I wonder then, if you know what that takes? Do you know the story, Earl, of how Richard obtained that name?"

"Of course—for the very discipline in strategy that you lack. He became Lionheart when he sacked the castle of Taillebourg in a mere two days. Over a rebellion, I might add, not unlike the one you here advocate."

"I don't deny his military successes. But he was called Lionheart before Tail-lebourg."

"It was Poitou, when he was but sixteen," creaked the voice of Robert de Vere, as proud as if the story were his own. "He rallied his barons to war, led the army himself. The boy became Lionheart that day, mark you."

Old men, all of them—worse than any foreign army. "Admirable, yes," Mar-ion replied, "but he was Lionheart before that. Does anyone here know where it started? Your Grace, I imagine you know?"

Prince John chewed his lip, giving a slow nod. "You can tell it."

A pause settled before she spoke. "He gave that name to himself."

John's eyebrows flashed upward, in confirmation.

"It was no heroic deed or battle, not at first. He simply wanted a grand name, and told an advisor to introduce him as such. Odd at first, yes, but nobody ques-tioned it. And he backed the name up with actions later, and everyone assumes what they assume."

Hereford, Oxford, and Essex, their mouths closed.

"So no, my kinship does not make me a Lionheart," Marion laughed, let-ting it roll into every word now. "If I want to be one, I simply decide to be. And what I decide today, what you find preposterous today, you will in time take as unbending truth. Power is not divinely granted, it comes to those who *stand up and take it*. Not to those who sit by and watch, waiting for someone else to show the way. And by my calculations, there are far too many people in this room content to sit and watch."

Her breath left her when Prince John stood, and the room stood with him.

"Sit," he said instantly, humbly. "I should . . . I should probably speak."

The hair on Marion's neck stood upright, and she swallowed to maintain her composure. "We are indeed eager to hear from you."

She stepped to the side, though the prince simply raised his hand for quiet.

Once silence was his, his arms dropped—but he still took a few moments to digest his thoughts. It was a transformation, Marion marveled. The brat was finally shedding his skin, to become the king he needed to be. The room itself awaited his every syllable.

"It's rather funny, if you think about it," Prince John chuckled. His words had a slow canter, but carried a casual grace. "You know, I was in the south of France around this time last year—Carcassonne, my first time there. My host bragged that he had one of the finest brothels in the country, and I'm not one to say no, of course. My entourage went ahead of me, to clear out any raff and make sure I was safe, you know how it is. It was a big deal for them—the owners of the brothel, that is—and they went above and beyond to welcome me. They had this sweet wine that was . . . well anyhow, it was a spectacular show, just for me, and then the time came for their whores to parade themselves for my choice."

He started to act the encounter out, demonstrating where the whores had come by, nudging chairs about to get it right, and Marion allowed herself to relax. The room ate up his every word, enraptured. It was an unusually salacious tale to follow her rallying call, but she had rallied them to John's hands, after all. And if the room felt comfortable hearing about John's sexual escapades in France, it was proof enough they would follow him as the natural leader he was.

"I sat down in a chair, which they had lined in satin and raised up onto wooden boxes to make a throne out of it, you see, and there were these boys with harps and flutes and strings, and the whores came out and they were all— every one of them now, not just in the parade, I realized, but everyone in the entire building, even the pretty girls that had already swooned over me—every one of them was *male*."

A laughter went around, which the prince nodded ferociously at.

"Exactly my reaction, yes! I laughed, until I realized it was not a joke at all! I was actually being quite offensive by laughing, because they were entirely serious. This was a whorehouse for homosexuals, as it were, and each of these boys was so very eager to be pricked by a prince!"

Marion laughed out loud, enjoying the new mirth of the room. Still sharing the space with him, she felt compelled to fill in some part of the conversation. "Do you think it was an honest mistake on the part of your host? Or was he trying to embarrass you?"

"Ehhh . . ." Prince John waffled his hand, "the former, I'd like to think, but that's not really the point. The point is that all of these people—these good people with good intentions, who had bent over backward to treat me well— were in for an utter disappointment. I had to somehow tell them I simply wasn't interested, despite the huge effort they had gone through to include me."

Marion's smile faded before she realized why.

"I'm in that male whorehouse again right now, and I'm afraid you're all in for a terrible disappointment."

She suddenly regretted her game with the chairs, as it left her nowhere to sit during what came next.

"You've got me entirely wrong. You all want to rally behind me to put me on the throne, and I don't know how to tell you that I don't want it. Do I like Will Longchamp? No, of course not, he's a prissy little bitch. We've been spatting back and forth for a year now with petty land grabs and the such. But I'm not interested in a war against him. My brother appointed him as Chancellor, and my brother is King, and by God he's going to stay King hopefully until well after I am dead. You think Longchamp is a bad leader? Wait until you see how bad things would be if I were in charge! I'd be terrible at it. At least Longchamp has the . . . strategic acuity for it all. I would just sort of . . . do whatever I want! Sorry. A bit too honest for the moment, but still. You all seem to be so angry with Longchamp for choosing to pay Richard's ransom, but you've got it all wrong. We met. Him and I. Longchamp didn't want to pay the ransom at all, he was in favor of giving me an army and having me march off to Austria to rescue Richard. But I would have been just as bad at leading an army as I would be at running a country. *I* was the one who demanded he pay the ransom."

Marion's stomach shrank into a very sharp coil.

"I came because I thought you simply wanted to replace Longchamp, which I would certainly enjoy. But you want to crown me? Under the assumption that I would refuse to pay this ransom? That . . . that is, no, no no no. No, I would sell the very land out from beneath you, this castle itself, to have my brother back all the sooner. So if you all want to rally together against your common enemy . . . I think . . ." he hissed in sharply, ". . . I think that enemy is . . . me?"

This silence, it was the worst kind.

Prince John sucked between his teeth, wincing as he took in the room.

A room full of people he had just labeled as his enemies.

"So . . . yes. So there's that. I think I'm going to leave."

With a reluctant clap of his hands, he did just that.

The chaos that erupted immediately afterward was the closest thing Marion had ever seen that could be described as actual hell.

SIR ROBERT FITZODO

NOTTINGHAM

THIS POOR DUMB GUARDSMAN wasn't dead, but he might never walk again without a limp. His name was Dillon Fellows—a young man with doughy, wideset features. Even in sleep, that gentle face grimaced as if he were reliving his attack in his dreams. Blood seeped through the bandages wrapped around his left thigh, which the cooks had already changed twice.

Robert had been there—by the Hounds Gate entrance of St. Peter's Square—when it happened. A figure, robed and hooded, had sprung from a window and loosed his arrows at the Guardsmen watching over the early mass. Dillon had taken the first arrow in the thigh while other arrows over-shot toward the crowd, fortunately without hitting anyone. A cowardly attack, meant to scare good people. Robert had chased the bowman off all on his own, protected the parishioners, and carried this poor young Guardsman back to the castle for help. He'd stayed by Dillon Fellows's side the whole time, but rather than be thanked for it—fuck them all—Lord Beneger de Wendenal had given him hell for helping Dillon rather than chasing Robin Hood down.

"He might have bled out if I hadn't brought him here," Robert said, looking down at the lad. He was mercifully asleep now, with no idea an audience had gathered around him, here in the castle's infirmary. "God-her-fucking-self knows where Robin Hood is now, but I don't regret my choice."

One of the cooks wrung out a bloody rag into a basin, and the Peveril whelp paled and turned away. Some pups were new to seeing freshly spilt blood, but Sir Robert FitzOdo had breached that gate more fucking years ago than he could count. Lord Beneger de Wendenal, at least, seemed more than comfort-able with handling the Guardsman's bloody discarded clothes he was inspect-ing.

"Look at that." Wendenal stood, holding the lad's belt up to the torchlight. "There's the mark of your Robin Hood."

Everyone leaned in to see for themselves, but Robert had seen it enough al-ready. The arrow had struck him in the hip, punching a clean hole through the man's leather baldric that Wendenal was currently fingering.

"I thought Robin Hood was supposed to be some sort of expert bowman," Peveril whined. "Was he running away when he got struck?"

"No, that was intentional, I guarantee it." Lord Wendenal admired the wounds, comparing the damaged belt to the blood spots on Dillon Fellows's unclothed leg. "This *is* the work of an expert. It kept our boy from pulling steel, see? Pinned his sword's hilt in place so it couldn't be drawn from the scabbard."

"And it also put an arrow in his hip," Quillen Peveril said with a weak smile, keeping his distance. "That couldn't have been too pleasant neither."

Robert was about as interested in Peveril's fickle humor as he was in sucking the man's cock.

"Why not kill him, then?" asked Jacelyn de Lacy. "And why him instead of FitzOdo, who was a more obvious target?"

Robert refused to be offended by that. "Well, who is he?"

"Common Guard," Peveril answered.

"I can fucking see that. If you don't know his name, just say you don't know."

The whelp frowned and made to retort some goddamned snark, but apparently thought better of it. Right choice, but probably not for the right reasons. He should've shut his mouth just for being in the presence of a knight, he should be saying *sir* every time he addressed Robert, he should show some fucking respect. But Peveril and the half-bitch niece were just like everyone else, all side glances and whispered barbs. Jokes, derision. Because they all assumed the same thing—that any knight left in England was a coward. They assumed a so-called "real knight" would be off fighting in the king's war.

Because fucking *pansy noble boys* like Quillen Peveril didn't know the first fuck about what it means to be a knight.

Lord Beneger stood and stretched his back, his eyes squinting outside at the glowing tips of the castle's battlements. It had been a long morning. "We might have prevented this, if the Sheriff had let me move on the Spotted Leopard. While we spend all our time preparing for this archery tournament, Scarlet is out there unopposed. And apparently," he did not hide a growl for Robert, "we can't even catch him when he sticks his neck out right in front of us."

The arrogance, to call Robert's compassion a mistake. But this Lord Beneger de Wendenal only saw what he wanted, and the man was obsessed with seeing failure.

Robert watched as the man's mouth made noises he mistook as wisdom, inventing new orders to hunt Robin Hood's already cold trail in St. Peter's Square. Lord Beneger de Wendenal was a direct man and stern, but his good traits ended there. He, too, saw Robert as some stooge, an ignorant grunt to use for heavy work. A failure. It was true that Robert had yet to claim a prisoner despite months of hunting, but this was a testament to his quarry's skills, not to Robert's shortcomings. They didn't even know exactly *who* they were chasing. Wendenal suspected that someone else was disguising themself as Robin Hood, but after dismissing Gilbert as an option, nobody had come up with a better suspect.

But it didn't matter. It was *Robin Hood* they chased, and one could not kill a name. Robin Hood was loved, and that was damned harder to fight than any swordsman. The fact that Lord Wendenal thought he could finish the hunt with nothing but rage guaranteed him to be the next man to look the fool. At least that wasn't Robert's role anymore.

"FitzOdo?" the lord barked. *Sir Robert FitzOdo,* a man of any worth should have said the full name. "You understand?"

"Aye," Robert grunted. He understood. He understood that Lord Wendenal intended to keep chasing the wrong clues, just as blind a strategy as the Sheriff's fucking archery tournament. And Robert understood more than that, too. He understood the many many leagues of difference between Lord Wendenal and King Henry. And only one of those men had touched his steel to Robert's shoulder, only one of those men had earned the words that Robert had sworn, on his knee.

"I pledge to serve you, above all others, in good faith and without deceit."

It was nigh twenty years ago that Robert had knelt and Sir Robert had risen. Most knights were highborn before they bent, but Robert had risen from nothing—youngest son of a poor tailor. Most knights swore their oaths before a local lord or a knight-commander if they were lucky, but Robert had knelt to the fucking king himself. He should have been a fucking legend.

But King Henry was dead, and all the damned decency of the world had gone with him. A good knight like Sir Robert was left to take orders from bitter barons and opportunistic nobodies. Robert was no member of the Nottingham Guard, he took no orders from Captain de Grendon and even fewer from Lord Wendenal. His sworn duty was to Roger de Busli of Tickhill Castle—*Red Roger*—who had given him the charge of bringing Robin Hood to Tickhill in chains. Robert worked *alongside* the Nottingham crew, not *with* it.

He had no obligation to do things their way.

Robert was happy to play the role of the dumb brute they saw in him—knowing better than to ever present more of himself than others assumed.

Hunting a man takes patience and attention to detail, the kind of groundwork Robert had been laying for months along with his men Derrick and Ronnell. *Chasing* Robin Hood, as Wendenal wanted, meant they'd always be behind him. Wendenal's team thought they could jaunt over to St. Peter's Square and sniff out Robin Hood's crumbs, and somehow magically end up in front of him. Thought they could catch a gopher by staring at the hole where it had last been seen, as if it would come back again. Daft twats.

So while the Black Guard went to ask every parishioner what they'd seen, FitzOdo would resume his own investigation. Specifically, looking in the places Robin Hood *hadn't* been seen.

He'd been following patterns: six taverns in Nottingham of late, each robbed and warned against selling to Guardsmen.

But one tavern, most notorious for serving them, was still mysteriously untouched.

THE TRIP TO JERUSALEM was built into the sandstone cliffside of Nottingham Castle's belly. Its wooden structure was slanted and mismatched, even though the building itself was rather new. It wasn't the closest tavern to the castle's entrance gate, but the fact that it was part of Castle Rock made it comfortable, a frequent destination for the Nottingham Guard. Some even preferred it to the barracks hall and were happy to leave the castle proper to dine here instead. Robert left Derrick and Ronnell outside to watch. Over the last few weeks he'd coincidentally earned the trust of the Trip's proprietor, who was the only other knight in Nottingham.

"Sir Robert FitzO-o-o-do," came his singsong voice, accompanied by a tankard raised in the air. Sir Richard-at-the-Lee's hair and beard were braided into competing tails—long brown-grey wisps that threatened to dip into every cup he poured. He waited behind his countertop, positioned in the middle of the room to let him serve those on all sides. But the Trip was empty of customers this morning, and Sir Richard hunched himself over a bowl of thick mealy slop. "A trifle early today! Have you been promoted to sun, come to let me know the day has begun?"

"Oh I see, you mean to anger me so that I'll cut out your tongue." Robert eased himself onto a stool at the counter. "A good strategy—it would make it far easier to eat the crap you have there." He eyed the porridge with suspicion.

"Fresh rat in it today," Sir Richard joked. "Actually, no, it's *last* week's rat. Want a bowl?"

He didn't. But he pulled out his coinpurse. "Take my money."

Sir Richard grinned and ladled out another serving from a copper pot on the ground. They broke their fast together, sharing unimportant stories and trading barbs at whomsoever they pleased. Robert wasn't precisely sure what he'd come to learn, so he meant to keep the conversation casual. It would have been a damned amateur to reveal what he wanted. If the Trip had any secrets to tell, it would be patience that brought them out—now that Robert knew to look for them.

"How's business then?"

"Wretched." Sir Richard scratched at the dirt on an empty horn of ale. "Less coin coming in, more going out. Damned ransom. I should have opened a whorehouse."

"Everyone has to eat."

"My purse would argue otherwise. Altogether too much money to buy King Richard back, I say. I keep explaining that we have a perfectly good Richard right here, and I'll do the job for only half the price!"

He laughed the same way he did every time he told that joke, showing his dark gums and missing teeth.

Robert probably would have loathed Sir Richard's company in any other scenario, but there would always be a common bond between those who had taken the knee. Sir Richard-at-the-Lee knew the same unspoken prejudice, the constant accusation in everyone's eyes as to why he wasn't proving himself out in the Holy Land and defending his king. The slander of *Coward Knight* had followed Robert for fifteen years, and the Crusade had brought it back for more. But Robert was simply obeying the orders of his liegelord Red Roger.

Sir Richard-at-the-Lee, on the other hand, had actively *refused* to join the Crusade. He was no man's knight now, which by many opinions made him no knight at all. But he was still the closest thing to a sworn brother that Robert had found in this city. Sir Richard wore his disgrace with pride, had even turned it into his livelihood. The very name of his inn was a joke—when asked why he had not answered the call to war, he would defiantly retort that he had indeed "made the Trip to Jerusalem."

"Another bout of ill news, then?" Sir Richard asked quietly, tucking a strand of rogue hair behind an ear. "Another Guardsman who won't be walking the walls tomorrow?"

"Not dead . . . but aye." Robert took a mouthful of the gruel. "Who told you?"

Sir Richard answered by raising an eyebrow toward the back of the Trip, where a few small alcoves honeycombed into the earthen wall. Each boasted a table, chairs, and a bit of privacy for those with business to conduct. One had a hulking dark shape in its middle, a lone occupant that Robert had not noticed upon entering.

"Far too early for him. Usually means he lost someone." Sir Richard lowered his voice. "Saw a lot of him last autumn."

Robert did not have to squint to identify the man. His size was sign enough, and even the dim light found ways to highlight the red in Simon FitzSimon's mane. The Scotsman led the training yard for the Nottingham Guard, and was known to volunteer himself on the occasional manhunt.

"Just an injury this time," Robert explained. "Young fellow, took an arrow in the thigh. But at St. Peter's, in front of a full crowd. Could have been anyone. Hell of a thing."

Sir Richard scowled, moving a few feet farther from Simon's earshot. "A lot of that lately. Tales of death and murder, I mean. They seem to frequent my counter even more often than the *rats*—" He stomped at the ground as one scampered away.

Robert frowned. "Anything tasty, then? In these stories?"

The man chewed his memories. "Some lord got gutted off the Sherwood Road not so long ago . . . him and his wife, too."

"Lord Brayden," Robert scoffed. "I was there. And I was the one what told you about it."

"Ah, so you were! What else . . . the guards at the Commons were sacked last week so the rabble could eat for free . . . a lot of fighting of late, too. People attacked for no reason, roughed up for the hell of it. People are on edge, afraid to step outside."

"Tell me something I don't know, Richard."

"Sorry." Sir Richard leaned back. "I only know what I hear."

"We've had some trouble with other taverns—busted windows, broken horns. See any faces you don't recognize lately?"

He sucked air through his teeth. "Nah. My clientele tends to be more on the *savory* side than the *un*. Take The Simons, for instance. Though I'll admit I'm glad for the coin, it's a shame he's here. Sorry about your friend's leg."

"Amen." Robert slid a few shillings across the table, more than was needed. "I'll buy him another. What's he drinking, wine? Mead? Just ale?"

Sir Richard barked in response. "Stick with ale for him! The Simons would have crushed your bones to jelly for offering him a southern drink. But if you want mead yourself, then I'm your man. Increasing hard to acquire of late, but at-the-Lee is at-your-service. Cheapest in town here, if you can even find it anywhere else."

"No thanks, ale's fine," Robert answered, quietly pocketing that information away. Whether it meant anything, he couldn't tell—but it was something *unique* about the Trip, which was exactly what he'd come to dig up. Maybe one piece of the puzzle, or maybe nothing. He could've asked more directly, but any barkeep was—by nature—untrustworthy with secrets. Which was the very reason Robert drank his shit small beer and ate his shittier porridge. Richard-at-the-Lee gave him a parting smile and took another gulp of his own porridge, letting it muck about in his whiskers as he swallowed it down. Robert found it a disgusting habit, though others found it endearing—earned the man his nickname of the *greenbeard*.

Robert carried both horns of ale toward the shadows at the back of the inn. While half the building was built proper, with a vaulted wooden ceiling that let the hearth smoke drift away, its other half was buried into the rock itself. Robert had to stoop as the sandstone cave loomed downward, giving the back tables of the inn the feeling of a rabbit's hole, or a stomach. Simon FitzSimon noted his approach and dipped his head in silent acknowledgment, but seemed less than interested in anything more.

"Top you off?" Robert offered, placing one horn at the edge of his table.

The master-at-arms raised his eyes to meet Robert's, then moved slowly back down to his own horn, still full to the brim.

Just this once, Robert chose to forgive the man his disrespect. It was no surprise the quartermaster hadn't stood at his presence, no surprise he hadn't said, *No, sir, thank you, sir.* Simon FitzSimon was one of the most respected men in the castle and several years Robert's senior, but he was still nothing more than an arms-trainer who should show due respect to a bound knight. But for this moment, Robert chose not to care.

Simon saw himself as father to every recruit that came through his yard. And this morning, one of those "sons" had been ambushed.

"You heard about this morning, then," Robert said.

The armsmaster's head nodded, slowly. "Dillon Fellows."

"Hell of a thing. I was there, I carried him to the castle."

Simon's lips tightened, a slow nod of his head. It said *thank you,* but it also said *you're not one of us.* It said *you get a pass this time.* It said *we're better off without you.*

"I know you don't care for me," Robert said, surprising himself with his frankness. "I know none of you do. You don't try to hide it. But I'm here. You have the only sober knight in Nottingham at your disposal, looking for the man who shot your boy. I'm on your side."

There was probably more to say, but he hadn't meant to start anything. Simon had never done him any particular wrong.

He moved to leave, but the Scotsman stopped him. "FitzOdo."

Simon slid his own horn a bit to the left and replaced it with the one Robert had brought. It was the tiniest of concessions.

"I don't know you enough not to care for you, but I can tell you something. Dillon Fellows. That name mean anything to you?"

Robert shook his head.

"His older brother Brian Fellows was killed in the autumn, murdered by the man who would then murder Roger de Lacy, while wearing Brian's tabard. Dillon cried like a babe at his brother's funeral, he'd only just joined the Guard then. His mother was there, begged Dillon to leave, begged me to let him. Dillon's not much of a Guardsman. Would've made a better stableboy, or a chair. But he stayed in the Guard, to do right by his brother. He watches at St. Peter's every morning, talks to the people on their way in, talked about his brother, you know? Not for himself, mind you, but to help other people, going through their own troubles. Gives out half his pay to those in need. Everyone there knows him by name, feels safer when he's around. Like he's family. They ought to put him on the pulpit. He's young and friendly, people love him—gives the Nottingham Guard a good name, you know? That doesn't happen much." Simon took a swig of the ale. "Did you know any of that?"

"No," Robert answered.

"That's why people don't care for you. You're not one of us, and you can't help that, but you don't *want* to be one of us. The Guard is a family. Literally, sometimes—brothers, fathers, and sons. It's something noble for those that could never be a knight. You don't eat with us, you don't drink with us, and those two goons of yours are like rabid curs."

You don't invite me to eat with you, Robert wanted to say.

You don't invite me to drink with you.

And Derrick and Ronnell are the only ones who treat me with respect.

He might have said as much, might not have. But a curious thing next, that drew his attention. The soft patter of bare feet on stone—a tiny mop of a thing, some dirty street boy, hurrying down the steps beside him toward the front door. The child left a trail of dirt in his wake, coming from a bucket that he carried with both hands.

Robert had come looking for anything unusual, and that ever counted. Might be nothing, might not. Whether he could even directly ask the greenbeard about it, he wasn't sure. But something in Robert FitzOdo's gut told him that just like that, he was in front of the gopher. How long it would take to show its head, though, he couldn't tell. That was the problem with groundwork like this—it was slow. And the archery tournament had established a deadline that couldn't be ignored.

So yes, he and his boys would continue to watch the Trip. But it didn't mean they could stop doing the other thing. That... that had to continue.

"Glad I came to talk to you," he said, and left The Simons to his drinks.

"... I observe my homage to him completely, against all persons, in good faith and without deceit." Robert had memorized the words long prior to kneeling. Years before, as a boy, he'd recited them in his dreams. They were better than prayers, because they were accountable on this earth, not the promise of the next. But he would eventually learn that simply knowing the words was meaningless. A thousand different interpretations lay buried in their phrases.

For instance. If he could only do his duty through deceit, which part of his vow should he break?

Fucking Nottingham. Robert had been late to the war here sixteen years ago. His duty was to King Henry the Elder, to defend the castle from his usurping sons. But in Henry's absence, was Robert's duty to protect his king, or to protect his king's lands? Were they equal? With an army between him and his duty, there was no way to break the siege lines from behind and get to the castle, not in good faith.

Not without deceit.

What name would they have called him had he sat idly by and waited for the war to be over, watched as his king's castle was sacked? The Waiting Knight? FitzOdo the Absent?

Instead he chose to act.

He infiltrated the army of Henry's youngest son, led by the traitor Earl of Derby, father of the current Sheriff William de Ferrers. Robert sabotaged the elder Ferrers's siege engines, and personally slew the knight-commander that was flooding the castle's walls. That was the act of FitzOdo the Brave, that was the act of the Warring Knight.

But he had acted in "poor faith," said his king, he'd succeeded through deceit. He'd broken his vows as a knight.

So he became FitzOdo the Coward.

The Shameless Knight.

King Henry transferred his scutage to Baron Roger de Busli, even then too fat for his station, who had held his battalion at bay a mile from the city's edges and waited for a victor. Red Roger they called him now, the Bloody Baron of Tickhill, whose every infamous act was secretly performed by his favorite pet knight.

Fucking Nottingham.

The city that ruined him.

THE RAIN CAME THAT night, pounding fiercely down upon a man who had once proudly knelt before the king, who had sworn to do his duty with diligence and honesty. Robert could barely see the wall beside him, and he knew surely if there was a God that She must have difficulty seeing down through the storm as well.

The rain was appropriate.

Beneger de Wendenal thought he could kill the gopher by screaming loudest into its tunnels.

While Sheriff Ferrers thought he could invite the thing out to dinner.

Robert knew the truth.

Flood the hole with water.

Turn its home against it.

"How do you want to handle it?" Derrick asked, half shouting through the downpour. They had returned to the Spotted Leopard just before the sky turned its hate upon them, before they had changed their respectable clothing for these fucking costumes.

"Same as ever," Robert ordered, "you take the lead, I'll let you know if I want to change pace."

He fidgeted at his smock, already soaked through, as if it mattered.

The problem, he had realized some time ago, was that nobody wanted to rat out the wonderful Robin Hood. He was friendly, he brought presents, he bought loyalties. It was an understandable trade when all he asked in return was a simple "Never seen him." The poorfolk were his shield, he used them as cover. He put them in danger.

But still they did his bidding. Still they hid his secrets, in plain sight.

"I mean how far do you want to take it, sir?" Derrick asked again, more importantly. "Am I still on a leash?"

Robert knew exactly what he was asking. Next to Derrick, his lean greyhound face flitting away from the rain, Ronnell checked his own costume. His weapons hidden in their folds. The hatchet. The bludgeon.

The Sheriff somehow thought the commonfolk would turn on Robin Hood when he was captured in the archery tournament. No, it would go the other way, unless his reputation changed. That's what Robert and his boys had been working on for months, slowly—but now they had to do so harder than ever. As much as they could, before the tournament.

Of course Robert had known who *Dillon Fellows* was, that's why he'd targeted the well-known young Guardsman. That's why they'd done it in front of a church mass—*the monster, Robin Hood*. Respect was a fickle thing, and it was easy to move from one side to another. An arrow to the thigh—courtesy of Derrick's bowmanship—and the people's sympathies moved slightly back toward the Nottingham Guard.

Robin Hood, whoever he was, needed his home turned against him. Robert was flooding the hole.

If the thief was indeed caught at the archery tournament, nobody would think twice about defending the man who chopped their hands and pinned them to the wall. Or if he escaped the tournament, it would only be a matter of time before he'd be flushed out by the very people he thought would protect him.

"Just check with me first," Robert said, hating every word.

"Yes, sir." Derrick's head bobbed.

At least he said sir.

Derrick flipped the hood over his head, leaving nothing but his sharp nose and smile. "After you, *Friar.*"

Robert knew a fucking thing or two about how easy it was to turn a man's reputation to filth.

He moved down the lane toward the Spotted Leopard, gritting his teeth for what would come next. He didn't even know if the tip they'd received that Robin Hood was a patron here was true or not—it didn't matter. "Robin Hood" would be there tonight, and he'd be exceedingly hard to please. Tomorrow, maybe another whorehouse. The next day, the Commons. St. Mary's, maybe. Every day until the tournament, until the people were slavering for Robin Hood's head.

The people had to learn, they had to realize they were hurting themselves by keeping Robin Hood safe. The more they began to fear him, the sooner this entire nightmare would be over, and Sir Robert FitzOdo could get the fuck out of this city for the last time.

Nobody could love a man who gave you a coin and then beat you.

Nobody could love a man who cut off the hands that helped him.

Nobody would hide a man who loosed arrows into crowds.

And if that meant putting on a costume and burning down a brothel, or whatever fucking worse was in store this night, then so goddamned be it.

PART V

RED AND RED

FORTY

QUILLEN PEVERIL

IF ST. MARY HAD anything to say about it, she likely would have stormed out of her church and shooed them all away.

Presumably.

Quill didn't really know much about her aside from the fact she was a saint, and that his companions this day—standing outside the great church's gaping front door—were anything but.

"We'd best hurry," Sir Robert FitzOdo growled, too anxious for his own skin. "These are precious seconds we're wasting."

His two lackeys, Derrick and Ronnell, both grunted something vaguely affirmative, as if the three of them amounted to even a single vote. It was possible the mere proximity of the church was a discomfort to them, burning their skin or the like.

"There's plenty of time," Lord Beneger answered, ever stoic, his eyes climbing the vertical lines of St. Mary's stonework to her great square steeple. Where most of the city had been filled with slapdash structures that turned Nottingham's normally straight roads into obstacle courses, the footprint of St. Mary's grounds was untouched by the encroaching city. She lay like a massive stone lion, daring the rest of the world to come closer, knowing it wouldn't. The largest structure outside of the castle itself, St. Mary's prompted a true sense of awe that hushed even their irreverent crew. "She's yet to ring nine, and we're not due until half past. Provided our information is accurate."

The answer was a glum mumble. "It's accurate."

It was difficult to tell which of them defiled the church more. The drunkard Coward Knight and his useless minions, the *Lord Death* and his lifelong sport of revenge, or the pudgy opportunist whose information they were reliant on.

"We'll see soon enough," Lord Beneger said.

"It's accurate," Rob o'the Fire repeated.

His round face had soft features and black bruises. Both begged for sympathy, but Quill had nothing but skepticism for the man. He was a Red Lion of little import by his own admission, and had come to the Nottingham Guard in the middle of the night, begging for amnesty in exchange for secrets.

Well, more accurately, *one* secret.

He knew how to catch the assassin Will Scarlet, so he claimed.

The last time an informant had brought them news, their opportunity had slipped by when the Sheriff refused to let them follow up upon it. They might have prevented the Spotted Leopard's fate—burnt now, at the hand of Robin

Hood's torch, three days earlier. So even though they had enough going on with the tournament today, Ben was not going to hesitate for a second on this Red Lion's information. The good gentleman o-the-Fire's hands were bound by rope, concealed under a folded woolen cloak he appeared to be carrying. Given the damp spit of the morning's charcoal clouds, it made the man look a right fool for not wearing the cloak—but since he was probably actually a right fool, it was all the same to him.

News like this was undoubtedly too good to be true. *"He may lead us to Will Scarlet,"* Quill had complained to Jacelyn de Lacy, *"but I'll bet my left nut that he gets something out of this, too."*

"I don't care if he gets to fuck the queen," Jacelyn had answered. *"So long as I get Scarlet."*

She was in St. Mary's now, absolving herself or whatever it was one was supposed to do, before they laid their trap. Jacelyn's sole purpose in joining the Nottingham Guard was to bring justice to her slain uncle, dead by Will Scarlet's hand. Quill was fuzzy with the details, but he imagined that everyone was allowed one bucket's worth of sin before he was expected to empty it out on the confessional floor. The fact that Jacelyn de Lacy had waited until the last moment to dump out her bucket spoke to how much sin she was merrily ready to do unto her uncle's murderer. The plan was just to arrest him, of course, but Jac was probably eager for things to go sideways, that she might end it her own way.

A part of him was jealous, that she'd get her moment. His thoughts lingered to the solemn table in his barracks room. The parchment and quill . . . and the letter to his father he had barely begun. He had sworn to write to his father and summon him to Nottingham, to make a claim against Ferrers for Sheriff, but every time he touched quill to ink, his fingers would not summon the words. Sending for his father felt like surrender, an admission that he could not handle this on his own. And how could he prove himself good enough to be Lord of the Peak one day, if he needed his father to sweep in and fix every problem? He'd burnt the first letter he started, and the second and third, until the sheer act of ignoring the table entirely felt like a victory.

And here they were, on the verge of capturing Will Scarlet. And more, given their plans at the archery tournament. The keel was righting, and though Quill could not claim to be its captain, he had his hands on the lines.

"Why are we waiting for her?" Ronnell burst out. "If she'd rather pray than catch criminals, we can do this without her."

"We very nearly did," Quill answered, before Ben could. "De Grendon didn't want her participating in this at all." She had a critical role to play at the St. Valentine's tournament today, and the captain didn't want anything to jeopardize her attendance. But according to their informant, it was the tournament itself that provided the opportunity they were about to seize.

"We wait," Ben answered. "There's nothing de Grendon, nor Ferrers, nor King Richard, nor God could do to keep Jacelyn from today's pursuit."

Derrick huffed. "Just wondering how much confessing she has left in her, is all."

Lord Beneger dismissed the comment with a slight wave. "I envy her. She's on the brink of her vengeance, and she's wise to tend to her soul first, to better enjoy it."

Even in Lord Beneger's cruelest scowls, there was always a slight sadness; some great weight that had long taken over his muscles. Jacelyn was purging her soul to better avenge her uncle, a man whom she had never even known in life. But Beneger de Wendenal mourned a *son*, his last surviving son. Quill hoped he never knew even a fraction of that grief.

"What about you?" Quill asked softly. "You'll have your revenge as well, no?"

"Perhaps." Lord Beneger's voice held as little enthusiasm as was possible. "There's no proof yet that Will Scarlet killed my son. He might deny it. Or there may be others. And *Robin Hood* might live on regardless. That's why I envy her. Her target is fully within her grasp. The only thing worse than the pain itself is to never find satisfaction. To know that your quarry has slipped away, like words in the wind. To never know what became of them, or what their actions did to them, if anything at all. She'll get hers, from Scarlet, today. But mine . . . mine is not so certain."

The Coward Knight reared his bald head into Rob o'the Fire's face. "This gang runt turned on Scarlet. After St. Peter's, and the brothel fire, and the Commons . . . the people are finally ready to turn to us, because they know we'll help him. *That's* what I've been working on for months—doing *good*, that is. Spreading the rightful name of the Guard. Helping people. You make fun of me all you want, but this today happened because of *me*."

Quill exchanged a confused glance with Ben. How FitzOdo thought that his daily routine of getting drunk was *"spreading the rightful name of the Guard,"* Quill didn't know. The man was probably just jealous that he couldn't claim this victory for himself.

Unlike FitzOdo, Quill knew better than to count his chickens before they shat in his lap.

Or something.

One thing at a time, Quill breathed. *First, Will Scarlet.*

JACELYN REJOINED THEM SHORTLY, apologized for her delay, and they heaved off.

South from St. Mary's, the ground dove down sharply toward the docks, though they took the Long Stair that offered a gradual ramp to the river's level. There were nine of them in total now, as two of Lord Beneger's Derbymen had joined them with their final member—a wary councilman named Gerome Artaud. The thin man was Will Scarlet's intended target, so Rob o'the Fire claimed, and had proven himself willing to participate in the reversal of his trap.

Their large company might have normally made for a conspicuous group by the docks had they not dressed down into the vulgar common trappings of laborers. Quill's neck protested at the rough edges of an ill-fitting tunic, which snagged awkwardly at the leather plating of his underarmor. He would have preferred a shirt of mailed chain, but its heft and noise ran an even greater risk of being discovered. They walked without purpose, in drifting clumps, lest any watchful gang member find cause to send warning of their arrival down the food chain.

Quill's eyes scanned the edges of the buildings and the hollows of windows, but found no sign of anyone paying them a single mind. It took only a few minutes for them to situate, scattered at convenient distances from the unimposing square shack of the harbormaster's office. It was stilted up above many of the other long storage houses, a bit removed from the river Trent but easily accessible from the main thoroughfare. A wooden staircase led to its doorway, and Artaud promised that inside was a single room with no other exit. Artaud alone was dressed in his normal garb, which was abnormal enough to be readily identifiable. The cut of his clothes was clean and foreign, and a distinctive velvet cap turned him into a literal target amongst any crowd.

Gerome Artaud strode with purpose up the stairs to his own office, accompanied by Lord Beneger and the two extra Derbymen—all three disguised in the tawdry rags of any docksman. Artaud was accustomed to traveling with three incognito bodyguards, so he explained, and Lord Beneger had chosen to use that device to their advantage.

At half past nine each day, Gerome Artaud ate a meal in his office alone, perusing the records of the day's imports. Those bodyguards would stand watch outside.

But this day, those bodyguards would be dismissed to attend the archery tournament.

So at half past nine this day—so Rob o'the Fire claimed—the assassin Will Scarlet had orders to enter the harbormaster's office and mutilate him.

He was less forthcoming with the *why* of it all, which felt as if they were being tricked into taking out the Red Lions' trash. If the gang was cleaning house and cutting ties with Scarlet, Quill didn't like doing their bidding. But as Jac said, it would be worth it if the day ended with Scarlet in chains.

Only half a minute or so passed before the three bodyguards emerged from the harbormaster's office again. They shook their master's hand before hustling away, hoping to make it up to the castle while there was still room to be found in the spectator stands for the afternoon's festivities. The man and his velvet cap re-entered his office, exposed and vulnerable.

At least, so it appeared to anyone watching.

The exchange of clothing had been done quickly inside the office, and the illusion was believable even to Quill. The man now beneath the velvet cap— alone in his crow's nest office awaiting Will Scarlet's arrival—was actually Lord

Beneger de Wendenal. Gerome Artaud was already gone, disguised as his own bodyguard, walking briskly back to the safety of the castle with his two Derby escorts.

The rest of them had but to wait, conspicuously clumped near the dockmaster's stairs, only a short run away. Once Will Scarlet appeared and entered the door to confront his prey, they could all close in behind him in a matter of seconds.

Quill's heart started beating faster, at the knowledge of what was coming. He had not seen Will Scarlet since the night of the massacre outside Bernesdale, where Quill had watched him turn some of the young men of the Guard into bloody ribbons. He still awoke some nights in a sweat, dreaming of that fight, wondering how he had survived the carnage. It seemed impossible that the world could put that man back in front of him again.

He tried to distract himself, by controlling what he could.

"If you make any unsolicited noise," he said casually to Rob o'the Fire, fastening the man's hands to a sturdy dock cleat with the excess rope, "if you give Will Scarlet any warning, or bring undue attention to us . . . if you bring your gangling friends down on our heads, or any bit of this goes differently than the way you've described . . . well. Well, I will certainly . . . I will be upset. I don't know that I have a threat for you. Jacelyn, can you make a threat for him?"

She didn't move a muscle. "We'll throw you in the river."

"*We'll throw you in the river,* is what we'll do." Quill raised his eyebrows in turn, hoping one of them was more menacing than the other. "Is that it? We'll throw him in the river?"

"His hands are tied, he'll drown. And it would be fast. For us, at least."

"That's very practical." Quill gave Rob's rope a solid tug. "You hear that? If you try to betray us, we'll treat you very practically. I was hoping for something with a bit more teeth. Bloody, something, you know. We'll cut your cock off, and feed it to you, something like that."

Jacelyn smiled, and Quill was certain he did not want to know why. "You men sure like threatening each other's members. Such a strange fascination."

He turned back to his captive. "I'm not going to cut your cock off, that sounds terrible. I'd have to grab your cock and try to cram it down your throat, that's a lot of cock handling. No, I'll . . . I'll cut your eyeball out. And then I'll take it and aim it back at you, so that you can see . . . exactly how foolish you look . . . without an eyeball."

Apparently his raging nerves were occupying all the brainpower he normally used for wit. Jac gave him a pathetic laugh. "I don't know how you've survived this long, Peveril."

He smiled at the insult, but then swallowed it down. He was on her bad side, her frozen side. "Sure you do," he answered. "We take the lot we're given and make it work for us. I imagine your days have been harder than mine."

If she meant to respond, she was interrupted by the appearance of a small man loping across the yard, headed directly to the base of the wooden stairs.

"*Here we go,*" Jac whispered, and Quill's bowels demanded to evacuate his body.

Their target stopped for only a second, risking one glance back before he climbed the stairs in daring, breathless bounds, and an absolutely unwelcome terror turned Quill's innards to stone. And whatever was coursing through him, he knew, was but a shaving of what must pump through Jacelyn's every breath. Though it was only a dozen stairs, the world had slowed such that it took hours for Scarlet to climb them.

When time returned to its cruel progression, a second figure darted across the thoroughfare behind Scarlet, bounding up the staircase a moment later.

"Who's that now?" Quill asked in a shock, and turned quickly to Rob o'the Fire to ask it again even faster. "*Whozzatnow?*"

"Fuck," Rob breathed, his beady eyes struggling to widen. "He was supposed to be alone. What's she doing here?"

"Push him in the river," Jac growled. She was probably serious.

Will Scarlet opened and closed the office door in a flash, while his skinny little companion leaned across the railing, guarding. Jacelyn lurched but didn't move. They'd all been ready to bolt the moment Scarlet was inside, but now they'd be spotted by his lookout on the rail.

Scarlet was alone with Lord Beneger.

"You said he'd be alone!" Quill shook his captive.

"What do we do?" Jacelyn whispered.

His heart smashed the words out before he could even think them. "If we move, she sees us, and she warns Scarlet." He craned his head to see if Fitz-Odo or his boys had reacted yet, but couldn't find them. *How many seconds had gone by? How long had Scarlet been in there?* "If we *don't* move," he continued, "then Ben's on his own. If we *do* move, at least we can get to him as soon as possible."

"Ben can handle Scarlet," Jacelyn muttered, though her jealousy was tangible. "But if we're spotted, he has to handle two of them."

Time, which had so recently frozen, now hurled past in furious clumps, impossible to track.

"But for how long?" he whispered back. His blood turned to fire. "He thinks we're coming, we should've already been there by now! If he's biding time, it's because he thinks we're coming!"

Good God, he was probably already dead.

"I'm going!" Quill decided, and was already running.

The staircase had seemed so close, and now he was horrified at how many steps it took for it to even draw near. And almost instantly, somehow before he was even truly at a stride, a shriek came from above. The girl who stood watch called out Will Scarlet's name and threw herself through the door, where Beneger was now outnumbered.

He felt
    every footstep,
        he took the stairs
           two at a time,
                but every moment was
a moment Lord Beneger was fighting for his life. Every time his boot met the
mud or a wooden step, it was a knife in Ben's gut, a blade in his chest.

They all crashed up the staircase at once, FitzOdo and Derrick and Ronnell
arriving from other directions, but Quill vaulted up first. His sword was in his
hands though he did not recall pulling it. He didn't wait to try the handle at the
top of the stairs, he greeted the door with the heel of his boot and burst into the
room at full speed.

Square, a desk in its middle, tiny slatted windows no body could squeeze through.
The girl to the right, clattering to the back wall. Two figures to the left. Quill's
eyes had not adjusted but he knew them by size. Lord Beneger stood tall, his
hands behind his back, where Will Scarlet was hiding. One arm reached out
from behind, high, where he held a fat dagger in a reverse grip. Its point was
directly downward, touching the soft of Ben's clavicle.

"Fuck, fuck, fuck!" Will Scarlet cursed, pulling Ben back the small amount
he could, away from the suddenly crowded entrance. The girl across from him
was young. She scampered up onto a large wooden chest to make distance as
the room instantly filled beyond capacity.

"Put it down!" screamed FitzOdo, or someone else, or all of them. Jacelyn
yelled it as well, she leveled her blade against the girl, who had whipped out a
small knife dangling from a thin rope.

"Fuck, I told you not to come!" Scarlet yelled at the girl, who continued to
scatter randomly, hoping to find some foothold or posture that would give her
an advantage. "Put that away, you're going to get yourself killed!"

"Kill the girl," FitzOdo demanded.

"Anybody fucking moves . . ." Will pierced over the commotion, ". . . and this
man is the first to die."

Quill locked eyes with Lord Beneger, by far the calmest in the room. His
chin was perked slightly up, as if to make it easier, as if to show how little
he feared the knife. Quill felt his own neck shrink away, what he imagined
would be a natural reaction to the touch of a blade. There was also blood,
blood on Ben's neck, but not his own. It flowed down from Will Scarlet's
hand. Whatever had already transpired before they entered, Lord Beneger
had done damage.

"As I was saying," Lord Beneger's voice was all gut, "there's no way out of
this."

"You'd better hope that's not true," Scarlet growled back at him, "or you
leave this world with me."

"Go on, then." FitzOdo pushed forward, lowering his weapon to get dangerously closer to Scarlet. "Kill him. You think it can't get any worse for you? Best

think that one over." For a moment there was a silence, the chaos of uncertainty had stilled into the edge of his words. "This is it for you either way, Scarlet. But we could end it quick, or we could take a few days." There was a raw truth in his voice that was black ice, and Quill knew that for the first time he was hearing the real Sir Robert FitzOdo. "I told Red Roger I'd bring him back a Robin Hood, and I mean to. If you're lucky, he'll give you the saw. Where we tie you upside down, hanging by your feet, splayed out, an' we take a saw. A good long saw, as you might use for a tree, and we start at your nethers and we go down, slowly, a few inches every hour—"

"FitzOdo!" Lord Beneger cut him off, nearly startling Scarlet. "That's enough of that."

"Oh," Scarlet said with some surprise, upon seeing FitzOdo's obedience. "I've got the bossman, do I? Things are looking up, Zinn."

"How's that?" the girl asked, still fidgeting.

"You want to talk about cutting off body parts?" Scarlet called out. "Let's start with bossman then. Tell them to leave, bossman." He shifted. His right arm slid away and came back again with a second knife, this one resting diagonally beneath Lord Beneger's nostril. "Tell them to leave or I'll carve off your nose."

Lord Beneger resisted, air spat from his teeth, but he made no noise.

"Fuck," Derrick muttered.

"Or maybe the ear." Scarlet shifted his blade to the side of Ben's head. "I can make you one of us."

"You'd have to cut his cock off to do that," FitzOdo returned. For the briefest of moments Quill met eyes with Jacelyn, reminded of how damned sick she was of men threatening to damage each other's cocks.

"Scarlet," Jacelyn said, calmly, with no threat to her voice. "Why is she here?"

"What?" he asked, repositioning slightly to look at her.

"It's Zinn, right?" she asked, though nobody confirmed. "Why'd you bring her on this?"

He looked at Jacelyn harder, and practically recoiled. "Fuck, your face."

She closed her eyes and let it pass. "You said you didn't want her here."

Scarlet glanced over at his young apprentice. "I told her not to come, but sometimes she's a stubborn little bitch, isn't she?"

"She sure is!" Zinn agreed.

"You know you can't get past us." Quill picked up Jacelyn's thread, anticipating where she was going. "Two against five, in close quarters, and one is a knight."

"Maybe I'd rather go out fighting," he sneered, "than let you put me on the gallows."

"I get that." Quill nodded. "But what about Zinn?"

The moment of hesitation told him they were on the right track.

Jacelyn continued. "If you go out fighting, as you say, then Zinn dies, too. Painfully, I might add. We're certainly not going to trade your life for *his*." She pointed at Ben with the tip of her sword, limply, as if he were entirely expendable. "So this is it for you. No matter what. But we don't have to kill the girl."

Scarlet didn't blink, he didn't breathe. "Goddammit," he said at last under his breath to Zinn. "I told you *not to come.*"

The two of them exchanged a few worried looks at each other. "You can take them," Zinn whispered.

"No," he returned, almost pleading. "I can't."

It might have even been touching if he wasn't a monster.

"Fine," Scarlet said with certainty. "You make a path and let her go. Once she's good and gone . . . and I mean *gone* gone, then I let bossman go. And then we see who walks out of here alive."

"What?" Quill reacted with genuine shock. "No, that's not . . . that's not how trading works. We don't want to kill you here, we want to take you alive. That's the trade. The little girl goes, and you give yourself up."

"That's not the trade," Will argued. "She goes free, and I let bossman free. One for one. Then we end this like men."

Like men.

Meaning with violence.

FitzOdo and his boys laughed at Scarlet's offer, they barked curses and tightened their grips on their weapons. But Jacelyn, apparently, knew better than to let this end in a bloodbath.

"Make a path!" she hollered, and took one step aside to help. Lord Beneger gave his silent agreement, and their bluster died down. Though their bodies were almost shoulder to shoulder, they somehow squeezed to create a channel between them, directly from the door to Zinn. She'd have to brush up against every one of them just to slide through.

"Leave your weapon there," Quill commanded the young girl.

"I need it," she breathed back, too stupid to realize the danger she was in.

"Then come back for it later. On the ground."

She did, she crouched and placed it gingerly down, seemingly terrified of what would happen the moment she was defenseless. For all the spitfire she had thrown, the girl's face was still that of a child, and it hid her horror poorly. Her eyes went big and wet and looked to Scarlet, but he was biting his lip. He refused to look at her.

The girl moved her foot twice, only to retreat each time. Skittish, like an animal on ice. When she finally consented to move she nearly ran, plunging herself into the gap, fearful of being stopped.

She was right to fear.

Quick as she was, Jacelyn was faster. She reached out with her left hand and grabbed the girl's hair, wrenching her neck around into submission. She moved her sword up to the girl's throat. Scarlet screamed bloody murder and made to plunge his knife down into Lord Beneger's neck, but he didn't. Quill closed his eyes, too horrified to watch Jacelyn kill the girl, not wanting to keep living in a world where that was possible.

"*Let's try this again!*" Jacelyn hissed. "You put your knives on the ground and you come with us willingly, or you watch these men rape her."

Quill gasped. All the air left the room, even FitzOdo reeled in shock. *She couldn't mean it*, it wasn't possible. *How far would she go to get her revenge?*

"They'll take turns with her," Jacelyn said, never breaking her gaze, "while I hold her down. I'd hate to miss out, so when it's my turn, I'll do it with a knife."

She was just trying to scare him, Quill tried to convince himself. But he knew now that he could never look at her again, without realizing that the dead half of her face was the kinder side.

Will Scarlet's jaw had dropped, his blade wavered. ". . . You wouldn't . . ."

"I'm sorry, does that shock you?" She gave him her full hate. "Do you think it matters *where* you stab someone? Would it be kinder if I put it in her belly first? Or her heart? That's how you butchered my uncle, isn't it?" At the confusion in his eyes, she curled even harsher. "My name is Jacelyn de Lacy. There's nothing I wouldn't do to pay you back for what you've done. *Drop. Your knives.*"

He did.

Quill tried to whisper *sorry* into Zinn's ear, but she pulled away and vanished out the door. Free from Scarlet's grasp, Lord Beneger returned to the rest of their group, massaging his neck. But he eyed Jacelyn as if he feared her more than Scarlet. FitzOdo leaned out the door to watch Zinn's flight, a genuine look of disappointment washing onto his face. As if Jac had gotten his hopes up, with the talk of rape. Bile rose in Quill's throat, he had to turn away. This room was full of monsters—the ones they had smuggled with them, hiding beneath their skin. It was too much to breathe.

Quill saw it first, but it was too late. Will Scarlet snatched one of his knives off the ground even as Ronnell kicked the other one away. With his free hand up to keep them at bay, Scarlet repositioned the knife up and against his own neck.

"You want me alive?" he asked, face red and purple and wrought in emotion. "If that's so important to you, then we make another trade. You let me walk out of here, or I kill myself. I won't go."

Quill's heart was no longer racing. Without the mist of the woods and the screams of battle, there was no great villainy in Will Scarlet, no mastermind. He was so clearly a pawn in the game of life; in every sense of the word, the man was a loser. Quill did not pity him that, but he saw now that his failures were his own, a natural conclusion to the pathetic waste that was his life. He wondered what miserable misadventures he'd endured in the last few months, what he had done to deserve the beating his face clearly boasted.

Jacelyn sheathed her sword. She probably didn't care at all if he cut his own throat out, but Quill did. They needed his answers, to pick up anyone else in his crew. Then, they needed to parade them through the streets, let the people see their faces, before hanging them all together. They had learned the hard way that it did no good to hang a stranger, lest the man's name live on beyond his years.

But Jacelyn didn't care about any of that. She wasn't here to secure Nottingham, or to make their city safer. She was only here because her uncle wasn't. Somehow, Quillen Peveril was the only one on this hunt who was honestly doing it for the betterment of the city.

"Put the knife down," he said.

"I won't go back to those cells." Scarlet started to push into his skin.

Lord Beneger just walked right up to him. "Yes, you will."

He slapped the knife from Scarlet's hand, smashed his knuckles into the thief's face, and that was that.

FORTY-ONE

JOHN LACKLAND

NOTTINGHAM CASTLE

"My most profound apologies," was a nice change of pace, though the man thought much of himself to describe his prowess at apologies thusly. Most people offered John their "humblest" apologies, which was second only to their "deepest" apologies, but John had never quite understood what exactly they were reaching into. He had little interest in anything that had to be scraped out of a man's soul. Particularly *this* man, this pot-bellied caricature, sweating through every one of his increasingly elaborate garments. "We did not know you were coming to Nottingham."

"Nor did I," John answered. He was still deciding if it was the right choice. Not even three months had passed since last he'd been here, for the funeral of the most recent Sheriff. He had never expected to return so soon, nor under such immediate circumstances. "We arrived late last night, without sending notice."

The castellan was flabbergasted. "Even still, you deserve every apology!" Each deeper and more profound than the last, no doubt. "I should have been notified of your arrival, and I promise you I shall punish the man who did not tell me!"

"I insist that you have him beaten," John said absently.

"Then so I shall, Your Grace."

"Although if you think on it, every man in the entire castle 'did not tell you.' So I suppose you should have every one of them beaten."

"Ah." The castellan's mouth plopped closed. "If that is your wish . . ."

"Nor did you tell yourself!" John added. "Perhaps you should start there."

"Ah." He twitched, not sure if that was a joke or not, until self-preservation clearly decided it must be. "Ah, very good! And you as well, then, Your Grace! You did not tell me, so I suppose I should beat you, as it were!"

John very much enjoyed giving the man his iciest stare.

"My most profound apologies—"

John waved him away, with just his fingertips. "I'm trying to get rid of you."

"Your Grace."

The castellan's exit was, no doubt, the swiftest and silentest run of the man's life.

Interactions such as these were the reason John preferred not to announce his arrivals, if ever he could avoid it. It was impossible to simply visit a city or a castle or a brothel without an arduous pomp being made of his appearance, full of inescapable conversations and niceties. Though for this particular journey, it was not privacy that prompted his secrecy—but necessity.

He was, geographically speaking, surrounded by traitors.

John's list of allies in northern England had become astonishingly shorter. That was his fault, admittedly, for openly labeling the members of that Huntingdon council as his enemies. He could have played along and spent months destroying them one by one from within, but he'd apparently suffered from a significant lapse of backhanded cunning that day. And now he was relatively alone in a section of the country that openly wanted to rebel against his brother the King. He'd selected Nottingham partially for his familiarity with it, but largely because it had not been represented by anyone at the council. Though that did not necessarily make Nottingham *safe*, it was at least *not hostile* to him—and he was in desperate need of gathering his thoughts long enough to figure out what to do next.

"Since I said no, they'll approach my nephew next," he said out loud, as if they had not already discussed it to death. Gay Wally stood at his side, on the battlements of the middle bailey, looking down at the defensive walls that segregated Nottingham Castle's three tiers. "And he'll say yes. They want someone to seize the throne in Richard's absence, and my nephew is both dumb and power hungry."

"He's five years old."

"That's what I just said."

It was *precisely* what Austria wanted. They never wanted England's money, they wanted England to eat herself alive. That's why John had convinced Longchamp to pay the infernal ransom in the first place, to avoid any of these petty schemings.

He looked out over the cascading baileys of the castle, constructed at increasingly high steppes within each other. A castle within a castle within a castle. "Built with true paranoia in mind," he said, appreciative. "It has never been taken?"

"It has been sieged several times but never successfully," Wally said beside him, probably blinking. "The city has burnt, yes, but the castle is impregnable."

John swallowed down the urge to comment on the many sexual obstacles of impregnating a castle.

"Which one of us should remind you?" asked Hadrian the Insolent. John trusted his surly swordarm exactly as far as he could pay him, which was fortunately quite far. That enormous amount of money also meant he could change Hadrian the Extortionist's title at the slightest whim.

"You have no authority over any castles in England," the man recited, because John had instructed them to do exactly that whenever it seemed even remotely possible he'd forgotten. "Your brother the king has forbidden it. Lest you do something like whatever it is you're lesting to do."

"I'm lesting to do little more than enjoy this archery tournament," John lied. "Didn't you know? I'm quite the enthusiast."

There was a great deal of commotion below, the makings of a tournament
that was starting shortly. The Captain of the Guard—whose name, Fulcher
de Grendon, was *fantastic*—had already explained that the tournament was
largely a ruse to capture a gang of thieves led by Robin Hood. John had met that
very man last year, and was surprised to hear how far events had escalated. The
timing of the tournament and his own curiosity were a perfect alibi—everyone
assumed he had arrived merely to be a spectator, which they were very welcome
to continue assuming.

"Do me a favor, Wally," he said. "And be clever."

"In any specific manner?"

"As Hadrian reminds me, I can't claim military right over any castles. Find
a way around that."

He could practically hear the boy blink.

FORTY-TWO

CAITLIN FITZSIMON

NOTTINGHAM CASTLE

CAITLIN SLIPPED HER ARM through the bend of Alfred Fawkes's elbow, both of them raising their longbows in the air with their free hands, welcoming the audience's roar.

And by God's almighty tits, did it ever feel good.

It was the opposite of their cave. It was the opposite of hiding. It was the opposite of pilfering in the goddamned shadows and slinking away. She made a full revolution, pivoting Alfie as she went, to take in the spectacle of the moment. From where they stood at the archers' line, there were spectators in nearly every direction—on their feet and waving a blizzard of colors, a dazzling sight like nothing she'd seen before. Noise and triumph, excitement and anticipation for the next round.

The stands for onlookers stretched down both sides of the archery range, which ended in the high battlement wall behind the row of straw targets, now riddled with painted arrows. At regular distances down the length of the range were heralds to make announcements—while off to the edges, entertainers made light with sideshows between bouts. Up on the wall high to their right, a group of actors spied the proceedings and shouted to their troupe outside the castle walls, who were reenacting the spectacle with added satire for those who weren't lucky enough to find space within the bailey. And even higher on the left, where the walls to the middle keep loomed, a box with several rows of seating had been built atop the battlement for the most "distinguished" viewers. Her father was unfortunately up there, and the Sheriff, too, but they weren't the important ones.

At the center of the front row, a surprise guest. An ignorant little thing called Prince John stood and applauded for Caitlin, Queen of the Lions.

"Watch this," she said at her full voice to Alfie, knowing that nobody could hear them while the crowd roared. "Fuck on you, Prince John!"

She bowed to the man up above as she said it, and the audience loved her for it.

Gentleman that he was, Alfie splayed his arms out to present his better half, urging the crowd to chant her colors. *Red and Red! Red and Red!* went the cry 'round the bailey, for Caitlin had just won her final qualifying round with an arrow that had not been a perfect shot, but carried enough strength to knock the wooden target onto its back.

"Welcome to the final ten." Alfie gave her arm a gentle squeeze.

"As if you had any doubt."

Ten archers remained from a hundred, and four of those were Red Lions. Counting the darling David of Doncaster as a fifth, a full half of them under Alfie's demesne. Ginger Twain and Ricard the Ruby had surprised everyone by lasting this long, but would be the first to admit they'd found more luck than talent. The other five was a pickleshot of nobodies that spanned the spectrum— from an old man with a grudge as sharp as his aim to an adolescent stableboy who screeched with elation every time his shot found its mark. But Alfred was undeniably the best of them, and his showmanship had earned the crowd's adoration from the very beginning.

However—best of the final ten did not mean he was best of the original hundred. After being eliminated in the first round, Dawn Dog brought a couple of his thickest-skulled seconds to "congratulate" each winner, with an emphasis on how easily the day's victor might find himself dead in an alley by morning. Those early standouts followed with mysteriously poor showings on their second rounds, clearing the path for more Lions to take the lead. And of course, there were dozens of others in Nottingham nursing broken fingers and sprained wrists who didn't show at all.

Even still, Cait was proud of their performance so far. It was almost— *almost*—like they actually deserved it.

"The final round now begins!" came the cry from on high, echoed every few seconds by the heralds down the line, and then by the actors on the wall in an outrageous falsetto. "Each archer will have only five arrows!"

Out on the range, new hay targets were being rearranged, and two bales had been lowered from the battlement above, suspended halfway up the wall by long stretches of rope. Five targets in total—three at varying distances on the field and the two smaller circular ones on the wall.

"These rules are ludicrous," the old man in their group complained. "I've been a part of many tournaments, and this is as poorly organized as they come. And no *class*..." he sneered at the eliminated competitors. How Cait failed to meet that criteria, she wasn't sure. "I mean, who *are* these people?"

The future Lord and Lady Fawkes, she wanted to tell him. They had tilted the scales in their favor as underhandedly as possible, but from this point forward, Alfie was going to be the legitimate winner.

"The sum of each mark..." came the announcements, "...will be compounded by the number of targets hit..."

Cait turned into Alfred's chest. "What does that mean?"

"That, I am not sure," he half chuckled.

The directions continued on, "...With consideration toward the difficulty of the target..."

She touched her nose to his sternum and took a deep breath. "You smell good."

"Liar." He smiled wide. "I smell like sweat."

"Like I said, then." She bit his arm. "You're going to win this, you know. Have you thought about how you'd like to celebrate?"

"Did you catch all that?" David of Doncaster interrupted, sidling up to them.

"I'm sorry?"

"The rules, that is."

She shrugged. "Sounded like a lot of counting."

"I had a hard time following it," David admitted. "But seems there's a bit of strategy to it all now. You could put your five arrows into the crowseye of the closest target, and have twenty-five points. Or you only put four there, and your fifth in the outer circle of a different target. Twenty-one points . . . but since you hit two different targets, your points count twice. So forty . . . forty-two points there."

Cait took a guess. "And if you spread your shots out to all five targets, then they count five times each?"

"Right, but the far targets are worth more, I think. I couldn't quite tell." He craned his neck around. "I'm glad I'm not in charge of adding it all up. Not sure what the best way to tackle this ought to be."

"Figure it out, then," she brayed, only half-joking. They'd put too much work into this to lose on account of snobby mathematics aimed at confusing them.

While David and Alfie discussed it, Cait took a moment to glance to the rows of eliminated competitors at the edges. Twelve more Lions were there, that her father had added to the lists. All fared better than they should have, but still hadn't lasted this far—including the whore Clorinda Rose. As much as Cait hated bitter little victories, that one tasted good. *You may be gorgeous,* she stared Clorinda down, *but that's all you'll ever have. You're a pair of lips and a loose hole, and nothing else.*

That wasn't the day's only victory so far, either. Cait had been busy at the range all morning, but Skinny Pink had brought the details on Will Scarlet. As planned, Rob o'the Fire had informed the Nottingham Guard, who stopped Scarlet from attacking Gerome Artaud just in time. The dockmaster knew his life was on the line now, so he'd finally be open to striking a deal. First pick of all the incoming mead in Nottingham meant the greenbeard would let the Lions have as much access to his back rooms as they wanted—and Zinn's old crew of children were already at work clearing them out. And then of course the side bonus, that Will Scarlet was in irons where he belonged. That spread a smile clear across Cait's face.

This day, this St. Valentine's Day, was for the lionhearts.

"Violet and Grey!" came the call, summoning the first archer to the line. Throughout the crowd, little flags with those colors sprung up, waving about furiously in the hands of their owners. There were ten colors in all, and every archer was assigned a combination of two. Their arrows were painted with a ring of each color halfway down the shaft—one wide, one thin—to keep track of their shots. Caitlin had claimed Red for both her colors, as she'd been lucky enough to pick early. Most of the Lions had claimed Red for at least one of theirs.

The Violet and Grey archer was a frumpy farmhand sort of man, quiet and unimposing, and round as the targets they were aiming at. He'd ignored Dawn Dog's first suggestion to lose gracefully, but Cait could see he was sweating far thicker than he ought to now. He took his time and sent one arrow at each of the five targets, though he missed the two high ones on the wall and fared poorly on two of the field targets. "Violet and Grey, fifteen points!"

The Amber and White archer followed, an old man who landed arrows into four of the targets, with a second ring shot in two of them. Forty points, apparently, and the crowd erupted with little amber-and-white flags. Most didn't know who they were rooting for, they'd simply purchased their favorite colors from the vendor stalls and were happy to scream for whoever bore them. To the masses, each archer was known solely by their colors. That was what the Red Lions were counting on—Alfred was as invisible as anybody here.

"Green and White, twenty-one points!"

The skinny waif who'd claimed green and white scowled, pointing at the single target he'd peppered with near-center marks, loudly complaining that he should've been ranked higher. He had opted to only take a single target. Cait recognized him from earlier, he was consistent at short distances and lousy from afar. Even after they'd thinned the herd, this waif didn't belong in the final ten. Half of the original hundred archers could have outshot this fellow beyond the closest target.

"Gold and Black, thirty points!"

They had gotten fairly lucky in that regard. Cait had watched scores of better archers eliminated in the early rounds, long before Dawn Dog or the others had a chance to scare them off. But the random selection had pitted the best marksmen against each other too early, weeding most of them out rather quickly. Twenty rounds of five archers each had taken most of the afternoon, with the highest scorers advancing from each bout. Cait's first group of five had all been amateurs, almost embarrassingly so. Those lucky pairings were further proof of the event's poor planning, and that fortune was theirs this day.

"Amber and Amber, six points!"

The eager stableboy had choked, he'd wasted his first three shots on the smallest target on the wall, missing each time. Cait could hear a growing round of complaints from those archers who'd been sidelined already. Grumbling that the stableboy should never have made it to the top ten, that he barely deserved to be in the tournament at all.

They weren't wrong, she had to admit.

Cait felt it in her stomach first.

They weren't wrong.

"Violet and Blue, twenty-five points!"

Alfred had dismissed the idea of any trap, because nobody knew their faces. Those with shorter hair wore caps that hid their trimmed ears, which the Guardsmen never questioned. None of them were notorious. Nobody could identify Alfred Fawkes as Robin Hood, or as Red Fox, or as anyone at all amongst a group of random archers.

But now that she thought on it, the groupings of the archers seemed unusually skewed to help them. As if they weren't the only ones who had stacked the deck for them to win.

Cait chewed on that. Wondered where it would lead.

There were honest contestants here, but no one important enough to complain when the odds were unnaturally against them. No one intelligent enough to argue the math. The colors for each group had been called from the nobles' box above. If someone had indeed orchestrated this, intentionally putting each of the Red Lions in a position where they were most likely to succeed, it could only happen if someone up there knew what each and every one of them looked like.

Coincidence, she argued against herself. *Things were going well because they'd planned it this way. And they'd been practicing at archery all week—they weren't half bad.*

That was vanity speaking. A flattered mark doesn't know he's being taken.

The Guardsmen hadn't bothered to check their ears.

"Alfred!" she whispered at him, but he shook her off. He was watching Ginger Twain make his shots, red-and-blue arrows. "Alfred, what if they know our faces?"

"What?"

He wasn't paying attention. Ginger's first arrow went wide, causing a brief panic amongst the crowd, then laughter at their own fear.

"What if someone gave us up?" she asked, her words demanding his attention.

"What? Who?" he tisked her away. Ginger's next arrow shot high down the range, hitting one of the far marks, but the arrow didn't stick, it tumbled down to the ground.

Her mind raced. "Clorinda, maybe. You know how she is, twelve ways of jealous. What if this was her play? What if she wanted revenge for being nothing but side trim?"

"You're being ridiculous," he said, and turned his head around in time to watch Ginger miss again.

She pulled him back. "Don't tell me I'm being ridiculous. Look at me, and think about it. Just *think about it.* Is it possible?"

He thought. The world kept moving behind him. Ginger settled for two easy shots on the nearby targets to the crowd's disappointment as Alfred Fawkes breathed out his preconceptions and considered the possibility that they'd already been betrayed.

"Scarlet's boys, maybe? No, David's here, and Arthur wouldn't send his friend up like that."

"Red and Blue . . ." came the announcement, down the line, six sets of heralds, and an epic pause before the second half.

". . . forty-one points!"

The ground tipped forward toward whatever was coming. Ginger Twain celebrated, oblivious to the fact that he hadn't earned his high score. Cait reeled to see if anyone else was alarmed. Alfie's face was clueless, but he leaned in so she could explain it to him.

"They made the math confusing, so they could group us together, regardless of our showing," she said. "Unless you honestly think Ginger was the best one so far."

The gallery of eliminated contestants showed signs of an uproar, but half of them were blindly cheering Ginger on while the rest were only barely confused or entirely uninterested. There was a murmur in the spectator stands, but those who waved red-and-blue pendants drowned them out with excitement. "Red and Green!" came the next call, summoning David of Doncaster to the firing line.

"Fresh arrows, mum," came a heavy voice behind her, and Cait turned directly into the face of a tall guard in Nottingham blue. He placed a handful of five arrows into her palm, two red rings painted around their shafts, and his other hand gripped the rim of a tall barrel of arrows. Only a lifetime of instincts kept her from buckling to fear.

He was wearing mail under his tabard.

He wasn't alone. Now that she knew to look for them, she spied them throughout the archers, collecting any extra arrows. The five in Cait's hand and the five placed in Alfred's would shortly be the entirety of their arsenal. David was nearly done already, he'd wasted no time in driving one arrow into each of the five targets, barely pausing between each pull.

"Red and Green," the heralds announced. "Sixty-one points!"

They called her colors next, and Cait stepped forward in a daze. Alfie whispered something to her, but it was lost. She no longer felt the shroud of anonymity, now it was as if every face in the castle saw exactly what she was. She stood naked in the middle of the archery range—naked, fat, and defenseless. Her bow's weight was unfamiliar, the arrows uncomfortable to her fingers. She pulled one to make her first shot but flinched, her eyes darting to the sidelines, unable to find Clorinda Rose.

She didn't even notice where her arrows landed, loosing one by one through the murk of a dream, her attention scattered everywhere else. On the guards in the crowd, on any commotion in the stalls, on the blinding sun that blocked her view of the spectators above. She searched for strangers, for blades, for anything out of place. Any reason to run now, any reason to hold onto her final arrow, but it was already gone. It eased from her fingertips, gone forever as easily as a secret. The crowd made noise, but she was still holding her breath.

"Red and Red, seventy-one points!"

One particular gord in the crowd drew her focus a third time, and finally she realized why. He'd been in the tournament earlier. He'd won his first round against four legitimate archers, and then choked in his second bout and lost to Ginger Twain. Now he was back, wearing Nottingham blue. Dawn Dog hadn't intimidated him, no. *He was a plant.* Probably one of many. To help eliminate the real competitors early, then fail.

Shit.

Had they done this to themselves?

Had Dawn Dog been threatening Guardsmen and not known it?

She didn't even watch as Alfred drew. The bear of a Guardsman stared her down as he crossed the field, he folded his arms and stood behind her, his lips hid a smile. Every other eye was watching Alfred Fawkes, except for this Guardsman. He had a job, and she was clearly it.

"Red and Gold," the heralds called.

"Eighty-one points," she whispered to the guard, though she hadn't even watched.

"Eighty-one points!" the heralds confirmed.

The bear man took a step forward, his hand wrapped around her bow. "Too bad," he said in a tone that screamed otherwise. The weapon became his, her shoulder became his. She flinched and his fingers tightened on her. "Don't fret. I'll let you know where to go next."

"The Red and Gold archer has competed with distinction . . ." Each sentence repeated sixfold upon itself as the heralds reached every ear in the bailey, the anticipation building and crashing into Caitlin as thunder, as waves, ". . . but there is another challenge before he can be claimed the victor!"

Alfred had stepped forward to the line, singular and powerfully nonchalant. For once, Cait couldn't tell if it was an act. *Had he figured it out, or did he think he genuinely won?* His signature red leather coat snapped as he turned to the crowd, encouraging their applause. Up in the nobility box, the Sheriff leaned out on the railing, clad in an ivory cloak.

"You have bested your peers . . . but now you face the best that Nottingham has to offer."

At field level, a crowd of Guardsmen entered, separated into lines, made a channel.

"We proudly present the pride of the Nottingham Guard, the finest archer in Nottinghamshire . . ."

A horse emerged through that gullet, draped in the blue-and-black trappings of the Guard, its rider held a recurve bow in one hand, held high in salute to the crowd.

". . . the niece of the late Sheriff Roger de Lacy! Every color, raise your flags to the Lace Jackal!"

She thundered past Cait into the middle of the field, drew an arrow from a quiver at her mount's side and launched it into the middle of the nearest target. It was an easy shot while standing, perhaps, but from horseback was something else entirely. The crowd erupted with excitement, all ten colors sizzled the air as this Lace Jackal rounded her horse down both sides of the range, welcoming the adulation.

The rider dismounted, a few guards rushed from the sidelines to take her horse and unbuckle her quiver. She wore the same pleated leather vestments of any common guard, dirtied and unadorned. Her black hair was gathered in a tail that barely contained its plume, her face was curiously solemn and still. If she took any joy in the attention, she did not show it.

"An expert bowman must do more than hit a target . . ." the Sheriff's words came down, ". . . an expert bowman must have speed as well as accuracy!" More guards—there were so many of them, Cait realized—had moved the three hay targets from the field to a single line hardly a quarter of the way down the range. "Let victory be given to whomsoever can hit these three targets the fastest! Red and Gold archer, you may make the first attempt."

The Lace Jackal handed her quiver to Alfred, whose confidence and performance was unshaken. He gave a deep and gallant bow to the woman before accepting the quiver. Cait could see him mouth words to her that were lost in the wind, but the woman neither laughed nor flinched. Alfred spent a few moments adjusting the quiver's belt to comfort, pulling an arrow from his hip and putting it back again in quick succession. He turned to each area of the audience and encouraged their applause, which they gave him heartily, and even Cait was compelled to yell out his name in support. His eyes did not find her, but they did glance up to the nobility box.

At the Sheriff, she realized. *He's marking a shot at the Sheriff.*

Had it come to this? If there was no backing out, was Alfie planning on punching forward? Creating enough chaos that they could hope to escape?

When Alfie moved, it was with shocking precision. His arm swept in one continuous fluid motion, never stopping, it pulled an arrow and slid it down the bow and released it at once, without holding, without aiming, and back at the quiver again without hesitation. *One and pull and two and pull and three,* he moved as smooth as silk, and each found its mark on the field, *thank God.* Not crowseyes, but central hits all of them. It was done as fast as Cait could imagine possible. The enthusiasm from the crowd fueled her relief, and she let herself smile as her Alfie turned and bowed, and laughed. This was the Red Fox in his glory, this was the Robin Hood he'd always wanted to be.

Even from afar, Cait could sense an unease in the nobles' box, and no proclamation came forth. *They did not think he could do it,* she realized, wondering how they were now desperately rearranging their plans. *And the crowd is now even more on his side, they cannot move against him now.*

Alfred bowed again, all the way to his toes, when he offered the Lace Jackal's quiver back to her. She returned no politesse but plucked three arrows, each one with a double ring of black painted round its shaft. Each arrow drooped lightly, held between her knuckles, and when she drew the bowstring back it was hardly a pull at all. She *flicked* all three, drawing each arrow on the outside of the string rather than the inner, in the blink of an eye. Cait was dumbfounded, it was more like a bizarre novelty performance than archery. It was very possible that all three arrows had been loosed before the first even found its mark. There was practically no force to each shot, but it was enough to prick their heads into each haybale.

The Lace Jackal did not flourish or cater to the crowd, she simply dropped her bow to the ground and walked off the range, victorious. For it they loved her even more, an uproar that brought weakness to Cait's knees.

"Red and Gold archer!" came the Sheriff's words, through the heralds' mouths. "Do you think you deserve another chance?"

Alfred's bow was in the air the moment the question ended. He shook it, his arm tall and strong, the crowd gave another round of excitement.

"Red and Gold archer!" came the heralds. "Do you think Tymon the Hammer deserves another chance?"

At this, Alfred lowered his longbow in confusion, and the crowd was unsure how to react.

"Red and Gold archer! . . . Do you think Asher of Radford deserves another chance? . . . Do you think the Preacher of Ropers Close deserves another chance?"

Cait tested the hand that still rested on her shoulder, but it tensed at her slightest twitch.

"Good people of Nottingham, you deserve an apology . . . This honest day's games and mirth has been invaded . . . By a criminal who does each of you dishonor . . . Who brings each of you danger! . . . This archer in red and gold is known by another name . . . A name that was not his to steal . . . The name of Robin Hood!"

Whatever joy the crowd had for Alfred curdled into spite and poison. *This is the moment,* she knew it had to be. Alfred had his bow and arrows still, he could launch them up to the Sheriff's box. The Lions would spring to action, cause a commotion. Wherever there were crowds, the Red Lions were at home. *This is the moment.*

"The Lord Brayden of York, his Lady Edith of York, Guardsman Dillon Fellows . . . these are but a few of the names of Robin Hood's victims . . . the poorfolk of the French Ward, whose hands he has taken . . . even the ladies of the night who deserved St. Mary's mercy . . . *do they deserve another chance?"*

Neither Alfred Fawkes nor any Red Lion had done any of those things.

Red-and-gold flags danced in the sky, this time not waved in celebration but thrown from the crowd in fury, they fluttered and fell to the earth.

They could get out of this, Cait knew it, *give us the signal.* She pivoted on the ball of her foot, she could break the guard's balance with her weight. *This is the moment,* but Alfred needed to start it. They needed to all act together, or they would be certainly taken down individually.

"It is a testament to the city that this false Robin Hood be captured . . . by the niece of the Sheriff whom he slew . . . a woman who has shown what true bravery is, what true heroism is . . . not by fighting against our city but by joining it!"

The Sheriff's voice was everywhere, amplified by the heralds, while Alfred was alone in the middle of the field, effectively muted by the crowd's boos. There was no denying his title, anyway. Clorinda had sold him out. The Sheriff knew exactly who he was, who all of them were. From the moment they had walked through the castle's gates.

This is the moment, it had to be. Alfred fingered an arrow. *Now.*

Every nuance that came next was familiar to her—despite the dread in her heart and the immediacy of the moment, she felt as drawn to him now as ever. The way a curious scent can recall a long-lost memory, his actions now reminded her, unbidden, of the first time they had lain with each other. Now it was his quiver that dropped to the ground, but then it had been his shirt. In his fingers now were three arrows, held limply, but then it had been a feather. He drew it smoothly down the bridge of the bow, fingers that had made that same graceful journey across her breasts. He held there, confident in his desire but still a gentleman who was asking for permission. Then he sprung as surely as an arrow itself, a man who knew exactly what he wanted.

Ironically, the similarities continued in that it was over in a second.

Then, it had been hilarious—when it was just the two of them to share that embarrassed moment. Now, the audience jeered at his pathetic attempt to copy the Lace Jackal's move. His three arrows flung impotently in the air, not one of them finding its mark. Because now, as then, he somehow thought he had something to prove.

The Lace Jackal returned with two Guardsmen at her side, holding chain and manacles.

"Citizens of Nottingham, your prince would have a word with you!"

All eyes flew up to the nobles' box. The sun had mercifully slunk behind a heavy cloud, and Cait could clearly see the prince vault from his chair onto the ledge, steadying himself on the pole of a bannerette. His toes teased over the lip and the forty-foot fall that invited him to the field.

"Nottingham!" the prince bellowed. Though the heralds repeated him, Cait could hear his actual voice. The audience hung on his words as they never had for the Sheriff. "This man is not Robin Hood. I met the real Robin Hood when he was alive." He spoke slowly, certain that his words were carried properly. "This is merely an impostor. It does us no good to put him in irons."

Caitlin's breath caught in her throat. Hope.

"He is simply the face of a greater enemy. He is proof that if we strike down one Robin Hood, another will take his place. Potential Robin Hoods hide amongst you, like a plague. They are a disease amongst the good people of this city. And it falls upon each and every one of you to be vigilant, to find the Robin Hood and refuse him sanctuary!"

That hope crumbled.

If only she had an arrow, she could pluck the prince from his perch, they could escape in the ensuing riot. Alfie was already restrained, but the arrows he'd shot, lying limply in the grass . . .

"Guardsmen!" Prince John called to the Lace Jackal and her companions. "Bind that man, but do not take him to the prisons. Strap him to the archery target."

She could slip the bear guard behind her. Run. Now now goddammit now.

Alfie didn't fight back, and Caitlin didn't run. The paw on her shoulder was heavier, or the ground was closer, or the world was over.

"To the nine finalists! You were robbed of your victory by this man, the same as Nottingham has been robbed of its security! It is not enough to sit idly by as traitors wreak havoc on this city! I ask each and every one of you to take arms against such villainy when you see it! You nine are now Nottingham's champions!"

The ground had the audacity to slide by beneath her feet, she was in a line now, with the others, the eight others. She found David of Doncaster and Ginger Twain and Ricard, but there was nothing in their eyes but the calm deadness of goats before the slaughter.

"Give them each a bow and arrow!"

Impossibly, the Guardsman pressed a longbow into her hands. He had to fold her fingers around it, she was too dazed to control herself. Four of them, four of the nine "champions," were loyal to her. She forced herself to focus. *Instead of hoping for a single arrow, they now had a total of four.* To feather the prince something fierce.

"Individually, the Robin Hood can beat any of you!" The prince was rallying the crowd. "That is what he is counting on! But together, we cannot be defeated! When we work together as a city, as one, then he has no power over us! He can only flourish so long as he terrorizes us! If we refuse to be afraid, if we refuse to be broken, then we are unstoppable!"

Her thumb and forefinger had the thin shaft of an arrow between them now, and across from her was Alfred Fawkes, arms chained wide across the hay target, his chest obscuring the crowseye in the middle.

His lips, *God, his lips trembled.*

He looked at nothing. As if he could not believe this was real. *Don't worry, love. This will be a sight for the ages.*

She glanced sidelong, but couldn't catch Ricard's eye.

Prince John. "On my mark, join your neighbor! Join your prince! Stand up against those that would divide us, stand up against their terrorism, stand up for Nottingham!"

Ginger Twain was sweating, but would not look at her.

"*For Nottingham!*" the other archers shouted.

"*For Nottingham!*" David added, meeker.

She tried Ricard again. His face a statue.

No matter. They'd follow her.

Alfie couldn't stop this anymore, it was up to Cait.

This is the moment.

"Ready, archers!"

They'd follow her. They were smart. They were just awaiting her signal. They needed someone to start it.

"Draw!"

And the rest of the Lions, they would follow suit.

Wouldn't they?

"Loose!"

And she didn't stop it.

She didn't send her arrow screaming up at the nobles' box, she didn't turn and bury it into the Guardsman behind her, or the Lace Jackal. The shame of it suffocated her. Her arrow soared absently to the left of Alfred, that was the sum of her courage. The sum of her leadership.

The other arrows punched a hole in Alfred's chest that burst bloody, his face contorted in utter shock. He didn't know how this had happened. *That was his dying thought*, it sickened her to think, *how did this happen? Why didn't anyone stop it? Why didn't Cait stop it?*

But as it turned out, Cait was a coward.

Her lover's head twitched a few times before it sunk forever into his chest, but she didn't look at him. She couldn't see anything through the tears. *They weren't even for him*, she knew already, *she was crying for herself.*

What a waste of life, this Caitlin.

"This is the punishment for those who seek to destroy us from within!" The prince was celebrating. "But as I said, citizens, it is not enough! The Robin Hood cannot survive on his own, he survives through the silence of others! Those who turn a blind eye! I understand that temptation, but in doing so you help the enemy! Doing nothing in the face of evil is as damaging as that evil itself!"

The Guardsmen ripped the arrows from Alfred's body, which sloughed to the ground. Blood stained the crowseye, all the way down.

"Guardsmen!" called the prince. "How many arrows found their mark?"

Some amount of work went into the counting. "Eight, my lord!"

"Eight! Eight of nine!"

"Whose arrow is missing?"

No.

She bit her lip. David and Ginger Twain and Ricard stared forward, mortified, *they had killed Alfred, they killed the man she loved.*

"Red and Red!"

"Bring her forward!" And the ground caught her, hands found her arms and dragged her, she tried to struggle but her legs didn't work anymore, they'd rightfully given up on her. "Any archer could have made that shot, especially these final nine champions! But Red and Red missed! She did not do her duty to this city. That is how we find them, friends! You find the Robin Hood by finding those who sit by in silence! Whomsoever sits on their hands while evil does its work is a friend to that evil! Silence is complicity! And let the punishment be equal, to those who let evil thrive!"

Something hit her cheek, wet, the Guardsman's spit. The grass scratched at her as they dragged her, she didn't start sobbing until Alfie's body was beneath her, his face mottled in blood and bewilderment. Cold manacles closed around her wrists, hay scratched the back of her neck, Alfie's blood wet her shoulder blades. Before her, the harsh emptiness of everything that she'd once known.

From above there was a riot, and she looked up, daring to hope. Something was happening on the ramparts, a throng of Guardsmen in a fight, holding back a mountain.

"No! That's my daughter!" her father screamed.

Help me, she prayed.

"The gates of the castle are locked!" The prince ignored the commotion. "The gates of the city are closed! Nobody leaves or enters the castle until we have flushed out all those who have supported the Robin Hood! Nobody leaves or enters our city until his stain is gone forever! It is time for good people to rise, to stand up, and cleanse your city of this filth!"

Across from her, downrange, eight archers nocked their arrows.

They didn't save Alfred. But they'd save her.

"We start with her," the prince bellowed, "but we do not stop until all of them are gone! My eight champions, loose your arrows on my mark. For Nottingham!"

Her father would stop it.

All eight, David and Ginger and Ricard included, repeated it. *"For Nottingham!"*

"Loose!"

Alfred.

Not one of them missed.

FORTY-THREE

ARTHUR A BLAND

NOTTINGHAM CASTLE

RIOT!

"*Fuck! Fuck! Fuck!*" Arthur recognized his own voice. "*Fuck!*"

Panic and fear were the only masters now, and they waged a holy fucking war. The moment eight arrows pierced Caitlin FitzSimon's chest, the crowd folded in on itself in chaos. All semblance of order burst like hot smoke, bodies screamed purposelessly in every direction. Arthur rushed to the edge of the crowd to press against the wooden supports of the spectator stands as the wave of people came. Half of them were terrified—*the gates of the castle are locked!*—and they went flying to the exits as if they might still find escape there. They trampled over each other with no care. Arthur pulled an older man to his feet who would've been crushed by the stampede, but it nearly bowled them both over. He reminded himself not to get killed doing something fucking idiotic.

But that half, the half that ran away, didn't scare Arthur nearly as much as the other half.

"*We do not stop until all of them are gone!*" the prince had decreed.

So the other half were *hunting*.

"He's one of them!" came a shriek, a thin old woman with her bony arm out-stretched, shoving her finger at the back of a man she was following through the confusion. "Him! Here! Here! I saw him, he's one of them!"

Her target was the big brute called the Dawn Dog. His face was terror-stricken but numb, as if he could ignore away the woman as well as everything else that was happening. But she attracted the attention of a nearby gord, who called for Dawn Dog to stop, and then for reinforcements. Dawn Dog panicked and plowed through the crowd.

Arthur didn't pause to see what became of him, but took the opportunity to move away, back toward the field, struggling through the panicked streams of human bodies. "Order, order!" called a herald with a ridiculous moustache, before being knocked from his feet, vanishing into the mob.

David, he focused as soon as he could, *he had to find David.*

David had been one of the final competitors before they'd singled out Red Fox for death, and he might have been identified as a Red Lion. Arthur could find no glimpse of him now, even though his blond mop should've stood tall amongst the crowd in the field. A cluster of gords had gathered around the bodies of Caitlin and Red Fox, swords drawn against the approaching masses. Maybe these were the rest of the Lions, maybe overwrought in anger or grief, meaning to collect the bodies of their leaders.

David had to be somewhere, and there was no chance he'd been arrested and taken away so quickly. He, too, must have ran, then. Arthur watched the fight growing in the field a second longer, just to be sure.

Not my concern, he told himself, wheeling around. The Lions were aiming to get themselves killed, and Arthur had no intention of going down with them. So much for all Will's plans. He wasn't even here—he was off on some secret mission with Zinn, while David was forced to compete. So Arthur had chosen to watch the St. Valentine's tourney with the rest of the commonfolk, he'd even bought stupid little fucking red-and-green flags to support his best friend.

"If you get yourself killed," Arthur had warned David beforehand, *"I'm going to kill you."*

Up above on the ramparts to the castle's second tier, things appeared to be equally fucked. The gords there were concentrated in a single undulating mass, fighting something or themselves. A brawl, sure as shit. The prince had not simply turned every citizen against his neighbor—by sentencing the daughter of the castle's armsmaster to death, he'd apparently started a civil war amongst the Guardsmen, too.

Anybody who follows him is going to drown.

Hells upon hells, Marion had been wrong.

They weren't drowning, they were burning alive.

"Here, here!" came a clear voice, and Arthur turned to see two fatherly men dragging a stranger, each pinning an arm behind their captive's back. "This one's working for Robin Hood, this one here!"

For a moment Arthur thought they were bringing the man to him, but he startled to realize he was nearly back to back with a heavyset gord. Arthur held his breath as he slid away, trying to keep his face hidden, daring only a single glance back to see which Lion had been caught. The gord tugged the captive's chin up to check his ear, allowing Arthur a clear view of a man he'd never seen before.

Not a Red Lion at all. The man protested his innocence, but the gord yanked his hair hard.

Not my concern, Arthur told himself.

And what did they think would happen? If silence was now punishable by eight arrows to the heart, then of course every man and woman in Nottingham was going to miraculously find a Robin Hood to turn in. Every idle suspicion, every domestic grudge, every sideways glance was now permission to beat a man brainless and drag him to the Nottingham Guard. It was pure anarchy, every depraved dog turning on its own just to stay alive.

David. Find David.

It was no coincidence that so many Red Lions had made it to the final round. The gords must have arranged it somehow, meant to group them together, capture them at once. David didn't deserve to be rounded up with the rest of them. But whether this madness was part of the gords' plans, or if it had interrupted it, Arthur didn't fucking know.

His shoulder jerked backward, spinning him around, and he brought his fist up to strike back. But it was just a young woman who'd stumbled into him, apologizing blindly, protecting her face now with both hands. She scrambled away, nearly tripping an older couple as she did, opening up a gap in the path where a round-faced fellow with wide eyes was staring right at Arthur.

"D'you see that?" the roundy asked his companion, as Arthur realized his clenched fist was still raised, ready to attack. "That man almost took that girl's head off!"

"You one of them?" the companion demanded, his black bushy eyebrows crashing together in the middle of his forehead. He didn't wait for an answer but drove closer. "Let me see your ears."

Arthur didn't think, he just reacted. As Bushy reached out, Arthur curled his middle and forefinger and jabbed their knuckles into the stranger's throat. He didn't wait—he grabbed the man's head with both hands and wrenched him up and backward, letting his legs kick out from under him as his forward momentum continued, and Arthur put all his strength into thrusting the man's skull down to the ground. Roundy reacted quickly, flailing his hands with open palms as if he were trying to grab Arthur's face, so Arthur snatched the man's forearm and pulled him off balance, opening his stomach for Arthur's knee. As air burst from Roundy's lungs, Arthur squatted and grabbed his thighs, hoisting them up and off the ground to send the fool down onto his back.

If Bushy had recovered by now, Arthur didn't wait to find out. A simple raised fist had attracted these two, so by starting a fight he'd just declared open season on himself.

He flung himself into the crowd that was still retreating to the gates, whose backs had been turned to the scuffle. Behind him came the shouts of would-be heroes, desperate for the opportunity in stopping him. *He was now their escape ticket.*

Quickly, quickly, elbows and turns, avoiding stares, behind a vendor stand, back again, into the crowd, against the wall, *fast, fast,* he had to catch his breath, but couldn't look out of place.

He'd traveled away from the archery range, in the market area now where he'd bought those damned red-and-green flags. The area was in complete disarray, most of the vendors who hadn't fled were just trying to protect their wares. The crowds to the south amassed at the main castle gates—where Guardsmen stood on boxes or the battlements above yelling futile orders into their midst. *If there was any escape from this hell, it wasn't that way.* Arthur backtracked, navigating the edges to return to the archery range.

At the first set of audience risers, Arthur spied a shallow walkway between its wooden beams and a cart that had previously sold skewers of meat. He ducked into its relative privacy, assuming it may lead to the far side of the risers, but fuck if it wasn't already occupied. Three young men in the dirty clogs of fieldhands had cornered a pretty young woman, who was waving one of the meat skewers about in defense. Her features were marred by a black handprint.

"Get the fuck out of here!" one of the bastards yelled upon seeing him, and Arthur was quick to comply.

Not my problem, he told himself. *He had to find David, before the guards did.*

A quick glance above told him everything he needed, and it only took a few seconds to hoist himself up the diagonal bracings of the stands. It put him at risk of being spotted, but once he hauled over the back railing he was at a good height to view the entire fuckfest. The risers themselves here were more or less deserted now, excepting a riot's mix of discarded hand flags. A fight now raged in the center of the archery range, gathered around the bodies of Caitlin FitzSimon and Alfred Fawkes.

But there was still no sign of David. He was taller than most, and blonder than most, and if he was anywhere to be found it shouldn't be this damned difficult.

Across the field, the opposite bank of spectator stands was thick with people. That structure had been built right up against the outer curtain wall, and the actors on top had apparently thrown down a rope to help people escape up to the walkway. Already Arthur could guess there were too many people trying to climb at once—there were twenty, thirty people already gathering below and more by the second, desperate to get up and away. *It wasn't a terrible option,* but farther along the walkway up top, two gords were already running toward the actors, shouting and pointing. *That path wouldn't last long.*

A scream crawled up from below.

Probably the girl with the meat skewer.

Not your problem.

Another scream.

Damn it, he scolded himself.

But still he hazarded a look down over the back rail of the stands. The young woman's top was now torn in half, exposing herself, and one of those men held a snatch of its pale fabric in his hand. Arthur turned around one final time in the hope of seeing David. *If David was hiding, he was safe.* If he was missing—arrested, or worse—then there was nothing Arthur could do about it. And if that was the case, then he'd feel a need most terrible to put his fist through something. And so, with no sign of his friend above, he submitted to getting himself in-*fucking*-volved below.

Maybe this could be a deal. If he saved the girl, then he'd deserve to get David back, too. A fair trade.

The first bastard crumpled into the mud as Arthur dropped on him. His feet landed firmly on the man's shoulders and he used that to roll off backward to a crouch, placing himself directly between the young woman and her other two shithole attackers.

The alley was long and thin, barely enough for two to stand side by side, which gave Arthur a distinct advantage in taking on multiple opponents. *Well not an "advantage,"* David probably would remind him. *Just not a "disadvantage." You're still outnumbered.* And he had no weapons. No swords had been allowed past the castle gates, and he'd even refrained from carrying a blade in his boot for fear of it being discovered. Now he wished he had it, because neither of the two remaining men shared his pristine sense of honesty.

"What the *fuck?!*" one bastard yelled, glancing up at the stands to see if any more men were about to drop on their heads. Unfortunately, Arthur was the only one dumb enough for that. This man had the square, pocked face of a brick, so that was his name now. Brick scrambled to pull a knife from his belt. "Who are you? You with her?"

"Not *with* her," Arthur raised his fists into a fighting stance, "just *in front* of her. Move along."

The man he'd landed on—*Mud,* of course—started stirring, earning himself a boot into his shoulder blades, and another faceful of muck.

"That girl's a thief," the second man said, a pug-ugly type with a roll of neck fat. "Watched her steal mesself, she's exactly who they lookin' for."

"Three of you, with knives, against a half-naked girl in an alley." Arthur repositioned his feet. "You're gonna try to claim moral superiority?"

"They've locked the gates, you fucker," accused Brick.

Neck Fat grunted in affirmation. "That girl's our way out of here."

"We turn her in, they let us through." His attitude shifted to a slightly happier brick. "You can come with us, f'you want."

"You can fuck yourselves!" the young woman shouted from behind.

Arthur didn't turn to check on her, for fear of giving an opportunity to strike. But he nodded slowly. "I'm inclined to agree with the lady. Best get a'fucking."

"He can't breathe!" Neck Fat yelled, pointing down to Mud. Arthur let up just a bit and the man spasmed, coughing out blood and muck and grabbing at his own throat. For one sickening moment, Arthur's heart twisted—it reminded him too much of the way Elena Gamwell had died, twisting and coughing on her own blood. Arthur had been forced to watch with a gag in his mouth and a blade at his throat, he felt that gag now, he couldn't swallow . . .

Mud's skull gave a rewarding crack when Arthur's boot found its temple, and he slapped the knife right out of Neck Fat's hands. He drove forward, unrelenting, swinging a fist toward Brick's face, but he only found air—the man ducked away to the right. Arthur reacted on instinct, he twisted and clipped his elbow out hard, finding the man's jaw, only barely softer than his namesake. He landed a foot into Brick's hip that meant to push him down to the ground, but he abandoned that in favor of grappling the man's arm with both hands. Brick still held his knife, and Arthur could certainly—

A sudden weight on his back smashed Arthur forward into Brick. He tried to hold onto the arm but lost it as he rolled over the man's back and came up in the slop. Right-side up, fortunately, but in danger. He pivoted on all fours and grabbed the nearest leg he could find with both hands, applying pressure at the knee to make it buckle and bring his enemy down to the ground with him. It was the brick, a very angry brick now, while Neck Fat was behind him searching for his lost blade in a cluster of trash. But Brick still had his knife, reeled it up high, and Arthur could do nothing but wonder why his grumpy little failure of a life wasn't flashing before his eyes as he held his hands out uselessly, as brick and blade came pounding down—

FORTY-FOUR

MARION FITZWALTER

HUNTINGDON CASTLE

THE CAVILING LORD SIMON de Senlis was young for a leader, Marion noted, but no less imposing for his youth. His outfit embellished the features he lacked—it boasted conservative fashion in the military style, and shoulders that rivaled his horse's. He looked a good deal more presentable than when last Marion had seen him, which was, admittedly, when they had snuck into his Grafham manor to steal from his treasury.

"I cannot allow such depravity to go unchecked," de Senlis insisted, almost as if he actually believed this was an ethical burden, rather than a political opportunity. "I cannot allow such corruption to fester so close to my home."

"Spare me your indignation, your incredulity," Lord Robert returned, keen on calling out the spectacle for what it was. "Get to your point, man."

Three days had passed since the council had crumbled in her hands. Each of its attendees—Marion's grandparents included—had fled Huntingdon's walls by nightfall, fearing whatever retribution Prince John would inevitably return with. None had yet come, but the news had clearly spread, as was evidenced by the day's arrival of de Senlis and his men.

Marion was part of a line at the front gates of Huntingdon, with Lord Robert at its center—a crisp green demicape across one shoulder that bore his shire's signature yellow hunting horn. That sigil also flew from atop long wooden poles carried by the bannermen at his sides. Her own modest dress featured a similar shade of the green, though she was uncomfortable with the loyalty it implied. Beside her, Amon's shield still flew the white swords of Essex. A dozen of Robert's men finished their line, blockading the entrance to Huntingdon Castle.

Across from them, their line was matched by Lord de Senlis and his host. The lord had brought nine men with him in full attire, a show of force that was disturbingly reminiscent of a battle formation. The main road was bordered on either side with yew trees, whose appreciable growth read less of beauty now and instead gave a spiderlike discomfort.

"My point is this." Lord Simon de Senlis's horse repositioned itself, though its rider kept a level gaze. "I demand you turn over the traitor, the outlaw known as Marion Fitzwalter, to my keeping. I will deliver her the justice that you seem incapable of offering."

"If the Lady Marion were a *traitor*, as you say," Lord Robert treated the word playfully, as though the concept were laughable, "then it would be your duty to bring her to your earl for punishment. I don't suppose you know who your earl is, do you? A handsome man, I hear, this Earl of Huntingdonshire?" His men laughed. "Your earl is already in possession of the traitor you describe. Why would I hand her over to you just for you to hand her over to me again? I think you may find yourself in this transaction, as in the world, quite inconsequential."

De Senlis waited his turn to speak. "Shall I sneak into your castle through an open window? Threaten to skewer your kitchen scullions, as you did mine? Or shall we try the novelty of dealing with each other honestly?"

Under better circumstances, Marion imagined she would find the Lord Simon de Senlis a respectable man. He carried himself with a practiced charm and took care in the construction of his speech. Education spoke to self-improvement, which forgave many the worser trait. But the worser trait, in this case, was calling for her head on a pike.

This was just the first fallout of her spectacular failure at the council. Each day brought the fear of punishment. If not the prince's men, then a contingent loyal to the Chancellor would arrive to dole out his consequences. Lord Simon de Senlis, though a tepid threat on his own, was simply the first bounty hunter.

"I'm not here to play games," de Senlis continued. "It is well known the Lady Marion held a concord of sedition within these walls, and you have ignored my petitions for her arrest. If you are unfit to do your duty as earl and bring punishment to an admitted traitor to the crown, then I take it upon myself to declare you as the witting accomplice you appear to be."

Marion swallowed hard and clenched her jaw. Earlier, she had reluctantly agreed to remain silent in this meeting, but for the life of her now she could not find any wisdom there.

"Ever ambitious, Simon." Lord Robert rolled his head side to side. "Suppose I pretend to be as innocent as you pretend to be outraged. What would you do with her? Bring her to the High Sheriff of Cambridgeshire and Huntingdonshire? Reginold de Argenton is a friend of mine, and will not entertain your groundless accusations. Again, you'll find your efficacy somewhat wanting."

"I have no interest in wasting Sheriff de Argenton's time. Treason should be meted by the Chancellor himself. The choice is yours to make, your lordship." De Senlis stiffened, though his tone carried no malice. "You can give the outlaw to me, or you can wait until I return with Chancellor Longchamp's men by my side. If I were you, I would consider heavily whether or not you will still be able to call the castle *yours* at the end of such a meeting."

The conversation, which was only barely an apt name for the meeting, concluded with a bit of posturing on both sides. It was, inarguably, a pleasant alternative to immediate bloodshed, which was a more common ending for the meetings Marion found herself involved in. Such violence was less frequent since Will Scarlet had left, but somehow it now seemed harder than ever to keep herself on the proper side of living.

"I think I don't like him very much," Lord Robert muttered as de Senlis's complement vanished amongst the sinews of the yew trees. "All he cares about is this castle, trying to revive his father's broken legacy."

Marion chewed on her lip. "Well, we *did* try to burglarize his manor."

"That's true." Lord Robert weighed the comment. "Alright, you've convinced me. I absolutely *hate* him."

THERE WERE DISCUSSIONS TO be had, obviously, but Marion preferred to avoid the castle for so many reasons. Only the least of which was that it served as the setting for her greatest embarrassment. Beyond that, she wanted to avoid the Countess Magdalena at all times, and she did not want to leave Amon behind, who was still forbidden to step foot within its walls. But mostly, she just wanted the simplicity of her old friends.

Their tents and shacks littered the spattering of villages that accompanied the Cook's Backwater. The stream was not big enough for game but served for most other purposes before meeting the Great Ouse at the base of the castle grounds. To her surprise, Lord Robert accompanied her, dismissing his retinue of men and horses back up the hill. His noble attire, while appropriate to give Simon de Senlis a talkdown, was comically out of place around John Little's humble fire. Robert gathered more than a few lingering watchers from the neighboring hovels, but he seemed quite comfortable eating with his hands and sharing ale.

"There's nothing for you to worry about," Robert mulled between sips. "I'm not handing you over to de Senlis, no matter how many men he brings back."

"I appreciate that," Marion smiled, "but you're missing the point."

"No."

John Little said it gruffly, though it might have been half belch. The entirety of his massive frame was focused intently on Marion.

She wasn't sure how to react. "What do you mean by that, John?"

"I mean *no*." His jaw sidled horizontally, his beard rippled. "No, you cannot turn yourself in."

"I never said I would."

"But you'll say it eventually. And the answer is no."

As soon as he said it, she realized it was true. It was the natural conclusion to this sordid tale.

"Turn herself in?" Robert asked with some confusion. "Why would she do that? We're more than capable of protecting her, and this situation is entirely my fault in the first place."

"That's not true," she insisted.

"Well, it might as well be. Maggie . . . she put you in a terrible position, which has caused no small amount of friction between us. You were my guest, and whatever happens to you as my guest falls upon me. I should have stopped what happened. I—"

Marion reached her hand out and closed it over Robert's forearm, forcefully enough to stop his sentence, but let it linger there. He meant well, but this wasn't his decision to make.

"Robert, please. I've already wasted enough energy being angry with your wife. The truth is, nothing that happened is anyone's fault but mine. The countess may have maneuvered me into an unfavorable position, but the leverage she held over me was entirely of my own making. The idea that you are responsible for me . . . well that implies I had no fault on my back when I came to you, which is anything but the truth."

Robert's eyes found hers, and whatever need to resist her seemed to melt away. John Little shook his head, giving her an unenviable stare. Even Tuck seemed to find the rare advantage of silence.

"But everything you've done—" Robert tried, but Marion just raised her hand.

"Everything I've done has been for the families I brought here. That's where this started, and I'm trying not to lose focus on that. Helping them was all I originally set out to do—it was never about overturning the law or replacing Sheriffs or Kings or inciting a rebellion. Now I've brought them here at great cost . . ." Her voice faltered.

Robert returned her grasp, giving her wrist a firm squeeze. "They're all under my protection."

"And I'm afraid I have put you in danger as well, Robert." She had to wipe the wetness from her eyes. "If the Chancellor names me traitor, you are right to fear he may claim your title, too."

"He's welcome to try."

"He is indeed," she said quite seriously. "And if he is successful then I think you're also right in assuming that Huntingdon would return to de Senlis. And what of my people then? Do you think Lord Simon de Senlis will suffer to have any *outlaws* living on his lands? How can I pay that price, or the price that you will suffer—that *anyone* will suffer—all simply so I can go on pretending that my actions of the last few years should have no consequences?"

The fire crackled, and offered no answer.

She thought achingly back to a time, so recently, when she had thought of running off with her grandfather in search of her next big hurdle. The idea that her people here in Huntingdon were so safe that she could leave them was an impossible dream now. Their fate, and Robert's, had become bound as one— and was on the opposite side of the wheel as her own.

"Are you asking us?" Tuck asked, his voice coarse. "Or telling us?"

"I'm *asking*," she answered, instantly offended. She was not the type to give orders, and it hurt that Tuck could even think she was uninterested in their opinions. It was everything she had argued against at the council—the horror of a world in which those in power acted in nobody's interests but their own. "I'm asking all of you. Even you, Amon."

"My lady." He bowed his head, but the inclusion clearly caught his surprise. She rarely consulted him for advice, despite their frequent proximity. It was not meant as an insult, she had once explained. *"I value your ideas greatly, Amon, but I will generally keep myself closed to your counsel. You will be as well known by my side as my own arm, but ours is not a partnership. If I ask for your advice once, then you would risk growing bitter when I do not ask it a second time, or when I disregard it. You are more than a protector to me, but we will both be the safer if my decisions are wholly mine to make."*

But she asked for it now. Maybe because she knew the extremity of her situation, or maybe because she guessed that he would soon no longer be able to provide his service to her.

"With respect, my lady," he said calmly, "you undervalue yourself. You brought fifty-four souls to this castle, and you would trade your safety for any one of them, because you are who you are. But you're worth a hundred of them. And that is not to speak poorly of any one of them—I include myself in that figure, and John and Tuck here. You're worth a hundred of us. And if there were actually a hundred of us to be sacrificed, you'd be worth a hundred more."

Her throat tightened, she could not respond.

She would like to think he was right.

But if she let these people suffer for her actions, she'd be worth nothing.

FORTY-FIVE

ARTHUR A BLAND

NOTTINGHAM CASTLE

"ONCE UPON A TIME," ARTHUR explained, having traded the entirety of this story for the pleasure of Zinn's silence for its duration, "there was a young man named Arthur."

She instantly broke their deal. "That's your name."

"I know that's my name. This story's about me."

"Then why are you pretending it's about someone else named Arthur?"

"I'm not. Shut the fuck up and listen."

This was one of their days with nothing to do, in the cramped little cupboard of Zinn's hovel off Plumptre Street, when she was recovering from the beating she'd taken at the whorehouse. Arthur's generosity with his own history was aided by a pilfered bottle of Portuguese red.

"Arthur made the same mistake that many young men make of labeling himself in terms of things he did not have. He did not have much food, so he was 'hungry'—and stole what he could from the people that raised him. Those people never complained, because they did not notice. He did not have any money, so he was 'poor'—and stole horseshoes from the stables to sell. Those horses never complained, because they were horses, and horses only complain about politics. He also did not have any God, so he was 'lonely'—and gave hell to those who did. God also never complained, because he was quite busy with being imaginary bullshit.

"Arthur survived like this for quite a while, an orphan boy raised by an entire community of neglect. He had no mothers to praise him but a hundred fathers to discipline him, and that would be a sad story if it weren't so fucking commonplace and boring. No, young Arthur was just like a hundred other hungry, poor, lonely people, excepting he had the decency to be named Arthur which, objectively, is the best name ever. The only thing special about Arthur was that he didn't die young, which made him exactly the same as everyone else alive, and only slightly more special than the dead."

HOT WHITE PAIN LASHED across his forehead and red filled his vision as Arthur went into rage. He sprang up out of Brick's grapple and smashed his skull into the man's jaw, he grabbed his wrist and twisted, wrenching the bastard's arm until the blade was aimed at himself, its tip was already bloodied from Arthur's brow. The brick tried to resist with both hands, but gave up to claw at Arthur's face.

Arthur didn't notice.

He put all his weight into a sudden push that jabbed the knife away from himself and into his would-be murderer's neck, just once, just barely. He went for a second stab, but Brick released his grip of the knife and barreled backward to probe his wound, which spurted hot blood out as they both tumbled to the ground again.

The knife landed between them, but closer to Arthur, and he didn't wait. He snatched it up and closed distance in one bound, falling down onto the man, slamming it into his brick chest thrice more, down to the hilt each time, only then pausing to wipe the blood from his own eyes and wince at the agony lancing across his brow. He had to wipe his eyes a second time, then again, but he couldn't tell if his hands were too bloody to help or if he was bleeding faster than he could wipe. By the time he leaned his head back into the sky, he was staring right into pug-ugly Neck Fat, who was screaming something—but the sound was from another world, underwater away. Arthur wondered if the man knew how stupid he sounded.

Arthur tried to stand but he fell backward. He raised his knife but it was gone, the pug ugly stood on top of him, his boot on Arthur's throat. Arthur made noises that should've been words while Neck Fat reached down to carve out his face.

Arthur's mouth filled with vomit.

> "Having little to tie him to one place, Arthur the young man grew into finding jobs that kept him wandering from town to town. He'd deliver foodstuffs and make trades between Redford and Sheffield, Leeds and Doncaster, always taking what he wanted from his cargo and finding every manner of unsavory diversion along the way. We shouldn't say he was happy doing this, because that was yet another thing he didn't have. Happiness."
>
> "He didn't have a penis?"
>
> "Shut up. He wasn't happy, but neither was he miserable—and up until this point he had definitely had a lot of miserable. So comparably, it was better. But the thing, the important thing of it all, is that Arthur kept on labeling himself by the things he didn't have. More specifically, the things he knew of that he didn't have. If only he'd known that he should've been labeling himself by the things he didn't know he didn't have, he wouldn't've had such a miserable time being miserable all the time. Do you follow?"
>
> Zinn shook her head no. "That makes no fucking sense."
>
> Arthur continued regardless.

He spat it out, the stinging taste of bile bringing him back to his senses. He would've wondered why he was still alive, but the pug-ugly's face had been made even pug-uglier by the thin metal skewer that pierced it from cheek to cheek, little bits of charred meat still dangling by the handle. Neck Fat's head twitched, his hands fumbled to make sense of what the girl had done to him, and why he couldn't open his mouth.

Arthur pushed himself up to his knees despite the heavy drunken weight that swirled through his senses. With his left hand steadying the pug-ugly's face, his right pulled the skewer back out the way it'd entered, and then up again through his pug-ugly nostrils, and eventually, hopefully, into whatever constituted his pug-ugly brain.

The body slumped backward, as Arthur probed the wound on his own brow again. More blood on his hands, his head was numb, his hands were shaking. The young woman was there, but sideways, or upside down. She clutched her torn clothes across herself, but her modesty was wasted since the world had chosen to go entirely blurry.

"Thank you," she probably said.

"Did he cut my head off?" Arthur asked back. Something about those words didn't sound right, or maybe it wasn't his voice at all. Again he tried to finger his head, certain there was a knife wound all the way across it, his brains seeping out. He surely didn't have long left.

"Cut your head off, sir?" she asked, leaning in. Her hair was a thousand pinpricks in the wound on his head, but her accent was the stuff of dreams. *That girl saved your life,* he knew, although he wouldn't be alive long to enjoy it. "I can't say to that, but you've got a nasty one here, that."

Arthur winced as she inspected him, testing out his eyebrows, wondering if there were still muscles up there that worked. "Did he cut my head off?" he asked again, since words weren't really his thing anymore.

"No," she scoffed. "You got lucky, there. I think his hilt got you more'n the blade. Not too deep." Her fingers brushed at his forehead, which was fortunately quite numb. "But you'll be ugly. Best get going. Don't want to be caught with no corpses right now, that's ever the truth."

"Wait," he said limply, since he was in love with her now, but he'd never really seen her face, and she disappeared and left him to tend to his own injury.

The urge to crumple and sleep was profound, but he remembered his bargain with the world. He'd saved the girl, which meant David had to be safe. He'd find David and they could limp out of here, and Arthur could die in peace outside the castle. *Or farther. Not in Nottingham.* He'd never wanted to leave the forest, and damned if he was going to fucking die here. If nothing else, he had to survive just long enough to get outside the city and die with some green around him.

There were water troughs not so far away, he remembered, and he knew he had to wash the blood off his head and his hands if he stood any chance of slogging along. When he emerged from the crannyway of the fight, there were still people running and calling out, but they were a thousand miles away. All Arthur wanted was the water.

One trough was overturned but the other was upright—he plunged his hands in first and scrubbed away at the blood, then pushed his entire face into its depths. That was as good as a slap across the cheek, it sprang his nerves to life and he came up sputtering. His head was still abuzz, but he grew the bravery to massage closer and closer to the wound on his head. Eventually his fingertips found soft tissue, but he seemed mostly intact. Most of the pain was above his right eye. He didn't go any farther, fearful that his fingers would plunge through down to the bone, or worse. He wondered what would happen if he poked his own brain, if he might lose all control of his body and shit his breeches. Even David would laugh at him for that.

He cupped water into his mouth, too, he'd almost forgotten about the vomit. The water was dank and bloody, but better than bile. *No wonder she hadn't fallen in love with me.* He'd been covered in blood and bork. *She called me ugly.*

A hideous crack split the air, followed swiftly by the horrible screams of too many people, and Arthur eased his head around to see it with startling clarity. The easternmost audience stand, where the actors had been hoisting people to safety, was *collapsing.* There were altogether too many bodies on it, all swarming over each other like a cluster of ants, and the structure beneath them buckled once and twice in a plume of dirt—as if it were some beast that opened its great mouth to eat them all alive. The tinder screamed from the pressure, snapping the rope that reached up above. The body of some poor sod was practically launched from the battlement like from a catapult, flung by the tension in the rope down into the mess of broken wood and bodies below.

Not my problem, he cursed to himself.

Maybe saving the girl wasn't enough. How many fingers had he broken in the last week? How many people had he hurt, that didn't deserve it? The way David wouldn't deserve it?

How many did he have to save to get David back?

"So one day, more'n a few years ago, Arthur was in Sheffield inventing clever new ways to be miserable, when someone else went and topped him at it. Arthur's cart, which was arguably the only thing he really owned, went missing. Not missing in the sense that you can't remember where you left it, and darn if it wasn't right next to your boots the whole time missing. No, missing in the sense that some feckless dickshit took it from exactly the place you left it. More of the stolen type of missing.

"So now Arthur, the man who never had anything, somehow had even less. All the money that wasn't his and the food that wasn't his and the weapons that weren't his were now the feckless dickshit's, which contributed mightily to Arthur's sense of miserable. He turned every alleyway in Sheffield upside down looking for the feckless dickshit, finding lots and lots of things like failure and fury and fuck all. For one of the first times in his life he truly deeply wished there were a God, specifically so that Arthur could blame Him rather than himself for his own fuckup. He eventually submitted to his poor luck and found his way to a stables in hopes of starting from scratch, or finding work to pay for dinner, but instead he found the aforementioned feckless dickshit."

"This story's crap," Zinn interrupted.

"Shut up, it's almost over. And you're supposed to be silent."

"It was a bad deal. I thought I wanted to know more about you, but I'm finding out that I really don't care."

"A deal's a deal."

"Fine. But you don't know how to tell stories. You're skipping all the action."

She pouted, but sat back to let it finish.

Not my problem, he repeated, staring at the wreckage.

Even as he started running, against every good decision, to *help.*

Not my problem!

People were everywhere—scrambling, crawling, climbing, screaming. Every flash of blond hair stole Arthur's attention, but it was never David. Some people were fleeing, terrified out of their wits. Arthur understood their panic, but still hated their cowardice. Women and children perhaps had cause to run, but there were men stronger and abler than Arthur without even a single knife wound in their heads who were running away.

But there was always that difference between men. Those whose instincts were to hide, and those whose instincts were to rise. Old Walter of Locksley had made that distinction, back at his family's castle, back before the world had found a way to shit upon itself. When Arthur and David had found themselves at the mercy of his hospitality, and treated like decent folk rather than thieves. Treated as if they were worth more than the worst of their luck. Arthur asked Walter once why he'd put his faith in the two of them, and he'd just laughed. As if the question didn't even make sense.

When Walter died and Locksley burnt, Arthur understood. Then, as now, some people ran into danger, and others looked out for themselves. There was a stunning similarity to it now, climbing through the rubble to do what he could. He weaved through the masses of the destroyed spectator stands, trying to find where he could do the most good, even though *good* wasn't a thing he'd ever much fancied before.

At first it was easy. The people at the edges needed a hand standing up, or a shoulder to lean upon, and Arthur was quick to help. Some he found standing around aghast, unsure how to assist, and Arthur gave them specific tasks. "Take her, walk her away, don't leave her." Or, "Talk with that man there, keep him talking, don't let him fall asleep."

But deeper in was the thick of the madness, bodies and bodies all writhing on themselves, screams from above and below. At a glance he could see some clearly broken legs, a few people that weren't moving at all. Others trapped underneath the wreckage. "Stand back!" he shouted the moment he saw the danger—the weight of helpers trying to get to the victims was pushing the splintered timbers down farther into the mess, only serving to crush the people trapped beneath.

They heeded his words, and he organized them to step off the debris and focus their efforts, first on those who could be easily cleared from the wreckage, and then on clearing what they could of the wreckage itself. The victims were hurried off toward the field to lie down, which helped settle some of the confusion and chaos. Arthur climbed down into the hole and found a horrified woman staring back at him, her chest pinned by a heavy support post. Her mouth was open, but it seemed she couldn't breathe enough to even call for help.

Ignoring every pain, Arthur straddled the beam, reaching his arms down and around it, but he simply wasn't strong enough to lift it. "Help!" he called, but everyone around was consumed with their own emergencies.

Arthur repositioned his feet and gripped it again. He didn't need to pick it up, he simply needed to relieve a little of the tension on her, that she might breathe, that she might wiggle out on her own. He bent low with his knees and then *pulled*, every muscle in his body screamed at the effort, and surely the beam eased up by a few fingerwidths, just barely. He couldn't spare the energy to look down, but he heard her gasp for air. She had only to slide out of the way now, before he lost his grip. His fingertips went raw and pain lanced down both his arms. There was no way to hoist the beam any higher, but he could hold onto it for just a little bit longer.

Just a little bit longer.

A pain seized in his chest, but he fought it, he dared a glance downward to see if she was clear yet.

She hadn't moved.

She still lay there gasping, eyes unfocused, unaware that she could squeeze out now, or unable. Arthur tried to yell at her, but his neck was clenched too tight, the sound only came out as a sputter. His knees started to wobble, he knew he couldn't keep this up for much longer. *If he dropped it now, she'd be dead.* Even if he tried to ease it back down to recuperate and find help . . . that wasn't an option. His legs were failing, there were only seconds before it fell.

His heart lurched as he felt it slip from his fingers.

> "Arthur chased the feckless dickshit all through the town. In and out of every building. Up the stairs and down the stairs. Through the fields and through the church. Around a tree and around a bush—how's that for action? Is this a better fucking story now? No. In the end he grabbed the feckless dickshit and threw him to the ground and meant to beat whatever feck he might still have in him. But he didn't. Because as he'd given chase, he realized that the feckless dickshit was actually very much like himself. They were about the same age, the same build, they were very equally matched when it came to chasing, and the dickshit had only stolen what he could to survive. So even as Arthur pinned the dickshit's arms to the ground with his legs and raised his fist in the air to turn his face into pulp, he knew he wasn't gonna do it. Because he finally realized the one thing he didn't have, that he didn't know he didn't have.
>
> "Someone like himself. Someone to be miserable with.
>
> "The moment I met David, that all changed. I've been very happy being miserable ever since."

"Because you two are fucking?" Zinn asked.

"No, you cunt."

"So what's the point of this story, I'm supposed to always remember that my enemies might be just like me?"

"Fuck, no, enemies are the worst, you should always kill them. The point is that you can't go it alone. You need someone like you. And I think that's us. I think you're a lot like us."

"I'm not like you." Zinn curled her defiance into her lip. "You're old and ugly."

"Goddamn," Arthur smiled with pride, "you're one feckless dickshit."

Arthur's eyes shot open as the weight of the beam went *up*, not down. Just in front of him was another man, his arms as thick as the wooden beam itself. Head to toe his dark skin was covered in hair and sweat and the goddamned blue quilted doublet of the Nottingham Guard. But he hoisted the beam up another few fingers and nodded to Arthur importantly.

The fact that he still had strength to move at all was a shock, but Arthur clambered down to the ground and slid his arm around the woman's waist. *Don't drop it on me,* he thought, but pulled her out from under the beam and to the safety of a few feet away. The wood made a sickening smash into the earth when the Guardsman let it drop, leaving nothing to the imagination as to what it would have done to a human.

"She alive?" the beastman asked, kneeling to investigate. Arthur tried not to look him in the face. If he were recognized now, he wouldn't stand a chance.

"I think so," Arthur grumbled. "Thank you."

"You know her?"

Arthur just shook his head sideways. *Go away.*

"Here," the guard said, and Arthur looked up to see him pull the blue cowl off his shoulder and over his head, and into Arthur's hands. "Cover her up."

Arthur's face must have shown his confusion, because the guard elaborated by way of brushing the woman's hair away on the right side of her face, exposing the scarred nub of her ear. "Don't let anyone see that. Dangerous thing to have right now, right?"

"Right," Arthur said, stunned. But he obeyed, and pulled the cowl over the woman's head, leaving its hood up to cover her incriminatingly clipped ear.

The beastman's face was heavy and certain, his eyes pinned Arthur to the spot.

"More important things than that, right now. Right?"

"Right," Arthur agreed again, swallowed.

"And we're all on the same side right now." Sweat dripped down his nose. "Right?"

Arthur. "Right."

Whoever this Guardsman was, he surely knew what Arthur was. "Good," he huffed. "Help me move her to the field, then let's get back at it. More to do."

Thankfully, it was only another ten minutes before it was over. Arthur bandied with a few other groups of men and moved about some of the remaining wood debris looking for more survivors, but most were already free of the rubble. Five deaths in all, dozens wounded, but the harrowing frenzy had dissipated into one of mutual aid. There was still an obvious commotion coming from the market stalls to the south and beyond—where no doubt the crowd was still trying to mob their way out of the castle gate—but here in the archery field, the chaos from earlier had thankfully found pause.

A man, kneeling next to an older woman, injured, whispered prayers. "Thank you, Lord, for sparing her."

Arthur shook his head in spite but walked away. *Your Lord didn't spare her. It was people like me or that Guardsman that saved her life. Where was your God when the structure collapsed?*

What sort of god would've let any of this happen at all?

This insanity had brought out both the best and worst in people, and all of it was born from within themselves, not from up above. It'd been a while now since Arthur had talked with Friar Tuck, but his empty words of advice came to mind now. Tuck had told Arthur to consider every good thing in the world when comparing to the bad, and was certain that his god would come out the stronger.

Not this day.

But still, Arthur had a curious compulsion to say *Thank God* when David of Doncaster milled through the field on his own.

They embraced instantly, but both recognized there was little time for emotion. The entire field had become a makeshift hospital now, and they found a patch on the ground to themselves where they could tend to their wounds and speak quietly. David tore off part of his tunic to make a wrap that went around Arthur's forehead, to keep his wound from collecting any more dirt. "How the fack did you do that to yourself?"

"I did it for love," he groaned, only mostly joking. He recounted aloud his fight behind the vendor stall, and of the young woman he'd rescued. "Didn't recognize her, though, and I haven't seen her again yet."

"You're picking an odd time to start courting."

Arthur flicked his friend's hand away. "She could be an ally, and that's something we need if we mean to get out of here. They said they saw her stealing, and that's our kind of folk. But she wasn't with the Lions." With the amount of time they'd spent with Nottingham's largest street gang of late, it was easy to forget that there were still smaller gangs that managed to survive as well. "The Red Lions have been betrayed. The guards knew exactly who to target in that contest."

"I noticed that, too," David mumbled. "Actually, Cait noticed it."

"Hm." Arthur felt a twinge of pity. "For all the good it did her. All her bluster about being a lion . . . which earned her eight arrows, right in the heart. We'd best be careful, or we might still get lionhearts ourselves."

David blinked a few times absently, then focused again. "With Fawkes and Caitlin gone, I don't even want to know what happens with the Lions now. It'll be anarchy. We've got to find Will and get out of Nottingham."

"And Zinn," Arthur added, somewhat surprised in himself.

David clicked his tongue. "And Zinn. They were on some errand together this morning for the Lions, so they're probably still together. But first, we have to get out. Castle gates are locked, and we have to assume any guard that gets a good look at us will recognize us. They mean to interrogate every man, woman, and child in this bailey until they're confident everyone with any affiliation to Red Fox or Robin Hood has been caught. We can't stay here."

Arthur looked south, to the vendor stalls. Beyond that, the gates, the crowd, the interrogations, the paranoia. "I imagine that'll get worse once they find those bodies I left behind the stands."

David didn't respond, his eyes were red and watery and somewhere else. A quick glance told Arthur all he needed—David was staring at the crimson splotch on the hay target that still stood at the center of the archery range. Caitlin and Alfred's bodies were no longer there, but their blood still soaked the ground.

David's face was afire with blame.

"Hey." Arthur put his hand on his friend's knee, but no response. "You did what you had to."

He tightened his lips and swallowed, but it was not an agreement.

"If you had refused, they would've killed you next. That's what happened to Caitlin. That's on them, you hear me?" He gave him a slight shake. "That's on them."

"I could've missed just a little. A foot to the side."

He was probably right. Caitlin's disobedience had been an arrow that blindly sailed wide of the target, an obvious refusal. David had the skills to put an arrow just shy of the target's chest instead. Nobody would have blamed him for being a bit wobbly under the circumstances.

But that wouldn't help him now. "They still would have died."

"But it wouldn't have been me." David's voice was small, as if it were hiding behind him. "It wouldn't have been my arrow."

"Hey." Arthur squeezed harder now, enough pressure to force David to look at him. "It may have come from your bow, but that wasn't your arrow none neither. The Sheriff of Nottingham sent that arrow. Prince John sent that arrow. Not you. They used you, like a tool, you're no more at fault than the bow itself. You can be mad as fucking sin that they used you like that, and you should be. But that's it. You didn't kill Alfred, you didn't kill Caitlin. They did. Take this . . . whatever it is you're feeling right now . . . whatever fucking pity or blame you have for yourself, and you aim it at something useful. Yeah?"

Arthur punched him in the chest for good measure, hoping it would make up for the right words that he clearly didn't have.

David nodded slowly. "I don't think I've ever killed anyone before."

"Fuck," Arthur said, because it was all there was to say. "You serious?"

"I think so. We've been in plenty of fights and close calls, and I've certainly meant to kill before, but I think today was my first."

Arthur grimaced. He had killed two, maybe three people within the last hour and hadn't even thought about it. *Why don't you feel bad about that?* Friar Tuck would probably ask, smiling with his crooked teeth and lopsided eyes. *You keep insisting that you don't need my Lord to have morality, but you don't flinch at taking life. Why is that?*

Because life isn't precious, he wanted to tell Tuck, and David, and the world. *Any fool can get born, and any fool can get dead. It takes a special fool to stay somewhere in between.* But David was softer than Arthur was, always had been, and it wouldn't do to poke that particular wound.

"That doesn't count as your first," he insisted, quite matter-of-factly. "Let's make your real first a good one, in helping to make this right. The Sheriff and the prince, yes? The Sheriff and the prince."

David finally came back down from the moment and gave Arthur the queerest look. "You're not . . . you're not saying we go kill the Sheriff and the prince, are you?"

Arthur laughed. "God, no! That'd be insane!"

"Because that would be insane."

"Yes. No, not right now!" He hadn't meant that at all, he'd only been trying to redirect his friend's anger. But the thought sent his mind tumbling into dangerous places. "Actually, *wait*. That might be brilliant."

David twitched, as if to get away. "You can't be serious."

"No, not about killing the Sheriff, no. But what about going *in*, into the middle bailey of the castle? Everyone's trying to get *out* right now, so the Nottingham Guard is watching the main gate very intently. How close you think they're watching the gate that goes up into the castle proper?"

"I don't know, and we're not going to find out," David said carefully, "because we're not insane."

"Just think it through." Arthur's thoughts raced. "Will's told us a dozen times about how they escaped from the prisons. That was in the next bailey up, not down here. He said that Arable led them to a storage larder where there was a postern door. No chance that'll be guarded right now, not while the gords are tearing themselves to pieces. We just have to find that gate."

"We *don't* just have to find it," David insisted, "because we're not insane enough to try that. You don't think they're going to notice two very insane people looking like us wandering up to the bailey gate? With everyone trying to escape, you think they'll let us walk in?"

"Not looking like us." Arthur smiled. "But if we take out two guards down here, and get their tabards and cowls . . ."

"Fack!" David kicked out. "Fack fack fack fuck fuck *fuck that might work.*"

FORTY-SIX

QUILLEN PEVERIL

NOTTINGHAM CASTLE

QUILLEN PEVERIL WAS THE greatest failure of a generation.

He had come to Nottingham for one singular reason—to determine if it was so unstable as to require intervention. Quill had *known* in his heart that it needed help, but he'd been too worried that his father would equate that failure with Quillen. He had selfishly hoped he could fix it himself via empty little acts like spying on Gilbert or stopping noblemen from shitting in the streets. He'd thought that sniping sarcasms from on high counted as a contribution.

Nottingham Castle was now eating itself alive, and Quill was the one that let it get this bad.

Swords were drawn, Guardsman against Guardsman, and absolutely nobody had any firm grasp of what was happening. In the middle of one group was Prince John and his handful of sentinel men, trying very desperately to remove themselves from the battlements to the safety of the higher keep. But between him and his destination was a red mountain of rage called The Simons, who had literally spent his entire life teaching people how to kill each other.

And half of those very people were on his side, screaming for vengeance for the quartermaster's murdered daughter.

The only reason the prince had not yet been torn to pieces and thrown over the walls was that there were just as many Guardsmen on his side. They weren't necessarily loyal to the prince; they simply happened to be nearest him when the riots began, and naturally obeyed when he started calling for protection. Those Guardsmen didn't know they'd be instantly squared off against their own friends. But they definitely knew that the prince's sentinels carried cross bows, and any Guardsman who tried to switch sides would undoubtedly have his morality rewarded by a quarrel in the back.

The reason Quill knew they thought all these things was because—of all the damnedest luck in the world—he was one of them.

"Stand down!" and "Move aside!" and "Get out of the way!" were all shouted liberally by members on both sides, and under any other circumstances they probably could have all calmed down and discussed things rationally. But Simon FitzSimon was screaming murder more primal than any animal, clawing his way through the men, forcing them to surge forward. Meanwhile, Prince John was prodding his crossbowmen to make progress as well, forcing both groups to roll and swell toward each other until the gap between them disappeared and Quill let out a masterful shriek.

The only saving grace now was that the Guardsmen, for the most part, didn't want to kill each other. Rather than a clash of swords, every man became a peacock—their arms and weapons brandished wide in a hopefully empty threat. But the distance between them shrank quickly. Someone's hand found Quill's face and he did his best to return the gesture, but the throng was compressing them together, and within seconds Quill had a mouthful of knuckles. Somewhere there was a guttural scream, perhaps the first legitimate injury, and the entire crowd flinched and rattled, and Quill *did not want to die this way.*

"Swords up!" he screamed, as soon as he maneuvered his mouth away from the stranger's fingers. "Swords up!"

He thrust his own tip to the sky, the only direction that was safe. There was not even elbow room enough to resheathe his weapon, but straight up there were no comrades to accidentally skewer.

"Swords up!" repeated the man whose fingers he'd tasted, mimicking the act, glancing his eyes around nervously to see if he would be killed for it. But thankfully, and against all recent precedent, the call for civility spread and weapons rose, rippling away from Quill. The brawl settled, if only slightly; the shouting was replaced by the long harrowing wail of Simon FitzSimon, trapped in his sea of students, lost to a world of grief.

"Guardsmen!" came a deep throaty roar, though Quill could not see its owner. "Stand down, fall in line!"

Finally their numbers spread out again, though the sounds of fighting did not abate. It came from below, over the lip of the battlement wall. Despite their orders to fall in, one by one their group realized what was happening in the archery field and they gathered at the ledge to watch. Whatever frenzied massacre they'd just avoided up here was already happening twentyfold throughout the lower bailey.

"Simons, I swear to you, you will have justice," came the voice again, and now Quill could see its owner, Captain Fulcher de Grendon, running to join them. He passed Prince John and his entourage, hurrying unmolested for the staircase to the highest bailey. "But first we have to get this castle in order! The prince has commanded a full lockdown of every castle gate and the city as well, and there are people *killing* each other down there!" He accentuated this point by thrusting a finger over the ledge at the mob that had converged at the outer castle gate. The Guardsmen normally posted there had retreated within the gatehouse's chamber, and were very likely praying that the doors would hold.

"You can fight each other tomorrow if you want." De Grendon pulled his hair back to fix its tail. "Right now, we have the Lord's work to do."

LATER, QUILL WOULD REMARK that *"we have the Lord's work to do"* was at once both a criminal understatement, and an insultingly accurate one. The work that needed to be done could only possibly be accomplished with divine intervention. There were few orders given as to exactly what form their *work* should come in, but the mutual recognition was that there were dozens of Guardsmen trapped in the lower bailey who'd been stationed there for the St. Valentine's tournament, and that they should be rescued until cooler minds prevailed.

Jacelyn de Lacy was one of them, Quill knew. She'd played her part in the tournament to perfection, but the prince's unexpected decree had fallen shortly after her final bout. Her persona of the Lace Jackal had likely earned her both admirers and haters, which put her in real danger. Quill only had loyalties to a few people in the Nottingham Guard, and she was one of them.

If Lord Beneger was accounted for, Quill would likely take whatever commands that man had to offer instead. But left to his own devices, Quill's brain somehow thought that his underweight, self-absorbed little self was the appropriate person to rescue a woman who was very likely impervious to even the concept of needing rescue.

Ferrers!—Quill cursed, pouring all the blame for this on the Sheriff's incapable shoulders. Quill had originally predicted that his archery tournament plan would be a failure; but that doubt had faltered a few days earlier when a beastly associate of the Red Lions surrendered himself to the Nottingham Guard. He asked for refuge in exchange for his firsthand knowledge of every gang member competing in the contest. Between him and the other informant, Rob o'the Fire, it seemed pretty clear that the Red Lions' ship was sinking and the rats were bailing out. So while the Nottingham Guard had already implemented a handful of tactics to weed out legitimate archers from victory, this Will Stutely fellow had sat on the battlements with Quill, singling out his old crewmates. De Grendon had been prepared to arrest them all, after their leader was publicly humiliated by Jacelyn de Lacy.

Until the prince surprised everyone by taking over.

And announced whatever abominations he thought proper.

And now, there was no telling up from down, much less right from wrong.

Upon arriving at the barbican down to the lower bailey, Quill instantly knew the job ahead of him was a nightmare—a horrified throng of people lay on the other side of the double portcullis. Normally left open for passage between the baileys, both gates had been lowered to keep the rabble out of the castle proper.

"Open the inner gate!" Quill demanded once the men at the wheels noticed him. He snapped his fingers to gather six or seven of the nearest Guardsmen to join him, to help in whatever madness lay on the other side. "We're going down, but only open this gate enough for us to crawl under, you understand?"

The gatemen's cowls bobbed, and a moment later the iron gates groaned under the turncock's latch, rumbling up foot by foot until Quill's group could scramble into the antechamber between the gates. Then the teeth of the portcullis bit down into the ground behind them.

What am I doing? He felt like a gladiator, awaiting his entrance to an arena where he was destined to die.

"Back away!" He slapped at the fingers of the citizens who were hoping to find some sort of escape this way. Their crowd retracted at the sight of the

Guardsmen's weapons, then farther and farther at Quill's commands. As they stepped back, one figure stepped forward—her unmistakably broken face a welcome relief indeed.

"Jac!" he gasped, waving her to approach. "I'm so glad to see you."

"Do you have Will Scarlet?" she asked, her good side as dead as her right.

"What?"

The second gate complained heavily against its counterweights, but jolted up, sliding between them. As the antechamber emptied of its men to go help below, Quill crouched and tugged Jacelyn de Lacy to join him on this side of safety.

"What do you mean?" he repeated the question.

"I mean, do you have Will Scarlet? Did he make it to the prisons?"

"I don't know . . ." They'd left him in Lord Beneger's custody after his capture, hastening to the archery tournament for the day's event. "Where else would he be?"

"He could be anywhere, until we find Ben," she huffed. "I'm going to check the prisons."

"No time for that," he urged her. "If he's there, he's there. If he's not, nothing you can do about it now. We have more important things at stake. *Ho!*" he called, noticing two injured Guardsmen limping up the lower bailey's ramp, trying to maneuver through the commonfolk. Quill looked up through the barbican's murder holes to shout at the men at the wheels. "Open the gate again, let these two in!"

Once more the iron groaned, up only a few feet, as Jacelyn and Quill both knelt to bring the two men into the antechamber. One had long blond hair and a look of absolute panic, the other boasted a vicious gash across his forehead and was covered in blood.

"You're safe," Quill said, trying to get a good look at the gash. "Get to the infirmary. You'll need some honey and egg whites to wash that out."

They nodded and huddled together, and Quill shouted again at the murder holes. "Open the inner gate, get these two some help!"

There was no response.

"Ho, is anyone up there?"

A moment later a silhouette covered the grate. "You, too, Peveril, get back up here." It was Captain de Grendon's voice.

"Just these two, Captain. I'm going down to help."

"No you're not," the captain responded. "Prince's orders. Nobody goes in or out."

"Not even Guardsmen?" Quill was incredulous.

"*Nobody.* He was extremely specific."

Quill looked back out through the bars, and the crowds of people trapped below, still rioting, still at each other's throats. He felt a sickening lurch of sympathy for the Guardsmen who had just crawled under that gate, now as trapped on its other side as the rest.

"Well you two are damned lucky then," he told the injured men, as the inner gate started its ascent. "What are your names?"

"Norman," they both answered in unison.

Quill had not expected that. "You're both named Norman?"

They stared back absently, as if the question were some sort of monster. Then a glance at each other, then back to him. Again, simultaneously, "Yes."

Probably new recruits. Probably wouldn't last the week. But right now, every man was worth his weight in gold. "Alright, Norman. Get Norman here taken care of, then get back out here. We need every able man we can get."

The less-injured Norman nodded, but turned back after only a few steps. "What about the postern door? We were . . . we were told to help guard it."

"Locked down tight," answered de Grendon, climbing down from the wheels. "Prince's men have everything."

"This is insane," Jacelyn answered. "The prince is insane."

"He might be." The captain nodded grimly. "But he's the prince."

SIR AMON SWIFT

HUNTINGDON

EACH NIGHT, AMON COMPOSED his thoughts onto paper, that he might sleep the better without them rattling so inside his head. On the rare night, he browsed through his own pages, hoping he had already forgotten more about the world than he knew now.

17ᵗʰ of November
I have rarely known a man to possess himself of rigid principle. I would argue that self-interests alone constitute a man, and his public moral doctrine bends to whatsoever aids him in their pursuit. That this self-deception is so readily mistaken for integrity is the foremost disease of our age.

NOT FOR THE FIRST time, Sir Amon Swift's thoughts drifted backward, wondering what life of leisure and respect should have been his. Had he known what misadventures lay in wait when the castellan Robert FitzWalter gave Amon the assignment of protecting his daughter years earlier, he may not have been so eager to accept the payment of his knight's fief. The protection of a young lady to the court should have been as docile a task as any, and should not have included any amount of foresthood galivanting or rebellions. While docility had never been high on Amon's wishes in life, he imagined that he could acclimate to it quickly.

As evening pulled herself over them, Lord Robert and Lady Marion took the shelter of Little John's hovel for privacy. More companions such as the Delaney brothers and Charley Dancer gathered by the fire, and discussion of de Senlis's ultimatum became impossible. Tuck tried to hide his bewilderment at watching Robert and Marion disappear together, but the growing connection between them was impossible to ignore. Amon chose to think nothing of it— Lord Robert had responsibilities as both an earl and a husband, and Marion knew better than to further complicate their already tenuous situation. The attraction between them was a natural result of the adventures they had shared, and nothing more. While the countess Magdalena had given them both slights, petty revenge was not in either of their natures.

"That was a kindness, what you said earlier," John Little shifted his weight toward Amon, "but Marion will never see herself as more important than anyone else. She wouldn't always be off trying to save everyone if she didn't think each one of them deserved it."

"I know," Amon answered. "But she asked my opinion, which I stated."

"She already carries the weight of every soul we've lost," Little sighed. "She wouldn't stand letting one more fall to protect her. She aims to turn herself over to this Lord Senlis, I tell you that plain."

"Well then oughtn't we find a way to talk her out of it?" Peetey Delaney asked. "She's done so much for everyone here. How can we let her sacrifice herself?"

"She'll argue that's not your decision to make," Little responded.

"Then we argue it is. We make a point of it."

"There's no stopping her from doing what she will," Tuck laughed mildly, "unless anyone plans on tying her up."

He meant it as a joke, but it was inarguably true. The only thing capable of pulling Marion away from Huntingdon now was a coil of rope and a heavy sack. Amon wondered where his duty would fall, if the Delaneys tried to abduct Marion for her own safety. To protect her from Lord Simon de Senlis.

12th of December

I have never met an evil man. Circumstance has brought me all manner of man and woman, and I use the male descriptor here for both, for ease rather than preference. I have met men ruled by petulance, by greed, by a numbing ambivalence to the consequences of their actions. Men taken to fanaticism, or ignorance, or to variations of both. I've known men whose actions could be described as cruel, I've known men with bones entwined in their beards who eat mud and claw at their own skin. I've met murderers and rapists whose disdain for themselves and the world led them to acts of depravity, but I've never met an evil man.

As a sworn knight, Amon shouldn't be in a situation where he would have to choose between fulfilling his vow or serving the law of the land. Thus far he had avoided any personal entanglement with the Nottingham Guard, and had not so much as unsheathed his sword against any enforcer of the king's law. Even now, Lord Robert's rule held authority in Huntingdon and Amon would be lawful to raise arms against an insubordinate lesser lord, regardless of de Senlis's justification.

But if the Chancellor were to present himself here and declare Marion a traitor, then Amon's situation would complicate. His very knighthood could be jeopardized by breaking the king's peace to defend her.

Marion had grown dear to Amon over the years, but his vows were not to abide by his endearments. Lady Marion Fitzwalter had made her own choices, which were often to hold the law with little respect. Amon's private priorities did not match hers.

28th of December

Mathematics teach us a principle of inverse proportionality—in which the value of one item decreases as the value of a second item increases, in equal portion. I would argue that the true value of any man is proportionally inverted

to that man's estimation of that value. The more a man professes his impor-
tance, the more certain it is that he is immediately replaceable. Knowledge
of this formula negates its application, of course, so I cannot appraise myself
with it. I would modestly hope that I might fare well. But in countless towns
I have found a crannyway, or church, or slum, or public house, or tavern,
where—based on the hearsay that often precedes me—some man tells me I
am worthless at best or an abomination at worst. Sometimes they have sought
to correct the problem of my existence personally. I am lucky to say they have
each failed, but I fear I will one day meet my fate at the edge of their prejudice.
While I do not advertise the details of my life, neither will I ever deny them.
Every one of these men . . . or any man in this world who considers himself so
flawless that he is compelled to condemn a perceived flaw in another . . . can
be held most rigorously to this principle of inverse proportionality.

BY AMON'S ASSESSMENT, LADY Marion had spent most of her life forging herself to compete in a world of men, a venture that by many accounts had led her
to act and conduct herself "like a man." Or a stereotypical man, at least—some
hypothetical warrior-hero who never showed fear. In most ways, Lady Marion
was more successful in portraying this farcical ideal than any male Amon had
ever known—himself most guiltily included. But earlier in the evening, when
he paid her his compliment, her eyes had widened and let loose their tears. In
moments such as those, he was humbled by the power of her womanhood. Her
capacity for care was beyond any other, which made her so very much stronger
than any man.

"Every soul *we've* lost," Charley Dancer spoke up, his head bobbing up between his gaunt collarbones. "That's what you said?"

Little grimaced. "What of it?"

"More lives have been lost than ours."

"What do you mean?"

Charley squirmed, seemingly afraid to contradict the group. "Well the Sheriff certainly, and Guardsmen, too. Do you suppose those weigh on her as well?"

John Little breathed in, and responded as kindly as possible. "Who have we
killed aside from those who meant to kill us?"

"The Sheriff," Amon answered instantly.

"Elena," Tuck added. "She put an arrow through a fellow's neck at Bernesdale."

"Who meant to cut Will in half." There was no concession in Little's voice.
"And this is after they killed Much, so I dare you to say they didn't have it
coming."

"Anyone before that?" Charley pushed. "I passed through Bernesdale 'fore I
joined you, I was told there were at least two dead Guardsmen."

Little huffed. "Just stories. I know I didn't kill anyone, and Alan didn't none,
neither. Will complained enough that he wished he had."

"Arthur, maybe?" Tuck considered. "Why does it matter?"

"Doesn't matter." Charley shook it off. "I just mean that perhaps Lady Marion has kept stock of both sides throughout this. Maybe she thinks it's better that she turns herself in now, to stop the bloodshed on *both* sides. Maybe she's not just looking to protect you, but good people that get caught in the mix of it all. I don't know."

Amon was surprised that no one objected to the idea of *good people* existing amongst their enemies, but neither did anyone seem to agree with Charley. The idea floated helpless in the air for a bit before dissipating to apathy.

"I don't know," he repeated. "I don't know how the score can ever be settled." He turned his head to Tuck. "I don't suppose your book can help us out?"

He didn't mean to, but Amon let a brief chortle escape. It seized the attention and he was forced to explain himself. "My apologies. I just don't think you'll find much in the Bible about killing—or revenge—that won't be awfully black and white."

Tuck nodded slowly. "I wouldn't say that's necessarily true. But what about *your* book, Amon? What does your book say about it?"

Amon laughed again, irritated the conversation had come his way. He wasn't interested in getting into a theological discussion at the moment.

"What book is that?" Charley asked.

Surprisingly, the frogman had an earnestness in his face that Amon warmed to. "You may actually like it. It's not like the Bible, not at all. But I do carry it and read from it to find answers. It's from a Roman philosopher named Marcianus Capella, titled *De septem disciplinis,* or the seven disciplines. It defines the seven intellectual pursuits of mankind." That was an oversimplification, but Amon preferred to keep his thoughts on the subject private. Many found it scandalous to disrespect the teachings of the Bible, which was not Amon's intent. "If you wish, I'd be happy to read to you from it, whenever is convenient for you."

"Hm." Charley's eyebrows popped. "And what does it say on this?"

Amon let the question linger. "It will say seven different things," he replied at last. "Depending on who you are when you read it, and which pursuits you currently struggle with."

Across the fire, Tuck smiled. "I think you'd find the same is true with the Bible if you gave it more consideration."

3rd of January
There can be no denial that some creator, whom we are compelled to call God, is responsible for this world and our ability to witness it. But of religion generally, and the Christ specifically, there is a stubborn desire to simplify this creator into a collection of rules and absolutes. Religion is the greatest affront to God, for it takes away His complexity. The creation of good and evil ignores the million brilliant shades between. Something as simple as murder, for instance, is aptly labeled evil, but has been sanctioned and condoned by reasonable men with moral intent for centuries. I myself suffer from characteristics that some call wickedness, but these are characteristics

endowed by my Creator. Can we believe in a God who demands perfection of His creations despite His own utter failings? No, the world has more than two options, I would say, which is consistently proven enough by its constant, rapturous, inimitable complexities.

EVENTUALLY, WHEN MOST HAD supped and left the campfire to tend to other needs, Lord Robert and Lady Marion remained still in John Little's hovel. More than two hours had passed, and Amon was left alone sipping small ale from a horn. At length he was joined by Miss Arable de Burel, who had come from the castle in search of Marion. Amon carefully explained their whereabouts, causing Arable to idle her time beside him at the fire. When offered a pull of ale, she politely refused.

Amon studied her closely. She drew closer to the fire, wincing as she wrapped a shawl tight about her chest.

"Do you mind if I ask you a most personal question, Miss de Burel?"

She smiled simply. "Only if you stop calling me that."

"Arable." Amon returned his eyes to the fire. "How many months?"

He felt her body freeze beside her, and she took a sharp inhalation through her nose. "I'm certain I don't know what you mean."

"You're beginning to show. How long has it been since you've had a monthly bleeding?"

"I don't—" She stood quickly as if to deny it, but stumbled slightly off balance and steadied herself on his shoulder. Amon rose with her and offered his support. What he found in her face was a frightened little girl, tears already gathered at the corners of her eyes. "I didn't want to believe it was true," she said as he lowered her back to her seat.

"You won't be able to hide it much longer. You've taken to wearing shawls, I noticed, but that bump will be larger than the shawl soon."

She bobbed her head softly, her face flush red and squeezed tight. Her hands found their way down to her slightly swollen belly, its roundness made more obvious as she traced its outline through her dress.

"Four months," she answered.

It was as Amon suspected. "I don't mean to pry into the particulars, but that is only slightly longer than you have been with us. You're certain, then?"

Again her head bobbed as an answer. "I haven't . . . yes, that is. That is the only explanation, there was no other . . . not since . . ." Her face dropped into her palms and she shook.

"Then the father . . ."

Another silent admission. William de Wendenal, the brief Sheriff of Nottingham—who had also been betrothed to the Lady Marion. Wendenal's and Robin of Locksley's deaths were a very tender subject that had proven an endless source of antagonism between the women for months. While that hostility had dissipated recently, Amon worried greatly what complexities the addition of a child might bring.

"For a long time I thought I was just tired from everything," Arable said. "I didn't think . . . I haven't had any sickness, you know."

"Not everyone does," Amon replied.

"How did you know?"

"I can see it in your face," he admitted. "And your . . . well, forgive my crudeness but there isn't another way to say it. There's been more sensitivity in your chest of late, yes? I notice the way you wince when you fold your arms."

Arable's hands moved to her breasts, unconsciously perhaps. Her emotion-wrought face somehow found a deeper shade of red. "I didn't think anyone would notice that. You know an awful lot on the subject."

At that, Amon could laugh. "I was my mother's only son. Ten sisters, if you can believe it. They joke that my father was lucky to have died before they grew of age. I saw six of them through ten childbirths. You'd be well challenged to find an aspect of it that would surprise me."

That earned a bit of laughter, and she straightened the errant curls of hair that had stuck themselves to her forehead. "No father? Just ten sisters, your mother, and you? That sounds like a trying time for a young man. I don't suppose . . . is that why you . . . er . . . ?"

Her mouth clamped tight before she made any further embarrassment of herself, but the question could not be unasked.

Whatever part of himself had warmed toward Arable in the moment turned sour and dark. "Is that why I *became a knight*? Is that what you meant to ask? Is that why I distinguished myself in Aquitaine against the usurper Henry's forces? Is it why I applied myself to studying the natural disciplines of the trivium? Is this what you were going to ask? Which of my achievements were you about to reference?"

Arable was appropriately speechless. Ten years ago he might have felt some shame at barraging her so hard, or for showing her no mercy while she was in such a vulnerable state herself. But he had never been given that same clemency. Ever since his first mistake of trusting an untrustworthy friend with that knowledge, it had followed him—and Lady Marion's infamy had only made it worse. Those who sought to define him solely by that one private bit of information thought he was always obliged to explain himself at any moment, in any circumstance. Even now, when Amon had chosen to approach Arable and extend her the support he knew she was lacking, even still her first instinct was to see him as a single adjective.

"I am so sorry," she said. "I just . . . I just don't really know how that works."

"Then you should educate yourself. Perhaps in something other than prejudice."

"I'm not . . ." She reeled. "Amon, this is me. You know me. You can't think—"

"I absolutely can." Amon stood to leave. "I have known you three months, Arable, and you strike me as a decent young woman who did not deserve my lady's distrust. But I have known others whom I would describe with much greater fondness, who I had known for many years, whose opinion of me turned quickly upon learning more about me. So no, I do not *know* you. You can never know what vices a person carries with them, and how it changes them into someone you've never seen before. You know nothing about me, and have never bothered to ask. Why on earth would I assume I can trust you with my secrets?"

22ⁿᵈ of January, 1192

It cannot be long now. The best of mankind always strives to improve it-self, ever moving toward greater understanding, greater knowledge, greater acceptance. As more people embrace the desire to study the human condition, the sooner the light of knowledge will chase out the shadows of fear and preju-dice from the collective soul. I doubt I will see it in my lifetime, because such bigotry is generational and seemingly impossible to uproot in a man. But one or two generations from now, it should no longer bear any taboo for a man to lay with another man. It will be as commonplace and unimportant as one's preference for breakfast. Fifty years, no more than a hundred, until humanity has improved its biases. It cannot be long now.

SIR AMON SWIFT DID his best to focus on the seven disciplines as he awaited Lady Marion. The night was clear, which let him trace the constellations of as-tronomy; and he practiced several mental examples of geometry and arithmetic as they pertained to the distances between the heavenly bodies. Rhetoric, logic, and grammar were trickier things to practice without instruments, and music was nearly impossible. Still, as he always did, he shifted his mind from disci-pline to discipline, always selecting that which he felt he had most neglected to keep his brain alert and curious. Charley Dancer ended up accompanying him for some length of time, and Amon found it relaxing to explain each discipline and how they related to each other. Charley did not seem to understand the no-tion of *De septem disciplinis*'s allegorical narrative, so Amon spoke only in broad terms. He was filled with the distinct notion that Charley was showing more kindness than true interest, but it was nonetheless rewarding to teach each con-cept rather than defend them.

It seemed ruthlessly late of night when Lady Marion and Lord Robert fi-nally rejoined the group. They both seemed startled that Amon was still await-ing them. "I am mortified," Marion apologized. "I took the opportunity to close my eyes, I had no idea you were waiting on me."

"It is no matter, my lady, I would wait on you asleep or awake just the same."

"But still." She blushed, taking stock of her hair and clothing. "You should get to sleep, Amon, I'll be returning to the castle."

"I will walk you to its gates, my lady. I can still, at least, do that."

Lord Robert remained unusually quiet as they ascended the hill. The night was dark as fresh ink, but Amon knew the path well and led his lady with cer-tainty. "May I ask if you came to a decision?"

"I have." Marion swallowed. "Though it does not seem to please anyone in-volved. If de Senlis or the Chancellor returns to Huntingdon to claim me, I intend on letting them. And I do not intend for there to be any more discussion on it."

The crispness of her words were aimed at Lord Robert, who remained stoic. "As you say, my lady."

"In that regard, Amon," she softened, "I will very likely not need your service for much longer. When the time comes, you will be released from your duty, and none of my crimes shall be reflected on you."

"That is most kind," he conceded. "But my charge is not yours to dismiss. So long as your father has paid for my fealty, I will defend you against any threat."

"It won't be a threat, Amon. It will be the law. You cannot challenge that."

"As you say, my lady."

Marion went on to promise that she would speak with the countess and allow Amon access to the castle again, but he had little ability to care for such things at the moment. He had expected Marion's answer, but somehow had not expected the wave of unfamiliar emotions it encouraged within himself. As uncertain as Lady Marion's course had always been, Amon had never been forced to consider what would become of his own, were she to leave him. He wondered if her father would issue him a new charge, or dismiss him for failing to protect her from herself.

He wondered if any other lord in England would have the strength of character to employ Amon at all.

He wondered what odd mercenary jobs he would be forced to take before being murdered by a backstabbing accomplice or a bigoted vagabond.

He wondered what shame would be left to throw at him, the only able-bodied knight in England who had been refused service in the war.

Marion and Robert left him at the gates of Huntingdon Castle, their silhouettes swallowed by the torches within.

14th of February

I have more to write tonight, on loyalty and its fickleness, or its steadfastness. I have not decided which yet. I find words are not mine to command at the moment. My thoughts remain elusive to the bitter confines of sentences.

BEFORE RETIRING, AMON FOUND the Delaney brothers again and pleaded a moment of their time. "There will come a moment, soon, I fear," he explained extemporaneously, "when Marion will need us in spite of herself. It may come at great risk to our health. I hope I will be able to rely upon you both to stand with me, if the need arises."

Peetey looked shocked. "We were just kidding about tying her up and dragging her out of here."

"I know," Amon answered. "Which is why I'm asking you to reconsider it."

PART VI

BAILEYKING

FORTY-SEVEN

JOHN LACKLAND

HIGH KEEP, NOTTINGHAM CASTLE

JOHN'S FIRST PRIORITY WAS to rearrange the furniture on the top floor of the keep. There were a total of eight rooms—one at each corner, and another in between each of those—connected by a narrow, square hallway. The central space, around which the hallway bent, was enclosed as part of the eighth room. This was the only bedroom of the lot, but its window was on the tower's eastern face, and John hated the intrusion of the sun in the morning. Both the sun and the endless groans of discontent masses were positively dreadful things to be awoken to.

This afternoon, he took reports about the happenings below along with a plate of too-salted ham. Only one dozen loyal men were at his disposal, who lived in blissful ignorance of the importance of their current task. They thought they were simply securing the high keep for his personal use. His sentinels were men of little acuity, best used for executing orders that had a lot of obvious verbs in them. If he'd told them what was really happening, they'd either demand more money or stab him in the back—both of which were admittedly wise moves.

On the other hand, they might have instructed the cooks to be more conservative with the salt if they truly knew what was at stake. It didn't matter how many quarried stones in the castle's walls stood between John and danger, if he could be felled by a single urinary stone.

He pushed the plate away. There were altogether too many ways to die. He refused to let a dead pig be his.

"Tell me about the sally." John demanded of Hadrian the Increasingly Bitter. His swordarm was less than thrilled to be cooped up in the keep tower when there was so much potential violence below he was missing out on.

"The sally?"

"The *postern gate*," he clarified. In France it was the *sally port*, and John was awfully sick of reminding people that his exile from England brought with it a slew of cultural oddities, like using the wrong words for the right things.

"It's well guarded. Well, it's guarded," answered Hadrian the Second-Guesser. "As guarded as anything can be, given."

"I want it sealed."

John wanted the world sealed.

If it were possible, he could seal himself into a stone crypt so that nobody could get to him for months, excepting the fact that he'd probably starve or suffocate and defeat the purpose. Altogether too many ways to die, and the world had all of its attention on a very small spot at the top of his skull.

John turned to look out the window. This northeastern corner solar boasted the only window wide enough that one could look down and see the entirety of the tiered castle baileys without dodging one's head around like a pervert outside a brothel. Ten chairs might normally have surrounded the room's long table, but each one individually was too short to use by the window. So John had rolled a wine barrel in from the adjacent room, which he turned into a chair, and he was now enjoying a glass of his favorite chair along with his least favorite news.

"Seal it. Nobody comes in. Nobody comes out."

Hadrian the Wise obeyed, because that's why he wasn't Hadrian the Unemployed.

"And send up Gay Wally," John added absently, peering into the seething crowds below and wondering if he was watching someone die.

Commonfolk were, unfortunately for them, the best cover to hide behind. Locks can be picked; castles, dismantled. Given enough time and resources, any intrepid assassin could outthink the traditional defenses at a prince's disposal. But there's no strategizing against chaos. If they wanted to come and find him, they'd have to navigate this storm he'd created. The mob below, which probably wanted him dead, was his greatest ally.

It took longer than expected, but eventually bootfalls came down the hall again, though heavier than Gay Wally could create. It was possible the boy—who lacked enough mass to leave an impression on the world, much less a commotion such as this—was stomping deliberately to announce his approach. Or, more likely, John had missed something, and he was about to be stabbed in the back.

Instead of his young advisor, John was faced with an aging man in pleated leather whose face was as hard and deep as the mortared stone walls around them.

John looked about for a weapon, and found nothing but his wine cup. He took some small solace in knowing that he could certainly drink the stranger to death.

"Lord Beneger de Wendenal, Your Grace."

The man did nothing to give the words any tone of disrespect, but still they sounded like a chore. Though he did not appear to be armed, John was anything but relieved. He'd already been briefed in detail by Wally about this particular man, specifically because of the question mark he represented.

John studied his visitor, hoping to divine some sense of his purpose. Wendenal was attractive—not in the conventional sense that might describe a half-naked, freshly bathed servant girl—but more in the sense that John was compelled to look at him. Wendenal's features *attracted* curiosity, and were thus *attractive*. He decided against explaining this beguiling fact and opted instead for, "And what the fuck are we doing here?"

"Three months ago," Wendenal's mouth answered, while his eyes sharpened, "my son was murdered in the next room."

John potentially stood better chances of survival if he pushed himself out the window. "That's a hell of a way to introduce yourself. I would have waited at least until *how are you?* before divulging that . . . morbid . . ." He had no finish to that sentence, and was a better man for it.

"I come on behalf of the Sheriff and the castellan. They sent me because they still have many things that you can take from them, and they're fearful that you'll do just that. While I have already lost everything of value."

"Except your life."

"I did not misspeak."

John's eyes, on their own, opened so wide they could have rolled right out. "You're really just such a delightful human," he answered, pleased he had not yet been murdered. "Thank you for cheering me up. Do sit."

He hoisted himself back onto his wine barrel, while Lord Beneger raised a single greying eyebrow at the heap of chairs piled dramatically in the corner. Procuring one seemed a bit too troubling for the dour lord, so he settled for setting himself on the edge of the long table. His willingness to comply hopefully meant good things for John's favorite pastime of still breathing.

"Wendenal, then?" John asked. "Your son was William. I only knew him for the final week of his life, but he was entertaining." That, too, he realized, was a poor adjective. It made it sound like William de Wendenal was a raconteur or a juggler, but the truth was that his very serious scrapings at the world *entertained* John. Perhaps it would be more suitable to say they *delighted* him, but he'd already used the word *delightful* and he didn't want to be thought of as an amateur conversationalist. "I would have preferred that he stay alive."

Lord Beneger de Wendenal did not seem to appreciate that this was one of the kindest things John had ever said about a person.

Still, he accepted it. "I would be in your debt, for anything you could tell me of that week."

John leaned forward. "Now you have my interest, as debts are my favorite things to collect. But come, you're not here for that. I imagine you've come to see whether or not I'm mad."

A brief silence passed that screamed confirmation. Wendenal's lips parted. "They used less conservative words downstairs."

John imagined exactly that. "Very good. Well then, Lord Beneger de Wendenal, I hope we can speak frankly. If you're amenable."

Wendenal blinked. "Amenable?"

"If you're *willing*, that is." He winced. "You don't know *amenable*?"

"No, I know the word."

"No?"

"That is, yes, I know the word."

"Not a great word." John considered. "Has the word *mean* right in the middle, makes it sound something less than friendly."

"Your Grace." Wendenal's lips recoiled at the phrase again, but he had nothing else to say.

"So." John kept the table between them. He was trapped in a room with a self-described angry man with nothing to lose, and Hadrian the Absent wasn't helping anything. "I've had my eye on you ever since I arrived. Important people and grudges are two of my favorite things, and you're both at once. But I'm not only interested in why you're here, but in why you *weren't* somewhere else."

That silence stomped about the room again, had a sip of wine, stomped some more.

John prodded the matter with his toe. "I myself have just come from a very particular meeting this week. With a very particular woman. Who was quite nearly your daughter-in-law."

"Marion Fitzwalter?"

John nodded. "My less-than-loyal cousin tried to use me as a flag of rebellion. I cannot imagine you weren't invited—you were practically family. Instead, I find you here in Nottingham, mucking about with that gargoyle girl. What would you have me make of that?"

"Marion Fitzwalter held a . . . rebel's council?" When liars pretend at surprise, their eyes squint as if to feign a thought—exactly as Beneger's did.

"Oh, thank goodness!" John bounded off the barrel. "Beneger, I love you."

Wendenal swallowed.

"So you *knew* about this council in Huntingdon," John emphasized his points by burying his fingernails into the wood surface, "and you chose *not* to attend. This is the best of all worlds, Beneger. You are a friend, you are . . . a friend. I won't forget this, you know. I make right by my friends, you know that."

In the coming conflict, he needed all his allies. And if Wendenal had not answered his own family's concord, then he was firmly a loyalist. Loyal to Richard, loyal to John, loyal to England.

The crowd outside chose that moment to swell, and the sounds of an angry mob drifted through the windows and lingered as an uninvited guest.

"What did you say about a *gargoyle girl?*"

"A Guardsman, or Guardswoman, so I'm told. You pick some curious circumstances to plow your mistress."

Wendenal blinked, slowly. "I'm not having any sort of relations with Jacelyn de Lacy."

"Oh, you should." John blew out his lips. "Scars actually add something, you know. History. Probably her father, and that makes them feisty lovers, every time. You should have relations all over her."

"What is happening here?" Wendenal practically snapped. "Why have you blockaded yourself in this tower? How long do you mean to keep the castle locked down?"

"Oh, indefinitely." John hesitated. That answer should have been obvious.

"I must ask why. What is your obsession with Robin Hood?"

"Nothing, outside of not wanting him to stick me full of holes." John was confused at the confusion. "I had no idea Robin Hood was still a problem in Nottingham until I arrived. He runs the local gangs, I'm told? And he's long been the right hand of my rebellious cousin Marion. I have no doubt she can reach me here, through him—and well, he is something famous at breaking into the castle and killing people. How many Sheriffs have they lost that way?"

Beneger didn't answer, and John remembered that one of those had been the man's son.

"You understand, then."

"The man who called himself Robin Hood is dead," the man said. "You saw to that, on the archery field. We also have Will Scarlet in custody, who murdered Roger de Lacy, and maybe my son as well."

"Listen to your own words, Wendenal," John said, returning to his wine. "There will always be another Robin Hood, if you keep on at it the way you have. I aim to put a definitive end to that."

The man stiffened, his first sign of antagonism. "By locking down the castle? And the city? Why not at least let the innocent people leave, rather than trap them in the bailey?" His face was full of terrifying intelligence, begging for answers. John was willing to give them. After all, he could not keep the rest secret for long.

"I promise you I'm not mad, Wendenal. Although it probably helps me, actually, for the others to fear my sanity. I'm not exactly concerned about their assessment of my character at the moment. As they have likely mentioned 'downstairs,' I am forbidden from claiming any military authority over a castle. But my advisors assure me that I am within my right to declare emergency *domestic* measures such as this. This Robin Hood business is a distraction—a convenient one, and one that must be seen through, yes—but hardly the entrée."

"Please, Your Grace. Enlighten me."

"This is about England's very *existence,* Lord de Wendenal."

The man on the other side of the table tried, unsuccessfully, to eat his own skull.

"Don't make that face," John scowled. "You'll apologize for that before this is through. I was *at* the council in Huntingdon, you know, I was their guest of honor. That's how I know you weren't there. I saw them with my own eyes. They sought to put me on England's throne, they wanted to abandon my brother to his Austrian captors and have me rule."

Once again, Wendenal's only response was a single blink.

"It wasn't the first time the offer was made." John explained his meeting the previous month with the two walrus men from France. "They wanted to support me, to insist that I take the crown in my brother's absence. They were very convincing. They would have me believe they could rally half of England's nobles to back my birthright . . . so long as I made certain concessions to Philip, of course."

"And this council in Huntingdon," Wendenal's jowls shook as he puzzled it out, "they, too, wanted you to claim the throne?"

"Hardly a coincidence. I would bet anything that France is behind it. Struggling earls like Henry de Bohun and his family . . . they all could have easily found sway in French coin. My cousin Marion is anything but incorruptible."

It took no great stretch of imagination to wonder what barons and earls across England would do to keep their power in times as financially desperate as these.

"So you refused."

"Of course. Fool that I am. If you were France, what would you do next?"

Beneger squinted, which was an incorrect answer.

"King Philip knows I have the better claim to England in Richard's absence, but mine is not the *only* claim. My nephew Arthur Plantagenet could claim his right—as son of an elder brother—but he would require significant backing to be considered legitimate. But he's a child, and gullible. Arthur's long been a ward of Philip. When France failed twice to recruit me, Arthur was an obvious fallback plan. The only thing standing between him and success is my head—which is, coincidentally, my very favorite one."

Wendenal was tracking. "And you think France will try to kill you here?"

"I think they'll try to kill me anywhere. I thought Nottingham would be safe, as it had sent no representative to the traitor's council. Derby's no good, it's still all wooden timber and I would make a tempting roast. Warwick was an option—I rather like the Earl Waleran de Beaumont, but his familial relations with Hereford are troubling, and he was at the council. So Nottingham it was."

Wendenal's eyes sharpened. "So you think Robin Hood's gang is trying to assassinate you, by Marion's order . . . in France's name . . . to crown Arthur as king . . . to France's benefit."

"You're deliberately making it sound implausible." John licked his lips. "And you'd be right, if you weren't so wrong."

Outside, a swell of noise.

Poor Wendenal, he truly had no idea how deep was the shit in which they were dancing. France was not going to hang all their plans on the hopes of a few hired killers. He deserved to know that which John had kept from everyone else.

"There is an army coming to England as we speak, Beneger. And it aims to destroy me."

The man's face did not budge.

"Oh, I know. And I'm the last person in the world who wants it to be true, but there are certain facts that do not disappear at the bottom of a bottle. I'm not some paranoid madman in a tower," he explained. "I'm literally England's last hope."

Wendenal inhaled deeply, his exhale full of judgment. "This army, it's coming to Nottingham?"

"Yes. It was gathering a week ago, I hear. My spies on the continent have kept me informed. Had I accepted Marion's offer, no doubt this French army would have been mine to command, in claiming the throne. Instead it will come for my head, to pave Arthur's path to the crown. The last report said they were gathering galleys to bring them across the channel. I imagine they'll reach our shores within a week. Two at the most."

He returned his gaze out the window, wondering what the hills beyond the city walls would look like with an army blanketed over them. Nottingham Castle had never fallen—but it had only ever been attacked by Englishmen, whose desires were to occupy, not destroy. This French army came with a singular purpose. A quick strike, to John's heart.

"Against an army, we can at least make a stand here. I've summoned as many of my own loyal men to the castle as I can. I'm glad to count you amongst them. If we thwart Philip's design and send him back to France, we can help secure peace for everyone. But if I am killed, then my nephew Arthur claims England's throne and you are all subject to King Philip. Richard will die in his cell and England's independence will be over. It might be hundreds of years again before she rises and unshackles herself from France, if ever."

"Then we should be preparing," Wendenal stammered. "These people in the baileys—"

"Are trifles. *Trifles,* Wendenal." He leveled his eyes on the man's curious face, desperate to find understanding. "The gates of the castle, and the city, must remain closed. No one passes through, we cannot provide them any opportunity. If an assassin finds a way to get to me . . . well then, I hope you've brushed up on your French lessons."

It was the world, on his shoulders.

"And if we succeed?" Wendenal's gruff voice faltered.

"Then we pay the damned ransom!" John blurted. Austria did more than capture England's king, they held the entire country hostage. "Austria knew that without Richard, England would fall into factions. And a people divided are most easily conquered. The answer—the only answer—is for Richard to return. Everything will be better if Richard returns."

"You don't want to be king?"

"Good God no, I'd literally—*literally! Look at all this!*—rather be dead."

Lord de Wendenal clicked his tongue. "How much of the ransom has been raised?"

John wished he had a better answer. "Not enough."

"I think that a lot of people," Wendenal said carefully, "view the payment of this ransom as weakness. They think that England will look weak for capitulating to Austria's demands."

"They're right," John sighed. "But it is still the best plan we have. Perhaps England can someday pay Austria back for this injustice, in time. In a decade, Richard can claim his revenge. But England has to survive this threat to make that possible."

"What about a rescue?" Wendenal asked, with a spark of light in his eye. "Could Richard be rescued?"

"I'd say you're too old for swashbuckling, Beneger."

"Not me, of course. But could it be arranged?"

If every idea in the world got in a line for John to judge in order of its merit, this one would be at the very end. "Yes . . . yes, of course! We simply raise an army, travel to Austria, find out where Richard is being held prisoner, siege the castle or whatever it is, and march back unmolested! You're brilliant, Beneger! Brilliant!"

The man sighed, letting the sarcasm slide. The brutal defeat that came with acceptance.

"This is the shit of reality, Wendenal." He passed his cup to the man, who raised his eyebrows and finally drank, and deeply. "This is real life."

FORTY-EIGHT

QUILLEN PEVERIL

MORNING, WHICH MIGHT NORMALLY bring tranquility, was only a promise of another day's horror. Quill found himself on the lip of the battlements again, vomiting over the edge. A physical pinching pain wound a creative path about his bowels, as though he'd accidentally swallowed some very angry animals who were eager to burrow an escape. Quill wiped his mouth with a rag, ignoring the feisty wind that threatened to carry him off the walkway. One side contained the small courtyard of the upper keep, the other led down to a fresh pile of vomit in the middle bailey. This was the entirety of his world now—the debatable safety of a cage upon a hill, and it promised to remain so until Prince John's madness exhausted itself.

An ocean of sound roiled over him, it swelled and pushed, the constant commotion of the lowest bailey. The citizens were still trapped there—hungry, cold, and increasingly angry. The management of it all was nearly nonexistent. Quill hastened to the Sheriff's office in the high keep, where gathered the men who intended on facing the day's emergencies. As Quill walked there, he kept one eye open for any small closet in which he might stow away for a quick year or two.

The vaulted room boasted thick columns, skinny windows, and a dozen prominent advisors who were already arguing as Quill joined them. A cursory glance confirmed that Prince John was mercifully absent. "He has secluded himself in the uppermost story of this keep," complained Hamon Glover, the rotund castellan whose eyes seemed desperate to pop out of his skull. "He will not even allow me access to him, he sends messages through his manservant. It is abominable!"

"He saw me," answered Lord Beneger.

"And no one since!" Glover spurted. "This castle is not his to command. Such were the stipulations of his exile, and now we are like to see why! He cannot deny my access—"

"He is claiming an emergency measure," Ben explained. "To deal with the domestic threat of Robin Hood. I don't know if there's any precedent for it, but it may be within his right."

The man harrumphed. "It is my privilege to protect this castle from any enemies, including those within its walls."

Ferrers, skulking by a column, uncurled his fingers. "Master Glover. Please."

Lord Beneger de Wendenal's voice carried a dire warning. "You would do well to give your words more consideration."

"I consider the prince a madman." Hamon Glover refused to back down. "I hear he goes on and on about French spies. Can you believe it?"

"He's welcome to stay locked up there." Captain de Grendon pounded the table twice. "He's the least of our concerns right now. Once we have peace you can all play prince and paupers, but right now I need help getting control of the castle, and control of the city. My men are a single short word away from tearing each other apart! FitzSimon has practically taken over the barracks, and I can't stop him if he tries to storm the upper keep."

"He won't *storm the upper keep,* they're Guardsmen—"

"The prince murdered FitzSimon's daughter!" De Grendon hit every letter of that statement, rightfully stunned it was a real sentence that could be spoken aloud. "For *nothing.* Because she missed. Because she refused to kill a man in cold blood. Frankly, I'd join The Simons if he wanted to raise hell. If my boys stay in that barracks with nothing to do, they're going to boil. And there's plenty of *goddamned work* to do, we just need to open the castle gates!"

"Prince John has forbade that," the Sheriff reminded them.

De Grendon's jaw locked. "Then let him come down here and defend that idea."

"There are innocent people trapped in the lower bailey," Quill tried to interject, "and not enough Guardsmen. It's probably worse in the city. The only people the prince has allowed to leave the bailey are those that are arrested—and then, only to be taken to a cell. The prisons can't even fit them all. Some people are turning *themselves* in now, falsely claiming to be associates of Robin Hood, just to get out of that bailey."

"I do not disagree with you." Ferrers scratched the tip of his nose. "But I cannot open the gates until the prince has commanded it."

De Grendon threw his hands in the air. "Then you're a fucking idiot."

William de Ferrers inhaled sharply but did not respond.

"We can't feed them," Quill pleaded. It was hardly his station to speak, but there was no propriety anymore. They were more like marooned survivors on an island, where titles were meaningless. "People are starting to go hungry out there. Hundreds of good citizens who came to watch a friendly archery contest, they'll soon be fighting each other to suck on bones. They will riot, they will kill our men, or our men will be forced to kill them, which is a burden they should not have to bear."

"Have you seen the chicken launcher?" de Grendon asked.

"Excuse me?" Glover startled.

"You can see it from the south-eastern corner of the bulwark," Quill explained. "Built on a rooftop across the way, someone's fashioned a sort of rudimentary catapult. For chickens."

The castellan's eyes bulged past credulity. "They're attacking my castle with poultry?"

"They're not attacking the castle." De Grendon dropped his face to his palm. "They're trying to feed their friends, and their family. The people on the inside are screaming for help, for food, and someone out there at least has the decency to try to feed them."

"I thought we *were* feeding them." The Sheriff directed this toward his castellan.

"We're trying," Master Glover puffed, "but there are hundreds of them, and you won't let us open the gates. The castle has reserves, but we normally bring in fresh food from the city. Without access to the bailey, we've resorted to lowering cooking pots down on ropes."

"One spilt this morning," Quill said, he'd seen it himself. "Must have burnt a dozen people. I was watching from above the bridge, useless. We have men down there that are trying to help, but it is *madness*. Surely the prince could understand our need to move supplies and Guardsmen between the baileys."

"There are no fucking Robin Hoods hiding in the soup!" De Grendon was at his wits' end.

With an almost unnoticeable calm, Ferrers responded, "I'm not an idiot."

"This is insanity," de Grendon roiled. "I won't let you endanger my men another minute. I'm ordering them to open those gates, and to hell with you and the prince's orders."

"*I'm not an idiot!*" the Sheriff snapped, suddenly standing aright and rigid, every muscle seething. "Don't you think I recognize the lunacy of this? What Prince John has demanded of us is reckless and ignorant, and I will authorize every possible action to alleviate its consequences, but I will not disobey his order. If you can think of alternatives to establishing peace in the lower bailey, or to feed the discontent, then offer them."

"We open the gates," the captain insisted. "That's the alternative."

"Think further than that, Fulcher." The two men locked eyes, but the captain seemed willing to hear the sheriff out. "Prince John can replace me at a moment's notice. If I upset him, he will no doubt appoint some underling in his entourage. If that happens, those people in the bailey will have no friends at all. Prince John can replace you, too, Captain, and very likely anyone who argues against him. I do not claim to understand why he has a sudden fascination with Nottingham or its gangs, but I know that we can only help this situation if we remain in power."

A heavy pause passed between them, made all the more painful by the muffled noises of the mob outside.

"If I am to be replaced, that can be on my head," Captain de Grendon decided. "But I am opening those gates."

"Captain, please." Lord Beneger did not shout it, he didn't need to. What the Sheriff lacked in presence, Lord Beneger had in his every breath. "The Sheriff has the right of this. If you open those gates now, you may help a few people immediately. But you put more people in greater danger in the long run. You would do us all a great disservice if you removed yourself from the board."

Quill cleared his throat. "If Prince John is the key to this, then why not appease him? He seeks to rid Nottingham of the scourge of Robin Hood? We already captured Will Scarlet, and the impostor Robin Hood was killed at the archery tournament. We have two informants from within the Red Lions—"

"Peveril." Ben raised his hand. "I tried that already. The prince isn't interested in results."

Quill couldn't even wrap his mind around what that sentence meant, like it was some linguistic riddle. "What do you mean?"

All eyes fell on the dread Lord de Wendenal. "It's not possible, really, to clean up every last trace of Robin Hood. FitzOdo tried, I tried . . . all we can do is pull at threads. There can always be a new gang that claims his title when the previous gang has died. There is no way to rout everyone involved. Prince John knows this. It doesn't matter how many people are arrested in the bailey, or in the city, it doesn't even matter how many of them are innocent. He's trying to kill the *idea* of Robin Hood. And to do that, he must stand by his word—by inflicting a terrifying punishment for anyone working against us, and a commensurate reward for anyone who works with us.

"These last two days have been terrible, yes, but they have only been two days. If he opens the gates now, then every future Robin Hood knows he can escape the prince's punishment just by waiting it out. But if this lockdown continues . . . not two days, not a week, but a *month* . . . or *longer* . . . well. The city will suffer greatly, yes, and they will fear *ever* suffering like that again. Prince John means to establish a punishment on this city so severe that no one will ever dare go Robin Hooding again. Not for a thousand years."

Captain de Grendon nodded solemnly. "And it doesn't matter who gets harmed in the meanwhile."

"Frankly," Beneger judged, "no, it doesn't. And he isn't wrong, either. It is a solid tactic, one that we disagree with because we find ourselves in the unenviable position of being harmed by it. But it will be effective. Eventually."

If the room was tense before, it now grew into alarm. The idea that their current predicament had only begun had clearly not occurred to most present. Quill felt his heart race, and wondered if this was what it was like, to look into death's maw. Surely he could find some way to get a message out of the castle, to finally summon his father . . . but this had already grown beyond his family's ability to help.

"But why does he care?" Ferrers asked nobody. "Why all that showmanship in killing Robin Hood on the field? These are not his problems to care about."

"French spies, apparently," Hamon Glover muttered.

"Sheriff." Beneger straightened himself. "We ought to speak privately."

The room stilled at the words of the only man who had spoken with Prince John since the riots began. Still they obeyed, although Beneger motioned for Quill to stay instead. Glover, the captain, and the dozen advisors who had watched all silently receded. Once they were gone, there was nothing but the grand emptiness of the room, and the ever-present noise of the mob outside, the new normal of the castle's heartbeat.

Eventually they were alone, the three of them. For the first time since Quill had known the man, Beneger de Wendenal appeared unsure of himself.

"There's much more to the prince's motives that I cannot tell the others. This business with eradicating Robin Hoods, the prince is just using it to keep himself safely barricaded in the castle. He believes that a French army is marching for Nottingham, to kill him."

He rolled out the details, and answered whatever questions he could, and then waited in silence as the Sheriff digested the information. Quill could hardly make sense of it himself.

Eventually, Ferrers spoke, with a startling genuineness in his tone. "It was not so long ago that you came storming into this room, ready to break my neck in half. And Peveril, you stood there, just as you are now, white as bone. I imagine none of us thought the world could get much more mad, could we?"

"I'm rarely wrong," Quill answered. "And always wish I wasn't."

"Hm." Ferrers spread his fingertips across the surface of his desk, one eye on Lord Beneger. "You're more adept at the larger political world than I. My ambitions have always been more . . . humble. Selfish, perhaps you could say, in that I care more about protecting what I have than adding to it. I suppose I learned from my father's failures."

Lord Beneger breathed sharply, once. If Quill did not know better, he would've thought it a display of emotion. When he did speak, the words came with great effort, made even more cautious by the empty chamber. "When I heard my son had been made Sheriff here, it was the proudest moment of my life. Your father would feel the same. It would be an understatement to say you've done well for yourself. You are very likely the youngest High Sheriff in history. This, then, is what you mean to protect?"

It was the Sheriff's turn to laugh. "No, no. I never pretended this would last." He stood now, his body more relaxed than before, perhaps free from the performance he normally affected. "Someone needed to step up in the wake of your son's murder, and my newfound earldom made me a natural fit. But I don't want this, I assure you. Don't forget that I'm young for an earl as well. You more than anyone can speak to how little my father was loved by his bannermen. I thought that a brief tenure as Sheriff might give me a bit more authority when I finally return to Derby. More credence."

"You wouldn't be wrong," Ben admitted.

But the Sheriff was somewhat absorbed in his own thoughts. He reached out and touched an ornament on the wall behind his desk, a decorative wreath fashioned out of different metals, intertwined with each other, and shaped into leaves. "I've already been here longer than I wanted. But as much as I may wish otherwise, this responsibility is mine. And I recognize that timid choices often spell defeat. If this army is coming, wouldn't he want to prepare for it?"

"He has summoned his own bannermen for that. I imagine they'll arrive within the week."

"And why didn't you mention this French army in front of the others?"

"The prince made me swear to keep his secret, until the first of his allies arrive. He doesn't trust anyone else. Until then, he thinks it plays in his favor if we all think him mad."

"Hm." Ferrers nodded. "Then why tell me?"

Beneger did not answer.

"Do you believe it's real?"

When, again, Ben remained silent, Quill raised his voice. "It sounds that Prince John thinks it is. Which makes it just as dangerous."

Ferrers laughed emptily. "Look at us. Three Derbymen, in charge of Nottingham's future." He breathed in deeply, as if he were testing every last muscle in his body. "This world of retribution is your expertise, Wendenal, not mine. If we have to take more drastic actions . . . what might they be?"

Quill bit his lip.

He was, quite possibly, asking if they needed to kill the prince.

Again, Lord Beneger did not have an answer. "I may need to think on that."

"Please do," he said, reaching out to straighten the wreath. "And soon. You can understand that we do not have the luxury of time to decide."

Wendenal nodded, and that was that. Though he did not move. After some time, he pointed at the wreath with one finger, and curious care. "An heirloom?" he asked.

"Of a sort. It's supposed to be a reminder, I believe, about mistakes."

"What's wrong with it?"

"Nothing." Ferrers traced the edges of the metal leaves with his fingers. "Something about the circle. About the mistakes we all make, and keep on making. It's not mine, I don't really know." He let his hand drop and repositioned to peer out the window. "Thank you, that is all."

FORTY-NINE

ARTHUR A BLAND

NOTTINGHAM CASTLE

ONE DAY AFTER PRINCE John seized Nottingham Castle, Arthur and David were still disguised as fucking gords, surrounded by more of them than Arthur could count. He was reminded of their first day in Nottingham, when he'd panicked from the claustrophobia of a city where a mere handful of guards might roam by a few times an hour. Now he was steeped in them, and his every nerve raged.

There was no opportunity for them to steal away for any privacy—barely enough even to share the occasional petrified glare with one another. They'd yet to discuss what in hells upon hells they were planning on doing, aside from the obvious answer of getting very fucking dead. The castle gords were all overworked, overcrowded, and struggling to wrap their little peanut gord brains around what was happening. Prince John had gone mad, so they all agreed, and would not let anyone enter or exit the castle—or even the lower bailey—until every last *Robin Hood* had been ferreted out into the light.

In short, none of this would be over until Arthur and David were dead.

He'd spent the first half day in the infirmary, being treated for the nasty wound that'd skinned most of his forehead a good ways thinner. David had been forced to leave him there to go do "guard things," and Arthur wished he knew any gods real enough to help his friend come back alive. But he could do nothing but complain, until he passed mercifully unconscious.

When he awoke the next morning, a full team of dray horses was pounding through his skull.

"I've found the postern door," David whispered, while helping him cut soup like they were a dying elderly couple. Other injured men were on the cots beside them, very likely pretending to be asleep just to spy on their act. "It's near a cage they call the Rabbit, in the southwest corner. It's never used, supposedly, and a storage larder was built around it some fifty years ago."

Arthur was impressed. "What did you do—kill the castle historian?"

David stifled a laugh. "You think we're the only ones who've thought about slipping out that way? People talk. The postern door leads to a small path cut into the rock, and a sharp climb down to the river. Apparently, the serving girls use it now and then to slip into town discreetly, to earn some extra penny."

"Hm." Arthur moved his head, testing its limits. The dray horses didn't like that, and resumed their pounding. "Alright, let's slip out with the whores. What's stopping us?"

"You being dead," David answered, and the patient next to them stirred slightly. They lowered their voices even further. "And Prince John's men. There's eighteen thousand things more important that need to be done in this castle, but somehow there's always two of the prince's guard watching that larder."

"Only two?" Arthur mulled it over. "We can handle that."

"Only if we're suicidal."

They looked at each other for an uncomfortable length of time.

"Which we're not," David said sternly.

"We surprise them. Same way we—" He went from a whisper to nearly breathless. "Same way we got these gord tabards."

David shook his head. It was hard to ignore that his cheeks were more sunken than normal. "Prince's men aren't dumb gords, I've seen them. They'd take us apart. And their only job is to *not* get surprised."

"Well we can't hide behind a cowl forever. You want to stay here until we're caught?"

"We've lucked out, actually. There was a class of new recruits in the castle when this happened. Those recruits all assume we're with the veteran Guardsmen, and the regular Guardsmen all assume we're with the recruits."

"Yes, we're so damned lucky," Arthur hissed, making a note to add this to Friar Tuck's abominable list of God's glorious bounty. "So you're saying we're trapped with *twice* the number of people who want to kill us?"

"Once you're ready, we'll give the postern a look." David dipped a dirty rag in a basin of water, stared at it as if he had no idea why he'd done so, and let it drop back in. "But I'll give you this. We're damned lucky we got out of that bailey when we did."

TWO DAYS AFTER PRINCE John seized Nottingham Castle, Arthur and David volunteered to walk the bulwark, which gave them the best opportunity to study the behavior of the prince's men around the postern door. The elevated walkway took them all around the perimeter of the middle bailey and up to the towers of the high keep's walls, then back down again. On the western leg of this walk, they'd tip their chins over the edge—where there was nothing but sheer stone wall, then cliffside—and tried not to imagine the damage such a fall might do to them. On the cityside eastern walk they always grew silent, watching the desperate huddles of spectators still confined in the great lower bailey beneath them. The people had spread out into small groups, at the commands of the gords there who were equally trapped by the curtain walls.

On each pass, Arthur would pick a cluster and squint, searching for the faces of any other Red Lions who'd been at the tournament. Ricard, or Clorinda. The Dawn Dog's size should make him easy to spot, but Arthur doubted he'd escaped after being fingered in the riots. The girl he'd saved with the meat skewer, she might still be down there.

"Are you looking because you're hoping they're safe?" David asked. "Or so you could turn them in for a chance to get out of here?"

Arthur didn't answer, because he hadn't much decided.

"I'm sure they've all been caught," he said instead. "Guards knew who to target during the tourney. The Red Lions were betrayed, but hell if I know who did it." A nasty little black nugget suddenly popped into his brain. "Though I know one little bitch who always thought her breeks weren't big enough . . ."

David shook his head. "Wasn't Zinn."

"Then why wasn't she here? A crowd that size, full of assholes buying little flags, it was a pickpocket's wet dream." Arthur didn't quite believe his own words. He'd finally come around to like the little critter, he just didn't have any better suspects. "Where was she?"

"She was with Will," David answered. "Ricard told me about it, at the tournament. They were supposed to attack that dockmaster we'd been tailing."

"Attack him?"

"I don't know. Threaten, maybe. Maybe worse. I guess they gave up on trying to get any dirt on him."

Arthur ground his jaw. He'd found plenty of dirt on that man—by the name of Saddle Maege—but refused to give it to the Lions. That refusal might have cost the man his damned life.

Fucking hell.

There were worse things in the world than guilt, but that didn't make it taste any better.

One of those "worse things" reared its head only a bit later that day. On their lap about the bulwark, they passed the curious *Lace Jackal*—the troll-faced archer who'd bested Red Fox in the last minutes of his life. Arthur and David kept their heads down, thankful for the stolen quilted hoods that obscured their faces. The Lace Jackal spoke with a skinny fop in a clean blue tabard, and Arthur nearly froze when he caught a critical snippet of information.

They'd captured Will Scarlet.

That quickened their pace.

Arthur wanted to tear the castle down with his bare hands. He had only stayed in this cuntolep of a city because Will had convinced them the tournament would change their luck. But with Will captured, and the Red Lions destroyed . . . there was no damned reason for Arthur to be anywhere near Nottingham.

Excepting a prince's orders and a locked gate.

"What the fack do we do now?" David asked, eyes wide, on the western half of their loop.

"I don't know," he answered, and those words had never been heavier.

At dinner that evening, they dared to approach a couple of gords who seemed on the more harmless side, to pry from them whatever information they could. Sebastien was a thin, fastidious fellow with a drawn face, and he eventually revealed that Will Scarlet had been arrested the very morning of the tournament. That likely meant he'd been captured while doing that damn dockmaster job with Zinn, and Arthur hated how much he cared to know it. One more thing for him to feel guilty about.

They spent fifteen minutes nodding at the religious ramblings of a puffy-faced half Spaniard named Matthias before he mentioned that Will Scarlet was being held in the prisons beneath their very feet. Those prisons were now swarming with people arrested from the lower bailey, well past its ability to house them. Some had been turned in by their fellow citizen and labeled a conspirator of Robin Hood, as Arthur had seen during the riots. Others had turned *themselves* in just to get the fuck out of the bailey.

Because some people in the bailey—particularly those who weren't willing or able to protect themselves—were starving.

The castle's cooks weren't prepared to feed such a mass, though they admittedly did what they could. There was food in the guards' barracks, where Arthur and David kept their hoods over their faces and ate the best meals they'd had since Locksley. But most of the other gords—not all, but *most*, shockingly—only ate half their meal and carried the rest out to the battlements, where it was lowered in buckets to the hungry mouths below. Both Sebastien and Matthias eventually left to do exactly that.

David suggested that they ought to do the same, but Arthur wouldn't have it. They needed their strength, and they'd be gone soon enough. One half-eaten meal wouldn't help anyone down below. Arthur and David needed to tend to themselves first.

At night, they watched the prince's men change shift at the postern. One man of the midnight watch had an angry bladder and took regular breaks, briefly leaving only one watchman on the door.

But attempting an escape that night would mean leaving Will Scarlet behind. Situated as they were, in disguise at the sole access point to the prisons, they were Will's only hope.

Arthur recognized the look in David's eye, because it was the same as his own. The both of them very much wanted to pretend the Will Scarlet problem was not a problem at all, and make their escape without him.

But if Arthur had told the Lions what he'd learned about Gerome Artaud as they'd asked—as *Scarlet* had asked—then Will would never have been on that job. He never would have been arrested.

So they planned, and they slept.

THREE DAYS AFTER PRINCE John seized Nottingham Castle, the postern door was no longer an option. The prince's men spent all morning barricading it with timber and clean blocks of sandstone that had been meant for renovating a wooden keep. By the time they were done, no weak bladder would ever give Arthur and David the time they needed to clear the way. It would take hours of labor for the two of them to move the obstacles, and wake half the castle in doing so. Arthur cursed the loss of its possibility with every expletive he knew, and a dozen more he didn't. The only way of leaving the castle unseen now was over the western battlement. It might be possible with the help of a damned long rope if they could find one, or they could do it with a simple jump and be rid of their hell forever.

Prince John's name was no longer spoken aloud in the castle. Instead he was referenced as simply *him* or by a solemn nod toward the highest keep, where his small figure could often be seen in the window of the top floor, looking down at the chaos he'd created.

FOUR DAYS AFTER PRINCE John seized Nottingham Castle, the grim reality of their new existence was beginning to set in. Not just for the two of them, but everyone. Rumors that the prince was more interested in punishing the city than catching Robin Hoods had spread like a rash. The commonfolk trapped in the lower bailey—who had by now earned the moniker of *baileyfolk*—began constructing shelters from the collapsed ruins of the spectator scaffolding. There were squarish structures rising in surprisingly organized rows through-out the archery range, and the entrance area where the vendors had sold their wares was dismantled and repurposed into fire pits. A few intrepid men used the available timber to raise an improvised ladder up to the outside curtain wall and attempt an escape, and they might've succeeded had they not proven too terrified to jump down the other side.

After that, the longer bulwark around the lower bailey was kept evenly populated with guards and crossbowmen. Arthur and David were conscripted to walk that duty, which afforded them none of the privacy the middle bailey ramparts had. They grouped with another pair of guards—two of the newest recruits, who were both named Henry. Arthur named them Henry Left and Henry Right, regardless of how they were standing. Mop-headed and fidgety, both of them, the Two Henries looked to Arthur and David for instruction, and now Arthur was training the future of the fucking Nottingham Guard.

The few staircases that descended from the curtain wall down to the bailey floor were blockaded and tightly guarded, and there was always at least one of the prince's men within eyesight. On one occasion, Arthur watched a Guard man named Timon sneakily reach down to hoist a friend from the bailey up over a blockade, only to be descended upon immediately by the prince's senti-nels. Both offenders were marched up to the high keep, and rumors held they both found themselves in the already packed prison tunnels not long after.

Nobody else tried to help those below slip up the cracks after that.

So the Guard lined the bulwark in a solemn row, as if they were protecting the castle from an invading horde—excepting the horde was on the inside of their walls. One could walk the full circumference of the lower bailey before ascending back up to the training yards, which made it easy for the bowmen to keep any hostility from brewing amongst the baileyfolk.

But not all were there for the show of force. Henry Left and Right volun-teered to pass messages over the wall from commonfolk gathered on the city side. Citizens would collect near the main entrance and shout messages up to the Guardsmen above, a few words at a time, who would then do their best to relay those words to their target. It sometimes took over an hour before the person could be found to hear his message, since all communication was done by simply yelling from the battlements to the people below. But the Henries claimed it was worth the effort, to help connect husbands to wives, parents to children, reassure them that the other was alive and well.

Not long after, other guards joined them.

On the evening of the fourth day, David volunteered for one of these jobs. And Arthur, of course, fucking followed him.

They passed messages that a father was missed, that his two-year-old son cried for his papa every night.

They passed messages that a wife had been robbed, and kicked from her own home.

They passed messages of violence and longing. Out in the city, there were too few Guardsmen to keep peace—they were all following their orders of keeping the roads into the city secure, that no soul could enter or leave.

So they passed messages that the gangs were taking over, rising up in the absence of the Red Lions. That they were selfish and violent.

Messages that a sister had gone missing.

That a mother had caught sick and had no one to care for her.

That a grandfather had tried to leave the city and been clubbed over the head, that he might not wake up.

Some of the messages were never heard, they were meant for someone who'd been taken to the prisons. Sometimes they weren't messages, but questions.

Is my brother in there?

Is my daughter alive?

When will my baby see her mother?

Some of those, they couldn't answer.

That night—late, late, that night—Arthur went to the postern door. It wasn't guarded anymore, because it was too impossible to use. He went alone, without David. He didn't go there to escape, he simply needed a location he knew would be deserted. He went there that he could have a moment's peace, that nobody would see him when he lowered himself carefully down into a ball and cried for the first time in more years than he could remember.

FIVE DAYS AFTER PRINCE John seized Nottingham Castle, there was an eruption of violence within the Nottingham Guard.

The castle's armsmaster was a great Scotsman called *The Simons*, who happened to be Caitlin FitzSimon's father. He'd withdrawn to his quarters in the barracks the very first day and never reemerged, which was the source of great concern. The question of Caitlin's loyalty and execution incited a brace of rumors, shattering the Guard into factions. Some believed the armsmaster was complicit in his daughter's crimes and had betrayed them all, while others believed she'd been innocent, murdered without cause. But everyone worried there were traitors within their ranks—spies from the gangs, or even a "Robin Hood" amongst them. And the prince's promise turned that fear into a spark, because everyone knew that the price of ignoring the slightest suspicion was the same punishment as being guilty. And that price was to earn a *lionheart*— eight arrows to the chest.

Arthur's guess that a Red Lion had defected was confirmed when the traitor was marched through the bailey into the captain's offices. Arthur and David arrived too late to see the man's face, but they got caught in the wake. A fight broke out when a small group of Guardsmen took it upon themselves to raid the captain's offices to execute the informant in the name of The Simons. That attempt ended with minimal violence, but it led to a heated debate about what should be done with the would-be executioners. Which led to a riot far more troublesome than the original scuffle.

Which led to the first death.

That same day, the first of the baileyfolk died of starvation.

Messages, that a grandmother was ill.

That someone trapped in the bailey had a new child, that it was healthy.

Arthur couldn't find the father to hear that message.

Six days after Prince John seized Nottingham Castle, people traveled through the gates of the castle for the first time since the archery tournament. This was not, however, an improvement. It was a group of thirty armed men bearing shields with red-and-white stripes, ringed in red-and-white circles, and matching livery. They were loyal to the Baron of Hornby, a man named Roger de Montbegon, who was in turn loyal to Prince John.

With their admission, the prince's forces in the castle tripled.

That afternoon they doubled again with a host from Worcester, led by two horse-faced brothers named Philip and Ralph. A smaller but fiercer—and holier—complement accompanied the Bishop of Coventry, an elephant man named Hugh de Nonant. Arthur didn't want to know these people's names, he didn't want to live a life where they mattered. But the politics and rumors were all that kept the castle alive, and it was becoming increasingly obvious that the men of the Nottingham Guard were exactly as valuable to the Prince of the High Keep as the baileyfolk below.

On the seventh day, violence engulfed the lower bailey. The baileyfolk had organized into two different camps—half that wanted to help the Guard and end their captivity peacefully, and half that wanted the predictably opposite. The fighting there went uninterrupted, as there were few in the Nottingham Guard who were willing to risk themselves to intervene. Not with mutiny in their own ranks. Not with the prince's growing army ready to cast them over the walls as well. Which meant the more violent of the two groups won, which was generally a bad sign.

Arthur and David kept passing messages back over the walls, that a little girl could no longer find her mother.

That a dockworker had had his teeth kicked in for a bite of bread.

That a group of men had slashed a girl's ear to turn her in as a gang member.

He was starting to recognize the voices, learn their stories.

The two-year-old who missed his father? He hadn't spoken in days now, and wouldn't eat, either.

The new baby whose father was unaccounted for? Something had gone wrong in childbirth, and her mother died a day later.

The questions? They no longer came to ask who was alive. They came to ask *why?*

Then they demanded it, in larger, angrier groups.

After that, the lords of Worcester placed their men on the battlements with crossbows, and put a stop to letting the commonfolk approach the castle at all. Arthur missed those messages, he felt for those whose stories now ended in the middle, that he'd never heard the end of.

That night there were sounds on the wind, of a desperate woman crying for help. Arthur and David had found a nook for themselves against the northwest wall. Down below the other side was the French Ward. The woman's calls for help went unanswered, and her cries turned to screams. Arthur could do nothing, the sounds came whistling through a thin hole in the wall, meant to drain rainwater. Arthur tried to imagine a scenario in which her wails were battle-cries, as she beat senseless whoever it was that was attacking her. But that fantasy vanished as her voice turned torturous, wrapped in a cruel harmony of men's laughter. He and David yelled back through the hole, but into the wind, muffled by stone, they knew they couldn't be heard. The sounds that followed . . . were too horrible to bear. They didn't sleep that night. They wept, the both of them, unabashedly. Arthur held David's hand until the noises stopped, and then longer.

Sebastien and Matthias had been nearby, and had borne that night as well. They were joined by a rabbity fellow named Stephen Quick and a brute more beard than man, called Morg. The six of them spoke in the morning, now bound by something terrible.

By noon, the six of them had become a dozen. Who wanted to do something. If they couldn't fight back, they could help. Find ways, any ways, anything.

The violence continued in the lower bailey, still unstopped by the Guard.

On the eighth day, there emerged a leader from the chaos below, who called himself the *baileyking*.

On the ninth, he was replaced rather bloodily by another.

Half a dozen more companies arrived in support of Prince John. They took over the barracks. The high keep and the upper bailey were now completely restricted from the men of the Nottingham Guard, who were forced to sleep twelve to a room meant for four. The only value the new armies brought was an abundance of fresh supplies, as they were clearly expecting to stay for an extended amount of time.

The prince was gathering his allies in preparation for something nobody understood. And the members of the Nottingham Guard, which Arthur and David had somehow come to identify themselves as, were effectively reduced to slave labor. They did the lowest work, they literally shoveled shit. They hoisted the new rations up over the walls—since passage through the lower bailey was obviously forbidden—and conspired to find ways to get some of it to the baileyfolk below.

Part of the stables was demolished to supply the wood for cranes to move supplies over the western wall. David noted to Arthur that this was finally a viable escape path. But by this time, it wasn't just "Arthur and David" anymore. They told themselves they were still trying to find a way to rescue Will Scarlet, but they hadn't talked about him in a week. In reality, they didn't want to abandon the other Guardsmen, who all wanted to find an end to this misery. Matthias prayed at every meal and never talked of *running away*. Morg pulled double duty to cover as the Henries continued passing letters over the wall, knowing they could get in trouble for it. These were men who wanted to do what little they could to make their tiny part of the planet a better place, instead of a worser one.

Two weeks after Prince John seized Nottingham Castle, Sheriff de Ferrers was replaced with a man of little humor, loyal to the prince, named William Brewer. This announcement was coupled with the strange realization that nobody had actually heard from the previous Sheriff in days. Rumors spread that Prince John had beaten him to death as an example, and thrown him out his window at the top of the high keep—which became an enviable idea, as it was the only guaranteed way out of the castle. It was even given a name . . . the *Ferrers Escape*.

In the third week, Stephen Quick attempted to escape the castle by shimmying down the crane ropes. He was arrested by the prince's army and vanished. The entirety of the Nottingham Guard was commanded to leave the middle bailey, to make room for all the prince's allies, and to "secure the peace" in the lower bailey. But they all knew the truth, that they were being corralled. Punished. Controlled.

That night, instead of obey these orders, Henry Left and Right held hands and took the Ferrers Escape over the western wall.

And one month after Prince John seized Nottingham Castle, word came that a foreign army had landed at the port of Sandwich to the southeast, and was marching north.

FIFTY

ARABLE DE BUREL

ARABLE HAD ONLY ONCE in her life witnessed the bizarre spectacle of an armed battalion, dressed and organized, rank and file, spread out across the countryside. For her, it brought a numbing sensation that made her want to slip even deeper into her own mind than normal. It was absolutely baffling that hundreds of other people had gathered for a single common purpose that she herself could never believe was important at all.

Sixteen years ago on a bright grey morning not unlike this one, it had been her father's battalion, and the last time she would ever see him. He had summoned his loyal bannermen to rally in the fields outside the Burel household, back when it existed, back when it was a distinguished manor and not an overgrown dirt hill. Lord Raymond de Burel said no goodbyes to her that day, too consumed with his duties as a liegelord to remember his duties as a father. And besides, he expected to be back shortly—after joining the army of the Third Earl of Derbyshire, William de Ferrers, and his quick campaign to seize the castle of Nottingham.

That battalion had marched off into the distance, which Arable had watched from the front balcony of their estate, having no words to describe the feeling of loss that drained her as it disappeared.

This day she stood on a different balcony high up in the Heart Tower of Huntingdon Castle, looking down upon a different battalion, of larger size and scope. They marshalled in the distance, the smoke from their fire pits giving a dark and industrious face to the countryside. There was a similar sickening sense of being the outsider, that all of these humans had mutually decided the correct thing to do with their lives was to be here, at this moment, for Arable to gaze down upon.

But this battalion was *coming,* not going.

This battalion was not led by her father. This battalion was led by Lord Simon de Senlis, and he had come to take the things in life that he had decided were his.

"He has more support than I thought," Lord Robert said glumly. It was heartbreaking to see the defeat in his face. As heavily as Arable had rolled her eyes at the earl swashing his rapier throughout the Senlis manor nearly two months earlier, she could not deny that his adventurous spirit was infectious.

Its absence practically deserved a funeral.

"They're on the wrong side of the Ouse if they mean to attack," the countess criticized, as if hers was the military expertise. It didn't matter which side of the river they were on, because Huntingdon wasn't going to mount a defense. There would be no battle. Lord Robert, to his own shame, knew he must hand Lady Marion Fitzwalter over to face charges of treason. And then he would, very likely, hand the castle over to its new owners.

And Arable would be unbound, again, left to the mercy of whichever cruel wind sought fit to blow her way.

"I don't see the Chancellor's banners," Magdalena continued, every muscle in her face raging against the captivity of her bones. "They have no authority here without him. Who are these people? De Senlis has gathered anyone with an axe to grind, hoping to mask the vacancy of his argument with the sheer *variety* of his followers. I see the Earl of *Chester* for Christ's sake, what on earth is *he* doing here?"

"It doesn't matter, dear," Robert grumbled. "We've lost."

He made no further explanation, and simply receded from the balcony's stone rail like a boat in a calm river. Arable felt a great sadness for that departure, but also a small admiration. Whatever the future held for him, Lord Robert was not shying away from it with futile delays. He had made his peace with his mistakes and was marching now to own them. Owning one's failures, Arable had learned time and time again, was better than owning nothing at all.

"This is all Marion's fault," the Countess Magdalena snapped into the wind. "I told him we shouldn't have welcomed her, and still he—"

"Shut up."

Arable inhaled, deeply, hoping to capture a fraction of the resolve Lord Robert had in this, the moment of his decline. Rather than scratch and spit and complain about its unjustness like the countess, Arable meant to keep her head held loftily high, all the way to the gallows if need be. After all, she had imagined a moment like this a thousand times. There was always a *someday* when Lord Beneger de Wendenal or his men would find her, and exact his vengeance upon her for the crime of being her father's daughter. She had proclaimed herself a Burel proudly for the world to recognize at the council, and she had no doubt that information had spread—especially now that there was nobody left to protect her.

If Simon de Senlis did not claim that easy prize for himself, it would come soon after.

Hopefully soon. She did not want to run again.

The lump seized Arable's throat, her chest froze. There was a small but unmistakably horrible difference in facing persecution now, compared to the last sixteen years. That critical distinction had made her first kick in Arable's belly only a few nights earlier.

"How dare you." The countess recoiled. Arable had already forgotten she'd told the woman to shut her mouth. "How *dare y*—"

"Rather easily," Arable answered, not caring to hide her scoff. "That's *how I dare*. It simply involves taking a risk, and bearing its consequences. You're not really familiar with that sort of accountability, are you?"

She leveled her eyes on the countess, for once refusing to shy away from her gaze. Everything about the woman read as a shallow performance now, rather than a commanding presence. From the calculated angles of her shoulders to the flaking skin around her pursed lips, Arable recognized Magdalena as an empty vessel, driven by an emptier soul.

"You arranged the council," Arable continued, "and let Marion hang for it. It was your idea, but you refused to back it for fear of your reputation. Well here it is, here's the price of your vanity—it's come to your castle walls to strip it away from you. You called for a rebellion you didn't believe in, because you saw advantage there, never intending to do any of the real work. This is what happens when you have no convictions, Countess. You *lose*."

The woman made noises, insolent exhalations, and then silence. Outside, on whichever side of the Great Ouse they damned well pleased, the battalion sounded its horns.

"Well," Magdalena swallowed, "you lose as well."

"I certainly do," Arable answered. "But I'm used to it, because I've risked everything before, over and over in fact. Whereas this is something new for you, isn't it? Talk to me in a decade, perhaps you'll be halfway to a decent person."

Down below, a small group was kicking up dust—a trio or so of riders from the battalion, approaching the bridge over the Ouse. The beginning of the end. Arable turned to leave the balcony, though she stopped one last time to study the desperate figure of Countess Magdalena de Bohun, arching her back as she clawed at the railing that, like the world, would not bend in her grasp.

"I realized something about you," Arable said, not caring at all that this would be a petty insult. "You were wed to Lord Robert nearly twenty years ago, were you not?"

"I was," she answered, turning her head just barely. "The moment I was of marrying age, my father—"

"Yes, you've told us a dozen times. The great Earl of Hereford, marrying his daughters out across the country to earls or their heirs. Lady Margery to the Earl of Warwickshire, Lady Maud to the Earl of Oxfordshire, and you . . . here."

"To the Earl of Huntingdonshire."

"Except he wasn't earl then."

The countess had absolutely no reaction.

"This was the Tower de Senlis then. Lord Robert's father was just another bannerman to the de Senlis family. That's what you were married into. I suppose you were wicked even then, weren't you? Imagine, the legendary Earl of Hereford, his daughters a prize for any man to fight over, and he could find no husband for you more prestigious than the son of an unimportant marcher lord. Nobody else would take you."

Magdalena swallowed. "I like to think my father knew that Lord Robert's family was on the rise."

"Yes." Arable smiled. "I imagine you would like to think that."

The air was split again by the sounds of horns, much closer now, announcing the arrival of the men below.

"You never belonged here," Arable finished. "You're finally returning to the life you deserve, one smothered in obscurity. The reason you're afraid of losing everything is because you don't have the skills to climb up again." She opened the door to re-enter the castle, and descend to meet their enemy. "Which is precisely why I'm *not* afraid."

THERE WAS A SINGLE complication.

"Lady Marion's not here." Friar Tuck folded his arms into his robes while John Little stood at his side, solemn as a stone angel.

"Good," Lord Robert answered. The entire castle was gathering, come to crowd the front gates, which Lord Robert intended on opening to their opponent very shortly. "I'd prefer to speak with de Senlis before she arrives. I may just be able to negotiate her safety, if she doesn't spoil it with any more nonsense of *turning herself in.*"

"That's not what I meant," Tuck replied. "She's not in the castle, she left in the night."

Arable was shocked, as were the others. "She ran?"

"Wasn't her choice, so don't blame her none," John explained. "Sir Amon and the Delaney brothers took her, by force mind you. An' I imagine she'll take all the three of them apart the moment she has a chance. But they left, an' wouldn't say where they meant to take her, only that there'd be no point in you giving chase an' that you'll never see her again."

Lord Robert looked positively devastated. "They *abducted* her?"

"For her own good," John answered defensively. "But yes."

On the other side of the gate, the herald horns sounded again.

For a few tense moments, Lord Robert stared blankly into the sky and Arable couldn't guess how he would react. Arable felt untethered herself, not sure if she should be furious at Amon, terrified for the danger it put on the rest of them, or just jealous she wasn't with them.

John Little held his hands up. "We didn't have a hand in it, my lord."

"I know," Robert answered, with no outburst at all. "I just would have liked to say goodbye to her. I'm glad she's safe. It's not as though de Senlis really cared about capturing her anyway. She was always just a means to get to me." He directed his men stationed at the wheels beside the gate. "Go on, open it. If nothing else, I'll get to enjoy the look on his face when I tell him he can't have his little prize.

"Oh! And also," he stuttered, realizing he had more profound responsibilities to deal with. He turned around and tried to address the crowd as one. "I apologize deeply for what is to come. You have all proven yourselves with distinction. It has been my deepest privilege to lead you, and my shame to have led you where I did. I seek nothing for my own well-being, but will negotiate for each of yours. You have my word."

He nodded once, twice, as if deciding those words were good enough. The crowd gave him little reaction, though not from any lack of sympathy. Eventually, Robert connected again with the gatemen, nodded, and the castle opened its mouth.

Slowly revealed before the entrance of Huntingdon Castle were six men on horseback. Arable took a moment to memorize it, knowing she would likely think back upon this image for many years to come, were she lucky enough to live so long. The riders were silhouetted by the glowing sky, one endless luminescent cloud with no distinction. Behind them, the makings of their war littered the countryside in the distance. The horses bore the sigils of Derbyshire, of Cheshire, and of Huntingdonshire—an insult that Lord Robert must surrender to a man bearing his own livery. But more than these facts, Arable remembered the disappointments. What ought to feel like an unforgettable grandeur was marred in the mundane. The gates wobbled as they caught upturned clods of mud. One of the horses sidestepped and tugged at its reins, and had to be led in a circle to return again. The ecstatic shriek of a young child playing within the courtyard, who did not understand what was happening. A flurry of gnats that hovered briefly by their heads, which they swatted away.

Historic moments were full of these, Arable had no doubt. The world continued in their midst, like the cloud of gnats, no matter what happened to the largest pieces.

"You've returned early, de Senlis!" Lord Robert bellowed, one last grasp at his showman's routine. "And brought so many of your friends! Hardly necessary."

"They're not here for you," de Senlis's voice returned, but not from the lead rider. As the horsemen made their way into the courtyard, Arable realized that de Senlis was at their edge, not their middle.

"I regret that the Lady Marion Fitzwalter is—"

"They're not here for her, either," de Senlis continued. "The Earl Robert of Huntingdonshire, may I present to you the Fourth Earl of Derbyshire, and High Sheriff of Nottinghamshire, Derbyshire, and her Royal Forests . . ."

Arable gasped.

". . . William de Ferrers."

The lead horse took a few extra steps forward, from which descended the same pockmarked weasel that had lurked around every one of Nottingham Castle's corners. The wretched son of the man who had led her father's army to their doom. Ferrers had claimed the title of Nottingham's Sheriff after William's death, a replacement so despicable that it boiled Arable's blood just to think upon. Now here he was, draped in a mud-splattered ivory cloak, extending his hand out in greeting to Lord Robert.

"Earl Robert, thank you for having us," he said, which were not at all the words that ought to precede a castle's seizure. "I wish that I could have sent word ahead of time, but when I explain our presence I'm sure you'll see that it was not an option."

Robert's lips sealed together, his neck clenched, and he shook Ferrers's hand. He stared until it was awkward that he had not responded, then his eyes flitted back to see if anybody else had any better idea how he should do so. Arable had nothing to offer. Robert settled for a wetting of his lips and a drawn-out, "Oh?"

Ferrers laughed. "I hope we did not alarm you, though I imagine no one enjoys waking up to the sight of an unannounced army outside their walls. I come to implore your aid, as one earl to another, and for your family's reputation specifically in capturing castles that would otherwise be considered impenetrable."

Lord Robert blinked. "You want me to show you how to capture my own castle?"

The Sheriff flinched slightly in confusion. "Not at all. I need you to capture mine."

That confusion infected the entire crowd now.

"Have you not heard?" Ferrers turned about, incredulous. "Prince John is mad. He's taken complete control of Nottingham, he's summoned his supporters from halfway across the country, garrisoning it for war. He's locked all entry and exit from both the castle and the city. My Sheriff's Guard have been practically deposed and thrown in with the commonfolk, starving and fighting in the bailey and the streets. I had to risk my life just to escape myself, and start gathering supporters to rise up against John's coup. Cheshire and Derbyshire stand at my side, and I'm hoping I can count on Huntingdonshire as well."

It was the sketch of the rabbit and the duck again. They had thought they were in the bottom of a pit, only to somehow realize they were actually on top of a mountain.

"You want us to fight against Prince John?" Robert asked.

"I've heard all about your council here," Ferrers explained. "And that Prince John labeled you all traitors for doing so. You have, so it seems, already rallied all the supporters we might need to take Nottingham back from him. You will need to mobilize at once. The longer we wait, the more he'll be prepared for us."

"You don't have enough . . ." Lord Robert struggled with the logistics, ". . . not to take Nottingham."

"What you see out there is merely a third of our forces. Earl Ranulph's forces in Cheshire are marching already, at his son's command, to match Derbyshire's host and then march on to Nottingham. Meanwhile, we'll convene with Rutland at Belvoir Castle, and then march west, to approach the city from opposite sides at once. How much time do you need to call your bannermen?"

Lord Robert appeared as stunned as he should be. A few minutes ago he had been prepared to surrender his life, and he was now asked to, effectively, lead the rebellion.

If Sir Amon only knew what he had dragged Marion away from, he'd feel awfully stupid.

Arable also suddenly regretted leaving Countess Magdalena with such harsh final words. She had been under the obvious assumption that they would never see each other again. But tomorrow's awkward apology was nothing compared to the prison cell she previously thought this day would hold for her.

"Two days," Lord Robert answered after deliberation with his captain. "We can send men to every major house by sundown, and they should need no more than a single day to rally their men and meet us here the day after tomorrow."

Ferrers's smile was not a weasel's grin, but some strange expression of genuine gratitude that Arable had never seen on him before. "Two days will suffice. Ranulph and I would beg your hospitality in the castle these two nights, and some of our entourage. Beneger, I assume you would prefer to stay with your men?"

The name reached across the empty air and stabbed Arable in the chest.

She had not even looked at the other riders, she'd been too shaken by Ferrers, and his news.

Now her blood turned to ice as she looked them over, and recognized every line of the face she had once considered as kind as a father, and then as cruel as the Devil's heart.

Lord Beneger de Wendenal.

Did she gasp? Did she scream? Did her soul tear itself from her body and flee, knowing the endless void was better than what must come now? What noise did she make that gave him cause to stare so directly back at her, his eyes wide, knowing, understanding not only who she was but how magnificently she'd been trapped?

Arable turned, and ran, though time slowed to a crawl and the air into tar.
She couldn't breathe it, she couldn't move through it.
Her foot dug into the mud, the strain of it was enormous.
She was not pushing herself off the round, no, her muscles pushed the entire world down and away.

She had imagined this moment a thousand times. She always knew he would catch her. She should have fled to France, she never should have stayed. She should have gone with her brothers, who had probably fallen at his hands years ago.
The last of the Burels, here before him, the end of his vengeance for his insurmountable rage.

He followed, he practically pounced down from his mount.

Was she moving? Had she even made it a single step yet?
There was nowhere to flee to, but she didn't need a destination.
She could fly up, back up to the Heart Tower, to the same balcony she had stood at that morning.
And she could keep flying after that.
It would be better, at her own hands, than his.

And better for her daughter, unnamed, unborn. Her death would not be his to
claim, there was no hell cruel enough for such a thing to be.

She did not look back, instead she saw the story of what was happening in
the faces of the people in front of her. Their wide-eyed horror, they backed
away from her, cleared a path.
Their eyes told Arable how close he was.
That he was gaining.
That he was upon her.
That it was over.

Hold her head loftily high, she had told herself so recently.
To the gallows with dignity.
Instead she wept, ugly and feral, when his massive arm reached around her
and caught her across the chest, stopping her flight, yanking her backward into
death. She screamed now, yes, she screamed everything she'd ever known, every
regret and love and fear came out at once, though she could not hear it, the only
sound was her own heartbeat, thundering through her blood like a mountain-
slide, every beat the last one she'd ever have.

And somehow, after this endless expanse of nothing, she was still there.
"Arable, my God, Arable . . ."
His arms around her.
Hugging her. And he, too, was crying.

FIFTY-ONE

MARION FITZWALTER

GIRTON, CAMBRIDGESHIRE

THE CARRIAGE DOOR SPLINTERED but did not break. It was, however, enough to sufficiently alarm Sir Amon into unlocking it, rather than let Marion damage the frame—or, more likely, her legs—in an attempt to smash her way out.

She spilt out of the carriage onto a once cobbled but now overgrown road, twisting her head in every direction in search of anything that might reveal their location. It was morning still, the fully covered sky glowed pale over long hills split evenly by the wide path. Off to one direction was a cozy village, a single church spire poking its head above the surrounding buildings to say hello.

"Where are we?" she demanded.

Amon closed his face and breathed carefully. "We're on the *Via Devana*. I believe that's Girton, and I also believe that's St. Andrew's church—"

"No." She didn't need more than the lone word to silence him. The two Delaney brothers had climbed down from the carriage bench, and were trying to will themselves out of existence. She ground her jaw and bore down upon Amon. "Where *are* we?"

Her knight gave an acquiescent gesture to the brothers, swallowed, and stood as tall as his lean frame ever had. "Two miles north of Cambridge."

Cambridgeshire.

She knew it. They were traveling south, not north. And Amon had lied to her.

"Shame." She seethed it, because she did not know what else to say. Amon made to explain himself, but she brought a fist up to her lips and he knew better than to test her fury. She had made it clear—unmistakably clear—that she intended on offering herself over to the Lord Simon de Senlis peacefully in exchange for her people's safety. If she was lucky, she might even have talked de Senlis down from trying to claim Lord Robert's earldom, at least for the time being. Amon had originally resisted the idea, but somehow she didn't question his last-minute change of heart. He had never lied to her before, but had now exhausted the entirety of that trust with a single act.

He had awoken her in the middle of the night with the Delaneys, explaining that John Little and the rest of the group meant to defend her when the time came. It was Amon's infinite wisdom—so he explained—that they steal away and travel to Simon de Senlis on their own, thusly preventing anyone else from being harmed. He'd used her deepest sympathies against her rather than trust in her judgment. He even said that Lord Robert would meet them on the road, that he had arranged for the carriage and horses. *Knowing that she'd want to see him.*

It was an absolute violation.

Marion had fought back tears for the first hour of that ride, at having missed the opportunity to say any farewells, knowing how John would blame himself for her need to vanish without them. She'd resolved herself to whatever grim future lay ahead, and at Amon's insistence she even managed to catch a bit of sleep, knowing how particularly arduous the coming day would be.

They broke their fast before dawn, they traveled farther as the sun warmed the clouds from above, and Marion cursed herself for not noticing it earlier. Despite the single endless blanket that covered the heavens, she should have recognized that the sun had risen on their *left* instead of their *right*. Once she asked the question, Amon grew silent.

When she discovered the carriage door was locked, she started kicking.

And now here she was, standing on an old Roman road, betrayed by those closest to her.

"You *lied* to me, Amon. You deceived me, against my explicit command—"

"My lady, I would remind you that my charge is to your father, not—"

"You have conducted yourself shamefully, ill-becoming of your knighthood—"

"I do not deny that, but I saw no other way—"

"No other way to what?" she snapped. "To get what *you* thought was best? Your *charge* is not to think, or to get things that you want, but to protect me. Which is your charge no longer, Amon, I dismiss you from your service."

"It is not yours to dismiss." His voice stayed soft, his eyes pleading. "My lady. I am protecting you, and I shall continue to protect you, whether it be at your father's employ or of my own volition."

She couldn't stand the sight of him at the moment, and turned upon the Delaney brothers. "Turn the carriage around, we're returning to Huntingdon immediately."

They both grimaced and looked at each other, then to Amon.

"Nick." She looked each of them in the eye. "Peter."

"This wasn't their idea," Amon defended them. "I solicited their help. But we are resolute to continue south, to the safety of your grandfather's lands in Essex."

"I'm not going to Essex." She made those words as clear as any that had ever been formed. "Simon de Senlis will turn Huntingdon upside down for me, he'll kick all our people out, they will be nomads again, and they cannot survive that a second time, *you know that.* You are damning all of them by . . . *absconding* with me like this, which makes you as much of a threat to their lives as anything we've faced. And how do you think I am going to respond to such a threat?"

"You're more important than that," Amon answered evenly.

"I'm taking your horse."

She moved directly for his mount, idling beside the two others that were harnessed to the carriage. But he placed himself directly in her path.

For years she had depended on him, something closer than a friend, though their bond was silent. Amon Swift was always by her side, a solemn truth as much a part of her as her own name. She knew his *smell,* of all the damnable things, the comforting scent of rosemary that was in the oil he used to keep his leather gloves from cracking. The long drawn lines of his face had always been gentle for her but hard for her enemies—and for the first time his jaw set in opposition against her.

"You stand in my way," she said, slowly. "You're physically stopping me."

He did not move.

"How far are you prepared to go with this, Amon?" She took a few steps closer, his height becoming more obvious until her nose practically touched his chest. She took a step to her right, and he countered. To her left, the same. "You'll block me now. Will you lay a hand on me next?"

She pushed into him, pressing her body into his as she tried to slip around him but his feet bit into the ground and he matched her. Using more of her shoulder, she tried to find some leverage at his ribs to force him to move ground. Failing at that, it came to elbows, and then to hands, where finally she successfully shoved him off his balance to stumble a foot away. In a reflex response, he reached out and grabbed her by the forearm.

"There it is," she breathed, even as his hands returned to his sides again. "Doesn't take much, does it? You've crossed that line once, you're willing to grab me. What's next, then? Will you strike me?"

"We cannot let you return to Huntingdon."

She slapped him across the face.

He did not respond. His hands were now frozen in their dangle.

"You'll have to hit me back if you want to stop me. I'm taking your horse, I'm returning to the castle, and I am saving my people."

His head shook slightly. "You're giving in to his demands, you're doing exactly what he—"

"I'm answering for my own crimes!" she shouted. "I am guilty, and I cannot let the others be punished for that guilt!"

"And I cannot let you make that decision."

She slapped him again. Then again. On the fourth she shoved him, made to slap him again, and he instinctively caught her midair.

"Stop it!" Nick Delaney was shouting, but all Marion's focus was on her once loyal knight. She could see his own surprise that he was still holding her wrist.

"One step at a time, Amon. How far will you go now that you've made your decision? How much more right do you think you are than me? Enough to restrain me, it seems. Enough to hurt me? Will you throw a sack over my head and tie me up before you let me walk away?" With her other hand, she reached down and wrapped her fingers around the hilt of his sword, sheathed at his belt. "Will you pull your blade on me? Tell me what your line is, because I guarantee you I'll go past it and more, to get back to Huntingdon and do the right thing. So you'd best decide now what your limit is. Will you kill me to prove you have the right of this?"

His hand met hers on the pommel, its pressure all aimed at keeping the blade sheathed.

"Didn't think it would come to this?" she continued. "Did you think I'd just suddenly agree with you and happily abandon all my responsibilities?"

"But that's exactly what you're doing," Peetey said. He'd positioned himself behind Amon, so that she could not ignore him. "Lady Marion, please listen. We talked about this, all night. At first I thought it was something villainous, too, to take you as we did, and God I'm sorry! But Amon's right. You have bigger responsibilities, that you can't walk away from."

"Things you've started," Nick joined in, "that reach across the whole country. That's more important."

"More important than the lives of—"

"Yes." Peetey didn't hesitate at all, as if the answer were insultingly obvious. "Listen, I can't pretend to understand even a tenth of what's at stake here. But I know that what happened at the council, successful or not, was important. And I know that if you get swept away by the first angry little lord who demands your head, that nobody will ever try anything like it again for a hundred years."

Off to the east, the bells at St. Andrew's marked the hour of nine. Peetey didn't continue until every last note was done, faded away into the blanket of sound from the north wind.

"You want to sacrifice yourself to save the rest of us, because—as you say— it's the right thing to do. And the fact that you're willing to do that is *why* we can't let you do it."

Nick tried to catch her eye. "You're a rare kind of person, and we need you at the front. That's the real reason they want to arrest you, because they know the kind of thing you can become."

"My lady," Amon said, still resolutely in front of her. "I mean no offense, but you think like a civilian. You think the best thing you can do is protect those beneath you at all costs. But a proper commander bears the burden of surviving his own—or *her* own—mistakes. It is easy, isn't it, to make a decision knowing you alone will shoulder the consequences? But a learned leader makes her decisions knowing that only others, often innocents, will pay the price of failure. It is a terrible thing, to survive unscathed when others suffer your choices. But we need you to be the person who is strong enough to do just that. Going to de Senlis is the weak choice, not the strong one."

"You want to make a real sacrifice?" Nick added, sidling beside the others. "The real sacrifice you can make ... ah dammit, Amon, how'd you phrase it earlier?"

"The real sacrifice is for you to give up your ability to sacrifice yourself for us. It will be far, far harder. But it's what we need from you."

Though she was still furious with Amon, it was hard to ignore the anguish on the Delaney brothers' faces. Their words were heartfelt, they trembled to even confront her like this. She could only imagine what bravery it must have taken for them to plan this thing out in the middle of the night. They wanted her to represent more than herself, to be the face of a movement, something to believe in. To show a better way, and to let her name become something powerful—which required it to be invulnerable.

They were asking of her everything she had asked of Robin.

They wanted her to be, in their own way, *Robin Hood.*

But well-meaning or not, they were still *wrong.* They had the advantage of being at her side, and simply did not want to lose her. "You can convince yourself this is noble," she said, "but it is a selfishness. When they throw women and children out of the castle to starve, do you think they will agree with your philosophy? When they take Lord Robert's castle from him, do you think his people will agree with you? When they—"

"That's already happened," Amon answered.

Her breath left her.

"De Senlis's army came to Huntingdon this morning. That's why we left before they arrived."

"We have to go back now!" She shoved him again, trying to claw through Amon's body to get to his horse, to ride before any more damage could be done. Amon had taken everything from her with his misplaced heroism, he couldn't understand that Lord Robert's stability meant more than a thousand Marions. Amon seemed to think she was some sort of savior, when she was nothing but a feeble voice in the wind, yelling things nobody wanted to hear.

Lord Robert would think she had abandoned him. After everything they had discussed, all their dreams of what an England might look like when the Chancellor's powers were curbed, they now had nothing. *And that night in the tent . . .*

With a start, Amon stepped aside, and she stumbled forward, suddenly unobstructed. Her thoughts were too wild to recollect, but her hands knew the work of finding the horse's saddle and checking her straps. But as she readied to heave herself up onto a horse she could barely reach, a rumble at the edge of her reason alarmed her.

Her three companions had not stepped aside because of anything she had done.

They each were looking south on the road, and Marion joined them in time with a few quick distant blurts from a short horn that announced the approach of a group of armed men on horseback. She startled, her winter's instincts still honed to fear any men on the road discovering them, but there was nowhere to hide. As the strangers grew closer, their details defined—they wore uniform pleated leather tunics and their horses were draped in chequered trappings, though they varied in color and she could distinguish no sigils.

Her fury with Amon paused as the four horsemen met them. "Clear the road!" the lead man shouted. "Move that carriage off to the town, and quickly!"

"And good morning to you!" Sir Amon replied, his hands out and open. "I am Sir Amon Swift, on business for the Earl of Essex, and here his granddaughter. Why do you ask us to clear the road?"

"Well met, sir," the man replied. "Didn't know there were any knights left behind. Well, you're welcome to stay on the road, but your earl's granddaughter will be trampled to death, so I'd still recommend you clear it." With little other explanation the men rode by, leaving them thoroughly untrampled.

Marion looked back down the road. She felt it in her feet before she noticed the shift in the air. The sky was ever grey, but off to the south and above the hills that obscured Cambridge, a soft white haze half the length of the horizon lingered.

"A fire?" Nick asked.

"No," Amon answered. "That's dust, kicked up from the road."

"Dust?" Peetey squinted at it. "What kicks up that much dust?"

Marion handed the horse's reins back to Amon. "An army."

FIFTY-TWO

QUILLEN PEVERIL

IT WAS A WIDE FLAT barge, a square raft cobbled together from mismatched wooden planks. From their larger skiff in the middle of the Trent, merchants tried to correct the barge's trajectory toward the docks with long poles, as best they could without coming closer. A stranger might think they kept their distance because Nottingham was afflicted with a contagion—which would not necessarily be wrong.

Quill added his voice to a symphony of meaningless directions shouted at the dockworkers, who were trying to steer the barge and its precious cargo. He stopped screaming when he realized his voice was being drowned out by Sir Robert FitzOdo's beside him, who was screaming something the opposite.

Quillen Peveril, self-acclaimed genius, was the only person to successfully orchestrate an escape from the castle's lockdown. His plan had only succeeded with the help of the Sheriff, as the point was to sneak Ferrers out of the city that he could rally the neighboring earls to take Nottingham back. It had required a massive coordination amongst sympathetic Guardsmen. In the silent span of half an hour they'd taken the colossal task of removing the unguarded blockade from the castle's postern door—just long enough for Ferrers and Wendenal to slip through, along with Quill and a few others. Those that remained behind risked themselves doubly by returning the blockade as it was, hoping the prince's sentries did not catch them.

But escaping the city walls had proven equally tricky. The entire city was on edge. Fights broke out at the slightest provocation. The only people allowed to pass through the city or castle gates were Prince John's loyal supporters, of which there were more and more every day. The arms of Gloucestershire and Worcestershire were everywhere; their men-at-arms had taken the duty of patrolling the city's gates, diligent to the point of ruthlessness. Trade was allowed via the wharfs only, not the city roads, which had given Quill his idea. He'd smuggled Beneger and Ferrers out in two empty wine barrels, which were supposed to be payment for a shipment of incoming food. Had there been a third barrel, Quill would have gone with them.

The river merchants must have discovered the slight, because the Worcester host clamped down on the dock trade the next day. Merchants were not allowed to berth at all now, but instead had to ridiculously remain in the middle of the river and send their wares by unmanned raft. The Worcester Guard sent payment back the same way, inspecting both cargoes, to make sure nobody dared another escape.

Two successful escapes, Quill ought to be congratulated. But he'd left himself behind, which felt like the opposite of a victory. And try as he might, he could not concoct any new reliable plan for a man to get in or out of the city without risking a quarrel in the back.

Which meant that Beneger and Ferrers had to be successful. They had to return with a host to confront John's coup, and *before* the French army arrived.

The city's only hope, riding on Quill's longshot.

"Unload!" the dockworkers cried, when the barge was finally tethered to the city-side docks. It was laden with nothing exotic—sacks of grain and vegetables—but it would go a long way to keeping the city alive.

"Let's go," Sir Robert FitzOdo grunted, at the same time that a hiss sliced the air and ended with a *thunk.* The hungry crowd recoiled in horror—a single flaming arrow had been shot into the barge's hold.

"Put it out!" Ronnell cried, while Quill searched for the perpetrator. There were endless claptrap wooden shacks that littered the wharfs, and any of a dozen windows might have hid the bowman. It didn't matter. Half the city seemed eager for more destruction. After the Red Lions' leaders were killed in the archery tournament, the other fledgling gangs had all gone to war—desperate to prove themselves the most ambitious, or at least the most brutal. Quill regretted now what they'd done to the Red Lions; that gang had likely been a stronger source of stability in Nottingham than Quill had ever realized. Their absence just added one more layer of chaos on top of an already over-flowing chaos cake.

It didn't matter. The Nottingham Guard didn't have the men or resources to stop every act of terrorism, while the men from Gloucester and Worcester cared only about stopping any traffic through the city, and not a thing for its inhabitants. They'd let the city starve before admitting a single stranger.

Because of that *other* thing. The *other half* of what kept the city on edge. The French army was coming, and everyone in the city knew that now.

What at first Quill had dismissed as a princely delusion, was now a rumor turned into horror. The only information coming into the city came with Prince John's new allies—and though none had yet seen this French menace, there was increasingly little doubt that it existed, and that it was headed for them. But directly in between the prince's stolen castle and the approaching French was the city itself. Nobody knew what the near future held for them, but everyone knew it would be bloody.

Quill no longer had any pride in his ability to predict the future. Frankly, he was too tired to even piece it all together. He could only hope that Beneger and Ferrers could make more sense of it, being on the outside now. Would they bother with their original plan, if reclaiming the castle meant losing it immediately afterward to the French? If they successfully took the castle back, would they then surrender Prince John to the French in exchange for the city's safety? Perhaps it would be better if the French arrived first and were weakened at the castle walls, that Ferrers and Beneger might attack the remnants from the rear—but at the cost of the city's sacking. The only thing Quillen Peveril knew for certain was that he should have seen all this coming, and had failed to act. It was Quill's sole misfortune to be the weather vane that had failed to announce the coming storm.

"Let's go," FitzOdo grunted a second time. "This place is fucked."

He meant the docks, but he'd accidentally described the whole city.

Quill almost protested, but the Worcester Guard had already swarmed the barge, put out the fire, and kept the crowd at bay. As far as they were concerned, everybody else was just part of the rabble. So Quill hastened to catch up with FitzOdo and his half-incompetent lackey Ronnell.

"Where's Derrick?" Quill asked, not really caring for the answer.

Ronnell answered by widening his eyes and shaking his head numbly, as if he was too overwhelmed to even attempt a guess. "The Trip, maybe?" FitzOdo's trio slept at the Trip to Jerusalem each night, and were rarely seen apart. The fact that one of FitzOdo's most loyal dogs might have abandoned him . . . that said everything.

Left to his own volition, Quill would prefer to lose FitzOdo as well, but they'd somehow become the highest-ranking members of the Nottingham Guard present in the city. Most had been at the tournament, but FitzOdo must have gone drinking before the lockdown started. So the Coward Knight and Quill the Nightwalker were now in charge of the few others that hadn't been in the castle. He did his best to keep them on their alert, to create repeatable processes, to establish rules they could depend on in the midst of absolute un-certainty. To prevent them from falling victim to their fears.

That, too, was a constant danger. Guardsmen saw threats in every corner. Paranoia turned every terrified citizen into an enemy in disguise, and hesita-tion could mean death. There was no tolerance for interfering with the Guard now—it didn't even make sense to "arrest" someone anymore. There was no access to the castle prisons, and the two city gaols were bursting past capacity. Quill had watched normally docile Guardsmen—cowlike boys with friendly temperaments, like Potter—beat citizens halfway to death out of fear. And as much as that haunted him, Quill couldn't even blame them. That, perhaps, was the third half of what kept the city on edge.

It didn't even matter that the math of three halves made no sense, because neither did the city. The world was apparently under no obligation to obey the rules of reason.

Quill followed FitzOdo up the Long Stair that led to the south side of Saint Mary's, watching the continued commotion on the docks below as they climbed. The barge had been besieged by a crowd of commonfolk who must have gotten past the Worcester Guard, but their weight unbalanced it. One cor-ner dipped into the river and then upended the other, dumping every last pre-cious sack of grain to the bottom of the Trent.

Quill had to stop, just for a moment, to digest the devastating loss of what that meant.

The cries from that crowd below carried up, but St. Mary herself could do nothing to get that grain back. There would be another merchant later, a fresh shipment, but it wouldn't be enough. Fewer boats were braving the journey to the doomed city of Nottingham. Rats knew well enough to flee a sinking ship—but every rat here was trapped inside the hull boards, and Quill was one of them.

The great church of St. Mary's had become the Guard's unofficial base, one of the safe shelters along with St. Stephen's down the west hill, and the Market Square. People flocked inside its courtyard walls for safety. Anywhere else in the city, it was every man for himself, and not enough Guardsmen available to even try to maintain order.

Today, as always, there was commotion billowing about St. Mary's perimeter walls—lines of commonfolk hoping for a portion of the food that had just sunk to the bottom of the Trent. That news wasn't going to be well received. Guardsmen were already struggling to keep a secure border at the church's entrance, while desperate folk tried to sneak their way in or outright rush the front double doors. The moment Quill had the church in sight, he was already at work commanding people to climb down, to settle down, to hunker down.

Down was, after all, the only direction to go anymore.

FitzOdo was less gentle, yanking and pulling people where he saw fit, and Ronnell followed after, snapping at those in FitzOdo's wake. They were nearly inside when *something* grabbed Quill's attention like a slap in the face. He startled and whipped his head around, looking for it again through the throng of churchgoers, without even realizing what he was looking for. It was the same frightening clarity of hearing one's own name spoken distinctly across a crowded room.

"Get along," FitzOdo demanded, but Quill grabbed the knight's arm and held him back, waiting for the crowd to open up just for a moment—*there*.

"What the fuck is that?" Quill asked. He didn't care for curse words, but he had to speak the language of FitzOdo.

"The fuck is what?"

"*That*."

Past the northwestern entrance to St. Mary's, a tiny doorway in the first stone building closed shut. It was the same as a thousand other entrances, excepting that this one bore a handprint next to its frame, notable for being painted in white.

A White Hand.

"You're worried about vandalism now?" FitzOdo laughed, prodding Ronnell to join him in doing so. "Or are you going to start arresting people for shitting in the streets again? Think it'll take a while!"

It took every bit of Quill's patience to detail the obvious connection between a painted white hand and Gilbert with the White Hand.

"What does it matter?" the knight balked. "We never found anything on him. And we got an army marching our way now. Past's about to get wiped clean."

"If Gilbert's innocent, then he's a Guardsman. And we could use every man we can get here. If he's not . . . well, half the city still thinks this is all Robin Hood's fault," Quill explained. "They think the prince still cares about catching every Robin Hood in the city. Could be the major victory we need to calm people down. Could . . . do some good."

"You're serious?" FitzOdo's bald head turned into all wrinkles. "'Sides, you think he's going to announce his hiding place by stamping his name on his front door for everyone to see?"

Quill bit his lip. "Does it hurt to go look?"

"It'll hurt when I slap some sense into you."

They might have argued more, but both of their eyes narrowed on a young man in a cloak who approached the door in question, placed his palm on the white hand, and whispered into its hinges.

"I'll be damned," FitzOdo breathed. "Good on you, Peveril."

"Try not to stare," Quill warned, watching out of the corner of his eye. They had to play this right, or risk spooking the stranger. "Let's see what happens next."

But Sir Robert FitzOdo was already three steps away. "Got a better idea."

Moments later the stranger's face was smashed into the wooden door, FitzOdo's meaty fingers wrapped around the man's skull like a melon. This instantly caused a dervish amongst the surrounding crowd, which Ronnell abated by flipping out a short bludgeon on a rope tether from his tunic, and making it very clear that he knew how to use it.

"What's in there?" FitzOdo demanded of the cloaked man, his mouth inches from the other's ear.

The man's voice was muffled. "Nothing!"

"You get one lie, and that was it. Lie to me again and we break your knees, both of them. What's in there?"

"The White Hand! The White Hand!" The man squirmed, pinned against the door. He was young, had a pudgy face, and was carrying something underneath his cloak that was apparently more important than trying to defend himself.

Quill edged closer. "What do you mean, the White Hand? Gilbert?"

"I don't know their names, maybe."

The use of the plural raised Quill's eyebrows. "Why are you here?"

"They say they can get you out of the city," the pudgy man whimpered. "Say they got caves that go all the way out. Say to go . . . go to St. Mary's and look for the White Hand, then knock and say the right phrase—oh! And to bring oil." He shrugged open his cloak to reveal a small but plump wineskin.

"Oil?"

"Dark down there," the man explained. "Oil's hard to come by. Say if you don't have oil, you get lost and never come out."

Whether Gilbert was truly involved with this, Quill could only guess. But it was no surprise that some gang had found profit in trying to smuggle people out of the city. It probably didn't even matter if they could actually do it—could be they were just leading the gullible and desperate down into a cistern for a fee, and then leaving them to die.

"We don't have time for it," FitzOdo growled. He snatched the wineskin and threw the man away, who recovered and ran furiously down the nearest alley. "This ought to put an end to it."

FitzOdo splashed the contents of the skin onto the mark of the White Hand, then drew his knife and tore a hole in the bag to empty over the door's edges. From his belt he produced a rectangle of flint, and a single knife slash summoned a spark that found its home in the oil. The door went up quickly, and Ronnell did not need to threaten anyone else to keep them from approaching the inferno.

THEY SPENT THE AFTERNOON at St. Mary's, corralling the masses, helping the clergy distribute what small amounts of food it had, and chasing off undesirables. The hours passed were marked only by the occasional toll of the steeple bells. The two o'clock hour sounded, and then some time later came two deep tones, followed by a curious long wait for the third, and then two more. Time itself had become unreliable.

The flaming door outside the courtyard walls had burnt ferociously for some of that time, belching up a vicious black smoke that occasionally swept into the front entrance of St. Mary's, to nobody's enjoyment. But only the door itself burnt—the rest of the building being made of stone—and eventually it settled down to a simmering grey stream. The entirety of the church reeked of the wooden char, and FitzOdo alone seemed to remain ignorant of the offense.

Out of that ashen wisp came a very young girl in a torn dress, who came directly for the three of them.

"'Scuse me sir," she said, trying to get the knight's attention. "Are you Sir Robert FitzOdo?"

"I am, girl," he answered with a smile, never one to turn down any amount of respect shown him.

"Are you Sir Robert FitzOdo?" she asked again.

"I said I was, are you looking for me?"

"Are you Sir Robert FitzOdo?"

"Oh, get off then."

She held out a small piece of fabric. "I have a message for you."

The moment it was in his hand she vanished, and Quill couldn't help but notice that she was particularly good at running without making a sound. "What's it say?" he asked.

"Nothing." FitzOdo shrugged, though something seemed to pass between him and Ronnell that Quill didn't understand.

On the fabric was scrawled a single world.

* * *

"Pities."

If there was one place in Nottingham that was most dangerous now, it was the northwestern slums of the French Ward. It had always been a pit of poverty and desperation, but with everyone terrified of anything *French* now, the borough had truly become the last option for those that couldn't survive the rest of the city.

The Pity Stables, or the *Pities*, were at its heart, and Quill had nothing but rancid memories and the taste of bile to recall his last visit there—prying chunks of desiccated hands from the wall. Despite the clamor of the city, the area around the Pity Stables was disturbingly quiet. As he stood there with Fitz-Odo and Ronnell, Quill had the unnerving sensation of spiders making their merriest way down his spine.

"No one around," Ronnell noted. "If someone wanted us to meet them here, they must be inside."

"We should've brought some more men," Quill complained. But FitzOdo had insisted the three of them could handle themselves, and echoed that notion now by striding down the dirt slope that led to the mouth of the old stablehouse.

"We'll check the sides," FitzOdo said with no other fanfare.

"Wait!" Quill gulped. "Do you mean to just . . . walk in there? We don't know who wanted us here, shouldn't we—"

"You wanted to *do some good,* Peveril?" FitzOdo rounded on him. "That comes with danger. Swallow your shit and act like you deserve half the uniform you're pissing in."

With that, he peeled off to the left and Ronnell took the right, leaving the world's most disappointing human—Quillen Peveril—to walk blindly into the open maw of this most indisputable trap.

As if to recap his entire life, Quill's mind flailed to understand how he'd arrived at this point, at this time, with this little to call his own. His was the weakest claim in the legendary Peveril family, dwarfed by the enormity of his father and siblings. His fate would be immortalized not by the annals of prestige, but by the shit-covered stables his feet were inexplicably moving him toward.

He wondered where he'd gone wrong. He thought perhaps he should have made some friends in life, rather than revel in criticizing those that might have become them. He wondered if Jacelyn de Lacy knew that he admired her—despite her behavior when they arrested Will Scarlet—and wished she had escaped the Nottingham baileys with him. She'd know what to do in a situation like this.

"Well, this is a stupid way to die," he announced loudly to the murderers waiting on the other side of the stable entrance. Having failed to come up with any of a thousand obvious alternatives, he marched himself inside.

His eyes needed a moment to adjust, but there was no hiding from the assault on his nose. The acrid stink of metal was in the air—*copper*—causing his eyes to tear up. There was no one else inside, despite the valuable shelter it offered the poor. Once the glow of the outside world had softened and he could open his eyes against the sting, he made sense of the image before him, knowing immediately that it would haunt him the rest of his days.

Yes, there was another hand nailed to the back wall of the Pities.

And a handswidth away from it, the arm from which it had been taken. This, too, was pinned in place with knives. Two of them. But the arm ended at the elbow.

The upper half of that severed arm was also there, pinned, again separated by a small gap of bare wood.

Beyond that, the torso.

All four limbs were accounted for, but certainly not intact. Each had been cut into pieces, splayed out, and nailed against the wall. Reassembled in this grotesque spectacle.

The head wore a hood, though it did not conceal the face. The long greyhound features were Derrick's, the third member of FitzOdo's regular trio.

Derrick had not simply been killed, he'd been *segmented.*

Quill did not have to count them to know there were exactly eight arrows that pierced the center of Derrick's chest. *Eight arrows* had become a slang in the streets after the archery tournament, a sign of the Robin Hood. *He deserves eight arrows,* one might say. Or one could flash a hand signal of *eight* to point out someone suspected of working with the traitors.

But these eight arrows had rings of white painted about them, a color that had not been used in the tournament. That same white paint was used for a handprint on Derrick's left breast, as well as the only thing in the room more prominent than the grisly display.

Spanning Derrick's arms from fingertip to fingertip—painted in large white letters with the central O making a ring around his decapitated head—was the word *IMPOSTOR.*

"Holy God Almighty," came Ronnell's voice, cracking. He stumbled in from the right entrance, his hands limply out as he took in the entirety of his friend's brutal murder.

FitzOdo had entered as well but said nothing, a grim alarm on his features. His eyes turned downward and his head cocked, aimed at the ground before Quill's feet. The straw there had been brushed aside, where in equally large letters was again painted the word *IMPOSTOR.* Quill was practically standing upon the second white handprint. He stepped to the side, fear finally lancing him through, wondering if they were all about to meet similar fates.

But nothing came, just the eerie sounds of the city outside, and the calm stupor of the Pities.

Ronnell was crying, ugly, heaving gasps that begged for pity.

But Quill's mind was finally working.

"Why call Derrick an impostor Robin Hood?" he asked at last. "What does that mean?"

"There's no meaning to it," FitzOdo said softly. "Gilbert's a madman."

Madman, yes. But calculating. This was the very definition of deliberate.

The second word, *IMPOSTOR,* on the ground before him.

Three times the little girl had asked *"Are you Sir Robert FitzOdo?"*

FitzOdo was supposed to be standing where Quill was now.

He raised his eyes to find the Coward Knight had already come to the same conclusion. Despite some smarter version of himself begging not to, Quill felt the missing puzzle pieces fall into place and demanded, "Why are they calling you an impostor Robin Hood?"

FitzOdo pulled steel.

FIFTY-THREE

ARABLE DE BUREL

BELVOIR CASTLE, RUTLANDSHIRE
SUNDAY, 22ND DAY OF MARCH

SOMEWHERE, SOME STUDIOUS SCHOLAR—who had not spent the majority of his life in fear of losing it—had probably calculated the precise distance to the horizon. Whatever number that was, it was exactly how far Arable could see in every direction. Belvoir Castle stood atop a large rolling pinnacle in a countryside that otherwise stretched flat for miles and miles. From above, she could discern the very geometry of the land, of fields parceled out with neat, clean edges, which she found somewhat comforting. When pulled far enough back, she thought, any single thing must seem terribly cute—and not worth any of the worry of those whose noses were constantly shoved into the dirt of it.

Far to the west, at the mercy of the clear morning sky but just barely hanging onto the world, were a few dark specks that marked the city and castle of Nottingham.

She might just be able to flick it, and knock it over the edge of the horizon and into whatever waited on the other side of the sky.

A male voice came from not so far away, but still too close. "That's Nottingham."

"Yes thank you for explaining that to me."

The view might have been beautiful if not for his presence. The black tendrils of his approach wrapped through every joy she might find in the scenery, tainting it. She had avoided talking to him, ignored his requests, hated even that he formed them as *requests*, as if to imply he was the reasonable one.

Until now, it was thankfully easy to keep him at bay, with all the insanity of the last few days. Bannermen from across Huntingdonshire answered Lord Robert's call to join the Earl Ferrers in his attempt to reclaim Nottingham Castle. Arable had volunteered herself to those arranging the daunting mechanics of this, such as organizing the camp followers and mobilizing enough food to keep them alive. Once Lord Robert's battalion was assembled, they marched north alongside the Derby host to join even more companies in the heart of Rutland, and Arable had simply vanished into the work.

Now they were met here, dozens and dozens of households arranged into terribly cute little squares, their encampments surrounding the hill of Belvoir Castle. Most of the fighting men were young farmhands—too weak to have joined the war and far shy for the title *soldier*—but they were the best that could be scavenged. At Belvoir they awaited the last promised companies to join them before marching on to Nottingham.

The city to which Arable had sworn she'd never return.

That alone ought to be enough for her to pull her hair out, to scratch her face to putty. But instead she also now had to deal with *this,* the man who begged her ear.

"I don't blame you," Lord Beneger de Wendenal said, as if there were any part of her that was worried that *he blamed her.* "And I understand why you don't want to talk to me. But I'm hoping at least you'll stay, while I talk."

She considered leaving immediately, for the sheer spite of it. She could climb down into the dank wine cellars beneath the castle's surface and enjoy a better view than any that contained *him.* But walking away now would only mean delaying this, and if it had to be done, then she could endure it. She'd suffered worse.

They were on a wide triangular stone battlement, across which the early morning sun cast his shadow near her feet. Even that was too intrusive for her taste. When it was obvious she was not going to leave, she heard his lips part.

"Do you know the story of this castle?" he asked, and she instantly rolled her eyes. "It's pronounced *beaver,* but it's spelled like *belle voir,* French for *beautiful sight.* William the Conqueror stood here, where we are, and said, *'Quelle belle voir!'* And so the name was chosen, but the English . . . well we don't care much for the French, do we? We kept the spelling, but without all those nasty French sounds. So, *Beaver* Castle."

He had probably hoped to lighten the mood.

When Arable finally answered him, she ground her voice into rubble. "Say what you came to say."

He inhaled, his feet shuffled. At last his voice returned, quieter. "I was told you were with William, in the end. If you ever find it in your heart, I would like very much to hear about that time. I had not seen him for several years, and did not even know he had returned. And so close to home. I don't know what my son's final days were like, and it eats me. It eats me as much as it did then, with George, and Hugo."

William's brothers—who had gotten themselves killed trying to escape from Arable's household sixteen years ago. That accident sparked Lord Beneger's rage and led him to decimate their family, their estate, their lives. She'd been fleeing his vengeance ever since.

"I'm thankful to you, Arable. I am. I know how much you meant to William . . . back then. There was a time when I would have liked very much to call you my daughter one day. William spoke of you often after the war, even though he knew it would infuriate me."

She didn't want to know that. She'd written her history already, and it involved a William who had abandoned her. She didn't need anything to soil those years.

"I know you must think me cruel. But your father was my friend once, you might remember. When Raymond betrayed his king, he betrayed our friendship, and he was responsible for the deaths of my sons."

"He wasn't there," she said shortly. "They died on their own. And it was *an accident.*"

"He swore to protect them." The voice took an edge. "That means there should have been no accidents. Raymond swore to protect them as his own, he embraced me in his arms, he swore to God that he'd see his own children harmed before mine. But those were empty words, and he marched himself to die in Nottingham, and George and Hugo suffered at his neglect and died for nothing. *For nothing.*"

Arable swallowed. Her eyes were focused on the distant black speck, and she could see nothing else. "And what did *my* family die for?" she demanded.

"For your father's betrayal, for his negligence." As if they were nothing, as if it were obvious. As if it were the color of the sky, he described. "Raymond swore harm unto his before mine, and so I took that payment. I did not come here to apologize for that. You should know better as a traitor's daughter than to think you are owed anything for his crimes."

Flick flick, the city off the horizon.

"But that was a long time ago. And as I said, I'm thankful for whatever company you gave William in his last days."

"You don't get to thank me for that. It wasn't for you."

He inhaled sharply as if to respond, but let it lie. "Fair enough."

The wind picked up a bit, but Arable did not avert her eyes from the single point she'd chosen to look at. She breathed in as the cold gust swelled around her, a massive blanket that cared nothing for their troubles.

"I understand you're with child."

With effort, she refrained from reaching down to touch her belly. Her bump was still slight, but it was a difficult thing to ignore.

"You have to understand." His voice was strained now. Disgusting, that he had the gall to display any sort of emotion at her. "I have no family left. My sons were taken from me, my wife died—well, you remember that. I never remarried. I have nothing to carry on my name. When my days are done, the name of Wendenal goes with me. You cannot imagine that burden, and what it has done to me, *what it has done to me . . .*"

His noise trailed off, his breath turned erratic, until he seemed to control himself.

"Everything I went through when I learned William died, all that grief and loss, moving from thinking your family is secure to having nothing . . . well, the opposite of that happened when I learned I had a grandchild."

Her skin shrank. To think he had any sort of *possession* of her baby was a new hell.

"I want to take care of you, Arable. I want to bring you to our home, I want to give my grandson everything in the world, everything. I want to repay you, for your loss, for what you've been through. Please let me do that."

She despised herself for hesitating. But she had felt those changes in herself lately, too. The shift in her own mind, some primal need to protect her baby— her *daughter*—no matter the cost to her. A life of comfort in a respected house would afford her daughter every opportunity that Arable should have had.

Compared to fleeing through the woods and getting caught up in everybody else's battles, there should have been no choice at all.

"You want to *repay me*," her mouth said, of its own, and she wondered where it was going. "For the loss of my family. My father, my mother, my brothers. My cousins, our attendants, our bannermen, their families, their fields, their futures . . . you want to repay *me* for that? As if I alone suffered? And by accepting your coin I say it's all even? You want me to speak for the hundreds of lives you ruined? How many of my family members did you hunt down? Have you killed my brothers? I honestly don't even know the full extent of what you've done to my family, do you understand that?"

He didn't answer.

"All this, you did it because two of your children made a mistake. You ruined generations of people as *your* repayment. And you think *my* repayment can be counted in gold crowns? I could live for a hundred years in your estate, my children could live for a hundred more, and your debt would not be paid."

A terse huff of air. "Your father betrayed the king."

"My father obeyed his earl."

"Who, himself, betrayed the king. Must we go round and round on this? War is war, your father lost. I will not bemoan the way of the world. By the laws of our King and our Lord, I owe you nothing. But I *choose* to repay you, Arable, and I think that should matter for something far more."

There was no point in discussing it any further. "I will never live with you. Nor will my daughter." She hoped to hurt him with that, she almost wanted to incite his rage, to goad him into violence, into finishing off his work. To prove himself the monster she knew he was.

But instead he sighed. "Very well. But I will give you coin. As much of it as I can. Whether you throw it away out of spite or put your child in comfort is on you. I hope you are not so bitter a thing as to actually harm a baby out of sheer insolence. I will see him cared for—or *her*, as you say—I will see that the child is given better security than your father gave my sons. I swear that, whether you want it or not, whether you *accept* it or not, I swear it nonetheless."

His footsteps receded, and only after it had been silent for a long time did she break her stare with the distant speck of Nottingham and take account of her surroundings. Doing so brought a lump to her chest and tears to her eyes, all the emotions she'd been holding back. In all her fantasies of how this interaction might go, she'd never played with this one. She'd always assumed he would hunt her, chase her, beat her to death. Something brutal and wicked. Occasionally she imagined him begging for her forgiveness, dying at the end of his life. But this *in between* was somehow worse. If he'd tried to kill her, then at least the world would finally understand his real nature.

But his offer to help her, without apology, was not something she could grapple. If it were just her, she could reject it without a thought. To debase herself and her family's memory by accepting his charity was unthinkable, she'd simply rather die.

But as a *mother,* something she was only barely beginning to grasp the concept of, she already knew that her dignity meant nothing if her baby's survival was on the line. She could debase herself to the ground and deeper, she could call Lord Beneger *Father* if it meant giving the life growing inside her a real future.

It wouldn't come to that, she swore.

After all, Lord Robert had not lost his earldom. She still had her new home in Huntingdon, and she would not have to even consider Lord Beneger's offer if everyone could simply outlast the very minor distraction of seizing Nottingham Castle from Prince John's forces without getting dead.

IN THAT REGARD, AT least, there was some startling news.

"You haven't heard, then?" asked the Sheriff of Rutland, William d'Albini. He wasn't a huge man, but he had two chins—the first smooth and white and the second red and prickled with short white hairs. He welcomed them in a circular room of the castle's main tower, a wide opulent space with high ceilings and painted windows.

"What have we not heard?" Ferrers asked, his eyes instantly suspicious.

"Let me put it this way." D'Albini lowered himself into a generous armchair. "I have thirty-three knights I can contribute to the march on Nottingham."

"*Thirty-three!*" gasped Ranulph, the Earl of Chester. His slack jowls flapped with incredulity. "My bannermen are nothing but farmers and stableboys, where on earth are you hiding thirty-three *knights?* Why didn't they answer the call to the Crusade?"

"They did." D'Albini's lips formed a rude smile.

"Deserters, then?" Lord Beneger asked. "We'd be better off without them. Their participation would make our cause look poorly. If we're to depose a prince, we cannot be seen as—"

"Not deserters." Behind now-steepled fingers, light danced in the Sheriff's eyes.

All about the room, nobody could understand his game. Arable frankly didn't even know why she was there at all, except that she had somehow become the surrogate version of Lady Marion ever since her disappearance. Another facsimile—the woman-who-was-not-Marion.

"You understand we march on Nottingham in two days?" Lord Robert asked, with his usual levity. "Because if you're about to tell us you've sent a letter to Jerusalem to kindly ask your knights to come home for this, I do think they'll be a trifle late."

"Oh, they'll be here." D'Albini laughed now, eager for anyone around the room to enjoy this half as much as he. "They'll be here by sundown, so I'm told."

"I think you'd better explain it, then." Lord Beneger shared no amusement. It would likely be the only time in her life that Arable found herself agreeing with him.

D'Albini repositioned his weight, bubbling only for himself. "Surely you've heard of the army that landed in Sandwich last week?"

"Rumors, nothing else," the Earl of Chester huffed. "The French wouldn't dare land an army here, it's preposterous. It's a lie, an empty excuse to let John seize the castle, for his own greed."

"No. Prince John believes it, with all his heart." Lord Beneger stood, cocking his head as if hoping to be challenged. "I spoke with him, and he was nothing short of shaken. He told me flatly, his spies have confirmed it. John thinks they're marching for Nottingham with one purpose—to kill him. To put Arthur Plantagenet on the throne, in Richard's absence."

Lord Robert chuckled, rapping his fingers on the table. "Then perhaps his *spies* are manipulating him. If so, I daresay he'll be surprised when *we* arrive at his doorstep instead of the French. Perhaps he won't put up a fight at all."

"Ah, but there *is* an army in England." D'Albini raised a single plump finger. "I have confirmed that myself. It landed in Sandwich ten days ago, and is marching north."

Robert reacted with his entire body. "It's real? Why hasn't the Chancellor organized a defense?"

"Oh the Chancellor knows all about it, as would you all if you hadn't been so consumed this last week rallying your forces." There was a joyous smile on d'Albini's face. "The army *does* exist, and it *is* headed directly to Nottingham. In fact, my scouts say it's larger even than anyone has been reporting."

Ferrers spasmed, clearly impatient with the riddle. "What are you hinting at then? If these rumors are true, it is half the reason for our urgency. If Prince John is still in Nottingham when the French arrive, they're like to destroy the whole city."

"You're asking all the right questions, except for one thing." D'Albini shook his head until he was certain everyone was waiting on his next syllables. "That army isn't French."

Well that silenced them all.

"Austrian, then?" Ranulph asked.

D'Albini roared with laughter, nearly choking on himself. He slapped the table and coughed out the rest of it. "No, no no no, go the other way!"

It came to Arable, but she was hesitant to say it, for fear of being ridiculously wrong. But when nobody else offered a guess, she cleared her throat. "The army . . . is English?"

"It's bloody *English!*" d'Albini exploded. "King Richard has been released from Austria, and he's come home!"

Every single jaw in the room dropped. Hell, Arable's daughter was still in the womb, and *her* damned jaw dropped.

"Released?" Ferrers echoed. "How?"

"The ransom is paid. In part by the Chancellor, and in part by Richard's mother—largely in the form of hostages to be held until the remainder of the ransom can be collected."

Most of the room had a laugh at that, but Arable could only marvel at it. What Eleanor of Aquitaine had done might well have ruined her. *What had the most powerful woman in the world sacrificed for her son?* But Arable knew, it was no more than any mother was prepared to do.

D'Albini continued, slapping his knees. "King Richard's back, and he hears his brother's been stealing castles while he's away. So he's bringing his army on up to stop him. They should be here by evening, come from the south road. You can see them already, actually, if you squint. Ergo, my thirty-three knights—if they weren't fool enough to get killed in the Holy Land—will be with them. And I imagine there ought to be several hundred more at Richard's side. And those are just the knights, of course! Probably a few thousand in archers, twice that again in footmen, and double it all in followers. How many men you think the Lionheart will even need to knock his littlest brother off his ass?"

FIFTY-FOUR

ARTHUR A BLAND

LOWER BAILEY, NOTTINGHAM CASTLE

DAVID'S FACE WAS CLOSER than it had ever been before. "We should have never come to this city," he whispered, and Arthur sure wished he'd fucking said as much a few months earlier.

"We should've left after Zinn caught me in the alley," Arthur counted on his fingers, "we should've left after the Red Lions said no, we should've left after Will chopped his damn ear off, or when Stutely abandoned us, or when Will broke that barmaid's finger—but now, *now* is when you change your mind?"

"I wanted to leave the whole time." David's face winced. "I thought *you* wanted to stay. I would've left if you'd brought it up."

"I will gut you."

Whispering was required, as there was no place to talk. There were exactly sixty-three members of the Nottingham Guard in the castle—well, sixty-*one*, since Arthur and David were technically impostors—and that number was going down. They were all confined to the lower bailey, just as much prisoners there as the baileyfolk. The highest two baileys of the castle proper were reserved for Prince John and his allies, readying themselves for the approaching French army. The prince was feverishly distrustful of the Nottingham Guard's ability to protect him—and admittedly, Arthur and David were a testament to how easy it was to infiltrate those ranks.

The more Arthur thought on it, the prince was probably actually being pretty reasonable.

The Nottingham Guard had claimed the south bend of the lower bailey, sharing it with those commonfolk who'd committed to help keep things orderly. They were at stark odds with the "baileyking," and those baileyfolk he'd incited to rebellion. They kept their distance in the north end of the bailey where the archery tournament had been held, where they had reassembled the remnants of the audience risers into a blockade that divided a quarter of the field into its own region. Their petulant leader had a real name now, at least—*Henry Russell*. He kept himself secluded in that barricade probably out of fear of being killed, just as he'd done to the previous baileyking.

From the bulwarks above, the Worcester crossbowmen could easily keep those rebels in line, but they apparently wanted to save their bolts for the war, whenever it came. Henry Russell refused all attempts at diplomacy, but had fortunately not incited any open conflict with the Nottingham Guard. The two groups were at a stalemate, living in an uneasy peace. The Guard had swords, but Henry Russell had archers—and the best in Nottingham, if the tournament was to be believed. It was like being trapped in a cave with a bear—it hadn't happened yet, but someone was going to get mauled.

"Latest on the French army is that they're close, they're gathered in Rutland," announced the captain, a stoic Midlander named Fulcher de Grendon. He was a lean man who kept his long hair in a tail, and had some supernatural ability to maintain his calm through all this madness. He alone amongst the Guard was allowed passage back up to the middle bailey, but only under an absurd amount of supervision. "I know Prince John isn't our favorite person of late, but if the French capture or kill him, then our children will be speaking French for the next thousand years."

"He got a plan for us?" asked Morg, one of the Guardsmen Arthur had grown close with.

"He does, but it's not a good one."

More grumbling at this. Arthur grumbled, too. He had no idea what to do with the fact that he considered himself part of the word *us*.

"Prince's men will line the battlements. The supply cranes are being converted, hopefully to keep some of the siege ladders off the walls. Nottingham Castle's never been taken before, but can't say the same for the lower bailey. Curtain wall's lower, and it's too long. So if the French manage a way over, they immediately become our responsibility."

The grumbles this time actually turned into laughter. Sebastien, who tended to stick close to Arthur most days, was first to complain. "There's not enough of us!"

Matthias joined in. "We'd be decimated!"

"The prince agrees," Fulcher said seriously. "So given the nature of the threat, he's calling on all proud Englishmen to raise a sword in defense of the castle. To that end, he'll be opening up the armory, and giving swords out to everyone here who can carry one."

"Oh that's fucking brilliant!" Arthur shouted, instantly earning an elbow to the ribs from David. But his outburst had earned him support, and suddenly there were a dozen other Guardsmen looking to him for a follow-up. "We're already all trapped in here, ready to tear each other's throats out, and the prince wants to give everyone swords? We'll all be fucking dead before the French get here!"

"Isn't my call," the captain answered. "As always, our job is to keep the peace."

"You think that baileyking's going to keep the peace?" Arthur yelled. It was one thing to be trapped with the bear, but another to be forced to go tickle it. "You think they'll just decide to do the right thing when the French come swarming over these walls? If the French get inside the castle, it'll be because *those* fuckers let them in! Then we're fighting two groups. It'll be a goddamned bloodbath."

The captain squinted at him over the crowd. "What's your name?"

Fuck. Arthur should've kept his mouth shut. He and David had befriended a number of the Guardsmen, but they'd kept their faces concealed around the captain. If anyone would know they weren't actual recruits, it'd probably be him.

"Arthur," he answered. They'd given up on using *Norman* a month ago. Completely unnecessarily, he added, "And this is David."

David whimpered.

"Well, Arthur may be right," the captain continued, but he spoke to the whole crowd. "And it'll be a risk we take. But what's the alternative? We go over there right now and kill them all? We can't arrest them, there's no secure place to put them. So we'd have to kill them, which means some of us die, too. You tell me which is smarter, to cut our ranks in half before the French get here? To kill off a potential ally? Or to trust they'll understand what's at stake when the French arrive? These are citizens of Nottingham, they're not monsters. They're over there barricaded up because they're trying to protect what little they have left. We're enemies now, but allies tomorrow."

"Someone ought to tell that to the baileyking," Arthur scoffed.

"You volunteering?"

Arthur had never prized himself much as a quick thinker. He'd always been happiest when there was a thing in front of him that needed to be punched, because that didn't usually require much in the way of thinking it out first. But in the half second after the captain's question, Arthur's mind did an impressive bout of gymnastics.

He knew the baileyking couldn't be trusted if they didn't come to an agreement first. He also knew it was in everyone's best interest for the baileyking to fight when the French came. And he also knew how two very specific feckless dickshits had already crossed that gap from previously hating the Guard to throwing in their lot with them. If Captain de Grendon went and talked to the baileyking, he'd use all the wrong goddamn words. But Arthur and David, they'd lived a few extra lives in the last few weeks. Hell, if they hadn't escaped to the middle bailey after the riots, they'd probably be holed up in the baileyking's barricade right now, getting ready to fight back. So if anyone knew how to think like them, and how to sway them, it was Arthur a-fucking-Bland.

"Goddammit, yes," he answered. "I'll do it."

He turned and walked north. No point in waiting for anyone to think they had the authority to approve it.

He struck himself instantly as some sort of tragic spectacle—what with the curtain wall on all sides, where the prince's men were looking down into the crucible of the bailey to see what would happen next. Here was the great fool Arthur a Bland, approaching like a pit fighter to meet his enemy on the other half of the arena. The commonfolk watched him walk through their camps, and the hideous wooden barricade wall grew larger as he approached. Perhaps the girl he'd rescued that first day was here, watching him, and he tugged the blue cowl off his head and let it drop to the ground in the idle hope she'd be impressed.

Jumping into alleys to protect girls had earned him the nasty gash across his head. How much more would he lose today just for trying to save the whole damn castle?

"What are you doing?" David's voice came, hustling to keep up with him.

"What the fuck am I doing." That was all the answer he had. "What the fuck am I doing."

"Are you feeling alright? Woozy, maybe? That wound doesn't look like it's getting any better."

Arthur absently reached up to touch the scabs of his forehead, which were at times either itchy or pussy. "Really?"

"It stinks," David said. "Then again, I don't know if that's a good sign or a bad sign."

Arthur looked at his friend. "When would it ever be a good sign for something to *stink?*"

David had no answer.

He kept walking. "What the fuck am I doing."

"Well you're not going without me," David said, keeping pace as they made their approach.

"Didn't want to die in the war, anyhow," Arthur said off-handedly. "Better to get that done with ahead of time."

"Agreed. 'Sides, this baileyking might actually recognize us. Figure he's one of the Red Lions?"

"Could be." Arthur hadn't really considered it. "Does that make it *more* or *less* likely he'll want to kill us?"

"I'd think *more,*" David answered, chewing it over. "Or maybe just a more *violent* death?"

"Well they've only got bows."

"Right." David snapped his fingers. "So they'll have to get creative. They could use the tips of the arrows to . . . sort of, scratch our skin off, bit by bit."

Arthur stopped. "What? These are the things you spend your time thinking about?"

He shrugged. "I think maybe you think I'm nicer than I really am."

Arthur was going to miss David, almost as much as he was going to miss being alive. "Actually, I *know* you're nicer than you really are."

David smiled, then frowned. "What does that even mean?"

"I don't know." Arthur turned back to the barricade. "Let's go die."

A group of appropriately burly men moved to meet them as they approached the wooden contraption, the same type of burly thug people that Arthur would normally feel most comfortable around. They carried some broken chunks of timber as crude weapons, while a few other gutterstock men and a sturdy woman stood atop the odd structure with longbows half-drawn.

"We've come to parley with Henry Russell," Arthur announced, not looking the men in the eyes. He instead looked for any sign of the baileyking, perhaps watching them from the open slats in the rubble.

"We don't talk to gords," grunted the nearest grunt.

"Yeeeah," David answered, picking at his dirty, quilted tabard, "we're not gords. Try not to judge us by these things."

"Just a talk. You can keep our swords. Fuck, you can take everything I've got, you want to take my goddamn *billies*? We just need a word." Arthur unbuckled his belt and let it slough off to the ground. Certainly wouldn't matter if these people gained a few blades now, they had no idea they were about to be armed to the teeth when the prince opened the armory to them.

Grunty motioned for them to step back and they did, then he crouched down cautiously to pick up the blade. As if even the most clever blacksmith in the world could concoct some sort of trap hidden inside a sword. He then—to nobody's surprise—grunted, and shuffled off to presumably get his mum's permission.

"Hi," Arthur said to the woman on top of the structure. She did not respond.

"Any idea what we're going to say to them?" David whispered.

"Not really," Arthur admitted. "Maybe I should cut my ear off?"

"Oh definitely." He nodded. "Works every time."

When Grunty returned he seemed a little more annoyed than earlier, probably because he wasn't going to get the opportunity to fill the two of them with arrows, or skin them alive, or whatever the fuck else David's weird fantasies were. Instead he led them, under the disapproving eyes of a wide variety of unfortunate assholes, around the backside of the barricade to a bit of overhanging wooden beams. The entire structure looked like it was simply balanced together, which was likely the case, and threatened to collapse and kill everyone inside at the first willful wind.

More baileyfolk rebels huddled inside—Arthur didn't recognize any faces, but he guessed many were members of the Red Lions or other gangs who'd never had their ears clipped. That was no surprise, that they'd end up here at odds with the Guard. After all, there were only two idiots in the whole world dumb enough to choose *joining* the Guard instead.

Henry Russell was shorter than anyone had a right to be who called himself *king*, but he had an athletic build and moved with confidence. A plume of blond hair bound by a leather strap detonated from the top of his head. Both his cheeks bore long stretches of war paint—bright red, like that used on the tourney arrows—that crisscrossed over his eyes, making it difficult to—

Arthur gasped, and flung a hand over his mouth when he realized it.

The baileyking walked forward out of the shadows to peer directly at Arthur's brow.

"God*damn*, what happened to your head?" asked Will Scarlet.

PART VII

THE SIEGE OF NOTTINGHAM CASTLE

FIFTY-FIVE

MARION FITZWALTER

NOTTINGHAM
TUESDAY, 24ᵀᴴ DAY OF MARCH

"Everything will be better *when King Richard returns.*"

That had been Marion's private belief for years. Her royal cousin had departed England mere months after his coronation, bleeding the country of its coin, its resources, its nobility, its knights, its manpower, its prestige. It was practically a cuckolder's con—seducing the entire country to trust him just long enough to marry him, only to vanish days later and take everything of value with him. He had left his bride—England—penniless, in favor of a dalliance with his mistress, the Holy Crusade. By that analogy, perhaps he was not the sort of husband England should wish back in her bed. But without him, England was being assaulted by carrion suitors, like the great Penelope in Odysseus's absence. Good husband or not, his return would scare off the scavengers.

"*Everything will be better when King Richard returns,*" she had reminded them at the council, along with the reality that his capture made that impossible. It was the very reason they had sided with one of those scavengers—conspiring to raise John to the throne, and seek alliances in the riven political world of Chancellor Longchamp. Everything would indeed be better if Richard *could* return, but instead they'd had to take things into their own hands.

But unbeknownst to any of them, it had already happened. Richard had been traded from Austria to the Holy Roman Empire, who accepted seventy percent of the ransom along with hostages and promises, and released Richard nearly two months ago. His armies had been traveling by foot ever since. All their fears and conspiracies had been meaningless. If only they'd known just to have patience. If only they'd waited for King Richard to return, to make the aforementioned everything better.

No more war tithe, no more ransom. No more gain for de Senlis to call for Marion's head. No more of the Chancellor's nepotism. Perhaps some of *Richard's* nepotism, but nobody was expecting heaven on earth. And, most importantly for their immediate circumstances, no more reason for Prince John to barricade himself in Nottingham Castle. King Richard had returned, and every last thing would be—inarguably—better.

Except here they were outside the city of Nottingham, having just discovered that not everybody actually believed he had returned.

"What do you mean they don't believe *I'm really me?*"

The King's question was met with an exasperated huff from the Archbishop of Canterbury. "I mean precisely that, Your Grace. They will not even entreat

to discuss it. They shouted at me from atop the city gates as if I were a burglar."
Hubert Walter was a careful man, the sort of proper English gentleman whose
every nuance spoke to his skills at diplomacy rather than villainy. He had been
freshly appointed to his position, a reward for his infinite service to Richard
during their long journey. "They accused me of being a French spy!"

Marion bit her lip at that. They were, after all, currently having this conversation in French—at Richard's preference. Were anyone from within Nottingham Castle able to listen in on this deliberation, they would think themselves
proven correct.

"Who else would I possibly be?" Richard asked, incredulous. He turned to a
soldier at his left. "Is it the beard?"

If anything, Richard was thinner than Marion remembered him, no doubt a
result of his time in captivity. And darker, certainly, given his long campaign in
Jerusalem. "Can we not demand a parley?" Marion suggested. "If Prince John
will simply come and meet his brother face-to-face, this nonsense would be
over."

"The envoy refused," Archbishop Walter answered with a chirp. "He said
the prince would not be so easily tricked to let our archers feather him, not even
to . . ."

Richard's eyebrows climbed halfway to his crown. "Go on."

The holiest man in the room swallowed. ". . . Not even to bare his arse at
you."

While the room recoiled in affected offense on Richard's behalf, he simply
rolled a smirk from one cheek to the other. He leaned closer to Marion. "He
might as well show his face then, we'd hardly know the difference."

She was glad to see that his irreverent humor had not been starved out of
him. She had only interacted with him a handful of times in her life, but she'd
always been impressed with his ability to make every interaction feel like a personal one, letting every person believe they shared a secret with their king. It
was the same charisma that had made Robin who he was—and *Robert, too,* she
realized, catching the earl's glance across the table—and at another time she
might unpuzzle why she was drawn to that quality so.

She wondered if other people ever described her the same way.

Robert, as if to answer, straightened his half cape and flashed her a comical
grimace.

"Prince John is under the impression we are a French army," Hubert summarized, "and rejects any compulsion to reconsider."

"Have they seen the banners?" Richard balked.

"They have," the archbishop's mouth pursed against a frustrated scowl,
"and they think it is part of the deception."

A sharp man with a sharper moustache—Sir William Marshal, Earl of
Pembroke—let out a long laugh, taking in the scope of the army that had been
assembled. His own sizable host was amongst them. "This would be the most
elaborate deception in history! They're mad to think as much."

Their armies had converged in the fields to the north of Nottingham's city walls. Their battalions sprawled long and wide, as if their numbers needed any exaggeration. The sigils of Derbyshire and Nottinghamshire were most prevalent, matched closely by Huntingdonshire and Cheshire, but dozens more mingled amongst them. Sheriff de Ferrers's original intention of reclaiming Nottingham Castle from John had practically become an afterthought, as this gathering was more a celebration of Richard's return—overrun with loyal lords eager to prove themselves by welcoming their king with startling obedience. Marion, too, had been overwhelmed with relief when she had chanced upon the army on the Roman road—letting it whisk her back north to discover that Robert had not lost his earldom at all, but joined forces with Derbyshire and Cheshire to march on Nottingham. With Richard's army added to theirs, it was ludicrous that Nottingham Castle thought it could defend itself from them.

A breeze lifted the flap of the command tent, beyond which lay thousands and thousands of good men, awaiting instruction.

"My brother is not mad," Richard said quietly, his face calculating. "If he truly believes we are a French army flying English banners, someone else must have put that idea in his head."

Marion sealed her lips as tightly as possible. She had no idea how the prince had concocted this idea about a French invasion, but there was no denying that her council in Huntingdon must have done something to push him toward paranoia. It was not an easy thing to pretend she did not carry some blame for all this, but with practice she could get good at it.

"It's not so surprising, is it?" asked the Earl of Chester, a man made round by both muscle and wealth. "Nobody believes the king has returned. John's allies have been rallying his call for almost a month—not just here, but all throughout England and France, too. Everybody knows that if they don't claim for John, they're essentially supporting young Arthur instead, who's a ward of King Philip! Given that choice, why *wouldn't* they pick John? Like it or not, these are fiercely loyal Englishmen before us, not a band of rebels. And they believe they are defending their new king."

"That's how it was in Tickhill," joined Hugh de Puiset, Bishop of Durham. "The baron there—de Busli—claimed in favor of John the moment he took Nottingham. When I told him Richard was returned, he practically threw me out of his castle. I had to bring two of de Busli's men to Belvoir to see for themselves, and they very nearly died on the spot."

"You say that to be funny," Richard raised a finger, "but that's happened, too. I'm told the commander of Mont St. Michel died of fright when he heard I'd been released. I did not realize I was so . . . terrifying."

"Perhaps we ought to prop you up outside the gates, then," suggested the archbishop. "And make this battle a unanimous victory."

"Battle?" Marion asked, more than a little out of turn. "There's not going to be a battle. This is a misunderstanding, not a coup."

Every human in the command tent stiffened, looking to each other. It was a game she'd seen a dozen times before, where the men of power each avoid being the one to explain to the woman what was happening, as if she could not figure it out.

"Do not underestimate the danger of a misunderstanding," Richard lectured, though not unkindly. "That is, after all, why we are here. I heard my brother was claiming castles, seizing power. If I had known he was simply defending himself from imaginary threats, I would not have bothered marching my armies here. Yet here we are, two idiots, screaming into the abyss."

"What of his followers? Do they deserve to die, for following orders?"

"For following my *brother's* orders over *mine?* Yes," Richard balked. "John at least has the excuse of ignorance. Those that stood at the gate today and turned the archbishop back are openly traitorous."

"And even if John genuinely thinks he's only defending himself," the Earl Ranulph said, "the people see it as a coup."

"So we let them sit in their castle until they're ready to come out and talk," Marion explained it back to him. "What we *don't* do is start trading English lives."

"Marion," the King spoke, before his supporters could jump on her. "I do not disagree with you. But nor can I allow the people to see me as weak. If they see my brother as rebelling and that my reaction is nothing beyond knocking on his door and walking away, then that coup suddenly becomes real. No, I must treat this as if it were real. And if my brother was actually making a grab at my throne in my absence, then my reaction would be swift. And violent."

Marion could scarcely believe it. "So your first act upon returning to England would be to slaughter your own people? Your men, gone for years, come home only to die a few miles from their families? Is that the kind of king you want to be?"

The eyes that met hers were cold, and for a brief moment she saw the result of his captivity there—a naked rage that refused to be controlled again. But Richard did not snap, he simply waited it out, then softened. "I will be the kind of king who brooks no revolts, especially from my own brother. We send our full force in, at first light, and we take the castle as quickly as possible."

Marion withheld a gasp, but he noticed it.

"I hate this no less than you!" he bellowed, daring anyone to argue. "Frankly, more of you here should share my cousin's horror. A little too eager for a bit of killing, I'd say, all of you. But if John will not parley with me, I see no alternative."

"There must be!" Marion's mind raced to find one. "John's no fool. If he were simply able to see you, face-to-face, he would relinquish the castle immediately! So while killing everyone between you and him would certainly be *effective,*" she hit the word sharply, challenging anyone to find joy in that prospect, "there's realistically only one person in that castle we actually care about."

William d'Albini fidgeted. "Don't make us guess, woman. What are you suggesting?"

She steeled herself against that word—*woman*. It was meant to paint whatever she said next in a poor shade. She'd borne it her entire life, but never grown accustomed to its sting. Most of Richard's advisors here were already skeptical of her presence—which admittedly was more a result of nobody telling her *no* rather than someone telling her *yes*.

But for now, she was in the room, and she intended on making the most of it. To Richard alone, she answered. "Use a scalpel, not an axe. Wait as long as you can to make your main assault—and in the meanwhile, send in a small force to infiltrate the castle and find Prince John. If he can be convinced you are who you are, all the better. If not, then he should be extracted and brought to see you in person."

The King snapped his fingers to seize attention, though he waited some time as he chewed the idea over. "I concur. But I cannot wait to start the assault. Come morning, they must see the wrath of their King, or think me coward. As a silver lining, I should think the chaos of the siege would only help this small force to find an opening in the castle's defenses."

Robert made eyes with Marion at this news and whistled. "So you'll siege the castle with the full strength of your Holy Crusaders . . . as a *diversion?*"

The King grimaced. "If we're lucky, then yes. If not . . . well, the siege will work, too. And I suppose my men could use some bloodshed. They've been cooped up for ages, waiting for me to get out of that damned castle. With a host of our size, there's no chance the siege will fail. But it may take a few days. So if the small force gets to my brother first, well then just think of all the English lives you'll have saved by doing so."

All the lives she'll have saved. That was not the currency in which she counted success. Marion could think of nothing but those who would die, meaning-lessly, between the prince's stubbornness and the king's reputation. It clawed through her belly like an animal. She'd spent months—*months!*—scraping for the survival of a hundred souls in the Sherwood . . . and now those kinds of numbers seemed trivial, mere grains of salt over a banquet of war.

"Very good," d'Albini chuckled. "And who is to lead this force?"

"I suppose it ought to fall on me," William de Ferrers answered, "as I know the city better than anyone else."

"No, you're Sheriff here, you need to be seen on the front lines, that the people know you're on the right of this," Richard answered. "If you're seen sneaking into your own city, it would read poorly. No, I need you at the van-guard. Ferrers, I hope you're better than your father at doing this."

"Well." The young Earl of Derby seemed to take it as a compliment. "I *am* still alive."

The other earls all volunteered to take on the special task, one by one, each boasting of some cunning attribute or past victory that made them an ideal candidate. Each begging for their king to trust them to carry out this, his first private request upon return to his country. But Marion felt it coming, a wave as strong as any ocean. She met Robert's eyes as he shook his head at the capitulat-ing barons, the poor fools. He knew it, too. None of them had the highest card.

Robert waited for Marion's silent approval before he addressed the King. "Your Grace, without Ferrers, we will need someone who knows the castle as well as he. We have a girl with us who worked as a servant in Nottingham Castle for years. We also have . . . the world experts at sneaking into the castle and . . . *finding* important men." It was kind of him to avoid the word *assassinating*. "And we also have people already positioned in the city, to help us."

That was a bit of an exaggeration, but in essence he was saying that *we have Robin Hoods.*

"And," Marion added, surprised he hadn't started with it, "thanks to the poor turnout of our recent council, every single one of our men knows exactly what Prince John looks like. No offense to you, Sheriff," she referred to d'Albini, "but I doubt your soldiers are so familiar with the prince's face. Had you answered the call to our council, perhaps. But your men would be sneaking around a castle full of John's influential supporters, hoping to find someone who 'looks important.' Whereas my crew," she hadn't used that word before, "we could die off down to a single man, and that man would still be able to finish the mission."

Her phrasing brought the tone down a bit. It was almost as if the others who had begged for the role hadn't considered how dangerous it would be.

"Very well. Huntingdon. Cousin." Richard nodded. "It's you."

"Stay with me a moment when we're done," the Archbishop of Canterbury added. "I have something that may aid you."

"See to it," the King finished. "The details are yours, but know that my campaign starts at first light, and does not stop until John has surrendered. Godspeed."

THEY DID NOT SPEAK as they followed the archbishop from the command tent, across the rolling farmlands of the hills outside the city, now flattened by an army's march. Robert did not so much as look back at her, but Marion knew every bit of his focus was upon her. It was the absences between them that spoke everything, the enormity of their silence. They did not look at each other, because they knew the other was there—and would be nowhere else.

They had not spoken of what happened that night in John Little's tent, because there was nothing to speak of. That is, nothing to put into words. Nothing that an observer could describe as salacious. They had spoken of her hopes of turning herself over to Lord Simon de Senlis, and he urged her to reconsider, and then the conversation had ended.

But when their words were done, they had not looked away from each other.

At first she'd almost found it comical, as if they were each waiting for the other to say one final thing. But as that silence lengthened, she knew neither of them would break it. At first her heart had raced with wonder, with anticipation, that they were on the verge of springing into an embrace . . . but with time it became more intimate than anything physical could ever be. The longer she looked into him, and he into her, the more she felt herself change, as if she were shedding layers of her very soul. At first she was aware only of the faces she was making, but then of her body, and eventually she was so relaxed she was aware of nothing but her own self-perceptions. At first, the lioness that Marion tried to present to the world. Then, the uncertain lady she knew others saw in her. Next, the terrified girl she saw in herself. Beneath that, just a human, just a heart, slowly sloughing off all the unfair trappings that she'd placed between herself and happiness. She was more naked than she'd ever been, letting Robert stare into her, with no pretense. In him she saw the same discarding of masks, from earl to husband to man, to *need*. They were just two souls, desperately in need of the connection with the other, lying a foot apart on the floor of a dirty tent. If it was hours that had passed that night, Marion would not be surprised. And both of them knew that while they had done nothing to violate Robert's marriage bonds—or Marion's grief—they had simultaneously done something far, far worse.

And so they walked together, bound together—*entwined,* beyond any ability to explain it. It eluded definition, but had somehow become an integral and precious part of her. When she tried to discard it—to chide herself for replacing her mourning for Robin with this new, adventurous thing—it somehow only nestled in deeper. When she tried to think of Robin now, it was always Robert standing next to him, the better man by far.

And each, as untouchable as the other.

THE ARCHBISHOP'S AID CAME in the form of a waif of a young woman, dirty and wide-eyed, clutching a young boy of similar description. Her name was Sarra Billinsgate—so the archbishop explained—and she had very recently escaped from the city.

"Nor is she the only one," he continued. "We've received a steady trickle of city refugees, who found us as soon as the army arrived. Most are, regretfully, being detained—for fear of inviting any of John's spies into our ranks. But I've spoken with this one personally, and am compelled to believe her."

The woman's breathing was short and strained, her grip on her son tight enough to leave a mark. Her neck was too skinny, her arms were nearly bone.

"See that she's fed," Marion ordered, crouching down to the balls of her feet, hoping to make a comforting face at the child. He buried his face away from her. "You're safe now, both of you. I know this must seem terrible—armies outside the city, and being detained. But I promise you you'll eat, and be protected, and that everything will get better from this point on. After all, King Richard is back!"

And about to siege your city.

If either reacted, it was with a nod so subtle it might as well have been nothing.

"Do you like it?" Robert smiled, flipping the end of his cape about, catching the boy's attention. "I could have one made for you, young sir. Would you like that?"

The boy looked to his mother, though still they said nothing.

"We understand the city gates are locked down, and no passage is permitted," Marion added. "We'd very much like to know how you got through them."

Sarra swallowed, perhaps to some pain. "I don't want to get anyone in trouble."

"Quite the opposite," Robert said. "If someone helped you get out, they may be able to help us get in. They may be the key to stopping this war before it begins."

After a look down at her son and a curt shake of her head, Sarra answered clearly. "They're called the White Hand. They're a gang, though that's not a very kind word for them. The Red Lions were all killed, and now there's a dozen gangs instead, the White Hand is one of them. Only they're trying to help people, help smuggle them out of the city."

"The *White Hand?*" Marion was surprised by the haunting phrase. "I don't suppose the name *Gilbert* means anything to you?"

Sarra seemed shocked to hear it. "That's him, he's their leader, yes. He's the one that led me and Hugh out."

Robert clearly sensed Marion's hesitation. "You know him?"

"Gilbert was part of Locksley, he stayed with us after the fire, but disappeared shortly after Robin joined us. He's something of a ghost story." She turned back to Sarra. "Did you see him? Did you talk to him? Tall, gaunt, and the glove?"

She nodded her head. "He's a good man, he was kind to us. His people leave their symbol throughout the city, a sign you can find for safety. There are caves under Nottingham, long tunnels, though you need a light to see. One reaches out far beyond the city gates, that's how he's been getting people out. So long as the prince's men don't see."

"Well this is only good news," Robert laughed. "We have a secret way into the city, run by a . . . friend? Or someone sympathetic, at least. Sarra, I know you've already been through more than anyone should have to endure, but could you do one thing more for your King? Could you lead us the way back to the entrance to this cave?"

She shook her head no before she had the bravery to say it, her mouth twisted hard to find some way to back out now. But even as she did, her son peeked out again, staring at Marion as hard as his little eyes could. His lips parted and a slight voice asked, "Are you Lady Marion?"

"I am." She smiled widely, though she was shocked to have been known. "You're a very smart boy, how did you know that?"

"We saw you last autumn," his answer came. "In Thorney. You were with Robin Hood."

"I was," she answered again, though her smile now was forced.

"There are a lot of Robin Hoods in the city now," he said, and gulped for air. "But everybody knows they're liars. Robin Hood's dead, isn't he?"

Unsure how to respond, Marion braved the truth. "He is."

"That's okay," the boy said matter-of-factly.

"Is it? Why is that?"

"Because you'll look after us."

Marion did an admirable job of not running very, very far away.

"I'll show you the entrance," Sarra said. "But not for your King. I'll do it for you."

"You're not going," Robert said, exactly one moment before she said the opposite.

"Of course I am," Marion answered. "It was my idea."

"You're not, it's too dangerous."

"Because I'm a woman?" Marion asked, shocked he would make the distinction. "You had no trouble taking me to Grafham."

"Because there wasn't going to be any killing there," he responded sharply. Behind him, the fields stretched far down the gentle hills to the city walls, above which the tiers of Nottingham Castle sat, climbing and wrapping around each other, daring them to come closer. The sky was full of heavy clumps of clouds, dark beasts turned brilliant gold at their edges. It would have been a perfect spring dusk if not for the promise of death that hovered around them.

Robert continued. "We will very likely have to kill a lot of people to get into that castle, so I can only afford to bring people who are very good at that. I already hate that we have to bring Arable along, but she's necessary. She knows the city, she knows the castle. She'll be enough."

"I know Gilbert, though, and she doesn't."

"Doesn't matter. Sounds like he's willing to help either way. You're staying here. Not because you're a woman, but because you're *you*."

"What is that supposed to mean?"

"You're *Lady Marion*, even that little boy knows who you are." He scratched at his cheeks, and shook his head. "You're too important to die in a cave under the city, or by some errant crossbow bolt in the middle of the fighting."

"I'm *too important*? You're an *Earl*, Robert, I'm just—"

"Stop it." He flinched and brought both his hands to his face, fidgeted, then they moved to her shoulders. As always, he didn't quite touch her, not quite. His palms hovered an inch away, he wouldn't cross that line. Which meant that it must have been her that moved first. In a moment her arms were around him, his hand on her jawline, drawing her in, her heart leapt into her throat, but he paused. Perhaps he was too breathless to continue, or perhaps he was aghast at the next boundary they thought they'd never cross. Perhaps waiting for her permission. Perhaps that's all he'd been doing that night in the tent.

But this time, the madness of all of it—*all of it*, the rebellion, and his damned insistence on facing an army on her behalf—it removed her every inhibition, her fingers found the laces of his doublet and she pulled him into her, thrilled that he met her just as forcefully, just as eagerly. His lips were thin, but confident, the stubble of his chin scratched her, and when his tongue parted her lips she lost herself, her fingers finding his hair, his elbow, she pulled his cape around her to be closer, to keep him, to keep him from going to the castle.

When they stopped to breathe, he touched his forehead to hers. "You're too important. And no, not just to me. You've started something, and you're going to see it through."

"What?" She couldn't keep track of what he was saying, continuing their conversation as if nothing had just happened. "You mean the council? It's over, it was a failure. King Richard is back."

"It wasn't a failure." His hands held her cheeks, he placed a single kiss on her brow, her eyelashes flicked against his skin. "You're the face of something now. And you're also King Richard's cousin. People were afraid to stand with you at the council, even though they knew you were right. Now that Richard's back, you're in favor again. People will . . . they'll kill just to be associated with you."

To be associated with you. There was a jealousy in those words, as if he found himself unworthy of such a role. "For what? I advocated for King John, who's now clearly a madman. I wanted to dethrone the Chancellor, whose reign is over now that Richard is back. What do they—"

"It doesn't stop there!" he said, his eyes imploring her. "You weren't just advocating that the Chancellor be controlled, you were advocating that *any* ruler be controlled. You convinced that room that even a king should have restrictions, that we can make an England where the people are not afraid of their rulers. Where those rulers are bound to follow the rules as well. And with a king like Richard at your side, *you can make that a reality.* You saw that. Before all our eyes, *you changed the King's mind.*"

"Barely—"

"Barely, yes, today. But tomorrow? That's why we can't risk you, Marion. You're tomorrow."

Suddenly the city and castle of Nottingham tumbled away from her feet. She was a thousand miles in the air and had no idea how she hadn't realized it. It was everything she'd been building on a small scale at Locksley, suddenly laid out before her, and all she had to do was grab the thread and keep pulling.

"So no, you don't get to risk your life crawling through a cave with me this afternoon. I'm not going to throw you over a horse and ride away like Amon did, but damn it—you have to start listening to the people you trust. Think of what Amon said to you. You're not allowed to sacrifice yourself anymore. He was right, Marion. This was your call, and we'll do it for you. You keep worrying about whether you can be anything like Robin Hood was, but you don't get it at all. Robin Hood was a king, yes, but king of his pond. But you, you're playing in the ocean. It's time that you act like it."

She felt her draw drop. She didn't feel like the *queen of an ocean.* She felt like a petty little girl who wanted the fleeting joy of kissing him again, without the guilt of what it meant for her memory of Robin, or for Robert's very living wife. She wanted to crawl into a tent with him and hide until the war was over, then crawl out and ask who had won. And the fact that she wanted these things, instead of the power—*she knew in her bones*—was the reason he was right.

"We'll bring you back the prince," he straightened, "or die trying. My lady."

FIFTY-SIX

ARABLE DE BUREL

NOTTINGHAM

ARABLE WAS REWALKING THE alleys of her own past, in every literal and metaphorical way she could fathom. Before her loomed the city of Nottingham and its castle—a chapter of her life to which she never wanted to return. Four months earlier she'd crossed this exact spot, horseback with John Little and Robin of Locksley, on a similar mission to sneak into the castle and stop the man in charge. They had stolen inside in the middle of the night, for reasons they all thought sickeningly noble at the time. Robin had died that night— she'd led him to his tomb.

Further back, sixteen years ago, her father might have shared this same spot, too. The parallels were nauseating. Then it was her father, Lord Raymond de Burel, leading his bannermen at the side of their earl, William de Ferrers, to siege Nottingham's Castle and *claim it for the king*. Now it was the daughter and the son of those same two misguided souls—Arable leading their group into the city, and the younger Ferrers at the charge to siege the castle. And *claim it for the king*.

Would that she could stand here, and whisper backward.

What went wrong? she might ask herself of four months ago. Had she learned anything from her failures that could keep her friends alive this time?

What went wrong? she might beg of her father, to know what she never would—what his final days had been like. Surging through the city streets, raising ladders over the castle walls. She would never know how he met his end, if it was with bravery or cowardice. Was it a quick blow to the head, or did he suffer? So it might go with his daughter, or any of them, slipping into a city that was ready to eat itself alive.

What was different? Was Arable insane to think any of it would go better this time? Or was she simply doomed to relive her own mistakes—and her father's—over and over again until one day she awoke to realize she'd been dead for a thousand years, trapped in some terrible purgatory?

No.

She was not the same woman who had fled Nottingham at the top of winter. Arable the servant had been the victim, fleeing. Lady de Burel had finally stopped running, ready to meet her enemies face on.

Or side by side. Lord Beneger de Wendenal crouched beside her by a ruined half wall, a divider between one field and the next. She found it easiest to accept his existence by remembering what had happened when last she was here. Since Arable was so good at bringing ruin to those around her, she could at least leverage that talent upon the one man who most deserved it.

They'd waited for dark, a waxing half-moon giving just enough light to guide their way. The bright fires and incessant clamor of Richard's armies was behind them, a gripping spectacle that was sure to attract every eye of the city's watchmen.

They were joined quickly by the two Delaney brothers, then Friar Tuck—eyes wide like a cat on ice. John Little had volunteered to come but their guide, Sarra, insisted he would never fit through the tunnels, and Tuck was the only one left who had ever known Gilbert. He kept his hood over his bald head, and he breathed short, shallow breaths, as if every hustle from hedgerow to hedgerow was the most daring act of his life. At their rear was Lord Robert, loping meaningfully through the barren fields, deep plow lines making obstacles of every step. Again he wore his half cape slung over one shoulder and carried a thin rapier rather than a proper sword, but somehow his intentions now seemed razor sharp rather than frivolous. His comfort actually took a bit of the edge off this wretched endeavor. Just before he reached the wall, he whipped out his blade and stabbed the air, letting loose a soft huff.

"Just in case," he said, throwing her a wink.

"That's enough of that." Lord Beneger made little attempt to lower his voice. "This is serious work."

"I know," Robert answered, reaching for something stashed in his belt. "That's why I brought my serious hat." The pointed thing went on, giving the silhouette of his head a single, fierce horn, aimed forward.

Nick Delaney snorted. "I hope this goes differently than Grafham."

"Of course it will," Robert replied. "For one, Simon de Senlis is *that* way," he pointed back to the army, then swiveled toward the city, "while we're going *that* way. So there's no way it can end the same way, is there?"

"Let's just hurry," Tuck said, his voice weak. "Sarra, please lead on."

The girl just stared at them, and for good reason. She was frightened out of her soul—she wanted desperately to be done with this task so she could return to her son. But she said nothing, simply dared a glance over the wall, then scurried sideways.

They followed her, staying low, keeping to the shadows if there were any available. They took every advantage of the low, god-angry clouds that wandered by and obscured the moonlight. There should have been watchmen here and there in the fields, keeping an eye out for raiders or wild dogs, but the farmlands were deserted. Now and then Arable saw abandoned tools, and she could only imagine their owner dropping them and fleeing at the sight of the encroaching army.

Horns sounded off to the north, repeated back to them after echoing against the city walls to the south. Lord Robert had requested as much, that the army make a ridiculous amount of noise this night. Not just to keep the city awake and alarmed, but as a distraction. To Arable, it felt like slipping around the outside of a great manor while a gala was being held within. She was almost embarrassed that she held a few of those memories at heart, that there was a time when her life had stakes smaller than the world.

Her belly lurched, and she had to slow. Her hands went to her side, as if she could calm her daughter inside—who was clearly no fan of her decision to run.

She had to pee, and hoped she would not get killed for something as stupid as that. She'd relieved herself before they'd left, but things like that apparently didn't matter at all to a pregnant body. She moved anyway, catching up, knowing that soiling herself would matter very little if she ended up dead.

Eventually they came to a cluster of trees that offered them privacy, and in the daylight it would have thrown its shade over a low stone well. Sarra scampered forward and touched the well's lip with her full palm, then turned back expectantly.

"This is it?" Lord Beneger asked, crouching to look down into its depths. The hole was hardly wide enough for a single person, if that was indeed where they were headed. Sarra had been right that John Little could not have gone any farther than this.

Her voice was a whisper. "There's a large crack just a bit down. It was hard to squeeze through, because of the angle, but it will open up after a dozen feet or so. Then it's a single long tunnel, most of the ways at least. I've shown you this far, I won't be much help beyond that."

"You've done more than enough." Robert reached out to her, but Sarra flinched away from his touch. She left without another word, fleeing back the way they came. She did not even bother to glance back at them.

"Poor soul," Robert said.

"She's probably thinking the same of us." Arable wished she were going that same direction.

"There will be more of her, if we fail at this," Beneger warned. "Wars only make three things—widows, orphans, and money."

"Money?" asked Tuck.

Beneger shrugged. "For the right side, at least."

"We can't risk a light until we're down there." Peetey was squinting into the well's mouth. "But I can't see anything. Which one of us is feeling the most nimble?"

At this Lord Beneger laughed, and cast a smug smile upon Robert.

"Alright," Robert submitted. "Someone hold my hat."

The going was slow, made even harder by the dark night, but Robert was able to suspend himself within the shaft of the well by sticking his feet out in opposite directions. They'd brought a good length of rope that Peetey anchored with his body, wrapped around Robert's waist in case he slipped. Eventually, after a good deal of pivoting and cursing, he claimed to find the crack Sarra had mentioned. A flurry of noise later, he found a way to slide himself into its shelf.

"It's small," he said, his voice muffled. "There are ... boards here? Planks. I need the light."

After a brief discussion they decided to risk it, hoping the light would be contained in the little cubby he'd found and not spill out to be seen like a beacon by the city watchmen. Nick lowered down one of their two iron lanterns, small things with walls of horn, and a single hinged door. The flint and candle were inside, and a small pouch of kindling, but what followed was a fairly laughable amount of time in which Robert tried, again and again, to get the flame to hold.

"We'll have a good view of the war, at least," Nick joked.

"We could just wait until a flaming arrow comes our way," Peetey followed, "and use that instead."

Eventually Robert found success and laughed at his failures, and the features of the well become immediately evident. It was not so far down to the water, and the south side indeed had a broken gullet where the stone had crumbled and exposed the bare earth behind it. In that crack was an open scar, curved diagonally, which seemed just wide enough for a human body to lean in—though uncomfortably at that.

"Not much of a tunnel." Tuck grimaced.

"So now maybe we can stop laughing at my fire-starting skills then," Robert answered. From his uncomfortable position, Arable was amazed he could do anything at all that required his hands. He pivoted the lantern to the other side of his body with some difficulty. "Looks like it's more of the same for a bit, then opens up. And I was right, there are some loose planks here . . ." again he twisted the shaft of light into the well's abyss, ". . . *there*. That's how they've been getting out."

Across from his opening was a slight ledge where the stones were uneven, marked by obvious scrapes across its lip. Repositioning himself, Robert manhandled the planks at his feet to reach across the gap and rest on that thin outcropping. They only barely held onto the stones by a fingerswidth or so, desperate to slip off and dunk a person into the well water below. Nick gave the first test by lowering himself as far as he possibly could before letting himself drop onto the planks, which bent but mercifully held his weight. Robert shimmied down the crack, and Nick followed, and one by one they crawled into the earth.

This is a nightmare, Arable told herself, letting her feet dangle over the edge. She didn't have the strength to suspend herself like the Delaneys did. This was no place for a woman in her condition. She eased her weight farther over the stone lip, her toes reaching out, desperate to find the wood before she was in free fall. But then she slid with a start and did not even have time to yelp. Her stomach lurched for a single hellish moment, but her feet touched the planks and Nick Delaney's arm was around her waist, and she'd never been more thankful.

"Are you alright?" he asked, with genuine concern.

"Oh, no," she answered, grabbing his arms with both hands. "That won't be an option for quite a while."

The crack's slant played with her senses. Losing all concept of balance, she had to slide on her back and shuffle her feet as if she were on the heavily banked edge of a cliff, excepting another cliff had already smashed into hers and was inches away. The sounds of her own breath and her heart were suddenly extremely close, and she tried not to think about the uncountable amount of earth lying above her, waiting to crush her like a pea. Nick kept his palm open for hers whenever he could, but soon he had to focus on himself instead.

Arable had been in storage caves and cellars before, but never anything like this. She felt like an insect navigating a tiny crevice between stones, and the air around her was suffocating. Her knees wobbled, but she forced herself forward.

Eventually it opened, the lantern was on the ground and played havoc with their shadows, and Arable fought to control her body. To her embarrassment she was shaking uncontrollably, and Nick sat her down to massage her shoulders and arms. Behind, Tuck sounded like he was having an even worse time of it than Arable had, but Peetey helped him through his every complaint. Once all six of them were in the little rock chamber, they caught their collective breath.

"I hope that was the hard part," Nick tried to laugh.

"We should move," Robert said, less joyful than he'd been earlier. "Even if they didn't see the light, we made a hell of a lot of noise. Swords hitting stone walls like that, that kind of sound travels."

"What if I stayed here?" Tuck suggested.

"Then you'd die *here* instead of *there*," Lord Beneger answered. "And in the dark."

That was enough for any of them. They lit the second lantern from the first, and made their way down a wormlike tunnel just barely too small for a person to ever stand upright. Again it was painfully slow going, given that there were only two lanterns for six of them, and the passage was unnavigable enough without the sickening sling of shadows tricking Arable's feet every second or so. The good news was that her daughter had already started reorganizing every one of Arable's internal organs, so the extra pain from stooping over was hardly even noticeable compared to the normal pain in her lower back. She tried to focus on her breathing, or her heartbeat, on anything she knew to be constant. Anything to avoid thinking of how much distance they actually had to cover in order to get past the city walls, and how little of it they had likely traveled so far.

There were forks now and then, which usually dead-ended quickly. They would send a single person down each one with a lantern for half a minute, crawling to check if it seemed viable. Generally, they decided that if a passage got smaller it was the wrong way, and if it got larger it must be the right one. Whether that was a good strategy or not, they couldn't tell. They traveled for what felt like forever, but was probably close to a full hour, and Arable ached viciously at all the hunching and squatting. There were times when they seemed doomed to wander the tunnels forever, and they began to question if they had somehow turned around and were backtracking on themselves. But eventually there came a larger chamber where they could at last stand up comfortably, stretch their agonizing muscles, and—apparently—get ambushed.

"Lotta noise yer making," came a female's voice. "Don't move, we've got crossbows."

Arable froze, certain of very little aside from the fact that she did not want to die down here. The proximity of the lanterns blinded them to anything beyond the ground immediately around them. Aside from the shift in echoes, there was no way of knowing how large this new chamber was, nor where the voice had come from. So the six of them stood motionless in their lone pool of light, a very easy target for whomsoever had been waiting in the dark.

"Are you with the White Hand?" Robert asked of the stranger, his hands raising gently in submission.

"Wow, you're bad at this," the voice returned with a slight laugh. "You *answer* the questions, we *ask* them, or else we shoot you with—"

"Who else is with you?" Beneger interrupted from the back of the group.

"I—what did I just say?"

"Gilbert?" Tuck stepped forward, making sure the light fell on his face. "Gilbert, are you out there?"

From slightly elsewhere a whistle pierced the room, made ever more hollow by the odd acoustics—such that it was almost impossible to tell where the sound ended and when the echoes had taken over. "Friar Tuck," came a soft, sonorous voice, unmistakably male but surprisingly delicate. "That is a surprise."

"Gilbert." The friar seemed relieved, though Arable could not say the same. From everything she had heard about the man, no one rested easier in his company. "Lady Marion sent us. She would have come herself, if she could. We know you've been smuggling people out of the city, and we need your help smuggling ourselves . . . *in*."

"What?" came the female's voice. "Why in God's crusty taint would anyone want to sneak themselves *into* Notts right now?"

"You'd have a point, Zinn," said Gilbert, "were these people anyone else. But I'll tell you once and once only—whatever they say, trust it as well as if I said it myself. They're good people."

"Fine." She seemed to shrug it off. "Don't matter much to me. By the way, we don't have no crossbows, we can't a-fucking-ford that."

Arable gasped when she saw him—mostly because he'd made no noise in traveling closer, but also because he chose to reach out with his single gloved hand first. Other than that, Gilbert's face was utterly normal, if a bit on the long and gaunt side. He exchanged a short shake with Tuck, which seemed a strangely friendly gesture compared to every rumor Arable had heard of the ghost man. He picked up the lantern and stepped back, aiming the light upon them. "I don't know your friends."

"I know. A lot has happened since you left," Tuck answered. "Hopefully there will be time enough for that later."

"Whacha mean to do in the city?" the girl named Zinn asked. She approached but stayed shy of the light, making it difficult for Arable to make out much more than her small frame. Just a thin little girl in tattered clothes, messing with the flop of her hair. Twelve, she guessed, both by her face and her attitude.

"Nothing," Robert answered. "But we need to pass through the city to get to the castle."

"Ooooh," Zinn shifted her weight side to side, "that's different. That's no small favor."

"I know the way into the castle," Arable explained. "But we don't know these caves. All we need is safe passage, and if you can help us get to the path to the postern gate without being seen, that would be helpful."

"No it wouldn't," Zinn returned with a satisfied smile, "because the postern's locked from the inside. There's only one way into the castle and we—*fucking hell!*" The girl suddenly spasmed and shoved Arable to the side, though she was not the target of the girl's anger. Tuck was elbowed aside just as carelessly, until Zinn stood nose to chest in front of Lord Beneger. A bright snap of the lantern reflected the blade she pulled from her belt—her right hand aimed it squarely at Beneger's breast, her other controlled a long coil of rope tied to the knife's handle.

"Steady now," was all Beneger said, backing into the curved cave wall.

"What's wrong?" Gilbert asked.

"I know this particular fuckface," Zinn snarled. "He works with FitzOdo. He's the one that nabbed Scarlet."

"*Will* Scarlet?" Arable gasped. "You know him? The same Will Scarlet?"

"I hope there aren't two of him," Zinn replied, but all her focus was on Beneger, who seemed rightfully wary of the knife at his heart. "I was just starting to like him when this royal dick fucker trapped us, nearly got me killed. He threated to let his men gang-rape me if Scarlet didn't turn himself over. But he did. Will Scarlet traded his life for mine."

Arable stared at Lord Beneger's sallow face. She had not previously thought it possible to hate the man any more.

"For what it's worth," Beneger said, carefully, "I did not personally make that threat. I was held at knifepoint—as I am now—and one of my men . . . well, a woman, actually, made that threat."

Arable didn't care. "*She's a child.*"

"No I'm not!" Zinn snapped. "But if I was, I'd be the child that's gonna fucking gut you."

Robert and the Delaney brothers both tensed, as if sensing the need to step in and stop her. Arable's instincts were more in line to help her push the blade in.

"Is Will Scarlet still alive?" Arable asked. "What about Arthur, and David?"

"I don't know," Zinn answered. "Haven't seen any of them since that day."

"Nor I. But you made the right choice to walk out of that room." Beneger paced his words slowly, his eyes locked on Zinn. "I don't know those other two, but Will Scarlet is as bad as they come. He's responsible for beating and butchering poorfolk across the city—oh, and killing noblemen in the woods. I saw what was left of Lord Brayden's wife with my own eyes. He's a monster. You dare throw the word *rape* at me, when you work with *him?*"

This was deeply troubling news, to say the least. Obviously Will was capable of rash acts, but Arable had a hard time believing the rest of it.

Zinn, apparently, was of similar mind. "He's not like that. The noblefolk in the woods were his, yes," Zinn said. "Though he said he just killed 'em. Didn't say anything else."

"Are you so sure that you know him? And what of Gilbert here, is he a blushing innocent as well?" Beneger addressed the White Hand directly. "Care to explain why you're away from your post, Guardsman?"

Another whirl of reactions. "Is that true?" Tuck asked, his face in bunches. "Gilbert, you joined the Nottingham Guard?"

"I did," his chilling voice whistled, "though my time with them is over. As for your other accusations, your aim is off. The mutilations in the French Ward, the attack at St. Peter's, the fire at the brothel . . . those were the work of Sir Robert FitzOdo, not Will Scarlet."

The name was vaguely familiar to Arable, but it apparently meant something more to Beneger. "Odo?"

"He'd been disguising himself as Robin Hood at night and doing such things, in his name, as it were. To get the people to turn against him."

Beneger's eyes narrowed. "What makes you think that?"

"I watched him do it." There was a quality to those words that Arable could not define, almost as if Gilbert had enjoyed doing so. "Maybe you would have seen it, too, if you hadn't been watching me instead. Wasn't my business, as it were, until recently. He's here in the city, and fancies himself something important. So I took his favorite toy and sliced it up as a warning, as a trap."

"His favorite . . . toy?"

"Some would call him a man."

Beneger huffed. "Derrick? Or Ronnell?"

"Probably."

Beneger shook his head, but his face betrayed his doubt. "If any of that were true, I would have known. He was under my command."

Gilbert did not seem to care at all if Beneger believed him. "We have another Guardsman with us, he'll vouch for the truth."

"Who is that?"

"His name is Quillen."

Another gasp from Beneger. "*Quillen's* with you?"

"Only very recently. FitzOdo tried to kill him, so we rescued him."

"So are you still . . . wait," Tuck stammered, clearly confused. "Whose side are you on, then?"

Gilbert smiled, his pupils utterly black. "Oh, Friar. As uncreative as ever."

"Alright, wait!" Robert held his hands out wide, begging for a moment of respite. "I don't know anything about any of you, but it seems pretty clear that none of you know anything about each other, either. There are seemingly sixteen thousand things that all of you need to discuss, and every one of you apparently hates each other, or at least *this guy*," he thumbed Beneger, "and I can't keep up with any of it. But the truth is that it doesn't matter, none of it matters, not a damned inch. There's a war out there, and come morning that army is going to storm through the city and smash it to pieces, and we're the only ones in a position to put a stop to it. We need to get into the castle, and you can all settle everything else once that's all over with."

"Zinn," Arable said, before anyone could contradict Robert. "I hate this man as much as you, probably more so. There's nothing I'd like to see more than you slam that knife straight into his heart. He ruined my entire life, my entire family. But Lord Robert is right. There's more at stake than revenge right now, and Lord Beneger is well known amongst the Nottingham Guard. He'll be instrumental in our ability to get what we need once we're inside the castle. He's respected, while the rest of us are . . . well, we're Robin Hood's gang, and that's how we'll be treated. So please, put that knife down. I've been where you are, I've been wronged and threatened and abused, and I can promise you one thing . . ."

Zinn hesitated, raising a crooked eyebrow at her.

Arable finished, "Payback feels just as good tomorrow as it does today."

After a bit of hesitation, her knife retreated. Tempers settled, and they all tenuously agreed to tiptoe around any conflicts they'd brought with them. They took a few minutes to catch up Zinn and Gilbert on the happenings outside, and of King Richard's return. The prospect of stopping the war before it began seemed to make a difference, and Zinn suddenly became a bit more co-operative.

"Alright, there's only one way into the castle right now," she said. "There's a tavern called the Trip to Jerusalem, built into the base of the sandstone the castle stands on. There are some tunnels in the back that worm up into the rock. Not sure if they actually go all the way up to the castle, but that's the theory. An' anyone bigger'n me'll have a hard time squeezing through."

"You've seen these yourself?" Robert asked.

"Sure as shit," she said, nodding. "My street crew was responsible for clearing them out."

"Then why don't you know if they go all the way up?" Lord Beneger asked.

"Not my fault!" Zinn snapped. "We could only get into the Trip when the greenbeard would let us, which wasn't often. Lions made a deal with him, trading mead and money—his inn gets a little edge, and the Lions got access to his tunnels. But they were small as shit, and needed to be dug out before anyone could use them."

"Which meant," Beneger probed, "you needed more and more mead?"

"Right. At first it was small stuff—smashing up other taverns on the days mead came into port so no one else would buy any, things like that. But that wasn't reliable. Red Fox hated that small shit, he wanted a big fix. Decided to blackmail the city dockmaster to get first access to all imports, and my crew was supposed to get information on him. But we got nothing."

Beneger smiled. "So you threatened him instead."

"We tried to," Zinn sneered, "until you interrupted us, and nabbed Will Scarlet."

"Don't blame that on me, girl," he replied. "One of your own sold you out."

"Stop it!" Arable interrupted. She was having enough trouble following without them ready to go at each other's throats again. "What matters is that the tunnels can only *probably* get us into the castle?"

The group exchanged uneasy looks. "We'll have to take our chances," Robert offered.

"Still, not as easy as that." Zinn's tone shifted into something smaller. "You got two problems to deal with 'fore you get there. First is that FitzOdo figured it out, too, and took over the Trip a few weeks back. Cunt. Don't know if he's tried to use the tunnels or not, big ol' ox, but he's guarding them. So if you're aiming into the castle, you have to go through him. And since FitzOdo was working for the good lord *dick fucker* here," she aimed her knife's tip at Beneger's chest, "there's no way we're letting them get close to each other."

"Oh, you don't have to worry about that," Beneger said. "If what you said about FitzOdo is true, I'll be the first one to put that damned dog down."

Arable had no qualms with any plan that put Beneger into dangerous places with people that wanted to kill him. "What's the second problem?" she asked.

Gilbert took this one. He smiled again, the lantern light turning the tips of his lips into a twisted devil's grin. "Why, you were followed."

FIFTEEN MINUTES LATER, GILBERT led them down a series of tunnels they had almost definitely been in before, ending in a large chamber lit with braziers and filled with furniture—practically a full tavern beneath the city's surface. There were only a few people lingering there, mostly as young as Zinn or younger. On a few of the craggy walls, a large white hand had been hastily painted.

"Used to be the Red Lions' main den," Zinn explained when Arable asked, "but they all decided to get dead, or join with someone else."

"Their leaders, at least," Beneger confirmed. "Prince John killed them at the archery tournament."

"Oh, that was all the prince's idea, was it?" Zinn twisted and gave him a squint of her face. "You didn't have *anything* to do with that, didehu?"

She purposefully swung his sword in a clumsy arc and let it bang against the ground. He had surrendered his weapon to her as proof of his good intentions, and she'd opted to use it as a walking cane—taking every opportunity to smash its edges into rocks for the delight of seeing him wince at its abuse.

Gilbert explained that they'd been going in the wrong direction in the tunnels before he'd stopped them, and might have been lost for a day trying to navigate the tunnels on their own. "We first noticed you crossing the fields," he explained. "We keep one lookout watching that well from the city, just in case it's compromised, as it were. It's the only opening we've found outside the city walls. Don't worry, I don't think the city guard saw you. We just happen to know where to look. Which is why we thought it odd when we noticed someone following you at a distance."

Someone had followed them, entering through the well and finding a better path into the city than they had, only to be caught by the "Children of the White Hand" here.

Gilbert climbed to another jagged shelf that split the middle of the curious underground chamber. There was no proper place to cage someone down here, so the captive was left to sit on the floor, his hands and feet both bound together and then to the iron foot of a nearby brazier that was too uncomfortably hot to be near. The man was skinny, had disheveled brown hair and large eyes with bags beneath them . . .

"Charley Dancer!" Nick Delaney shouted with relief. "What'd you follow us for?"

"He's with us, you can cut him free," Robert quickly added.

But Arable was lost, in his features . . .

"Don't touch him!" she shouted, before anyone could follow Robert's command. She crouched down on the balls of her feet to look him in the face, and a resigned look overwhelmed him as he realized his long deception was finally over.

"What is it?" Tuck asked.

She sucked in air. "His name's not Charley."

Arable's mind reeled to figure it out. She had thought it strange that she'd never actually met Charley Dancer during their time in the Sherwood, but John Little had dismissed it as a quirk of them both preferring their own privacy over the group. She'd thought that the frogman hated her—blamed her for their group's trouble—and she'd been content to let him always skulk away from her presence, dismissing him entirely. Ever since they made it to Huntingdon, she'd spent most of her time in the castle while the group camped by the Cook's Backwater . . . but even that wasn't enough to explain it. No, "Charley" must have put a massive effort into making sure they never interacted—for she surely would have turned him in for who he was, if ever she'd bothered to look past his beard and into the eyes of a man she'd known, when she was still a servant in Nottingham Castle.

The betrayal of it was sharp, sharper than every other reason they all had to kill each other. She felt invaded, lied to—and whether this defensiveness was just part of the changes in her body, she didn't care. She was one breath away from grabbing the sword from Zinn's hand and cutting this impostor in two.

The prisoner smiled sheepishly, a wide grin she'd seen a hundred times, mocking her utter ignorance of how long he had deceived her, right under her nose. His emotion made a choking seize in his throat that had always been his version of laughter.

"Hi, Bellara," he said, recalling their old game together.

She wasn't interested in playing with the Guardsman. "Hi, Bolt."

FIFTY-SEVEN

ARTHUR A BLAND

NOTTINGHAM CASTLE

"HOLY, HOLY, HOLY SHIT." Arthur hugged Will Scarlet close the very instant the tunnel down to the prisons gave them any privacy. He was too exhausted to laugh—it had been damned difficult to keep a straight face for the last day, pretending they didn't know each other. David's arms wrapped around them both, he squeaked in celebration.

"*'Holy shit?'*" Will choked, his joy muffled by their embrace. "Since when do you believe in holy anything?"

"I believe in holy fucking everything now," Arthur answered, happy to pray to any god Tuck wanted him to pray to. "There's no other way to explain any of this."

If the sky had opened up and rained goats down on them, it wouldn't have been half as strange as the last day. After discovering Will was the bailey-king, Arthur and David became the official envoys between him and the Nottingham Guard. Their insurmountable task was to broker a peace in the lower bailey—which was actually the easy part. Because at the same time, they had to ensure that nobody in the Nottingham Guard discovered that *Henry Russell* was an invented name, and that Will Scarlet had never made it to his gaol cell. He'd altered his appearance as much as possible—gathered his hair into a tail that sprouted from the top of his head, and covered his face in red streaks from the archery paint buckets—but there were certainly some Guardsmen like the Lace Jackal who might recognize him on closer inspection, as Arthur had. So they'd claimed that *Henry Russell* refused to deal with anyone besides Arthur and David, turning the two of them into goddamned heroes amongst the Nottingham Guard.

Meanwhile, Arthur and David's real identities as Will's old crew had to remain hidden to most of Will's new crew, or else the truce would hold no water. Some of Will's rebels had been Red Lions and understood the absolute fucking insanity of their situation—but for the others, Will had to pretend they were indeed insolent *gords* that he obviously hated and would rather kill than give a damned peace treaty.

The three of them juggled all those secrets with straight faces, pretending to yell at each other in front of the others, keeping up a ruse of hostility to satisfy both sides' need for aggression. It was a joke beyond anything Arthur had ever kept before. Through it all, they hammered out a truce. Of course, the arrival of the French army outside the city walls made that part easier.

Everyone was on edge, and the preparations for a siege were in full swing.

The necessity of the truce—and the Guard's willingness to do anything to unite the bailey—was the only reason the three of them were allowed *here*—back into the middle bailey, and down into the catacombs of the gaols beneath the castle. At the entranceway, they stole the first opportunity to finally talk amongst themselves freely.

"*Holy holy holy shit . . .*" and so on.

"We thought you were dead!" David exclaimed, shaking Will by the shoulders. "Second time you've done that to us, I'll have you know."

"I probably should be," Will admitted with a smile. "They knocked me out cold when they arrested me. Locked me in a cage in the gatehouse so they wouldn't be late for the archery tournament. If I'd made it down here," he thumbed the gates that led below, "well . . . that'd be something else."

David whistled a sad note.

"Not gonna lie," Will continued, "wasn't sure you'd be so happy to see me."

Arthur opened his mouth to answer, but didn't. After everything that had gone so fucking wrong in the last month, he'd practically forgotten about the fight he'd had with Will. Over a barmaid's finger. A *finger* seemed a damned small thing to worry about now.

"Well," Will finished, despite their hesitation, "I was damn glad to see you two."

"My fault, that you got captured," Arthur said, surprised at how much he needed to get it off his chest. "You were right, Will, I should have done what you asked."

"Fuck that," he replied. "I shouldn't have asked it. Breaking arms for the Red Lions? Look at where it got them."

"Not just that." Arthur scratched at his beard, knowing he'd regret it if he didn't say it. "I found information on that fop with the velvet hat, but I didn't give it to them. You never would have been set up like you was, if I'd just done as I was told."

Scarlet's eyes flicked back and forth, his breath held. Arthur steeled himself for a punch in the jaw—he deserved it. Maybe worse.

"We stayed, for you," David added, probably trying to help. "When we heard you were captured, we thought . . . well we didn't do anything, but we thought about it."

Eventually, Will touched the tunnel walls beside him, gently. "Listen. Nobody's fault but mine what happened to me. And we all came out alright, didn't we?"

Arthur had to laugh. Nothing about their situation could really be called *alright,* but there was admittedly plenty of room still for it to get worse.

"So who's Henry Russell?" David asked.

"Just a name. Needed something generic. You two kept your own names?"

"We did . . ." Arthur shrugged. "Wasn't feeling very creative."

"How the hell'd you sneak in with the gords?"

"Same way you did last year," he answered, though he was surprised at his new aversion to the word *gords.* "Stole a tabard and waltzed into the castle."

"Good on you." Will seemed impressed. "And you didn't kill the Sheriff afterward? Not even once?"

"No, that's how they caught you, remember?" David poked his chest. "We decided to do the opposite of that, and it worked out pretty well."

"Huh." Will wobbled his head. "I'll try that next time."

Looking down the maw of the prison tunnel, Arthur jangled the key ring in his hand. One of those keys, which the captain of the Guard had placed squarely in his palm, would unlock the gate before them. If he'd known, when choosing sides in the Sherwood Forest months earlier, that he'd end up joining the Nottingham Guard and being trusted with the keys to the fucking city . . .

"How many are down there?" David asked.

"Most of the Red Lions," Will answered. "They were picked up pretty quickly in the riots, and moved down to the gaols. With Alfie and Cait gone, they'll follow me. Especially if I'm the one that sets them free."

Arthur was uneasy at the thought, but they needed every able-bodied man they could get. The final deal of their fake negotiations was to open the prisons. Captain de Grendon needed every man in Nottingham to fight in her defense, so he conceded that *Henry Russell* and his men would be forgiven of any crimes if they joined forces against the French. That included everyone who'd been arrested in the riots as well. So here they were, ready to release all the *Robin Hoods* and sympathizers and the like who'd been held captive this last month, to arm them with swords and shields and stand them before the French army.

It was going to be a hell of a time.

Arthur grasped the key, enjoying its cold edge. "That's good. We'll need them."

"It'll give them a fighting chance at least." Will grimaced. "But we can probably get a dozen Lions, maybe more, to join with us. That I can guarantee. Then we can make a break for it."

Arthur fingered the iron key between his thumb and forefinger. "What do you mean?"

"We've been building a rope ladder, hidden under the rubble of the spectator stands. When the fighting starts, we can probably get to the south wall." Will nodded his head. "Sling it over, and get the fuck out of here."

There was a small nick in the key halfway down its shaft, Arthur's thumb graced over it over and over. The callus on his finger was too thick for the sharp metal, but again and again he rubbed his flesh over the barb. Someday, a dozen years from now, when this key broke in a lock, it would start at that little nick.

"What about the army?" Arthur asked, staring at their own bootprints in the dirt.

"They're mostly to the north. Even if they see us, I don't think they'll worry about us," Will laughed. "But all the same, faster we get away from them, the better."

The key ring felt heavier now, he had to hold it with both hands.

"And the city?" David asked.

"Dawn Dog told me there's tunnels that go past the walls. So if we get him, or any of the other Lions who know about it, we're golden."

Will wasn't answering the right questions.

"We made this deal . . ." Arthur paced his words out, not sure he wanted to reach the end of this thought, what would happen when he got there, ". . . so that we can get these people out of gaol, and help defend the castle."

"Exactly! Which most of them will do." Will smiled. "They'll never notice we're gone."

Arthur sighed. "Will, don't you think . . ." he glanced up to David, whose worried features gave him the strength to keep going, ". . . don't you think this is bigger than us now?"

He might as well have been speaking another language. Will's face twisted, as if he literally couldn't understand the words.

"There's a French army out there," Arthur continued. "They're trying to sack the city, siege the castle, and kill Prince John. And if they do it . . . there's no more England. The throne goes to Arthur. He's got a good name, admittedly . . ." he earned a laugh from David with that, ". . . but he's a child, a ward of the French. This is . . . this isn't about us and the Sheriff or the Guard or any of that bullshit anymore. This is everything, Will."

Will Scarlet squinted back, as if he'd misunderstood. "This is *everything*? There's '*no more England*'? What are you talking about? They're not going to . . . sink the whole country into the ocean! God's heel, the world will not collapse in on itself. All it means is that somebody else will own all the castles we never get invited to anyway, so it'll be somebody else that hates us instead of the current people who hate us. They're not going to rampage the lands and kill every Englishman. They're just going to tax us. That's not exactly a big difference."

David shuffled his feet. "But Prince John, he's the rightful heir . . ."

Muffled sounds floated up from the tunnel on the other side of the gate, still locked. Will ignored them. "What do you care about Prince John?"

"Nothing, but I . . . I care that we're not ruled by the French."

"Why?" Will's eyes were wary now. "Because everything was so good before? Hell, maybe the French will run it better."

Arthur winced. "Are you serious?"

"I don't know." Will shrugged it off. "But neither do you, that's the point. We can't control any of this. Look at all these people, all these armies ready to start off against each other. You think a dozen of us can stop that? No. I don't want to get killed in someone else's war. Doesn't matter if it's the French or the English who win. You know—you *know*, deep down—nothing's going to change. *Nothing*. It doesn't matter who's on top, it's always shit for the people on the bottom. A little bit of chaos might even help us, people like us can ride that shit. Look. *Look*. We came to Nottingham to recruit some men. You kept on complaining that we weren't doing that, and *now we can*. The Red Lions will follow me now—they'll have to!—their city's about to be destroyed! We get out of Nottingham, we go find the others. We win. It's everything we wanted."

Everything we wanted.

Arthur didn't have a clue what that meant anymore.

He looked at his old friend, wondering what that path meant. What it meant to pursue a selfish victory. This was Will Scarlet, his hair plumed out like a peacock, red paint cracking over his face, the gruesome nub of his mutilated ear exposed to the world. The scar across his chest from Zinn's rope dart, visible under his open neckline. The memory of Elena haunting him everywhere he went. This was the collection of things he'd gathered to *get what he wanted.*

Anyone who follows him is going to drown.

Arthur had his scars, too, the wide crusty gash that still wept across his forehead, but he'd never regretted it. The wound he'd received for trying to help someone else, instead of himself.

And the other scars, the far far worse scars, where his skin was smooth and healthy. The *absence* of scars, that he might have earned while helping someone who needed him. The bruises he should have earned, if he'd refused to break that cobber's face. The broken bones he might have taken if he'd fought *for* people rather than stand idly by. The woman who cried on the other side of the wall. The many, many messages over the battlements. The times when he looked away, or said *"not my problem."*

Arthur still had skin to scar, which meant he hadn't yet done enough.

"A lot of people are going to die," he said.

"So we should aim not to be one of them—"

Arthur raised his hand, begging a moment to collect himself. "Listen, I've never thought much about myself. Not in any important way, you know? I'm just . . . I'm just trying to get from one thing to the next, and not be too miserable along the way. Found a couple of people I like, and consider myself lucky for it." He met eyes with David, whose every strained wrinkle spoke to his same struggle. "I thought we could just skitter through life, keep our heads down, and let the bigger things be handled by bigger people. But, *fuck.* I mean, just look at us.

Both Will Scarlet and his peacock hair looked back.

"Will, you organized a hundred people in the middle of *madness,* to defend themselves, with everything against you. With nothing but a fake name. Just your personality, you literally became king! Me and David . . . you know, we just decide to do the right thing every now and then, and somehow people follow us. We suddenly stand out in the Guard because we're willing to put ourselves out there. It doesn't take . . . heroes, you know? It just takes someone who's willing to do the work. Because there's so many people out there who won't take that step, who would rather be in the background, because they think other people will handle it. Well guess what, *we're those other people.* We're fucking . . . we're fucking *capable,* you know?"

It might have actually taken that long for Will to realize where this was going. "Are you saying you want to stay? You want to actually fight in this war?"

"No," Arthur said. He absolutely did not want that. "But I'm saying we *should*."

"Will, you can go, if you want," David added quickly, his voice weak. "I get it. You've been through hell, Will. The Nottingham Guard captured you, you've had it worse than us down there. And if anyone recognizes you, I mean, you killed the Sheriff, you can't risk that. I get it. But they're not . . . bad. The guards. They're just people. And they're on the shit end of everything, too. And the people in the city . . ."

"They need us," Arthur finished his friend's thought.

The messages they'd passed. The lives disrupted, ruined, thrown upside down, or lost entirely. People who needed the strength of others to protect them, and who were let down. Women, and children, trapped in the bailey—now carrying a sword and shield they had no idea how to use, waiting for the French wave to break through. These weren't the people who ought to be in charge of defending their city. Like it or not, that job was for people like Arthur.

"I'm good at smashing things, Will. Damn it, I'm exactly where I'm supposed to be. This city is going to be wrecked. We can help that. I don't know if we'll make a difference, I don't know if it'll matter once all hell breaks loose, but I know what'll happen if we're *not* here."

"Honestly, I'm thinking of Zinn," David said, with no embarrassment. "Girl like her, pro'ly never knew her parents, she's grown up unloved and unwanted, and she's had to scratch her way for every little thing she has. That little wooden hovel of hers, full of knick-knacks, that's her *life*. An army's about to march right through it, going to destroy everything she has . . . and we're thinking about walking away? I bet you she'll be out there with that little knife whip of hers, doing everything she can, pro'ly get skewered in a heartbeat, because she loves this city. While we'll be . . ." David's voice caught, ". . . what, sneaking out the back door?"

"And the same goes for these prisoners we're about to release," Arthur added, looking down past the bars, fingering that same nub on the key until it hurt. "Those Red Lions, especially. I didn't like them at first, but *damn,* they love this city. You're going to try to convince them to leave and watch it burn? I don't think they'll follow you."

David nodded. "And frankly, we need them here."

"Alright."

"So if you want to go, we can . . ." Arthur didn't even register that Will had agreed.

"Alright," he said again, nodding his head. "You're right."

Arthur blinked away some piece of shit wetness that'd come to his eyes. "Really?"

"Yeah." Will reached up and tugged at the leather tie, letting his hair gently fall back on both sides of his face. "I'm just making this up as I go along. I'm in no rush to go back to Marion. Hell, I don't think I'm interested in that at all. I miss John, and Arable, but . . . that's it. But if we're not going there, then I don't know what else the plan would be anyway. So maybe it's this. Why not."

"You'll stay, too?" David asked, rubbing his cheeks. "Not worried you'll be recognized?"

He shrugged. "We'll figure it out."

Arthur was relieved, of course, but he had to ask. "What about . . . what do you mean you've been making it up as you go along?"

That smile. "That's the only thing I've ever been good at."

"Yeah, but—" He glanced at David to check that he was equally confused. "You always said you had a plan, that we were going to rally your forces . . . raise gangs across the county . . . live like kings. You sold us on that, you said you knew what you were doing."

Will's lips clamped together, his hands flopped down, his body sagged. "Yeah, well. I mean, what do you want me to say? I wanted to do those things, yes, but no there was never a *plan*. The plan was to figure it out."

If there were time to do so, Arthur would have mourned that. Mourned the man that he once thought Will Scarlet was. The man he'd believed in, and argued for. He bit it off. There was no point in wasting time with disappointment now. After the war, if any of them survived, he'd deal with whether or not his future and Will Scarlet's were still the same thing. But he'd spent the better part of a day convincing people with far greater differences that it was time to rally together, and he'd be the first fool to think that didn't apply to him, too.

So he clapped Scarlet on the shoulders. "I think you ought to just go stand on the curtain wall in front of the army, and cut your other ear off," he said with a smile. "And yell out, *if I can do this to myself, what you do think I'm going to do to you?*"

Will laughed. "Well, I don't know French. So they might just think I'm insane."

"You think they'll figure it out that fast?" David asked, finally relaxing.

They each chuckled, but that laughter died at the sound of far-off horns. Not one or two horns, not a few riders announcing an approach, no. This started as a dozen, then joined by a dozen more, then doubled again, and again. A hundred horns in a hundred notes—more, a thousand maybe—all joining together raucously, jumping on each other, and beneath it a roar unlike anything Arthur had ever heard. Like a flock of birds taking flight, but trapped in a box. The sound of the French army rising, laughing, delighting in their ability to put everyone in the castle on edge. The horns didn't die down but moved in waves, joined by others as the previous wave settled. There would be no sleep this night, the invaders would see to it.

And come morning, blood.

Arthur put the iron key into the hole. They would need every man, every damned one.

FIFTY-EIGHT

ARABLE DE BUREL

NOTTINGHAM CITY TUNNELS

"I SWEAR, I CAME to help," lied the man who wasn't Charley Dancer.

"He's a Guardsman." Arable fumed, the world had shrunk such that she could see nothing but Bolt's face, hidden beneath his ragged long hair and thin beard. Later she might realize that she had become the sole focus of the cavern, drawing the interest of every single one of Gilbert's followers toward the brazier. But for now all she saw was a traitor. "Not just *any* Guardsman, he was part of Captain Gisbourne's private regiment. He's lying to you."

"I've never lied about it," Bolt answered. The muscles in his face spasmed, as if he hoped to blink out of existence. "I just never told anyone neither."

"Arable, are you sure?" came Tuck's voice, and his hand found her shoulder. "Charley's been with us since . . . well, since before you. He was one of the first to join after Bernesdale, which was . . . four or five *months* ago. He's been with us all through the winter, he's starved with us, he's helped us survive. If he were some sort of spy . . . are you sure?"

"He joined with *us*," Peetey added, nudging his brother. "He found us in Bernesdale. That'd be a long time to keep up a lie."

"Arable." Tuck almost laughed at it. After all, what was one woman's certainty against three men's opinions? "Are you *sure*?"

She twisted to give him a lifetime's worth of spite. "*Ask me if I'm sure again.*"

His eyes shrunk into his skull, and the friar retreated.

"I've never seen him before," Gilbert said idly, crouching down to inspect Bolt like he was some intriguing species of insect. "And I was in the Black Guard."

"Well *I* haven't seen *you* before, either," Bolt eyed Gilbert up and down, "but I'm not calling *you* a liar. When did you join? After I left?"

Gilbert's voice grew curious. "Four or five months ago. Just after Bernesdale." His eyes widened. "Do you suppose we traded lives?"

"Charley, is this true?" Lord Robert asked. "You were a Guardsman? You don't deny that?"

"I don't." His neck pulled in like a turtle. "And honestly—*honestly*—you're right to be suspicious. When I volunteered, I meant to hide who I was. I wanted revenge."

"Revenge?" Beneger perked up, his favorite word spoken.

Bolt nodded. "Robin Hood killed my best friend."

"Reginold." Arable had been there at the funeral pyre, along with most of the castle. Reginold of Dunmow and his so-called *little brother* Bolt had once been her favorite friends in the Nottingham Guard. They'd welcomed her and included her in their games, they'd flirted playfully—they'd been *kind*. Before de Lacy was killed, before William had returned, before all this. Before all *this*. Before the Nottingham Guard turned on her, before Gisbourne abused her, tricked her, used her. *But Reginold had died before all that,* she remembered, *and Bolt had left immediately after the pyre.*

He looked at her, his face soft, his mouth twisted into a knot and pulled away. "I left the Guard after Reg died. I didn't know what to do. I just . . . wandered for a bit, but I knew what I wanted. I wanted to kill whoever killed him. And I didn't care if I had to die to do it. I didn't have anyone else, you know, Reg was the only one who ever looked after me. I went to Bernesdale, where we'd been ambushed. We'd just been guarding the road and Reg went off to take a shit, and then some boy jumped out of nowhere. As soon as I moved to find him, someone hit me in the back of the head. When I woke up, they told me that Reg was dead. His head was smashed in, he was laying in his own shit."

"I remember you," Tuck said, shock in his voice. "Much distracted you, and . . . and I think Will knocked you out? I don't remember anyone dying, though. I forget who went after the second guard . . . Arthur, probably?"

"Well, it happened." Bolt's face was a simple slough. "And when I went back, I found the Delaney brothers. Them and a few others who were talking about finding Robin Hood and joining him, and that was that."

Peetey, rightfully, appeared to be mortified by that knowledge.

"Are you trying to make it worse for yourself?" Zinn laughed at Bolt. "I think he's making it worse for himself."

"But I didn't *do anything*." Bolt coughed, pulling against his restraints. "I thought Robin Hood's gang would be full of evil . . . murderers, and monsters, you know? But they weren't. They were just *people*. And I'll admit it, I'll *admit it*, at first I only idled my time because I didn't know who killed Reg, and I wanted to be sure. I couldn't exactly just ask everyone about it. Not to mention that when Arable joined, I had to hide half the time, keep to the edges, not let her get a good look at me. But the longer I stayed, the more . . . I don't know. The less I wanted to do it. And eventually the friends I made became real, and I found that I cared. And I tried to help. Like I'm trying now."

Arable laughed at his attempt at sympathy. "You want us to believe you just—what, *changed your mind?*"

"Yes." His wide face folded. "Is that so impossible? Didn't you do the same?"

"What?"

"You lived in the castle, you were friends with the Sheriff, and they trust *you*. Why can't the same be true with me?"

"I didn't lie to them!" she answered, shocked he was pretending their situations were equitable. "I was up front with everything, and still they didn't trust me! Most of them still don't. While you sneak in, under false pretenses, you lie about your name, you lie about—"

"Charley's my real name," he interrupted her. "Reg called me Bolt, and it stuck, but my name's Charley Dancer. Always has been."

She had no response.

"You said you were in the Captain's Regiment, too?" Bolt motioned up to Gilbert. "But now you're helping them? What's the difference? What does it matter who I was before I came to join you? Aside from the fact that I can *help you*, it's why I followed you! I know this city, I know the castle, I probably even know the Guardsmen you'll come across. I volunteered to come originally but Lord Robert said no, on account of my leg, so I followed you instead. Figured you couldn't turn me away once I was here. I'm not just a cripple, I'm not trying to kill you. I just want to help."

The rest of the group, too, was at a loss.

Zinn leaned close to Arable. "The leg didn't tip you off?" she asked at half breath.

"More than one person in the world can have a limp," she defended herself, but it was an embarrassing oversight. Perhaps her time with Bolt had normalized the affliction so much that she hardly even noticed it in Charley.

"I never loved the Guard," he continued. "It's just where I ended up. I grew up in the streets. When the war came sixteen years ago, I ended up in the wrong place—in between the castle walls and the army. I climbed the siege ladders just to keep from being trampled. I jumped off on the other side and broke my leg, but Reginold found me, he protected me, and he took me under his wing. He was the only reason I stayed. Once he was killed . . ." His sentence drifted away, he bit at his lip and fought back tears.

If Arable did not feel so very betrayed, she might have been swayed by it. *But might it be the truth?* Could he really have spent so long with them if he still meant to do them harm? Would he have suffered for so long, when there had been so many opportunities to turn against them?

"Why did you hide from me?" she asked. "If you'd had a change of heart, as you say, why not reveal yourself? You're only telling the truth now because you've been caught."

His lips trembled, his fingers reached forward, his froglike face stretched and contorted, and when he finally spoke it was with great difficulty. "Why didn't *you* tell me who *you* were?"

She had not expected that. "What?"

"You hid your name, too, in Nottingham, didn't you?" he squeaked. "I thought you were just a servant girl, I didn't . . . I didn't know you were a *lady*. But you were doing the same thing I was, weren't you? Hiding who you were, to protect yourself?"

"But I wasn't secretly trying to kill someone," she answered back. "I was just trying to survive."

"And that's all I'm doing now," Bolt replied. "And trying to make up for things."

Arable shook her head, she could not overcome the sense of being lied to. But he was saying all the right things. And like it or not, her mind was drawn to a similar moment of her own, cowering in the Sherwood, awaiting judgment from Robin and the rest of the group as to whether or not she was trustworthy. Whether or not she was a spy. There was nothing she could say that could convince them otherwise, when all of the facts pointed against her.

But Bolt had *literally* come to spy on them. Of course he would say all the right things, he'd been preparing for this moment for months.

Or maybe she was just on edge because she had to *pee again.*

"Arable," Tuck said with some humility, "I believe him. Charley's been nothing but helpful. We trusted you, we took that chance. I don't see any reason why we shouldn't do the same with him."

"He's been useful before, and we need every friend we can get," Lord Robert added. "Now is hardly the time to be picky about our allies. Look at this group—nobody here trusts each other! By that account, I'd say Charley fits in perfectly."

They were asking for her permission. Her history with him had apparently turned her into an authority on the matter. She didn't want to make that call. She didn't want it to be on her head when Bolt revealed his true nature, and turned them in. She had nothing beyond a gut instinct to say no. But Lord Robert was right. The stakes were too high, the world was about to be on fire and all their petty differences from the past were meaningless next to the threat of this war. Hell, she was standing next to *Beneger de Wendenal,* of all people. Surely little Bolt was nothing compared to that vile insult.

"Dammit," she relented. "Life can't get any stranger."

WELL, IT COULD GET a *little* stranger.

Almost all the members of Gilbert's crew were Zinn's age—children, effectively. Most seemed to look to Zinn for their commands, though Arable got the impression that this group was only recently created out of a number of smaller gangs, possibly rivals, that had little more than their age in common. Frankly, it seemed they'd attached themselves to Gilbert without his consent, and the only other adult in the group was a thin Guardsman.

They met him in another chamber, much smaller than the previous one, which smelled strongly of both beer and ash.

"Glad you're alive," Beneger greeted the man.

"I'm glad you've returned," he replied, giving Lord Beneger a firm handshake. This was the Guardsman who'd discovered FitzOdo's true nature and was nearly killed for it, but Arable didn't recognize him until she heard his full name—Quillen Peveril.

"My goodness." Arable could barely keep up with the day's surprises. "I *know* you."

"I'm so sorry for you," Quillen answered, apparently by instinct, and then squinted at her face. It was no surprise he wouldn't remember her, but there was no denying it. His pinched, beady eyes and tall nose were the same features she'd seen on him when he'd been a much younger boy.

"Your father is the Lord of the Peak," she stated, recalling long-lost memories. "My father took us to visit him once, it must have been twenty years ago or more."

"Oh I would have been a boy, then, less than ten at least. And I made that much of an impression on you?"

"Well you got lost in the caves beneath the castle. Our entire family spent the night searching for you."

"Ah." Quillen's mouth opened in embarrassment. "I'm glad to hear I'm still famous for that."

Arable had to laugh, to think she would find the same boy twenty years later in another cave. But the grand caverns beneath Peveril Castle were nothing like these sandstone tunnels. Beneath the Peak was an underground lake, and caves as expansive as the mountain itself. Arable remembered marveling at it as a young lady, enjoying the way her voice echoed endlessly in that space, calling for their host's son, *"Quillen! Quillen!"*

It was a curiously small world.

"I doubt I'd remember you otherwise," she said. "I was the one who found you. You'd slipped down a little crevasse that nobody else could fit down."

"My God," he said, eyes widening. "I *do* remember you. I haven't thought on that in . . . I don't remember your name, though?"

"Arable." She extended her hand.

"Quill." He took it, and the room erupted in laughter.

"Keep your pants on," Lord Beneger chuckled. "We're in the middle of a war."

"What?" Quillen startled. "I was just saying hello."

Arable looked at the others—Tuck and Lord Robert, particularly—who seemed equally amused. "For Christ's sake," she scolded them. "Is that honestly all you ever think about?"

Heaven forbid a man and a woman exchange pleasantries without some other motivation. It was an absolute wonder that anything in the world ever happened at all, when men could become so instantly distracted by even the faintest hint of sex.

They caught Quillen up on the circumstances of their presence, who returned with some grim news. "Well there's no way into the castle tonight, might as well get some rest and try in the morning."

"It has to be tonight," Lord Robert answered. "The fighting starts tomorrow."

"Well tomorrow *is* as soon as it's possible," he replied. "FitzOdo has taken over the Trip to Jerusalem, and they're there tonight. There's no getting inside as long as he's there."

Tuck scratched at his beard. "Is he using the tunnels, then, to go back and forth into the castle?"

"He never mentioned those tunnels to me," Quillen answered.

"He's too big," Zinn added. "Me and mine had a hard enough time in there. Unless he's been spending his nights digging away."

"We sneak in during the night, then," Beneger suggested. "Deal with him while he's asleep. They're not expecting us."

"*You*, no," Quillen huffed. "But he's on his highest guard. He thinks Gilbert is trying to kill him, mostly because of the fact that Gilbert is very much trying to kill him."

All eyes moved to Gilbert, who did absolutely nothing to deny it.

"I was wrong about him," Quillen explained to Lord Beneger. "FitzOdo was the one doing unspeakable things as Robin Hood, and we never suspected him. All while we were tracking Gilbert—I made a mess of that. Gilbert . . . uh, well I don't want to speak for you, but he means to make FitzOdo pay. He killed Derrick, and probably would have killed Ronnell and FitzOdo, too, if he didn't stop to save me instead. They've been protecting themselves in the Trip since."

"And he never leaves?" Arable asked.

"Oh, he leaves all the time, but never without a large group of supporters. And only during the day. Not sure what he does, really. But either way, once he's holed in for the night, we can't get to him. They're ready to be attacked."

"So we have to wait," Arable agreed. "We can sneak in when he leaves."

"People are going to start dying tomorrow," Lord Robert said, though his tone implied that he knew there was nothing to be done about that. "Marion wanted us to stop this war *before* it started."

"He's a knight, right?" asked Tuck. "Why not trust him to do the right thing? We can go talk to him, explain what's happening."

The cavern hushed. It was nice to think of a world in which it would be that easy.

"Do we really want to risk everything on that?" Beneger asked. "On the good will of a man who's been chopping hands off commonfolk for fun?"

"Not him," Charley whispered. "Trust me. *'Do the right thing?'* That's not Fitz-Odo."

Even Tuck seemed to understand.

"One problem," Lord Robert said. "Even if we can sneak past him when he leaves, that would be a one-way passage. That only works if we're able to convince Prince John to surrender of his own accord."

"If not," added Beneger, "we have to drag the prince out by force. And if Fitz-Odo hears us coming back into the Trip through those tunnels with a screaming prince in our hands, that'll be the end of that."

Arable closed her eyes. Nobody wanted to imagine what that scenario looked like.

"We'll have to split up." Beneger stretched his arms. "When FitzOdo leaves, half of us tend to him. The other half get into the castle, as fast as possible, to find the prince. After we take out FitzOdo, we can secure the Trip for ourselves, in case you need it to bring the prince out again. If enough of us survive Fitz-Odo, maybe we can follow behind and help, too."

That was met by silence. There were dark and heavy boulders in that sentence, such that none of them knew how to grapple. Both paths seemed equally suicidal.

"What if we can't do all that?" Nick asked.

"Then we all die, I expect," Beneger said. "Did you think this was going to be easy?"

FIFTY-NINE

ARTHUR A BLAND

"NO, THANK YOU!" DAVID shouted over the castle walls.

But the French army still approached.

"It was worth a shot," he said, and absently fingered the feathers of his arrows. It was unlike him to display such amateur behavior—Arthur had seen his friend scold other men for exactly such a thing. *"Are your arrows still in your quiver?"* David had asked one of the Red Lions when they'd been practicing at their archery. *"Yes? Then stop touching them. They'll be there still if you need them."*

But they'd never done *this* before. They'd never seen *this*. It was as if the world itself had ended, it was so impossible to imagine life ever being normal again. The earth was moving, rolling, screaming. The French army was as wide as the goddamned horizon, its noise was more than anything that could even count as sound. Arthur felt it in his bones, in his heart, it pounded through him like a sudden crack of thunder, except it never ended, never settled.

They stood on the battlement of the lower bailey, as did every other competent archer in the castle, as did every other half-competent archer, as did every other incompetent slug who could be made to hold a bow, as did a few other people even more useless like Arthur himself. They stood shoulder to shoulder, Nottingham Guardsmen next to soldiers from Gloucester and Worcester, next to villagefolk and baileyfolk, next to Will Scarlet's men, next to liars like himself and David. Some had their own bows, some had those from the castle armory, some had nothing. David had his own personal quiver slung at his legs, while most relied on barrels or page boys prepared to run across the battlements and replenish any bowman who ran low.

And the French army still approached.

They hadn't slept, the French had seen to that. Horns had blasted all through the night. "But that means they didn't sleep, either, right?" Arthur asked his friend. "That had to hurt them as much as us, right?"

David squinted back at him. "Is that . . . is that supposed to change our strategy in some way?"

"I don't know," Arthur answered, because he didn't know anything anymore. "Sure. You can shoot your arrows into the ground, so that if they try to lie down and fall asleep they'll be very uncomfortable."

"I think I'll aim for their bodies," David replied without humor.

Arthur didn't know what to say. He didn't know what he was supposed to say, if there was anything at all that was expected of people in circumstances like this aside from waiting and dying. He wiped the sweat from his brow only to find something slick and oily. His wound was weeping again.

"That's not a good color," David said, sparing him a glance.

Arthur smelled his fingers and wished he hadn't. Admittedly, he felt as if he had a bit of a fever, too. "Not the top of the day's worries."

Arthur's fault, that they were here. He'd convinced Will to stay and fight, argued that the three of them were somehow *special,* that they were the sort of people others looked up to. But now he knew how profoundly wrong he was. They were just three bodies, three of a thousand who would die, meaninglessly, and soon. They weren't helping anyone by being here—except the French, who could gloat over three bodies more.

"Will was right, we should've left," he whispered, watching the army collide with the city walls. The decision had been made to abandon the defense of the city. Nottingham's perimeter was too long, impossible to defend against an army of this size. Instead Prince John commanded them to make their stand at the castle, which was far more defensible. If there was anyone still left guarding the city gates, they had no effect. The unfathomable mob of the French army barely flinched as it passed into the city, as if the walls weren't even there—there was only the slightest sense of bottlenecking before they were in the streets.

For some reason, Arthur thought the streets would slow them. He'd thought the people of the city would ambush the army, bursting from their doors and windows with knives and clubs, beating the invaders senseless from the advantage of their close quarters. He'd wanted to see the throng stall and swell, recoiling in horror, not knowing how to react to a populace that refused to be overridden. At least a slight delay, at least slow them down. At least tell the French that they meant not to lie on their backs and spread their legs.

But the army flowed through the streets and alleys like melted butter—if anything, their approach went faster, rushing through the seemingly abandoned city of Nottingham.

"Why won't they defend themselves?" he asked aloud. "Why are we fighting if they won't fight for themselves?"

What had happened? Why was Arthur left to defend this city when those who lived here were cowering in their homes? *What the fuck was he doing here?*

Panic grabbed him. *He was trapped.* There was no getting out of the castle now, he hadn't realized it until this moment, there was no last-minute escape anymore, there was no chance of using Will's rope ladder now, nothing but the ground beneath him tilting steeper and steeper still—steeper until the beast, war.

He reeled, Guardsmen all around him. These people . . . *why was he beside them now?* Only a few months ago they'd hunted him, captured him, put him on his knees—he'd watched silently as Elena had died. *Some of those men were with him now.* They weren't going to defend him, not if he was injured, they didn't care about him . . .

Behind him, down in the bailey, a mob of fucking *civilians.* Will Scarlet, leading his men in training exercises, making them repeat the same moves, even now, stepping in formation. The same practices that Robin of Locksley had taught them, now applied to commonfolk who'd never swung a sword before. Will barked out numbers and orders, keeping them alert, sharp. It was better than waiting on edge, Will had explained—better than letting the dread seep into their muscles and freeze them. If they could keep moving, keep practicing up until the very moment the army broke through the walls, then they'd hardly notice the difference between when they were practicing and when they were dying.

Arthur had convinced them all to stay.

The rest of the Nottingham Guard was behind them—*behind them.*

"Oh God." His voice crept out of his lips. "We're all going to die."

Thunder, thunder, down the streets it pounded, beating, mauling, smashing the air into pieces and back again, thunder thunder, fuck the king and fuck the prince and fuck the city, thunder thunder.

Out beyond the castle, in the empty expanse between the stone curtain wall and the first of the city's buildings, the army arrived at the foot of the castle. Massive tower shields formed a front line, red crosses and blue stars and green fields and mud and spears, horns, calling, screaming, and in their middle a cluster of raised banners, red fields with golden lions, their standards bursting up where the noise was loudest, until it bulged out to the front of the lines like a bubble, where paraded a man mounted on a horse with a warcrown and mail, flanked by an entourage.

"There is all the proof you need!" called out a man who'd been given command of this legion of archers, someone important or other from Worcester, but Arthur couldn't remember his name now. Hell, Arthur could scarcely remember his *own* name. The commander screamed, "They parade an impostor before us dressed as a king, as if we are foolish enough to bow down! Are we to believe the real King would march to the front line? Perhaps in France where they have no wit at all, but this is England! This is Nottingham! Ten crowns to the first man who can feather that French asshole with English plu—"

David released his arrow before the man finished, and a shocked hush followed its flight. The army was still far, almost too far for any bow to reach, but David carried a strong yew longbow and his arms had spent their life preparing for a distance shot such as this. The arrow flew high and straight, perhaps unnoticed by the French, its arc smooth and perfect and then cut down to slice through the morning air.

Though he did not hit the Frenchman pretending to be king, his arrow found the neck of a soldier nearby, who spasmed and fell. Around him, the French army recoiled and pulled back, surely having thought they were still too far away to be struck.

David's face—the man who could find laughter in everything, who was ever the light that kept Arthur fighting—was as stone serious as he'd ever been. There was no drop of doubt in his harsh lines, no regret, just a grim determination that put Arthur's earlier panic to shame.

The Frenchman across the expanse, stumbling down to the ground in blood, that was David's first kill.

The Worcester captain did not call *Loose* but Arthur—and every other proud Englishman alive—screamed bloody hellfire, and the sky went dark with English arrows.

SIXTY

QUILLEN PEVERIL

THE ROAR CAME FROM the north, an overwhelming noise that was in some ways reminiscent of the crowd at the archery tournament, excepting the minor difference that this was a hundred times louder and also all the killing.

Actually, then—Quill corrected his own assessment—*not so different after all.*

They emerged from the tunnels by St. Mary's, through the same doorway FitzOdo had scorched to cinders. Their boots sunk through the fresh ash and left an obvious trail as they ducked around the outer edge of the church's courtyard. From there they had intended on sticking to alleys to avoid being seen, but the main street that led down the hill to the west was utterly deserted. They walked it warily, wide-eyed in the hands of a city the likes of which Quill had never seen before. While Lord Beneger made some comments about *"the calm before the storm"* that had the vague scent of wisdom to them, Quill could not find any calm in the empty city. *Normal* was calm. People, going about their business, *that* was calm.

This, this was walking a knife's edge. Every second of it.

At the bottom of the hill they felt a touch safer, less like they were sticking their necks up for attention. They passed the smaller steeple of St. Nicholas and found that its doors, too, were closed—barricaded, even—with nothing at all to indicate there was anyone inside. "I would have thought people would gather in the churches for safety."

"You really don't know this city then, do ya?" the girl, Zinn, mocked him. "Underground's the only safe place to be right now."

"The tunnels, you mean?"

"Some." She shrugged. "Almost every building'll have some sort of cave for storage."

"Do they all connect to each other?" the friar asked.

Zinn shook her head. "Most don't."

Quill considered it. The people thought they were under attack from an invading French army, and rightfully feared what came with that. Sacking, pillaging, raping. They didn't believe that it truly was King Richard at their walls—frankly, Quill was still struggling with that truth himself. But the people were terrified, and it was easier to defend a hole in the ground than a building full of things an army might find tasty or valuable. "How many are there?"

Again, Zinn shrugged off the question. "Caves? Who knows? More than anyone knows of, no doubt."

It gave Quill hope, at least, that the tunnels in the Trip to Jerusalem truly did connect all the way to the castle.

It was not so long later that they found themselves concealed behind a ramshackle shelter bridging an alley across from the Trip, where they settled in for some time. The roar of the battle was louder here—the inn was built into the very base of the sandstone cliffs that shortly turned into castle wall to the north, and the front gates farther up. It was there that the battle had started, though they had yet to see it.

"How do we know if FitzOdo is still inside?" Lord Beneger complained. "He might already have joined the line. We should have been here earlier."

"We were," was Zinn's response, and she took to ascending the wooden structure around them with both alarming dexterity and little explanation. Since he was largely indebted to her and Gilbert for saving his life, Quill generally forgave her worse habits of thinking she was the most important thing in the world. Once she was high enough, she knocked lightly on the wooden shutters of a window on the second story of the alley, which creaked open slightly. "They still in there?" she whispered.

"They're still in there," came a muffled response, and it closed again.

"There ya go." She smiled back down. "We put eyes on her last night, because we're not . . . what's the right word? . . . *slaggin' idiots.*"

"That *is* the right word," the Earl of Huntingdon said. "I checked."

"Fucking hell," Beneger swore under his breath. "I hope you'll treat this all a bit more seriously when the fighting begins."

"They *are* taking it seriously," Tuck scolded, before anyone had the chance to fling some barb back at the man. "Different people react in different ways. I guarantee you every one of us is shitting our breeks."

"*I'm* not," Zinn answered from above, her legs dangling off the wooden beam. "Took care of that this mornin'. Always shit *before* a fight."

If they'd been forced to wait for long like this—the ten of them all at odds and uncomfortable, unsure they were even doing the right thing—they might have eventually torn each other to pieces. But fortunately, it was not so long before the front door of the Trip to Jerusalem jarred open and belched out a small mob of men. They were dressed simply, though a few had padded leather vests, or tattered blue tabards, and all carried their weapons at the ready as they ran with purpose across the street's gullet. A dozen men, Quill guessed, and there was no mistaking the bald head of Sir Robert FitzOdo at their center. He alone bore a steel chest plate and mail sleeves, and carried a black spiked mace instead of a sword.

Quill's heart quickened just at the sight of him, recalling the fury in the Coward Knight's face when he realized his game was up. With his lackey Derrick vivisected on the stables wall, *IMPOSTOR* about his head, FitzOdo had nearly cut Quill in two. The idea of running *toward* that monster of a man rather than *away* was enough to turn Quill's stomach inside out several times over. "Where do you suppose he's going?" he whispered.

"To his grave," Beneger answered. "Alright then, fighters with me. The rest of you, Godspeed. Find the prince."

They divided into their groups, as discussed. Arable, Charley, and the twin brothers would use the Trip to sneak into the castle, while Zinn and their friar stayed behind to watch its entrance. Meanwhile, Beneger meant to hunt down FitzOdo to prevent him from returning to the inn, with the help of Gilbert and the earl Robert. Somehow, Quill fit into this latter category of *fighters*. He had originally protested as much, but Beneger made a point of it. *"You should be there when we kill FitzOdo,"* he'd insisted. *"It'll be good for you."*

And he *did* want to see this through. FitzOdo had deceived Quill for months as he chased down the wrong leads. He'd been utterly blind to it right up until the moment Gilbert spelled it out for him with literal writing on a literal wall. Quill's days of considering himself the family genius might just be over.

And so they split up, making hasty farewells and *good lucks.* "It was nice to re-meet you," Quill said to Arable, having no connection to the others headed to the inn. "I hope you don't die."

Her face confirmed exactly how stupid a thing that was to say.

"Protect yourself, Arable," Lord Beneger said, more an order than a wish. "If Charley knows the castle as well as he says he does, then you stay inside the tunnels until it's safe."

"Fuck you, I hope you die," Arable returned. She left without hesitation, leading the others across the cobbled road to the entrance of the Trip to Jerusalem. Zinn cackled silently at Beneger as she followed, going so far as to actually point her finger and hold her belly.

Quill was compelled to comment on the queer exchange but there was no time—FitzOdo's men were already disappearing up the street, closer to the sounds of war, and Beneger prompted them to follow. Quill took a moment to wish he was the sort of person who might find comfort in prayer at a time like this, and then followed the others so that they could all meet a very ungentlemanly death together.

SOME PHYSICIAN MIGHT FIND an academic curiosity in what went through Quillen Peveril's mind as he trudged along at the back of their foursome. Given the imminent likeliness of his life's end, his brain was drawn toward daydreaming of his possible futures. Perhaps it was some sort of primitive animal instinct intended to keep him brave and inspired, but Quill found it incredibly distracting. He clearly should have been focusing on how best to move silently and keep strangers' swords away from his innards, but all he could think about was whether he ought to ask Arable de Burel to marry him once this was over.

He knew there wasn't any rational causality to the thought, like *I'm hungry and therefore I should eat,* but logic had been evicted from Nottingham and he was not beholden to its laws. It didn't matter that he'd only shared a handful of sentences with the woman, nor that those sentences were mostly about an embarrassing event from his childhood. The only facts relevant to Quill's horror-soaked brain were that they were both of comparable age, unwed, and knew each other's names—which surely comprised a romance. After all, she was born a lady but her family had lost everything, while Quill's family was well known. She would be a fool not to take such an offer. And one day, when Quill finally proved himself to his father, he might become the Lord of the Peak himself, and Arable was surely wise enough to see that. She was, by all accounts, incredibly lucky to have recognized him.

With exactly that milk-sopped lunacy clouding his thoughts, he stepped directly into a puddle in the middle of the road with a loud splash, tripped as he tried to correct himself, and fell to the ground in something that would be best described as the absolute opposite of silence.

Ahead of him, Beneger and Robert both cursed and threw themselves at the closest building to hide, which Gilbert had also done with an offensive grace. Quill was left alone on his hands and knees, reaching out for the sword he had dropped which could not possibly be retrieved quietly, staring up and down the street at the two trailing members of FitzOdo's entourage who had heard the commotion and turned around to get some murdering done upon him.

Having already been noticed, Quill panicked and scrambled for his sword, which only skittered farther away, and by the time he got a knee underneath himself to make a second grab, one of the two attackers was nearly upon him. But shockingly, it was an unarmed hand that extended, palm up, accompanied by the fairly unmurderous question of: "Need a hand?"

Quill assumed the man—a deeply tanned fellow with wide-set eyes and a disheveled mop—was just being chivalrous and preferred to do his killing on armed enemies, so he refused the help and found his way back to his feet on his own. The man responded by patting his back and urging him along. Around the same time, a few nearby buildings opened their doors as one or two more men slipped into the street and encouraged Quill to hurry.

Now badly outnumbered, he took their command and ran forward, making eye contact with his original companions who were extremely visible from behind. They, too, were welcomed by the newcomers, who continued to trickle into the street. Each had a weapon, each looked like they knew what to do with it, and each one did their best to stay quiet and follow the path of FitzOdo's gang. If Quill didn't know better—which he coincidentally did not—he would have thought that every one of them had the same intent of catching up to FitzOdo and confronting him. Soon enough, the four of them were running along with half a dozen armed strangers, having very little idea as to what was happening.

When they rounded a few final corners, they'd caught up to the rear of FitzOdo's group, which had now tripled in size. His bald head was easy to find, bobbing at their center and leading them forward. The men at the front of the group would pause at select doorways and knock quickly—always two short knocks, then a pause, then two more—while the rest of the group ran forward.

Half a minute after each knock, that door would open and a man would barrel into the street, running to catch up with the mob. *They were calling out their men,* he realized, *and Quill and the others had been mistaken as allies.*

They rushed on, their noise now impossible to hear beneath the din of the army a few streets to the north. They finally stopped at a waist-high makeshift barricade in the center of a wider street. Most of the men were swarming past it on either side, but a few were gathered behind it, kneeling in preparation. Beyond the barricade, down a short straight lane, was a sight that took Quill's breath away. *The army.* This path led directly to it; there was a wall of men pushing slowly to the left, shields held above their heads, and their noise had taken on a stunning new clarity.

Quill and the others stopped behind the barricade, and found themselves face-to-face with Sir Robert FitzOdo.

"Lord Beneger!" the man exclaimed with surprise, even relief. But upon seeing Quill, a flash of rage overcame him—and when he recognized Gilbert, he perhaps understood what was happening. He tensed but did not attack, shifting his gaze from one of them to another.

Sweat accumulated in Quill's palms as he repositioned the grip on his sword. He hated this man, from his wet bald head to his bulbous nose, his scabby ears. FitzOdo had betrayed them all, masquerading as a *Robin Hood* in the night to torment the poorfolk, and had very nearly killed Quill for that discovery. As his nerves flared to see the man again, so close, he knew that Lord Beneger was right. He wanted to be here for this, he needed to watch the man receive his due.

"Whatever you're here for," the Coward Knight said with caution, "it can wait."

The sounds of the army moved through the earth itself, Quill could feel it in his feet.

"What the hell are you doing?" Lord Beneger demanded.

"We're fighting back," FitzOdo answered, and turned just briefly enough to direct a few of his men forward, down the sides of the lane. "We're going to fuck the French in the ass."

"Those aren't the French!" Lord Robert hissed. "That's King Richard out there!"

FitzOdo's mask curled, and he turned to look down the lane. Quill might easily have thrust his sword's point into the man's neck then and there, but the knight's lack of concern was disarming.

"Those are Englishmen!" Robert continued. "That's your king out there, sir."

"The fuck does it matter who it is?" FitzOdo growled back at them. "They're here for the city, and we don't mean to let them."

Beneger shook his head. "They're here for Prince John, no more."

"Tell that to them!" He pointed one meaty finger down the lane. "The city's being destroyed, and the castle needs our help."

That much, sadly, was true. King Richard's men thought they were quelling a rebellion, that Prince John was throwing a coup. And by helping him, Nottingham had become their enemy.

Still, honor was hardly in FitzOdo's character. "Since when do you care about the city?" Quill forced himself to a full voice. "You've been chopping hands and burning buildings and beating innocent people, now you think you're one of them?"

A single furious moment passed as FitzOdo realized his secret was out; but rather than deny it, he claimed it fully. "I did that for a reason, whelp, one you could never understand. The people were putting their faith in *Robin Hood* rather than the Guard, and where the fuck is he now? I brought them back to us, back to trusting that they're safe when they see a Guard tabard, which is the only reason they're willing to follow me now. I've got half the city ready to fight back, ready for my signal." He placed his mace on the ground and reached out to another man, who had a couple of strong longbows and a full sheaf of arrows. "Robin Hood split this city in half, but *I* brought it back together. You really give two shits about the way I did it, in the face of *this?*"

He nodded, took an arrow from the bag, and signaled the men next to him to do the same.

Down the lane, his men had concealed themselves against the sides of the road. While the army attempted to siege the castle walls to the west, FitzOdo meant to attack their flank here, luring them down the lane to deal with a small group of archers, while the bulk of his men waited to ambush from the sides. No doubt a dozen similar traps were waiting elsewhere, and FitzOdo could retreat through half the city and pick off soldiers all the way.

"That is King Richard's army," Robert said again, perhaps realizing as he said it how little it mattered. "We're trying to help them."

"Love Richard all you want." FitzOdo nocked an arrow. "But if you think those soldiers are going to give a single fuck who you are then you're even dumber than you look."

Quill looked to Beneger and the earl for support. Even the silent Gilbert seemed perplexed as to exactly what it was they were supposed to do now.

"If you're in the city, best get your nose underground," FitzOdo sneered. "But if you're up here and have a weapon drawn, you'd better as fuck be fighting for the same thing I am."

Sir Robert FitzOdo stood up, as did his four companions who'd been kneeling at the barricade beside them, and they pulled the cords of their bows back to their noses.

"*Nottingham!*" the knight screamed, and they loosed their arrows.

At the army's flank, two soldiers fell and those around them startled, turned, and pulled away from the main company to respond to the threat, while every single thing that Quill had ever known for certain in life threw its arms in the air and scattered.

SIXTY-ONE

THE BEAST, WAR

FUCKING HELL, EDWARD STRONG was closer now to his home in Preston than he had been in five long years, and he damned well wasn't going to die here in the slop-bracken streets of Nottingham. His nerves flared as he stepped over Sutton's flailing body—who was still struggling to figure out why there was an arrow embedded in his ribs. Edward had to leave him, swinging his shield to protect himself from whatever pissant city archers had done the wicked thing. He called for Gregory and Doran Grand who were both already one step ahead of him, creating a spear formation to peel off from the main assault and deal with the attackers down this side street.

Not here, he swore. That wouldn't be his fate.

He'd spent too long on the wrong half of the world fighting for Richard's lost war just to be killed by some hapless traitor at home. He meant to see his wife soon, and his daughter, Tilda, who was but two years old when he'd left. He felt a light *thunk* smack against his shield, but it was thick alderwood that had held up against months of strong Saracen bows, while these attackers were probably spitting warped arrows with makeshift weapons. King Richard had promised them a quick fight against an unprepared city, that there'd be spoils, too—which he could bring back to his family. Tilda had loved that straw doll as a baby, perhaps he'd find a new one for her in some respectable house here, a proper doll.

Gregory and Doran leaned into a run toward a shoddy barricade strewn across the street and Edward followed—until his ankle caught against something and he toppled forward, his arm wrenching as his shield bit into the ground. *Damn it!* he cursed as he twisted to free himself from whatever had tripped him, just in time to see a group of strangers *behind him, no,* and a hairy face that screamed with fury as he swung a blade down between Edward's eyes.

A CROSSBOW BOLT SHATTERED against the crenellated castle wall just beside Ricard the Ruby's face, and he froze for only an instant. Had it flown a few inches closer, he would be *plus court d'une tête, mais* luck was on his side today. The French crossbowmen would need time to wrench their locks back, and Ricard could let fly five or six arrows before that. He peered down—the French army was crossing the divide between their front lines and the castle walls, gathered in columns of men with their shields above their heads. They were very likely protecting the wooden ladders he'd seen built earlier in the morning.

"Take them down!" screamed the captain de Worcester, pointing his finger at the colorful leather sigils covering the French shields, but Ricard *avait les meilleures idées.*

Even with bodkin points and gravity on their side, they could do little more than feather those shields, which wouldn't stop the advance. Instead Ricard aimed true for the crossbowmen, who would soon let forth another volley to give the ladders cover. His first arrow fell short but his second and third found their homes.

"*C'est moi,*" he whispered, every Frenchman a reminder of why he could never return home. "*Je suis ici.*"

He flung another at a man cranking his shaft back—who was quickly eclipsed by another with a crossbow at the ready. The unnatural clatter of their triggers shocked Ricard—he had not realized they'd staggered their bowmen into two ranks. The castle wall around him erupted in splinters and chunks of rock, and he did not have enough time to curse as he was jolted back, his vision went blank, and he felt himself topple into *la nuit noire . . .*

JOHN OF ST. ALBANS gasped as an arrow landed before his feet, and his lips said a prayer on their own. The front of the siege ladder weighed down his shoulders and his shield balanced on top of it, so all he could see was the dirt a foot ahead of him. The noise of the war echoed in unnatural ways, balanced by his own rancid breath. *That tooth has rotted,* he knew. He'd barely seen any fighting in their last city siege at Acre, and had felt like an impostor for the better part of a year. Now he wished he were in the rear ranks again—this wasn't worth it. He prayed to St. Albans that he would not be made martyr himself, and tried to think of summer nights by Daya's side, memories of safety and comfort that could protect him more than his stolen shield.

At the commander's whistle he knelt and shifted to the side of the ladder, planting its foot on the ground in conjunction with Alain across from him. His shield had not shifted for more than a second when he felt a smash across his entire body, a wet slap that pounded his senses, followed instantly by *a million searing pinpricks* that drove miles beneath his skin. He screamed as the boiling oil turned every inch of his skin to blister, and his last thought was of Daya, turning her face away in horror at the sight of him.

RONNELL OF BLYTHE SWUNG hard and smacked the Frenchman's shield wide, opening just so—that he could plunge his sword into the man's open armpit. He heaved forward with the action, pushing the blade deeper as the blood poured out, and kicked the body free again as it slumped to the ground. But his eyes were on Sir Robert FitzOdo back at the barricade, and the men who had joined him there. *Wendenal and Peveril,* he recognized first, but at the sight of the *pigfucking* white glove beside them his blood hardened. *Nothing, no army, no god,* could keep Ronnell from Gilbert this time.

He ran, twisted, slashing his weapon down *and through* the back of another Frenchman's head, who had yet to realize the trap. The skull opened, spewing hair and meat and purple pulp into a pile—*a practice swing, for Gilbert,* Ronnell swore. That traitor had fucking *dissected* his brother Derrick. He swore now on their mother's grave that he'd split the man in half as many times as it took until Gilbert could no longer be identified as human. *Because he wasn't.*

There was a Frenchman's body on the ground before the wooden wall, and Ronnell used it to vault over—*no,* he lost his footing and smashed his face into the wood instead, he felt a crack in his jaw and teeth and a numbness smothered him, and then *mother no, no, not before Gilbert, not now* but there was something new inside him, blistering cold steel plying his ribs apart, pinning him down, *no mother no*

JACELYN DE LACY PEELED the arrows from between her knuckles, springing them into men *who had not killed her uncle.* Five ladders, from her viewpoint, had now found their footing on the north side of the curtain wall and were ascended by scores of men *who had not killed her uncle.* She directed the nearest kitchen cooks to pour their pots over the battlement edge, where more ladders had arrived, carried by a cluster of men *who had not killed her uncle.* It didn't matter that Will Scarlet was captured. It had done nothing to quell the stone rage that lived beneath her muscles. She pawed out another fistful of arrows and waited at the wall's edge for her next chance.

Jacelyn did not intend on dying before she saw her uncle's murderer hang, so she meant to survive this. She moved and let loose her arrows, but the wooden ladder before her was already at its peak and falling toward the battlement. *Low walls,* she cursed the entire castle, and when its wooden planks met stone she knew there was no pushing it away again. But they'd planned for this. A coil of rope was nearby with a barbed grapple, which she flung down until it clattered against one of the ladder's rungs. Its other end stretched to the fulcrum arm of the nearest converted crane. "Make yourself useful!" she shouted to the crowd of men below, who scrambled for the turncock wheel that would pull the entire blasted thing up and over the wall before it was used. Jacelyn and the archers next to her just needed to pick off any men who were weighing the ladders down.

She made brief eye contact with the archer next to her, whose eyes flicked. Even in the middle of this hellforsaken war, this stranger's eyes flicked.

They all flick. With only one eye that could see, it was always so obvious to Jacelyn when someone's attention glanced over to her dead side. Gilbert was the only man whose eyes had never flicked.

Somewhat happily, she enjoyed that the soldier's eye was quickly replaced with a crossbow bolt from below, and he *flicked* himself right off the wall, backward into the bailey.

HENRY FLEETFOOT WAS NOT the first to the top of the ladder, but he was first of his company, which was enough to finally prove his name. He'd been mocked for months for being the last to finish their march north from Austria, but here he was ahead of every one of his companions, vaulting over the top battlements of Nottingham Castle. The archers on the wall were already retreating or pulling their short arms, but Henry had his at the ready. He lunged forward at a man but found nothing but air, and before he could reposition the man swung his bow—*his bow! Which wasn't fair at all*—into Henry's nose and he felt a burst of copper, then something moved *beneath his chin* and the next breath he took was all blood, his neck was cold, and he was certain his company was laughing at him again. His feet slipped through the rocks and darkness devoured him.

KELLE WAS ALREADY CRYING, but she found the smooth handle of the knife and pulled it from the wool bundle. *"It's worth more than everything I've ever owned,"* her papa had explained to her, before he left for the war. *"But don't sell it unless you have no choice. I'd rather you have it when you need it."* She traced her fingers over the spiderthin black ripples in the knife's blade. *Damascus steel,* her papa had called it, and just touching it made her feel invincible. She was old enough to know what the army would do to anyone who fought back as they sacked the city, just as she knew that she was not quite young enough anymore for her youth to protect her from them. Kelle glanced out the window, though she could hear it all—louder than she knew anything could be. An endless throng was dismantling her home and the buildings around it, tearing the wood planks apart with their hands and swords. The stone buildings were just being pillaged, while every wooden hovel was being destroyed. *"For the ladders,"* her brother had explained before he'd leapt from the window to fight back. His body was still there on the street where the army had marched right over him. *But he didn't know about the Damascus knife,* and she gripped it harder with both hands, even as her stomach lurched, even as the wall across from her, her *bedroom,* where Kelle had gone to sleep every night for a year—it ripped open and men were there hacking at its timber. She held the knife out in front of her and screamed her papa's name.

A ROAR WENT UP from the northern wall, and Roana twisted with the others to look. "What is it?" she asked.

"I don't know," the older woman answered. "But nothing we can do about it."

Roana saw commotion at the top of the battlements, but little more than that. The French had gotten to the top, she guessed, at the farthest point before the bulwark dead-ended into the taller walls of the middle bailey. Everywhere else the invaders had climbed, they'd been beset upon on both sides by the wall's defenders—but here, they only had to fight in one direction. "Hell," she said, before the old woman grabbed her and tugged her forward.

There was little else for her to do. She ran with the trio she'd been assigned and found another body to haul away. She'd never ran so much in her life. The moment that their first archer had fallen over the battlements back into the bailey, they'd been moving. Four of them grabbing each fallen soldier by their limbs, praying they wouldn't recognize his face, and dragging him to the back of the baileyground. Taking any weapons, and armor. At first they looked for coinpurses, too. Now they just took a breath, and ran again.

SEBASTIEN CLUTCHED HIS BELLY, hoping he could keep the blood inside, his guts inside. He curled into a ball and prayed to every name he knew and looked up as people flooded over him, streaming over the wall, and he prayed and he prayed and his hands were so very wet.

NISSA LOCKED THE DOOR, but she could see the stream of soldiers passing by the Bell turn and look in, gaping, mouths open and hungry. Thirsty, weren't they, and her inn was an easy target. She felt the weight of the cleaver in her hands, good for taking heads off birds but she wasn't aiming to cook anything in the kitchen this day. Ollie wasn't back yet, and wouldn't be now, not with the Market Square filled as it was with the worst type of customer.

"Keep your gawkin'," she muttered at the next solider who paused to peer through the wooden slats. The gangs had already had their fill of the Bell, and she wasn't lying down a third time. The first one—she swore, she spat—the first one would lose his hand, as God was her witness.

A shake of the door, a knock, a slam. Fingers, next, prodding into the cracks where once had been her window, and that was good enough for her. She swung and three fingertips were hers now, bouncing from the fat of her blade like giblets. "Come on then," she growled at the screams on the other side. The door slammed, the door slammed, the lock bulged, broke, and Nissa started swinging.

WILLEM THE GENTLE FLED. The barricade had been overwhelmed, and the French were now sacking the city rather than focusing on the castle. *You brought this on yourself,* he knew, flying down the lane, his lungs bursting with fire. This was all his fault, he knew it. God was damning him for what he'd done—*for what that crazed bastard Korben had made him do*—but as many times as he'd prayed for repentance he knew it wouldn't matter. He'd never trusted Korben, but he'd never trusted any of the men he'd been paired with for those damned smuggle jobs.

On their way back from York, they'd come across that carriage off the side of the road outside Nottingham, and found two nobles murdered inside.

Willem had said they ought to bury them. But Korben had other intentions, and Willem had been too afraid . . . afraid of what Korben would do if he tried to stop it. *What he'd done to the woman,* it chilled Willem every time he closed his eyes, and the fact that he'd *helped,* had dragged the woman out of the carriage that Korben could do the thing, was the reason he was damned now, the reason that God had sent an entire army to burn Nottingham to ash for what he'd done.

"FUCK YOU," THE FRENCHMAN grunted as Henry Three-Face drove his sword through his guts. The blade stuck and he tried to pull it out, but the man twisted and brought them both down to the ground. Henry's back was exposed as more of them pushed forward onto the battlement. Again he tried to wrench his weapon out but there was no room now, so he let it go, wrapped his fingers around the man's throat, and squeezed.

"Fuck you!" the man said again, his fingers crawling up Henry's arms, trying to find his own face. They wrapped into his beard and pulled and the pain made Henry wince, but he wouldn't let go. Even as he stared into the man's face, almost certain, *almost dreadfully certain* that he recognized those features, and it wasn't until after the man went limp that it occurred to him that he said *"Fuck you"* in English, not French. Before Henry could realize what that meant there were hands on his legs and his shoulders and suddenly the ground was gone, the castle walls threw themselves away. He'd been flung over the battlement, and never had a chance to tell anyone what he knew.

"OUR TURN," DAWN DOG yelled as the first group of Frenchmen made it down the inner stairs alive, finally setting foot in the lower bailey. Will Scarlet—or *Henry Russell,* as he was hiding himself—had held them back until now, forcing them to watch as the battlements were overrun. Archers didn't know but one way to kill a man, and once the enemy was within ten feet they'd chosen to die rather than do anything useful with their final moments of life. But still Scarlet had held them back, letting the prince's men do a fine job of fucking the whole castle for the rest of them.

But now there were people that needed dying in the bailey itself, and Dawn Dog had a double-headed battle axe that was itching to get its first bleeding.

For a full month they'd been kept inside the castle's walls and then the prisons, and Dawn was eager to let every goddamned inch of his fury about that out upon the first fucking French skull he could find. And then the second, and the third, and if he was lucky, a couple dozen more.

"Hold!" Will Scarlet screamed, but Dawn Dog was at a run, as was the first Frenchman who'd seen him, and Dawn pulled his axe high and swung it clean and *damn* but if the Frenchman's head didn't pop right off. Dawn didn't even wait, he carried the weight and swung the axe wide again, loving its heft, loving how it felt in his hands, and he buried its head right into the chest of the next man—mail shirt and all. Blood splattered his face and he smiled wide and he knew he was born for this, for this goddamned moment. No more *street rabbles* and *bullshit*. Dawn was born to kill, and he was going to prove how exceptionally good he was at it.

At the base of the staircase, the enemy could only come down one at a time, which was exactly how quickly Dawn could kill them. With every swing—the top of the head, the ribs, across the belly, clean through a leg, and then down straight into the neck—he paid the world back. For the mockery of his real name, for his sister's rape, for Lorna who'd loved him but slept with a Guardsman anyway. For his parents for deserting him, for his uncle for *that night,* for the sickness that had taken Peat-Pete, for the dreams and feelings he still had that he wished he didn't. Blood flew, muscle rent at his command, and he never really felt the blows that took him down, because they were too many. All he knew was that eventually his body stopped, he told his arms to swing again but they were limp at his sides and his lip was dangling open. This time the blood was his own, and the ground rose to meet him, and the world had its last fickle laugh at the Dawn Dog.

ROBERT SEIZED THE OPPORTUNITY and slid his epee back through his leather frog, that he had both his hands free to direct the men around him. "Grab those shields," he pointed at the fallen cluster of attackers—*Englishmen,* though FitzOdo and his forces would never believe it—and ordered a few more men to follow.

"What are you doing?" Beneger asked from behind, lingering back to keep an eye on as much as possible.

"Trying to save some lives," Robert answered. "If FitzOdo moves, follow him. I'll catch up."

Until they could corner FitzOdo, Robert could at least try to keep the casualties low. He'd left King Richard's command tent yesterday with a promise to make things better, and here he was amongst the city's defenders, fighting against some of the very men he'd shared that tent with.

"We need to stay on FitzOdo," said the thin Guardsman, Peveril, while practically tugging on Robert's cape. *FitzOdo, to protect Arable. Arable, to finish Marion's plan. Marion, for the promise he'd made her.* But even still, Robert could not watch the bloodshed of so many innocent parties and do *nothing.*

"I'm right behind," he assured Peveril, then returned to the men who were gathering up their shields. "Watch me, watch me!" he yelled, pushing their shoulders so that they overlapped, trying in the span of a few seconds to explain the strength of a shield wall to a bunch of terrified citizens. If they focused on defense, fewer people would die.

Robert tried to get his bearings. FitzOdo was still near, Beneger and Peveril waiting for him to rejoin them. Gilbert . . . Gilbert was nowhere to be seen.

KEEP CALM, LAURENCE REPEATED to himself. *Don't scream. Analyze.* The soldiers around him were all lost to the frenzy and commotion, which is how they would get killed. Laurence was smarter than that, he'd studied under the Earl of Chester for years, and while he knew that his men found his youth to be a source of weakness, Laurence had proven himself with strategy. He walked carefully rather than ran, he controlled his breath that he would not exhaust himself in minutes. He had even pushed soft wax into his ears to keep the clamor from alarming him, outwitting his body's natural instincts. *The gate,* that was his goal, and he would earn Earl Ranulph's favor this day by opening the castle gates for the rest of the army. The great bailey on the inside of the curtain wall was filled with the castle's defenders, but Laurence could tell at a glance that the front lines were full of civilian fodder, while the castle guard was gathered at the rear. *Cowards,* Laurence allowed himself a moment of judgment. It wasn't enough that Prince John had declared war against his brother, but he meant to throw away as many innocent lives as he could for his own folly.

Laurence quickly calculated how many men he needed to push to the castle gatehouse—sadly, they would be overwhelmed if he tried to make that attempt now. He would not spread his men thin too early, not when every passing minute brought reinforcements over the ladders to help with the fighting in the bailey. A quick whistle and he commanded his men to form a perimeter and hold, making a line with their shields that the second rank could reach over for killing blows. The throng of civilians approached but was unsure how to attack, which was all the better as far as Laurence was concerned. This was his moment to flourish, and prove the quality of his character.

The man in front of him suddenly crumpled with a sickening crack. Laurence glanced up at the taller walls of the middle bailey on his right, and the glowing sky made a crystal silhouette of a half-dozen shapes—stones, thrown from the wall itself by defenders higher above—that filled the sky and rained down upon him.

"GOD'S TITS, WHAT ARE they waiting for?" Percy asked. He twisted to look at the back of the bailey, where the Nottingham gords were still waiting, some on *horseback,* for Christ's sake, and had yet to join the fray.

"Well, Ginger," Will Scarlet answered, still using his gang name from a gang that was all but dead, "they're waiting for us to die first."

"I should have fucking stayed in my cell," Percy grumbled back. They could have all waited for this whole thing to be over underground. Those gords weren't interested in fighting side by side, they were hanging back until every last baileyman was dead.

"We need to give them a reason to fight earlier," Scarlet answered. "Come with me."

JONAS SMASHED FORWARD WITH his shield, then sliced with the sword. And again. And again. They were making no ground, but giving it. Noise, screams, blood, the cobbles of Nottingham's streets slick with gore. They'd killed enough of the French to amass a line of shields, and now they were an impenetrable wall. And the longer they lasted, the more people were drawn to help them, crawling back up onto the streets from their hiding places. *Fighting back.* Nottingham wouldn't go down easily, not so long as there were men like Sir Robert FitzOdo to show them the way to victory.

Sword. Shield. Sword. It didn't matter if he found flesh with each jab, it kept the French at bay, ducking behind their own shield wall. And while there was no surfeit to be found in staying smashed at each other endlessly, it gave the others a chance to get high. Sir Robert and his bowmen simply had to climb the nearest buildings and fire down into the French side, and their shield wall would crumple. There was nothing stronger than a shield wall, Jonas knew, but that was in an open field. Here in the streets, the advantage was elevation.

"Fall back!" came the shout, but from *behind.*

"No!" Jonas yelled instantly, nudging the man next to him with an elbow. "Stay in line!"

"Fall back!" it came again, and Jonas braved one second to glance back, where Sir Robert's bald head was easily seen, his sword in the air. "Fall back!"

No, but Jonas could do nothing. Even the slightest hesitation and a gap in their wall broke, splintered. The men behind him retreated and he no longer had their weight to support him. The Frenchman before him shoved and he stumbled. *It would be a rout if they ran.* Jonas had seen this, in Normandy, he was older than FitzOdo, but he thought that—

JEFFEREY THE COBBER DIDN'T want to die like this, rolled into a ball as the French overran the barricade. Somehow his mind flushed with the song he'd been working on, and he felt the dangle of the lyrics he'd been missing to finish it with, but he couldn't grab that thread, his hands over his face, boots smashing into them, he felt his skull crunch.

WHITE BLINDING AGONY, ALL down his spine, the rim of the shield had smashed *through* his teeth, Asher raised his own to defend himself, but his arm was too light, it wasn't there, his arm was gone, missing from the elbow, the shield came back into his face a second time.

MATTHIAS TOOK TWO STEPS, staring at the holes in his chest, weeping blood. *Weeping like Mary had wept,* he closed his eyes and prayed but the Lord wasn't there anymore, He had slipped from Matthias's body through these new openings. Some spiked mace had opened him up, pumping blood, his hands couldn't keep it back, and with a single startling clarity he knew there was no Lord to welcome him in heaven now. His lifetime of piety had not been to any God that cared about him, no, it had been obedience to men who had sold him lies . . .

ROSLYN'S VISION WENT GREY as the soldier squeezed her neck, and she welcomed it. She had known she would not survive this, but she had little else to live for anyway. Rather than fight for air she spent her last few seconds driving her thumbs into her attacker's skull, piercing his eyes, feeling them puncture and goop onto her hands, and she smiled as she felt the Lord's hand lift her from her body and into the white, where her family lay waiting.

"THERE'S FIGHTING IN THE streets," William de Ferrers commented, pointing back east to the open plaza of Market Square.

"No matter," the Sheriff d'Albini answered. "Cheshire is over the walls, and the archers' defense is falling back. We'll have the whole of the bailey by the afternoon, I think."

"You ought to be proud," the King said, offering William a smug smile from atop his horse. "Your father tried to do this and failed. Here we've done it with nothing more than the better part of a morning."

"As you say, Your Grace," William answered the unkind compliment. "Though you also have the better part of the country's army, while my father had only Derbyshire at his side."

"Then that was his error," Richard replied. "Or does it not occur to you that it is planning alone that decides the battle? Our planning was correct, so the castle will be ours. The bailey by the end of the day, I agree, Rutland. We'll need machinery for the second bailey, though."

"We'll have mangonels and petraries by the morning," came the Lord Simon de Senlis, whom Ferrers hardly thought prominent enough to answer the question. "I've set the entirety of my men on to help your architects."

"Good," the King clipped, and turned his horse. "Let me know any developments. Shall we lunch?"

AN AXEHEAD OPENED CLORINDA Rose's stomach and everything but her love for the world spilt out.

CAPTAIN FULCHER DE GRENDON sent Henry Russell running, not sure if he had agreed to his own suicide. But everything the so-called baileyking had said made sense, or at least whatever sense was left to be made in a world as upside down as the hell they were currently living in.

"Lances, and grapples!" he commanded, urging his mount forward. There were a dozen wooden tourney lances still wrapped in linen that had been brought for the archery tournament and never used. They were shorter than full lances and had blunt tips, but most of the Nottingham Guard had little training in their use anyway, and so would be better served with their size. Outside the curtain wall, it was mostly French men-at-arms waiting to climb the ladders now. Fulch believed in Russell's advice—a conroi erupting from the gates of the castle would cause terror in the front lines of the French army, who were in no way prepared for a mounted assault. Fulch could lead his men out and destroy a handful of the siege ladders and still get back within the gates before the French had any idea what to do with themselves. The battlements were being overwhelmed by the sheer quantity of soldiers flooding up onto the bulwark, and Worcester's men were losing ground. They could no longer hoist ladders with the fulcrum arms from the inside. They could only send reinforcements via the infrequent stairs up to the walk, while the French were joining from any of a dozen ladder points. Eventually, the fighting in the bailey would come down to attrition. But if the Guard could destroy even a few more of those ladders from the *other* side, then Russell's men could keep the soldiers controlled and bottlenecked at the stairs down from the wall—turning their disadvantage in offense into an advantage of defense.

It was risky, of course, because it meant opening the gates—the very thing the enemy was trying to do themselves. But it was also the exact reason the move might catch them by surprise.

"Stay by me!" Fulch ordered, then yelled up to the last pocket of longbowmen that were holding their ground on the battlements. "And give us cover!"

THE GUARDSMEN AT THE BARBICAN were sympathetic, they opened the portcullis with just a single, knowing nod. Nobody was supposed to pass through the baileys, but Simon FitzSimon had been denied his due for too long. Some vermin, some gang-scraping cunt had sold lies about Simon's daughter to get her killed, and Nottingham's limpwrist new captain had the audacity to *protect* that filth. Still in the captain's quarters, living in practical luxury compared to the shit of the rest of the castle. Simon's boys had tried to get to that piece of shit, *Will Stutely*, when this all began, but they were in the minority. That was a month ago, a month of injustice. Now, with the war raging, there was a clear path for Simon to smash in the captain's door and shred the villain's neck to sinew and bone.

Behind him, the sounds of war. He knew he should care. He knew he could never drink enough of Sir Richard's small ale to make up for the lives being lost as he walked away from it. His boys were his boys, they could take care of themselves, he'd seen to that. But his girl was his girl. He could never do enough to protect Cait, precious little Cait, he'd never close his eyes without seeing her smiling eyes as a two-year-old, and also her body convulsing on the archery target. The captain's office was up in the quarter keep. If Gisbourne were still alive, he would have delivered Stutely to Simon on a platter. No, it would have never happened in the first place. Gisbourne would have known better.

Men tried to stop him. The prince's men. Simon didn't stop. He moved one with his hands. He might have punched the other. Or thrown him? Didn't matter. He never stopped looking forward. Up the stairs, into the quarter keep, up to the captain's door. He didn't check the lock. He kicked it once, it shuddered, didn't open. Again, nothing. Locked, from the outside. To keep Stutely in.

But Simon knew where to find an axe.

"THIS IS NEEDLESSLY DANGEROUS," Amon chastised Lady Marion, "and I implore you again to return to the camp."

She didn't respond. It had been King Richard's prerogative to position his command post ludicrously close to the front lines, and Amon wondered if he would see his king killed this day for the price of his hubris. But it was not his charge to defend the King.

"I disagree." Marion did not turn. "I know that you will do everything in your power to defend me, sir." He felt the chill of the word *sir*, and how much it meant for her to refrain from using his name. She still held a divisive grudge for what he had done to her. "And so I choose to place myself here in the city, *exactly* so that the danger to you will be greater."

At that she gave him the full icy force of her gaze, and some small piece of Amon's heart broke. With time, as does all things, her bitterness would mend. It was a difficult thing to think she truly wished him bodily harm, but here they were at the King's side, in full view of the castle's wall and the grotesque display of the day's carnage. Surrounded on all sides by the allied companies, he had every reason to expect their safety. But there were pockets of civil resistance throughout the city, and it was not unthinkable that they might quickly find themselves in such an ambush.

"I hope you understand that, given the circumstances, I would consider it my duty—once again—to take you forcibly from this building, to return to a place I can guarantee your safety."

"You would abduct me again." Marion's voice was cruel, she closed her cloak as she watched the melee unfold from the second-story balcony of the inn. "Well go on, then, why don't you try?"

"Because I respect your slightest opinion," he answered, in sincerity, "more than my gravest fact."

If that had any sway over her, it was lost to a new din. A roar went up from the front lines, and Amon watched with some surprise that the front gates of the lower bailey were lurching open. He had not expected Richard's armies to claim that prize so early in the day, and it was clear that the men-at-arms around it were equally unprepared. They broke into random clumps, abandoning their previous posts to fly at the widening maw, opportunists seizing the chance at a fresh kill. It was equally shocking to watch those men smashed aside as a cavalry charge burst out of the gates, lances dropping low and shattering against shields, flattening a dozen men to the earth in a heartbeat, and a dozen more a moment later. "They're leading a sortie," he marveled. "Against the entire army."

And it wasn't just the horses. The moment the cavalry was clear of the gates, a mob followed them. Men on foot, not in uniform, screaming a wild bestial noise, set loose upon the nearest ranks like a pack of wolves.

SKINNY PINK SCREAMED BLOODY murder and charged with the rest of them. *The gate was open!* There was finally an escape from the bailey, all they had to do was fight their way out. They were a raging stampede, the swell drew him toward the enemy . . . carried like a wave in the ocean. His mother had told him not to get involved with those gang boys. She'd begged him. She'd threatened to kill herself if ever he got hurt. A spear thrust into the gap between the two men in front of him, its blade snagging his shoulder, he begged his mother for forgiveness, for help.

POTTER SPEARED HIS LANCE through the open rungs of the siege ladder and urged his horse away, just as de Grendon had ordered. The strain twisted the ladder until its tip slipped off the battlement walls above, and it skidded down the face of the wall, crashing into the next ladder in its path. Potter screamed something victorious and raised his fist in the air. His riding skills had never been great, and he'd never so much as touched a lance before, but this Common Guardsman was the goddamned savior of Nottingham. He reared his horse to return to the gates, but the French lines—who had recoiled from them barely a minute ago—was all too close now. Potter dropped the lance and reached for his sword, but his horse bucked, and Potter could not keep himself asaddle as he slid sickeningly off, his horse falling on top of him.

JOHN LITTLE SHUT THE door behind him, ignoring Marion's pleas. He could guard this door for her better on the outside than the inside. The mob escaping the castle was coming their way, but they appeared to be looking more for escape than quarrel. John Little could see to it that nobody chose this building as their hideaway. Not with Marion inside. She was too important now.

At first he held his staff out, warning those that came too close.

Then he pushed into them.

When the first man made an obvious choice to engage, John struck his quarterstaff out for the man's chest. Wheeled it around, caught the man's wild swing of a sword. Another was behind him.

He screamed, for everyone they'd lost so far, and John Little didn't mind so much if he'd be next on that list, if his place there kept Marion off it. He was too old for this. Maybe it was better this way. He swung again, cracked a man's jaw, waited for the next, they swarmed toward him.

SIMON DE SENLIS SPURRED his horse around. The gates were closing again, having belched out the castle's defenders, and let none in. He kicked his heels in, and called to his bearers. They could reposition closer, around the curve of the gatehouse's tower. In case it opened again.

GILBERT MADE IT BACK TO the Trip to Jerusalem, and reached his hand out to the Zinn girl, didn't he? The friar watched as she took it, incredulous, and Gilbert led her away. *There's nothing we can do now*, he told her, *but see to our own.*

WILL STUTELY SMASHED THE moment there was a head to strike. Someone was breaking the door down with an axe, screaming hell at him. He didn't wait to find out who it was. The broken table leg cracked when it found skull, and Stutely swung again. Blood splattered his face, matted the wild red mane of the intruder. The man stuttered and fell, but Stutely swung again, three times even after the body had hit the floor, until he heard the skull crack open, and then three times more.

He stared at the open door.

Out there, everyone was dying. Because of what he'd done.

He'd never meant for that. He was just trying to do what he thought was right.

He closed the door. He wanted to lock himself in again.

A shattered hole in the door, rimmed in blood, let in the sounds of Nottingham.

Everyone—*everyone*—out there, wanted him dead.

Stutely grabbed his beard, curled into a ball, and wept.

FOR NOTHING, FOR FOLLOWING his orders, for standing in the wrong place, a kind man lost his life—and with it, his chance to ever teach his son the things he had learned, about anger and how it was a poison.

FOR NOTHING, FOR SOME other man's ambition, some forgettable man, a mother's son was sliced open. Her tortured years of raising him alone, of the things she'd sacrificed for herself, her years of poverty that he would not starve, her nightly tears at her own inadequacy, wasted in a dash of crimson in the battlefield.

FOR NOTHING, FOR GLORY, whatever the hell that was, a friend and a lover—who was never quite good enough at either—tumbled from his horse and out of himself. What good had it been, wondering at the stars, practicing his disciplines, debating the philosophies of the ancient Greeks, and studying the economics of spice routes? All he had been, all he had wanted to be, was nothing to the steel blade that pierced him above the sternum.

FOR NOTHING, FOR A piece of earth a few feet farther than another, a hundred thousand wishes wisped away.

FOR NOTHING, FOR DIRT, for one man to say that he claimed it, a grieving father was finally gone himself, would never wake to the memory of the empty impression in the bassinette again, but as he fell he knew he would miss it more than anything else.

FOR NOTHING, FOR NOTHING, for nothing, a hundred sons became a hundred griefs, and a hundred more, and their memories, stacked up upon each other, hundreds of lifetimes of love and needs, amounted to little more than a film of dirt that, too, blew away, for nothing.

SIXTY-TWO

ARABLE DE BUREL

THE TRIP TO JERUSALEM

IF THE FIRST TUNNEL under the walls of the city was terrifying, this then was some arcane hell. This wasn't a tunnel. This wasn't a passage. Perhaps a hare might think it useful, but to a human it was madness. They had to crawl, but *crawl* was not even fit to describe this—as one could *crawl* on one's hands and knees, which would have been a luxury here. It would be more accurate to say that Arable was *slithering*, with her elbows trapped by her navel and her fists punching herself in the chin with every few inches she was able to nudge forward.

Perhaps on a flat surface, or through grass, this might have been slightly less torturous. But the rough stones scraped her arms, and her sleeves were doing little to protect her. And it was anything but straight or smooth, its incline was often grueling and even the slightest of advancement came only at laborious cost. The only advantage of the tiny confines was that she did not fear sliding backward onto Nick Delaney, because she could simply inhale a full breath and her lungs would expand and wedge her safely in place. Such was how tight it was.

Oh, and pitch black.

"You, then, share the same lunacy as the Red Lions," the innkeeper of the Trip to Jerusalem had answered, an aging man knighted Sir Richard-at-the-Lee. Zinn referred to him as the *greenbeard*, and he seemed more than willing to honor his part of whatever bargain he'd made with the Red Lions. *"But I'll tell you the same thing I told them, that you can pay me all the honey in England and there's still nothing I can do about the size of the hole."* He had led them to the second story of his inn, into a secluded dining space that was all cave, and drew back a tapestry to reveal a honeycomb pocket. *"Not sure why I even bother hiding the thing, since no fool would ever think to climb themselves in there."*

Except the Red Lions. They'd been using Zinn and other children to climb in with spades and scrape away at its sides in the hopes of one day making it a possible secret entrance to the castle. Whether it even connected all the way in, the greenbeard didn't know. That thought was more horrifying than anything else—the idea that she'd eventually come to a dead end, and they'd have to crawl out again *backward*.

Zinn was the smallest of them, but she stayed behind—her chopped ear would get her killed if she made it into the castle. So Arable led, the Delaneys next, and Bolt struggling behind them.

There was no movement in the air. She was sweating through her every article of clothing. The air was the same temperature as her breath, and disturbingly stale. Any moment she truly thought upon how absolutely trapped she was—unable to move her arms, or to twist, or to breathe freely, or ever to be out of this hell if she wanted to—she felt panic claw out her heart and she started to sob. Not a cry of sadness or loss, but a wail, a horror that knew no bounds, her teeth would chatter, and she had to prop her feet up to keep herself from sliding. She wanted to flail her arms berserk, and she could already feel the deep bruises caused by her fitful spasms.

Nick's voice floated up toward her in the utter inky black. "Breathe, Arable, breathe. You're strong, you're stronger than this. Don't think about it. Imagine the rocks are gone. There's sky above you, and we're just playing a game. *Breathe.*"

The only thing that *telling her to breathe* would do was make it more likely she would punch his face the moment they were clear of this. She knew he meant well, but now was not the time to coddle her.

"If I can do it, you can do it," came Bolt's voice from farther back, and that—surprisingly—helped. Not because it made her *believe in herself,* but because she knew that the faster she went, the harder it would be for his lame leg to keep up. If "Charley Dancer" got lost in this tomb beneath the castle, then one good thing had happened this day. And it must have been harder on the Delaneys, too, being wider than her, but they refused to show their misery.

It was impossible to know how long they burrowed. Arable had to stop often, the strain on her body was too much. She worried desperately about what damage she was doing to herself, *to her daughter.* And there was obviously no chance for the others to squeeze past her and forage forward, so they were all stuck at her piteous pace. The first few times she stopped to rest they encouraged her to keep going, but after a while she simply said, "We're stopping," and they did not argue. She would lie there, bury her head into her forearms with her eyes closed, and try desperately to control her breathing, to slow her heart, to ignore her circumstances. To think on better times, until she could muster up the motivation to move rather than to die.

She tried to picture her daughter in her womb, similarly confined, unable to move, in darkness. It wasn't the same thing, not by a long shot, but it helped to put herself in the mind of her baby. She felt a connection that reminded her why she needed her heart to keep pumping, her lungs to keep breathing. And eventually, *eventually,* she would slide one elbow up a few more inches and pull her body forward, returning to the endless, unbearable, claustrophobic shuffle through crumbled stone and rubble.

There was a point, surely hours and hours in, when the noises became slightly different and Arable tilted her head carefully up and did not hit it on rock for the one-thousandth time. She pushed against the ground and found the roof of the tunnel here was slightly higher, and she released another cry as she rolled over and finally stretched her arms out. The pain was nearly crippling, but it felt wondrous to unbend them again. Her muscles trembled uncontrollably, and she lay on her back, and her lungs heaved for great desperate gobs of air.

"It opens a bit," she gasped, hearing Nick crawl in behind her, also exploding in huffs of relief and agony. But he kept moving, shuffling around her, she could hear his hands patting out the circumference of the little cavern.

"Don't try standing," he said, "but we can all sit here, at least. Let's catch our breath."

Arable cried again this time, and fingers fumbled against her leg to find her hand, which she held tightly. She had no doubt it was Nick, and she thought back to the idea not so long ago that the man had developed feelings for her. And here she was, trapped in a coffin with him and Bolt as well, who a year ago had almost certainly harbored an infatuation of his own, and perhaps still did. The world had a cruel way of putting people together.

"I'm pregnant," she blurted out in desperation, having absolutely no filter on her thoughts.

"And you just found out?" Peetey answered. It wasn't really that funny, but Arable was a raw nerve and she bellowed in laughter, as did the others. They were so desolate, their emotions so extreme, that any shift could send all four of them careening from one mania to another with little effort.

They waited and took turns stretching, untying their boots and emptying out the loose rocks, and trying in vain to find any words to describe their terrible plight. "I would trade anything to be in the other group," Nick mumbled.

That had been a contentious debate. Men like Lord Beneger and Quill had knowledge that would have been useful once inside the castle, but they were also the most capable of managing the threat of Sir Robert FitzOdo. Essentially, Arable and her four companions were the *least* useful at both tasks, which is why it fell on their unqualified shoulders to handle the little thing of ending the war. They had thought this would be an actual tunnel, that they could jaunt up in a few minutes and pop magically into the castle. The other group even thought they might catch up if they could deal with FitzOdo quickly.

There was no *quickly* in here. The others were hours behind, if they were still alive at all.

And the war—the war they thought they could put a swift end to—had been waging for all that time. While they rested, here in the black belly of the rock, more and more died.

"I assume I'm not the only one," Arable fought to regain her voice, "who's thought about how this cuts our options in half?"

There was a bit of silence. It was Bolt who eventually asked, "How do you mean?"

"Our job is to find Prince John, and convince him that it truly is King Richard out there," she answered. "And, if that fails, to *extract* him. Which is obviously where you two come in, I don't think I would be of any use there. Hopefully you have an idea on how to do that?"

"I didn't want to think about it much, either," Nick answered, squeezing her hand. "But I imagine it meant smashing something heavy over the prince's head and dragging him around a bit."

Arable grimaced at the thought. "I was picturing something more like a gag and tying his hands together, but the point is the same. Can you imagine trying to drag an unconscious body, or a person who doesn't want to go, back down this tunnel?"

Another silence clearly meant no.

"So if Prince John doesn't believe us, well then I don't know what we do." She laughed at this, because she had nothing else to feel. "Aside from die. I suppose we just sit and wait to die."

"Frankly, that sounds better than ever coming back this way," Nick said, and gave her knee a gentle squeeze.

The idea that the Nottingham gangs had arranged to use this crawlspace was laughable. That this was some sort of "ingenious plan" for ferreting people in and out of the castle was ludicrous. But at the same time, it was a mortifying comment on how difficult it would be to get into the castle otherwise. She thought back on her winter's escape from the castle through the postern door with Will Scarlet and Elena, and how insanely easy that was in comparison. But without that path, this wormhole proved that Castle Rock truly was as impenetrable as its reputation claimed.

Unless one had a king's army. Perhaps the siege was already over. Eventually they might poke their heads out of the ground to discover that it had all ended hours ago.

They slogged on.

Nick offered to go first this time, even to come back and report what he'd found, but nobody wanted to be left alone in the absolute dark. And Arable was the smallest of them, and it made little sense to put their largest person first in case they bottlenecked in a hole through which he could not fit. So Arable led again, and she cried again, and she wished that literally every single thing in her entire life had gone slightly differently if it meant things would not have led her to this inhuman misery.

After another hour, or longer, she felt certain that all their hopes were dashed. The tunnel had ended, as it had always seemed like to do, and her breathing became erratic and she knew she was about to dive off the edge of sanity. She kicked her legs in fury and realized there was a pocket of air above her a few feet back, and returning to it she was able—with great effort—to squeeze upward into a vertical shaft, and her fingers probed higher. The rush of blood was invigorating, to stand up again, and her fingertips found a few smoother lines in the rock. "This is mason work," she whispered with excitement. "We're getting close."

That rush gave her the energy she needed for the last—and most brutal—climb, ascending a chimneylike flue between the quarried stone and the unforgiving cave wall. They took this section one at a time, for if her legs gave out and she fell, they would all break their bones upon each other, and Arable was categorically uninterested in finding out which one of them would turn to cannibalism first. In the end she guessed it was thirty or forty feet up, but by far the most exhausting thing she'd ever done, always barely keeping her body suspended in the air by applying pressure to both sides of the ragged flue.

At the ledge it turned to a horizontal crawl again, and her muscles found relief. Another mole tunnel, yes, but at the end was the faintest of light—a tiny speck of soft amber.

There was room at last to shuffle, too, and wide enough that two might uncomfortably do so side by side. She stayed to give a hand to Nick behind her, and then moved down toward the light. Bolt needed the most help in the ascent, his leg being more hindrance than ever, and he needed a few minutes to recover as his chest seized and his muscles cramped. At long last Arable drew him with her down the tunnel, that they might recognize where the light was coming from.

The tunnel chomped down one last time into the tightest crawlspace yet, but this was just a single rock to squeeze beneath and then a drop down. On the opposite side was a full tunnel, a real and honest man-made passage, and they were emerging into it by dropping in from its ceiling. A lantern flickered from a dozen paces away, and Arable looked around for an easy method of slipping down from their stony lip.

"Shit," Bolt whispered beside her.

"What?"

"This is the gaols."

She looked again, and he was right. She had thought perhaps it was part of the wine cellars, but she recognized now the iron bars glinting a lantern's edge to the right. "*Shit.*"

"What's wrong?" Nick whispered from behind.

"This is a dead end after all," Bolt said back to them. "We're in the prisons. There's no way out from here, not without the keys."

"We came all this way," Peetey whispered, "just to end in a prison cell? Why would the Red Lions want that?"

"They weren't trying to get *into* the castle," Arable sighed, piecing it together, they were trying to get people out. That explains . . . Lord Beneger said that one of the Red Lions had turned traitor, which is how Will Scarlet came to be arrested. That must have been part of the plan. They *wanted* him to be arrested, so they could test their tunnel and see if they could break him out."

"Not a very nice way to do it," Nick mumbled.

"I didn't get the impression they liked him much," Peetey answered.

They lingered in silence a bit, staring over the lip down into the gaol tunnel.

"Well," Nick stammered, "we'll just have to figure it out."

"Figure it out?" Arable replied. "The Red Lions *figured it out,* that's what this whole tunnel is for! If they went through all this work to get someone out of the prisons, what makes you think we can just *figure out* a new way in the next hour?"

She didn't want to go back any more than the rest of them—the sheer thought of it made her muscles throb anew. But if they dropped into that tunnel, they might literally be trapping themselves.

"It's strange," Bolt said by the exit hole, then clicked his tongue and listened for its echoed response. "I don't hear anything. Sounds deserted."

"That *is* strange," Peetey huffed. "Gilbert said the prisons had been filled to the brim, twice and twice again."

Bolt looked at her, perhaps asking permission to continue, and Arable shook her head no. But he slipped his legs over the sandstone lip, eased his hips over, clung to Nick's arms for another foot or so, then dropped into the gaols.

Madness. Absolute madness.

With help, Arable dipped over the rock ledge and stumbled down to the ground. She might have landed better had her legs not been so fatigued, so she consented to slump down and just collapse under the exhaustion. There was a bit of movement to the air at last, and her sweat welcomed the cooler air. Her arms covered in goose pimples, while her bowels screamed to be released. One by one the Delaneys landed next to her, descending from the curious hole above them. It was practically invisible from below—just a ribbon of cave wall that rolled along the tunnel, that nobody would ever suspect held a nearly un-navigable hole. She was also unsure any of them could figure a way back up to it without a ladder—but again, these were problems for another time.

"This is downright eerie," Bolt said again, leading them down the next tunnel, careful to make no sound. "Something's wrong. Never seen the gaols empty."

Eventually, they moved. Every cluster of cells they passed was indeed vacant, the doors swung open. There was at long last another noise, like a far-off waterfall, muffled by a thousand miles. She'd been here before, *exactly here,* when she'd helped free Will and Elena. It had been easy enough to open the individual cells, as each key was slung from a ring nearby. The trick was to get out of the prisons themselves, which she knew required a different key on both sides simultaneously. Arable had stolen Captain Gisbourne's ring, which he'd left behind—*purposefully,* she reminded herself with bitterness—but she'd discarded that ring long ago, thinking there would never be a reason to need it again. How she wished she'd held onto it now, that she might save the day with a fortuitous reveal.

"I'll go to the entrance," Bolt offered. "Could be I'll know the men there. If they recognize me, they may let me out."

"Or you'll turn us all in," Arable muttered.

"Arable," he responded, a shiver overcoming his shoulders. He turned to look at her, his wide eyes bulging with intensity. "On Reginold's life, I swear, I mean to help."

She had no answer. It didn't matter if she trusted him, because he was their only hope. He scampered off down the tunnel and up an incline, which she recognized as leading to the main slope up to the middle bailey.

Nottingham Castle. She had never wanted to be here again.

And to think she was trying to *save it,* of all things. She ought to just sit here and let King Richard's armies raze it to the ground. Turn to rubble every stone and memory—of Roger de Lacy, of William de Wendenal, of her father and the discolored rock in St. Nicholas's yard that represented his grave. There was nothing for her in Nottingham, and there never would be.

But here she was still, because she was the dumbest girl God had ever made.

I hope you're better than me, she prayed for her daughter. *I hope I can give you a life that will never involve anything as terrible as all this.*

"Surprise," Bolt said, poking his head around the corner again.

"What did you find?"

"The gate's wide open." He shrugged, shaking his head back and forth. "We're clear."

SIXTY-THREE

ARTHUR A BLAND

LOWER BAILEY, NOTTINGHAM CASTLE

"Go, go, go, go!" Arthur led the men at a crouch as long as seemed reasonable, then they broke into a run. Back onto the battlements from which they'd previously retreated. The fighting was now outside the curtain wall—both the mounted Nottingham Guardsmen and the bulk of Will Scarlet's *baileyfolk* had streamed out the front gates to bring the battle to the French line. This distraction had successfully slowed the stream of soldiers climbing the siege ladders, and gave the archers a chance to reclaim ground. Arthur was a shit shot with a bow, but when the French were shoulder to shoulder as they were, it didn't take much skill to find a fucking target.

"Down!" he yelled again, and the eight Guardsmen ahead of them took a knee. They each held a tall shield that they angled as they knelt, giving the archers a few perfect seconds to shoot over their heads. Arthur let his arrow fly and knew it sailed shy to the right of their target, but he pulled another arrow and compensated to the left. His middle fingers were bleeding from the hemp cord, and he silently reminded himself to never make fun of David's fancy archery glove again. As soon as the second wave of arrows had flown, he screamed for the shield men again, who raised their defense and ran another dozen paces forward.

"Pull with both your arms," David said, beside him, hunching his head until their next opportunity.

Arthur stared at his friend until those words made sense, which was never.

"You're just holding your bow out with your left hand," David explained, "and pulling the string with your right."

"That's how you shoot a fucking bow!" He couldn't believe David thought this was the proper time for a lesson in archery finesse.

"But your right arm is tiring, isn't it?"

"My whole body is fucking tiring!"

"Start with your bow at the center of your body," he demonstrated as best he could, given that they were shuffling behind a rampaging shield line, "and push it forward with your left just as much as you're pulling back with your right. Don't shoot this time, watch me."

"Down!" Arthur would have yelled either way, but Arthur knelt along with the shield men and watched David as the arrows flew. He loosed three arrows in the time it'd taken Arthur to do two, and still had enough time to flash him a reassuring face between each one, showing him his proper bow placement.

"Do you see the difference?" David asked when the shields went up again, and they started nudging forward.

"No," Arthur said, honestly. It looked exactly like every other damned person who'd ever shot an arrow, excepting David's smug little face.

"It'll keep your aim in line," he continued. "Right now you're yanking the string back and missing your target."

"Fucking hell." He shook his head. How David was able to keep track of Arthur's form during the midst of this madness was so far beyond him. "I thought you said you'd never killed anyone before!"

What rippled beneath his friend's skin had no humor. "Well, I've quick become an expert."

When the shields went down again Arthur stood and tried this new technique, giving his muscles equal weight as if he were tearing a giant wishbone in two. The end result was an arrow that sprung far to his left and down into the bailey—thankfully finding nothing but mud, but Arthur nearly exploded with anger. "I'm doing it my way!" He pulled another arrow and flung it into the dwindling group of Frenchmen. He felt a painful searing slice in his fingertips as this arrow too flew wide, and he cursed every damned thing that'd ever been bold enough to bother existing in his path. He was useless up here. He needed a sword and a Frenchman close enough to stab with it.

"We've got this covered." David nudged him away. "Get back down to Will."

"*Henry*," Arthur corrected him.

"Go!"

He clambered backward, looking down into the bailey in search of Will Scarlet. He hadn't left the castle with the rest of the baileyfolk—frankly, Arthur wasn't sure that was even part of Will's plan at all. But when the castle gates opened for the first time in a month, those baileyfolk had seized the opportunity to fight their way out. He wondered how many even engaged the French at all, or if they fled south down the castle walls until they ran out of army to fight and could escape, finally, back into the city. Find their families. If they still lived.

Wherever they'd gone, the tactic had worked. As the cranes grappled a few more siege ladders up and over the walls, the French had fewer opportunities to reclimb onto the battlements. It took twenty men and women below to spin the turncocks, even with the tall wooden fulcrum arms they'd built to make it easier. If the curtain wall had been any higher, then it might not have been possible at all. But there were already a dozen stolen French ladders cluttering up the bailey, and it didn't seem that the invaders had built many more than they'd used on their first wave.

Arthur practically ran down the open stone staircase into the bailey. The enemy that had already made it below was grouped in one massive cluster on the north end now, held in place by the Worcester garrison, but Arthur could see they were struggling to contain them. He spotted a heavy spiked mace lying on the ground between him and that throng, and felt a burst of dark joy. David may be good with arrows, but Arthur—Arthur was good at clobbering things. Swords were nice but they required such . . . aim. But a mace, all it wanted was to smash things to pulp, and Arthur very coincidentally wanted the exact same thing.

It was surprising how quickly his senses—and humor—had returned to him, once the tide of battle had changed. The first few hours had been like nothing he'd ever experienced. Pure blistering white fear had turned his bones into fire, and when the French topped the walls and slowly started gaining ground he'd been overcome with a singular clarity of action that had been intoxicating. Men were killed all around him at times, but not Arthur. Perhaps he started to believe in his own words, that the three of them were indeed special in this rabble, but it prompted him to lose himself in the mania of it all—something like the fabled euphoria of a long-distance runner, where time sped by and blurred together and his muscles could not tire. It was hard to tell how long that lasted, but now that the French were being beaten back, he felt the slow, cold normality sink in, which made the world all the easier to laugh at. In normal speed, Arthur looked at the throng of enemy soldiers and knew he just had to smash his mace into each of their heads, and fuck all if that wasn't the easiest thing he'd ever been asked to do.

"Arthur!" came a voice, and he was quickly joined by Will Scarlet, the red paint on his face marred with sludge and blood. He carried a tower shield with a red cross on it, scarred with deep axe gouges. It was nearly as tall as he was.

"Perfect," Arthur said, waving Will closer. "Let's do this together. Make room for me, I swing, then fall back. Over and over until they're dead."

Will made a couple of quick pointed breaths. "All of them?"

"Do you think we should keep a few alive?"

"No, you're right." Scarlet smiled. "All of them."

They ran into the line where it was thinnest, Will pounding forward hidden entirely by the shield, pushing against the first man he could find, then turning into a slim profile. Arthur filled the gap, wheeled the heavy mace up and down, and smashed a man's helmet in, bursting blood out the front of his crushed skull. Will closed the shield and backed up.

They could save Nottingham, the three of them. They'd united the Guard and the baileyfolk. They'd negotiated for the release of the prisoners who had joined the fray. The defenders of the castle were three times what they would've been without them. *Let the prince and his men stay in the baileys above.* He laughed, swung, killed, retreated. *Let them look down at the real heroes here.* Smash, skull, gore, meat. *Captain of the Guard, Arthur a Bland.* Swing, pound, bone, crack. *Bend the knee, Sir Arthur a Bland, Sir Arthur of Nottingham.* Black, crunch, pulp, pop! *Prince Arthur! King Arthur! Here's your God, Tuck, here's the God you'll never meet, a God of death, a God of Gods!*

Around him, the screams, the screams, the screams of victory.

The French were dead, only a pile of bodies, moaning and begging for mercy, which they would not find. Nottingham Guard next to Red Lion next to poor-folk next to nobleman all there, raising their weapons, roaring, roaring.

He turned his attention up to the battlements, and found the archers there rejoicing, too. He spotted David—always easy to find in a crowd, thanks to his height and golden locks—who raised his bow in victory. They waved at each other, and Arthur laughed that he was so damned lucky to be alive at a time when such a thing as this was possible.

"That's just the first wave," Will was saying, trying to dampen Arthur's cele-bration.

"Bring another!" Arthur shouted in his face, heaving the weight of the bloody mace from hand to hand. "I've got more in me!"

He was met by Will's curious expression, which carried with it a hesitation. As if he did not recognize Arthur, and perhaps he didn't. Arthur had never expected to be here, embracing the city he'd hated, and the Guardsmen he'd despised, and himself . . . who he'd never been exactly fond of. But defending the city felt good, as good a thing as ever he'd done. There were still people that needed him, and damn but he still had room for scars.

David joined them shortly, and pressed a skin of water into Arthur's chest. "Drink."

He did, amazed that he hadn't realized how parched he was. Leave it to Da-vid, always the saint to whatever-it-was-that-Arthur-was, to think of bringing him water even at a time like this.

"Facking fack," David said, cracking his neck, "that was lunacy."

"I hope some of them got through alive," Will said, looking deeply at the front gates of the castle, where his allies had escaped. "Sad that they have a bet-ter chance out there than in here."

Arthur couldn't follow his logic. "What do you mean?"

"The prisoners," Will answered. "At least out there they might get out of this alive. In here . . ."

"What're you talking about?" Arthur balked. "We got them out of the gaols."

Will scoffed. "You think that'll matter when this is over? If this is ever over."

Arthur hadn't thought about it at all. His mind hadn't really grasped the concept of what anything would be like afterward. Would the captain's offer of pardons stand? Would the prisoners be sent back below to pay for whatever crimes the prince thought they should be punished for? Would he and David be captured once their faces were finally recognized? Did he even want to stay?

Or did the world just go back to the way it was, thieving in the forest, with the Sheriff building little posts in the Sherwood to search for them? That was an impossible world, it was forever ago.

And if he had a choice, which side would Arthur be on?

"What *do* we do after this?" David asked him quietly.

"I don't know." He clasped his friend's shoulder, unable to bear that burden at the moment. "But it'll start with drinking."

"That, I can agree with."

"You know I thought of something earlier," Arthur added, remembering a stray thought. "When we left Marion's group, you said that we ought to stop running and build a castle instead. Well here it is, David, you got your castle."

David's thin smile had a bit of pride in it.

At that, a commotion at the front gates aroused their attention. *"Open the gates!"* came a hurried call. *"Captain Grendon!"* They all turned to the main entrance, where a dozen men rushed forward to lift the massive timber barrels from their iron locks. It was a good sign, that the French must've retracted far enough that they felt safe to briefly open the gates again. The Nottingham Guard came streaming forward, whooping at the return of their captain.

The moment the gate heaved open, a single body appeared in its gap. It was Captain de Grendon alright—horseless, nursing an injured arm, covered head to heel in blood. He had led the mounted assault out of the gates, to break the bases of the siege ladders, which was how they'd claimed this first victory. Arthur had assumed nobody on that assault would come back alive, but here he was—the heroic captain, returning to his castle. Battered, beaten—but walking, and victorious. That's how Arthur wanted to end this day, too.

"Close the gates!" came another command, and the ground thundered.

"Hurry!"

It was hard to tell because he was limping, but Captain de Grendon was *running*.

"They're English!" the captain screamed, then his back exploded with arrows and he fell into the slop.

The gates screamed on their hinges nearly shut when a roar sounded from the other side, and the mouth of the castle was suddenly blocked by a horseman who swung his blade down into the heads of the men who were pulling the gate closed. Then another horse squeezed into the gap, a renewed struggle, until the gates lurched a second time . . . this time *opening*. A dozen horses burst through the entrance at full gallop, pounding over Fulcher de Grendon's body with little care. The earth shook with their mass, and more were coming, more, not just more—the entire fucking army. It grabbed Arthur by his bones and throttled him, he turned and ran, unable to speak, to scream, he could only count the number of steps between himself and the barbican up to the second bailey and he knew he could not make it in time.

This is the tale of a boy that was angry with the world.

Will Scarlet on his right side, David of Doncaster on his left, they ran. There was no way to plug that hole, no way to close the gates again. Just like that, the lower bailey was lost. Up on the ramparts the archers scrambled to shoot down into the attackers, but down here there were just people ready to be trampled. They couldn't fight *this*.

Nobody ever taught him that his hands could be used as
anything but fists.

Screams, again, this time the dying. Arthur wondered pitifully if the people behind him might slow the horses down with their bodies. Might buy him a few extra seconds of life.

So he smashed the world, to make it as ugly as he thought it was.
As ugly as he thought himself.

Up ahead, the slope and the bridge up to the barbican, where the portcullis was already being lowered. It stopped a few feet off the ground—low enough for people to scramble beneath, but impossible for a horse. The men who manned the gates knew the danger, and a small group of spearmen had already come out with shields to make a wall, to let as many people through before the horses got to them. Arthur prayed he would get there in time. He didn't even realize he was praying, but he asked God for help more times in thirty seconds than in thirty years.

One day the angry boy met another boy, whose hands were open, not closed.
The angry boy had never seen such a thing before.
Didn't know hands could do that.

The crowd around the portcullis was huge, a hundred people desperately trying to duck beneath it to safety, and the spearmen expanded to keep them protected. Some joined that group, though armed only with swords they fared little chance against mounted attacks. Arthur ran past the shield line, astonished he was alive, pushing forward, urging, he could hear the riot of violence behind him. The archers, too, were retreating from the curtain wall, back to the doorways that led up to the middle bailey barracks. He cursed whoever had given the command to open the gates for the captain, who didn't think the French could rush it in time.

The angry boy used his fists on the new boy, because it was
the only language he spoke.

After ducking under the iron teeth of the gate, Arthur helped Will Scarlet do the same, but his stomach lurched when David was not there. He turned and looked through the grate's wide squares, but David was not nearby. Damned damned David of Doncaster, always easy to spot in a crowd, he was still down at the foot of the hill with four other men. They'd picked up one of the siege ladders and had turned it into a fence, keeping the charging horses at bay.

And the new boy, bleeding, welcomed the angry boy still,
with open hands.

Because that was the only language he spoke, too.

Arthur screamed his name, as others flooded under the gate. They even raised it up a few more feet that the crowd could escape faster. But some were still behind, fighting back, or creating a blockade with David. David had probably called Arthur's name, asking for him to help, and he hadn't heard. Or maybe David had just gone, because that was who he was. It was his instinct to help before ever looking after himself. It was that thing Arthur had thought he'd found, the urge to help—but here he was, realizing it wasn't *in him* yet.

He could *talk* about it, but it wasn't in his bones. David . . . David did it just as natural as breathing.

In time, the angry boy learned to open his hands, and with it
he opened his heart.

The makeshift hovels that the baileyfolk had built from the broken spectator stands, they were obstacles for the horses, too. The siege ladders quickly turned those obstacles into dead ends. They'd accidentally made a maze. And from above, some quick-thinking shitheads in the middle bailey started throwing barrels down, small casks full of oil, that shattered and splashed open amongst all that wooden claptrap. *Bam bam bam,* the barrels fell with sickening noise, even over the roar of everything else, and quickly followed by a hail of arrows, their heads lit ablaze, and where they found wood and oil the flames took quickly.

One of those barrels, sent by some horse-fucking Guardsman who thought he was saving the day—Arthur watched as it crashed squarely over his friend David's head.

When the new boy died, the angry boy's heart closed into a stone fist.

Arthur was carried backward by the crowd, away from the portcullis. The world had lost all color except the orange of flame. The gate slammed down, its hideous iron scream putting an end to the day's fight. More arrows rained down from above. The structures of the lower bailey billowed into a massive column, the black smoke encompassing the entire bailey, choking the attackers and forcing them back. The French had conquered the bailey but couldn't use it, not now, not until the fires were out. Anyone who tried to stay in that inferno would be burnt to cinders.

Arthur didn't move from the inner gate, despite the heat, despite Will Scarlet's attempts to pry his bleeding fingers off those iron bars. His eyes were locked on the black shape that was once his only friend.

And when the angry boy smashed the world again, it was all the worse.
Because it was no longer the only language he knew,
it was now the language he chose.

SIXTY-FOUR

QUILLEN PEVERIL

THE SKY WAS BLACK, though it was but only midafternoon. Quillen covered his mouth and nose with his jerkin whenever they were outside, and his eyes stung from the ash in the air. None of them knew what exactly to make of the raging smoke that erupted still from the castle's first bailey, but not one of them was naïve enough to think that the castle being on fire could count as a good thing.

He was still paired with Lord Beneger and the earl Robert of Huntingdon, though they had lost Gilbert some time ago in one of the many instances when they'd been separated from Sir Robert FitzOdo. Their day was spent in waves of attack and retreat, running at sometimes breakneck speeds through the streets parallel to those the main English army occupied, trying to keep up with Fitz-Odo and his mobilized pockets of followers in the city. At times the three of them fought reluctantly alongside those citizens just to keep near FitzOdo, at other times they worked against them—notifying the army that they were about to be assaulted, in the hopes of dissuading any more needless killing. More than a few times Quill stopped to wonder what exactly their mission had devolved into.

"Why not head back to the Trip to Jerusalem?" he asked at the next opportunity. "We can secure it now, and defend it if FitzOdo comes back later."

"There are only three of us, Peveril." Lord Beneger was clearly loath to explain himself. "You've seen how many followers FitzOdo has. We can't defend that tavern from him if he comes back to it. Our only chance is stop him out here."

"Then let's just stab him already!" They'd been near FitzOdo all day, sometimes fighting side by side.

Beneger shook his head. "If we confront him while he's with his people, they'll eviscerate us. But if we can isolate him, then we can control him. That's the key to winning your battles, Peveril. Only participate in fights you know you can win."

Lord Robert's bated breath told Quill that he was having similar doubts.

"Arable might need us," Quill argued. "They might already be back. This wasn't the plan."

"The plan was to stop FitzOdo, to clear a path for her."

"Killing the knight doesn't change anything." Lord Robert's voice was careful. "If his followers all go back to the Trip later, as you say, they'll still overwhelm us—with or without him. But if we go back now, at least we can be there if Arable's group is successful."

Lord Beneger's brow hardened on them. "If we go back, our only strategy is to hope for the best. Out here, we have our best opportunity to strike."

"Ben," Quill said, not even meaning to be so informal, "FitzOdo did a lot of things in the name of Robin Hood, but he wasn't . . ."

The look he received was as good as a slap in the face.

"*Don't,*" was all Beneger said. But Quill couldn't help but wonder if they were chasing FitzOdo for the wrong reasons. If Beneger had become so obsessed with hunting down his son's murderer that he could not see the folly in what they were doing now. The Grieving Father of Nottingham was already beyond fatigued by their day of skirmishes he was ill suited for. The man was on the wrong side of age to strike fear into the hearts of anyone who did not know him. It was his reputation and name that made people give him his leave, but in the midst of a melee with strangers he was just an older man with silvering hair—quite the easy combatant at a glance. Quill recalled with unease his first encounter with Lord Beneger in the spiral stairwell, where he had broken his knife against the stone wall. His best days were behind him, and still he pushed on.

This was a man driven to a single goal. And it was not the right one.

Quill was about to suggest to Lord Robert that they leave Beneger to his revenge, when the earl pointed a finger through the grey haze of the street. "There."

FitzOdo was retreating from the group he'd met. He was carrying a heavy glaive now, and the awkward dimensions of the massive axe prevented him from running.

"He's leaving them."

"And heading toward the Trip," Beneger added. "What did I tell you? It's now, then."

Quill cursed under his breath.

Even though they'd been more or less hoping for this opportunity for hours, Quill had been leaning toward the *less.* He'd hoped the war would take care of the FitzOdo problem on its own. Not to mention that Quill had never sparred anyone with a glaive before, and he was fairly certain his head might pop itself off just to save the trouble.

But instead he loped through the crooked alley to the left, where they hoped to intercept the Coward Knight on his way back to the inn.

There was a compelling part of Quill that wanted to raise his hands and claim privilege—that he could walk away and return to a home of comfort in Derby, leaving this mess to the commonfolk and soldiers who were much better prepared for killing and dying. But both his companions had more prestige than he, and showed no signs of hesitation. Huntingdon was an *earl,* for God's sake, and here he was leaping through city streets like some sort of brazen vigilante. It was the coward in Quill that made him want to flee, he knew that. He knew it, he accepted it, he'd happily write home about it and scream it from the rooftops if it meant he didn't have to hold any of his innards in his hands this day.

When they rounded the corner into a small squarish plaza, the behemoth shape of Sir Robert FitzOdo was standing in wait, expecting them, the long cleavered blade of his polearm held at a casual but dangerous angle. His voice, unnaturally deep. "Made your decision finally, did you?"

"FitzOdo," Lord Beneger said, catching his breath. "You have crimes to answer for."

"And you think now's the time for the answering, then?" The knight's lips pulled back into a farcical grin. "Oh, because I'm alone. You've been following me all day, but *justice* waits until you think you have the advantage, does it? Fickle thing, your justice."

Beneger swallowed. "You have abused your power for months. Your only charge in this city was to track down Robin Hood, and instead you—"

"Robin Hood's dead!" FitzOdo howled. "Anybody can pretend to be him, because there is no Robin Hood. He's a whisper in the night, he's a fucking myth. You can't catch a myth, you can only change its details. That's what I did. I did the impossible—I killed a dead man. And in so doing, I saved this fucking city."

Quill couldn't hide his laugh. He pointed at the black smoke that made a dark canopy, streaming over the buildings around them. "It doesn't look saved to me."

"Shut your cunt mouth, Peveril."

He did.

"A few months ago," the knight continued, "nobody in this city would have lifted a finger in defense of it. They would have thought their precious *Robin Hood* would do it for them. Well, where was he today?"

As if to make a point on it, a curl of wind whistled through the alley, bringing with it specks of glowing ash.

"Exactly. I taught the people to stand up for themselves, and that's what we did today. This city should be sacked, but instead it's intact. The words you should be looking for are *thank you*."

"If you are so certain you've acted honorably," the earl Robert said, defiantly flipping his half cape over his shoulder, exposing the hilt of his rapier, "then submit yourself to us. We shall hear the full account of your actions. Perhaps the King himself will judge in your favor."

FitzOdo's jaw hardened, his eyes made a very obvious summation of the earl. "Well there's the thing. I did *not* act honorably. After all, I'm the *Coward Knight*, aren't I? I earned that name here, in these streets, when I infiltrated the last army that tried to siege the castle. Saved the city then, too, and labeled with *dishonor*. But you know what? I don't need your respect. I don't need the pissant King's respect either. The only worthy man I know is King Henry, and I've done him proud, rest his soul, in this fetid shit world he left behind. So go fuck yourselves with your *honorable*. And get out of my way so I can save some more lives."

Metal on metal, Robert and Beneger drew their weapons. Quill did the same a moment later, his delay earning a new barrel of laughter from FitzOdo.

"You're mad at me for killing a few people," he chuckled, "and yet you insist on adding yourselves to that list?"

"You kill us, it will be in a fair fight," Beneger said evenly. "But you tortured the innocent. Beat them, burnt them, murdered them. You don't deserve to be in the Black Guard, much less to be called a knight. If you will not come with us willingly, we'll take you by force, FitzOdo."

"*Say my fucking name!*" the bald knight snapped. "I'm a goddamned knight, I knelt before the King himself, you will say *fucking sir* when you address me!"

Oh, Quill sometimes hated himself, because he couldn't keep from saying it.

"Very well. Fucking Sir it is."

Like a raging bull, the battle began with a kick in the dirt. Fucking Sir dashed his feet in fury through a pile of ash that had already rained down, causing the three of them to recoil. A second later the plume was split by the heft of his axehead, forcing them to startle backward and give the monster space. Beneger, in their middle, split distance with the earl and signaled Quill to circle sideways, that they could surround him. It seemed an obvious advantage to Quill, even with his rudimentary knowledge of the finer points of killing things—and three against one seemed like the type of mathematics that ought to settle the fight easily.

Instead, FitzOdo somehow threatened all of them at once. The long pole of his glaive meant he was always poised against two of them, and he flicked constantly at the third, daring an attack. Beneger made a couple feints with his sword but FitzOdo practically snarled them off, while the earl seemed more interested in making light footwork than risking any sort of attack. Quill was left waiting for an opening—surely FitzOdo's bare back would present itself eventually, and then it was simply a matter of stabbing it with his stabstick.

FitzOdo attacked first, a swing that started at Robert and ended at Beneger, and Quill tried to leap forward into the gap, but the glaive was already rounding and came careening low in a slice that Quill only avoided by throwing his legs backward; which had the predictable effect of landing him stomachwise on the ground. He panicked and rolled, only barely able to hold onto his sword as he did so, expecting his body to neatly split in two as FitzOdo came for a second round. But Ben distracted him, and the first shrill howls of steel on steel split the air as Quill scrambled to get his feet under him again.

A series of cracks continued as FitzOdo struck forward violently, again and again, pushing Beneger backward. Beneger managed to parry the thick blade's thrusts to alternating sides as he retreated, but it was obvious there was more force behind those strikes than Beneger could handle. Quill ran forward along with Robert to engage him from behind, but the man had clearly anticipated that. He pivoted and flung his weapon up at both of them—Robert wisely ducked to the side, while Quill brought his sword up on instinct and felt the impact rock his entire body. His arms were flung wildly against his own face and he was pushed backward, his forearms reverberating with the violence of the attack.

And suddenly his sternum cracked and he collapsed to the ground.

FitzOdo had struck him square in the chest with the wooden end of his long handle, which was the only reason he was not dead yet. But his vision rippled with bright lights and stars and hot lances sliced through his ribs when he tried to inhale. *My ribs are broken,* Quill gasped, *I can't breathe.* He groaned and grabbed at his chest, kicking himself backward on the ground with his feet, gulping down air in short shallow bursts. His hands were quivering uncontrollably, and he grabbed his entire chest as if to keep it from sliding apart in halves.

He could only watch, in agony, as FitzOdo stomped the ground again with his unreasonably thick legs, punched forward with his glaive held horizontally in his hands, and then charged Lord Beneger de Wendenal. Once, twice, Ben's sword made contact with the cleaver but only accidentally, and then the huge protruding tooth of the glaive was in his side and Ben screamed, falling back with the momentum of the blows. Quill had to blink to make certain what had happened; it looked like Ben had taken the blade mostly in the armpit. It was very possible the man's arm was halfway severed at the shoulder, and he clutched the wound in his left hand, blood seeping through his fingers.

Lord Beneger was going to die, and Quill was going to watch it happen.

And then he was probably going to die as well.

It had barely been a minute, and FitzOdo had dispatched two of them. So much for mathematics.

"It occurs to me," the Earl of Huntingdon's voice was calm, baiting FitzOdo to turn around before finishing Beneger off, "that you don't know who I am."

"You're a corpse," the knight said. "You just don't know it yet."

"I suppose that's true for everyone," the earl laughed. "But in life, we share a given name of Robert, though my title is the Earl of Huntingdon."

"Huh." FitzOdo frowned. "Don't think I've ever killed an earl before."

"So you *don't* know who I am." He reached down and slowly draped his fingers through the ash on the ground, then pulled up a handful that he rubbed into his palms. "It's no surprise, nobody really does. After I became earl, that was the only title anyone cared about. The same way you probably want people to remember you for whatever it is you did in the Kings' War, I wish people remembered me for my laurels, too."

"And what's that?" FitzOdo smiled. "Longest shit streak?"

"Yes, but let's not change the subject. No, I'm *not* my father's firstborn son. I shouldn't have inherited the earldom, my older brother should have had it." He clapped his hands several times, pleased with the puff of grey smoke they made. He flexed his fingers, he stretched his arms. "But I distinguished myself in tournaments for years, so much so that my name became famous. People came from halfway across the country if they heard I was going to be in a tilt, or a melee, simply to watch my fighting style. You don't know it, sir, but you are squaring off against the Champion of Salisbury, the Champion of Canterbury, and of Kent."

At this he whipped his rapier out again, deadly level and parallel with the ground, one foot planted firmly forward in a deep thrust.

FitzOdo seemed only barely amused. "Never heard of you."

"Nor I, you." He moved again, backward, angling sideways, his boots silently slipping past each other like cat's paws, his other hand holding the tip of his demicape out gingerly as he danced. "You know, a lot of people who've never heard of me make fun of me for this weapon. Say it's too light, that it's a dandy's toy, and not made for proper combat. And it's true, I think its blade would snap if you so much as touched it with that monstrous thing."

The wooden pole of the glaive pounded the ground.

"Her name is *Tesoro*. An epee isn't much good for cutting, but she's good for making little, tiny holes. And by the end of this, you'll be full of them. And if you'd ever seen me fight before, you'd be smart enough to surrender right now."

Quill wondered if the earl was bluffing. Perhaps trying to give himself, or Ben, some time to recover. But watching the man move now, his muscles expertly trained, the sinews in his arms seemed purpose-made, and Quill believed every word of it. The man was as graceful as water, but he wasted not even a single drop of energy. His thin frame and needle blade made a striking silhouette compared to the ox of FitzOdo and his two-handed glaive, and Quill could not help but marvel.

FitzOdo clearly meant to make short work of the duel. He swung wide and level with his glaive at full extension, then wheeled it around to slice down two times and into a brutal thrust forward, the way he had gored Lord Beneger. But at every swing the earl sidestepped, leaned, hopped nimbly away, and then danced himself in a long sweep to safety.

The knight shuddered to regain his momentum, but when his face reeled back on his opponent it was full of shock. "*Ffffucker...*"

"Three," the earl Robert said, nodding his head slightly. "How many would you like?"

Quill hadn't even realized that the earl had jabbed his rapier's tip out during each of his evasions, and FitzOdo clasped his hand over his thigh, where a small circle of blood marked an injury. Where the others were, Quill was not sure.

In rage the knight attacked again. This time the earl flipped his cape up off his shoulder and swatted its heavy fabric at the glaive's blade, more effective than any shield at quelling its bite. He turned under the man's arm and pricked the inside of FitzOdo's chest, high up where his plating left him unprotected. The axe came around again and found nothing, again and again, flurries of ash rose to surround them as they spun, the bullfighter and the bull.

Quill was well shy of recovered and he could not yet inhale without agony, but the commotion of the fight was traveling away. He took the chance to half crawl his way over to Lord Beneger. The man was on his back, controlling his breaths into short bursts, his hand clasped at his armpit.

"Let me see," Quill said, and met Ben's eyes. There was fear there, maybe the first time he'd seen the man with anything but a stoic certainty.

His clothes were sopped with blood, torn open enough that Quill could see the wound beneath. It was less in the armpit than he thought, and mercifully in the arm itself rather than his chest. Still, a thick flap of muscle was opened wide, and Quill bit down against his nausea as he kneaded the meat back in place and folded the man's arm against his chest. "Keep pressure here. I think you could be sewn up again," he said, as if he had any real knowledge on it, "but you're losing blood. We've got to take care of you fast. Let me wrap you, we'll get out of here."

"FitzOdo . . ." Beneger murmured.

"Will wait. This first." He glanced backward at the two Roberts, continuing as they were before. The earl spent most of his time trip-stepping and baiting the knight, but never attempting any attack. He only reacted and found another place to prick the tip of his rapier, in an arm, a leg, only an inch or so in, but the knight was clearly fatiguing at the accumulation of tiny wounds.

Quill tore his own shirt over his head and then into strips, which wrapped around Lord Beneger's arm. Before the last loop he found a short but sturdy stick nearby and included it under the wrappings. Once the last tie was done, he gave Beneger a warning before twisting the stick like a lever, tightening the straps clearly past the point of comfort. "Hold this," he said, putting Beneger's good hand on the stick. "Keep it there."

He helped the man up, but frankly had no idea where to go. There were normally physickers in the Parliament Ward, but there was an army between them and there, even if they weren't in hiding. The castle was burning, and there was no way Ben could survive the tunnels to get back out to the King's camps. If there were other options, Quill didn't know them.

FitzOdo yelled, and Quill turned his attention back to the fight. The knight was close to the earl and suddenly *threw* his glaive with both hands out directly into the earl's face. Unprepared for such an audacious attack, Robert's rapier whipped out wildly, but the wooden pole still knocked him back, and a second later FitzOdo's empty hands reached out—the left grabbed the earl by the throat, and the right smashed into his face.

And again.

It was hard to say this was a *punch.* If Quill punched someone, the reaction would be a giggle. This was more like a battering ram. The third punch left the Earl of Huntingdon with blood bursting from his nose and lips. His legs were weak, and when FitzOdo let go, the man slumped to the ground like a rag doll.

Goddamn, this Coward Knight was everything Quill hated about the world. Men who thought their strength was the measure of how right they were. Men who defined themselves in terms of how much pain they could inflict on others, or take upon themselves.

Quillen Peveril was no good at hurting other people, and even worse at being hurt, which is why he was so reluctant to impose himself into the troubles of the world. But watching a meat mountain smash the face of a graceful lord made Quill know one thing, with absolutely no doubt. That between himself and Fucking Sir Robert FitzOdo, Quill was the infinitely better man.

The knight tried to bend down to retrieve his weapon, but winced at the attempt. He was spotted all over, like a pox, with little blood roses. The earl had crippled the man, and while Quill was not much of a threat to anything besides ignorance, he was fairly certain he had enough wits about him to take out an unarmed man who was already bleeding out. The earl had done the hard work, Quill just had to finish him off.

And so the youngest son of the great Peveril family, famous only for getting lost in the caves of the Peak, who had since identified himself solely by the quantity of things he *did not do,* chose to act. He left Lord Beneger leaning against a wall, picked up his sword, and screamed at his opponent. "FitzOdo!"

The beast turned, his mouth gaping, trying to determine who had the temerity to challenge him.

Quill looked forward to telling his children about this someday. When he was Lord of the Peak, head of Peveril Castle. Perhaps with his wife Arable. Their children would know that the scourge of Nottingham was felled by a man a quarter his size, who was very likely pissing himself just to do so.

Perhaps he'd leave that part out of the story.

"Surrender yourself," Quill threatened.

"Fuck you," FitzOdo spat. And despite his injuries, he reached down, grabbed his weapon off the ground, and made a riotous charge at Quill that he had not expected.

Quill tried to strategize but there was no time, he held his sword out in front of him as if the man might simply impale himself, felt his sword batted away and flung from his hands, then the blade swung and there was only a single moment of pain before the dark.

SIXTY-FIVE

ARABLE DE BUREL

MIDDLE BAILEY, NOTTINGHAM CASTLE

THEY WERE ANYTHING BUT alone now in the castle gaols. An hour ago the first voices had come from the ramp downward, prompting them to quickly scramble and hide. But the visitors were seemingly normal citizens—refugees that now filled every hallway and cell. Women and children largely, and some elderly. The catacombs had clearly been identified as the safest place in the castle during the siege, and was now being used to shelter those who were not immediately useful in the castle's defense. Arable overheard that the lower bailey had been evacuated, which explained all the people. It was now under control of King Richard's armies, though everyone was still obstinately under the impression that it was the French King Philip in disguise. The bailey and the barbican had apparently been set on fire to delay their advance, and the fighting was likely over for the day. But tomorrow they would no doubt commence on sieging the second bailey.

Despite their best efforts, they'd failed to stop the first day of the war. Arable hoped to never know how many people fought and died today. Particularly in the last hour, while they waited for Charley to return, hoping he'd learned how to get to Prince John.

"I thought Castle Rock was impenetrable," Nick whispered.

"It is," she explained. "But the lower bailey isn't Castle Rock. Its curtain wall is long and not very tall, and I'm not surprised an army of Richard's size could overwhelm it. But the Rock up to the second bailey is something else. Those walls are three times as high, and there's significantly less of it to defend. We should be safe up here."

"Excepting the fact that we're actually with the invaders, and we're surrounded by the enemy."

"Oh yes, of course, except that."

When Charley Dancer finally returned, he looked very much like the young man Arable had once known. He'd donned a quilted blue tabard of the Nottingham Guard—though it was slightly too large for him—and had even scraped off his beard leaving a semblance of his smoother, more familiar face. Earlier, he'd convinced them he could move around the castle undisturbed. But most of the time he'd been gone, Arable and the Delaney brothers had spent wondering if he'd turned traitor.

Or, as Arable was quick to remind them, turned traitor *again*.

"They were tricky to get, but I have clothes for you all," he said, laying a bundle onto the ground. "Yours has a hood, Arable, so nobody will recognize you."

Her hands instinctively reached up to her cheeks, feeling the scars on either side. If any member of the Nottingham Guard were to see her, she knew exactly how long she would last. The fact that Bolt had considered this was a second surprise.

"I found a couple of Guardsmen I used to know," he explained, pinching at his borrowed tabard. "I just told them I'd been on a special task in York the last few months, and returned just before all this. With everything going on, they didn't question it. Glad to see me, actually."

"What about the prince?" Nick asked, looking doubtfully at the tabard he'd been handed. "And wait, what's this?"

"Extras." Bolt gave a sheepish smile. "Keep your heads down, you two can pass as Guardsmen."

"No no no." Peetey shoved the bundle back at him. "That's insane."

His brother agreed. "That's a terrible idea. We can go as we are. There are plenty of commonfolk up there."

"And they're all being brought down to hide in here," Bolt countered. "Top-side it's shoulder to shoulder, Guardsmen not just from Nottingham but soldiers from all Prince John's allies. If you want to blend in, you need to look like you're ready to defend the castle. Arable's one thing, but a couple of . . . healthy men like you . . ."

Arable hated it. She had hoped they could sneak into the high keep undetected, darting from building to building and using the servants' hallways. But if there truly were as many men-at-arms as Bolt described, then she admittedly had no better ideas.

"We are going to get killed," Peetey said slowly, pulling the tabard over his head.

"It might work." Nick tried to sound hopeful. "This is how Will got in last year, isn't it? He always said that they *dressed up as gords* and nobody looked at them twice."

"That was when nobody had a reason to doubt them," Arable warned. "We'll be doing it while everyone's on their highest alert."

"Not to mention that they already fell for that trick once. Only an absolute idiot would think it would work a second time."

"It's all I have." Bolt put his hands out wide. "I'm not saying it's a good plan, but I don't see anyone with a better one."

Arable ground her knuckles together, wiping her fingertips hard until the dirt came out in dark little rolls. Her elbows and forearms were red and raw from their crawl through the tunnels. *But she wasn't dying,* and there were a lot of people outside that were. All in all, the next part should be the easy one. All they had to do was get from the gaol tunnels to the ramp up to the highest bailey without anyone looking at them too closely.

"It's just a matter of moving confidently, like we have a purpose."

She had spent two years as a servant in this castle, and the only time anyone had ever thought to question her was when she'd been idling about with nothing to do.

"Best do it now, then," Peetey said with a swallow.

"Anybody need a moment to make their peace?" she asked.

They chuckled at this.

"I'm serious," she followed. "This could very likely go the wrong way. If you need a moment, if you need to pray, or just . . . get yourself in the right place for this, then take it now." They stared at her for a moment, unsure what to make of her suggestion. But rather than joke, they each nodded gravely and closed their eyes.

Arable was not taking her own advice on this.

She wasn't going to die.

She was resolute against it, and this moment of silence she took—with her eyes closed, penitent—was to make certain the world understood that it could not claim her today. She thought back with shame on the sense of hopelessness she'd succumbed to upon first seeing Lord Beneger at Huntingdon Castle, when she had fled. When she'd thought of throwing herself from the top of the Heart Tower. In the heat of that moment, she'd somehow thought that death was the best choice for her and her unborn daughter. More than a few times since then, that raw, icy memory had brought her to tears. No, she would *live* for her daughter, *live* no matter the cost. She had to remember that—to keep herself from giving in to such dark temptations again. Her daughter deserved a life. She deserved a *name*.

Admittedly, Arable had refrained from thinking of one yet, specifically so that she would never have to mourn it.

She didn't know if Nick or Peetey Delaney had anything similar to keep them motivated, but she hoped for their sakes they did.

The walk from the gaols to the stairs up to the keep—if they could accomplish it unmolested—should take no more than a minute or two. After that, there was still the tricky thing of finding Prince John and convincing him of the impossible, but for now there were just two simple minutes they had to get past. "Let's go," she said, as casually as if they were taking a stroll down to the river, and slipped her hood up and over her face.

They moved quickly, kept their heads down. She poured her concentration into making her posture seem confident. As they emerged from the tunnels she had to squint to keep the brightness of the sky from blinding her, and even still she was almost unable to stifle a gasp at the sight that greeted them. There were black snakes winding through the air, converging into great clouds above as the fires over the battlement's edge raged on. But more shocking than that was the crowd here—to say it was *shoulder to shoulder* was only barely an exaggeration. Camps filled every open space, soldiers in a wide array of uniforms were tending to their weapons, cooking meals out of their helmets, dressing wounds, nursing their feet, waxing their bowcords, or any of a hundred other tasks. The idea that Arable could quickly barrel through to the barracks kitchen as she'd planned was an absolute impossibility. She darted her eyes for another option—rounding to the south larder, perhaps, but then she'd have to risk the main commons of—

"Arable?"

Directly in front of her, literally seconds after emerging from secrecy, she'd already run into someone who recognized her. Kyle Morgan, affectionately known as Morg, had once been the kind of lovable mountain that was as terrifying to his enemies as he was comforting to his friends. The wary tilt of his head told him which of the two he now considered her.

His hand moved slightly to the weapon at his side as he repeated, *"Arable?"*

Later, in the history of the world's worst lies, Arable would need to file her feeble response of: "No, I'm not."

His face squinted, not in doubt that she was right, but in doubt that any human could think to use that as an excuse. Eyes darting to the Delaney brothers and their stolen tabards, Morg fumed. "Who the *fuck* are you two?"

She knew it was a terrible idea.

"Morg!" Bolt exploded, and slipped between them, pushing into Morg's belly and wrapping him in a hug. *Go,* he mouthed to her—then took to playfully punching Morg in the chest and laughing far too loudly about it.

He hesitated. "Bolt? What are you doing here?"

"Don't worry, she's with me, there's so much I have to tell you!"

Again he glared at Arable, and she took the cue. She grabbed both Delaney brothers by a fist of their stolen tabards and cut hard to the left, slipping into single file to make a path through the crowd that was disinterestedly watching the commotion of Bolt's now public reunion.

That trick wouldn't work a second time.

Five seconds in, and one of the four of them was gone.

A few hard eyes followed them but Arable mumbled a terse *"Make a path,"* leveraging the Guardsmen's bred instincts for obedience. It only needed to work long enough to disappear, and let Bolt's distraction win the contest of interest. She abandoned any hope of making it closer to the high keep, and opted instead for a direct line to the rear entrance of the maids' quarters. It was the wrong way, but they needed to get out of this crowd—and she hoped it would at least be empty, as there were clearly a thousand tasks outside that the girls ought to be tending to.

They crossed a wafting air coming from the kitchens, and the smell of roast meat instantly brought her mouth to water. Arable wondered how long it had been since she'd eaten. *Perhaps there would be time to steal a bite of something from the adjoining quarters.* She didn't even look back as she flung open the familiar wooden door and tucked under the worn stone arches that had been her home for so long. Thankfully, it was mostly empty now except for one young girl who was curled in a bed crying, and Arable hated herself for yelling so harshly at her to make herself scant, which she quickly did.

"Shit, that's a lot of soldiers," Nick exhaled, kneeling down on a bed to regain his composure.

But there was not even time enough for a reply. The door behind them opened again violently, and two men entered—one in a Nottingham Guard's tabard, the other in a mismatch of pieces and a fat knife held out in readiness.

Both Delaneys sprung to their feet and drew their swords to block the small corridor. "Get to the keep!" Peetey whispered at her, and turned to give her whatever small amount of time they might.

Arable couldn't watch. *Too quickly, they were losing too quickly,* she cursed, biting her knuckles, but she turned and ran. *Three down, and now there was only her.*

"Arable!" yelled a voice she distantly recognized, and she knew she should not have come. She'd wrecked the whole thing, and doomed the castle as well.

But she risked a glance back and the Delaneys were not fighting—instead they laughed, and the clatter of swords was not of steel on steel but of sheathing them away to safety. Arable was halfway out of the room before she realized it. It took a long, incredulous moment to register that the dirty, mismatched man was in fact Will Scarlet. And the grim Guardsman . . . Arthur a Bland.

Relief overwhelmed her, and she let herself pool down onto the ground and heave. She had only absently hoped they would be so lucky to find their missing people while in Nottingham, assuming it more likely that they'd long moved on to something else. Seeing both of their faces now was the most uplifting thing she could fathom.

Which didn't last long. "Where's David?" she asked.

Arthur's eyes were only half-open—and they didn't really look at her, but through her.

SHE NEEDED A MINUTE. She wept. She'd been fond of David, he had kindness in him, and humility, and so it was no surprise that the war would pluck him off the world. She knew he wasn't the only one who died, but in this moment he was a surrogate for everyone she knew. Every bated breath worrying about every single last person, the tension of that dread all came out for David. She mourned him, yes, but also she mourned for those who might die still—Marion, Lord Robert, Arthur, Will, John Little, Tuck, anyone who had proven themselves to be made of stuff soft enough that the world would want to rip them apart.

That David's death was so recent made it doubly difficult. If Will had led his men out of Nottingham a month ago and then died quietly in the forest after deserting them, it might have felt different. But David of Doncaster died *defending the castle,* and barely an hour earlier, while Arable had been crawling through the rocks to save them all. She wished she could have crawled faster. She could've taken fewer breaks, been stronger. It wasn't her fault, she knew that deep down, but nor did she want to blame herself for anyone else yet to come. *If she had the strength to stand,* she swore solemnly, *then she had the strength to keep going.*

Arthur was a statue, who said nothing, and added very little to their reunion aside from existing. But Will was a relief to see, despite the torturous evidence of his latest hardships displayed across his face. He had bruises and cuts all over, and half his ear looked torn and burnt. She chided herself for staring at it. Too many people had stared at her own scars. Even though she knew Will would probably boast of each injury, she deeply knew that nobody should be made to feel an object of pity.

But there was not much time to catch up on all they'd missed. Arable explained about King Richard's army, and the color drained from Will Scarlet's face. After the full account, he just shook his head. "Fighting the Sheriff was one thing, but does this . . . does this make us *traitors?*"

"You might easily be tried as one, along with everyone else in this castle," she answered. "That's why we need to get to Prince John, and tell him what we know."

"Well you'll never get to him," Will answered. "Nobody passes into the top bailey but his men. So unless you can scale the outside of that keep with nobody noticing, you'll need another method."

It said a lot that Arable actually considered it for a moment.

Will shook his head. "No offense, but you had the wrong plan. This is precisely why you need someone like me."

"You have something?" she asked. "Another way in?"

"Listen, this isn't sneakthieving—you can't use tactics meant to keep you hidden when you're trying to get to the very top. Not when the top is doing everything possible to protect himself. So work it out. There's only one way up to the tower, so that's what we have to use. And Prince John only lets things enter if he wants them to. So we have to be that."

Arable didn't follow. "We have to be what?"

"Something that he wants." He nodded, scratching at his dark blond beard. "And thankfully, we are exactly that. We're Robin Hood."

It broke her heart to hear it. *He meant for them to turn themselves in.* If that was a reasonable plan, they could have done it before any of this, before the fighting even began. Everyone who'd already died would have been killed in vain if they did this. And they'd come so far, and were so close—literally yards away from the prince's tower—*just to surrender now?*

"What if it doesn't work?" She gaped. "That's an all-or-nothing gamble. No going back, no second chances."

He didn't flinch. But he searched her eyes, and she could swear that his whole soul was there for the world to see. He looked tired, beaten—grieving. "You tell me. Is it really that important that we talk to the prince? Can we just sit this one out?"

Arable had been wondering the same thing all day. But David's death had clinched it. "We can't. Yes, it's that important."

"Then this is the only way."

Will turned to Arthur for approval, who made no noise, no reaction. His face was dead.

"Hell, I wasn't going to last much longer up here anyway." Will shrugged. "Down in the lower bailey I had more of a chance, but too many gords up here know my face. If I'm going out, let's make it worth it."

Arable bit back a tear, and shifted to the Delaneys. "I'll go, but not you two. Stay hidden, if you can. If we fail, at least you can . . ." She was going to say *try something else,* but she was already certain this was the last option. "At least you can tell the others we tried."

Nick and Peetey chewed their lips, but consented without argument.

Arable reached out for Will's hand.

"I'll go, too," came Arthur's voice. "For David."

SIXTY-SIX

JOHN LACKLAND

THE BREAD, BEING HARD as a rock, would suffice. John gave himself a running start and threw the inedible chunk as far as he could, only slightly hurting his arm in doing so. The ominous cocket flew out the window and into the world where nobody could ever break a tooth in trying to eat it, soaring and falling for ever and ever. If he closed one eye and ignored the scale, perhaps its unforgiving crust would land on King Philip's front lines and smash them to pulp. The bread that ended the war. *Le pain* of pain. It was only fair, after all—Philip had been throwing rocks at John's castle all day long, the least John could do is throw one back.

There were three French mangonels now, constructed overnight, that launched their stones at Nottingham's upper walls. John had been doubly and triply assured by several men that the French could batter the middle bailey for a month and still it would not help them claim it. But a third of the castle had been lost in a *single day,* which made John want to throttle the necks of people who made assurances until they were a bit deader than he started.

Crack! Crack! Crack!

In rapid succession the latest barrage hit, which John watched from his window. The siege machinery rested on the hill north of the castle, in the middle of the French camps. They were close enough that John could count the banners, if he were more inclined toward boredom. He had to admire the audacity of the tactic—pretending that they were Richard! With fake sigils and everything! It was a lie so bold it might have worked on someone less inclined toward outlandish pranks himself. But John could see through the ruse, so now the French apparently intended on taking Nottingham down, three stones at a time.

The faces of the walls had taken the brunt of the assault, causing rubble to fall down into the lowest bailey where Philip's men were easy targets for the archers above. Some buildings in the second bailey had taken damage as well— the castle garrison was currently clearing away the ruins of a collapsed wall of a stables. The only casualties were little more than broken windows, chipped edifices, endless annoyance, and lost sleep.

The fires below had petered out over the night into grey wisps in the morning, now fully exhausted. There were more oil casks in their arsenal, but John had ordered his sergeants to save them for the next time Philip tried to raise larger siege ladders all the way up to the middle bailey catwalks. At this point, it was simply a game of numbers. If Nottingham had enough resources to survive a prolonged siege, then Philip would give up when his armies became too burdensome to feed. Otherwise, John would end up as one more name on the list of his dead brothers who had never been king.

"Which is fine with me," he said to the open window. "God keep me a prince. Still, a *living* prince would be preferable . . ."

Crack! Crack! Crack!

The top of the chapel in the second bailey took a stone and slumped onto itself, which seemed an appropriate response to John having used the word *God*. He reminded himself to pray to himself instead, as he was ever more reliable at delivering the things that made him happy.

He took an early dinner at the urging of the bishop Hugh de Nonant, whose resolve might have been the day's only real loss. The brothers from Worcester had livelier spirits but were both uglier than the other, which made it difficult to enjoy any conversation with them that required eye contact. The proud Roger de Montbegon remained his stuffy self and insisted on making stuffier reports about the casualties, the diminishing reserve of arrow sheaves in the armory, and dire predictions of how long their food would last. None of it was much fun to listen to.

"Did you see the gallows?" asked the bishop, his voice whisper thin as if the thing were a beast that might be lurking behind the door.

"Of course I did," John replied. It had been erected just out of arrow's range to the north, where the French commanders had hanged men captured from the previous day's sortie. "And by blanching so, you play into their hand. Philip hopes both to entertain his men, and intimidate us. By being intimidated, Nonant, you do their work for them. So smile and choose—as I do—to find it entertaining as well, before I punish you for being a French sympathizer."

"Entertaining?" The man huffed and heaved himself into a stupor. "You find the execution of our men to be a source of amusement?"

"I find everything to be a source of amusement," John answered dryly. "The alternative must surely mean I am less like me and more like you, and there is already too many of you in the world by one."

The bishop's mouth puckered, a dying fish. John, in a rare moment he hoped never to repeat, regretted his words. These men were his allies, and he had precious few of them.

"Settle," he laughed, refilling the man's wine. "Do forgive me my black humor. It's my way, as it were—last son of the king, humor was the only distinguishing mark I could make in the world. I'm unaccustomed to having the weight of the world revolve around whether or not I'm alive, especially when so many people involved apparently wish I were not."

"As you say, Your Grace." Montbegon made a curt end of it, and revealed a ledger that meant he was prepared to vomit out more numbers that John could not possibly do anything about.

Crack! Crack! Crack! They all turned their attention slightly to the window, but not a single boulder smashed through it to pulverize them to gore and gristle. Instead, a great sigh of disappointment came from below, and John wondered what was crushed to cause such a curious reaction. "We need to relax for a bit. I doubt there are any actors or musicians in the castle, but are there at least any matters to tend to that have any importance less than *the death of all things?*"

"In need of a distraction?" asked the ugly Worcester brother. "Is that why you emptied your wine out the window earlier today?"

John was flattered. "I didn't realize anyone noticed that."

"I did," said the other brother, the ugly one. "It landed in your nephew's camp! He was furious, he thought you were mocking him!"

"Oh." John winced. Gilbert de Clare was his *wife's* nephew, although John loved Isabel just as much as he'd loved the wine he'd thrown out. But family was family, so the good Earl of Hertford had brought a small complement of men to help John defend Nottingham. "I'll make it up to him someday, if we all do a good job of living so long. If it makes a difference, I was trying to hit King Philip."

"With wine? From the high keep?" gasped the first Worcester brother, the ugly one. "And here I defended you when they said you were mad!"

"Don't bother." John waved his fingers with some intentional mischief. "Let them think that. Keep me mad, keep me mad. Until Richard returns, heaven keep me mad! The last thing I need is more people wanting me to be king!"

It was a perilous game to play. The French wanted to kill him, that Arthur Plantagenet could be king in Richard's absence. John needed to avoid that, but not at the price of becoming king himself. He didn't want to become the lesser of two evils, he had to be exactly as unfavorable as a French invasion force.

Perhaps I should actually go mad, he thought. *It would be a lot easier than pretending at it.*

"I may have a good distraction for you, Your Grace," suggested William Brewer. The loyal Sheriff of Devon had come a long way for his promotion to High Sheriff, and he might actually keep it if Nottingham stood long enough. "My men captured a trio of saboteurs yesterday, who claimed that they were—collectively—*Robin Hood.*"

John wrapped his mind around the logic of such a statement. "Contortionists, then? What of it? I thought we had lanced that particular boil with the archery tournament. How can there still be any of them left?"

"Well, the curious part is they turned themselves in." Brewer's tone implied he legitimately found it intriguing. "And more—in exchange, they only wanted one thing. Which was to parley with you. We denied them of course, and locked them in the kennels. I only bring it up now because we were having a laugh about it last night. If you're in need of entertainment . . ."

"Perhaps." John considered it. They likely wanted a parley just to piss and moan about what John had done at the tournament.

Then again, watching other people piss and moan about things he'd done *was* a fairly delightful thing to watch.

"After dinner, if there's time," he said.

Crack! Crack! Crack!

* * *

"IS IT A GAME?" John clapped his hands together, more delighted than he ought to be at the arrival of these three dour strangers. He wished he could blame the wine, but there had not been nearly enough of the stuff—which tasted too strongly of vinegar, anyway—for him to be drunk. He'd long ago calculated the volume of wine it took to make him slap-happy, which was exactly one glass more than *a lot* and one fewer than *a shit lot*. He had not come even close to that number tonight, so he regretfully agreed that he might just be the sort of person who gets giddy at the thought of games.

"I'm to unpuzzle which one of these is really Robin Hood?" he asked, giving each of the captives a cursory glance. *Not the girl, obviously.* He'd met the original Robin Hood once, and—

"We're all Robin Hood," the girl interrupted his thoughts.

"Oh hush!" He waved her off. "Let me try it in silence first, before I ask you questions." The short one had the wild haggard look of a starved hermit, albeit a very angry one with war paint crusting at the edges of his face. The other was a solemn man—Scottish, maybe—with a nasty swath of red scabbing across his forehead. He was the only one of the three who would not look John in the eye. *The least likely choice,* he considered, which probably made him the leading contender.

"This is not a game," the woman tried again, and John answered by snapping his fingers at the Guardsman behind her, who knocked the back of her head just hard enough for her to recognize how much harder he might do so next time.

The three of them were in a line, on their knees, hands bound behind their backs. They'd been brought up here to the Sheriff's office, after John's late evening of minor drinking and betting on where the catapult strikes would land next. *"We have to enjoy our situation,"* he'd explained to his cajoling guests. *"Otherwise, we become prisoners."*

He bit his lip and gave them a second look. What subtle tells might lie in their clothing? Would darker skin imply time spent outdoors, or would the forest's canopy keep their skin protected where a city dweller's might tan? *The woman,* he considered her again. She was far dirtier than the other two, and she appeared to have two straight scars down her cheeks. *There was a story there,* he knew. Usually meant they were like unbroken colts in bed. *She was pretty, too.* He knelt to get a better sense of her—then realized he'd had these very same thoughts before.

"You recognize me now?" she asked, a half flinch backward at the Guardsman who'd pushed her. "I was at the council in Huntingdon. My name is Lady Arable de Burel."

"I remember," John said with a slight curiosity. "You caused a bit of a commotion. That was well done. I did enjoy that. But a lady with no family nor lands is hardly a lady, no? And you're saying you're also Robin Hood?"

"Anyone can be Robin Hood," answered the short hermit. "But if you're looking to use that name to punish someone, then you can punish me. I'm the Robin Hood that killed Sheriff de Lacy last year. In this building. Snuck right past this room and up the stairs. Name's Will Scarlet."

John didn't know if he was supposed to be impressed by that. "Oh," he said instead. "My, you sound dangerous, *Scarlet*." He looked at the sullen one and asked, "What about you, which Robin Hood are you?"

The question bounced off his face and landed forgotten on the ground.

"Ah, you're the mute one."

"We have been kept in shackles for over a day," the woman, Arable, complained. "We only turned ourselves in that we could speak with you, because we have urgent news that will stop this siege and end this war. Every life lost today was done so needlessly."

"We don't take commands from prisoners," William Brewer interrupted. "Assassins, in particular."

"No need for excuses," John calmed him. The *crack crack crack* of boulders crashing through the stone battlements outside was all the explanation necessary. "You know, there was a time when I quite enjoyed the idea of a Robin Hood running around. But not one of you is the Robin Hood I actually met. And your rebellion in Huntingdon announced that you want to overthrow my brother, Richard the King. That's treason. So I can't think of a single reason why I would believe anything you've come here to tell me."

John preferred it when women—particularly those with pretty faces, and *particularly* particularly those with mysterious scars—batted their eyes at him and bit their lower lips. So it was a little unarming when Arable flared her nostrils instead, cocked her head in annoyance, and said with half-bored eyes, "Your brother the King is outside, you *fucking idiot*."

Well, at least he had his answer. By the wild-eyed stupor the other two men gave her, leaning away as if to save themselves, John knew he'd found the real Robin Hood.

"We both know that's the King of France out there," John returned carefully, dismissing the Guardsman who was silently asking if he should club her unconscious. "My brother is still in an Austrian prison."

"You honestly think that?" She was undeterred. "You think France has costumed ten thousand men and banners to match half the counties in England, and hoped you wouldn't notice the difference?"

"Oh, I know some of them are real," John laughed. "Everyone at your traitor's council would naturally back Philip when he came for my head. But the bulk of that army is French, dear, come to put a child on the throne so he can be France's puppet. The English traitors out there seek to profit from that arrangement. If Richard had miraculously escaped from prison and brought his army home, do you really think his first act would be to march here and wage war on his brother? That's the thing about a lie, it's not a very good one if it unravels the first time someone asks the word *why*."

"He thinks *you're* the traitor," came Scarlet. "He thinks you've claimed the castle for your own power in his absence—so yes, first thing he does when he comes home is remind the people who's in charge. It's what *I* would do."

"Ah." John snapped his fingers, having realized the game. He turned to his advisors, the few who were still left at the periphery of the room. "This is all for *their* benefit! You're hoping to plant a little seed of doubt in one of their minds— turn them against me. Which is, after all," he smiled wide, intentionally making light of the otherwise sound strategy, "what *I* would do."

"Send them away," Arable said, all too quickly.

John was practiced at not showing any surprise, but he had no immediate answer for this.

"Send them all from the room, see if our story changes."

"So you can overwhelm me?" John tried to laugh. "I have no doubt you'd love to be in a room alone with me."

"Oh God's teeth," moaned Scarlet. "Is every possible thing we can say a trick now? I promise you we're not clever enough for that. Fucking look at us!"

He tugged on his restraints, a look of genuine agitation pumping into the veins of his forehead, his arms.

What game were they playing after all? John worried. It is the liar who says he has nothing in his hand. They were here before him, as they wanted. They'd turned themselves in, as they wanted. Whatever John's next move was, it was very possibly exactly what they wanted as well. They were a puzzlebox, for certain, and probably one that had either no solution, or many that were equally disastrous.

"Give me the room," he commanded. For fear of alarming his allies, he added, "I won't waste your time with this prattle. You all need your rest, I'll handle these children."

He stood his ground as they moved past him—the brothers Worcester, his nephew, the bishop, the new Sheriff, the castellan, their subordinates. Some made gracious exits, others were a bit too silent, but one by one they left until there was nothing but John and three strangers, bound to each other and the pillar in the room, kneeling, and scheming.

"You know, the real Robin Hood was a loyal kingsman," he told them, recalling Locksley's obstinate love of Richard. "And here you are, ready to abandon him and give the country to France. What has Philip offered you? I'll double it."

"Nothing," she said, her face tired. "We are loyal to Richard still, because he's right *there*." She turned her head pointedly at the window, then back again. "We were on your side, too, you might remember. That was the point of the council—not to be disloyal to Richard, but to be loyal to you. I don't know what's possessed you to think France has come for you, but you're mistaken. And that mistake is quickly turning you into England's most incompetent villain."

Villain. That was theatrical.

But there was nobody else around. There was nobody for her to perform to. *She didn't honestly think this would work?*

"And you want me . . . what, you want me to open the gates to welcome my brother in? You think I'll surrender the whole castle based on your little lie? Oh dear." He swallowed. "Is my reputation truly so rank that you think I'd fall for any bit of this?"

"Get out there!" Scarlet yelled, hot and fast. "Look for yourself! He's right on the other side of the walls!"

"So Philip's crossbowmen can take my head off as soon as I peek out?" He laughed. "No thank you. I'll tell you what—if his armies retreat, I'll allow your king inside the castle walls, alone, unaccompanied, that I can look on him with my own eyes. If he is who you say he is, he should have no issue with this, no?"

The captives looked at each other, a look of doubt shared between them.

"Exactly," John finished.

"That's an unreasonable demand, and you know it," Arable grumbled.

"You like games, then?" Scarlet asked.

John didn't answer, but was intrigued just enough to let him continue.

"What if we're telling the truth? Think of it like a war game, a riddle. If you were outside an ally's castle but he didn't believe it was you, how could you prove yourself? You wouldn't go into their castle unattended, not against an army full of half-dead Guardsmen eager to make a name for themselves, no. What's your next choice? Tell us what the safe option is. You clearly won't trust anything we suggest, so we'll take your suggestion instead. Figure it out, you're such a fucking clever fellow."

"Now you want me to do your work for you." John picked up another piece of the bread from the table. Perchance it would do the same damage to a skull that a real rock might. "But you're going about this the wrong way, all of you. Well, the two of you who are talking, at least. The grim fellow, he's here for . . . what? Decoration?"

"What do you mean *the wrong way?*" Arable asked before the mute could respond.

"Well, you're telling me *what* to do and *how* to do it," he answered, looking around the table for something sharper. He might need to hurt them, intimidate them, maybe torture one of them to discover what they were hiding. "But that's not how you sell an idea. You have to make me *feel* something first. Either you make me feel good, then provide me something to make me feel that way again—or you make me feel bad, and then offer the remedy. Now it just so happens that I'm an unfeeling monster, and you'd be unsuccessful even if you *weren't* the worst con artists in the world. But you *have* told me one important thing. Your presence here alone means that Philip wants the siege to end quickly, which means he's worried he can't win. Which means that I *can* win, and am thus even less likely to take your—"

"Holy fuck!" Will Scarlet interrupted, and John realized with a small surprise that he hadn't been interrupted by anybody in a very long time. "Shut the fuck up!"

"You need a *why?*" Arable pushed. "Because it will save hundreds, maybe thousands of English lives. Englishmen are killing Englishmen out there. You're worried about the King of France? Well he's sitting back laughing while we kill each other right now! You're making a bloodbath of your brother's return home—the return that you claim you *wanted!*"

That was curious. He stared at her, wondering what her feeble little world and its feeble little players were like. A small sense of jealousy there, for her horizon that was within her reach. John wished he could be so small.

"*Arable,*" he said. "That means *plowable,* doesn't it?"

She blinked. "What?"

"Who cares about *lives,* Arable? Who cares about your hundreds or thousands of lives? Those aren't the stakes I deal with. Oh, certainly, I understand why you might care, since you're one of the lives in question. But if you want me to explain myself, don't pretend we play at the same table. At the level of princes and kings, we don't gamble for mere lives, we gamble for the very breath of the country. That's what I'm betting on. Lives . . . lives are just currency, we trade them like you might trade shillings. Everybody dies. Usually in some wretched way or another. At least in a battle, they'll die with some dignity. You want me to sacrifice England for a handful of people who will just go and die somewhere else anyway? What would be the point? Why would I risk myself for something so insignificant?"

Her reaction was unique, perhaps he'd genuinely hurt her. There might even have been tears in her eyes, though he'd done nothing other than try to expand her perspective.

"What's the point?" she asked, her voice choking. "Why are you doing any of this in the first place if there's no point? Why do you care if Philip runs England—if that's what you really think is going to happen—if life and death are so meaningless to you? Why did you even wake this morning, if the world is such an inconvenience? Why would I . . ." she faltered, bit her lip, looked down and then up again, ". . . why would I bring my daughter into this world if all I thought about was how she was going to die? I want her to *live,* I want her to love every bit of this world that you seem to despise. I want her to do better than I did—better than *you* did, most of all. I want her to meet whatever bitter thing it was that turned your soul so callous, and I want her to laugh at it. To laugh it right out of existence, and replace it with joy, and fascination, in every single second of her life. In the good and the bad. I want her to hurt when others hurt, I want her to care when others care, I want her to feel—everything, everything there is to feel. Delight and loss and misjudgment and forgiveness, every emotion we don't even have a name for . . . to keep her from becoming *you.* You're right, you shouldn't be king. Because you're the worst of us. I want my daughter to see you as I see you—as a warning!—while she's still young enough to choose to become something better. And to help shape the world into something where men like you are no more. Not because we've killed them all off, no, but because no little boy would ever choose to grow up and become you. A world where it wouldn't even make sense for someone like you to exist in the first place."

Of all of it, John was oddly insulted by this one phrase. "What do you mean, *men like me?*"

She chewed on that a bit, before deciding. "*Spectators.*"

He'd never been called that before.

She leaned into it. "*Audience members.*"

Nor that.

"How am I an audience member?" he asked, worried she'd mistaken him for some other handsome prince. "I've rallied half the country to my side to defend ourselves against a foreign threat. You think that's an example of *inactivity?*"

"How many children do you have?" she asked.

Probably a litter of bastards, but he knew what she meant. "None."

"And why not?"

His mouth opened, but it was such a ridiculous—

"*That* face, right there." She thrust her chin forward at him. "*That* shrug. That's what makes you a spectator. For you, the world is just a thing to entertain you as your years pass by. You're a bystander. What a tragedy, that you have the rare power to improve people's lives, but you're too selfish to even understand why you should do so. Of course you don't have any children, because you think this world is for *you*. But you're wrong. It's for my daughter. And as soon as she's born, it will be for *her* daughter. You think you're so enlightened, to play at the big table, to proclaim that lives have no value—but you're the reason *why* they have no value! Because spectators like you are in control."

Her mouth opened again as if she had more to say, but she shook her head and seemed to give up. She wasn't even talking to him, he thought, not really. She was reacting to something else, maybe a lifetime of something elses. A long history of *spectators* and *bystanders* in her past, but not John, no. An *audience member*, as she had described it, would never have lifted a finger to begin with. But still, John's feet carried him slowly to the window. The army's campfires littered the northern hill as far as he could see. Of its own will, the first bit of his resolve cracked and raised an eyebrow at that enemy with renewed curiosity.

What if she wasn't lying?

What if that truly was Richard?

What if he was making it worse?

"I would need you to prove it," his lips said. He stared into a world that waited on him.

"Go out and meet him then," Scarlet answered.

"You know I can't."

"Send someone else. Someone who will recognize King Richard."

As if he had not thought of that days ago. "There's nobody I could send that could not be bought with enough coin."

"Then it has to be you."

If he left the castle, and it *was* Philip, he'd be killed. "You know I can't."

"*Hey!*"

John turned to realize the mute redhead had finally chosen to speak, and it was just possible that John had never seen a man so full of fury in his entire life. His words clawed their way from his throat, one at a time, with nearly insurmountable difficulty.

"My best friend died for you yesterday. He saved a lot of lives doing so, and he had *no* power, *no* name, *no* money. Don't you fucking dare complain about the things you *can't do*. Quit your whining and *figure your shit out!*"

John probably should have been insulted, but the man had an accidental point. If there was anyone in the world who could outsmart this problem, John was certainly the one to do so. And even though the key words—*no power, no name, no money*—came from the redhead, it was Prince John Lackland, unwitting heir to England's throne, who took those pieces and turned them into a plan.

SIXTY-SEVEN

CHARLEY DANCER

THE KENNELS, NOTTINGHAM CASTLE

THE DOGS BARKED, BUT Charley Dancer touched his fist to the cold cage bars, and their bared teeth and riot quickly turned to whimpers and wet noses on his knuckles.

"You remember me," he cooed, slipping his hand between the iron to stroke their ears. He'd often taken his dinner down here when he wanted to get away, and would throw scraps to the hunting dogs. Back when he was a Guardsman. Dogs didn't care what was happening now, or what had happened since. They welcomed him back blindly, slapping their tongues into his palm, letting him grab back and tug them around playfully. Good girls.

With their barking settled, the sounds of war still raged in the background. Sharp snaps of stones shattering against the bailey walls. The permanent rumble in the ground, in the bones of the castle. Companies of crossbowmen and archers, repositioning and loosing volleys as the invaders below vied for advantage. Horns in the distance.

Charley scratched the pup's black fur, all around her ears. He used to know each of their names, but not anymore.

"Charley?"

Good pup, though, she deserved to be scratched.

"Charley, is that you?"

Iron on iron in the next kennel over, where Arthur a Bland was kept. Rusted manacles bound his hands behind his back, and to the cage wall. Restraints that hadn't been used as long as Charley had been in the Guard. Their only real purpose was to keep a prisoner from taking his own life. But for men like Arthur, no precaution was too much. Manacles it was.

"They're preparing," Charley said, giving the dog his last attention. "Prince John is going to go out in the morning. I don't know how you convinced him, but I think we did it."

"Arable did most of it," Arthur said, heavily. "Don't know what happens to us afterward, though."

"Don't know," Charley confirmed. "Maybe the King will show you mercy, for helping to stop this. If it works."

Arthur's feet shuffled. "I doubt it. What about you? Are you . . . are you in the Guard again?"

Charley looked down at his stolen tabard, tugged at it with one of his hands. It was the same size as he'd always worn, but it didn't fit anymore. "You're not surprised to see me like this," he said.

"Arable told us," Arthur confirmed. "Before we met the prince."

After that meeting, Arable and the others had been separated, held now in three different places. In case they were "conspiring something." Arable in the high tower, Scarlet in the Rabbit, and Arthur here in the kennels. The rest of the castle was at work—mitigating damage, preparing for tomorrow—and the kennel master had broken a leg in the siege and lay in the infirmary. Charley had all the time in the world here, nobody would come to check on the dogs at a time like this.

So he dug in his pocket, pulled out the key to the cages with two fingers, displayed it proudly.

"Holy fuck me, Charley."

The cage door opened with a shrill creak after the lock gave, and Charley swung inside and shut it behind himself. Sat down on the muck and straw floor, Arthur opposite him. It smelled of piss and shit, the straw hadn't been changed in a while. Arthur twisted and nodded his head at the manacles that bound his hands behind his back, as best he could. As if Charley had simply forgotten that he was still locked in place.

But Charley hadn't forgotten.

If there was any point to all this, it was that he *hadn't forgotten.*

Charley clicked his tongue. "What did Arable say about me?"

"Hm?" Arthur grunted again. "A bit. Said . . . you used to be a gord, but you ran away from them and joined with us?"

That was kind of her. She could have said so much more, but she'd hidden the worst parts. A large part of him thought maybe he really could join the Guard again. After revealing himself to Morg, so many of the old Guardsmen had already accepted his return. But once this was all over, once things settled down, they'd ask exactly where he'd been for months. How he came to be back. The same old battle lines would return, and what Charley'd done could not be overlooked. Joining the outlaws in the forest, for longer than he could justify as an act of conspiracy. And frankly, longer than he himself could pretend was an act. And then the manacles would be for him.

He wished he could stay, he did.

He missed Nottingham, and those familiar faces in the Guard, he did.

But it was also no lie, what he'd told Arable. That he'd grown fond of Marion's Men. Touched, by outcasts who'd accepted him without questions. The great fatherly John Little, protector and guide. The endless help of the Delaney brothers. And of course Arable. Charley was now a man ever between two worlds, very likely welcome in neither. But the better odds were with the outlaws, who might still take him. *Might.* Begrudgingly.

"I get it," Arthur said, once it was clear Charley was not about to unbind him. "Not sure, are you? If you set me free, you'll get in trouble, right? Not sure you want to make that choice?"

Charley had to laugh at that. There wasn't really a choice to be made.

"I was in the Captain's Regiment," he explained, as if Arthur could understand what those words meant. Charley had to fight an iron choke in his throat to get the words out. "We're the ones that fought with you at Locksley Castle last year. And then again at Bernesdale."

A moment of silence.

"No shit?"

Charley nodded.

Or maybe Charley's head alone remained motionless, in a world that at last nodded to him.

There was only a single lantern in the space, on the front side of the cages, throwing deep black shadows across the stone walls and Arthur's face. Even half devoured by the black, his pupils shined. *What those eyes had seen. What those hands had done.*

Charley continued. "Last year in Bernesdale, I was standing guard at the south road, where you and your group arrived. I was with my friend. My only real friend. He went into the woods to relieve himself, and then a little boy appeared in front of me. I hobbled down from my ox cart to see who he was, and then I woke up an hour later. You had ambushed us."

It sounded so simple when he described it that way. Frankly, the details were still hazy. It was like remembering a dream, he could barely even recall the boy. He had no memory of being attacked.

"You did a good job of it."

More silence. Maybe Arthur knew where this was headed.

"My friend," Charley continued, "you killed."

Reginold of Dunmow.

Charley didn't say his name, he knew it wouldn't make a difference. Arthur didn't know the name. None of them did. He was just a guard, just some guard. A *gord,* as they joked. They bashed in Reg's skull while he was shitting in the woods.

Charley had seen what was left of him.

His pants around his ankles, sitting in his own shit, his cock out, the most embarrassing way a man could die.

His forehead, caved in.

His fingers, still twitching.

Reginold was the smartest man Charley had ever known. Even when they were both young men, Reg had been unusually sharp. He liked to play with words, move them around, break them apart to find their secrets. He was fascinated by their origins, by Latin roots and bastardizations. He could dissect a word into pieces and build new ones, better ones, that made more sense. The two of them would use those with each other, a private little language only ever spoken by two people, now lost to the world.

Charley's years in the Guard were often marked by abuse—he'd been smaller than most, weaker than most, and his lame leg somehow made people want to push him down rather than lift him up. He'd never understood that instinct. Charley had only ever wanted to help people, it was why he put up with it all. Reginold of Dunmow had stood between him and every hurled insult, every unwarranted shove in the dining hall. Though they'd risen the ranks together, Charley always knew it was Reginold doing the rising, Charley just holding on. After Gisbourne invited them into the Captain's Regiment, the insults stopped. But Reg never stopped protecting him.

He'd been the one to give Charley the name of Bolt. He knew that both *Charley* and *Dancer* were "weak" names, and there were already too many ways for others to make fun of him. His size, his leg. But *Bolt* was a weapon, fast and sure. *Bolt* was a sudden strike, never expected. *Bolt* was a threat, a warning. *Bolt* said *you have misjudged me. Bolt* said *surprise.*

"Surprise," said Bolt.

Arthur's mouth opened. "Life's shit sometimes, innit?"

Said the bully, when he was finally cornered.

Said the strong man to the weak one.

"So you've been hiding this . . ." Arthur's eyes calculated. "You've been with us for months."

"I just wanted to be sure." Charley's neck seized with laughter. It sounded silly now. "I wanted to be sure I killed the right person. Took a long time to find out for sure. Hard to get any details about Bernesdale, nobody would talk of anything but Much. Nobody cared about the Guardsmen who died there." Every time he'd brought it up with Will Scarlet, or John Little, they'd avoided it. But one by one, he'd narrowed it down. "For a long time I was afraid it was Elena, or Alan. If it was them, I'd never get to do this."

A deep breath, to enjoy it.

"But it wasn't them," Charley finished. "It was *you.*"

He'd been anticipating this moment for a long time—too long, far too long—but had never actually let himself visualize it. He didn't want to daydream about the way he'd do it, he knew the fantasy would taste too good, that it would dull his drive. He didn't want it if it wasn't real. In his imagination, things only ever led up to this point. When he confronted Reg's murderer—and then he pushed the thoughts away, to black. To numb. A block he'd built, so the real thing would have nothing to compare to.

He didn't want any chance of this being disappointing. If Arthur didn't beg for mercy, if he didn't profess his dying rage, if he didn't cry like a baby. Charley had no expectations, no demands. This would be exactly, and everything, that it was—and nothing that it wasn't.

But in all his planning, he'd never dreamed of anything as convenient as this. Arthur, hands already bound, chained to a wall, *in Nottingham*. It was poetry. Charley didn't have to overwhelm him, or attack in his sleep, or use poison. He wasn't strong enough to beat Arthur in a fair fight, he knew that. But here he was, wrapped up like a gift. And nobody else around. Nobody else waiting. Nobody who cared.

"I told Arable that I originally joined with Robin's gang hoping to get revenge, and that was true," Charley explained. "I also told her that my desire for revenge disappeared after I spent time with you all. That . . . that was not true."

Charley's hands went to his belt, his thumb fingering the hilt of the knife he'd carried with him for months now. Reg's knife.

Maybe Arthur realized why he was still chained to a wall. Why he wouldn't get a chance to fight, or defend himself. At least he would know *why* he died. Reg never even got that.

God, it felt good—the look in Arthur's eyes—when Charley unsheathed the knife.

SIXTY-EIGHT

ARTHUR A BLAND

THE KENNELS, NOTTINGHAM CASTLE

In one hand, the key. The other, the knife.

Arthur didn't struggle, didn't kick back. He couldn't make any distance between himself and Charley Dancer. He was pinned, bound, defenseless. His heart hammered in his chest like it never had during the war. With a sword, a mace, even a fucking bow—well then it would be his own fault if he lost. But like this he had only one weapon, and though he'd rarely used it before, it kept him calm. Charley had every advantage, but Arthur had something better—the truth.

"I don't think I killed your friend."

Charley laughed. "You think I didn't make certain? I talked to *everyone*. John Little confirmed it was you." He made a point of that with the knife, looking down its length with one eye. "You know, only two Guardsmen died at Bernesdale. Elena put an arrow through one of them. All I needed was to find the one person in your group who also killed someone that day. I know everyone who was there, I've pieced the whole thing back together, what happened after I was knocked out. Nobody else killed anyone. And you're the only one I never got to talk to."

"I didn't kill anyone that day, either," Arthur said, shaking his head. He tried to recall the details of that day, searching for another explanation. He remembered *wishing* he'd killed someone, but he'd never even come close. They'd arrived in Bernesdale from the Sherwood Road, come across a couple of Guardsmen blocking the way . . . "I remember it. I remember you, too, now, actually. Much distracted you, then Will knocked you on the back of the head with the butt of his knives. I *do* remember that." Arthur had even helped drag Charley off the road. "But I didn't go off to take care of your friend. John Little did that."

"Horseshit!" Charley coughed. "I talked to John. He didn't kill anyone. He had no reason to lie to me about that, like you do now."

"He might *believe* he didn't kill anyone," Arthur answered. "But nor does he know his own strength. I swear, Charley, I swear on whatever you want to find holy, it wasn't me. John followed the other man into the woods. Said he gave him a *lovetap* with his staff. Maybe he thought he just knocked your friend out, but . . . but maybe he hit too hard. I don't think he knew, Charley. I don't think he meant to kill him."

"You liar," Charley said, his grip around the knife tightened, his face lilted away. "John Little has been nothing but kind to me. He wouldn't . . ."

"As I said," Arthur kept his tone low, "he didn't know."

A long, slow second passed, and a thousand heartbeats.

"You liar," he said again.

Arthur's thoughts spiraled into the previous month, of hiding in the Nottingham Guard and the perpetual edge on his nerves—the daily fear that they'd be discovered. Arthur had borne it terribly, he'd felt his temper shorten, his wits wither. Charley had been through all that, for four times as long. And where Arthur had David there to calm him, Charley had the opposite. The *absence* of his friend, to enrage him further, every day. In Charley's skulk, Arthur saw the wicked screw that his own life might still shrivel into.

All for one death, which refused to let go of those who mourned it.

"My God, Charley," Arthur could hardly even say it, "for *months?* For one person? Through all this, all this madness . . . how many more people have died since then? Holy fuck, how many have died just here at the castle in the last few days? How much has changed since then? And you've done all this . . . just for something we don't even remember?"

"*I* remember." Charley's neck clenched. "*I do.*"

"I see that." Arthur's head dropped. "I see that you remember. I'm just saying . . . think about all the people whose lives have been destroyed. Should every one of them seek their vengeance, every one go to the lengths you've gone through, just for a little payback? What kind of world is that? For an *accident,* Charley? For something John didn't even mean to do?"

Charley's head turned again, his back to the lantern, his features vanished into shadow. "Reginold was my best friend."

Those words hit home. Because Arthur knew, he *knew* the hell that had shaped Charley's every choice.

"You understand, don't you?" Charley asked. "You and David."

A stone sank in Arthur's gut.

"That was *an accident,* too, right?"

Arthur's vision dipped, all he could see was David's body again, black, unmoving, as the oil casks fell.

"Arable told me," Charley continued. "An *accident.* Defenders from the second bailey, throwing oil casks, to start a fire. To slow the attackers down. To get more people out."

"One landed on David," Arthur finished. "And that's it. That's fucking it."

"Someone threw it." Charley clearly hoped the words would claw at him. "Some person was responsible. Threw too early. He knew there were people down there, he didn't care. Cared about himself. What if he was here? What if we talked to every man we could, found the one who threw that exact oil cask? The one who killed your best friend. What would you do to him?"

An urge rose in Arthur, too dark to ignore, intimate but unnamable. He had killed so many in the fight for the bailey, over and over, but nobody since David's death. He'd had no chance to punish the world for what it had done to him. As long as his target was a nobody—a faceless *thing* that had done him wrong—then yes, he could see himself killing it. But if he put any face on that thing, the story changed. Whoever it was, like John Little, had not meant to do it.

But delivered, tied up, on a platter? Like Arthur was now? When nobody would know, with no god to judge him, and no consequences?

"I don't know," he said at last. "I'd like to think I wouldn't do *this*."

"Then you're lying to yourself." Charley leaned forward and readied his knife.

"But wait!" Arthur flinched back this time. He could see the pain twitching beneath Charley's face, worming beneath his skin. He knew what bargain Charley was making with himself, and failing at. "Don't. I didn't kill your friend."

Charley hesitated. "I shouldn't have told you."

And that, that wasn't fucking fair at all. If Charley meant to continue forward, meant to return to the group and seek his vengeance upon John Little, then Arthur had to die. "You think I'll warn him."

And of course he would.

"I get it," Arthur continued. "If you really want to go forward, kill John . . . then yeah, you have to kill me now. I can't make any promises you could believe, I get it. But Charley. *Charley,* you can choose not to. Marion's Men and the Nottingham Guard, chasing each other, over and over, for what? How'd it start? An accident? What does that roll into? How many people die just because . . . just because we can't let things go?"

David's body, burning.

"There's no letting this go," Charley said.

"There has to be," Arthur pleaded, pushing away his own thoughts. "Someone, at some point, has to back down. Has to say, this is *bullshit*. Put an end to it. Who better than us? Who better than we, who've seen both sides? I honestly— I'm not lying now, I know you think I am—I honestly came to care for some of the men in the Guard. A month ago I thought you were all pissant whores, would've killed any of you on the spot, until I spent time here. I put the tabard on as a disguise at first, yes—but only at first. When the war came, I defended this city, and its people, for the same reason you do. We're no different, Charley."

David, holding the ladder.

Charley closed his eyes, shook his head.

Arthur swallowed. "Honestly, I close my eyes, I still think David's alive. Think he's going to come around that corner and whistle at me. I don't know what it's going to do to me. But I see what it's done to you, and I don't want that. I don't want it, and David wouldn't have wanted it for me none neither. He was always quick to help people, he died doing it. Maybe I can help you, then, Charley. Maybe we can help each other."

David, laughing with Zinn.

Fuck, Arthur struggled against his pain. He, too, wanted to break the world in half. But then he considered what David would've wanted for him. If this was the person David would've wanted him to become.

"Maybe we can make a peace," Arthur said. "Listen, you've spent time with us. You've changed. Me and David, here in the Guard, we changed, too. When David died . . ." his stomach seized, he almost had to stop, "when David died, everything he'd gone through was for *nothing*. Nothing. At least I can carry forward, where he couldn't. Make sure our time here amounts to something. I can't lose what we gained here. Nobody would ever know the things we did, the people we helped. The people we didn't. How fucking unfair would that be?"

He thought of the messages they'd passed over the Nottingham walls, connecting loved ones. And of the stories that had ended in the middle, with no end. That couldn't happen with him. It was too unfair, too unfair by far, to think that everything they'd gone through would vanish like that. It had to be for some reason.

"I've got more amends to make, Charley. I've got to, for David's sake. The people I killed in the last few days, thinking they were the French . . ." a boulder now, his guts, one he would always carry, "I don't know how to even begin to fix that. It would take me a thousand years. I'm glad David never found out we were killing Englishmen, it would have destroyed him. All this fucking madness, there's got to be an end to it, Charley! We have a chance to end this cycle. If you kill me, then it goes back to how it was, and we learn *nothing*. But stopping it all, finding peace, wouldn't that be better than revenge? For your friend, and for mine?"

The world was blurry, but for Charley's uncertain face.

"I need to think," Charley gasped, and dropped to the ground and crossed his legs.

One hand, the key. One hand, the knife.

Charley stared, into the dirty straw on the floor. He was emotionless, as if waiting for any whim to take him in one direction or another. Arthur had no more words, he'd used them all. He was certain they weren't good enough, he'd never been good at those damned things. But it was all he had, all he had left in the entire fucking world.

For some time, there was nothing, just a quiet emptiness between them that was, at least, better than the rage that had held Arthur for the last few days.

He didn't know what he saw in Charley. An outlaw, a Guardsman. A victim, a murderer.

The key, the knife.

They stared at each other until the lantern's oil gave out, as the sounds of war outside swelled and settled, as the air turned cold and colder. So long that Arthur's eyelids eventually became heavy.

"I'm going to trust you," Arthur said at last, his throat raw and pained, and he let his eyes close.

That was something he could thank David for. In the face of the worst, David had always chosen to trust.

Bound before a man who wanted to kill him, Arthur chose to do the same.

SIXTY-NINE

CHARLEY DANCER

THE KENNELS, NOTTINGHAM CASTLE

HOURS LATER, CHARLEY DANCER rolled up off the floor and crossed to Arthur, who was still asleep, arms still chained behind him to the wall. He plunged Reg's knife down into Arthur's neck and chest a dozen times, then a dozen more. The dogs' barking covered Arthur's gurgled screams until he thrashed his last, then Bolt went back to the far end of the cell, curled into a ball, and fell asleep.

SEVENTY

JOHN LACKLAND

NOTTINGHAM ·
FRIDAY, 27ᵀᴴ DAY OF MARCH

NO POWER, NO NAME, no money.

Well, no power or money, at least. John was borrowing a stranger's name—he took that of Nottingham's captain, who'd died in the first day of the siege. For today's purposes, John was now *Fulcher de Grendon*. An ugly name, made for old Scandinavian folklore with heroes and dragons. He was hoping that the rank of captain would make him just important enough to avoid being hanged by the French host, and also not *so* important for him to be *definitely* hanged.

It was the morning of the third day of the siege, and the man who claimed to be King Richard consented to a meeting. Two men from the castle could safely go and speak with him. In disguise, John could visit the French army and see their trap for himself, assuming nobody recognized his dirtied face under the captain's hood and tabard. He had no doubt they would offer to promote him from captain to baron if he returned to convince the great Prince John to surrender. Today he was just the proverbial messenger, whom no one was wicked enough to kill.

The portcullis in the barbican ground open, charred timbers crumbling to clouds of ash around it. The lower bailey had been emptied of the enemy for this parley, but everywhere the scorched earth stank of soot. A hundred archers lined the battlements above him, but once he left the outer curtain wall he'd be unprotected, at the mercy of the army on the northern hill.

He walked through that gate, with Will Scarlet at his right.

Scarlet, who'd selected the pseudonym of *Henry Russell* for this venture, had his hands bound in front of him inside his cloak. John insisted upon it. If he truly was about to walk into this most uncunning of traps—if King Philip was going to pepper him with crossbow bolts the moment he was in range—then at least one of these Robin Hoods would die by his side. If John was going to meet his end today, he would at least do so on his own terms—with a heart full of lovely petty revenge.

Two liars, heading out of the castle to meet a third.

The remnants of wooden structures were nothing but gnarled black husks, there were great swaths of ash on the inner walls that crawled up toward the castle proper. A few small snakes of grey flitted to life in the occasional wind. And bodies. There were bodies, some burnt, some not. Some dismembered, some not. Some were already eaten by birds, some looked as if they might blink awake, stand, and walk away. John wondered absently if they were real people, with real problems. He preferred his view from the tower.

From above, the walls of Nottingham were packed shoulder to shoulder, watching their long walk.

"Did you really kill the last Sheriff?" John asked his unlikely companion.

"I did."

"Huh." Ahead, the open gates of the outer curtain wall. "What compelled you to do such a thing?"

"I wanted things to be better."

On the other side of the gates, a blinding blanket of sky.

"And were they?" John asked. "Were they better, afterward?"

Will Scarlet, Henry Russell, Robin Hood—whoever he was—ground his jaw and spoke no more.

Through the gates, outside of the castle for the first time in six weeks, John felt alarmingly naked. He had nothing but a borrowed tabard and a dead man's name to protect him now. No power, no name, no money—a fun trick, to dabble anon in anonymity. But it came with no walls, no allies, no politics. No escape route aside from his admittedly silver tongue.

The scope of the army was a sight beyond description. As the horizon grew, so did it. His eyes strained to understand it, there were eye muscles at play that had never focused on such a thing. A trio of French riders came to meet them. They brandished banners and shields with Richard's lions rampant on a red field, even believably distressed. Their English, too, was notably convincing, though they were likely part of the English traitors. They kept their distance as they escorted John and Scarlet to the enemy line, as if the two of them posed a threat to their thousands.

Every eye in every direction was upon him.

Actually, John realized he could rather enjoy this. As much as he didn't want to be the center of the country, he admittedly loved being the center of attention. And that center was a blisteringly small pinpoint on the top of his head. That Arable girl was wrong, more wrong than she would ever know. John was, in fact, the only damned human in the thousands of them present that was *not* a spectator.

The terrain pushed up, their boots slipped in the beaten, mud-soaked earth. They pushed onto their knees to climb past the first lines of soldiers, then more, then more, then more. The siege engines that had hurled boulder after boulder for two days lay quiet to the left, to the right were the first tents striped in bold colors. John paid none of them heed—he instead studied the ground visible behind horses' legs, and the edges of tents, and the shadows peeking around any obstacle. For the trap, for the Frenchmen, for the axe to fall.

The snippets of conversation around him were all still unnervingly English.

John decided to ignore that fact for a few minutes longer.

Eventually there was a larger tent than the rest, with larger guards, and a larger sense of impending death. Time refused to slow for him to enjoy the details of it, and soon enough he and the friendly assassin next to him were standing in front of a large collection of angry men with grizzled beards and crossed arms. The stink was impressive. One man, front and center—with sleepy eyes and a set jaw—was introduced as the King of England, Richard the Lionheart.

"Well?" the man asked. "Am I him? What do you think?"

John's stomach twisted so hard it turned his guts into diamonds.

Beside him, Will Scarlet repeated the question. "Is that the King?"

John swallowed.

"No. No it's not."

Scarlet's face turned bone white and his mouth opened, but John gave him a calming touch on his forearm. Then he pointed a finger at a nearby soldier at lazy attention near the back of the command tent, bearded, with a mail coif making an oval of his familiar face.

"But *that*," John said, "*that's* the King."

John didn't know if his brother recognized him in return. If he did, then it was perhaps all the more insulting when the actual Richard replied with a simple, "You may go back freely."

They did.

And so the war ended with a sigh, with John left to wonder at the fascinating and prickly hollow new sensation of what it was like to be so spectacularly wrong about something.

PART VIII

LIAR'S NAIL

SEVENTY-ONE

MARION FITZWALTER

MARION HAD BEEN RIGHT *when she said that everything would be better when King Richard returned.* What she had not known was what the cost to get there would be.

She did not fight the lump in her throat nor the tears in her eyes as she wandered the castle's apron. Here, the fighting had been heaviest. The air was ribboned with white and black smoke still, and unidentifiable acrid odors. Here the ladders had been raised, even as arrows and hot oil came down from above. Here Richard's armies had engaged with the defenders' sortie when the gates had opened, and here they lay still. Men who did not hate each other, men who did not even disagree with each other—just men unfortunate enough to be on opposite sides of an epic misunderstanding.

As early as yesterday, this was the most dangerous place in Nottinghamshire. Now, Marion needed little more than a heavy cloak and her riding boots to stand safely in the mud that had cost so many lives.

Both the castle host and Richard's allies tended the battlefield. Commonfolk picked their way like ghosts, looking for loved ones. Bodies were solemnly gathered onto carts and carried away. Knights would receive proper burials, no doubt, but footmen would likely share a communal grave. Men who had killed each other would now lie next to each other. The dirt didn't care for which side they'd fought.

The dead would never see the better England that Richard's return promised. They'd suffered the worst of his absence, of the Chancellor's corruption, and the verge of civil war. To think of how close they'd come to seeing daylight on the other side of their long night was more than Marion could bear. She already knew that she would spend months unraveling her own role in what had happened, and whether she could have avoided such unnecessary loss. Marion had yet to fully believe what the others told her—that she was headed toward something greater—but if they were right, it was her duty to grow from this. To make the future truly better.

But her thoughts were decidedly less lofty at the moment.

Robert was still unaccounted for.

Arable was still unaccounted for.

The Delaneys.

Ahead of her, a corpse of a young man lay on his stomach, a short axe wedged between his shoulder blades. Based on his position, he must have been fleeing when he was killed. His weapon—she assumed it was his, at least—lay a foot from his hands, not a single drop of blood on it.

"We should not be here, my lady," Sir Amon said from atop his horse, picking a careful path behind her. "It's not safe."

"Oh to hell with *safe*." She did not bother to turn back. "Do you think one is going to wake up and attack me?"

"This area is not secured," he answered. "There's no knowing who is left in the city with a grudge to bear. And the dead bring disease, my lady, you would be—"

"Nowhere in the world is safe," she cut him off. "I should think this has proven the point."

The immediacy of the war had been her excuse to avoid this next conversation. Now that it was over, there was no point in delaying it. And with such tangible proof of her responsibilities around her, she was ashamed to have even put it off.

"You're selfish, Amon," she said. "Do you know that?"

He held back a slight gasp. *Good.* She'd meant to hurt him. "I have given much of myself for your safety, my lady. It pains me to hear that you do not recognize that."

She ignored his protest. "You see the world only in terms of your *charge*. In whether or not something is safe for me, not whether it's inherently right. That's why you abducted me, it's how you convinced yourself it was honorable to do so. I won't be in need of your service any longer."

"My charge is not—"

"I know." She'd heard it before. "It's my father's to decide. I'll be writing him a letter today to demand that he discharge you, and replace you with someone else. There are, after all, a great many other knights suddenly returned to England in need of retainer."

His horse shuffled in the mud behind her. She wouldn't look at him. There were too many bodies here, of young men who deserved her pity so very much more than he.

"As you say. But I will continue to watch over you until—"

"If I see you, I'll cut my arm open." She knelt down and picked the unbloodied sword from the ground, held its point to her wrist. "Do you understand? If you care about my safety so much, then know that the closer you are to me, the more damage I will do to myself. So protect me, then, by removing yourself from my sight."

She wasn't proud of dismissing him so, but she had no emotion to spare for him.

The soldier with the axe in his back, Marion didn't know him. But at the same time, she knew him a thousand times. He was everyone she was fighting for, and everyone whose fate she did not yet know. He was all her responsibilities, and especially those she'd shied away from. Her thoughts turned to Will Scarlet, whom she'd once been so eager to cut out of her life. It had been a profound shock to see him again in King Richard's command tent, side by side with Prince John of all people—and Marion was apparently the only person who had recognized either of them. She would give a great many things to learn what bizarre events had placed the two of them in that moment. Despite all her frustrations from the winter, she was dying to find out what had happened on Will's half of their diverged road. She *missed* him, and perhaps, too, the adventurous side of her past that had vanished along with him. She wanted the opportunity to say farewell to both of those. Maybe even to apologize. But the world was rarely so tidy as to allow her that opportunity. She doubted she'd ever get that closure.

But whatever had happened to Will Scarlet, that, too, was her responsibility. To see to it that it never had to happen again.

Amon's horse huffed and moved away, but Marion focused on the dead man on the ground until his every horrid feature was memorized. She wasn't sure if she was happy that Amon left, or even more disappointed in him. But if ever there was a good time to clean the slate, this was it.

Each body here, there was no knowing what brought them to Nottingham. Some had followed their king's orders to Jerusalem and back, some had marched for their liegelord, some had defended their city, their castle, because they didn't know of another way. Because their leaders only knew how to solve their disputes by spilling blood. Because it was the way they saw the world. Like Amon, they could only think of solutions that fit their skills.

Hammers, all of them, who thought they could pound the world until it was made of nails.

SHE STORMED RIGHT PAST the line of noblemen waiting for a word with their King, which stretched the length of the war camp. Men who were vying for his recognition, men who wanted to remind him they were here on this day. Men who wanted land from their rivals, positions for their children. Men who had risked the lives of those beneath them, whose loss they would never mourn. Marion Fitzwalter refused to wait patiently behind men who wanted to profit from the dead, and be congratulated for it.

When she reached the entrance flaps to the command tent, a pair of foolhardy sentinels blocked her way. If she thought back upon it later, she would never remember what—if anything—she said to move them. Perhaps an entire life of suppressed rage had been funneled into a single cold glare, which set the two guards succinctly back to their places.

Within, she took the cup of wine from whatever capitulating nobleman was in front of the King, and wordlessly turned it over to spill into the dirt at their feet. Soon enough the room was empty.

"We need to change," she said.

If there was any justification to all this, it was to place her in this exact spot, for her to say those exact words, and she would not leave King Richard's command tent until he dealt with the enormity of her demand.

"Who are you, again?" Richard joked, in French.

She changed languages, her first and final concession. "I said, cousin, we need to change."

"What are we changing?"

"England."

And she told him why. She told him everything she'd told the others at the council in Huntingdon, and everything she'd learned since. She finally had the words that had just been whispers back at Locksley Castle, and now she could scream them. It was not enough for Richard to return, if the country just limped on as it always had. Its people needed protection beyond the unbridled whims of their masters. The earls and barons of England needed to be held accountable, as did her kings and princes—and Lady Marion Fitzwalter was not going to leave the room until her cousin, her King, who had finally returned, agreed to actually make it better.

At some point in her tirade, his face softened. His defenses lowered, he started genuinely listening, and he asked her to slow down. "Tell me more."

MUSIC PLAYED THAT NIGHT. Not just in King Richard's camp, but all throughout Nottingham. The city streets that had been black as pitch the last few nights now glowed, pouring their warmth up to light their stone and timber faces. A celebration of victory was shared by both sides—though Marion wondered how many truly understood the details. It didn't matter. *They were alive,* and King Richard was returned to them, and that was enough to be joyful. All the death and animosity of yesterday was forgiven now. Amongst all the other things they discussed, Marion had also persuaded Richard to be lenient to John's allies—who had only been following orders, and genuinely thought they were defending their country from the French. It was the first war in history, she reckoned, where there had been no losers.

None save the dead, of course. And those that mourned them.

She returned to Huntingdon's campsite to find its main tent bustling more than she would have expected. It was almost too full for her to even approach, but she found her way within and spotted John Little in the throng.

"What is it?" she asked, managing a path close to him.

"Oh, Marion." He embraced her with both arms. "They found Lord Robert."

Her heart leapt at his maddeningly vague words. "Alive?"

"Alive, yes, sorry!" he chuckled, realizing his mistake. "Though maybe just barely."

Marion ground her jaw and stared at him. My but she loved John Little, but he had a talent for sharing emotions before facts.

"He's in the corner." John gestured. "How did it go with the King?"

She paused, touching his shoulder as she thought on that.

"It went well," she said, and felt the awesome relief of being able to say it aloud. John's face lit up, his cheeks drawn tight in an expansive smile, and he turned away to hug the nearest people he could find, whether they wanted it or not.

There was a cot in the rear of the tent, and decency kept the crowd a few feet away from its occupant. It pained Marion that there were no better accommodations to be given him, but half the city had become a hospital and still there was not room enough. Robert lay propped up on the cot, looking anything but comfortable. His face—*his face*—she gasped, was a mess of black and purple, bloated around his eyes and lips, which had split wide and wore open wounds. Marion might not have recognized him at all if she'd not been told who he was.

She knelt beside him and put her hands to her face by instinct, then second-guessed herself. Certainly he would not want to know how wretched he looked, and she shouldn't be the one to reveal it. Instead she clamped her lips tight and craned her head into his eyeline, giving a disapproving frown.

"That's not the face I sent you off with," she grumbled. "What did you do with your old one? I thought it looked better on you."

"Sorry, my lady," the earl whispered, the tips of his lips curling slightly upward. "I think it may still be attached to that knight's fist. I'll retrieve it for you if you ask me to, but maybe not until tomorrow?"

"Shhh." She placed a hand on his chest. "You did it."

He returned an ugly cackle and a chunk of black snorted from his nostrils. "Oh, I didn't do anything. I was just along for the ride, and came out none too well for it. Arable went into the castle, she's the one that did it."

Marion turned, hoping perhaps Arable was nearby, but found only Friar Tuck. "Anyone else?" she asked him, afraid of the answer.

"Not yet," Tuck said, bowing his head.

Marion returned her attention to Robert. She tried not to imagine how he'd received those injuries. He'd gone into the city in her stead, refusing to let her risk herself. It was possible that the Delaney brothers and Arable had been killed long before they accomplished their mission, and that the war had ceased entirely on its own. Perhaps it was Will Scarlet who had stopped the war, or Prince John had come to his senses without any help at all, and the only thing Marion had contributed was to make the pile of the dead a little higher.

Cold fingers entwined with her own, and she was pulled from her dark thoughts.

"I know what you're doing," came Robert's coarse voice. "Don't. It's not on you."

"It *is* on me." She squeezed his hand. "But that's alright. That's the point. I want it to be on me."

It was Robert who had taught her that, after all. And Amon, misguided as he may have been. Marion's burden was that of leadership now, which meant she *needed* to feel every loss, every injury, in order to know the weight of her every decision. The moment she grew numb to the consequences of her actions would be the day she turned into the very thing she fought against. She would not play with people's lives the way others move numbers in a ledger.

Which reminded her. "I spoke with the king, Robert, and he was interested in our ideas. We can make some progress, real progress, on all the things we wanted."

"That's good." He smiled. "While we were sneaking into the city, you were trapped talking politics with the King? Sounds like you had it worse after all."

She had to blink away a tear, just at the joy of seeing his humor intact. "Well, since you won't let me join you on your mad adventures, then I can at least handle the big things."

His fingers stretched farther, taking her wrist. "That's a deal. You manage the king parts, I'll take care of the getting-our-face-beaten-in parts."

She laughed for him. "That's a deal."

"And no more Robin Hooding," he added, with something more serious in his eye.

The name no longer brought the immediate pain it once had. Now it was just a stone in her belly. She pursed her lips, refusing to let another tear come. "Agreed. You know, when Robin died we realized the best part of Robin Hood was that it didn't matter who he was. That *anybody* could be Robin Hood."

Robert's thumb traced her wrist, back and forth. "But?"

"But you know what the worst part was?" She looked into him. "That *anybody* could be Robin Hood."

Bruised and beaten, his eyes were gentle, and he understood. Some instinct recognized that private smile and Marion wanted to lose herself, but modesty forced her to withdraw her hand. She was all too aware of the number of eyes on them, and the impropriety of their closeness. She would have liked to kiss that hand, to touch his face, but not with an audience. There was too much at stake, she chided herself, to follow such adolescent urges. She wasn't quite sure where she stood right now, but she had the ear of the King—and it would do poorly for her to be too friendly with a married earl.

On the other hand, she considered, *who the fuck cares?*

She leaned forward and kissed him on the lips, holding his head softly with both hands. His skin was puffy and swollen, his lips thicker than before, her nose scratched against a hard scab, and she didn't mind any of it one bit. Robert did not flinch in shock, nor smile his way through this one. His other hand floated up to find the fabric of her dress, pulling her gently closer. Marion didn't know what this meant, and didn't want to know. For the moment, it was what her heart wanted, it was a thank-you, it was relief and celebration. Yesterday none of them had any reason to think they had any future at all, so today they could all of them live as if the future was anything they wanted it to be.

And at last—*at last*—they were in a position to actually build that future, rather than simply survive it.

The war was over, Richard was returned, and there was no need for anyone else to die in Nottingham.

SEVENTY-TWO

WILL SCARLET

NOTTINGHAM

"ARE WE LEAVING NOTTINGHAM?" Elena asked. She hugged her knees to her chest, rocking forward and back beside Will on the gentle wooden slope of the rooftop, keeping him company as he watched the ramshackle buildings of Plumptre Street across the way.

"*I'm* leaving Nottingham," he answered her, picking at another clump of dirt caked into his boots. "But you? You're dead."

She snorted and flicked her braid over her shoulder, the one with the twine in it. Even when she was alive, she'd never let him get away with using facts against her. "You're dead, too, lover. Sooner you come to terms with that, sooner we can get back to having some fun."

She nestled closer to him, slipped her hand down his chest, under his belt, her cold fingers finding him waiting for her. That satisfied hum she always gave.

"Go away," he told her, and himself, and stood. He didn't want to wait any longer, but he had yet to see any sign of Arthur, or Arable, or Zinn. He'd been waiting here, watching Zinn's hovel on Plumptre Street, for a day. Surely Arthur would return here if he were freed. Surely Zinn would show up here on her own. As of yet, neither had.

It was possible they were still locked up in the castle. Will had become an object of fascination after returning with the news that King Richard was really King Richard. Every prominent man in the castle wanted to speak with *Henry Russell* to learn what had happened, as the prince returned to his seclusion in the tower. One by one he spoke with them in the Sheriff's office, and piece by piece the castle crumbled into chaos as John's allies dissembled around him. Somebody probably was supposed to remember that Will was a criminal, that he should have been on a noose. Somebody probably was supposed to guard him, and lock his door between visitors. Instead, while the castle reeled in relief at the prince's surrender, Will Scarlet just walked the fuck out of Nottingham Castle's newly opened gates like he was going for a Sunday stroll.

But in so doing, he'd left his companions behind.

"I have to know they're alright," he said.

"Suit yourself," Elena cackled, tied a noose around her neck, and jumped off the edge.

He gave one last hard look at Zinn's door before resolving to climb down. He didn't even know if there was any point in waiting. Arthur would probably want to return to Marion anyway, just like he'd wanted ever since they came to the city. As Arable had described it, the rest of their old group was doing *"just fine in Huntingdon."* Marion had been right all along—she'd brought her people safety, while Will's ideas had descended into a spiral of failures. Stutely had abandoned them, and David was dead. Nottingham had beaten them all senseless, broken them.

Will couldn't stay in the city . . . but neither could he go back with the others.

"They can't domesticate you," Elena said, next to him again, sharpening a blade.

There was no life for him in Huntingdon, no honest life.

"That's not who we are," she said, firing an arrow off the rooftop. It struck a man in the chest below, who screamed, and Elena shot him again.

He shook it off and descended by the wooden scaffolds on the edge of the building. He'd hoped to see John Little and Tuck again after all this, he'd wanted them to say they were wrong about him. He wanted to tell them the unlikely story of the time he walked between two armies, side by side with the prince to meet the King—the true story of how the gangling runt Will Scarlet ended the war. But after that, what place was there for him in the real world? Not at dinner tables and castles. Not policy and politesse. Not for Ten Bell Will.

His skills mingled less than kindly with others.

"Where are we going?" Elena asked, tiptoeing along the roof across the street.

"You know where we're going. You're in my head."

"I know," she said, walking backward in front of him now, her hair undone and wild, half flowing over her face. "I just like talking to you."

"You don't get the things you like," he told her. He had to be firm with her, it was the only way. "Not anymore. Not since you killed yourself."

"I fucked Rob o' the Fire." She touched herself between her legs. "And he was better than you."

The plank eventually turned to splinters in his hands, shredded scraps of wood, his palms bled and blistered. He had found the wood on the ground, he had beaten the stone wall beside him until he couldn't hear her, couldn't think of her, but never until he couldn't remember her.

There were other sounds behind his heartbeat, behind his labored breaths, and if he waited long enough he might recognize it as singing. The city was celebrating the peaceful ending to a relatively short siege, and the return of King Richard meant a return to normality. Will both envied and despised these people, since it took so little to please them.

AS MUCH AS HE hated to go back there, he took comfort in knowing it would be the very last time. He took the long path, down by the southern wharfs on Leen Side, and then a serpentine route through Dodson Yard, then The Peach and the Pear, around and between Severn's and Ten Bell, where he'd scrapped a hundred times, a hundred years ago, with poor Freddy Fawkes. He glanced down Knotted Alley to see if any young lovers were tying their ribbons together, wondering how long it had been since his own had been cut down and stolen away on the bottom of someone's boot. He wasn't normally one for nostalgia, but then he was never one for swearing absolutes, either.

And Will would never, swear to God, return to Nottingham.

"That's where we met." Elena pointed at a stone wall, which was not where they met. She ran to it at full speed, diving at the last second to meet it face first, her neck snapping.

He walked faster, and took a direct path for the caves just north of Red Lion Square.

The squeeze was not as difficult as it had been even two months ago, meaning he was skinnier now than he realized. He didn't need a lantern on the inside, he just kept his hands out to the cavern walls, knowing the long slope down, and where it led.

"Maybe we can find your ear down there," she said. "Maybe I can find a real man to fuck, too."

He punched the wall, didn't care at the torn flesh on his knuckles. They were raw and cramped already from the war, and nobody cared what happened to them, to him.

The light that crawled up the tunnels was brighter than normal, orange eating up the ripples of the cave's sides, drawing him in. When he made the last curve that brought him into the foot of the Lions Den, he knew why. The Red Lions were gone, which apparently meant it was time to burn them and their things. If any had survived after mobbing the siege ladders, they weren't here now.

Alfred's piecemeal throne was ablaze in the middle of the room, an earthy smoke blooming upward to disperse against the ceiling of the cavern, whisking away into little eddies that revealed the many wormhole openings that led to the world above. Around the effigy were a dozen children, laughing and tossing things in, daring each other to get closer, pushing the weaker ones and cackling when they ran.

"I dare you to sit on it," Elena said, pulling her shirt off over her head, dancing in silhouette.

His presence did not go unnoted. The shit rolled downhill as each skinny gang child found someone skinnier and younger than himself to do the dirty work of telling whoever was in charge that Will was here. Eventually the lowliest little waif was found, who kicked up a pout about having to leave the fire, and slumped off as if every footstep held all the world's unfairness. Scarlet admired that little waif. He, too, had been the bottom of the chain once upon a time. That little skiver had an entire unspoilt life ahead of him, full of poor decisions to leap into, and opportunities to demolish. Elena raised her glass to the little man. "Make a mess of it, life," she said, and downed the drink.

"Oh no," she continued, coughing blood into her palms. "This happens every time . . ."

Will looked elsewhere. The shadows of the dancing children painted the walls in profane caricatures. Most of the room's previous decorations were gone—stolen, probably—and replaced with giant lumpy drawings of hands in white paint. The *"Children of the White Hand,"* Arable had described them, though Will doubted they'd last long. After a pillar like the Red Lions was toppled, it would probably be a year of in-fighting before the gangs were ever organized and stable again. Part of him wanted to stay and pick up those pieces. He knew how to use that chaos to his advantage, it was where he was comfortable.

Elena slipped her hand into his and squeezed it. "But I'm here."

"But you're here," he said back to her.

This was his last night in Nottingham.

When the waif returned he had a visitor in tow, and it was exactly who Will had hoped it would be. Zinn wore a long split coat now over her normal ragged outfit—just reminiscent enough of Alfred Fawkes to invite comparison, but still distinctly her own. Elena nodded in approval. "She knows what she's doing."

"What the fuck ya doin' here?" Zinn screamed, stamping her feet. "You goddamn slag."

It was good to see her. It was good to know she'd survived after fleeing from the dockmaster's office, when Will had surrendered himself for her life. Good to see she'd continued her habit of rising.

Good to know Will was still capable of caring.

"But she'll get killed here," Elena said, and demonstrated by stabbing Much through the neck.

"I'm hoping you've seen Arthur," Will said. "I'm here—"

"I can't fucking believe it." Zinn threw her hands in the air, turned back to look at something Will couldn't make out, before the fire. She flicked the tails of her coat out and flopped down onto a shelf of the rock, her shoulders slumped in defeat. "I'm sorry. I really am."

"Sorry for what?"

"You shouldn't'a come."

A larger shape came into focus now behind her, moving with a careful gait. "I do like being right," came an older voice, male. Its owner's name was only on the tip of Will's memory, but his nerves recalled the danger of its tone. "And I knew you'd come."

"He's been waiting for you here," Zinn explained. "I told him to fuck himself, that you weren't dumb enough to come here. Way to fucking prove me wrong."

"Oooh, I know you." It snapped into place. Will squinted at the stranger. "Didn't I put a knife to your neck last time?"

"You did do that," confirmed Lord Beneger de Wendenal. "Though I also put a fist through your face, so do you really want to gloat about *last times*?"

Elena laughed at that. He hated that she was right.

But Wendenal did not look like he had the strength to put a fist through anything at the moment. One arm was trapped tight to his chest in a sling, and his face was pale and sickly. "You're a man eager to die," the man said, "and yet you refuse to do so. I wonder if you're still interested in that duel?"

Will laughed, because every word the man said was truer than the last. "Oh, gladly." His twins were long lost to some Nottingham armory, but there would never be a day when Will Scarlet needed a blade to take out an old man who was both one-armed and unarmed.

A whistle to his right stopped that thought cold, as another figure revealed itself from the edge of the room. She held a bow limply in one hand, three arrows dripped from the fingers of the other, and the harsh orange light revealed only the dead half of her face.

Will had spent most of his life taking his chances against impossible odds, but his gut sank into the floor at the prospect of going up against the Lace Jackal. The woman who had bested Freddy at the archery tournament, the woman who had threatened to let Zinn be gang-raped when last they'd met. The woman whose uncle died at Will's hands.

Elena covered Much's eyes and withdrew to an alcove.

"Zinn," Will said with caution, wondering if he had any allies. "Are you hiding anyone else here who wants to kill me?"

"Don't blame me for steppin' in yer own shit." She clicked the heels of her boots on the ground.

The Lace Jackal had barely moved. Her frame was at once full of energy, ready to spring at a thought, and impressively relaxed. Both her eyes were half-slit, one full of an unfathomable fury, the other with apathy. They were, Will could not disagree, the two most common impressions he left on people.

"You'll answer me first, though." Lord Wendenal coughed. "Did you kill my son?"

At that, Will could be surprised. "Your son? No." He tried to recall his few interactions with the late William de Wendenal. "I met him a handful of times, can't say I liked him much. But no. That was Robin. Far as I know."

"As a father, I beg you," Lord Wendenal's eyes were suddenly wet, "to tell me the truth. I've been side by side with many of your old crew this last week, and never asked them, not once, because I knew they would lie. Or protect you. I have come a long way to know this one thing, do not deny it to me. I ask again. Did you kill my son?"

Will didn't have it in him to bite or bark. "I did not. I swear it."

Lord Wendenal's eyes closed, but he almost seemed to expect the answer. "I'm told Locksley did not go to the castle alone the night my son was killed. If not you, then who?"

"John, and Arable," Will answered, maybe too quickly. "But neither ever saw your son. Arable stayed outside the castle, and John got separated from Robin and retreated." They had both recounted their stories a dozen times, for those who wanted to know what happened that night. "It was Robin—and Robin alone—that did it. And he's dead."

The grieving father of Nottingham stared, the muscles at the corner of his lips tensing. Eventually he inhaled a long unsatisfied breath, and withdrew. "He's yours, then, Jacelyn. I envy you."

She did not respond to him, she'd simply been waiting her turn. "You killed my uncle."

It wasn't a question. And this one, Will could hardly deny. Will hadn't seen the Sheriff of Nottingham as *an uncle* then. He wasn't anyone's family, he wasn't any one thing besides the reason Much was dead. He and Elena, they'd both buried their knives into Roger de Lacy's chest half a dozen times, thinking they'd changed the world.

"I did," he said.

The gesture was practically a flick, her two hands glanced apart like she was peeling an onion, but it sprung the first arrow from her bow and stuck it in Will's thigh—high, just barely below his hip—and his leg crumpled beneath him. The pain of his kneecap hitting the rock floor was almost worse than the puncture, and he clasped both hands over the wound in agony. His muscles quivered as the sting made white lightning of his nerves, while he gave the arrow a gentle nudge and found that it could move. He eased it out of the hole in his muscle, thankful that its head had a leaf shape instead of barbs. He smashed his palm over the wound, wincing as blood came to meet him, while his other hand turned the arrow around and held it out at her, as if he were ready to fence with it.

"F-f-fuck," he said. He meant to say something else, something far more clever, but the pain was overwhelming. He'd never been shot with an arrow before, and it was shocking how deep the pain was. Any second now, he'd probably have another matching wound in his other leg.

"Stop it!" came Zinn's voice, and Will blinked away his shivers. Zinn stepped in front of him, blocking Jacelyn de Lacy's next shot. Will tried to yell at her, but his throat was still clenched tight. "You said you weren't going to kill him."

"No I didn't." Lord Wendenal's head tilted. He exchanged a confused look with the Jackal. "We didn't say that at all."

"Oh." Zinn seemed surprised. "Well . . . don't kill him."

"That's . . . that's why we're here."

"Oh."

She let her little hook knife drop from her hand. It bobbed a few inches above the ground, held by the tether still wrapped around her palm. A twist of her wrist and it started a circle, slow, floating in front of her as if it might somehow intercept the next arrow.

"Knock it, Zinn!" Will yelled, furious how difficult it was to breathe. "Get out of the way!"

"Naw, they're in *my* house," Zinn replied. A twitch of her head sent her hair flopping over the shaved half of her skull. "They want to kill you topside, that's one thing. But not down here."

Will spared a glance over to the other children, who had stopped their dance around the fire and stood closer now, watching.

Elena stood up and bounded over to them. "Oh goodness, how many Muches get to die today?"

She spun like a dancer in a minstrel show, a knife in each hand, slicing through their throats as she span, a great red ribbon of blood swirling around her as she moved until it became a sphere that obscured her, though her laughter only grew louder.

"*No!*" he yelled, and against all good sense Will rolled up and struggled to his feet, keeping all his weight on his right foot. He threw the arrow at Zinn's back, which tumbled uselessly but got her attention. When she met his eyes her lips parted, her weapon slowed. "No. Not you. Not any of them. God, what would be the *point?*"

This last word he screamed, it came back at him from down the halls a few times until there was nothing in the room but the crackling throne.

"They kill me, you kill them, they kill you, someone else kills them, again and again, it doesn't matter, it doesn't fucking matter! Where does it end? Whose revenge goes last? Fuck, the world doesn't care, it just doesn't. This war, this fucking war, didn't give the first damn what we want from the world, not one hot goddamn. And soon as it's over here we are again, pointing steel at each other and crying vengeance. Stand down, Zinn. I've got to die, that's obvious. But let's end it there. Let's just . . . let's just end it there."

Zinn's eyes widened as if she'd never heard that kind of idea before. Maybe she hadn't. Maybe nobody had ever told her that you don't *have* to fight back. Maybe nobody ever told her that a slight can go unpunished. Maybe nobody ever explained strength to her as anything other than a thing she didn't have. Maybe she was raised thinking the only way to succeed was for others to fail, and that the reason she hurt was that other people didn't. Maybe, just maybe, she would finally learn something new. With her nose in the mud of the Nottingham streets, she could only think in terms of left and right.

Maybe nobody had ever taught her the direction of *up*.

Elena touched Will's chin, she drew him down calmly, she sat with her legs crossed and invited him to join her. So he did. It was an odd thing, knowing it was the last time he would ever sit down. It was the most relaxing feeling he'd ever known. His feet would never carry his weight—or the weight of all his mistakes—ever again. He crossed his legs, too, letting the blood flow from his wound. He smiled with Elena, whose eyes were full of tears. His thigh was numb, but his heart . . . his heart, damn it, for the first time in a while, it was joyful.

"Hoping to make your peace?" the Jackal asked, a sneer in her lip. "Or maybe hoping I'll think twice if you seem remorseful? I won't. You stabbed my uncle to death in his office, wearing a Guardsman's tabard. You're the reason there's a hell."

She lowered her bow to the ground and drew a curious weapon from her side, a heavy sword that did not end with a point but a wide, flat edge. This was not a blade made for fighting, it was designed for the singular purpose of separating a man's head from his shoulders. Will shrugged. It was as good a way as any.

Beside her, Beneger de Wendenal's face was haunted, and Will knew why.

"You don't know how your son died," Will said, with actual sympathy. "And you probably never will."

Wendenal shook his head, just barely. *What a monstrous thing.*

"At least you were there for me." Elena tugged Will's fingertip. He had that. Elena had been in his arms, until the very end. And suddenly he wanted to apologize to Marion, too, who would never know how Robin died. He wondered what that had done to her, and whether he could've been more understanding. Too late now.

"I'm sorry," he said to Wendenal, and meant it. He looked to the Jackal. Jacelyn. "I can tell *you*, at least. It went quickly, for your uncle. He wasn't scared—or if he was, he was scared for *us*. He tried to protect us. Even with his final breaths, he seemed more worried about what it meant for us than himself. I hated him then, you know. I thought he was the reason I was hurting. But it doesn't really work like that."

Jacelyn exhaled from her nose.

"What was he like?" Will asked.

"Who?"

"Your uncle. Roger de Lacy."

The muscles in her neck clenched. "I don't know. I never met him."

It took a few seconds for Will to really understand that, and then he laughed.

"I only knew him through letters," Jacelyn continued, her voice oddly disconnected from her body. "And even still, he was my favorite of my family. He didn't talk down to me. Every letter felt like we were . . . conspirators together. He didn't pity me. Actually . . ." Her breath haltered. "Actually I memorized one of his letters. He said, '*I have heard tell of your affliction, and I am truly sorry. I can think of no greater handicap in this world than to be related to your mother. What a cruel hand you have been dealt.*'"

Exactly half her face rippled with emotion.

"Is it a burn wound?" Will asked.

She shook her head, her focus on the ground. "Just born this way."

"And that's why you liked your uncle? Because he never saw your face?"

She didn't answer, though she did look him in the eye.

"Come on," Elena said. "Stop talking. I'm waiting for you."

"My family didn't trust him," Jacelyn said. "I never had an opportunity to thank him for treating me with decency. That was my first regret in life. My second, was playing any part in releasing you from prison."

Will laughed again, thinking of that escape last November. Arable, bringing them the keys, fleeing Nottingham—victorious. No idea they were being followed. "We thought we were so clever. We thought we were free."

"Losing you was like losing him again," she said, and twisted the heft of her weapon.

"So . . . is having me here," he asked, just on instinct, "like having him back again?"

She stared at him for a long time, so long that he almost forgot which one of her eyes actually worked.

"No." The blade returned to her side, she picked up her bow, and she walked away without looking back even once.

Lord Wendenal called her name twice, but in a dozen steps she was out of the chamber.

Will didn't breathe until her footsteps were gone, until her presence might have just been a dream. Wendenal's eyes narrowed on him, as if he were trying to calculate what the trick was. And then, with just as little warning as Jacelyn de Lacy, he turned away. He watched the flames in silence for a bit, oblivious that Will was still there bleeding on the floor, and then wandered off toward another exit, with absolutely no urgency.

Will sighed. "Well *somebody* better kill me."

"*I* could kill you," Zinn offered.

She slapped his shoulder, and eased him onto his back, raising his foot up. She tore into his leggings with her knife and cut away to expose the wound, but Will could do very little besides stare up at the pulsing rock shadows on the ceiling of the cave. His thoughts were blank and patient.

"Hurry up," Elena begged him. "I miss you."

"I can sew this up," was Zinn's voice.

Will doubted he'd be around long enough. His leg was cold, his fingers tingled.

"I'll fuck every man you've ever killed if you don't come to me right now."

"No you won't," Will answered.

"What?"

"Let me go," he told her.

"You're a job, old man," Zinn said. Her hair tickled his nose. He didn't even realize his eyes had closed. "I can't believe you're not dead."

"Give me a few minutes," Will promised. "I won't disappoint."

She laughed. "What, you think you're dying? You took an arrow to the leg, you idiot. Stop being dramatic. And if you don't want a limp for the rest of your life, *stop fidgeting.*"

Elena shrugged. "What do I know?"

"You should get out of Nottingham," Will said, to Zinn. "Gangs won't be safe for a while, they'll eat each other up trying to fill the void."

"One step ahead of you," she answered. "Gilbert said the same thing."

"Gilbert?"

"Yeah, he's down here, too. Me an' him an' a dozen of these runts. We weren't planning on sticking around, so thanks for your brilliant old man advice." She tied the strap around his thigh so tight he grunted. "Why'd you come, anyhow?"

He opened his eyes to look at her, her and her beautiful, arrogant spite at the world, a costume that was ready to crack open. Underneath all that snark, the real Zinn was waiting somewhere. "I came for you," he said to that person.

"Take care of him," Elena whispered to Zinn, and took Much's hand.

Zinn rolled her eyes, momentarily full of that insolent rage of hers. "Please. I don't need you to rescue me."

"No." He reached out and caught her elbow. "You don't get it. I need *you*
                                                         to
                                            rescue *me*."

SEVENTY-THREE

BENEGER DE WENDENAL

NOTTINGHAM

BEN'S RETURN TO THE castle was marked by a queer feeling, a sensation that Nottingham was muted to him. While commotion was everywhere, and every pocket was populated thrice-over more than would have been uncomfortable, Ben viewed it all as if through a tunnel. He'd left the traitor Will Scarlet alive, and in so doing had mentally turned the page on this city. The cobbled streets through which he had so recently led armed charges were now rendered a waste of his time. This city's people would go on with their lives and heal from this madness, as would Ben. But Ben would do so in Derbyshire, and had every desire to leave as soon as possible.

This city, to his shame, had beaten him for its third and final time.

But there were requirements, of course. Tomorrow was Sunday, and King Richard would spend the day in a public council, meeting with all those who had grievances to bear. There were men who would receive punishments—others, laurels—and it was generally frowned upon to leave the city before the king had sorted it all out. But Ben was drawn to consider it. His only reasons for being here were gone, leaving him a stranger in a place he despised.

He looked down at his arm, confined in the wraps of his sling. His entire hand was numb to sensation, and seemed to be getting worse. Ben had seen too many injuries in his life to hope that this would end with anything short of him losing the limb. The physicker had told him to give it a few days, and wait until it started to stink or turn black to make the decision. By then, Ben would be home, at least. Nottingham wouldn't claim that piece of him.

Passing through the burnt barbican to the middle bailey, he paused in heavy consideration. His son had died in this castle. Too recently. He'd undoubtedly crossed this gateway dozens of times. But there was no way to feel him. The distance of a few months was as permanent as a thousand years. It was worse than being alone, the sense that these halls had history forever out of his reach.

The training yard—a squarish dirt field at the mouth of the barracks—was now a makeshift hospital. Tents of various plumage had been erected to give cover to a field of bedrolls and cots, where the injured lay indistinguishable from the dead. He walked down the aisles and found his way toward one specific cot in the back, to say his goodbyes. The shifting colors and streaks of sunlight through the canvas canopies were reminiscent of a market or bazaar, as if Ben were here to barter and purchase an injured soldier.

Quillen Peveril was still unconscious, his thin frame hiding little more than his bones. His weak jawline, his sloppy hair—it was hard to believe that Ben owed the man his life.

In the cot adjacent, a fellow soldier gave a nod in welcome.

"Has he awoken?" Ben asked.

The soldier shook his head. His colors were that of the Worcester Guard, and he cradled an arm that now ended in a stump and bloody linen. His hand had been crushed by falling debris from the siege engine attacks, then amputated halfway past the elbow.

Peveril likely could have died as well. The gash across his chest was swollen and bruised, but it was not a hole. Why Sir Robert FitzOdo had left any of them to live, Ben didn't know. He could have opened Quill's chest like an oyster, splitting his ribs apart with a single blow, and then finished Ben off, too. Instead the Coward Knight had walked away the moment there was nobody left standing to fight him. He'd shown mercy. Perhaps it was why Ben walked away from Will Scarlet. Perhaps it was why he was walking away from the city, and from *Robin Hood,* and from his son's death. Even though Peveril had defended Ben from the knight's axe—the debt of his life also lay abominably in FitzOdo's clemency.

Others would continue that fight, maybe. FitzOdo's crimes were made known; Ben had seen to that, at least. The next captain, the next somebody, would bear that torch.

"If you're here when he wakes," Ben asked of the neighboring soldier, "tell him I was here, and that I owe him. Lord Beneger de Wendenal is his man, if he needs it. I'll be at my estate in Derbyshire."

"And if he doesn't wake?" the soldier asked.

Ben looked down on Peveril, skinny and dirty, his lips parted and drooling like a child. Though he wished it didn't, it reminded him of his sons. All three. "Then the world will be worser for it."

The world was already worser for it. Every day, worser, the only direction the world had ever known. *Life was nothing more than riding that slope down, to see how long you could hold on before it was your turn.*

Just outside the colorful canopies, Ben spotted Nottingham's castellan, Hamon Glover. Glover surveyed the yard with a sincere interest, and was very likely responsible for its existence in the first place. Ben gave the man a curt greeting and farewell, mostly as a courtesy.

"Are you leaving us?" the castellan asked, before Ben could avoid the conversation. "Ahead of Richard's announcements?"

"I'll stay, but only just," he answered. "I'd rather take my leave with haste."

The thick man fidgeted. "Understandable."

Ben would have walked on, but curiosity stayed him. "Have you heard any sign of FitzOdo?"

"Sir Robert?" Glover gave a quick scan of the hospital, all while shaking his head. "I'm afraid not. Though my attention has been . . . pulled in many directions of late."

"Of course."

"And what of—if you don't mind my asking—what of Robin Hood, then?" Glover straightened the ties of his heavy cloak, which threatened to rip at the strain. "Have you completed your investigation?"

"Robin Hood is dead." Ben looked out toward the horizon, where the sun was already making its way to Derby. "But he'll only stay that way if we ignore him. He's only as strong as we make him. I imagine there will always be another Robin Hood now, his idea is too compelling to those with nowhere else to turn. He'll be remade, in one form or another, and there's nothing we can do about it. Nor should we. Ignore him, I say, that is the summation of my investigation. Only if you chase him down, can his power grow."

Glover's lips pursed in consideration, but seemed to think nothing more of it. "Back to your home, then?"

"Yes." Ben could smile at last, on that. There was one shining hope that had come of all this. "I'm to be a grandfather! I need to build a crib, and I've never been happier to say such a thing." Whether Arable would accept the gift, he didn't know. But that was not in his power to control, while building the thing was.

"Then congratulations." Glover bowed respectfully. "Good to see a bit of God's smile in the middle of this. Is it . . . a *grandfather*, you say?"

Ben answered what the man wouldn't ask. "My son wasn't Sheriff for long, but he did at least one thing right while he was here."

Tears came to his eyes, not from thinking on William, but solely from the act of smiling. It had been a while.

"Sheriff de Wendenal was a good man." Glover's face beamed. "I don't know that I ever said this, but you have my deepest condolences for . . . for such a terrible loss."

Ben had closed that door. "Thank you," was all he could reply.

"It was my privilege to prepare him for the funeral myself. I would have no one else see him in such a state."

He leaned away, eager to end the conversation. "Thank you," he repeated. "That could not have been easy."

"As I said, I considered it an honor."

Ben laughed at the misunderstanding. "I meant because of his wounds."

"How do you mean?"

"Just that. I mean it must have been difficult, given his wounds."

"There were no wounds, your lordship," Glover answered. "Did the Sheriff not tell you? It was poison that took him—a woman's weapon. Your son was a handsome man, even in death."

Oh, if Ben were still looking through a tunnel, that tunnel shred itself to ash and thrust him back to the forefront of rage. The sky boiled and burst. Ben pushed hot iron through his heart and welcomed its old familiar burn.

He reached out and touched Hamon Glover's shoulder. "Do you have any rope?"

* * *

WILLIAM DE FERRERS WAS in the Sheriff's office on the second story of the high keep. Ben's every footstep turned the castle stone to molten lead, a scorched path more ruinous than anything the catapults had done.

"Are you still Sheriff, then?" His breath pumped steam.

"Lord Wendenal," was the answer from this creature, this thing, the son of an earl who had chosen vanity over honor, who had only grown so far as his father's ankles. "That shall be determined tomorrow. William Brewer has stood aside until Richard—"

Ben's fist, a glove of gold and grief, split the whelp William de Ferrers's face in two.

He did not need both hands for this. He could reach through Ferrers's brittle skeleton and pull out his soul, screaming, with only a single hand. The one in the sling would be jealous, yes, but jealousy passed with time, while vengeance . . . vengeance was immortal.

"What in—" Ferrers did not utter another word before Ben struck him again. His body careened backward and over the top of his own desk, scuttling away for distance he would never get. It was in this very room that Ben had first confronted him, strangled him, but he had pulled back. This city offered little in the way of second chances, but this one Ben could correct.

"Guardsmen!" Ferrers sputtered, wiping his bloody lips with the back of his hand.

"They're busy."

"Lord Wendenal!"

"*How did my son die?*"

A crystal clarity snapped Ferrers's face to attention for just a moment, and Ben knew he was right, in his bones, in the darkest pit of him that he thought he could never fill again. "I told you," Ferrers lied, "Robin of Locksley and Will Scarlet killed him."

"What you told me," Ben unshouldered the heavy bag he'd brought along, let it land on the desk, "was that his *'wounds were grievous.'* That he fought *'as well as any man ever has.'* But he did not die in a fight, did he? It was poison, was it not?"

Ferrers held one hand up. "I don't believe I phrased it that way, and if I was misunderstood—"

Ben laughed, from his gut, so sharply that Ferrers's jaw chomped shut in the middle of his desperate evasion. "You phrased it *exactly* that way, you worm. You were describing to a father the final moments of his last son. Those words were seared into my mind as surely as if I had burnt them into my flesh."

"A mistake, I assure you." Ferrers's head lilted. "We told that to the people . . . we wanted the story of your son fighting, to make him . . . to make him a hero!"

"Will Scarlet was never in the castle that night." Ben leveled his eyes on the man. "You *lied* to me, Ferrers. You lied to me so that you could *use* me."

He should have trusted his own instincts months ago, when he came here. He knew then that it was this spindly cretin to blame for William's death. He should have squeezed the boy's throat longer, harder, he never should have let any morsel of doubt in. It was vanity alone that had stayed his hand, the fear that William had fallen to such a weakling as this. The lure of *Robin Hood* somehow validated his son's death, that only some mythical villain could be strong enough to defeat a Wendenal. Ben had chased ghosts through Nottingham, had even helped Ferrers escape from the castle and recruit allies to return to it. He'd trusted the story of William's death, for exactly the reasons that Ferrers had concocted it—because it was heroic. That lie placed Ben by his side, *by his son's murderer's side,* blind to the truth, the cruelest thing one can do to a grieving parent.

"I meant to protect you, your lordship," Ferrers capitulated, still maneuvering to keep the desk between them. "I thought it better to give you a good memory of your son's death, to remember him as brave in his final moments. I was trying to be kind to you—"

No part of Ben could entertain such excuses. Instead he tugged at the buckle of the bag on the desk with his good hand and flung its leather flap open, revealing its contents. Ferrers again stopped midsentence, his throat passed an absurdly large swallow.

"Do you remember what I said I'd do if I discovered you had lied to me?"

Ferrers stopped shifting, his body was likely frozen in terror. His eyes darted around the room, probably hoping to find a weapon. If Ferrers found a knife, it was not unreasonable to think he could overwhelm Ben. Ferrers was just a frail little thing, but Ben was admittedly beyond his best years, and crippled now, too. Despite this, there was not a single seed of doubt in his mind. "I told you I'd throw you out that window," he swore it now, as a promise fulfilled, "with a rope around your neck."

He'd already tied the noose in the thick braided rope that Hamon Glover had procured. And anyone who had raised three boys knew exactly how to carry a struggling child with only a single hand. Hell, he could carry three of Ferrers and still not break a sweat.

Ferrers's body shook, his voice trembled. "I am your Sheriff . . ."

"You're not, actually." Ben pulled the coils of rope out, until he found the iron hook of its other end. "Prince John declared his man Brewer as your replacement. Perhaps Richard will reverse that tomorrow, but for this exact day . . . no, you're not."

"I am still your earl."

"Yes, but I don't care."

He thrust the hook through the heavy breach hinges of the office door and gave it a satisfied tug. *Beneger the Revenger,* he'd heard that name go around. *Lord Death.* He was happy to live up to that standard now. It was a fitting circle to close—if it had to happen, it was almost appropriate that this insolent pup had been the one to take William's life. The elder Ferrers was responsible for the death of his first two sons, and Ben could now settle that score.

"Wait," the dead man stalled. "It's true, I lied, I lied about your son. But Lord Wendenal, you must understand. William was a *traitor*. He conspired *with* Robin of Locksley to take power in Nottingham, he was involved in de Lacy's assassination. I have done everything I can to hide these facts, for the sake of stability, so that your son would not be dishonored in death! This much is true, Lord Wendenal, I swear it. I hate to say it, and it brings me no joy to tell it to you, but your son betrayed his country in a coup of power! And you are on the verge of following him, and destroying your family's name forever."

Most of it fell on deaf ears, there was no excuse Ferrers could concoct that could pierce the armor of Ben's lifetime of rage. But that final nugget, it made a tiny crack. His grandson was soon to enter the world, to carry on the name of Wendenal. If it was discovered that Ben murdered Ferrers here, then the new family he'd just gained might suffer for it.

On the other hand, he'd made a promise. On his son's life.

"Who poisoned him?" Ben demanded.

Because that was the only piece of information that mattered.

Ferrers, after a moment's deduction, ran.

There was a small servant's door in the side of the room, but he never made it. Ben met him halfway there, yanking the back of his neck like a dog, then quickly repositioned to reach around under one of Ferrers's arms and grab his hair. From here he could pull him any direction he wanted, and he dragged him back to the center of the room and pounded his face into the oak table. He released his grip and smashed his fist into the back of Ferrers's skull, rewarded with a shiver that went through the murderer's body.

Ben pulled out the loop of rope and slipped it over the top of Ferrers's head. The boy's arms were already weak to respond, and flailed now at trying to fight against the noose. Ben snatched the man's hand and grabbed a finger, any finger, and snapped it with a single violent motion backward. Ferrers screamed, his hand quivered, and Ben walked a few feet to the left to open the large iron casing of the window. A single lever eased it from its locked housing and it swung inward, letting the cool breeze of the world rush in, making havoc of the paper piles on the desk, but filling the office of the Sheriff of Nottingham with much-needed fresh air.

Ferrers was standing, but too dazed to move. His face was black and spattered in blood, he cradled his broken hand with the other, his mouth was dangling open uselessly. Ben didn't ask him for final words, or to admit his crime, or to prepare himself for God. Instead he bent to fold the man over his back, stood to heft him over his shoulder. It was easy, surprisingly easy, to throw him out the window and watch the rope snap taut a moment later.

And finally, *finally*, Ben knelt down and cried for his baby boy.

ARABLE DE BUREL

"THANK YOU FOR COMING," she sighed.

"Oh, I had nothing better to do." John Little's smile stretched across his full wide face. He winked and took a respectful step backward, clasping his hands over one another across his belly.

Arable lowered herself to her knees and considered the discolored stone. The square steeple of St. Nicholas cast a shadow across the cracked marker, surrounded by other gravestones in the enclosed burial plot beside the church. While every other marker had a name and a date, this curious little cobble was just a mistake. Perhaps someone had thrown it over the wall a dozen years earlier, and it had been accidentally pushed into the earth. But for Arable, it was the only remnant of her father, Lord Raymond de Burel.

"He would've been a good grandfather," she said, letting her fingers touch its surface.

John let a deferent moment pass. "Have you thought of a name?"

"Not yet," she whispered, which was only half-true. For a son she had a few options—of the various men who had made a difference in her years. It would be appropriate to give *Raymond* a new life, but it seemed even more fitting to give Roger de Lacy that honor. *Robin* might be a contender, too, if not for all its complicated baggage. *David, perhaps.* But for a daughter, she had nothing. There simply weren't enough women who had mattered to her. There were only creatures like the sisters Lady Margery and the Countess Magdalena, which made Arable wonder if power turned all women into such destructive beasts. She prayed that would not be the case with Marion. And despite their newly repaired relationship, Arable wasn't exactly going to name her daughter after the woman that William nearly married. The only woman who'd been strong enough to pull Arable out of her difficult times and force her to flourish was named *Arable*, but she didn't want to spend the next few years tisking a child with her own name.

So, no. "Not yet," she repeated, kissed her fingers, and pressed them to the stone. She had not thought she'd ever be here again, but was glad to have a chance to say goodbye.

"My wife's name was Marley," John suggested. "It was a good name, I think, and she hasn't used it in a while."

That warmed her. "I'll think on it," she laughed. He was hardly the first person to give her a suggestion. Tuck had offered a couple of saints' names, while Lord Robert had insisted she consider *Tesoro*—which was Italian for *treasure*, and also apparently the name of his rapier that had broken in battle. She owed him much, but certainly not *that* much.

John offered her a hand and they left the gravesite, rejoining the main road that followed the curve of the castle's outer wall, a block to the west. Up the hill to the northeast they would come to the long Market Square, where King Richard was holding his open court for the day's declarations.

"How was Will?" John asked as they walked.

"Hard to say." She shrugged. Will Scarlet would always be a man of extremes. "But I'd like to say he was doing better. He needs *things to do,* you know? And in Nottingham . . . I think he had a lot to do, at least. He didn't seem as selfish. Not *better,* perhaps. But headed there."

"That's good." John nodded. "I hated to see him suffer."

"Nobody's seen him since the siege ended, nor Arthur. Charley said they're not in the prisons, either," she added. "They must have found a chance to sneak out. You haven't heard from them, then?"

Little shook his head.

"Maybe they'll head to Huntingdon." She smiled to a young woman they passed, who was sweeping ashes into a small basin. "It's still dangerous for them both here, so maybe they'll come join us there."

The next few steps were silent, which meant that John doubted the idea. She couldn't blame him—she didn't believe it herself.

"That's a shame about David, though," John said at last, his voice low. "And Charley. It's still hard to think of him as a Guardsman, little frog 'at he is. I never would have known, not for my life. But . . . you say he's trustworthy?"

"He is." She was surprised to say it. She had thought Charley might have opted to stay behind, but he'd sought them out again and was eager to return to Huntingdon with the others. "He did right by us. You have nothing to worry about."

"That's good." John nodded seriously, as if this one thing might redeem all the rest of it. "I always liked him."

"And Will and Arthur . . . they'll show up eventually, I think. Once this gets all settled."

"Woof." John flashed his eyebrows as they rounded a corner that led to the Market Square. It was packed with humans all eager to catch a glimpse of the proceedings. Heralds stood at every block or so, standing on hastily made wooden platforms, repeating each proclamation of the day. "I think we'll be back in Huntingdon and die of old age long before this ever 'gets all settled.'"

He squeezed her shoulder and grinned, then barked some curt words at the people before them in the crowd to make a hole, and they wormed their way down the streets to eventually return to the celebration.

KING RICHARD SAT IN THE middle of a row of mismatched tallback chairs on an elevated stage at the east end of the Square, flanked by several swaying standards and banners bearing his sigil—three lions rampant on a red field. Arable assumed those beside him were his lieutenants, though she only recognized half their symbols and fewer of their faces. Prince John was amongst them, though near the end of the row. His placement was simultaneously a show of forgiveness as well as an absolute reprimand.

A good deal of the day went by unnotably, and the crowds shifted frequently as people came to watch for some time before realizing they did not understand any of what was being discussed. There were some auctions for smaller plots of land whose owners had been unfortunately killed, but there was little excitement and often few buyers in those sales. Prince John's most prestigious allies were punished with diplomacy alone, which much disappointed a crowd that had rather hoped to see some bloodshed for whichever side they thought was more in the wrong. Some charges of misconduct were raised against the Archbishop of York, which Richard eventually dismissed, though the Bishop of Coventry was not as lucky. Arable paid closer attention when she heard the name of *William d'Albini*—the Sheriff of Rutland who had once refused them hospitality as they crossed his borders—but he was receiving favor rather than disparagement. Rutland was rewarded the lands of Roger de Montbegon, who had sided with John—and so on and so on, to nobody's surprise or interest.

There was one bit of news that was met with varying reactions, at Richard's announcement of a new tax—which he called a *carucage*. Nobody else seemed to be thrilled at the idea of a *new tax*, but Arable lit up and slapped John's shoulders. "That's Marion!" she squeaked. "That was her idea, and Richard is using it!"

"*Carucage?*" John struggled with the word. "Never heard of it."

"It's a representative tax, in which a landholder is taxed based on the size of his land, rather than a fixed percentage."

"Oh," John answered, though he clearly did not understand. "And that's better, is it?"

"Well," they weren't in the best environment for a lesson on economics, "for some, yes. How much land do you own, after all?"

"None."

"Well there you go."

John beamed. "I *like* it."

"It's not exactly a fix," Arable explained, "but it's a start. More important, it means Richard really will listen to Marion. It's everything she wanted, everything she was working for. She can finally help us from the top down, rather than the bottom up."

This, at least, John understood, and his face nearly choked with pride. "Maybe someday she'll actually get a seat up there."

Now *that* was a radical idea. "One step at a time, John."

He gave her an elbow, his whole heart flush in his face. "Well, of course! Don't you know? That's how walking forward works."

One step at a time.

They stayed for a while and watched. They purchased some apples and a rind of cheese from a salty old vendor who was doing very well for himself in this crowd. Most had taken a seat, turning the day's event into a city-wide picnic—which was such an impossible thing to believe, given how recently there had been full-fledged warfare in this very same plaza. If she looked for it, she could probably find blood stains in the cobbles and stone walls. That ghost of violence was ignored in favor of a bit of relaxation and the enjoyment of King Richard's presence in Nottingham, which would undoubtedly be a story many a child would hear for decades. That was how the world moved on, Arable recognized. By letting the past slide by. By choosing the promise of the future.

The biggest repercussions of the war had already been announced in the morning, when the King declared his brother John's punishment. This came in the form of Richard's proclamation of his nephew Arthur as his official heir—which frankly did not seem to be much of a punishment at all to the prince. Arable had met the man in person and found not a single stitch of his body that ever wanted the burden of being king—despite what everyone seemed to think of him, or however they misinterpreted his seizure of the castle.

Ironically, Prince John had been correct all along. King Richard made his declarations in French, which were then translated by an attendant and repeated by the heralds. Which meant that at the end of the day, after all the misunderstandings and conspiracies, John had indeed been defending Nottingham from a French-led army intent on making Arthur Plantagenet the next king after all.

Arable enjoyed that joke immensely, even if nobody else did.

The difference, of course, was that King Richard was young, healthy, and—most importantly—not in a prison. Therefore, he had many years to make a more legitimate heir. Neither his nephew nor his brother would ever rule, and England could finally start healing. *Long Live the King*, after all, wasn't an endorsement of the King—it was merely a recognition that things were generally more peaceful when nobody was fighting for the throne.

As the proceedings continued, John Little made his own improvised translations to Richard's French, whispering them to Arable. "I hereby declare," he announced at a half voice, imitating the king's wide gestures, "that I have . . . two hands!"

Arable laughed and nudged him.

"Furthermore, *this* hand," he mimicked as the King raised one higher in the air, "is my favorite! It is a good kingly hand, do you not agree?"

The audience applauded for the king's magnificent hand, and Arable burst in laughter.

And so on.

Sometime in the afternoon, the name of *Sir Robert FitzOdo* caught their attention, and Arable sat up and craned her neck at the stage. "In recognition of his acts of valor and courage in defense of the city . . ." the heralds were saying, and Arable spotted the bald knight before the King, one knee on the ground.

"How about that," she marveled. She'd never interacted with the man herself, but the stories Lord Beneger and Robert had recounted were certainly not of a man who deserved any royal laurels.

"... *Hero of Nottingham,* to receive land in the Sherwood, and dispensation ..."

"Hero of Nottingham?" John asked, harshly. "Wasn't FitzOdo the one that gave Lord Robert's face that bruising?"

"I can't imagine he'll be pleased with that," she replied, straining to understand what else was being said. "But that's the way of the world, I suppose."

It was not as if they could rush the stage and explain the worser things the man had done. That which had happened before the siege might as well have been a lifetime ago. King Richard was washing the slate, and perhaps it was wise to set the new table with more heroes than villains. It would be a wondrous change of pace.

It was not terribly long after that when her own name was called by the heralds.

"Did I hear that right?" John raised an eyebrow at her.

"That sounded like me," she said, equally perplexed.

"Well go on, girl!" he roared. "Don't want to miss out on becoming a *Hero of Nottingham!*"

Her name had just been one of many listed to be called in the next hour, and she waited with another crowd by the side of the stage for them to be acknowledged one by one. Most of the important dignitaries had been doled out their gifts first thing in the morning, so she waited mostly with minor commanders from armies on both sides, or lesser landowners who expected some small reward. Marion and Lord Robert's names were also announced, though they had a slightly more prestigious waiting area where Arable was not allowed.

Eventually, she was summoned by a little shrew of a man in a motley of purple checkers, who ushered her clerically toward the stage. And then Arable de Burel was—against all likeliness—kneeling just feet away from Richard the Lionheart, King of England.

After a bit of consultation with his advisor, he turned his warm face to her. "Arable, you speak French," he said in his preferred language, "which is good, as I would have you hear this from me directly. I understand you are with child, yes, and that the father is William de Wendenal?"

She bowed her head. "Yes, Your Grace."

"Stand, please." When he smiled, it was as if she could see the very reason he was king. "I cannot ask a pregnant woman to bow to me. I knew William, as I'm sure you know. I was very close to him. It grieves me to hear of his death, more than I think I could ever quite express. He was a loyal and good man, and I was a better King with him by my side. Many a night passed in which I wondered if it was wrong of me to send him home, him and Robin both. Perhaps I could have avoided capture in Austria if they had still been with me!"

His advisors laughed, though Arable did not know what to say aside from, "Thank you, Your Grace."

"I've also been informed of your own difficulties, Arable, and I wish to help."

She focused and hoped to memorize what came next, that she could tell it to her daughter someday. The day that King Richard returned and everything—as Marion had promised at the council—became better.

"Unfortunately, this comes with some bad news as well. I'm sorry to tell you that William's father—your child's grandfather—is dead."

Lord Beneger . . . Arable wasn't sure what to do with that information. A few weeks ago it would have brought her nothing but relief, though now their relationship had become more complicated. "I had not heard that," she replied. "I knew he'd been injured, but I was told he was likely to survive his wounds."

"Regretfully, this wasn't in battle." The King looked to his advisors. "He was murdered yesterday."

"I was witness to it," came a hoarse voice, and Arable found its owner. She had not noticed that William de Ferrers was amongst Richard's council, possibly because his face was so swollen and distorted. One of his hands was bandaged into a thick ball. More linens were wrapped around his neck, ineffectively concealed by a green kerchief. But his tight curly hair and ivory cloak were his alone. He stood, though with extreme difficulty. "It was Robin Hood."

"Robin Hood?" Arable asked aloud. There was no one left to claim that title, except for Will Scarlet, who was currently unaccounted for.

Ferrers simply nodded. "Robin Hood. He and his men came into my office while Lord Beneger was visiting me. We were discussing his son, actually, when they attacked. Robin Hood forced a noose around my neck and threw me from the window." His good hand scratched at the cloth around his throat, which explained his gravelly voice. "I was very lucky that my neck did not break, and luckier still there were men on the battlements who saw me, and cut me down before I strangled. We rushed back to my office, but it was regretfully too late for Lord Beneger. Robin Hood and his men had killed him, and were long gone."

"My God." Arable could hardly understand it. Robin Hood and his men . . . Scarlet and Arthur . . . and Gilbert, perhaps? Zinn's crew? Who else hated Lord Beneger? She'd never cared for Ferrers and would have loved to see him thrown out a window, but she had no idea who to thank for that. As for Lord Beneger, she had yet to understand what emotions were going to burrow up later about his murder.

"My men are investigating," King Richard assured her, "but in the meantime, you have your grief to tend to. However, as I'm sure you are aware, Lord Beneger had no other legitimate heir, but he does have considerable affairs. Though you were not married to William, I'm told you were important to him. As my debt to William, then, I use my prerogative. If your child proves to be male, he shall inherit all his grandfather's land and titles. If not, I would urge you to marry quickly, to secure your household."

She was utterly bewildered. Your household.

"What are you saying?"

Richard, this strange man with a crown and a gentle face, reached out for her hand. "I'm saying that you have my friendship, Lady Arable de Burel, Countess de Wendenal. And I hope your future is brighter than your past."

ARABLE REMAINED AT THE ceremony in a stupor for some time, offered a seat in one of the finer spectator galleries that had been erected nearby. There seemed to be an endless number of affluent men who were now eager to offer her a chair and congratulations. Later she might realize they had begun the time-honored dance of the nobility—courting those with power in the hopes of adding it to their own. It was not chivalry that gave her a cushion to sit upon, but greed. But for the moment, Arable did not care in the slightest. If these capitulating men sought to be considered as a potential suitor, that was their mistake to make. For none of them knew her, nor what she had been through.

Countess de Wendenal needed nobody's help.

Such a strange thing, she could hardly wrap her mind around it. She'd spent half her life in fear of Lord Beneger, the man who'd eradicated every last Burel from England, who'd decimated their estate down to rubble. Now, instead, it was the Wendenals who were extinct—and the last surviving Burel had control of their titles. She thought about dismantling the Wendenal manor as a fair balance, but that felt like a selfish sort of petty revenge. Revenge was Beneger's game, no. The Wendenal manor would stand. She could change the name, of course, but something felt appropriate about keeping it, that her title as its steward would become her trophy. A testament to what she had endured, and overcome.

Though her daughter would decidedly still be a *Burel*.

At length, Arable spotted some of her friends in the crowd—John Little caught her gaze and gave a flummoxed bow, which she could only purse her lips at and shake off. The Delaney brothers each doffed their cap to her, though Nick's smile was one of both admiration and loss. Perhaps they would consider coming with her to the Wendenal estate and leave Huntingdon behind. Though Huntingdon's castle was far grander than anything she'd just inherited, there was no pretending any of them felt at home there. Instead, Arable could give Marion's group a true place they belonged, without the watchful eye of the Countess Magdalena, and without the sense of indebtedness.

Arable's home would be a haven for all. She'd never been to Locksley, but she wanted it to be all the things that John Little and Marion described about that place, and more.

Eventually there were more names she recognized summoned to the King. "Lord Robert, Earl of Huntingdon!"

Robert assembled forward and bowed, his half cape pulled dramatically to the side with one arm. His face, however, looked much like Ferrers's. Robert had taken a gruesome beating at the hands of Sir Robert FitzOdo—the *Hero of Nottingham*—in the battles for the city streets, and it would be some time before his charming smile was seen again. He had very likely watched FitzOdo's commendation, Arable considered. That must have been difficult for Robert.

"Huntingdon," King Richard acknowledged the earl, and then stepped sideways to consult with an advisor who was furiously shuffling about some ledgers. They consulted for a short time before Richard waved his hand in understanding, and turned back to Robert with something akin to disappointment. "I've heard much of the exploits of Huntingdon, of late. My coinmaster would remind me that you were negligent in your dues toward paying my ransom." This he accented with a comical frown.

"That is true, Your Grace," Robert returned lightly, "though not for want of effort. I am most pleased to see that you have returned to us, regardless of Huntingdon's missing share. Perhaps we can repay you in another way?"

"Mm. Perhaps." The king made a nondescript signal to his advisor. "My mother traded many important men as hostages instead of ransom payment, and we still have a good deal of money to raise in that regard."

"Indeed, Your Grace."

"But what concerns me more is the account of a particular council you held recently at your castle . . . ?"

The hubbub about the stage died down, as all eyes found themselves falling askance upon the Lord Robert. "We did hold a council, Your Grace," he continued carefully, sensing the shift in mood. "We feared that King Philip of France was moving against you, and so we discussed this as a potential threat to your throne."

"King Philip?" Richard asked. "That's a lofty target for an earl's purview."

"It was merely a discussion, Your Grace."

"My brother tells me you were working *for* King Philip, not *against* him."

If there was still any chatter to be silenced, it fell away now.

"With respect, His Grace the prince has misunderstood our intentions."

"They meant to put me on the throne," Prince John declared, standing from his chair at the end of the stage. "There was nothing to misunderstand."

"Which would mean," the king picked up the thought, "the removal of myself."

Lord Robert glanced sideways for help, but found none. Nobody else of any notoriety had actually arrived at the council, so there was none here to either share the blame or defend him. Certainly not a lowly, newly bestowed countess like Arable.

Robert's voice quivered. "You were captured, your fate unknown. We sought only to protect England, to do as we believe you would have wished us to."

"My fate was anything but *unknown*. It was quite explicitly known to all." Richard drew back his sleeves, ringed in golden fur, to reveal his bare wrists. They were red and raw, the wounds were clear from any distance. "I sat chained in an Austrian prison for months, awaiting the ransom from my country. A ransom to which you did not contribute, all while conspiring with your allies to denounce me and leave me to rot. And you would claim this is what I would have *wished* of you?"

Arable's heart was pounding, but indecision crippled her. If she spoke to defend him, she might be casting her lot in with his, whatever that may be. And it was highly unlikely she had anything to add that would sway the king's accusation. But Lord Robert had rescued them all, and was now about to suffer for it, with nobody to stand by his side.

"Your Grace, I fought for you," Robert pleaded, confusion in his voice. "My bannermen rode by your side, we bled and died for you here. I myself took your trusted command and infiltrated the city to stop this war—what . . . what else would you ask of me to prove my loyalty?"

"Consistency." Richard's voice was bemused. "Your loyalty means nothing if it only exists while I am nearby."

An exasperated sigh drew from Robert's bruised lips. "Of course, Your Grace. I throw myself to your mercy, and pledge that Huntingdon is ever your friend. This misunderstanding is solely my failing, but I have delivered you—"

"There you are again, Huntingdon, you say one thing but do another."

Robert shook his head. "I don't understand, Your Grace."

"You say you throw yourself at my mercy, but still you kneel there, unmoved. If you are a man of your word, then I invite you to prove it. Throw yourself, then, at my feet."

This was met with a few snickers that were quickly hushed, while Richard splayed his fingers out to demonstrate the empty space before him.

"You want me to . . . you ask me to *throw myself* at the floor?"

"Exactly that."

Robert looked about uneasily, brushing his sleeves flat and tidying himself. When it seemed clear the King did not mean to retract this unusual demand, Robert swallowed, pulled back on his haunches, and dove limply to land on his belly before the King. The stage erupted in laughter, and Arable's stomach twisted with embarrassment for the man. There was no need for such belittlement, but it was an utter relief as an alternative to something worse.

"Robert of Huntingdon, I strip you of the title of earl, and demand that you surrender yourself to my custody until Chancellor Longchamp has decided what to do with you."

Arable gasped, but threw a hand over her mouth.

From the sides of the stage, several royal Guardsmen in red-and-gold tabards moved forward and lowered their long pikes in line with Lord Robert, who struggled to right himself, stammering for words. "Wait!" he cried, but one of the Guardsmen turned his pike around and punched its flat end into Robert's stomach. The crowd exploded in joy at the display of violence. Tears jumped to Arable's eyes—for Robert's mistreatment, but even more so for the number of people who watched it in laughter, letting their cruelest side show.

The King continued with an insulting nonchalance. "I award the earldom of Huntingdonshire to Lord Simon de Senlis, fourth of his name. The de Senlis house has proudly led Huntingdon for generations, and Lord Simon proved himself with distinction in the battlefield outside these castle walls. Lord Simon, you have my absolute faith in your position."

"Thank you, Your Grace," replied de Senlis, who had risen simply from his chair not so far away from Arable, and sat down again with the contemptible smile of a man whose every plot had come to fruition.

Beside him, beaming with pride, the Countess Magdalena de Bohun.

Watching her husband's ruin, with a single cocked eyebrow.

"Richard!" came a cry from Arable's left, and the crowd shifted to see Marion, her face red and furious, who was clearly freeing herself from two other attendants who must have been trying to keep her from interrupting. *Thank God*, Arable exhaled. Marion repeated the King's name like a mother scolding a child, and the shocked murmurs of her impudence rippled through the spectators.

But at this, it was Arable's turn to laugh.

They had no idea what they were about to witness.

They thought Richard was a Lionheart? Then Lady Marion Fitzwalter was a *dragon*.

"I will vouch for Lord Robert's loyalty," she announced, her every syllable on the precipice of derision. "He had nothing to do with the arrangement of the council in Huntingdon. I can gladly explain it—though I assure you, its details are far short of scandalous."

The crowd gave an uncertain grumble. *Let them, then*. Arable adjusted her seat to watch with pride. *Let them be surprised.*

King Richard angled his head and smiled, gesturing grandly to Marion. "My cousin," he introduced her to the crowd, "whose name, I understand, is well known in these parts."

Marion ground her jaw, eyeing the King with precision. Her voice lowered. "We discussed this."

"We did discuss this, cousin. Or rather, you discussed it with me, before I had any other knowledge of it, and I took your version as truth. But since then I have been informed not by one or several but by *dozens* of my loyal advisors that your council in Huntingdon was anything but short on scandal, and that you and Lord Robert were behind its orchestration."

That was preposterous, Arable thought. *It was his wife, the Countess Magdalena. She planned it all, then abandoned us, forced us to carry her burden.*

"As I said, I can explain—"

"It has been explained, cousin. I also understand that politics is not the only bed in which you two have become entangled."

Marion's jaw dropped.

King Richard nodded to his men. "Take my cousin into custody as well," he ordered them, "where she will remain until charges are levied against her, for conspiracy against her king, to be tried as a traitor to the crown and country."

"No!" Arable screamed, but it was lost in the crowd's reaction, and there was suddenly a hand on her shoulder. She panicked and reeled—the man reaching to her from the row behind had an old, spotted face, but one that was familiar.

"Sit down, Arable," urged Waleran de Beaumont, the Earl of Warwick. The husband of Margery d'Oily, sister of Magdalena. He'd been Roger de Lacy's friend, he'd fled from Nottingham last autumn when Prince John turned on him, just as he'd vanished from the council in Huntingdon after the prince's arrival. And now he was here, his wild eyebrows pointed in a furious warning. "There's nothing you can do. Not from here. Not right now."

"They're innocent!" she whispered back to him.

"I know they are," the earl hissed back. "But this isn't a court, this is *theater.* And you're a player now, like it or not. Keep your head low, and you may survive to play in the next act."

He tugged her to be seated, though he kept a firm but respectful hold of her shoulder.

Arable turned back to the stage—*the stage, by God*—as Richard was calling for his men to remove Marion by force.

Where was Amon? Arable strained to look. *Why was he not there to protect her?*

"Marion!" Lord Robert screamed, still on his knees, until he shoved at the nearest Guardsman and stole a sword from the man's scabbard, wielding it back wide. More blades were drawn, Arable's heart stopped—

"No, Robert!" But Marion was surrounded by men in red tabards, their pikes leveled to make a cage around her, while others moved forward and drew their swords against Robert. "Don't fight! Put your sword—"

The first ring of steel on steel shattered the tension in the crowd. Like a hot bubble of oil it burst, and sent ecstasy in its wake. The city had suffered the clamor of war merely days ago, but the shrill cry of combat now brought the city to bloodlust. The crowd in the Market Square was at its feet, pulsing, cheering, as city Guardsmen flooded forward to join the fray.

In their own stalls, the other nobility were alarmed but not fleeing. Arable tried to rise again, while Waleran's grip on her elbow only tightened. *"Do not help them,"* he pleaded. *"Think of your child!"*

And he was right.

She did nothing.

She did nothing, as Robert swung his sword at the men with pikes, parrying their long thrusts but finding no room to get close enough for an attack of his own.

She did nothing, as he was beaten backward, spinning and stepping deftly over low attacks, as he spun and saw the crowd gathering below, where more Guardsmen had cut off his escape.

She did nothing, as he threw his cape around an incoming pikehead, redirecting it and lunging at its owner, even as another pike came in and punched a hole in the fabric, which tore in half as he wheeled away.

She did nothing, as Robert's name was screamed from the far end of the stage, where the two Delaney brothers had suddenly appeared, waving wildly, shouldering a few of the unaware Guardsmen from their post and off the platform, creating an opening.

She did nothing, as Robert flew, bounding across the stage in a few graceful leaps. Nothing, as he dove off the edge and slashed his weapon at a pole beside him, toppling a red banner of Lionheart to slow down his pursuers. Nothing, as he vanished into the crowd, calling to Marion, promising to return for her.

Nothing, as the Delaney brothers stumbled to catch up with him, to escape as well, suddenly confronted by Richard's quickly recuperated private guard.

Nothing, when the sharp tip of a pike plunged into Nick Delaney's chest.

Nothing, despite the urge to keel over.

Nothing, as Peetey crumpled to the ground beside his brother, too awe-struck to defend himself when a sword came down into his neck.

Nothing, despite her every instinct, nothing.

She did nothing as Marion's dream fell to pieces, as her friends were dis-sembled.

"No refuge, no mercy!" King Richard called to the crowd. "Not to those who would take advantage of England in her king's absence! England is united against the thief, against the outlaw, against the subversionist! Loyalty to England!"

The crowd—especially those closest to Arable—responded, "*Loyalty to England!*"

"Say it," Waleran whispered next to her. "You don't have to mean it."

She did nothing—but neither did she cry out in terror, nor panic. No, not anymore. She did not look for an exit this time, she did not even think to hide. She did nothing now . . . so that she could be ready, someday, when the moment was right. If her muscles tensed, it was not in fear.

Arable de Burel was steel, poised for the fight.

Because while the Countess de Wendenal's first official actions could out-wardly be described as doing nothing, her inner thoughts for what came next were afire with the decidedly treasonous.

Prince John stood by his brother on the stage. "Loyalty to Richard!"

She joined the chorus. "*Loyalty to Richard!*"

Each word, a lie.

ACKNOWLEDGMENTS

Much of this list is retroactive gratitude for people who worked on
this book's predecessor, *Nottingham*, whom I may have not met
until it was too late to change its acknowledgments.

For both that book and this one, I continually owe
my profound thanks . . .

To all my readers, thank you deeply for spending your time with me and these
(very many) pages. Whether you enjoyed them or not, I hope you found
that time worthwhile. After all, inspiration doesn't just come from
the things you love, but from the things you don't . . .
which is what compelled me to write this series in the first place.

To my editor *Bess Cozby*, for being a die-hard evangelist of this series,
who not only always knows how to shape it into its best form,
but is also particularly good into tricking me into thinking
I came up with each idea myself.

To my agent *Jim McCarthy*, who is endlessly kind and understanding
and has quite curiously not slapped me hard across the face even once,
despite the fact that I have very likely deserved it.

To everyone at Tor/Forge Books (regardless of whether they had a hand
in this book, because they're all just fantastic), and specifically to
*Linda Quinton, Fritz Foy, Lucille Rettino, Patrick Canfield, Lauren Levite,
Sarah Reidy, Caroline Perny, Jamie Stafford-Hill, Peter Lutjen,*
and *Lauren Brenzy*. Also to *Matie Argiropoulos* and *Dakota Cohen*
of Macmillan Audio, and, of course, the spectacular audiobook
performances for *Nottingham* by *Raphael Corkhill* and *Marisa Calin*,
who have become the voices in my head when I write.

To the team at Penguin Random House Australia for bringing me
to the other side of the world, particularly to *Beverley Cousins,
Caitlin Jokovic,* and *Madison Garratt*.

To my wife, *Cassie*, for once again suffering the worst of
keeping the child distracted so I could write.

To the child, *Ryland*, except no. Quite the opposite. This book exists
literally *no* thanks to you. You have in fact done everything in your

three-year-old power to pull me away from writing for so-called critical activities like bulding train tracks, sword-fighting, wrestling with the sleepy monster, and trips to "The Grilled Cheese Store" (which, sorry to blow your mind, isn't even its real name). You seem to be actively working against me, which means I hereby declare you my mortal enemy. I know you can't read this yet, but someday you will—and when that day comes, know that you had best arm yourself with the nearest foam sword you can find, for I am very likely standing right behind you and I have been planning this moment for years.

To the cast of the original stage production of *The Legend of Robin Hood*, whose unforgettable performances continue as my inspiration for their characters. Particularly to those whose roles continued into this book: *Elisa Richter, Andrea Dennison-Laufer, Jaycob Hunter, David Chorley, Larry Creagan, Ryan Young, Gabriel Robins, Evan Green, Rob Downs,* and *Kyle Hawkins.* But yes, also to those who I so brutally murdered in the previous book: *Frank Tryon, Michael Keeney, Scott Keister, Sabrina Ianacone, Glenn Freeze, Jeremy Krasovic,* and *Bryce Wieth.* And, of course, the crew and contributors: *Lauren Shoemaker, Brian and Heidi Newell, Amber Robins, Amanda Zukle,* and *Sarah Haase.*

To the many wonderful new writer friends I've made along the way, in every stage of their own journeys, who are far too numerous to try to list here; and particularly to those in the *Debut Authors '19* group for creating a community of people all in need of each other's advice, experience, and shoulders (both for boosting and for crying).

Finally, to Talisker scotch whisky, who I include here solely in the hopes they will send me a free bottle. Or, you know, any other scotch distillery that would like to beat them to it.

AUTHOR'S NOTE

This is a work of fiction, inspired in equal parts by history and folklore.

It is faithful to neither.

(This note contains spoilers, so if you're just casually browsing through the book and found this, I suggest you wait and read it after you've finished.)

The return of King Richard to England and his immediate siege of Nottingham Castle is fairly well documented and occurred very closely to the manner depicted in this novel. The three-day duration and specific timeline of the siege, the identities of the allies on both sides, and the epic misunderstanding of the defenders believing they were under attack by the French have all been re-created as faithfully as possible. Even the names of the two men who finally came to meet with King Richard—Fulcher de Grendon and Henry Russell—are accurate (although almost nothing is known of either of these two men aside from their names, so I've obviously taken the liberty of shoehorning our own heroes into these roles). Like the first book in this series, I've also leveraged some revisionism in looking at the historical figures of John Lackland and King Richard, choosing to find alternative justifications for John's behavior when he was—by all reliable historical accounts—just a terrible person. Likewise with Richard, I prefer to find the darker side of the legendary Lionheart, in order to bring both of these figures closer to a middle ground that we can comprehend.

The council in Huntingdon was entirely my own creation, though eagle-eyed historians may notice that all the invited barons to Marion's council (the ones who did not show up) will eventually become the twenty-five signatories of the Magna Carta against King John a decade or so later. That's right, Marion started that. Fight me.

There is one egregious historical error which I must confess. You may have noticed that the year of this book was only mentioned once, and for intentional reason. The first book was set in late 1191 which would set this book in early 1192, but the actual siege of Nottingham did not take place until early 1194. I retained the calendar dates of all events, but have quite brazenly moved the entire thing by two years, so that it would better suit the fictional narrative and characters established. In reality, Richard sat in an Austrian prison for about a year before being traded to the Holy Roman Emperor Henry VI and held there for another year. The effort to raise his ransom obviously lasted significantly longer than the few months described in this novel. I was hoping nobody would notice this change, so it's probably a bad idea for me to mention it now. This is, I presume, why I don't get invited to all the raging historical fiction writer parties.

And, of course, there are endless historical details that I've either ignored, bent, or outright changed in order to best fit our characters' journey into this famous event. I am less interested in perfect historical accuracy than I am in exploring human themes. I used the canvas of the siege of Nottingham to put enemies in situations where they are forced to become allies, allies forced to become enemies, and to look at the many different ways that revenge can play out and what it does or doesn't do once achieved. Along the way I was happy to continue deconstructing the Robin Hood legend into pieces to make fun of its most ridiculous parts, and then have fun pitting all the pieces against each other along the way.

With any luck, there's more to come.